Before
Carreña

By
K GERARD MARTIN

Shouldercat Books

Before Carreña
Copyright © 2010 by K Gerard Martin

Cover art including photo of rural road in Ontario, Canada taken on March 18, 1989 is copyright © 2010 by K Gerard Martin

ISBN 978-1-935816-00-3

Published by Shouldercat Books, Kenosha, WI 53140

2010.0715.A

Contents

Contents

CHAPTER 1

Introduction

What is language? Is it the utterance of vocal sounds to form words? Is it the collection of alphabetic symbols strung together to form printed sentences? Or perhaps it is the visual dance performed by a bee to the hive for directions to honey.

Language is the difference between the etchings from a boulder dragged along the ground and the etchings of a poet on his parchment. It is the difference between a meteorite colliding into a crater and a waiter delivering the bill to a patron. It is a record not of what has happened, but of how to interpret and act based on what has happened, is happening, and could happen.

Language is life. Without it, none could exist. Life owes its existence to the language of RNA and DNA—stored language handed down from parents so that children may read and create life processes.

A spoken language lives from moment to moment, captured only by memory, or more recently in human history by audio recording devices. Written language, however, has enjoyed a much longer life, allowing people thousands of years ago to communicate with us today. Language crosses boundaries of time and is therefore timeless, much like DNA which carries the language of life through millions of years.

Humans differ from most animals on this earth in that we have a specialty in communicating with each other through language. From the humble beginnings of learning the alphabet in kindergarten to the complex creation of term papers at the university level, humans excel at language. Our command of language in written form has improved from a high rate of illiteracy a mere few hundred years ago to a majority literacy rate today. Humans excel at written language.

I am such a human. Born in 1967 in Atlanta, Georgia, I grew up in a time before the home computer and the internet, where the only means one had for reading was the newspaper, magazine, or book—obtained from the library, school, or book store. Writing was performed by hand—in print or cursive—or with a typewriter with an electric one being preferred. Writing was time-consuming and error-prone unless one worked hard to minimize mistakes. Hands cramped from writing, and manual typewriters dealt heavy resistance against the pinky keystrokes of *q, a, z, p,* semicolon, and question mark. Checking spelling required a sharp eye and access to a dictionary. Checking grammar required the eyes of the well-trained editor that most folks could not afford.

And so, as a young boy growing up in Georgia who was more interested in the developing technology of the day than the static print found in books, what little I wrote reflected my mental skills of the moment in time.

Before Carreña is a book about that young K Gerard Martin, not so much a biography through matter-of-fact reporting, but a mental biography of how his brain strung together thoughts and transferred them to the written word. The timeframe spans from 1976 to 1995*, a period where the author aged from eight years of age to twenty-eight. The author is me—I am writing this now, though I speak to you of the future, because my present is your past, but this is language—it always speaks to the future.

And why is this book named *Before Carreña*? What's *Carreña*? *Carreña* is a book series I started in 2007—twelve years after my last efforts at the short stories of *Fictionnaire* (more on *Fictionnaire* in a bit). During those twelve years, I made two attempts at a novel but could not complete them. I may return to the second attempt someday, but for now my

---

Part II of Futures was completed in 2010, but I do not count this toward the timeframe since Futures was already started and needed completion.

goal is to arrange this compendium of older works for *Before Carreña* and to expand on my *Carreña* book series.

The first and last chapters of this book (one and eleven) are written in the modern time of this book's publication. All intervening chapters (two through ten) were written in the time as noted by their dates. My modern-publication-day comments appear in braces [ ] for the intervening chapters, except for picture captions. And now, I will provide summaries for the intervening chapters.

Early Years

Chapter Two begins with the image of a letter sent to my maternal grandfather, showing my transition from printing to cursive. I was only eight years of age (almost nine) at the time and had little knowledge of the world or of writing. The year was 1976, but little did I know that forty-two days after writing that letter, my perception of the world would change forever. On March 28, 1976, I witnessed the death of my older sister by a passing car as she crossed the street. While I did not write specifically about this event, a curious oddity about her death plagued me for years and influenced my thoughts in the form of dualities. Where did this concept of dualities come from? She died at the age of eleven years and eleven days on the eleventh hour of the day. Two numeric ones together—eleven— become the duality of two lines. It was this eleven event that pushed my sense of dualities in *Carreña*. But this book is *Before Carreña*, so let me continue with my summaries.

High School, Sophomore Year

English was never my favorite subject in school. I felt more comfortable with the order and predictability of mathematics. But English was required as were the writing assignments. I read little fiction on my own, and I had no grace in expressing my thoughts. It should come as no surprise that my first SAT score in English was a meager 470 (out of 800), and my second SAT score for English was 490. My classmates (who I considered my equals) had significantly higher English scores—why was mine so low? The answer, according to my friends, was simple—I didn't read enough. Looking back, I see (in these writings) a struggling adolescent brain.

The play was based on my study of *Julius Caesar* in English class and was used to fulfill a "multimedia" requirement where students grouped together and performed some form of entertainment for the class that highlighted whatever we were learning. I wrote the play for my group, and we performed it in front of the class with no costumes and by reading the script. Coincidentally, someone really *was* standing outside the hallway at the end of the play, he really did look inside, and he reacted self-consciously when we referred to him, though the play was already written without expectation of him being there.

High School, Junior Year

The fall of 1983 marked the beginning of my junior year in high school. Most of my writing was for something my English teacher called, "Free writing." "Free writing" was a way to earn extra credit by submitting weekly writing without fear of receiving red marks from grammar mistakes. Most of my fiction in high school was written during this period, and when my junior year ended, my high-school fiction writing ended as well.

The Late 80s

I wrote little fiction, certainly not the kind that stands alone. I did, however, write many letters to a good friend of mine from Marquette University. I wrote about many things and many feelings. I include a few snippets here as a snapshot into what those years were like. The first snippet, a game, was a dream of mine. The second snippet was not directed toward my friend, but toward perceived failings in parts of society of the day.

Fictionnaire Nos. 1–5

Fictionnaire was my attempt at producing a magazine-like collection of short stories. *Fictionnaire* was never officially published (until now) but rather was distributed among a small group of friends. My thinking was that each edition would sport a number of short stories and one novella. I felt I could improve my story-writing technique with the *Fictionnaire* format with the hopes of someday being able to write a full-length novel.

These short stories were inspired by things around me of the day—people, news media, and available fiction. I created the stories on my personal computer and printed out a master copy onto 8½ x 11 inch paper in landscape and booklet mode such that each final page would be 5½ x 8½ inches. I designed a cover and photocopied the master. I cut the photocopies in half and placed the pages in order. Silicone was the glue of choice—this held the pages and cover together at the spine.

Only four *Fictionnaire* editions were physically produced. The fifth edition was never completed—until now. For this book—*Before Carreña*—I finished the incomplete short story of *Fictionnaire No. 5—Futures.*

CHAPTER 2

Early Years

Dear Grampa Mac.   Feb, 15, 1976
I'm having lunch now. It is 1:30 in the afternoon. I hope you and Gramma are having fun. We had a nice time on Valentines day. I'm now in the third grade. I will be in the fourth grade in August. I can write every cursive letter in the alphabette. A B C D E F G H I J K L M N O P Q R S T U V W X Y Z a b c d e f g h i j k l m n o p q r s t u v w x y z
Those are my cursive letters.
From Kenny Martin

P. S. Send me a letter back.

January 4, 1979

A lot of time I try to understand a lot of how the adult world works. It is hard, but I don't think I can quite touch on a lot of things that adults understand. I just will have to wait until people tell me. Such things are like propaganda, loans, insurance, etc. and a lot of things. I'm 11 years old. I will be 12 on March 20th. It seems like I can understand what to do but how to do it? It is hard for a person my age to get the important factors. I also try to understand the teenage world. You have to get a job (a good one) and a lot of other things you couldn't before, you can now, but you don't have much time. The teenage stage seems very pressured. There must be an answer to a lot of the problems.

January 4, 1979

The Woman with a Cane

There was once a woman with a cane.
And a very horrible pain.
She took a bus,
And made a fuss,
And never returned again.

Sometimes I feel that man's brain isn't very powerful at all. In fact, a lot of things I think about are so complex to the brain that I can't comprehend it. Such as does the universe go on or stop? I can't comprehend how it can go on yet if it stopped there had to be something on the other side. How high or low does temperature go? You see! The same thing. That proves man's brain is limited. I can only understand certain things. Sometimes I can't understand how to understand.

January 5, 1979

Today in lunch I received a poor banana. I went back and exchanged it for a better one. She showed me one. I said, "Well." She said, "Oh, pick any one you want." I picked a small one. I tried to open it, but I couldn't. I wanted another one. The lady said, "Let me try." Then she said, "I can't open it!" I went back to my chair cracking up laughing!

January 5, 1979

If something is old, is it bad?
If it's old and must be moved that is sad.
Why should good things be considered bad?
That makes the owner very mad.
Some people say, "That's show biz."
But it's really more of a quiz.
There is a thing mostly used by a lover,
"Don't judge a book by its cover."
This saying should always be used,
Then the object won't be "losed."

Feb.25,1979

Today is Sunday. It is very cloudy outside. I am typing anything to help me get practiced up on it. So it doesn't matter if this does-n't make sense. Tomorrow the United States will have a solar eclipse. It will be the last one for the U.S. in this century. So far I haven't messed up on the typing. In the last sentence I messed up on the word "the". Well I guess that is all I want to say.

Typed by,
Kenneth Martin

The author in 1979

CHAPTER 3

High School, Sophomore Year

A Fire of Lamp Oil Experiment
September 7, 1982

My experiment started out by obtaining the materials I needed. I used a small dish-like pan to hold the oil, sticks, and pennies. The matches and other items were gotten.

I started a fire by lighting some slivers of wood and placing them in the pan. As the fire began to grow, I added some oil. The oil heated up and soon became aflame.

I proceeded to attempt to melt in some way a few cent pieces. As I was placing the penny in with some pliers, a sudden shift of wind blew the flames toward my fingers and me. My hand was quickly withdrawn. As I noted the singed hairs on my fingers, the smoke was coming at me. I smelled like burning flesh.

I retrieved the cent piece and placed it on a burning piece of wood. The colors of the cent turned into all kinds of wavy images. The cent then started to get larger. It also seemed to turn into a dirty-bronze appearance.

I stopped the fire and cooled the cent. It did indeed expand! Not only that, when I broke it in pieces, the inside was a silver color instead of copper. Thus, my experiment was useful.

The Death of Two Lovers
January 24, 1983

On the first day of spring, Albert asked his girlfriend, Molly, to go on a date to the movies. She accepted, and soon the lovers were on their way, in Albert's car, to the drive-in.

After the movie, the couple went walking in some woods together to be alone. As they approached a cliff, the girl spoke.

"Eek! I certainly wouldn't want to fall down there. Let's go back now."

"Ok."

But as they turned around, a man jumped toward Albert, attacking him. She screamed as he tried to avoid the jumps of this man. The man missed and went sailing off over the cliff. Before he fell, he grabbed the edge of Albert's coat, pulling Albert with him. Furiously, the boyfriend tried to fight the hand off. It was useless. The man was cursed for pulling the jacket as Molly screamed in horrible shock.

The two disappeared from sight and sound. Molly cried and returned to Albert's car. She called both parents and explained what happened.

She went to school the next day, much to the surprise of everyone. Wherever she went, people asked her about the accident. She only felt worse. Her true love was gone. To make matters worse, a rumor was started that Molly killed Albert to get even with him and made up this story.

She could not handle it. The pressure was so great that she decided to join her love forever. She jumped off the cliff, leaving the cruel world behind.

What Makes a Person Good?
January 26, 1983

People have variable personalities, but I find that a person who is understanding and not having an overly big personality is good. Someone who knows what they're talking about but never brags is definitely good. I find people with an interesting or unique characteristic are nice to be around. People don't have to have large amounts of money to be good, but looks in all aspects contribute to the person. Usually the personality dictates what the person will wear and his facet. Someone that you can talk to and trust him in keeping secrets instead of spreading it around like hot gossip is good. Also someone who won't laugh at one's ideas or try to change things that he likes and one does not like.

Obituary of Kenneth Martin
1983

Kenneth Martin, 80, born 1967.

Kenneth Martin died in Grady Memorial Hospital of poisoning on August 16, 2047. His death was quiet and peaceful.

Martin graduated from Georgia Tech and worked as a computer programmer/repairer for forty-two years. One of his most famous programs was, "North Pole," a three-dimensional holographic video game that was popular for almost six years.

He is survived by Mrs. Kenneth Martin, Jack Martin, Rosel Martin Jones, Cindy Martin Blackmoore, and Hugh Martin.

Funeral services are to be held on August 20, 2047 at Oakland Cemetery.

A Bicycle Ride
February 21, 1983

On May 29, 1982, I decided to set off on a journey to North DeKalb Mall. Such a trip required some planning of mine, so I went to Nancy Guinn Library.

After locking my bike up, I went inside and pulled out an in-depth map of the entire Metro-Atlanta area from a shelf. My plan was to find a short but not very busy path to my destination.

After spending some time looking and thinking, I found the path I was looking for. I wrote down the instructions for both going to and coming back. I figured that it would take me about three hours each way on bike.

At 12:00, I got on my bike and began pedaling the slow miles past me. I had a quick pace at first, but my legs soon told me to slow down. It was a sunny day, just a bit hot for a bicycle ride.

About thirty minutes into my ride, I suddenly noticed that somewhere in my travel, I made a wrong turn, causing me to go in a circle. I corrected the error, but it cost me an additional thirty minutes.

About an hour later, I found myself well along on Rockbridge Road. I began to notice my skin being slowly cooked by the sun.

My arrival could not have been at a worse time. The parking lot was full of cars, but I managed to find a pole to lock my bike up at.

As I entered the mall, I found myself starting to wander around looking at all of the interesting and fascinating things. A quick glance at my watch told me to go to the shop that I had come for. The coin shop.

Inside were a multitude of coins in every place to look but the ceiling. I was dazzled for a second, but I decided to just buy some coin folders.

I left the mall and proceeded home when my stomach reminded me that I had not had any food since leaving home. I stopped off at a convenience store, bought a quart of milk, drank it, and continued on my journey home. About twenty minutes later, my legs were renewed with energy from the milk.

The sun continued to cook me. My journey seemed to last forever, but when I reached Conyers, I knew I could rest.

At home, I washed up, and after a plate of food, I set down in my journal the events of the day. One noticeable factor that I recorded was that even though I spent six hours on the bike, my legs were not sore.

Comparison of <u>Good Earth</u>
February 1983

In the filmstrip, Wang Lung was not very muscular or dark-skinned as he was in the book. The first house in the filmstrip did not seem at all like the one in the book. The one in the filmstrip seemed better.

O-lan in the filmstrip was not as short and stocky as I thought she would be. Lotus was not as thin and delicate as I thought she would be.

The Earth is Bad
February 18, 1983

The earth that Wang Lung owned and worked was definitely more harm than good.

During the years of small harvest, the land had many problems. First, during years of little water, the land was difficult to plow. Water had to be taken to the crops to keep them alive.

On the other side of the coin, a year with soggy land can be just as bad. It was difficult to plow for the reason that the plow and ox got stuck. The crops could not grow well.

In the years of constant large harvests, the land caused greed in many ways. The sons of Wang Lung did not know what it was to be poor. Thus the richness of the land led them to laziness. Wang Lung also became lazy when a flood came to the land, thus causing him to become "a dirty old man."

Thus are the reasons, in good harvest and bad, why the land is bad.

Book Critique
April 17, 1983

1) The Hobbit
2) Tolkien, J. R. R.
3) 287 p.
4) Romantic book, Adventure book
5) Bilbo, the hobbit, is drawn into a quest for the treasure of Smaug, the great dragon.

6) (a) 9. Tolkien uses the finding of the ring, battles with spiders, and escaping from the Elvenking to prepare Bilbo for Smaug and the Battle of Five Armies.

6) (b) 7. Although the main characters are developed, there are so many dwarves that one can get confused while reading.

6) (c) 10. Everything is described in detail. Setting is also slightly different in the way it is seen by each other. For example: Gollum can easily see in the dark, but Bilbo cannot.

6) (d) 5. It seems rather difficult to find a theme. However, a possible theme is, "One does not always know what a person can really be like."

6) (e) 10. Tolkien's style of witty and off-hand writing makes a reader fascinated and more comfortable than other authors.

6) (f) 9. Since 1937 when the first publication came out, this book has been very popular. This caused Tolkien to write, "The Lord of the Rings." People like a book where they can escape from the world and live in fantasy times.

6) (g) 8. The book is well liked by many but seems strange to others. Since it is an imaginary world, it would seem ridiculous to bother reading about to many people.

7) The best highlight was when the last light of the setting sun shone upon the keyhole, thus letting the adventurers get in the mountain.

8) The worst point that I can think of is probably when the adventurers went through Mirkwood. Not much happened.

9) I think that people sixth grade and up who have a good imagination should read it.

10) This book is so enjoyable that I have a hard time putting it down when I read it.

[Teacher's comment] *Your writing of each paragraph is good, but you need transition between paragraphs to avoid a choppy, listing approach. B.*

Spring 1983

(Narrator) It is February 15. The people of Rome are gathered to welcome Caesar whose triumphant return from Spain coincides with the festival of Lupercalia.

(Mike, Marullus)- You sir, what trade are you?

(PETER, Commoner)- A mender of soles, sir.

(MIKE, Marullus)- You are a cobbler, aren't you?

(PETER, Commoner)- Truly, sir, all that I live by is with the awl; I meddle with no trademan's matters nor women's matters, but with awl. I am, indeed, sir, a surgeon to old shoes; when they are in great danger, I recover them.

(MIKE, Marullus)- Why do you lead these men about the streets?

(PETER, Commoner)- Truly, sir, to wear out their shoes to get myself into more business.

(Narrator) The triumphal procession appears, trumpets flourish...

(KEN, Soothsayer)- Caesar!

(MIKE, Caesar)- Ha! Who calls?

(KEN, Soothsayer)- Beware the tides of March.

(MIKE, Caesar)- Don't you mean, "The ides of March?"

(KEN, Soothsayer)- Caesar! Beware the sides of March!

(MIKE, Caesar)- Surely you mean, "The ides of March."

(KEN, Soothsayer)- If I'd have meant the ides of March, I'd have said, "The ides of March."

(Narrator) The trumpets flourish; the procession and the crowd go. Brutus and Cassius remain behind.

(Cassius is drinking wine.)

(KEN, Cassius)- I was born free of Caesar; (Slurp) so were you. (Slurp) Now we both have to bend down for him (Slurp).

(MIKE, Brutus)- Cassius, have you been to the vineyard market?

(KEN, Cassius)- Why do you ask (Slurp)?

(MIKE, Brutus)- It looks to me like you are drinking wine! Is this part of the celebration?

(KEN, Cassius)- No, I am an alcoholic. (Slurp) My! This wine tastes good!

(MIKE, Brutus)- Another great shout! I do think that these applauses are for some new honors being heaped on Caesar.

(Narrator) Casca enters.

(Peter, Casca)- You pulled me aside by the cloak, sir. Would you speak with me?

(MIKE, Brutus)-Tell me what happened.

PETER-(Casca)-Well the sun got up at seven, the commoners...

Mike-(Brutus)- That isn't what I mean. What were the applauses about?

PETER-(Casca)- Well, the crown was offered to Caesar three times, but he refused it each time.

A month has gone by since Cassius talked to Brutus about Caesar.

KEN-(Cassius)-I know well that Caesar is to be crowned king tomorrow. In no way can I <u>stand</u> to live with that man alive.

PETER-(Casca)- But surely the wine that you drink each day is giving you a hangover that is affecting your senses.

Ken-(Cassius)- No, but perhaps if I could...(Ken drops his script.)

PETER-(Casca)- You dropped something, Cassius. Are you going to pick it up, or will I do it for you?

Ken-(Casca)- I have it (He picks it up.) It must be my nerves.

PETER-(Casca)- See, you aren't in the mood for murder.

Ken-(Cassius)- No, but Brutus can do it for me.

Cinna comes in.

PETER-(Cinna)-What is your problem, Cassius?

Ken-(Cassius)- Perhaps too much brandy. Actually, I want you to take this letter to the house of Brutus and throw it in the window.

It is a few hours later. Brutus is in a secluded corner of his garden. He has spent a wakeful night, and now he begins to walk restlessly back and forth.

Mike-(Brutus)- It must be by Caesar's death; and for my part, I have no personal grudge against him. But for the public, he would be crowned, and that might change things.

PETER-(Lucius)- Searching for the matches, I found...

Mike-(Brutus)- Lucius, there are no things in Rome known as "matches," all right?

PETER-(Lucius)- I found this paper. The flint that I was looking for was to light a candle.

Mike-(Brutus) That should be an interesting paper. "Brutus, you are sleeping; awake! Speak, strike, redress!"

In come the conspirators. Cassius comes up to greet Brutus.

Ken-(Cassius)- Hello, Brutus. I hope that we are not bothering your roof?

Mike-(Brutus)- What does my roof have to do with this play?

Ken-(Cassius)-Nothing. But I have come on some important things in mind.

Mike-(Brutus)- I am convinced that for the good of the people, Caesar must fall.

Ken-(Cassius)- I am of the same opinion, but I think that Antony should also share that fate.

Mike-(Brutus)- No. that would be too bloody. Antony is but a limb of Caesar, and with the fall of Caesar, Antony shall also fall.

Ken-(Cassius) Yet I fear that Antony has a great love for Caesar. Antony must fall at the same time.

Mike-(Brutus)- Peace! Count the clock.

Ken-(Cassius) It is time to go. However, don't forget that there are no striking clocks around here.

It is early morning on the ides of March. Several hours have passed since the conspirators met in the house of Brutus. Caesar is now speaking to himself in his house.

Mike-(Caesar)- Nor heaven nor earth have been at rest tonight. Three times Calpurnia in her sleep cried out, "Help! Ho! They murder Caesar!" Who's within?

Ken-(Servant)- My lord? What is your will?

Mike-(Caesar)- Go bid the priests do present sacrifice and bring me their opinions of success.

Ken-(Servant)- Why should I?

Mike-(Caesar)- Because the script says so.

After a while, the servant returns.

Mike-(Caesar)- What do the augurers say?

Servant(Ken)- First, they asked me how I was doing, and then...

Mike-(Caesar)- Not that! Tell me what is to happen to me.

Ken-(Servant)- They would not have you stir today.

Mike-(Caesar)- Staying at home today would be more dangerous than anything that I have ever done.

(Narrator) Servant leaves. Decius enters.

(KEN, Decius)- The senators wish to crown you today.

(MIKE, Caesar)- Yes, I shall come. (Mike pretends to catch a fly in the air. His fist is closed and he puts his fist next to his ear, trying to listen to the fly.)

(KEN, Decius)- Begging your pardon, Caesar, but what are you doing?

(MIKE, Caesar)- Aghn. I caught a fly, a Mediterranean fly.

(He lets the fly go.)

(KEN, Decius)-Scubidy.

(Narrator) Today, the ides of March, Caesar is to meet the Senators.

(MIKE, Caesar)- The ides of March are come.

(KEN, Soothsayer)- Aye, Caesar; but not gone.

(Mike, Caesar)- Well, Brutus, I'm glad to see you here. Am I to receive my crown now?

(KEN, BRUTUS)- You are in for a great surprise, Caesar!

(Narrator) Brutus shoots Caesar with a gun. Caesar is hit and falls to the ground.

(MIKE, Caesar)- And you Brutus. Rome never had any guns.

(Caesar falls to the ground, dead.)

(Narrator) We cannot do the rest of this play with Mike on the floor, so we will bring him back to life.

(Mike gets up off of the floor.)

(MIKE, Brutus)- Here Caesar shall lie bleeding while Rome is freed.

(KEN, Cassius)- And now, Brutus shall lead; and we will grace his heals with the most boldest and best hearts of Rome.

(Narrator) Cassius leaves, Antony enters.

(MIKE, Brutus)- Welcome Mark Antony.

(KEN, Antony)- I don't know why you shot Caesar with the gun that doesn't exist. However, I would like to shake your hand.

(MIKE, Brutus)- Shake your own hand. As for me...

(Mike stares at another fly that is approaching Ken. Ken notices it and tries to catch it. Mike watches Ken catch it, then slap it against his leg.)

(Narrator) We don't have time for this playing. Please continue with the play.

(KEN, Antony)- Yes, Brutus. It is time for your speech to the mob.

(MIKE, Brutus)- Hear me for my cause, and be silent, that you may hear; believe me for mine honor, and respect my honor. Censure me in your wisdom, and awake your senses, that you may not fall asleep while I speak. Had you rather that Caesar was living, and all of you slaves? Well, then scoobidy!

(Narrator) Brutus leaves and Antony speaks.

(KEN, Antony)- Friends, Romans, countrymen, and zeros, lend me your ears. I come to bury Caesar, not to raise him. For Brutus is an honorable man. Three times on the Lupercal I presented Caesar the crown, and he refused each time. Is this an over-ambitious man? But Brutus and Cassius deserve to be wronged for Caesar's death.

(KEN, Antony)- Good friends, sweet friends, let me not stir you up to such a sudden flood of mutiny. They that have done this deed are honorable; what private griefs they have, alas, I know not, that made them do it; they are wise and honorable, and will, no doubt, with reasons answer you.

(Narrator) In enters the servant.

(PETER, Servant)- Sir, Octavius is already come to Rome.

(KEN, Antony)-Where is he?

(PETER, Servant)- I just told you that he is in Rome.

(KEN, Antony)- I mean what part of Rome is he in?

(PETER, Servant)- He and Lepidus are at Caesar's house.

(KEN, Antony)- And thither will I straight to visit him. He comes upon a wish. Fortune is merry, and in this mood will give us anything.

(PETER, Servant)- I heard him say, Brutus and Cassius have ridden like madmen through the gates of Rome.

(KEN, Antony)- Belike they had some notice of the people, how I had moved them. Bring me to Octavius.

(Narrator) For many months after Caesar's death in March, 44 B.C., chaos has reigned in Rome. Mark Antony has attempted to make himself virtual dictator of Rome but has been opposed by young Octavius Caesar, the grandnephew and the political heir of Julius Caesar; and a devastating civil war has broken out.

(KEN, Antony)- These many, then, shall die; their names are marked.

(MIKE, Octavius)- I do consent to that. We have the listing of the people to be on Death Row. Do you have something for poison ivy?

(KEN, Antony)- No, I don't. You might want to go down to the herb shop and get something.

(Narrator, to the actors) Roman Herbs has a sale on Calamine lotion.

(KEN, Antony)-Octavius, listen great things, Brutus and Cassius are gathering forces and strengthening themselves. Therefore let our alliance be combined, our means stretched, and let us go sit in council how dangers may be discovered.

(MIKE, Octavius)- Let us do so, for we have many enemies (He points to Prance's office) and some that smile have in their hearts, I fear, millions of mischiefs.

(Narrator) Several months have passed since the members of the second triumvirate made their plans. Far from Rome, Brutus awaits the arrival of Cassius, whose actions have so troubled Brutus that he has asked him here for a conference.

(MIKE, Brutus)- Hark! Who goes there?

(KEN, Cassius)- Stand ho!

(MIKE, Brutus)- Stand what?

(KEN, Cassius)- Stand ho?

(MIKE, Brutus)- Where?

(KEN, Cassius)- On Peachtree street.

(Narrator) Alien spacecraft lands outside of Brutus' tent.

(MIKE, Brutus)- Cassius, did you hear a strange noise outside?

(KEN, Cassius)- Brutus, you must be daydreaming.

(MIKE, Brutus)- I'm not daydreaming! I am certain that I heard something that sounded like a flying saucer.

(KEN, Cassius)- Now that you mention it, I did hear something. It might be some message from the Gods, or perhaps Caesar's ghost is haunting us!

(Peter, Alien)- All right you sleazy Romans! Don't move or I'll blast you with my lazer pistol.

(MIKE, Brutus)- But I'm the noblest Roman. How can you be doing this?

(PETER, Alien)- I'm doing it. I don't care who you are, what I say, goes!

(KEN, Cassius)- I believe you are in the wrong play or the wrong century.

(PETER, Alien)- Why don't you just shut up. As of now I'm taking both of you prisoners. (He escorts them out in the hall.)

(Narrator) The scene changes to the battle field of Philippi. There is a great commotion because Brutus and Cassius have mysteriously disappeared.

(MIKE, Octavius)- Brutus! Cassius! Antony have you seen Brutus or Cassius? Antony? (Antony enters and is rubbing sleep out of his eyes.)

(KEN, Antony)- I haven't seen anything today except for these past few minutes.

(MIKE, Octavius)- What's wrong? Had something in your eye?

(KEN, Antony)- (He yawns.) No, I've been sleeping. What's your yelling been about?

(MIKE, Octavius)- I've been practicing my yodeling. Just kidding you. Actually, I've been looking and calling for Brutus and Cassius.

(KEN, Antony)- Oh, they were on the eleven o'clock news. Claim is that they were taken away in a space craft.

(MIKE, Octavius)- I think that you had too much wine last night, Antony.

(Narrator, to the actors) What eleven o'clock news are you talking about?

(KEN, Antony)- Why, the news on TV.

(Narrator to Antony) There are no TVs in Rome.

(KEN, Antony)- But my house is not in Rome!

(MIKE, Octavius)- O.K. Buckwheat.

(Peter begins to use his fingers as a pretend gun. He pretends to shoot various things and uses sound effects to make it realistic.)

(KEN, Antony)- As far as I see it, since Brutus and Cassius are obviously gone, we can rule the rest of Rome.

(MIKE, Octavius)- You mean I can rule Rome, and all of it, too.

(Peter shoots his gun at Ken and creates a terrific sound effect.)

(MIKE, Octavius)- Antony, what are you doing? (Ken falls to the ground as Peter's shot cripples him.)

(KEN, Antony)- Someone shot me with a gun, and guns don't even exist!

(Peter blows the end of the imaginary revolver and pats it.)

(MIKE, Octavius)- Get off the ground, you old crip!

(KEN, Antony)- Say the magic word, and I will.

(MIKE, Octavius)- Scoobidy!

(Ken springs to his feet.)

(MIKE, Octavius)- Did you see that guy outside the doorway?

(Ken looks in that direction.)

(KEN)- I don't see anybody out there. (He turns back around.)

(MIKE)- I could have sworn that I saw someone out there.

(KEN)- I wish you wouldn't swear.

(MIKE)- There he is again! He is peeking in and ducks his head when you look in that direction.

(KEN)- I think that you have had too much classwork. By the way, how have you been doing in your classes?

(MIKE)- All right, I guess. What about you?

(KEN)- This class right here has been giving me little time for studying in my other classes, with all the stories and poems we have had to read. Do you have any last things to say?

(PETER)- I do. I'm glad to get this multi-media project done.

(MIKE)- So am I.

CHAPTER 4

High School: Junior Year

The Thankless Child
August 29, 1983

"Spare the rod and spoil the child." That is a well-known quote from Proverbs. How important that can be when children grow up.

A thankless child is also known to many as a "brat." This child can hurt the parents in many ways such as financially, emotionally, and reputation-wise.

Financially, the child always wants money or merchandise. When he/she learns of another brother or sister that gets something nice, the thankless child is envious and feels ill-treated, thus wanting more.

Emotionally, the child can upset the parents quite a bit and give them a hard time. Stolen items can result if the parents refuse to give money. Constant pleas for money drain the parents of income, thus forcing the parents to have a lower standard of living. That could be quite depressing.

Reputation-wise, the neighbors of the family may hear gossip or see arguments out in the yard or even hear yelling. Many neighbors dislike such things and would not associate with the troubled family.

In conclusion, one can see the importance of strict discipline in an attempt to prevent the thankless child.

[Teacher's comment] *You certainly, unlike most, understand the logic behind developing an idea in a composition.*

The Race
September 1, 1983

Ben Franklin once said, "Wasted time is lost money." In sports, business, and everyday competitive life, time can make a difference.

With this knowledge, I prepared for the start. I slowly rolled my ten-speed racer to the starting line. With a nervous heart, I put my right foot in the toe clip of the pedal. Time seemed to stretch toward infinity as I anxiously awaited the gun noise.

Bang! I was off! With all my might, I accelerated to twenty miles per hour. My competitors were staying with me. Some started to gain, others were rapidly falling behind. I knew that to win, I would have to be the fastest.

Wump! My front tire hit something in the road. As my tire deflated, I knew I was in trouble. The thoughts of a lost game raced through my brain as I quickly took off my tire. The hole was big enough, but with fortune I dug out a patch from my repair kit that was capable of working.

Ten minutes elapsed when I returned to the road. My position had slipped from near first to dead last. I had lost hope when suddenly it started to rain. My first reaction was one of despair. Yet with the cool drops, I became replenished with a new vigor that surprised me.

Evidently, my competitors were not used to this weather. My training in wet weather seemed to be paying off as I slowly but surely began to pass my opponents.

The rain began to fall more heavily. The lack of fenders on my bike caused me to become soaked. The water splattered in my eyes as I approached the leader.

The rain continued. I grew weary. My gain was slowing up. Up ahead, I could see the finish line. The last leg began.

I sprinted on. My opponent was riding a parallel course, keeping the same speed as I was. We were stalemated. The line grew closer. I wondered what would become of this deadlock.

My opponent surged ahead. In desperation, I tried to follow, but my legs were weak with exhaustion. Then he cut in front of me. At that same instant, he seemed to lose his balance.

Pang! My opponent crashed in front of me. There was no way for me to avoid him. With a crash, my bike and I fell to the ground.

Pain. An indescribable amount raced through my left arm. I tried to get up and walk, but exhaustion overtook me. Then everything went black.

I seemed to be in a dark, deep hole, looking up, up, up. There seemed to be a light, a faint light, but growing stronger. Closer and closer I came to the top, then finally I did.

I opened my eyes. At that moment, I knew I was in a hospital. My left arm was in a cast. I felt lonely and anxious for news.

In walked Aaron, my trainer. At my request, he filled me in on what happened. I pricked up an ear with intensity.

Apparently, my opponent who crashed was on stimulants. The drug lost its effectiveness. Thus, he collapsed from exhaustion. The bikes were severely damaged and became inoperative. My opponent was disqualified, and I became the winner. I didn't know it at the time, but my crash hurled me over the finish line. All in all, I was glad to be alive.

[Teacher's comment] *Neat narrative! Are you a biker? This reminds me of the movie "Breaking Away." You'd like that.*

The Passing of Kogem Kethmarl
(From the book A Biography of Kogem Kethmarl)
September 8, 1983

It was on a Saturday morning that I went to my friend's house. His name was Kogem Kethmarl. I rang Kogem's doorbell, but I got no answer. This seemed strange since Kogem always was home on Saturday mornings.

I was opening the screen door when I noticed a note in the door. It read:

"Dearest Ken,

"By the time you read this, I will be far away. I have come down with a rare disease that is incurable and will kill me in a few days. I know that you would rather me stay here and go to a hospital, but I want to die in peace. My will is in the safe that is in my room. You know the combination. Farewell Ken!

Kogem Kethmarl"

I hurriedly unlocked the front door and ran to his room. I opened the safe with the combination 6-10-83. It suddenly struck me that the combination was the same as yesterday's date. Perhaps that was the day he left.

For the present, I turned back to the thought of the will. I pulled it out and read it carefully. With a shock, I learned that all he owned was to go to me. Even his huge collection of arcade games was to go to me.

I realized, however, that since Kogem disappeared, it would take years before I could get one penny. It was this, and the hope of seeing Kogem alive again, that caused me to search for him.

My problem was this: Which direction and how far did Kogem go? His car was still here, so I assumed he either went on foot, or he got a ride somehow. I thought the latter more probable. This led me to believe that perhaps there were some clues about the house.

I checked around the house. The living room was organized and neat; no clues there. Therefore, I decided to check the kitchen. On the counter, I found a sheet of paper with train schedules on it. One was circled. It was the train to Clarksdale. Evidently, he left last night, around nine of the clock.

I raced out of the house, keeping enough sense to lock it up. I jumped in my car and sped off toward Clarksdale. First though, I would have to stop at a service station to get filled up.

Clarksdale was a two-hour drive. After paying five dollars for gasoline, I drove off in pursuit of Kogem. Along the way, I noticed dark clouds above gathering closer to my position. The dread of rain occurred to me.

Within minutes, I found myself in a deluge. My wildly running windshield wipers could not keep track with the gallons of water that poured constantly upon my windshield. I had to slow my car down with the visibility reduced. This went on for an hour, though it seemed longer to me.

Finally, the rain let up. I turned the wipers off and increased my speed up to the speed limit. I came up to an interstate highway and proceeded to take it.

The time passed, and I finally reached Clarksdale. I went to the train station in hopes of finding some clue. I asked the service clerk if he saw anyone by the name of Kogem Kethmarl.

"Kogem Kethmarl? I don't believe I remember such a person."

"Thanks anyway," I said. I decided to sit on a bench to gather my thoughts. As I tried to figure out what to do, a drunk man approached me and sat down.

"Do you know who I saw, Buddy?" he inquired.

As he talked, I ignored him, seeing how he could not speak coherently. I concentrated on my next plan of action.

"Strange lookin' fellow. Looked like he needed a shave and wash-up. He was in such a hurry that he bumped into me:

"'Hey, old man, get out of my way,' he said. I asked him what his name was and he told me 'Kogem Kethmarl'."

At the name of "Kogem Kethmarl," I was wakened up out of my thoughts. I quickly had him repeat the name and the story. The drunk told me also that Kogem left toward Mapleview Cemetery.

After getting directions, I rushed to Mapleview Cemetery. I walked about in search of some signs. I noticed a grave dug, but no casket was in it. I looked all about me for Kogem, but I found no trace.

I was suddenly attacked, by whom I did not know. He was on my back, hanging on to my neck. He attempted to strangle me, but I responded with some elbow jabs. He fell to the ground clutching his abdomen when I realized that this man was Kogem Kethmarl.

"Kogem!" I exclaimed.

"You wretched fool! Can't leave people alone, can you? Always badgering me. Well! You shall dearly pay for this!"

Thus, we were engaged in combat. I wondered what came over Kogem. The sickness must have almost overcome him. Somehow, the fight would have to end. It did.

I decided at last to make a break for it. I threw Kogem on the ground and started running. Just as I took my third stride, I heard a loud groan from Kogem. I immediately turned around to see if he was all right. I was able to hear his last words.

"Forgive me my friend, but a madness overcame me. I now go to my father, and my father's fathers. Your friendship was proven when you followed me. May you live long and prosper. Farewell!"

Thus passed Kogem son of Crogem Kethmarl. Sadness overcame me, and I wept for hours it seemed. I finally got the courage to take the corpse and give it a proper funeral. Never again on earth did I see Kogem Kethmarl alive.

[Teacher's comment] *Wow! This is quite a tale. Did you make it all up?*

Winter Comes
September 15, 1983

The coming of an autumn breeze,
Brings pollen that makes one sneeze.
The cool air that rushes by,
Is refreshing and nice, oh my!
The leaves fall, yellow and red,
Forming nature's noisy bed.
The birds are leaving, quick and soon,
At dusk I see them pass the moon.

The grass is dry, thin, and gray;
It hopes for rain some coming day.
The snow will come, the people will hum,
If they pass an old poor bum.

At nights I feel a coming storm,
As thoughts begin to take a form.
These thoughts are what the winter may be,
Looking ahead so far to see.

The warmth is gone,
The wood is sawn,
I want to make,
A bluish cake.

And for what reason I don't know,
But if I did I'd surely show,
That winter time may not be bad,
But to many people it is quite sad.

[Teacher's comment] *Neat! You're not only an excellent prose writer, but a poet, too. My, my.*

An Extract of Riddles
(From Riddles Renew *by Kenneth Martin)*

I cripple the old, I bring on the cold;
I make great gains, I bring on the rains;
I don't know how, but I'm ever-present now.
What am I?

I creep into your bed, I lurk among the dead;
I cover the earth half the time, I'm in a dime.
People seem to fear to know, when I grow.
What am I?

I bring life, I kill like a knife;
I cover the sun, I'm moved by the sun;
I have a great girth as I cover the earth.
What am I?

I hold you down, I carry you 'round;
The strong I've built, the towers I tilt;
A pendulum I move, the rivers I move.
What am I?

I make you comfortable, I make you uncomfortable;
I crack streets, I produce heats;
I am inside and out beside.
What am I?

I bond two people, I break two people;
I'm given a lot, I cannot be bought;
I'm important, however, 'cause I last forever.
What am I?

Answers: Time, Darkness, Water, Gravity, Temperature, and Love.

[Teacher's comment] *I love them all, but especially the last one!*

On Education and Study

More and more people are looking at school systems with disappointment. States tend to feel that schools are not doing well enough and education must be improved.

The only way would seem to be an increase in the quality of facilities and teachers. But it is the students who are going to have to improve. This is an important fact, because if students do not try to improve, education will not be as good.

There are students who are looking for a system of getting good grades. There is a large amount of literature on this subject, but much of it tends to contradict other methods.

I have recently been experimenting with various forms of study methods. Most of the kinds I have tried require that I preread the material, listen in class and take notes, then at home review and learn the next section. The problem is that such methods require large amounts of time, writing, and thinking. One can easily quit due to mental exhaustion.

I must look for a new method now, along with some others I know. I do not know if students would like a class, however, that taught students a method and required them to use it. That is a very poor way of learning if it does not work for some students.

[Teacher's comment] *We do need more incentive for smart folks to join the teaching ranks! From what I've read, some plans are being considered to do just that. I won't be too soon!! Keep experimenting! You'll find the best method for you.*

The Arcade Game Debate

In the past few years, more and more people have been spending more and more money to play video games. People who look upon arcade games with disfavor see the games as a threat to the good habit development of youths.

The people who play these games see things differently. These people enjoy the ability to participate in some fantasy world. They like to relax from the problems and hardships of ordinary life. They view it as recreation and a way to meet new friends.

People opposed to these games think participants foolish. They consider it a waste of money. Their argument is this: After playing a game and spending your money, what have you gained? What have you sacrificed for the money and time?

These people opposed would like to ban children from playing the games. The key to the issue is this: Is the kid getting poorer grades as a result of playing games instead of doing homework? Is the kid becoming so addicted that his mind thinks and yearns for the game and nothing else?

One thing I would like to point out is this: Kids generally do not like doing homework. Many do not do homework and find something else to do. Many times this meant joining a gang and roaming the streets. Arcades get them off the street and develop their coordination. Thus, arcades seem to have some useful purpose after all. But the debates continue.

[Teacher's comment] *Have you read the reports that the games may be visually (mentally?) damaging? Are you a fanatic?*

The Age of Computers

Computers are becoming more and more of a way of life. People who make them are making money, those who buy them usually have some use for them. So where does that put the people who know little if anything about computers?

Confusion is growing more and more about computers. Many people think of well-known science fiction novels when computers are mentioned. Will computers some day take over the world? Authorities say "no" to this. They think of it being impossible since a computer is a machine and does only what the programmer tells it to do. But I think that the possibilities of computers could be as limitless as the universe.

In this day and age, computers are used for games, business applications, and home use. What does the future hold? How will the human race be affected by computers? What about other areas of technology such as space? Space travel has been regarded with excitement. But now? It seems to have lost its fascination. Computers, I think, will probably be as common as a television set. Its fascination will wear off. This may take many years.

Hopefully, humans will not live in a society where books are replaced by computer chips, and teachers replaced by computerized robots. I hope we will not be reduced to the same level or a lower level than machines.

[Teacher's comment] *I hope not, too! I believe the fascination will wear off—at least to some extent.*

Thoughts of Food

Food is the thing that keeps us living, and a pleasure it is to eat it. I find it a thrill to eat certain foods, especially when one knows it is nutritious. For instance, every breakfast I eat contains two fried eggs, one bacon piece, three pieces of toast, and a glass of orange juice. In this meal, I just cannot get over the superb taste of the eggs.

One of my favorite dishes for dinner is spaghetti with small meatballs. Whenever my mother makes this dish, I eat my plate clean and ask for more. Barbeque pork is a meat I really enjoy. I don't know what I'd do if it were substituted for the meatballs. I'd probably go crazy over it.

Whenever I'm hungry, really hungry, I especially appreciate good food. Even mediocre food takes on a new appeal when I'm hungry.

Take rice, for example. I used to never eat school rice. When I got more hungry, though, I decided to try it. I liked it and still do.

Desserts are very appealing to me. When I visited my grandparents up north on a lake, desserts were served right after the meal. They were pies. But the pies varied from evening to evening. Putting ice cream with my pie increased the pleasure of eating the pie.

With new products and new styles coming in, food will always be a luxury.

[Teacher's comment] *I eat yogurt and Grape Nuts for breakfast most mornings.* [Regarding barbeque pork] *That's what I cooked on my grill this weekend for my family.*

Combatting Depression

Depression bothers me from time to time. It stems from anxiety of things that have happened and will happen. This does not do well for me, so I have been experimenting with various things to combat depression.

The thing that I need is something that will take my mind off of these worries and turn them into only slight concerns. Therefore, I need to find something that will make me think about *it* rather than worries.

Solutions can be found! Recently, I played three straight hours of Donkey Kong. This made me forget all about school (where my worries come from) and think about how well I did in Donkey Kong. I felt happy when I went to school for the first time in 1½ years. This effect wore off after four days.

Getting a job has helped me some. My theory in getting it is to, first, get my mind off of school, and second, get money to play some video games. Since my experiment has shown video games beneficial, I will play them to improve my mental health.

So, depression can be subdued by doing some entertaining and relaxing thing so much that one thinks more about the entertainment than the worries.

[Teacher's comment] *I'll have to remember that when the dreaded Big D strikes me, as it inevitably does sometimes. 1st quarter free writing = A.*

Chapter 12
(From the Diary of Kogem Kethmarl)

I went down to the new arcade in town, the "Fantasy Fun Arcade." There were many games there, some old, some quite new. The newest one, "Warrior," was the game in popular demand. There were twenty people lined up to play it. I got tokens first, then I played some less popular games before trying Warrior.

One game there was called, "North Pole." I played a game and did quite well. The object of "North Pole" was to guide one's jet sled around and destroy everything in sight. I sat in a chair, which represented the sled, and raced around or so it seemed. Holographic images zoomed past me, and the enemy ships looked real and terrifying. Using controls on the chair, I could turn my sled around and zoom in another direction.

I finished playing the game and decided to play "Warrior." I first waited an hour, then it was my turn at last. I got inside a dome with a moveable floor. If I walked, the floor would move under me. I started playing. This was the best holographic game I had ever seen. I seemed to be wearing a medieval suit of armor. I carried a sword, and I was out in the wilderness. The computer controlling all of these images was a newly developed one that revolutionized computers in speed and capability.

Out in a forest, I walked about, when suddenly I heard a faint but audible noise. An approaching goblin. I took my trusty bow and fired two arrows at the goblin. Both missed as the goblin closed in on me. I drew my sword and swung wildly at the goblin. The goblin threw a flail at my legs and tripped me up. The goblin was upon me. End of my first man.

My second man took me to a plain. I walked until I found a cave. The cave had some inscriptions on the door. I recognized them and spoke the word "Asuki." It was a magical door to be sure. As it opened, I heard some hawks behind me. I ran into the cave and shut the door.

I was in a corridor, eight feet high and six feet wide. A dim light was ahead so I followed it. I suddenly felt webs, pulled my sword out, and saw a spider. The sword shone with a dazzling light. The spider was huge and tricky in movements. It jumped on me, but with a mighty swing of my sword, I killed it. My bonus points were rung up, and I proceeded to the next section.

I entered a door. There was an eerie noise in this room. There was a man sitting on a throne, and he spoke.

"Welcome to the Kingdom of Gharr. To become a warrior, you must pass the tests of the Qeltil. Prepare!"

My bow and arrows disappeared. I was left with my sword. Suddenly, white lightning bolts shot toward me from his right armrest. I vigorously swung my sword in the air to repel those bolts. A pit opened behind me. The noise startled me, and a bolt hit me. I fell in a pit, far, far down. Man #2 was used. I had one chance left with my last man.

(To be continued)

[Teacher's comment] *Are you going to patent your inventions to make your million? Perhaps you should!*

In an effort to catch up on "Free Writing" I shall be writing two weeks worth each week until I am caught up.

Chapter 13

The pit had a tunnel running horizontally. I had never gotten to this part of the game program. A threatening noise of snakes lay ahead. Ahead was the only way out. I walked cautiously, using my cracked and bent sword to test areas in front of me.

I was dismayed when my sword hit what appeared to be a dead end. The tunnel was dark and damp. I frantically searched for something, but nothing would happen. The noise of snakes was now obvious to me to be a bluff. I angrily threw my sword across the room since there was nothing else to do.

Wang wang wang wang wang! My sword went through the wall! I went up to the wall, but my hand would not go through. Then it occurred to me. The object to go through must be airborne when contact with the wall is made. I paced backward four steps, took a deep breath, got a running start, and jumped. The view changed in a flash. The floor had come up, so I fell to my knees. I was back in the room. But my sword was not on me. Bolts of lightning came at me, and my game was over.

I walked out as the next person in line went in. I looked at the clock and noticed that fifteen minutes had passed. Video games can certainly eat up your time, I thought.

Then I heard a scream. It came from inside the "Warrior" game. I rushed back and the managers were calling an ambulance, clearing the crowd out, and assisting the poor person in that electronic monster.

The machine was going out of control. When the door was opened, the machine was producing all of the most horror-paralyzing images anyone had ever seen. Some people tried to unplug it, but the machine was emitting pain-waves everywhere. The closer one got to the machine, the more the pain-waves hurt.

Finally, the local power company cut the power to the building. It was safe to go in. I went home, because I had had enough. I turned on our TV. There was a special meeting of all the town officials discussing what had happened. With much confusion and time, it was decided to ban all video arcade games. Word spread of the events to the rest of the nation, and the debates began. The issue was taken to the Supreme Court. After some days, the court proclaimed video games as being a physical, mental, and emotional hazard to people's health. All industries making these games were banned from any more sales. Many went bankrupt. All this was over some computer that went out of control.

The End

[Teacher's comment] *They have <u>proven</u> them to be somewhat harmful to eyesight, haven't they?*

The Car Paranoia

One night on my way home, I was travelling along the expressway at about 10:00. Travelling at a "cool" 60 mph, I was gradually passing some cars. I was within three miles of Conyers when I noticed some car behind me flash its headlights by switching from low beam to high beam and back and forth. I noticed this and became curious as to why this person was doing this. I thought of all the things my car could not be doing right. The lights were on. Trunk was shut. Everything seemed all right.

I started speeding up in hopes of getting away from this car. I got up to 65 mph. I gained only small ground. I decided that I would get off at Sigman Road instead of West Avenue or Salem Gate.

He got off too. I quickly turned left to cross the bridge and passed by Buddy's. Normally, I would have turned right in order to get to town. I decided, however, that since that might be common, I would simply continue straight until I reached Winn Dixie.

As I approached the traffic light at the intersection of Sigman and Covington Highway, the light turned yellow. I jammed the accelerator to the floor to get through the light. The suspected pursuer was caught at the light as I sped at 50 mph to get a big distance between us. In my mirror, I noticed that when he stopped, he did not put his turn signal on for turning either direction.

I continued on and made the out-of-the-way journey home. I have never seen that car, but sometimes I wonder if that car really pursued me, or it was my imagination.

[Teacher's comment] *That happened to me once with a trucker when I was returning from a night class at UGA.*

Inflation

Recessions bring much sadness to many people. When times are bad, people feel the effects of it. When there is a recession, people blame it on something: inflation, the national debt, unemployment, the President, taxes, or what jobs are available now. Of course there are a lot of other factors. People see prices rise and less money for themselves. The dollar becomes worth less and less.

When good times come along, either people forget about inflation and take for granted what they have, or they still think they have not completely gotten out of it. I personally think that we are in good times now, but a recession in future years is coming.

Many people think that once we get out or finish getting out of this recession, we won't have inflation again. May I point out that this country has been having recessions since its creation. It has pretty much been going up, down, up, down, etc. So why should we think that inflation will never come back this time? We will continually get recessions.

All I can say about life, then, is this: one should recognize and enjoy the good times and make the best of the bad times.

[Teacher's comment] *Are we allowed to gripe, though?*

The 40 Mile Ride

When I was at the end of my ninth-grade year, I decided to start collecting coins. I could not find any coin dealers in Conyers, so I decided to make a trip to North DeKalb Mall.

First, I went to the public library and charted the roads I would use to go to North DeKalb Mall. Since I was going on bike, I had to pick some small roads.

I started at noon. The day was hot. As I bicycled along, I thought the trip would be easy since I was going in mid-gear for a good bit of the first part. However, as I began to tire, I tried to rest my legs as much as possible, such as when I went down hills.

Then it happened. I got lost. I went the wrong direction. At a crucial intersection, I turned right instead of left. This caused me to wander in circles at the north-west edge of Rockdale County. After a thirty minute delay, I got back on course for Atlanta.

I ran into trouble again when a certain road name that I was looking for was given to more than one road. This only cost me ten minutes. After this, I got on Rockbridge and travelled for a few hours. After a while, I got thirsty, so I stopped at a convenience store and bought a soft drink.

I finally arrived at North DeKalb at 3:00 and stayed 'till 3:30. I only bought a few things. On my way back, I felt my legs cry for energy. So I stopped and got a carton of milk. I finally got home, weary, and sun-burned. I accomplished something, but it was at least a week before I was totally healed.

[Teacher's comment] *Whew! That made me tired reading about it.*

My Dream

One night many weeks ago, I dreamed that I went back into time. Back, back, back to the early 1920s. I was wondering where I was. A city I was in, and wandering was I to find some food. I was hungry, and I did not realize that I was dreaming.

As I passed the shops, I was amazed at the extremely low prices on things. I pulled out my wallet, but no money was in it. Depressed, I sat on a bench and looked at the ground. I saw an ant busily carrying a dead bug. He had found a feast, I was still in search of one. Noon turned to afternoon which turned to evening then darkness. I fell asleep on the bench.

I woke and found myself in a nice warm bed (still part of the original dream, not awake in reality). I had a few sheets, and the mattress was not too bad. The room was bare; the floor, made of wood. I sat up in my bed as the morning sunshine warmed my feet.

In stepped a man. Presently he talked and said:

"Well, well. Had a good night's rest? Breakfast is ready if you want some."

I eagerly accepted. I walked with him to the dining room. I told him my name and age. Upon inquiring why I was on the streets, I answered that I had run away from my mean parents. (This is not true, but how could I tell him I had gone back in time?)

The maid brought in breakfast, and I hungrily began. As I gobbled my pancakes, the man (who obviously was the owner of the house) spoke.

"Master Ken, I would like to introduce you to my daughter, Caroline. Caroline, this is Master Ken Martin."

She said "Good morning" and at the same moment I looked up and said "Hello."

The "o" in "Hello" was cut short. I was struck by her beauty, and she captured my heart immediately. In order not to seem unusual, I quickly forced myself to look at my food and resume eating.

Her father finished and left, explaining that he had to go to work. He said I was free to stay at his house all day, and he would be back in the evening.

The radio was on. The announcer spoke and said that Hoover was elected President. I mumbled, "Of course he would," but Caroline heard me.

"How were you sure?"

Caught, I revealed some knowledge, "I can predict the future. For example, this country will go through a Great Depression starting in 1929 when the stock market will crash in October. We will go to war in 1941 against Germany, Italy, and Japan, then…"

"Goodness gracious! How could you know these things? It seems hardly likely that they will come true."

I knew I was right, but I could not argue with her. Her voice seemed to hypnotise me. If she were to command me to jump off a house, I would do it. Enchanted, I talked the best I could with my love for her growing every minute. We talked about many things, and I was getting to know Caroline quite well.

All of a sudden, a blinding white light came through the window. I closed my eyes by reflex, but when I opened them, I was back to the real world. I sat in bed and realized I would never see Caroline again, even if she never really existed. It was as if she had died. I became quite sad, and it took a few days before I was able to get her out of my mind.

[Teacher's comment] *This reminds me of a movie called "Somewhere in Time." This is almost what happens in the movie.*

The Well

I had a dream one night that I was looking for someone, who it was I did not know. It was a chilling cold day. I was tired and thirsty when suddenly I saw an arrangement of boards. I moved them aside and found myself looking at what used to be a well. The well had a cemented, brick side and measured six feet in diameter. As I peered down, calling for anyone, a sudden and strong gust of wind blew me in the back. I almost lost my balance. In my over-reaction to regain balance, I lost my grip and fell, fell, fell, CRASH! I hit broken branches and frozen earth. Pain overcame me, and I cried out.

The sun faded, the wind howled, and I was there, lying in pain and fearing to move. After some efforts, I scrambled off the branches and rested on a clear spot, sore, but scared. Death was on every side of me, the darkness was ready to consume me, and I reviewed my inevitable outcome: DEATH! A heavy blow pierced my heart. I became shocked and depressed. I never was more serious in my life. I scratched at some ice in order to occupy myself.

Clouds above rolled by as evening approached. I made feeble attempts to yell for help, but my weakness hindered me. I finally just turned my head toward the wall, closed my eyes, and gave up in despair. The cold was on me; I was freezing to death. Feeling left me, and my mind was soon to go. Suddenly, a blinding white light filled around me everywhere. "I must be in heaven," I thought. I heard my name called. I thought that God was calling me. He asked me to open my eyes, and I felt him shake me.

"Get up, get up."

It was my brother, waking me from sleep. The light was on, and I fell on the floor from my bunk bed. In the process, I landed on a shoe. I realized how my dream was affected by real environmental factors. I was glad to be alive but was still cold. The reason for this was found out soon enough; a window was open.

"How did that happen," my brother inquired, but I realized instantly how it got open.

[Teacher's comment] *Did this really happen?!*

The Fire
(By the way, the last Free Writing was purely fiction.)

While visiting my relatives in Michigan in the country, our van needed repair. My dad proceeded to open up the van and figure out what was wrong and what to do. I was washing dishes (no running water) in a large pan, when suddenly I heard my father.

"Help, help!"

A flash came to me that the van had fallen on him. His next words proved me wrong (fortunately!).

"Water, bring some water!"

I had no time to think. As quickly as I could, I took most everything out of the rinse pan and rushed outside. There I saw the woods starting to catch on fire. I heaved the water in the middle of it, putting it out.

The crisis was not over. The fire had been shot out from the inside of the van. (There is a hood cover on the inside to allow easy access). Up came my grandfather with a pail of water, and as he came I began moving away from the van, fearing it would explode like in the movies.

The fire in the van was small. "Get a dipper, get a dipper." A dipper is like a ladle and is used for getting water, but it is a little bigger. Too late. My grandfather splashed water on the fire, putting out the fire, but it also got my father and a lot of the van wet.

The crisis was over. My dad had 1st degree burns on his leg (can't remember which one). Part of the inside of the van was burnt, and a plastic foot mat was melted. We all discussed the crisis. My sisters, mother, and grandmother helped by trying to put out the woods fire before I came. In fact, as I raced out of the cottage, I went right by where the pails of water were kept and didn't think to use them. Worst of all, no one thought to use the emergency fire extinguisher kept by the door.

Now to the big question. What caused the fire? According to my dad, he tried to start the van but with no success. He poured a little gas down the carburetor from a can and started the van. A spark flew, and the gasoline was on fire. My dad threw the can of fire in the woods, getting some on himself and the car, then called for help.

In retrospect, we were very lucky to all come out as well off as we did. One good thing about the fire is that it makes a good story. On our way back, I mentioned it several times. Even now, it is a good story for this free writing.

[Teacher's comment] *And this one is true? I'm counting the 3rd page from last week to make this two. 2nd quarter free writing = A.*

Care and Up-keep of a Brain

The human brain must receive proper attention to its needs to keep it running smoothly and efficiently. The brain, being an organ, must be taken care of as any other organ is. Important factors contributing to the health of a brain are physical exercise, proper nutrition, and adequate rest.

Many-a-time one will see a jogger on a road. What motivates this jogger? As researchers have proven, strenuous exercise done in a "relaxed" and fun fashion creates a sense of well-being. This relaxes and refreshes the person's brain, making him ready to do some active thinking.

What good is exercise without proper nutrition? Without good nutrition, the body starves for the nutrients. The brain is included in the body, thus it starves, too. A brain deprived of essential nutrients cannot run properly, like a car that is given the wrong oil or gas. This reduced efficiency negates the healing effects of exercise and sleep.

Sleep! Of course every brain needs sleep, for with all exercise comes a period of reset. Lack of sleep dulls the mind. Information and thoughts are clouded up as if some soreness from exercise had not completely gone away. Long-term effects of this make one depressed and less intelligent.

To conclude, care and up-keep of one's brain is necessary for good health. Proper exercise, followed by rest, and balanced by proper nutrition, are necessary to the proper care of one's brain.

[Teacher's comment] *This is good! It could be excellent if more fully developed. I can imagine reading this in a magazine if you'd prescribed kinds of good exercise, amounts of nutrients, and a sleep prescription.*

School Discipline

How many times does one see a student in the hallway during class? During my D.S. [Directed Study] classes, I frequently see students in the hall. I have noticed that teachers rarely, if ever, check for a hall pass. In fact, once last year I was going to my locker because I forgot a book. I had no pass, and Mr. Prance was going to pass me. I worried, but all Mr. Prance did was to say, "Hello."

Frequently during 6th period I notice people in the parking lot five and ten minutes before the bell rings. There are even people in the halls, many are from Heritage. Even I am guilty of wandering and going to the parking lot early. Yet no one checks. No one wants to or has time to check people for passes either. So how can this be dealt with effectively?

Another problem is with lunch. The method of confining students to the lunch room has its merits, but some people still go in the hall, minutes before or after the teacher leaves. Certainly a mistake that the administration made was when it enforced the rule before explaining the problem and threatening action. This was done when lunch trays were left, why not now? Will we stay on this system forever? Even though we have started a new semester, we are still on the same lunch policy.

Certainly discipline has its problems, and the administrators are hard-put to find the solutions.

[Teacher's comment] [Regarding how can this be dealt with effectively] *I don't know! Do you have a suggestion? We had student hall monitors in my high school days.* [In response to the question of staying on this system forever] *I don't know.*

Strange Coincidence

One day last year when I was looking for a job, I heard that Ms. King had a job available. She told me that Western Steer had a job opening, and she gave me a card to let the manager there know about my asking of a job.

When I decided to go to Western Steer, my mother drove me. We went along 138 going south until we came to the turn-off left down the road by Dan's Amoco. We waited in the left turn lane as the light shone red. My mother and I were looking at the cars in front of us that were going the opposite way. In fact, their light had just turned green, and the line of them started out when CRASH!

A car attempted to turn off of the expressway ramp onto 138 when it hit a van that had started to go when the light turned green.

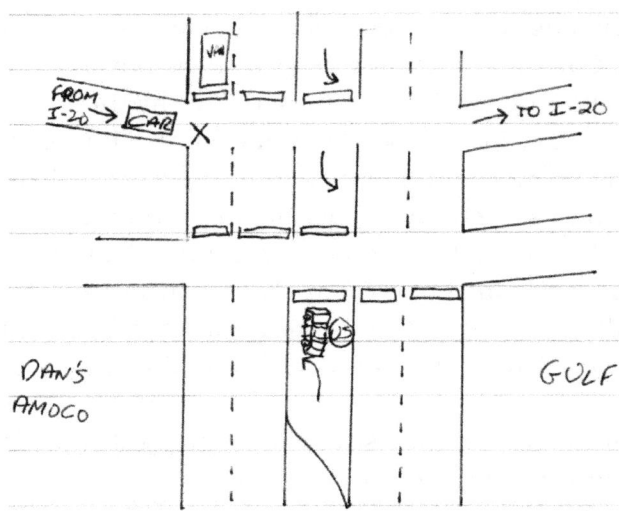

In the drawing, the two vehicles collided at point 'X'. It was a lucky thing that my mother and I had seen this accident. Yet it was strange to be actually looking at the cars as they collided. I and my mother are positive that the car was at fault.

I didn't get the job, but I did witness the accident and helped the police with their accident report.

[Teacher's comment regarding a lucky thing] *You mean lucky for the police?*

The Complex World

Today's society is filled with all kinds of technology that can boggle the mind. Anything from computers to fuel-injected cars to brain surgery to the space shuttle. Many-a-time I have wished for a vacation to the past when there was less complexity. That could be possible by going on a camping trip, but even on a camping trip one might hear over the radio about some Soviet talks on nuclear weapons or some other fact that relates to modern society. To be responsible for simpler things and enjoy a simple life has been an aim of mine, but the necessity of getting a job to keep up with the world can interfere with this goal. Many-a-time I have thought of certain jobs that would be more enjoyable than what my present career is taking me to. To illustrate upon this further let me use myself as an example.

I am planning to go to college to educate myself in the field of computers and electronics. If successful, I should have a good paying job. However, other people may be trying to get the job I want. This would cause considerable competition and possibly someone's career. It would be a burden to learn something so complex that one can hardly do anything really useful without overly taxing one's brain. I have heard of certain coaches that have "burned out." This could happen in any field, but fields that require one to use one's brain to the extent of exhaustion can influence the fate of that person more than some ordinary job.

If I were to pick some job that I could barely live on financially yet really enjoy, I would be happier in the long-run. These jobs that I am thinking of would probably serve society more than some high-paying job that would serve me. Or would it serve me better? The love of money is said to be the root of all evil, but others could say that man is the root, or Satan is the root. I must consider the benefits of money over happiness. I could be happy by using money to buy things, but I have found that the more money one has, the more money one wants, or similarly, the more things a person gets, the more things a person wants. Therefore, a high-paying job might not make me that much better off than a low-paying job, and if this low-paying job makes me happier, perhaps I should pick that job.

[Teacher's comment] *How right you are! I love Thoreau's line: "A man is rich in proportion to the number of things he can afford to let alone."*

Accidents of Cars

Many people have died in some car accidents through no fault of their own in the past few years. Most people agree that traffic accidents are the problem. Most people don't realize how important it is to know how dangerous it can be until one of our close friends or relatives dies in such a wreck. It makes the outlook of driving seem gloomy.

The worst part of this whole business is when the commotion dies down temporarily, no one changes the way they drive. Everyone still drives the same way they always did before, thinking, "Ah, it will never happen to me." Then when they barely miss being killed, they reconsider.

Most of us think that we're so experienced and so safety conscious that we could avoid a head-on collision or whatever. But people aren't that good, and mistakes do happen, and alcohol exists, plus cars are so fragile now-a-days to make them so fuel-efficient.

So what to do? Little can be done by an individual. No matter who the driver is, every driver is taking a risk of death every time he/she gets behind a wheel.

[Teacher's comment] *How right you are!* [Response to what to do] *Ban the automobile? Go back to horses and bicycles?*

The Change

Loinier Beaucoup lived in a small town. He was 23 years and made a living off of selling computer products. He enjoyed his work and made a tidy amount of money off of it. He was married to a homely girl who could cook, sew, clean the house, and just about any useful house-thing. The couple lived in a spacious yet comfortable house. They had no children, but they planned for them in the future.

One day as Loinier travelled to work, he ran into a snowstorm. He waited out the snow, but this cost him two hours. This caused Loinier to open his shop late. This proved to be unfortunate since he was expecting a special customer. The customer's name was Attendre Longtemps. Attendre was furious at the delay, but Loinier tried to calm him down. Attendre, however, refused to do business with Loinier, and he left Loinier. After Attendre left, Loinier noticed a small watch that had been apparently left behind by Attendre. Loinier tried to catch Attendre, but he was nowhere to be seen. Loinier opened the watch. On the inside was inscribed, *"Parlez le mot 'ami' et entrez dans le chateau d'Attendre."* Loinier translated the sentence from French. It said, "Speak the word 'friend' and enter into the castle of Attendre."

Now it is curious to say that Attendre had no castle, and that Attendre was constantly leaving his watch to people who he disliked and wanted to get rid of. Loinier did not know this. He went ahead and said, *"ami."* The watch glowed and turned to hot grease. With a cry, Loinier dropped the grease and furiously held his blackened hand. He now was in some dungeon that was damp, dark, and filled with the smell of dung. Loinier gasped for air as the acrid vapors from the cracks in the wall subdued him. Loinier felt himself falling and remembered nothing more.

As Loinier awoke, he found that he was extremely hungry. He noticed something else, too. His clothes were a bit too big for him. Loinier looked at his watch to see the time. He met an unpleasant surprise. His watch registered that it was seven years before what it was supposed to be. Loinier suddenly realized that he was now sixteen instead of twenty-three. He was no longer in a dungeon but rather in an alley in a street about ten blocks from where his business was or was supposed to have been. Loinier thought about the date he was at and understood that according to his past history, he was supposed to be in school.

Loinier thought that if he really had to live his life over again, he would be at a great advantage. He could make some corrections to his high-school years that could benefit his career. Loinier went to his high-school, the Gaetheioaueum High School. Loinier found that he could remarkably remember his daily routine quite well. He opened his locker to find the papers of someone else. Did time goof? Was Loinier replaced by someone else? It seemed so. Loinier took the opportunity to leave school and search himself for his next plan of action.

As he was thinking of this on campus, he accidently bumped into a young girl by the name of Fleurette du Soleil. By habit, Loinier said, "Excuse—" He never said, "me," because he was struck by the charm and enchantment of Fleurette. Fleurette was struck by the same arrow of cupid, and both realized in seconds what they were doing. Fleurette immediately began speaking.

"Oh, it was my fault anyway. I don't remember seeing you before. What is your name?"

"My name is Loinier Beaucoup, and may I inquire as to your name?"

"My name is Fleurette du Soleil. When did you come to this school?"

Loinier was at a loss for words when Fleurette asked this question since he was not officially alive. Loinier decided to change the subject by saying that he was in a hurry to get to one of the computer labs.

"Do you use computers too? That is strange that we have never met. I go there almost every day to work on programs. Did you bring a disk with you?"

Loinier by luck did. They went to the lab together and got acquainted. Both had many things in common and began seeing each other in the lab each morning before school. However, one day Fleurette did not show up. Loinier became anxious. He later learned that Fleurette had been in an automobile accident and was in critical condition. She was on the brink of death, and Loinier was at the mercy of God. Finally after a tormenting weekend, Fleurette's doctor came to Loinier and gave him some grave news.

"Mr. Beaucoup, I have some news of Fleurette. I am afraid that she is—"

(Continued next week.)

[Teacher's comment] *My, my, you do stop at a suspenseful point. You've certainly packed a lot of action in the short beginning to your story!*

The Change: Part II

"Rat-tat-tat-tat-tat!" The bullets of a machine gun rang out. Attendre had somehow caught up to Loinier. Loinier jumped for his life. He ran out of the building, sneaked off to the woods, and made plans for his next action. He recounted the events that had just taken place. The doctor came, bullets rang everywhere, and here he was. How did Attendre find him? What happened to the doctor? Or was it a real doctor? It suddenly came to Loinier that that was not a real doctor, but it was a trap instead to perhaps allow Attendre to kill him. "But what of Fleurette?" he thought. Loinier decided to investigate upon what happened to Fleurette.

After days, Loinier found that Fleurette was not injured, but she was missing. A false article written in the paper was found by the police when they had no accident report on the accident. "Attendre's doing, I bet!" It occurred to Loinier that Fleurette was a captive and was in danger. "But why? How could he have figured out that we both know each other? Unless he was spying, he could not know. That's it. He is getting back at me in this way of stealing Fleurette from me." Loinier was intelligent and right as well. This was an unfortunate fact, and once again Loinier found the reality of pain to flare up.

Hours became days, days became weeks, and weeks became years. Loinier was on the edge of rage and still no word of Fleurette. Then Loinier disappeared. It was strange, because Attendre did not know what happened to him. Fleurette was alive in the captivity of Attendre, who abused and amused her. Fleurette could not take it, but she was helpless. It was at this point that Attendre was getting impatient and was thinking of getting rid of Fleurette and searching again for Loinier. Attendre made plans to secretly dump Fleurette in the river. He decided to attach a heavy weight to her to keep her from floating in the river. Fleurette heard of this and became frightened. She desperately tried to think of some way to escape. An idea took place. She remembered reading *The Count of Monte Cristo* where Dantes escaped by cutting loose his bonds that would have carried him to the bottom. She anxiously looked for some knife. She found her purse. It was empty. She looked in her secret pocket and found her pair of scissors. The pair was small, being only for her nails, but it was her only hope. She hid them in her braids and hoped for the best.

Early morning while Fleurette was still asleep (or so Attendre thought), Attendre attached the heavy weight to Fleurette and drove her to the Bridge of Hauoleon. Off she was pushed, and Fleurette held her breath (she was only pretending to be asleep). After hearing a splash, Attendre left, while far below Fleurette was struggling to cut the ropes. She almost cut the last rope when the scissors slipped! Death seemed certain as she was quickly running out of air and space before she hit bottom. The scissors began falling away. A moment more and her chances would be dashed. Her hands went out for them, but the scissors were deflected and went out of reach behind her back. She hit bottom. Death seemed certain. Her lungs were screaming for air. Above her, the scissors came down slowly. Her patience was running out along with her life. She grabbed them, cut the rope, and pushed up to the surface. She treaded water for a few seconds before swimming to shore. Once she reached shore, she flung herself upon the ground and rested for what seemed a long time.

By noon, Fleurette was tired and hungry. She walked along a small highway, not knowing where she was or where she was going. She tried to hitch-hike, but there were no cars around. She was out in the country. Then a car appeared in the distance. It gradually got closer and closer until it almost passed her when it stopped. A young man of twenty-two or so opened the door. He was wearing sunglasses and wore a hat. Fleurette was scared but decided that a ride was better than dying in the desert heat. She got in and the two sped off in the distance.

"Well, young lady, what are you doing in the middle of nowhere?"

"You wouldn't believe me if I told you, but I have escaped from an evil man who for some reason I don't know has been holding me prisoner."

"You're right, I don't believe you," actually he did, but he did not want to seem like he was sarcastic, "but where are you going, pretty lady?"

"I really don't know. Could you tell me where Daetheoum is?"

"Whoaaaaaah! That city is eighty miles from here! That's a bit out of the way. Maybe I could drop you off in some other city where you could contact someone who could get you where you want to go."

"I didn't realize that I was so far away. Well, I thank you for giving me a ride."

It was not long before they arrived at Ravoelueth. Before Fleurette left, she asked what the driver's name was out of curiosity.

"Why Fleurette du Soleil, don't you know?"

How did he know who she was? The thought of Attendre flashed through her mind. The driver removed his glasses. Then, Fleurette knew who it was. It was...

(Continued next week.)

[Teacher's comment] *You've done well at building up your reader's curiosity!*

The Change: Part III

"Loinier, Loinier!" Both embraced for several minutes before talking to each other.

"But Loinier, why didn't you tell me who you were when I first got a ride?"

"At that point, I was afraid that Attendre was following me, and I did not wish to worry you. We managed to get far enough away so that hopefully Attendre will not find us. However, let's not waste time here where Attendre can find us. Get in the car, and we will relocate."

"But what about my life in Daetheoum? Won't I miss it?"

"I assure you, you will be much safer with me than to go back to that city. My next plan of action is to catch a plane and get across the country for the best of both of us."

"I have so many questions to ask you, Loinier. Where did you go all that time? Where have you gotten all this money from? How are you so familiar with all of these places? Who is Attendre, and what does he have to do with you or even me for that matter? And what is so important about—"

"Wait a minute!! These questions and many more will be answered on the plane, where we will have ample time to talk. Right now we must concentrate on getting there in secret."

No sooner had Loinier spoken, Fleurette noticed a car behind Loinier's. It had been with them since the city of Ravoelueth. She told Loinier, who was stricken with terror. In desperation, he accelerated the car, turned off onto side roads, and tried at all lengths to lose that car. To their horror it followed them in hot pursuit. Loinier cut a corner quickly with a lot of skidding and squealing wheels. The car behind began catching up to Loinier, and very soon it would be parallel to them.

"Hold on, Fleurette, I'm about to do a fancy maneuver!"

Loinier hit the brakes hard with the other car speeding past. Before the other car could slow down, Loinier had turned around and had started to go the other way. Loinier had a good three hundred yard lead when the other car had finally turned around. With this advantage, Loinier picked a small road that was practically hidden from view from the main road. Loinier pulled up a hundred feet, hoping that the other car would pass by. It did, and after waiting thirty seconds, Loinier pulled out and went the other way. He continued at a high speed to get away from the other car as far as possible.

"That was close! Where to now?"

"I should have known that Attendre would come after us. I was too careless at Ravoelueth. I think that the airport is now a dangerous place to go, at least the one in Hassexburg. I think that we should travel by car until we get out of state. That means another three hundred fifty-six miles. It should take us about five hours and fifty-six minutes. And the nearest airport after that is another two hundred miles. That is a total of nine hours and fifteen minutes. Since it is already 6:00 pm, we will have to spend the night at a hotel. But first, what about some dinner?"

Fleurette, being famished with hunger, heartily agreed. They stopped off at a nice restaurant, and they spent an hour eating. The first thirty minutes, the two ate to satisfy their hunger. Fleurette had many questions, so she began asking them.

"Now Loinier, you have been getting more and more of a mystery. Don't try to evade my questioning this time, because I am bursting with curiosity. For starters, tell me about where you were born, what you have done, and all about this person Attendre."

Loinier told his history up to his sixteenth year, not saying anything about afterward, when he finally got to the critical part of who Attendre was.

"I now come to the part that you will not believe, so why should I bother to tell you?"

"I'm a lot smarter than most girls, and after what I've been through, I'm willing to believe anything."

"All right. The reason we have never met before is that I have travelled back in time to what is now. I was living in the future, but some device of Attendre's made me come back in time. Attendre is a sly and cunning person who gets angry easily and will frequently seek some revenge. The day that I was transported back into time began like this: I awoke to find a cold day, and while I was travelling to work, I got caught in a snowstorm."

"How many years in the future was, or will this be?"

"Seven years or around that. I had Attendre scheduled for a meeting that morning, but the snow made me late. Attendre got angry and left in a huff. He left a watch that I was going to return, but I was too late. It had some writing on it, and I read it. It was a riddle, and I solved it. I found myself in a terrible place. I passed out, and when I came to, I was in the town of Daetheoum."

"That does seem hard to believe, but not impossible. I have read about the possibilities of travelling in time, but most of it was theory and conjecture. But what about Attendre's actions of kidnapping me and following you? How are you so wealthy now?"

"Attendre was angry at me but even angrier because by travelling back in time, I destroyed his watch. He was using you as bait to lure me into his trap. I realized this and left the city to build up some wealth. Since I know what the economy will be like, I can and did invest in stocks and valuables that I knew would rise. Thus I was able to earn a large amount of money in a very short time."

"Was it then by coincidence that you happened to see me and pick me up?"

"Actually, I was—"

Loinier choked on some food in his anxiousness to reveal his news. Fleurette tried to help him, but it was a serious thing. It looked for certain that Loinier would not make it. Or would he?

(Continued next week.)

[Teacher's comment] *He needs the Heimlich maneuver! Your endings are of the nature of soap operas which hook people.*

(*The Change: Part IV will appear next week at its usual time. Now for an NBC World update...*)

A Wet Day in the Sun

This past Wednesday, I had soccer practice on a hot afternoon on the practice football field. I was dribbling the soccer ball around a defender when all of a sudden I heard a gushing sound of water. Someone had tried to get a drink of water from the hose when the faucet broke. Everyone looked in amazement at the forty-foot geyser. Some of us went up to the water, some stayed in the field. Attempts were made to cut off the water, but in the process someone turned the sprinklers on. This got many people on the field angry as well as wet. Some people even tried to cover it up, but the water was too strong. Other people played in the water, getting some relief from the sun. Finally, Coach Kerlin sent Scott McCord up to the school to cut the water off. Meanwhile, we were still playing in the water. We put a soccer ball on it, and the ball went up twenty-five feet. We put a hat on it, and the hat went up thirty-five feet. All the water made parts very muddy. After awhile, the water began dying down. As it got lower, it got muddier, and unfit to drink. Now there's no water to drink. We get thirsty, and there's no water to drink. There's a creek, but it's composed of sewer waste. Mike Bowden and David Jones slipped on those places on the field that got wet from the sprinklers.

[Teacher's comments] *A true story? I never know with you.*

The Change: Final Episode

Fortunately, someone close by had taken a course in first-aid. Thus, Loinier was saved. He then began explaining to Fleurette that he had found out about Attendre's plans and was looking for Fleurette. He did not know whether she was dead or alive and disguised himself so that if Attendre noticed him, he (Attendre) would not recognize him.

So time passed, and the two went off to a hotel to spend the night. They rented separate rooms, for Loinier was a moral and just person. So it was as the night passed. Fleurette had a fitful night, tossing and turning while getting little rest. She finally woke with a start as the full moon peered in at her through the window. It was sinking westward, and soon it would be dawn. Fleurette walked to the window and looked out. The outside was dark and gloomy. No sound penetrated the darkness, and Fleurette was uncomfortable. She returned to bed, and she slept 'till late morning.

"Rise and shine, for today we go to our new place of settlement."

Fleurette opened her eyes and peered at the clock.

"Why, it's 10:30. I did not realize it was so late."

"I have everything ready. All that now awaits is for you to get ready. Is thirty minutes a long enough time? Perhaps an hour will do. In any event, why not meet me in the restaurant at 11:30 for late breakfast or an early lunch?"

"All right."

Loinier made arrangements, and soon Fleurette walked in. She was flamboyant and radiant, with a smile that could pierce a man's soul. So it was that Loinier found himself as usual.

"Yes, I know you are worried, but soon we'll be far away."

"How did you know what I was thinking about?" questioned Fleurette.

"I guessed as much from your expression."

"Where exactly are you taking me, and what do you intend to do with me?"

"Well, I expected we could live in a house in a small town, but as for you, I..." Here, the words got choked in his throat, and he hardly could speak. Fleurette looked at him with an inquisitive look. "I...you...this is hard to say, but maybe I can get it out." Loinier got down to a whisper and was losing his voice.

"Yes, what is it?" said Fleurette, half-guessing what Loinier was going to say. Fleurette began to shake him.

"Loinier, Loinier! It's getting late! Will you get up?"

"Get up?!?"

"Yes, or you'll be late for work."

Loinier closed his eyes then opened them. It was his wife after all. He had been dreaming.

"Your breakfast is ready, but there's a terrible blizzard. What did you say? You've been mumbling like that all night!"

"Oh no! This is terrible. What shall I do? A blizzard? Are you sure? Let's see, what's today? That's right, Attendre Longtemps is to meet me today, that scoundrel. I know! I shall take the day off!"

The End

I am I

I am I, and I be I.
I live, I see, I watch and cry.
I, me, my, I have an eye.
My eyes see why I do not die.
Why should I go lie to my,
Myself, I mean, but do not try.

To see me be really mean.
We see thee, he be me,
The tree leaves leaves contentily,
We three bees see three tea trees.
Please be the freebie, the key,
She cleans, she eases the bumblebee.

Oh no blow-Joe! Show some snow.
Row the boat, lower your woe.
Mow no snow, oh hoe and grow.
So don't know crows, though also.
Although a bow and arrow show,
Don't throw stone over the moat.

I am I, and I be I.
I live, I see, I watch and cry.
I, me, my, I have a pie.
My pie and I sigh quite right.
Why do I write so nice,
I must try my fine wine lines.

.   .   .   .

Day is day, but night lights bright.
A song for now, but beer tastes right.
I learn for now, but I forget later.
I remember your lesson, I'm school's worst hater.

We studied for class, we partied all night,
I enjoyed the park, we stayed up 'till light.
I am calm today, I'm wild later on,
Our society teaches well, what's good is gone.

.   .   .   .

Good, light, well, moral,
Bad, dark, sick, immoral,
Are what we use to live our lives.

A car, a house, a school, a dollar,
A company, a bank, a government, a person,
Are what we use to live our lives.

Life, murder, piety, guilt,
Death, restore, sin, innocence,
Are what we use to live our lives.

This man, this woman, this girl, this boy,
This earth, this universe, this god, this poem,
Are what will live to use our lives.

.   .   .   .

My friend of friends, I say,
Is one to spend time with today.
We share together,
We grow together.
We make good days out of bad.

We really never let the other sad.
But on one point in time,
We will stop our rhyme.
We will not be close,
We will forget glucose.
For one of us will leave,
And the other, a sigh shall heave.

. . . .

It is of time, form, and place,
It will never be prejudice of race.
It is, was, and will be,
It can and always sees thee.
What can I do? What can I do?
I'm joking, of course, saying hulla-bulloe.

. . . .

The leaf, the branch, they live apart
The hand, the arm, they'll never depart.
Water, sun, air, and fire,
Life, health, rest, and desire.

I know of him, I know of her,
You told me this, you want a fir.
It reaches out for the life,
We reach out to you for life.

Are trees alone, is sun without fire?
Are people alone, do we evoke desire.
What do we do unlike the trees?
Nothing more different than a hive of bees.

. . . .

She is a flower of flowers,
Fresh from some April showers.

She is energetic, full of life
Many wish to make her their wife.

But my view of her is one of joy,
For she is envied by many-a-boy.
Her hair is golden gold,
As the sunbeams of a day warm or cold.
Her face, her eyes,
They tell no lies.
She controls me completely, she has my heart,
She pulls me, taunts me, I wish not to part.

Enchantment, a daze, hypnotism, awe,
She commands me with these, la-ha.
Her voice, is the pleasant melody.
Of a playing harp, o well o dee!

But if I had the nerve to ask her out,
Would I be sure, be sure, without a doubt?
I leave her be, she's wrong for me,
She abuses her power, like a parasitic flower.

She loses her power over me,
She's too flaunty and flirty.
So what am I saying today?
My theme is simple, yet hard to say.

[Teacher's comment] *My, this is quite a combination of profoundness and silliness!*

The River Goes Ever On

The River goes ever on and on,
Through forests green and valleys deep,
It crosses regions big and stron'
It sometimes slows down to a creep.

I sail on it, I swim in it,
I enjoy the nature's beauty clean.
It flows so fast, it hardly lasts,
I remember well the things I've seen.

'Till one day steamboats roamed the place,
Full of people, full of waste,
The river turned gray with evil things,
It ceased to be what it should be.

The river goes ever on and on,
Hither it flows, thither it dies,
Now comes the time of no-belong,
Yet no one hears the river's cries.

. . . .

I know this place, I camped here fine,
I grew and lived, I did eat and dine.
I lived alone, I was solid to the bone,
The feeling of living had a pleasant tone.

I left from there, to seek a life
Full of reward, something for strife.
I met a lady full of charms,
She came to me with outstretched arms.

We lived together, we lived as one,
We shared our lives, we had some fun.
Then tragedy took her away,
I wept for her for many-a-day.

Now time has come for me to go
Back to the place I once did know,
But shadows get longer every day,
I knew that I could never stay.

. . . .

A day is here,
Time for some beer.
To have some fun,
To tell a pun.
To work no more
To sleep and snore
To eat and eat
And ignore the heat.
But what will we,
What will we be?
Nothing, nothing,
Could not be something.

.   .   .   .

I seem to be living in a world alone.
My view of life is a different tone.
My friends, my peers, all do the same,
Yet in my point of view, it's all a game.

They do these things, they ask me why,
I don't do what they do for a high.
They find me strange, they put me apart.
They scorn, ridicule, and heavy my heart.

Who am I, what am I?
Why should I do or die?
I'll do what I want for me,
And be the best person I can possibly be.

[Teacher's comment] [Regarding the scorn] *Ignore them!* [Regarding being the best person] *That's the correct attitude!*

I Journeyed Back in Time

I journeyed back in time with the aid of a special watch. I went back a few years to a recent time I was familiar with.

Carter was president, inflation was double-digit, and I wanted to make some quick money.

There was a contest that challenged anyone to solve a mystery from a mystery book, and the first person to solve it would win $1,000,000. I was excited, and I sent in the correct answer knowing I would soon be rich.

Well, a check came in the mail for $1,000,000 and along with it, a man from the IRS. He informed me of the taxes on it, "In your tax bracket, it's only 70%."

Now I was $700,000 poorer. Then State taxes were due, and FICA as well. I now had about $230,000 which was a substantially less amount than what I grossed. That meant that I kept 23% of my pay, and those wretched politicians got the other 77%. Of course I was angry, but the law was the law. I thought of starting my own business, but property tax, income tax, and sales tax would take a chunk out of my profits. I was sick of taxes. I wanted to invest in something that would not be taxed and the government could not keep their eye on. Well, I could always buy a house. All this thought of money suddenly disappeared when I regained consciousness. It was only a dream, but the thought of government taxes has always plagued me.

[Teacher's comment] *It not only plagues me in my dreams but in reality.*

Getting a Job

As this school year began in 1983, I decided that I needed a source of income. I had many expenses and thought that if I had a job, my problems would be solved. My friend, Peter Moritz, had a job at Mrs. Winner's, and I decided to try a fast food restaurant.

Peter and I went to Krystal, Burger King, Mrs. Winner's, and Dairy Queen to get application forms. Burger King didn't have any. And I had recently gotten an interview for a job at

McDonald's. I got an interview at Mrs. Winner's, but I didn't get hired. Then in late October, I was told that someone from Dairy Queen had called a couple of weeks earlier. I got angry and called Dairy Queen. I got an interview on Wednesday and began work Thursday.

A job! I began at 5:00 pm with two girls and another boy who had also been hired. We clocked in on the register, then we were shown the various surroundings for an hour. We next got a break for fifteen minutes that we were paid for. Next, the two girls went up front to learn how to work while that boy and I went in back to cook. We were taught how to make hamburgers, hot dogs, BBQs, fish, and chickens. We learned how to close; we closed at 10:00.

I worked Thursday, Friday, Saturday, and Sunday. The pay period ended Monday, and we were paid Friday. My first pay check was about $70.00. I bought many new things and got many expenses paid off.

Next pay check was net $163.00. The other cook and one of the new girls were fired; two of us remained from the original group. I worked many hours and found myself not getting enough time for homework. My grades went downhill; my grades in math, English, U.S. history, and Chemistry II were at stake. I found myself borrowing time from some subjects to study for others.

I decided to quit. I informed a manager my desire to quit. My employer called me up and asked me what the problem was. What we finally worked out was that I would keep my job but only work Friday, Saturday, and Sunday. It worked well, but the damage had been done. I borrowed too much time from chemistry to compensate for my other classes. Final result, Chemistry II went from an "A" to a "B". Math and U.S. history both barely made "A's". I had an 89.25 in math, but I negotiated with Mrs. Sammons to get an "A". U.S. history was an 89.5.

Things went smoothly for a while. Soccer practice started, so I came in later on Friday. Then one week, two cooks quit just like that. The other girl who was still working who was hired the same time as I also quit. I was the only one left hired from my group. I was also faced with the possibility of having to cook more often.

My boss then hired three cooks in a matter of days. One worked during the afternoon, the other two in the evenings. My job became even more important when I decided to go to Newberry College in the summer. No more could I freely spend my money. I saved money; I got about $100 every two weeks.

I started playing in some soccer games, which lowered my income. I paid for my lunches at school and also paid for gasoline to drive. Insurance came up. It was only $95 for me to pay, but combined with lower income, I found myself not making any gains for one month.

I recently began making gains again. I sent in a notice of resignation a week ago declaring that I will resign effective June 6, 1984. My work at Dairy Queen has been profitable, even if I still get paid $3.35/hour.

[Teacher's comment] *You resigned, then, to go to Newberry?*

On Learning

How should we learn? In a classroom with books and a teacher? Darwin said that it was best for people to learn through experience. Stick a book in front of a student, and he'll probably push it aside. Put a puzzle in front of him, and he may be there for hours.

Most of my learning has come from school, true. However, I have learned something quickest on my own when I wanted to. When I first knew of the computer in our school in 1982, I was curious. I took a book home, read it the whole weekend, and came to school writing programs. I learned a remarkable amount of information in a small time.

Sometimes during the summer I'll go to the Nancy Guinn Library and mosey around. Then I'll see a catchy title and end up spending a couple of hours reading a book. Or I might see many old magazines bound together. I would go through that and learn of our history. Or the New York Times with massive amounts of information. I went to Oxford of Emory and went in their library. It's times like those when I like to learn, but it must be interesting. Going to school and sitting in the same rooms, learning something that is not made very interesting, and I could care less. It can get quite boring. What really gets me is that our high school is deprived of many courses that I would be willing to take that are educational in a specific field but would never make. Truly, our math and science departments are lacking. I'm leaving to go to Oxford for joint enrollment next year because there are no more maths here for me to take.

[Teacher's comment] *I sympathize, believe me, but you and I are more curious than the mass of men. Public schooling is designed, unfortunately but of necessity, for the masses.*

4th quarter free writing = A. I heard you comment one day that you did free writing for the grade. Nonetheless, I'm glad you were motivated to do it. I've enjoyed reading your thoughts and the products of your imagination.

CHAPTER 5

The Late 80s

Swimming Pool Game
September 25, 1988

I was playing a game with another person in a swimming-pool environment. The
two of us were in a room with a referee
starting the game. I looked at the person;
the person looked at me. The game started,
and we started mildly attacking each other.
If I became more violent, he became less so;
if I calmed down, he became more violent.
So I once became very calm; he started going crazy with rage. He broke off from me,
went over to the other side of the room, and

The author in 1988

began pounding on the floor. I became drowsy; with each hit
on the floor, the tables, chairs and other furniture shook more
and more. As I nearly fell asleep, the referee ran over to the
crazed person, held him to the ground, and subdued the fit to
prevent eternity from blowing up. The shock waves grew less;
the furniture stopped shaking. We finally came up out of the
water, and the ref said, "Wanna play again?"

I thought there was only one room, but there was one next
door. The second room represented the way the other person
saw things, the first room represented the way I saw things. I
asked the other person why he had the fit; he asked me the
same question. You see, he saw me having the fit from his
point of view. So when I thought I was calm, I was actually

angry? Maybe. To see what really happened, I looked for the third room, the referee's point of view. I couldn't find it.

Letter from K Gerard Martin
November 2, 1989

There! See that room down there? That's the last one on this floor. Let's open the door and see what's inside. Hmmm. There are eight tables with nothing but a book on each one... no, wait! One table doesn't have a book on it. How strange, the tables are identical; each book is approximately the same size with the same plain cover. As I walk around the room, I take notice of the book titles.

This is a strange collection of books to be sure. Where is that book from table #6? Surely there must be one that belongs to that table. After all, the other tables have books. Well, maybe there was no book for that table. Why complain? Maybe people are going to be using these tables, and one will be empty.

Whatever the case, let's walk around the room again. It seems that each of these books is open to a particular page. I can almost believe some of the stuff that is written on these pages, but there are some subtle flaws imbedded in the paragraphs. What about the table with no book? Well, let's see... there appears to be a small pile of ash on the table. Let's look closer...the ashes are actually burnt pieces of paper. Let's pick one up. Oops! It's crumbling. Ok, maybe I can read the burnt paper without touching it. What does that say? "How to Burn a Book."

Can I get immunized against the pathogenic environment that surrounds me? I don't wanna get sick again, that stupor that keeps me from doing things during the day and the malaise that keeps me tossing and turning during the sleepless nights. What did you say? It's normal to be stupid? I don't agree. What do you mean, I'm wrong? Since when did you become an authority? Those certificates on the wall? Yeah, I see 'em, what about 'em? Those papers are proof? Bull, no certificate is gonna tell me what to do. I know you're reciting this from p. 666 of your book. Can't you throw away your book? No, I didn't think you could understand. You may think it's nonsense, but it isn't. Yeah, you ignore me, ignore the truth. Go on, hide in your book. Yeah, bye. What? No, I ain't gonna spoon feed you anymore.

Yeah, you think the world is flat? Why don't you try walking to the edge before you come up with this fool notion? But no, you must try to put an explanation to anything and everything whether you understand it or not. If you can't find an explanation then the thing doesn't exist, right? So you complete your book and live your life by it. Worse, you attempt to teach your children to follow the same book you've set for yourself. It is bad enough that the kids have to put up with the flaws of your book; it's worse that you ingrain the idea that your kids must live by a book. So your kids reject your book then search in a confused state for a book that suits them. Or maybe your kids try to write their own, their moral code. Can we show you something different than following a book? Probably not, since one of your major rules is to believe in a book. Don't quote verses to me. Are you speaking from your own thoughts and feelings, or are you reciting some lines that you memorized in grammar school? Put aside your rules that tie you down to your life and think for a moment, think and contemplate the possibilities with me. Don't give me this have-to-do-this or have-to-do-that, or that you can't do this or that. You lost me again? Who cares? Forget it, just go on your path toward death. Keep your disease to yourself.

Tribal Rituals
June 1, 1990

The two observers came to the edge of the cliff and rested. The first observer, Josh, unstrapped his gear and rested it beside some loose rocks while the second observer, Aaron, pulled out his binoculars and leisurely panned the distant valley.

"Interesting," remarked Aaron as Josh sipped water from his canteen.

"What do you see?"

"Just beyond the river is a tribe of some sort. They're quite primitive by our standards, yet their methods of interaction are interesting."

A cool, clean breeze rustled through Aaron's grey beard as he spoke. Josh pulled out his binoculars and looked in the same direction as Aaron, adjusting his focus as the tribe came into view.

"What unusual creatures," Josh said. "They resemble our people yet behave more primitively. Note how they stay close to the fire—"

"The grey-and-black-fur being seems to travel around quite a bit while the others work on their various little projects," noted Aaron.

"That red-spotted being doesn't seem to be working on a project like the others. It's watching the others and communicating with a black-fur being. The pair seems to have isolated itself. The grey-and-black-fur being is making rounds to all the other beings except for the isolated pair."

"Oh my!" the observers said in unison.

"The red-spotted creature just took a branch from the fire and threw it at his fellow being," Aaron added.

"Should we intervene?"

"No," cautioned Aaron, "we are here to observe, not interfere. Whatever happens on this planet must happen on its own."

The observers spent several hours peering across the expanse, studying the behavioral patterns of the tribe. Their vantage point provided an excellent view while giving good protection from being seen. The isolated pair, however, drew much attention from the observer's eyes, and their actions were studied closely.

"Look Aaron, beyond the tribal group, a large herd is stampeding across the plains."

"Incredible! Their vibrations can be felt from here. Yet the tribe is unaware of the herd. If you've noticed, the tribe hasn't journeyed beyond a local radius."

"Skies are darkening, Aaron. It seems there's some lightning in the distance. Could be a thunderstorm..."

"The winds are picking up," said Josh. "The tribe is scattering for cover. Maybe we should look for cover ourselves."

"Wait, just a few moments more. I want to see the end of the conflicts."

"Aaron, it's pouring rain! Let's find some cover."

"Ok, lead the way."

The travellers made their way along the narrow, winding path for several moments. The wind whipped rain in all directions as the travellers made their way toward a small cave. With their artificial light, the travellers checked the cave for other creatures before making themselves comfortable. The cave was shallow—there was nothing else in it.

"Set the lantern in the middle—we'll use it to provide some heat," instructed Aaron.

As Josh set the lantern on the cavern floor, Aaron pulled some foodstuff from his backpack.

"Here, try some of this," said Aaron as he passed some food-stuff to Josh.

"What is it?"

"It's some preserved *bushador* meat from our home planet. I'd been saving it for an unusual circumstance. Also, try some of this."

Aaron passed a small bottle to Josh.

"It's *keeradil* wine."

"Mmm, delicious. I miss the food from home. The food on this planet doesn't have the energy or the pleasurable taste of our food."

"It's good to see you appreciate the delicacies of home. Tell me, what were your impressions of the animals we've seen today?"

"The small, flying creatures we saw earlier were uncommonly lively and friendly to us. I somewhat enjoyed our visit with them. However, I was disappointed with the behavior of the tribe. For all the things the tribe seems to do, it can be destructive to other animals and to its own kind. And yet the tribe is best at manipulating its environment. I'm surprised a species with such abilities is wasting its time with such negative ways."

"They seem to participate in strange rituals," Josh explained, "where they throw various feints, jabs, blocks, then turn right around and hug their opponent. For a few moments they dance around the fire in a merry chant, the next minute they're taking branches from the fire and attacking each other. Such irrationality and misdirection. The tribe is quite unstable."

"It's getting late," said Aaron. "We should get some sleep before tomorrow's journey."

Aaron and Josh unfolded dry cloths and placed them on the floor. There they slept as a subsiding storm passed into the night.

The next morning, the travellers arose and packed their things after a not-too-restful night. Upon leaving the cave, they welcomed the sunshine and whistled cheerfully as they embraced the new adventures of the day.

Spring 1992

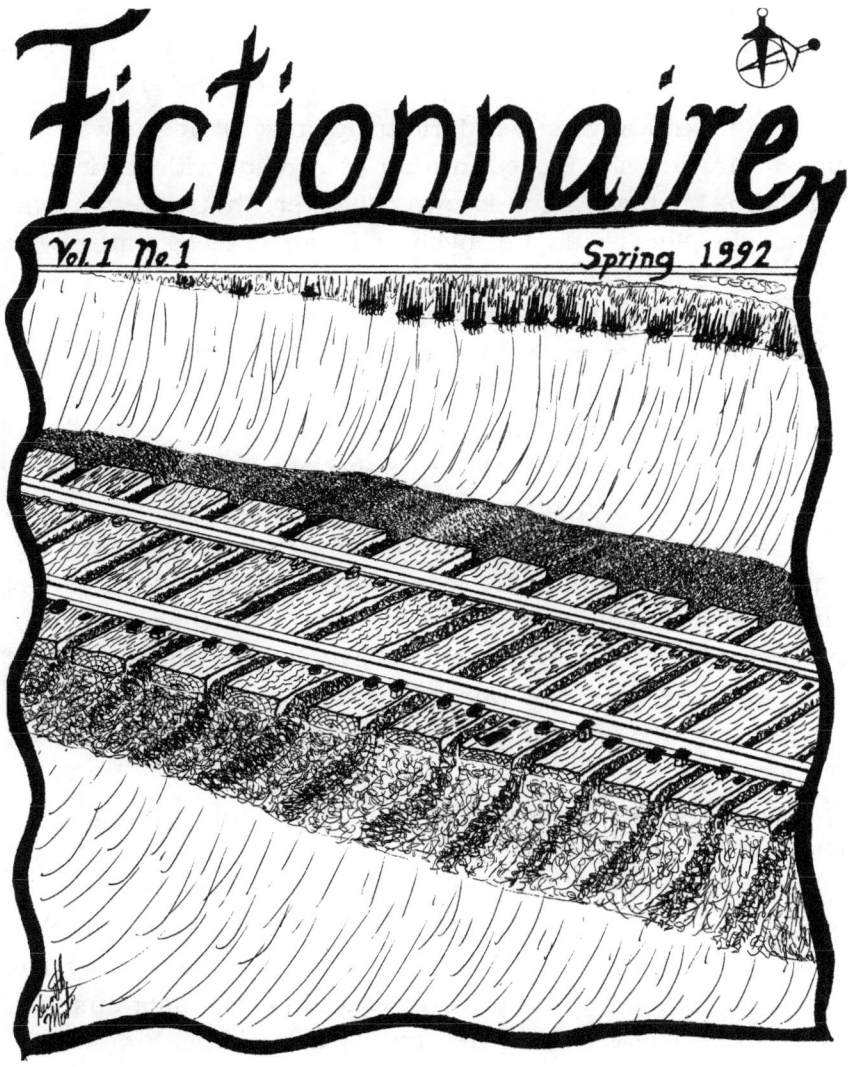

The Cat from Hell

March 4, 1992

It is unknown whether Maria truly knew what she was getting into when she moved into an apartment with a friend in Ypsilanti, Michigan. It is known, however, that once she was settled in, she would be involved in an endless battle with ...The Cat from Hell.

We don't usually think of cats as being especially troublesome. On the contrary, cats tend to be very quiet and clean pets. No barking, no daily walks—cats take care of themselves and on the average are pleasant, gentle beasts.

Somewhere in humankind's subconscious is a living terror, evoked by the thoughts of lions, leopards, tigers, and cheetahs hunting down large prey with cunning speed and agility. These cats have ferocious fangs and claws, capable of slicing and shredding meat faster than a butcher or a meat processor. Their appetites include virtually all living animals of size, and the cats will pursue their prey until the prey is caught—no tree or boundary can stop them (except for water, perhaps).

Domestic cats are thus rooted in this venue although to a lesser extent. Every once in a blue moon, however, one cat will inherit the instincts and cunning of the larger cats. So it is with...The Cat from Hell.

Maria, fast asleep in her bed is sharply awakened by The Cat from Hell as he pounces on her toes. Maria, delirious with rage, grabs The Cat from Hell by his tail, swings him several times around her head (as a warbled meow sounds from The Cat), then with a final swing whips him through the window, at least she thinks he is through the window. With a devilish grin, The Cat from Hell gyrates his legs at the last second, bounces off the window, then does a back flip onto Maria's bed and pounces straight for the offending hand. Maria takes her other hand and pounds The Cat several times then kicks him out the door. The Cat from Hell comes back, jumping onto Maria. While still in the air, Maria deflects The Cat with her pillow. The Cat from Hell falls then jumps again. A second time Maria hits The Cat with her pillow. A third. A fourth. Finally, Maria jumps up and chases The Cat from Hell, swinging her pillow at him several times while The Cat runs across the floor, up over the furniture, along the counter, over the stove (where his hairs are singed by a late-night snack being prepared by Maria's roommate), then up the wall where he clings in a corner next to the ceiling, just barely out of Maria's reach. She throws the pillow at The Cat, but he sticks like glue. Again she throws. The Cat from Hell doesn't budge. Satisfied, Maria returns to sleep.

The next morning, Maria's roommate asks what Maria did to The Cat. "Nothing," Maria replies. "Then why is he stuck up in a corner? He won't come down." Maria chuckles all the way to work, almost forcing a scrawny salesman dude off the road. Another car has one of those yellow, diamond-shaped signs hanging in the back window which reads, "I love lively cats." Maria pulls around the car and cuts it off, forcing it into a snow bank. "I wonder," she says, "if I didn't let that car off too easy."

On the way home she sees a cat running to the edge of the road. Instead of avoiding it, Maria purposely leaves the road, jumps over a ditch, slaloms around three trees, and drives through a bush to run over the cat. Then she drives around a fourth tree and realizes she's on a different road, a short cut. "I saved a good mile running over the kitty. Have to do that more often."

The Cat from Hell is undaunted, and though Maria is a greater being, The Cat vows revenge (although even I was surprised to hear cats had such an ability. Perhaps they don't really, but The Cat from Hell, well...). Still stuck in the corner, The Cat jumps onto Maria as she walks in, sinking his fangs into Maria's right arm. Maria instinctively closes the door on The Cat's tail, which briefly reminds The Cat from Hell that he's a domestic cat and not a cougar.

After stitching herself up, Maria realizes The Cat from Hell is still stuck in the door, the tail being firmly wedged into the frame. The Cat from Hell hisses and growls (rare in a cat) and is suddenly freed when Maria's roommate enters. At this point, Maria is more than slightly offended by The Cat, and she attempts to voice her irritation regarding The Cat (to her roommate) when The Cat plays hurt and practically pouts at the roommate's feet.

"Aw, poor little kitty," says the roommate (also known by some as Miss R), "how on earth did you get hurt?" While Maria is waiting to get her word in, The Cat from Hell slowly looks over at Maria, whose expression turns from "a voiced concern" to "a very angry Maria for being made the guilty one." Maria's face turns harsh, and The Cat cowers in Miss R's arms.

"What have you done to my poor kitty?" Miss R snaps at Maria.

"Me? It was your cat—THE Cat. He—"

"You should know better than to hurt my poor kitty. You're bigger than he." As Miss R stares coldly at Maria, The Cat from Hell shows a more aggressive face to Maria, unknown to Miss R.

"Look, see?" Maria says, pointing to The Cat. As Miss R turns to look at The Cat, he cowers and plays innocent.

"See? I certainly do see! My kitty is frightened to death—and it looks like you hurt his tail. You're paying for the vet bill, Maria."

With that, Miss R stomps into her room with The Cat in arms. Before vanishing from sight, The Cat from Hell gives Maria a devilish smile in triumph. With a last effort, Maria hurls a banana at The Cat, only to watch it land on Miss R's head.

"You're skating on thin ice, girl."

Maria calmly hums to herself as she draws a picture of The Cat. As she prepares dinner, she "accidentally-on-purpose" lets the gas burner ignite the picture into complete flames. The ashes sprinkle gently over the chili (tonight's supper), and Maria takes a sip. Mmmmmmmmm.

Sugar for You, Carrots for Me

March 8, 1992

Walk with me, I cannot run.
Talk for me, I cannot speak.
A simple cry is the voice I make,
Who shall decide the path I take?

I suppose I never gave much thought to the unfortunate ones, thinking a bad thing was to buy a music album and after a few go-rounds decide it as poor artistry. I'd seen the television commercials showing the South American poor and thinking little of it. Why shouldn't the government of those countries better themselves? Don't the donations to those "help groups" go mainly for the paper-pushers? No matter, to prove my point (as part of a bet with a drinking buddy of mine), I sent a $1 donation to the Oversees Relief Foundation (ORF).

It was a joke for certain, and I laughed heartily as I put my airmail stamp on the envelope. I was certain I'd never hear from the people again—a case of beer was riding on it. A week passed, then two. I was victorious, I knew, but to be safe we'd agreed on a six-week turnaround time. My buddy had originally suggested five, but I was foolishly generous and went the extra seven days.

It was my undoing. I cursed myself, I'm positive, but my buddy thought otherwise.

"You plain lost!" he said in jubilation.

"Can you believe it?" I asked in surprise. "They actually responded to my one-dollar donation. The cost for postage plus the administrative fee is more than that! It just doesn't make sense."

"You're a generous person, both to them and to me. Thanks for the case of brews."

"Yeah, yeah, yeah. My wife will get 'em for you. I just can't figure it."

"Well don't just stand there like a bump on a log. Open the letter."

"This? Junk mail. It goes with the empty brewski cans—in the *garr-bazh*." I tossed the unopened envelope toward the can. Buddy caught it at the last second.

"C'mon. You paid the dollar, after all. Let's see...ooooooh, boy, 'Thank you for your contribution to ORF. Your money goes toward—'"

"Ok, ok. You've proved your point. Look, I'll get the brews for you myself. You won. You wanna watch the game on TV or not?"

"Aw, they're asking you to sponsor a child," Buddy said while continuing to look through the literature.

"Talk about rubbing it in. The game—"

Buddy wouldn't let up.

"'Leesha is six and needs a sponsor to help her get adequate food and medicine so she can stay in school. She likes to draw and is very spirited considering her surroundings. Leesha's younger sister, Juanita, is four and likes to draw too. Juanita would like to be a ballerina when she grows up, but her hopes will die unless she gets a sponsor.'"

"They go after you the same way, every one of 'em," I shot back. "They try to make you feel guilty, like you're blessed or something." I wasn't going to let some sob story rattle my bones.

"'Fifty cents a day will make the difference between hope and despair for Leesha and Juanita. That's only $3.50 a week, hardly enough to buy a loaf of bread and a quart of milk in the States.' You know, they're right—$3.50 is just pocket change these days. Just think, you supported Leesha and Juanita for two whole days. How happy they must have been! I almost wish I were in your shoes."

"Take 'em!" I said, tossing my shoes to him.

"Funny guy. You haven't heard a word I've said, have you?"

"Sure I have. I gave you my shoes, didn't I?"

"No, about Leesha and Juanita. You and the Mrs. could be foster parents. Didn't you say you wanted children?"

"Yeah, but I want my own, not some I don't even know. Kids living in some poor country—I don't even wanna hear about their problems. We got enough here as it is. The economy, the crime—"

"Hi, Buddy," said my wife as she walked in. "I thought you boys were gonna watch the game." She was drying off a saucer dish.

"We're just going over—" I tried to say, but Buddy cut me off.

"Did you see the photo?" Buddy was winding up.

"Photo? What photo?" She walked over and looked. "Ooooo, look at them. Aw, they're so cute!"

"Leesha and Juanita—ole Romeo here is sponsoring them," Buddy said, motioning toward me.

"All right, that's enough. I've had it with this 'sponsorship' crap. This was just a plain and simple bet. You won. It's as simple as that. Now, if you're gonna keep makin' a fuss about it all, I think YOU should sponsor the two South Americans. Just one more thing..." I ran to the fridge and back. "Here's your beer. Now why don't you just take the beer and the Latinos and go home."

I left Buddy standing there and walked in the living room, turned on the television, and watched the game. I briefly heard Buddy's voice in the background then silence. My wife stood in the doorway for a moment, wanted to say something to me, but she didn't. She went back to her dishes.

"It's one big scam," I tried to explain to my wife later.

"Of course," she said at the dinner table.

"Besides, I'm not responsible for other countries' problems. I'm but one person. We have enough to worry about here at home."

"Absolutely," she concurred.

"You're just saying that, aren't you? Like Buddy, I bet you think I'm stodgy. Don't you?"

"Oh honey," she said, walking over to me. "Don't be silly. Besides, I have some good news." She sat next to me in a side chair.

"Good news? Did we win the lottery?"

"Much better than that. We're going to have a baby!"

I sat in silence.

"This is a surprise. When did you find out?"

"Yesterday afternoon at the doctor's. I was a little concerned because I was late. Then I was feeling a little sick—the flu, remember? We're going to have a baby! I'm so happy! Aren't you happy, dear?"

"A baby. Well, I suppose it's about time."

"Oh silly, at least pretend you're happy." The wife was very ecstatic, I was melancholy. I wasn't particularly excited about a new family member, but some things in life gotta be done, so I supposed it was my turn.

"Well, it will be good to have a little person around."

"I knew you were happy." She gave me a hug.

Within the next few weeks I had insisted the wife have the fetus tested for various anomalies. I was very suspicious when the doctor wanted to test me as well.

"What is it, doc?" I asked. The wife and I were seated in his office.

"There's good news and bad news."

"Oh really?" I asked. "What's the good news?"

"Due to advanced technology, we were able to test for a very wide range of possible problems. Unfortunately we found one. Your unborn son has CF."

"CF?"

"Cystic fibrosis."

"How serious is this?" I asked. "I mean, what will our son expect to go through?"

"Your son can expect to have difficulty breathing. Also, he will have a hard time absorbing nutrients properly. This is due to the abnormally thick mucus which will develop in his respiratory and gastrointestinal tracts. He also will be highly susceptible to respiratory infections."

"There must be some mistake. How can you be sure?" the wife asked.

"I suppose there is a chance for a miracle, and with modern therapeutic methods one could almost believe in miracles, but I assure you, your baby has CF. Chromosome 7 contains the defective gene, and both parents must have a defective copy of it. That's why we made the additional tests—to confirm the condition."

"Are you saying we're defective?" I retorted.

"Now be calm. It's quite common for people to carry recessive genes. Only by some rare bad luck do these things happen. With modern treatment, there's a fifty percent chance your boy will live to age thirty."

"Fifty percent? So if he's lucky, he'll live to thirty. If not he'll die—probably in childhood." I was upset.

"It's not that bad. Research is very close to providing a cure. Although treated CF patients would be carriers, they could enjoy perfectly normal lives. There's a good chance this cure will come about during the course of your son's lifetime."

"And if not?" I asked. "If not, he'll fight a daily struggle to survive."

Enraged, I left with the wife. She was in tears and sobbed the entire way home. I slouched in my easy chair, staring into space. The wife came in.

"Why? Why have we been cursed?" I blurted out.

"I don't care what the doctor says," she said. "I'm gonna have this baby, and we'll work out everything."

"Are you crazy?" I couldn't believe what she was saying. "Do you realize what that means? The insurance won't cover the medical payments for CF. Hell, my sanity won't hold up. There's only one option—we'll have to have an abortion and try again."

"Kill my baby? What are you, a murderer?"

"Is it murder? When a mother dog discovers one of her pups is deformed, does she nurture it and take care of it? No, she digs a hole and buries the pup alive. We're not talking about killing a self-sufficient baby—it's just a fetus inside of you, incapable of living on its own at this point. Can you feel right about bringing pain into this world for everyone involved? That baby will require constant attention and will never get better."

"But the doctor said there's hope," she said.

"Yeah, like he can wave a magic wand and make the world a perfect place. The world isn't perfect, dear. We can't have this baby. Say, where are you going?"

"I'm leaving you."

"What?? You are NOT leaving. Don't lose your head. Give yourself a day or two to cool off."

"Forget it. I'm leaving!"

I couldn't believe it. She left me. Just like that, she left me. I spent a week trying to figure out what had happened. Maybe I was wrong, maybe I was too cruel. Naw, it was her. To make matters worse, ORF continued sending me literature, asking for further contributions. I then realized the wife had sponsored some South American twins behind my back. That was just like her. I tore the request to shreds and burned it.

After a month, I realized the problem wasn't going away. Each day that passed meant the fetus was developing more and more. In time she'd have the baby. It was futile to change her mind—I would have to sacrifice my dreams and put up with a CF baby.

"I'm sorry," I said to her over the phone. "After much soul searching, I've come to realize how inhuman I was. You were right," I said. She was hesitant at first, and it took a few more phone calls to convince her of my sincerity. I wasn't really sincere, but I had to do something to get her back. Eventually, she moved back in.

Trying not to cause any further tension, I had paid the monthly contribution for ORF, and every so often I received progress reports on the twins as well as receiving some of their artwork. I had set those aside, and the wife resumed the contributions following her return.

The wife's labor was average in length, I'm told, and she was in some pain until the doctor gave her a spinal. The baby cried and cried, and though the wife was allowed to hold him for a few minutes, the baby was rushed off to intensive care to clean out his lungs.

"What's his name?" we were asked.

"Bert Andrew Franklin," the wife said. I wondered how many years of torture we'd asked for.

The first month was rough. I took a week off from work to help get things going. The wife's mother came down and helped after my vacation time was used up, and we joined a CF support group. I didn't realize how many others had the same feelings as I regarding the difficulties. After several more months, I learned to accept my situation, though I had to take on a weekend job to pay for the medication (which wasn't as bad as I'd first imagined).

As the doctor had warned, Lil' Bert had a difficult time during the flu season. During his first winter, he was constantly sick, and several times we took him to emerg. On the surface, I showed genuine concern for Lil' Bert's health, but in the back of my mind I hoped he would be taken away quickly, and each trip to the hospital was another opportunity for Lil' Bert to say goodbye. However, he had a will to survive which surprised me.

His first birthday passed, then his second, his third. Lil' Bert wasn't so little anymore, and he was learning to speak and to draw, including some crayon work on the living room wall. I wanted to spank him but didn't want the wife to see me—Bert was too fragile to handle any kind of significant shock. However, I did manage to convince him to draw something on some paper, and I sent the paper to the South American twins. The twins in turn sent us some of their artwork and even wrote some short messages in English.

Bert celebrated his sixth birthday with unusual coughing and a fever. The wife took him to our family doctor who in turn sent Bert to the hospital. Bert had come down with viral pneumonia, and a secondary staph infection had set in. Bert was on several different antibiotics, but the years of being on them had allowed staph bacteria to evolve with an immunity to the antibodies. Bert was fighting a desperate struggle. The bacteria grew rapidly, and as the wife and I stood by his hospital bed, Bert died.

For the first time since the wife was pregnant, I was sorry to see Bert die. I know, after I had first learned of Bert's CF, I wanted him dead. But after the years of work and the few joyful moments Bert gave us, I was sorry it came to an end. There would be no one again like Bert—he, like everyone else, is unique.

What would have been Bert's seventh birthday passed, empty. The wife couldn't stop crying, and I kept staring out the window, wondering, just wondering.

An interesting letter came from the CF support group which I was about to throw away (since it was no longer necessary), but I decided against it and opened the envelope.

"This year the U.S. Post Office is doing a special stamp series on children in need. Drawings from such children will be submitted, and a random selection of drawings will be printed for the Christmas season."

It seemed rather worthless with Bert being gone. I couldn't bear to part with any of his artwork—each one was too precious. I read the letter a second time. I paused, thinking. A thought occurred, and I searched through my old letters looking for something, anything to send to the Post Office. In a letter from the South American twins, I found what I was looking for.

A Grand-Mawl Visit

March 9, 1992

Let me introduce my family. My name is Jacob Richardson. My wife, Helen, joins me with my two sons, Bobby and Johnny. The boys are six and five, respectively. Helen and I are in our young thirties. We recently purchased a four-bedroom house in a removed subdivision. Life has been good for my small family, and up to this point things have gone quite well.

One summer, Helen asked if we might visit my parents. She had only seen them once at our wedding, and since that happy day of my life, only I would visit my parents—Helen would take the boys and visit her parents (who live ten miles west of mine). Helen could never understand my insistence of solely visiting my parents.

"We should visit them as a family for a change, don't you think dear?" she asked.

"I really wish you'd reconsider," I cautioned. "My parents—well, they're my parents."

"And I have parents. You've met mine. I've met yours. I think your parents are nice enough people, at least that's the impression I got when I met them. C'mon, what do you say?"

"Ok. Two days. Then we're off for the summer resort."

"Two days? Well I suppose it will have to do. I was hoping maybe three—"

"No. Two."

"Ok, ok!"

It was settled. Bobby and Johnny would see their grandparents, and Helen would see her parents-in-law. Perhaps I was clinging onto old feelings—the ones I'd had from childhood. It was silly, really, 'cause Helen and I were mature adults.

The trip. As in other years, Bobby and Johnny seemingly needed to make bathroom stops every twenty miles, and at other times were asking, "How much farther?" Helen, on the other hand, was a true god-send. She managed to keep the boys somewhat in control, and when I grew fatigued from driving, she took over. It's only an eight-hour drive to my parents' house, but I can't drive the whole way on my own, not like I used to when I was twenty (and boy were those the days, but that's a different story). So Helen drove during the middle stretch, and I drove the last half-hour (seeing as I knew the way best).

I tried sneaking along the driveway quietly, but my parents have a loose concrete slab which makes an audible "chunk" as a car drives over. It's the automatic doorbell.

"Well hallo, 'dere Jacob!" My mother couldn't wait, she was so excited. Flapping her jaw and waving her arms, she lumbered across the lawn to greet us.

"Hi, Maw. Just got in," I said, trying to be short.

"And ya brought da fam-lee. What a shur-prizh!"

The family jumped out of the car quickly.

"Maw, you remember my wife, Helen? Then there are the boys, Bobby and Johnny. Boys, say hello to your grandmaw."

"Hi, grandmawl," they said in unison.

"Johnny and Bobby. Or is it Bobby and Johnny? Ya boyzh look sho much alike. And Helen. How are ya, shweetie?"

"I'm fine, thank you. Should I call you Mother? Mom?"

"Maw, I'm maw to you, grandmaw to the boyzh, right boyzh?"

"Yes, Grandmawl." The boys kept adding the "l" to "Grandma," but matter it not.

"Well come on in. I 'shpect y'all wanna eat." Maw led us inside with a wildly waving arm and a hurried gait.

"Actually, we ate just half an hour ago," commented Helen. It was a casual comment, and Helen thought nothing of it until...

"What do ya mean? Jacob? Is this true?" She gave me her worst scolding look. Maw's relaxed voice turned a bit cold and crisp.

"Maw, I told you we were eating out before arriving," I said, defending unsuspecting Helen.

"Nonsense. There's nothin' better than a home-cooked meal. What happened, boay, did Helen tell you to go out? You know better."

I didn't think it possible, but Maw was the same as before I'd left home. Helen looked at me with surprise and nearly laughed (thinking it all a joke).

"Pappy, they're here," Maw called out.

"Well, well, now. How're ye doing there, Jacob? And Helen, it's been a long time. These are the young-uns?"

"Yep, Pappy, that's them," Maw said, cutting us off. Bobby and Johnny started exploring the house. "Hey, you too. Get back here," Maw called out, but the boys couldn't be bothered. "Boy I tell ya, in my day I'd get a horse whipping for not answering an elder. Jacob, don't you discipline your boys enough?"

"My boys are quite good. Helen and I give them lots of love, which is as good as anything."

"Poppycock. 'Spare the rod and spoil the child,' my mother used to say. Those boys could use a switchin' every now and a-gin. Keep 'em on their toes."

Helen and I sat down in the living room, though I could tell Maw was disappointed. She wanted us to eat, but I was too tired to do much but loaf. Paw sat down in his easy-chair with pipe and newspaper in hand, and Maw sat in her favorite rocking chair. Presently, she struck up a conversation with Helen while faint voices from the boys hummed in the distance. Maw and Paw lived in the same house where I grew up. It was mid-sized with modest furnishings, but years of sunlight had bleached the carpet and parts of the couch. As Maw eagerly questioned Helen, I glanced around the room. Not much had changed, though dust seemed to accumulate on the flat surfaces. Suddenly, Helen sneezed, not just once but several times.

"Hey there, are you catchin' cold?" Maw asked. Paw looked up from his paper.

"No, I don't think so. It must be the du—"

"Well it certainly sounded like evil spirits to me. Hold on a second, I'll be right back."

"All right, dear?" I asked, quietly.

"I don't know. I think maybe it's a little dusty," she replied.

"More like a lot dusty. Doesn't look like this house has been dusted in years."

"Here you are, sweetie. I have a home remedy for things like this—it'll put you back to normal quicker than lightning. Open wide!"

Maw held a medicine bottle in one hand, and a big, soup-sized spoon filled with a cherry-colored medicine in the other.

"Really, I'm fine."

"Nonsense. You're obviously catchin' a bug. Take it!"

"Jacob, explain to your mother how—"

"Jacob doesn't have to explain anything. Drink up or else!" Maw had cut me off again. She was very determined to get her way. Reluctantly, Helen swallowed the medicine. Her face turned green instantly as I could tell the medicine had a horrible taste.

"There, good girl," said Maw.

"Yech," said Helen. She clutched her throat for a moment then put a hand to her stomach.

"So how long ya stayin', Jacob?" Maw asked.

Helen had originally suggested two days (which meant sleeping over one or two nights). However, I could tell Helen's demeanor had changed, and she would have left then and there if common courtesy wouldn't have been violated.

"Well," I started, "we planned on staying tonight and tomorrow. The day after tomorrow, we want an early start."

"A day-n-a-half? Why, you'll miss your sister, Angie, who's comin' into town. She just divorced her second husband, don't you know, and she'll be comin' in three days. Couldn't you stay a week so you two could visit? She really misses you and hardly ever gets to see you. Won't you stay?"

"Well..." I said, trying to smooth the reply. Helen gave me a dirty look, as if to say she'd kill me if I agreed to a week.

"It's all settled. A week. Angie will be so happy. Now, I'll have to go shopping tomorrow to get some things. Helen, you *will* be a dear and go with me. Thank you. And Jacob, I'm sure

Pappy has some projects around the house he'd like for you to do, isn't that right, Pappy?"

"What dear?" he said foggily. He was engrossed in the paper. Maw slapped the paper away.

"Pay attention when I'm talkin' to you. I said, don't you have some projects around the house for Jacob to do?"

"Oh, sure. Sure thing. Bright and early tomorrow."

"Your parents really *are* off their rockers," Helen started to say as we readied for sleep.

"Shhh. Don't say that too loudly. The walls are paper-thin," I cautioned.

"Are we really staying a week? Why don't we just leave tomorrow—make up some excuse and be on our way?"

"What would you have me say?" I asked her. "That work called and asked me to be back a week early?"

"That's not a bad idea. Work would seem relaxing compared to this," a little knock at the door, "who could that be?" Helen said, going up to the door and letting Johnny in. "What's the matter, dear?"

"Mommy, something's wrong with Bobby. He keeps tossing and turning and gasping for breath," Johnny explained.

Helen motioned me out of bed, and we walked over to where Johnny and Bobby were set up for the night. Sure enough, Johnny was struggling as Bobby had described.

"I...I can't breathe," Johnny tried to say. "I itch all over." A gentle moonbeam shone on his confused face.

"What's goin' on here?" came a voice as the lights went on. Everyone but Maw squinted the light out. "That boy's got da az-ma, don't he? Just like you when you were a boy, Jacob. I'll get that home brew I used to use back then. That'll cure you, Johnny."

"Now wait a minute," interrupted Helen. "I've seen this on my nursing rounds—Johnny is having an allergic reaction. What kind of bed is he sleeping on?"

"Why nothing but the best," came back Maw, as if Helen had no right talking like that. "A feather pillow, cotton sheets, and a wool blanket. Nothin' but the best."

"That settles it. We should get him to the hospital immediately, Jacob. He's ready to go into systemic anaphylaxis."

"He'll be fine," came back Maw with her medicine bottle and soup-sized spoon. "Just take this."

Helen couldn't stop the lightning movements of Maw. She had the medicine down Johnny's throat quicker than you could say, "Jack Sprat," and was busily rubbing some strong-smelling jelly on Johnny's chest. A couple of pillows were re-arranged to prop Johnny's head up, and in a few minutes he was asleep.

"Works every time," said Maw. Helen moved toward Johnny to examine him, but Maw pulled her away. "No girly, don't bother the young-un now. Let him sleep. And you should get back to sleep too."

Helen was quite upset, and I less so, but Maw pushed us back into our room for the night. I could tell Helen was agitated, but I asked her to wait 'till morning, then we'd inform Maw we were leaving. Helen gave a sigh of relief, and we fell asleep.

Sometime during the night, Helen writhed in pain, clutching her right calf. "Cramp," she mumbled as she pounded her fist against the contracted muscle. I spent half an hour massaging the sore calf before she could get to sleep. I didn't dare get up for aspirin for fear of Maw coming in and making a big fuss.

"Rise 'n shine! Rise 'n shine. Get up you two," shouted Maw at 5 am. "Git up now." She kept going around the house, then started banging her largest spoon against a skillet as she made the rounds. As she passed our room, she opened the door and banged the skillet several times. "Up 'n at 'em!"

"What time is it?" yawned Helen dreamily as she rolled over toward me. I didn't have to look at the clock—I knew Maw's tactics.

"Five. It's five in the morning."

"What is she doing?" Helen complained to me. "She's like...controlling our every movement. I'm getting a headache. Let's call it off now."

"Oh, she's just trying to be helpful. Besides, we can't leave without a breakfast. I'll make a phone call back home and pretend an emergency occurred at work. Then we'll go home."

Breakfast went smoothly enough as I got up to make the phone call. As I picked up the receiver, I noticed it was dead. I searched around for the phone wire to ensure its connection when Maw came in.

"Whatcha lookin' for, Jacob?"

"I'm trying to get your phone working," I replied.

"It'll do you no good. No phones."

"What?"

"We had a tiff with one of 'dem operators at the phone company, and we decided to drop service. Trying to call someone?"

"Yeah, I'm supposed to check in at work to make sure the computer is working fine."

"I knew I raised you right—always a hard worker, even when on vacation. Relax Jacob, enjoy yourself."

"No really, I gotta call in—"

"Now you sit yerself back down and finish yer breakfast. Gotta have food for the long day's work." Maw just wouldn't let up. Before I could utter another word, she was in the other room. "Git yerself together, Helen, we're goin' to the store," I heard her say in the background.

"Haven't you told her yet?" Helen mumbled to me upon walking in.

"No, the phone doesn't work, and—"

"What's holding you up, girly?" yelled Maw.

"If you don't do something, I will," said Helen. She was getting angry at me.

"Look, I'll tell her, just give me some time."

"She's going to drag me to the store if you don't tell her now," came back Helen.

"Ok, tell her. I'll gather the kids together."

I rushed over to Bobby and Johnny, helping them pack when the walls shook.

"WHAT?" bellowed Maw. She marched quickly to my location. "What is this, Jacob? What's this nonsense about leaving?"

"I'm sorry, Maw, but we gotta. Our plans will be—"

"Plans nothing! Angie will be here in the next few days, and I won't hear of you missing her." Maw was very upset. I carried the boys' suitcases out to the car while Maw followed.

"Really, I had no intention of staying that long," I said.

"Is that so? You led me on to think otherwise. Well, we'll see about this, right here and now." She stomped off, and in my free moment I made a dash for the car. Amazingly, Helen had grabbed the other suitcases and had the trunk open. With blinding speed I threw the cases in, put the boys in back, and jumped into the front while Helen jumped in her side. As I fought to get the right key in, Maw came out.

"Start the car," said Helen. I was mesmerized by Maw. "Start the car!" urged Helen.

"Listen here, Jacob," yelled Maw as she approached. "Don't let that Helen boss you around. You're my boy. Listen to me. Stay awhile."

Helen was going insane. "Start the car, NOW!"

It was too late. Maw had opened my door and pulled me out. "You're making a big mistake," Maw said.

"Not on your life, sister," came back Helen. She jumped out my door, shoved Maw back, threw me in through the driver's side, and I landed in the passenger seat. Helen jumped in, closed the door, locked it, turned on the car, and while Maw clawed at the car, Helen pushed the shifter into reverse and popped the clutch, squealing the tires and forcing Maw to follow, which she did (which amazed me—I didn't think Maw could run so quickly). The boys were cheering Helen on, saying, "Yeah Mommy, push the pedal to the metal!" Helen hit the brakes and made a quick Y-turn with all four tires in harmonious squeal. In the same motion, she had the car in first, more tire squealing, and we were gone, knocking over my parents' mailbox on the way.

Helen's eyes were determined and focused dead ahead—she didn't even flinch. After the initial shock, I opened my mouth to speak, hesitated, then decided against it. The boys were still saying, "Go Mommy, go!" when she said, "Sometimes it's best not to talk too much."

Aside the Rushing Water

March 10, 1992

Greta was perhaps seven years old as she sat on the stream's bank, watching the water flow past. She was but a lone figure, small, and fair-skinned. She threw a single pebble into the stream. Plop. Ripples travelled for a few feet before dissolving. Next, she threw a stick and watched it float slowly by.

This was one of Greta's few quiet spots. From behind she could hear the yells and screams come from her house, where she knew her parents were fighting yet again. She had no brothers, no sisters, and no real friends (certainly no one to reassure her that her situation was anything but normal). More yells. Sounds of breaking glass. Greta threw a leaf into the water—it too floated by. Another scream. Greta threw a pebble into the stream—plop. Plop, onto Greta's head. Another plop. Drops from heaven came down, and it began to rain. Greta didn't care, and seeing how no one bothered to call her in, she stayed outside and threw more pebbles, sticks, and leaves into the stream. The yells grew stronger then died down. The screams stopped. A moment later, squealing tires left fresh rubber on Greta's driveway as an angry father drove away.

Greta was a quiet girl sitting by the stream. At times she wished life were as peaceful as the water rushing past or the water sprinkling on her forehead. It was not to be. Greta lived with violence, a violence she could neither understand nor accept, and her only means of existence, her only means of survival came when sitting next to the stream.

A swift hand grabbed her from the back, the swift hand of a police officer. Several squad cars parked in front of Greta's house as she was taken through the back yard and placed in the back seat of a car. Many people of supposed importance walked through the yard, some even stepping on Greta's mother's precious flowers. Greta yelled out to them, but only deaf ears listened—Greta was alone.

Greta couldn't understand why she was no longer allowed to live at home. An Aunt picked her up and tried bringing her up according to the strict rules of her house, but Greta could not grow—inside she was dead. Officially, Greta was told her mother had gone to heaven, and Father had driven off, never to be seen again.

Greta wished to be with her mother, the only person she felt close to. "Mommy," she would say to herself before going to sleep each night, "I wanna be with you in heaven." Greta thought perhaps she heard a voice saying, "yes," but she couldn't be sure. She dreamed of her mother nightly only to wake up and find she was really gone.

Never could Greta conform to her aunt's rules. Repeatedly she received punishments for failures. Greta was alone.

One wintry day, Greta discovered her aunt's pill bottles, her tranquilizers. Greta knew her aunt called them "sleeping pills," and Greta thought how nice it would be to go to sleep and see her mother in Heaven. On the way home from school, Greta crossed a wooden bridge overlooking a stream, the stream that ran behind her house. Several ice rafts floated by. The barren trees moved with but a murmur in the wind. The sun was going to sleep early, too early. Light faded. Greta swallowed the bottle's contents, stepped over the railing, and took a step into the air, falling several feet into the icy waters below. The sun set, the air grew still, and Greta joined her mother—in Hell.

Cries of the Marmalade Kitten

March 19, 1992

One.

I was only seven when Father died. The accident, the mourning, and the funeral left Henry Stradt six feet under the earth's surface, resting in a concrete-enclosed casket. Death was unknown to me until that day—I imagined other people could die, but not anyone from my family. It's difficult to remember those times—as I said, I was only seven.

My only memories of Father center around our time in the back yard. On some days we'd play with our dog, Ginger, and her puppies. Other days he'd help me build sand castles in the box he'd built especially for me when I was three. Then there were days he'd tell me stories whilst I swung on the swing set. Some were about gallant knights in a faraway land fighting battles against organized empires. This led to the tales of Robin Hood, and Father would change his voice as if he were Mr. Hood himself. He'd swing his arm as if holding a sword, and speak of taking from the rich to feed the poor.

Often on the weekends we'd go to the park. I used to get sick to my stomach on the ride where I'd go 'round and 'round, so I didn't ride that one too much. The swings were fun, because I could go much higher than the one at home. I guess the best part was the nature trails along a path I know has a different purpose, but Father would tell his own tales, often making things up on the spot. There were these posts along the way with numbers, and at each one Father would pause and say something like, "Here stood Prince Wellyman when approached by Gelzireeb the Black. Gelzireeb attacked first, slashing his sword at the Prince but missed and gashed this rock." He would then point to a rather large rock that did in fact look like a sword had gashed it. Other things in the woods he would include—the flying squirrels were given their flight when the Prince's wizard, Mizerin, cast a spell on the hundred squirrels which were captured by Gelzireeb's brother, Takireeb the Red, and were to be slaughtered needlessly as Takireeb's show of power. The squirrels took flight from near death and attacked Takireeb, sending him over a cliff. Gelzireeb was upset and sought revenge on the Prince but was driven away when the Prince called out to his mountain eagles.

In our last outings, Father actually became Prince Wellyman, and I Mizerin the Wizard. I carried a short stick as a magic wand; Father carried a large limb as a sword. Together, we fought the evil of the forest, making friends with the animals along the way. We'd save our instruments for each outing, and I grew quite fond of my magic wand.

Some children are afraid of the dark when they go to sleep. I was reassured, because Father would tuck me in and ask me to cast a spell to clear the night air of evil spirits. I waved my wand in the air a few times and cast the spirits out. Father kissed me goodnight, and I dreamed of adventures in faraway England.

Mother, on the other hand, spent her days cleaning house and feeding us. She was always working hard, and always very tired. When Father would come home, I'd see little of her, just as I would then see little of my two older brothers, Han and Phil. Father never spent the time with them as he did with me. Han and Phil were fraternal twins, each four when I was born, so being eleven when I was seven; and always getting into trouble or so I thought. Sometimes when I was thought to be asleep, I could hear their whimperings two rooms down broken by the occasional smack of leather on their skins. I never learned what they did to earn the whippings, and I never asked.

I can remember the final month before Father's death. It was December. I had finished my first half-year of second grade and was sitting by the fire when my mother hurriedly answered the phone. She was a little worried about Father, and I was sad too—he had promised to take me out to ice cream after dinner. Dinner was over, and bedtime had gone by without Mother saying a word to me. Han and Phil were in the basement, I think. I'm not sure what they were doing—up to no good I suppose.

Mother was silent on the phone then screamed. Her screams reverberated up and down my spine, causing goose bumps to cover my skin. I shivered and moved closer to the fire, warming my hands. I'd never heard her scream like that, ever. Mother's screams changed to cries, then wails. She slumped down in a chair and sobbed for several minutes. Frightened, I gingerly walked over to her.

"What's the matter, Mommy?"

She moaned again and gathered me quickly in her arms, holding onto me for dear life. Mother didn't speak—she kept sobbing and holding me. I could feel her shake in misery, and I was scared. What was wrong? Why couldn't she tell me? I would cry when I fell and scraped my knees, but Father or Mother wouldn't cry when they got hurt. Usually I'd hear them say words I didn't understand, and their faces would show they'd been hurt, but they'd be fine after a few minutes.

"Billy," she said after some time, "it's your father." I knew something was horribly wrong and was afraid to hear more. Her tone changed: "Henry! No, no, no, don't leave me like this!"

Mother ran off to her room while I stood next to the phone, thinking I was in some sort of dream. Several people came by shortly afterward (including a police officer), and I heard the official announcement—Father was dead. I didn't learn the details of the accident at the time—but I think Han and Phil knew. They didn't cry though; they had sadistic smiles on their faces. I was sad, confused, and angry.

The casket was closed, so the last time I saw my father was the morning of his death before he left for work. I didn't know caskets were usually open to allow the surviving family a last look at the deceased. I learned that later, much later. Throughout the funeral, Phil and Han acted as if it were a party, running around and making lots of noise. Mother had fainted five or six times since the initial shock and was nearly insane with distress. I, though previously a talkative and lively child, had completely withdrawn into a silent boy, communicating only by my tears and whimperings.

There weren't many people at the funeral—mostly adult people I didn't know and some relatives from Father's side. Mother was an only child, so only her mother could attend (her father had died when she was sixteen). Heavy snow slowed the procession's progress from the funeral home to the cemetery. Han and Phil were throwing snowballs at each other while I watched the final moments of Father's vault being lowered into his grave.

"Good-bye, Prince Wellyman."

Two.

I don't think Mother was ever the same. We stayed in our suburban house for a bit, but Mother was forced to find work. No longer could we afford the niceties we had before. Mother sold the cars and caught rides into town. She sold her prized china, sold her silver, her jewelry—nearly everything. In six months the house was for sale, in nine we lived in the city. Mother spoke less, baked less, and lived less.

Meanwhile, Han and Phil acted as if they were in paradise. After school they'd wander about the neighborhood—Mother had two jobs and was never home 'till late—and often I was home by myself. I was scared much of the time, but Mother couldn't afford to have someone take care of us, and in one of the few times she really spoke to us, she stressed the need NOT to let anyone know she wasn't around to watch us.

Our apartment had but two bedrooms. Phil and Han were in one, while I slept on a sleeping bag on the floor of Mother's room. As winter approached, the apartment became colder— Mother couldn't afford much for heat. I'd wrap my sleeping bag around me and sit in a corner, sit, sit, sit. I did a lot of daydreaming, harkening back to my journeys in the woods with Father, reliving my role as the wizard.

My eighth birthday (October 2nd) came and went—Mother had forgotten, or perhaps she was ashamed she didn't have the money for gifts. It was remembered at school in the form of eight paddle smacks on my rear. I was in the third grade, and the kids were generally rougher than the ones I knew from the suburbs. One girl, Melinda Glover, gave me a book when no one was looking—*Winnie the Pooh*. Melinda smiled when she gave it to me, and I thanked her, which was more said than the last sixth months spoken at home.

I had something new to do when I came home from school—reading. Although only in the third grade, I discovered reading was the one way I could escape my misery and jump into the pages so to speak, whether it be with Hansel and Gretel or the many other stories we read in class. Often I'd read ahead in the workbook and learn more difficult words. Reading was the only class where I excelled.

I became Christopher Robin, and my best friend was Pooh. I reread Melinda's gift over and over again. After a few months, the book was engraved in my head, and I would see the pages as I drifted to sleep each night.

Christmas was just as miserable as my birthday. Mother had the day off from work, but she slept most of the day while Han and Phil ran off to look for a Christmas tree. Several hours had passed before they returned with a small cedar tree they'd cut down from the small woods next to our school. I went up to touch it, but Han pulled me back forcefully.

"Don't go near our tree," he shouted at me. "Why don't you go outside and get out of our way?" It had begun.

I think it was February when I slipped outside during recess and got a bloody nose. I was a frail boy in those days, not having much to eat. I spent half an hour in the nurse's office trying to make it stop. It was then I decided I didn't want to go out for recess anymore. I pleaded with my teacher to let me stay in the library, and seeing my distraught condition she agreed. The library was better for me since there were fewer children in there during recess. I found myself jumping into other books, living the lives of *Encyclopedia Brown* or the *Hardy Boys*. The librarian, Ms. Miller, was very helpful when I asked her if there were any more *Encyclopedia Brown* books. I think she ordered more on my behalf, because I came in one day and there were more of the collection on the shelf.

As I said, my school lunches were my largest meals. We were on the free lunch program, and I ate as much as possible to the point of asking fellow classmates for their peas and carrots, or lima beans, or spinach, which they eagerly gave to me. Often I'd put a roll or Twinkie in my pocket and save it for home. Other times I'd put chicken or turkey scraps in a sandwich bag I saved for such a purpose and ate what I thought was a king's meal at home.

I was coming home from school on April 1st when a fat classmate made some funny April Fool's joke, and seeing how I didn't laugh, he promptly beat me up. I lay on the ground for a few moments, stunned with a bloody nose, then cried my way in a run for home. The next day at school I asked Ms. Miller if she knew of any other way to get to Douglas Street (where I lived), and she showed me a map of the area. It was then I noticed the woods behind the school provided an alternate route.

That afternoon, I made the trip through the woods. It was scary, because I didn't know the right way through. There was a path I followed at first, but it forked, and I took the left path which led me several blocks past my home. The second afternoon I took the right path, but that wasn't good either. The third afternoon I took the left path but made a new path, cutting through several bushes and much plant growth. That's when I got poison ivy. It itched and itched and nearly drove me crazy, but after a week it was gone, and I learned to avoid the infamous three-leafed plant.

I think it was May when Mother decided I could no longer spend the nights in her room. I was upset and didn't want to move in with Han and Phil, but she gave me no choice. Han and Phil grinned from ear to ear while I moved my things. I didn't have much, just a sleeping bag, a pillow, my *Winnie* books, and a couple of *Encyclopedia Brown* books borrowed from the school library. Han and Phil had bunk beds, Mother had a bed, and I was the only one without. I asked Mother if I could sleep on the living room couch, but she wouldn't hear of it.

The next few weeks went very badly in Han and Phil's room. I came home one day to find one of my Winnie books in an unflushed soiled toilet bowl, the other in pieces, its pages torn and scattered throughout the apartment. I screamed when I came home, I threatened to tell Mother what they'd done, but Han and Phil had other plans.

Over the years I've tried to forget everything Han and Phil did to me. The memories were just too difficult to bear, but I suppose I need to take one last look at it all to set things straight in my mind, that it was them and not me.

"You've done something wrong," Han would start. "When you do wrong, you are punished. This is your punishment."

"That's right," Phil continued, "Mother has put us in charge of you while she's gone. You forgot to put your sleeping bag away this morning." Phil came up to me, grabbed me by the collar, and lifted me in the air. "Are you going to put your sleeping bag away tomorrow morning?"

"Yes," I said in a strangulated voice.

"Promise?" Phil asked.

"Promise."

"Ok," Han said. "We're letting you off this time. Next time you won't be so lucky."

Phil released me, and I crumpled to the ground. I started sobbing when a sharp pain attacked my side.

"None of that sissy stuff," Phil said after his pointed boot jabbed my side. "Are you a girl or what?"

I stiffened up and stared him in the eye, but inside I was crying. I seemed to choke on the inside, to the point where I nearly vomited or suffocated, I wasn't sure which. Slowly, I reached for a single page from the *Winnie* books. I gazed at a picture showing a stuck Pooh looked on by Rabbit.

"Ow," I said, "you're hurting me." Phil's foot wedged my fingers against the floor.

"What do you think you're doing? You're not reading that garbage, are you?"

"M-m-ma-my book."

"Forget it. It's history. And unless you clean up this mess, you'll be history."

At first I couldn't believe what had happened. I wanted to tell Mother, but she was never around, seemingly, and Han and Phil had threatened to "punish" me if I didn't keep quiet. It became important, then, to avoid them as much as possible.

Three.

It seems as soon as I found something to cling onto, some-one or something ripped it away from me and took a part of me away as well—like a tree being uprooted, the roots cling on to much earth, and some roots are left behind.

Anxiety gripped me as my third grade school year came to a close. I wasn't sure how I'd survive the summer with Han and Phil at my throat. I didn't mind their kicking to wake me up during those last school mornings, because I knew school provided a safe haven for me (their classes were on a distant wing from mine).

My walk through the woods gave me another escape I needed before returning home. Sometimes I'd whistle and car-ry a stick along, kicking an occasional pine cone or skipping off a fallen tree. Just a little bit from my path grew a zillion small blue flowers, and I'd pick one each day, plucking a leaf and reciting an old chestnut I'd heard in school, "She loves me, she loves me not." Somehow I managed to end up with "she loves me" which was ironic considering my circumstan-ces. Melinda Glover was the closest thing to a "love," but I think that was a passing fancy. I was grateful for the books, though. Sometimes I wonder where she is these days...

Part of my "chores" assigned to me by Han and Phil was to fetch the afternoon paper and bring it inside. Now, Mother couldn't afford a subscription, and I pointed this out, but after a couple of ear boxings, Han suggested I "borrow" the neighbor's paper on a permanent basis. I told him it was stealing, but he replied with another boxing.

"That's what you'll get if you don't bring one home," he said, and my thieving career had begun.

The first month was easy—I simply reached down for the Thompsons' paper and stuffed it casually in my bag. It was too early for them to be home, so I didn't think anything of taking their paper again on the last day of school. Easy, I thought, until a German shepherd careened around the house with silent speed and took the paper and my hand in his jaws. He took me completely by surprise, and out of wild fear I swung my bag at his face, trying to free my hand. I grunted, being too much in shock to scream, and after the third blow the dog tried maneuvering his jaw to engulf my arm, but with that my bloodied hand slipped free. I ran three steps, but he caught my pants, ripping them apart. Another blow with the bag, and a second. He let go of the pants but took the bag and paper and ran around triumphantly to the Thompsons' back yard with the same blinding speed as he came.

The hand hurt badly, too badly for me to look. The paper was gone, the bag gone, and I stood there wondering what I was to do. The warm blood flowing off my hand reminded me of the moment, and I tried wrapping a portion of my shirt around it while speeding home. Han and Phil cursed up a storm.

"You good for nothing dweezil! Where's the damn paper? What happened to your bag? What the hell did you do to your hand? Don't stand in here, you're making a mess! Stand outside until your frickin' hand stops leakin' blood."

The pain in my hand was unbelievable. It swelled, and it wouldn't stop bleeding. I felt a little tired, so I sat on the steps. Some pigeons cooed above, a train was roaring in the distance, and the moon was half full in the sky. I wished for someone to come along and help me, but it was quiet, very quiet. It was warm outside, warm enough for a T-shirt and jeans, but I suddenly felt cold and dizzy before the world went black.

"Father?" I said when my eyes opened. The blurred view of a man cleared, and I realized I was looking at a doctor.

"There there, you've taken a bad injury to your hand."

"Where am I?"

"You're at Central Memorial Hospital. What's your name?"

I froze, like a cat who'd been spotted by a predator.

"Pulse has jumped to 220 over 190," blurted a nearby nurse. "Heart beat is erratic."

"Father!" I screamed, denying my past bad memories, believing Father to be alive, calling for the only person who'd been close to me. "Father," my voice trailed after the nurse stuck a needle in my arm.

Was I sleeping? My body continued being tense, but I felt paralyzed—I couldn't scream though wanted to, couldn't move though wanted, couldn't see but could hear. Voices seemed distant but audible.

"A strange case," said one. "He has only a mild concussion, but the loss of blood may have caused brain damage."

"He's obviously delirious," said another.

"But for this long?" said the first. "No, something else is at work here, some emotional trauma being amplified by his physical trauma. Give him some time. Meanwhile, see if you can ID him."

I jumped with a start, ready to yell again at the doctor, but he was gone. Nurse too, she was gone. With the exception of the other patient in the room (on the other side of a curtain), I was alone. I looked briefly at my surroundings, I remember, but the specifics of the room were a blur, a blur but not the corner chair on which rested my clothes, neatly folded one atop another. Pulling the needle out from my arm proved painful, but a keen sense of survival instincts displaced my rational mind, forcing me into a highly aggressive mode.

Escape through the door was fruitless, as a peep around through the doorway showed me. Clothes on, a quick look through the window, an indistinguishable comment from the other patient, and I was out, down, clinging, gripping, sliding, and plop! on a refuse of aborted fetuses—a smelly venture it was.

I wasn't sure where I was nor was I sure where to go. I was in the city but in a part I'd never seen. Striking up courage, I asked a passerby how to get to Douglas Street. Passerby paused, looked at me quizzically, then gave directions resulting in a two-mile journey from the hospital.

"The runaway is back," Phil said to me upon my arrival home. He called over his shoulder, "Hey Ma, the runaway— he's back."

I shook for a moment, seeing the gleam in Phil's eyes, but Mother's presence reassured me briefly, that was until…

"Boy, where'd you get to? Get in here this minute! I've heard how you've been a bad boy—and to run away! That does it. Into the bathroom with your clothes off!"

She yanked me by arm into the bathroom, and while she forcibly removed my pants, Han appeared with a hairbrush. Mother whipped the brush's flat side against my buttocks numerous times while I screamed in pain.

"Shut up!" she said. "Unless you want me to keep going, shut up! Now get in the shower."

While the shower's roar washed away the fetal smell, I could hear Han and Phil laughing in the distance. My sobs slowed, and I came to realize perhaps I was the bad boy— Mother apparently believed it so. From then on I was determined to behave "as a good boy" and make the best of my situation. "I will obey," I thought, picking at several stitches in my hand.

Two weeks were lost in the hospital, but I made up for it with numerous favors for Han and Phil. Mother had taken on a part-time summer job to supplement earnings, leaving us home alone more often than not. Han and Phil were happy for my willing servitude, and I found some sort of strange satisfaction from a job appreciated. A paper every day, lunch and snacks prepared on demand, television station changed periodically, beds made in the morning, items carried from one room to another—the list continued to build. I avoided painful situations for a month, but it couldn't last for long. Han and Phil were bickering over me as if deciding who would get to use my services for the day. In the end they came to a truce, though over several fights, and were so much enraged by each other (but unable to take it out on each other much more), they took their frustration out on me. No longer was I the helpful servant, I had become the local punching bag.

Han began with outdoor activities. He'd created a primitive spear from bamboo and needed a way to challenge his accuracy.

"Walk," he said to me during a rainy August day. "Walk unless you wanna be hit by this."

Walking behind me, he threw the spear toward my heals, missing quite often but once nudging my shoe. "Oooo," he said as if he'd done a good thing. I continued walking, Phil gave a call from the screen door, and I turned around in pause, finding the spear on its way in my foot. It wasn't terribly sharp, fortunately, but it did pierce my shoe and partially puncture my foot, leaving me with bleeding and pain.

"Dammit, Han," Phil said, "now he's no good to me. Get away from him."

Phil came running up to me with a towel and bandaged my wound. I thought it strange—here these two had been torturing me, and Phil was helping me? It was a nice thing to be sure, but I couldn't understand how someone who could hurt me could also help me. Phil had me sit in a chair during his ownership time. We struck up a chess game (his decision) several times, though Phil won all.

I think there were other minor incidents, but Han and Phil alternated between calling me into service, torturing me, and babying me. I suppose I must've found comfort in the new stability, because I didn't feel as bad off. Mother was rarely around, which was good considering my most vivid memory of her with the hair brush.

Perhaps I'm spending too much time describing my childhood memories. I suppose every person has the feeling of wanting to get away from home as soon as possible—like the bird ready to take flight and make its own. Whatever the case, I avoided them as much as possible, spending the last years of elementary school withdrawn.

One day while walking home through the woods (I was in seventh grade, I think), I ran into Han, Phil, and their friends. They were smoking something, but I wasn't sure what. Realizing my mistake, I attempted to sidetrack the issue, but it was too late. One of the friends saw me and shouted curses. I ran for my life, but in a few steps someone had grabbed me from behind.

"So, you decided to snoop on us, huh?" said a familiar voice. It was Phil. "Boy are you in for it now!"

"Hey Phil," a voice said, "who's the little twerp?"

"It's my bratty brother—a real dweeb."

"Yeah," added Han. "You're in for it now, Billy-brat."

Phil had twisted my arms behind my back to the point of excruciating pain (for me) and forced me forward through a part of the woods I hadn't seen. We walked for some time 'till I grew tired and fell. Phil dragged me along while Han kicked— that got me up on my feet. Shortly, we stopped at a steep drop. A stream had cut through the forest floor. Over the ledge lay a smashed assortment of boulders, some jagged and some smooth. There must have been a good twenty feet of air from the ledge where we stood to the boulders.

"Jump," yelled Phil. I squirmed around trying to get free, but Phil slapped me back.

"Jump," he repeated, "or I'll push you."

"Hey Phil, we've had our fun. Let the kid go."

"Shut up," Phil retorted. Looking back at me, Phil said with a finality, "That's it, you asked for it!"

I had never contemplated dying until that moment. As I slipped from the ledge, I felt my life being thrown out of control. I was both furious at my brothers and stricken white with fear. I tensed then curled—instinct threw my arms in gyrating motions near the end but to little effect—I lay frozen on two jagged boulders, my body racked with pain but too over-whelmed to move. Within seconds I blacked out.

Four.

Death, or so I thought. Somehow I had avoided it again. I don't know how long I'd lain on the rocks—was it hours? Days? I was parched upon regaining consciousness, and pain was my only companion—a lonely thought. My left leg and left arm were in severe pain (being swollen), and a knot had devel-oped on my head (which throbbed to no end). Gingerly, I crawled a few feet, pausing for a moment to regain composure. The struggle to move was enormous. I suppose hours must have passed before I was able to get to soft earth (next to the stream) and rest. After another moment, I sipped water from the stream, but it proved heavily polluted. Another moment later, and I'd found a stick as a cane which allowed biped travel.

I stopped short. Looking around, I realized I couldn't re-member where I was. Not only that, I couldn't remember how I'd gotten there or even my identity. I knew I must've had am-nesia and was lucky to remember English (at least I thought—I'm no expert on concussions).

"Now what do I do?" I said aloud, half hoping to hear a re-ply. There was none, save from a passing eagle far above. No humans within ear-shot (or eye-shot). No direction. No hope? Bah!

"Onward," I said, knowing I couldn't stay around with an empty belly. Shadows grew long from a dying sun as I left the woods and entered an urban setting. Hobbling, I was able to make my way to a dumpster behind a grocery store. There I found some food though rummaging was necessary to avoid the spoils. I was thankful for the meager meal I could make but was frightened at the prospect of finding a place to sleep. Should I have gone to the police? Being unable to remember made the decision more difficult—what if I'd committed some crime and was to be arrested? I decided it best to wait a day or two, see how things went, and in the worst circumstance go to the police with my problem. Meantime, I made my way to a small park and slept behind some bushes.

Sleep was difficult. The pain had worsened, the earthen floor was harsh, and I was scared. Scared? You betcha! I imagined all sorts of evil things, from being eaten by a bear (or wolf) to being bitten by a black widow spider. Then what if someone would come along? I shut my eyes and prayed I'd make it to morning.

I suppose I dozed off several times during the night after waking up with a start. Once I thought I saw a light being shone around the park while hearing voices nearby, but I froze in fear. I wanted to cry, but I was too dehydrated. A mosquito kept buzzing near my ear and irritating me to no end. At least it didn't rain.

I spent a week sleeping in the park and eating from the dumpster. A water spigot in the park provided sanitized water, I learned, and a nearby stream provided bathing (though it also drew the mosquitoes). There was a small pavilion with a bathroom facility in the middle of the grounds, but I avoided that unless use was absolutely necessary. My left leg and arm were still swollen, though the pain had subsided. The lights I'd seen the first night returned the following nights at roughly the same time. Local police made the rounds to ensure no one was in the park. I remained well hidden during those times.

I was able to keep track of the days by glancing at the newspaper stand each day. That's how I knew it was a Saturday night when I had unexpected visitors in the park. I had retired to my usual sleeping place (which was well hidden from view but provided a view of the main park grounds), the police had made their nightly rounds, then perhaps twenty minutes later my acute hearing picked up people scuffling through the grounds. The group made their way to a corner and briefly left my sight.

I don't know if the park had some strange acoustic effects or if my hearing had simply become exceptionally keen, but I heard the group chanting, and their voices would rise then fade like the passing of the wind. At times the group seemed uncomfortably close, at others quite distant. I suppose the chanting continued for ten minutes or so—it was difficult to tell without a watch. Suddenly the chanting stopped, and I waited "for the other shoe to drop." Then a single voice murmured for a minute, another moment of silence, then a short, shrill shriek pierced the night, causing night animals to scurry. Though a hot summer night, I shivered, and a vague memory of me hugging someone came to mind. After a few moments, I realized the memory was of me hugging my mother after hearing of my father's death.

The chanting started again but was different. I also thought I heard percussion instruments clinking in sync with the chanting, but it was a windy night and I half asleep—anything was possible. The chanting continued as I fell into deep sleep.

A loud explosion and bright flashes of light startled me in the night's middle. As heavy water drops pierced my clothing, I realized I was caught in the middle of a thunderstorm. Again the acoustics of the park played havoc with me—each thunder-shot sent me cringing in shock, as if an electric eel had whipped against my legs. I headed for the pavilion as quickly as I could, using the brief lightning blasts to see. I was only a few steps on the way when I became completely drenched. I splashed through mud puddles and was constantly flicking water from my hair to see. Getting to the pavilion seemed to take hours, but in fact it perhaps took three minutes. Upon arrival I went for the bathroom (as additional protection from the storm) but slammed into a locked door. That's right. It was locked nightly.

"Who is that?" a feeble voice called. I yelled briefly in fear, and the feeble voice yelled back.

"Hello?" I said, trying to calm my nerves. A quick lightning flash revealed a figure hunched under a picnic table in the pavilion's middle. The bathrooms were at the end (where I was). The thunder followed and shook me again. No reply.

"Hello?" I said again, being extremely bold. Another brief pause.

"Please," said the figure, "go away." I realized the voice was feminine.

"I just wanna stay dry," I said back. The wind whipped the rain in several directions, leaving all but a few places soaked. I was in one of the soaked places.

"Go away," pleaded the figure again.

"I just wanna stay dry," I reiterated. I crawled toward the dry, middle picnic tables.

"Stay back!" she said, her voice getting stronger. She backed up like a frightened cat, almost hissing at me.

"I won't hurt you," I said, lowering my voice. I stopped two picnic tables away. "See? This is as far as I'll go."

She froze and I too. Another flash of lightning. Another. We looked at each other, waiting for the other to make a move, not trusting, no trust.

"Please," she said finally, "don't hurt me."

"I won't," I said.

We must've watched each other like that for another hour. The storm raged on, and I could tell she was frightened by it, but she held her ground, trembling. For a moment I thought she wouldn't bother me as I put my head down to rest. Strangely, the storm was subsiding, and my eyes closed to the fading flashes and low rumbles. I half fancied hearing the chanting I'd heard earlier with percussions fading in and out. The chanting was rhythmic and hypnotic, and I imagined being on a train instead. Then the same shriek I'd heard before came back, and I opened my eyes with a start. I looked up just in time to see the once frightened figure now hunched over me with knife in hand ready to stab. She came down with the knife, but I rolled over in time then turned around and came behind her, grabbed her arm (forcing the knife's release), and twisted it behind her back.

"Ow!" she yelled.

"What's going on?"

"Let me go! You're hurting me!"

"And what were you going to do to me?" I said, wrestling for control of her other arm. She writhed around in a desperate struggle. I tried reaching for the knife, but her nails dug deep into my face, forcing me to recoil and move ten feet from her. She snapped around with knife back in hand and held her ground.

"Stay back," she warned.

"Hey," I said with a quivering voice. "Take it easy."

"Stay back or I'll kill you!"

I tried reasoning with her: "Look, I have no intention of hurting you."

"They all say that," she interjected.

"If you please, I'll just be on my way..." I started walking backward slowly, preparing to get away. The storm had let up, so there was no worry about getting rained upon (though I was still wet).

"Just wait right there. I don't trust you. You just might come back and kill me."

I considered running, but it would have been hopeless with my injured leg (still healing from the accident). I sat down.

"Ok, I'm not going anywhere. Say, why don't you put the knife away? There's no need—"

"Shut up. You think I'm stupid or something? Don't you think I know what you're up to?"

I was puzzled. What was she talking about? "Perhaps you could fill me in. What am I up to?"

"Smarty. That innocent routine won't work with me. You're one of them, a scout for the group. Well, you're not getting out of this alive. I know what would happen if I let you get back to the cult—you'd make sacrifice of me, that's for sure!"

"Cult? Group? Look, I know I shouldn't be out here like this, but I'm on my own, see? Do I look like I'm with a group?"

The world was growing lighter. Dawn approached. She squinted in my direction, trying to get a good look at me. There was a pause.

"I'm out here on my own. But I did hear some strange chanting earlier. Is that why you're here?" For some reason I thought I'd said the wrong thing. She stirred for a moment then lowered her knife a bit.

"No," she said, her voice a bit relaxed. "I thought you were."

"Then you're not with a group?" I asked, trying to speak in her fashion.

"No. I'm on my own."

Could this be true? As hard as it is to believe, I thought I was the only person in the world who was in hiding, living like a critter. But to bump into another person on the run was astonishing.

"Did you run away?" I asked.

"Did you?" she asked back.

I was still having problems remembering, but somehow I figured I must have run away or wanted to very badly. If only I could remember.

"What's your name?" I asked. That was a mistake. As soon as she'd answer, she'd ask my name. What was my name?

"Katy Liz Hackles. What's yours?" The knife was completely withdrawn. Katy sat on a picnic table while I remained sitting on the pavilion floor. C'mon brain, what's my name? If I told her I couldn't remember, she'd become very suspicious, possibly even kill me. I had to say something and fast.

"Willibee," I blurted out.

"Willibee?" she said, puzzled. "Willibee what?"

"Willibee Runnan," I said, making something up in a confused mind. For some reason, it didn't sound like a real name. Why didn't I say "Jake Smith" or something easy like that?

"You mean, 'Will he be running?' What kind of name is that? You ARE one of them, aren't you?" The knife came back into plain view, and she tensed up for the kill.

"Yes, I mean no, I mean—"

"What DO you mean?" she challenged.

"Half a minute," I pleaded, shaking. "Lemme 'splain."

"I'll 'splain you to Spain if you don't tell the truth."

"Ok. Fact is, I had this bad accident a week ago. Can't remember how it happened or who I am. See the bump on my head?" She peered through the dawn. "Also hurt my leg and arm. See how they're still swollen? My clothes—they're all I got. All I know is I was in some woods and wasn't sure what to do. I've been hangin' out here for a week, hoping I'd get my memory back."

"You have been hurt, haven't you?" she said, putting the knife away again and taking a closer look.

"Yeah."

"You can't remember anything?" she asked.

"Not until tonight."

"And what was that?"

"That I remembered?"

"Yeah."

"During the chanting, I heard a shriek. Then I remembered hugging my mother after something horrible had happened. That's all."

"You heard the chanting?"

"Yeah. Did you?"

Her face froze. By now the sun was peeping through the trees. I could see how she was wet from the storm—like a drowned rat. Her hair was long and blond, and her face had a bluish bruise.

"I heard it. I saw it. It was them, the cult. Over there," she said, pointing to the corner where I'd heard the group go the night before. "Over there."

Five.

"Now wait. I don't think you should go over there," I yelled. I was a moment late. Katy had already left, aside my warnings. I watched her run over to the corner then disappear from sight. I knew that spot was evil, and I dared not tread its ground. I hesitated, then hearing a foreign voice, I fled for cover. I paused, waiting for some sign of good or ill. Unfortunately, ill was the day's agenda. I heard another scream, but instead of being quickly silenced, the scream carried, faded, then echoed throughout the woods.

It was Katy.

"Leave me alone," she screamed. "Help!"

"Come back here," said a scraggly voice. "I just wanna be your friend."

Katy was momentarily in sight, and I could see her struggling with a scraggly person (though creature would be more apt). Primitive instinct held me at bay, but then I remembered she was like me—a runaway, someone who decided living in the wild was infinitely preferable to living at home. I felt some sort of obligation to help (least of all to stop the screams which were driving me insane with pain).

The guy never saw the leg coming from behind and under, which struck his genitalia. He crumpled to his knees for a second while I lunged at him with Katy's knife (which I found on my stealth run but ten yards away). Instinctively, his hand attempted to block the slash, but his palms paid dearly. Writhing in pain, he jumped back once then fell on his back. Another slash landed along his throat, silencing his last cry and his last breath.

Katy and I were alone.

In the few seconds of my attack, she had limped a little ways off the path. Blood was everywhere—on the man, on the grass, the knife, my hands, and on Katy's leg.

"Katy," I cried, "are you ok?"

"Stay back!" she scowled. "I knew you were one of them."

"No, I'm not one of them. You ran off, then I heard his voice."

"Get away!" she screamed.

"I hid, but I heard you screaming. Katy, I know who you are."

"You don't know anything about me. How could you?" Her screaming turned into tears then a muffled sob.

"You're a runaway. Just like me, you're a runaway."

For the first time, I acknowledged the truth. Like her, I was running from something. A grey picture of two older brothers hurting me flashed through my mind then faded. It was coming back, but slowly. I glanced around quickly. Still quiet.

"What are you running from, Willibee?" she asked through her sobs.

"I can't remember. I had some sort of accident. Listen, we gotta get out of here!"

Katy suppressed her tears and slowly made her way past me, staring at the knife. Dazed, I watched her go through the dead man's pockets. She pulled out a wallet and placed it in her pocket.

"Help me push him into the river."

"What?" I asked incredulously.

"C'mon! We don't have much time."

Setting the knife aside, I walked over to a frightened but determined Katy Liz Hackles.

"One, two, three!" and the corpse was in motion, picked up speed as it rolled clear down to the river, splashed in, then slowly floated away.

"Let's go!" she whispered/screamed. "Wait. My knapsack." She disappeared for a moment then returned. "Ok." Katy made a run into the woods, past a newly dead cat, up a hill (with me hobbling as fast as I could), around a bend, then down around and down. We went up again then onto some railroad tracks. Both sides were banked with trees and provided ample cover from all but a passing locomotive.

"Katy, wait up!" I nearly fell on my face from exhaustion. She stopped, turned around, then ran back for me.

"Just a little farther, just enough to get out of earshot."

"I think we are out of earshot. Besides, do you know where we're going?"

"I saw these tracks on my way through. They have to go somewhere. Just a bit more and we can rest."

I hobbled hobbled hobbled along the tracks tracks tracks past the ties, coal, and stones. Pain seared through my legs and forced an uncontrollable stop. I dragged myself to a small log set from the tracks where Katy was seated.

"I thought I was bad off. Look at your poor leg."

"It's just a cut. I'll be ok."

"Let me take a look," I said.

"No, stay back!"

"Look," I came back. "If we're gonna survive, we gotta work together. We've made it this far together. Now let's take a look! We can't have you bleeding to death on us."

"You're not gonna hurt me, are you? I saw you back there—you killed one of them!"

"No." I didn't know much about healing, but I did know about clotting wounds, from where I couldn't remember. "It doesn't look bad. Your jeans took most of the edge off the attack."

"And look at you. Blood all over yourself."

She was right. My hands and shirt were covered with the man's blood. I had killed another person, and his blood was on my hands. Full shock set in, and I realized I was in trouble—murder. That person would never walk again, never breathe again. I was responsible. I was answerable.

"If someone else were to look at me, what do you suppose they'd think?"

"That you're hurt?" she offered.

"And when they discover I'm not?"

"It doesn't look good. Here, put this on." She reached inside her knapsack and pulled out a clean T-shirt.

"Are you kidding? Me, wear a girl's shirt? Forget it!"

"It's not just a girl's shirt," she said. "A guy can wear it too. If you don't wear it—"

"I'll go without. It's plenty warm as it is," I said.

"Yeah, warm enough to burn your skin. Put the shirt on."

The shirt landed at my feet. Placing the knife on the rail and removing my soiled shirt, I briefly examined Katy's T-shirt before wearing it.

"It's a bit small," I mentioned.

"You better get rid of the bloodied shirt."

She said this as I picked up the shirt and tossed it behind a small bush. When I returned, the knife was gone.

"Hey, you took the knife!"

"It's my knife," she said. "Besides, you won't be needing it anymore."

"And you will? For what? Stabbing me in my sleep?"

"I didn't know you then," she said.

"And you do now?"

"Look, I thought you were one of them. I'm still not sure who you are, but I'm glad you killed that man. By the way, what are those marks on your back?"

"Marks?"

"Yeah, if I didn't know better, I'd say they were..."

"Were what? Come on, tell me."

"No," she said, "it's just a guess."

"Then guess. What is it?"

"Scars. From a whip it looks like."

I stood there a moment trying to figure it out. Whip marks? From what? Nothing made sense; nothing could be remembered. A faint rustling came from a nearby thicket.

"Shhhhh. Did you hear that?"

"Hear what?" I asked. I couldn't hear anything specific. But Katy must have heard a quiet meow.

"There it is again. Here, kitty, kitty, kitty," Katy called. I was a little confused, but out of the thicket came a small, orange-striped kitten.

"Well will you look at that—an orange cat," I said, trying to be funny.

"It's a marmalade kitten. What are you doing out here, poor little kitty?" she asked the kitten. The kitten would only meow back.

"It looks rather thin, even for a kitten," I said.

"It's probably hungry," said Katy. She reached into her knapsack and pulled out a can of tuna. Wielding the knife with skill, she punched the can open. "Here, kitty, have some tuna."

"You're giving your food to an animal? What a waste," I lamented.

"The poor thing is starved. Besides, we're all loners, and I think we should help each other." The kitten meowed once more then ate the tuna quickly.

"You mean take the kitten with us? Are you crazy?" I asked.

"No, but I am taking the kitten with me. You can go on your own merry way, now. I won't be a bother to you anymore." She picked up the kitten and walked down the tracks. I stood there for a moment watching her. Then I ran.

"Wait up a minute," I said, a little out of breath. "Where are you going?"

"It's none of your business. You see, I don't really trust you, even if you helped me, and although you seem ok on the outside, well, I don't think I could really trust anyone at this point, except a harmless creature like this kitten."

"Look, I won't hurt you. I...I..." I struggled for a moment as a memory flashed through my head.

"You what?" she said, turning toward me. "What is it?"

My face went blank for a moment, then I spoke, "I remembered something, a bit vague, but something."

"What is it?" she said, a little curious. We continued walking down the tracks with the kitten in her arms.

"A corner of a room. I'm sitting there with a blanket, keeping warm. That's all I can remember."

"The whip marks and now a cold corner—you could be making those up for all I know. Every guy I've met has lied to me at one time or another."

"Believe me, I'd do anything to remember," I said.

"Ok, why don't you hold the kitten," she said, handing it to me.

"It's so small."

"Not it, he. I'm going to call him Alexander for being so noble and brave. Brave enough to venture into the wild, as we are. But he's gotten away from something, I can tell."

"So what happened back there? Why were you attacked? What do you know about the chanting?" I asked.

A grey shadow passed over Katy's face, then it lifted. She opened her mouth to speak, paused, closed it, another pause, then spoke.

"Some sort of cult. They were close to my hiding place last night. Close, but they didn't see me, at least I didn't think so. There were about seven of them, each wearing some strange clothing and ornaments—devil worshippers, and dancing around a person tied to a tree. Need I say more?"

"But something else must have happened. What else did you see?" I asked.

"They chanted, yes, striking various percussion instruments, candles everywhere, then with a sudden strike the leader took a large knife and buried it into his victim, the one tied to the tree. I couldn't bear to look after seeing that. I heard a scream, but it was muffled through a...what do you call them...some sort of bandanna or cloth around the person's mouth."

"I moved away quietly, but I caught the eye of one cult member, if only for an instant. That was the same one who caught me this morning. You see, I was going back for my knapsack, which I had mistakenly left behind."

"This victim," I said, "I didn't see anything this morning."

"It was gone, the candles, the dead person—everything. I can't prove anything. Maybe I dreamt it. No, it happened. Later, I went to the pavilion when I heard the thunder."

"What about you?" I asked. "Huh? Why are you out here?"

There was a long silence, perhaps for five or ten minutes. Alexander was purring quietly in my arms as we continued to trudge along the tracks.

"I guess it doesn't matter that I don't know you well enough. Heck, if I did know you better, I probably couldn't go through with the story, my life," she started. She looked down as she spoke, not looking up once, not even at me.

"Ok, I'm listening," I said.

"My parents—well, I can't live with them anymore. Maybe I'm foolish, sometimes I wonder what other families are like, if they're like mine...he'll never hurt me again."

"He?"

"My father. No, I don't want to think about it."

"Katy, he can't do anything to you now. You're free."

"Am I? I may be physically free, but my spirit, my soul—it's imprisoned, imprisoned by the memories of what he did to me. My mother—she wouldn't do anything, not even call the police. When I told her the things he did, she told me to be quiet and not cause a problem. Father had a bad temper. Look at my wrists."

We had stopped walking. I put the kitten down for a moment and looked at Katy's wrists. Scars encircled both.

"What are these from?" She picked up the kitten, and we continued walking.

"Rope burns."

She was quiet for another five minutes. I wanted to know more but was afraid to ask.

"He," she started, "would tie my wrists to the bedposts and...rape me."

That was it, the bomb exploded. I expected her to complain of various beatings and some-such, but to hear this—it made me sick. Somehow, I knew that nothing that had happened to me, remembered or not, could come close to what Katy had suffered—not just pain, but complete and absolute humiliation. In a way I felt guilty too, because being a male I knew I had the same capability as Katy's father. Would I grow up and do the same thing? Could it happen to me? I shuddered at the thought and would have slit my throat rather than do such a thing. I didn't though, didn't slit my throat. We continued walking.

"I was hurt in several places, both physically and mentally. After the first time, I felt victimized, but I also felt dirty, as if it were somehow my fault."

The first time? What had this girl been through?

"He would beat me at other times, or threaten to beat me, saying if I told someone, I could not expect to see my eighteenth birthday. He had me thinking I deserved everything that came to me, but you know, I think he was wrong, I know he was. But what I don't know is why—why did he do those things? It couldn't have been just 'punishment.' Compared to what my friends did, I was good—I caused no trouble. But it didn't seem to matter whether I was good or bad—punishment always came."

"I overheard him with Mother one night. I was surprised to hear him beating her as well. She was in tears, promising not to do 'it' again. He was mad, saying she deserved it since she couldn't have any more children. He kept repeating that over and over, and it made me think. I mean, I was an only child, and maybe that's why she couldn't have more children. But I'll never forgive Father. He had no right to take out his frustrations on us. So I left—I packed a few things and left. I vowed never to let any man hit me again, not him or anyone."

So that was it. I couldn't imagine Katy being raped, though. I looked at her, and she didn't seem like the kind of girl who would get raped. I guess I always envisioned some sleazy girl from the streets getting raped, but not someone like Katy. She was more of a plain but nice looking person.

We walked in silence for the rest of the morning. Just after noon, the clouds cleared. Katy stopped for a moment, handed Alexander to me, and pulled out a hat.

"I don't wanna get burned," she said. I almost laughed, but the seriousness of her statement hit me as several more flashbacks came to mind. The more I thought about what she'd said, the more I could remember what had happened to me.

"I'm getting hungry," I said. "Would you mind sharing any food you might have?"

"I'm afraid the tuna was the last of it. We'll have to get some food. How much money do you have?"

I checked my pockets. "None."

"None? How have you been surviving? By the grace of God?"

"Almost. Stealing food from the dumpster behind a grocery store. It's been tough this past week."

"And before that?"

"Before that I can't remember. I know I awoke on some jagged rocks next to a stream, and I was in great pain. I don't know how I got there—whether it was from severe exhaustion or from a fall—I don't know, but I suspect I fell somehow."

"So actually, you're suffering from amnesia. Not a real runaway, just unsure of what to do. Don't you think you should try to find your home?" she asked.

"I have this feeling that home is not the place to be, at least not for me. I've been getting some flashbacks, memories of my past, and they aren't pleasant. Say, we're coming up to a small town. Little York, population 2600."

In a few minutes more we left the tracks and sat under a tree in a small but secluded park. As we rested our tired feet in the cool of the shade, we continued to talk. Alexander walked off to a nearby puddle and drank.

"How old are you, Katy?"

"Fourteen. What about you, Willibee? What is your real name?"

Voices echoed in my mind, but they were distorted and warbled, like listening to some warped record being played in a tunnel. The one thing I could hear was...Billy. Calls for Billy. Billy do this, Billy do that, Billy where are you?

"Billy. At least I think my name is Billy. That's about as much as I can piece together."

"And how old are you, Billy?"

"Good question. I would guess the same age as you—fourteen, though I could be wrong. There is one thing, though. We need food."

"Well," she started, "let's see what we have here."

She pulled out the wallet from the attack and rummaged through it.

"We could get into big trouble if we're caught."

"You mean if you're caught. And I'd say no more, if I were you. Ears can be everywhere. Let me see—a driver's license, social security card, library card, a ticket stub to a movie—how much money does he have?"

"A thief you are," I commented.

"I'd rather be a living thief than a dead saint. I think I'm going to be ok. Here, Alexander," the kitten meowed a few times while running to her. "Nice kitty. Well, Billy, I think I'll be on my way. Good luck to you, and thank you for helping me."

"Wait a minute. I thought we had an understanding." I was perplexed.

"Only that we can't live with our folks. But I can't trust anyone right now, maybe Alexander, but that's about it. I gotta do this on my own. I've had a hard life, and I don't want to take any more chances."

"You're taking a chance now. Risking everything, that is, just being on your own at such an age. What if we're caught—underage and all? Hmmm?"

"*We* won't get caught. You might, but I don't plan on it. But, seeing as you're in a bad way, you might as well have this," she said, handing me the wallet. She had obviously removed most of the money but left a twenty note inside. "The ID cards are worthless to me, and I can spare the twenty."

"Where will you go? What will you do? Katy, it's a lonely world out here and brutal. We're in the same boat, can't you see this? If we work together, we'll have a better chance. Katy, you gotta listen to me."

"We've been through this already. I've made up my mind. And you know, the last person who said, 'You gotta listen to me,' was my father, and look at the kind of person he was. How do I know you won't attack me, steal my things, or even kill me? I'm sorry, I wish I could say, 'yes,' but I can't. Not yet. Good luck, Billy."

It was useless. She walked off without turning back. I could hear some soft cries from Alexander, her marmalade kitten, as she left. I sat there for a few more moments then left.

Six.

The next few years were slow and uneventful for me. I guess I spent eight or nine months riding the railroad with other hobos, drifting aimlessly around. In that time I managed to get most of my memory back, enough to know I was better off moving around than going back home. I grew quite a bit which surprised me considering my poor diet. I didn't save any money—the twenty dollars Katy gave me went rather quickly for food. The wallet was sold, but I kept the stranger's driver's license and social security card. Those turned into my tickets to early freedom.

After several close brushes with death, I left the rails and looked for work using Anton Briggs as my new name. I settled in a mid-sized city called Parkersville and roamed it for several days, scouting it out. Checking the stores, I saw no "Help Wanted" signs. I ate at several soup kitchens and slept at a homeless shelter while donating plasma twice a week for some quick cash. After four weeks, I landed a job as a cook for the Hungry Jim Steak House. I was supplied with a uniform which was good considering I had no clothes except what was on my back. Getting a job and making money was a new thrill, although I was a bit nervous about posing as Anton.

Anton Briggs, the guy I killed,
A few years back to save a girl.
Her name was Katy, she nearly smitten,
Then heard the cries of the marmalade kitten.

The marmalade kitten, the marmalade kitten;
She heard the cries of the marmalade kitten.

I chanted this to myself over and over as I worked, which helped a lot considering how badly my legs ached afterward. After a month of work, I was able to get a small apartment. It was nothing fancy—one bedroom/living room, a kitchenette, and a bathroom. I had no furniture, but to have my own place at last, well, quite simply it was pure heaven. I never knew how pleasant a hot shower could be. Being able to afford food was another delicacy—and a refrigerator to keep milk and ice cream—it was just incredible.

I saved old boxes from work and used them to construct some shelving in my apartment, where I placed my uniform, my two pairs of pants, my three T-shirts, underwear, and socks. I slept on the floor the first month then purchased an inflatable foam mattress. With no television and no radio, I took to walking around the streets and shopping centers in my free time. I couldn't afford to buy anything or do anything like see the movies, but at least I had some sense of stability.

Six months of working at the Hungry Jim Steak House got on my nerves. Perhaps I had become less desperate about the job, but I found the managers were intolerable, and at times I came home with burns during a hectic evening. It was time to get a better job, but my search proved nothing. Finally, I landed a job as bagger at a grocery store and was much happier. With the Steak House crisis over, I soon grew bored with my free time. Every Sunday I picked up a newspaper to read up on the city and look for ideas. What kind of ideas? I didn't know, but the paper was as good a place as any. A month after I started buying the paper, I bought a spiral notebook and started writing my thoughts down. At first I just doodled, making silly pictures which had no meaning, but it was a good way to pass the time.

The bagger job lasted a few months, then I was promoted to the meat department where I made a good bit more money. It was a bit scary at first with the saws and cutters, in fact a worker there told me of the person I was replacing who lost his arm in a saw. I tried not to think about it.

I couldn't help but wonder what had happened to Katy. The wonder kept gnawing which drove me to look for her. I started with Little York, the place I'd last seen her. From store to store I asked around, but no one could recall a Katy Hackles or her kitten. Feeling badly for not following her way back when, I travelled on to the next city—River Bend. It was a bit larger than Little York, and I hoped and prayed it contained some clue of her existence.

Searching for Katy proved more difficult than I'd originally envisioned. After spending six cold months of bus trips, train trips, and cab rides—all paid for with my spare money, I was ready to give up.

"Maybe she went back home," I thought. It *was* a possibility, but in the back of my mind I had a feeling it wasn't true, couldn't be true. She *had* to be out there somewhere.

Spring brought new life into the trees and birds, and it brought new hope in my search. I purchased newspapers, searched phone books, and continued to ask around. I thought of other ways to find her—newspaper ads, city directories? Perhaps she had lied to me, was her name really Katy Liz Hackles?

Sitting on a bench waiting for a bus one Saturday, I kept feeling I was close, very close but was missing something, some clue. What had I overlooked? The sun was setting, and in a nearby tree several birds were fluttering around here and there. Some swooped close to the ground, landed, then flew back up. Next to the tree, squirrels were hopping around, digging up nuts. A man across the street walked his dog past me. In a few minutes he was out of sight. As the last rays of a setting sun waned, I could hear the familiar roar of a bus's engine draw near. It was my bus.

The squirrels scurried away, the birds kept swooping, and as I turned one last time, I saw them swooping down over a cat, who occasionally lifted a paw at the cackling birds on each pass. Thinking nothing of it, I picked up my bag and waited behind two people. The first person boarded, I heard a faint meow behind; the second boarded, I felt a cold chill as if something was familiar; then I walked up the steps, and while the driver inspected my ticket, I turned around to see an orange-striped cat climbing up the tree.

"Hey buddy, what's it gonna be?" the driver called out as I rushed out the bus and at the tree.

"Go on," I said, waving my arm. With that he was gone, my ride back to Parkersville was gone, the sun was gone, the birds gone, the cat gone, dog-gone! Dog-gone it, what was I supposed to do? As it turned out, the cat came down after five minutes of fruitless ventures. I checked his coat carefully as he meowed—marmalade.

"So it's you," I said. "Alexander, the marmalade kitten. Only you're not a kitten anymore, you're a cat." I think he must have recognized me because he came up to me and let me pet him. "Meow," he said in his distinctive voice.

"Ok," I said, as if he could understand me, "we'll see where you go tonight. Do you live around here?"

"Meow, meow," was his only reply.

"Kinda hard getting information out of you," I said. "Ah well, the night is young, and it *is* Saturday. We'll just play Cat and Mouse, only I'm the cat and you're the mouse."

"Meow," he said. I got up and walked back to the bench, but as I did so he followed me and jumped on my lap.

"Hey, I'm supposed to follow you, not the other way around. Tell me, Alexander, where is she?"

"*She* is right behind you, wondering what you're doing with *her* cat. And how do you know his name is Alexander?"

"The same way I know you must be Katy Hackles," I said, turning around. Only it wasn't her, it was some other young lady.

"No, no, I'm not Liz. No one calls her Katy anymore. Who are you?"

"An old friend," I said, hoping not to be too rude. "And to whom do I have the pleasure of addressing?"

"What? You sure ain't from 'round here! You mean my name, don't you? I'm Sally, Liz's roommate. She's out workin' tonight, and I'm giving her cat some air. Nice kitty, come here kitty, kitty, kitty, kitty!"

Alexander ran up to her and jumped into her arms as she brought him up to her chest.

"Nice cat, isn't he?" she said. "Well, it's time I went back in. It's dark, and we're tired, aren't we Alexxie?" She nuzzled her nose against the cat's.

"Wait, Sally. I need to see Katy, er Liz."

"Like I said, she's working tonight. Again, who are you?"

"I'm..." It had been quite a while since I had gone by my true name, "...Billy Stradt, though she probably knows me better as Willibee. Couldn't you tell me where she lives so I could visit her?"

Sally looked me over with a suspicious eye. "Hmmm," she said. "Does she have your phone number?"

"No, of course not. Say...ok, how 'bout this? I'll write down my phone number, give it to you, and you can give it to her. Then she can call me? Or you could give me her number. That would be better."

"No," Sally said, "you just give me your number, and I'll give it to her."

I hurriedly pulled out a pen and pad of paper from my bag. In seconds, the paper was in Sally's hand.

"Hmm. This is a Parkersville exchange. Long distance."

"Oh, she can call me collect. Please, it's important," I urged.

"Ok, I'll give it to her. Bye."

With that Sally was gone. I considered following her to see where she was going, but in the minute I considered, she was completely out of sight.

Several weeks passed. Nothing. I had the feeling Katy had ignored me, or perhaps she had never received the note. One evening while I was writing in my journal, the phone rang. At first I thought it was my boss from work, wanting me to come in for some overtime. I picked it up anyway. It was her.

"Katy, how are you?" I asked. It was a polite nothing.

"Doin' ok. My roommate gave me your number a couple of weeks ago, but I forgot. So it's you, Billy. How did you find me?"

"That's a long story, I'm afraid, but let's just say it was Alexander who caught my eye. He's all grown up, though."

"Yeah, it's been a couple of years since you last saw him. He's more playful than ever, getting into all sorts of mischief when I'm at work. My roommate, Sally—oh that's right, you two have met—anyway, she tries to keep him out of trouble."

"I'd really like to see you, Katy. I know it's a strange thing to say, but I didn't know what to do after you went your way and I mine. Have you seen any of your family since leaving home?"

"No. You?"

"Nope. I keep wondering, though, what's happened to them since I left."

"I guess this means you have your memory back."

"Yes, most of it anyway. There are a few missing pieces, though. What do you say, Katy, to dinner sometime? Nothing fancy, just a chance to talk about things."

"Well, I don't know, I work most every day, and I'm so tired when I get home. Sometimes I work double shift. And weekends, that's the worst."

"C'mon. My treat. Just a little dinner. Please? Pleazzzzzze?"

"Ok, ok," she said, giving in finally. "I think I'm off this coming up Sunday, at least around dinner time. Where did you have in mind?"

"Seems like I saw a nice little diner there in East Lankton. 'Patty's Kitchen.' Sound familiar?"

"Yeah," said Katy, showing a little excitement. "I know where that is. Ok. 'Patty's Kitchen'."

"Is seven too early?"

"No, seven should be fine. I guess I'll meet you there then, right?"

"Right. Ok. Seven o'clock pm at 'Patty's Kitchen' on Sunday. Great. See you then."

"All-righty. Bye."

"Bye."

Five seconds after replacing the receiver, I jumped up with a fist in the air, shouting, "Yes!" A pounding from the neighbors reminded me to be more quiet. But I had my date with Katy, and I drooled with anticipation.

Seven.

"Which brings me to this diner," I said, just summing up what I had done during the past couple of years. Katy and I were nibbling on our sandwiches we'd ordered and sipping our sodas.

"You have been through a lot, haven't you?" she said. "That was one strange night and day, though, when we met in the park. I can remember how terrified I was during the storm.

All on my own, and already I'd encountered worse stuff than I'd ever imagined. I never thought I'd be here talking with you, though. After I left you in Little York, you were just another person, another shadow who faded away."

"I'm also afraid my life was less eventful though less stressful than yours since Little York. I travelled a bit 'till I came here, East Lankton. I spent a couple of days on the street, but I looked through the paper for a place to say. Several ads for female roommates were posted, and after checking out the location of each, I decided on my current address—with Sally. She was very nice to me, even when I was honest about my being underage. She offered to help me find work, and with that I agreed to room with her. Being fourteen was a bit young, but I lied on my applications, saying I was sixteen, and I eventually got a job as a waitress. That job lasted about a year and a half, then I turned sixteen for real."

"The waitress job was hard on my back, my legs, and my feet. I was able to quit that and get a job in the department store in the women's clothing section. A couple of months ago, I moved to the cosmetic section, and now I help ladies select their colors and their makeup."

"Their colors?" I asked.

"Yes, every woman has her own set of colors which best enhances her appearance. I look best with winter colors, for example."

That explained why I thought Katy looked much more mature than just a couple of years. Not only had she grown, she'd spent more time making herself look good.

"Well I must say, you're the warmest and nicest winter I've ever met." Katy smiled but suppressed it. She didn't smile too much around strangers or at least people she didn't know very well.

"I guess I was surprised to hear you were in town," she continued. "I mean, I had quite forgotten about you, being mainly thankful I was away from my parents and on my own. Sally and I get along very well, and I've been quite happy since working at the department store."

"Do you ever think about them, though?" I asked. "I know you say you'd never go back, but don't you wonder if they've been looking for you since you left?"

"Yes, I mean no. Sort of. No, I try not to think of them. However, they have been looking for me, I know it. That's why I've been going by 'Liz' to throw them off. They've shown a flyer around with an old picture of me with blond hair. It's turned brown, and I no longer wear it long as in the photo. They're looking for a girl; I'm now a young lady."

She was all that and more.

"I'd like to see you again," I said as we left the diner.

"I don't know. This is very sudden for me, and I'm just now getting adjusted to my new life."

"I know, but I enjoy being with you. You're easy to talk to— I can say my mind and not worry about being criticized for being me. Please, what do you say? Next weekend?"

"Next weekend? Well, er, I don't know, it—"

"Just say yes," I urged. I could tell she was debating it, part of her saying "yes" and part "no." I needed the full "yes."

"In East Lankton? I can't make it up to Parkersville that easily. I don't have a car, and I don't like the buses."

"Yes here, in East Lankton. I'll walk you to your apartment."

As we walked back, we finalized plans to meet the next weekend at her apartment. Before she went through the lobby door, she kissed me on the cheek and said, "Goodnight."

During the next few months, I would not refer to our gatherings as "dates," but rather as "social visits." Our relationship was more or less a friendship on the outside, but on the inside I was boiling, wanting to take her and smother her with affection. I held back, though, not wanting to look aggressive or domineering. We had fun anyway, going to the fair, seeing some movies (she likes the drama/romance, whereas I prefer the horror films), and taking strolls along the beach to soak in the air and speaking whatever crossed our minds.

Neither of us acknowledged it to the other openly, but we were seeing each other. When Sally mentioned how the "love bug" had bitten Katy and me, Katy shrugged it off, saying I was just a good friend. It was perfectly innocent fun, and I savored it as much as possible, writing my most personal thoughts in my journal.

A couple of years had passed, and I felt the time was now or never to make my move. We were both of age, so why not pop the magical question? Before doing so, I rushed to the jewelry shop to find a moderately expensive but nice diamond ring. One day as we were walking down the beach, we joked about the possibility of...

"Yeah, do you think I would consider it?" I said.

"Probably not, you're the independent type, Mr. Studley, the guy who's on the trail for another *fe-male*. I don't think anyone could tie you down," she said.

"Yeah, but what about you? I'm sure some poor lost soul has thrown the question at you once or twice."

"Just once. And yes, he was a fool to think I would consider it. You know me, do I look like the marrying type?"

"I think you'd take 'Divorce' as your new last name," I joked.

"That's a good one," she replied, "but this one guy—I was working behind the counter, and he kept walking by. I mean, no guy keeps walking through the cosmetics—most are embarrassed to be even close to the ladies' section. He was strange, though. Every Saturday I worked, he'd come around and around, and eventually he tried striking up a conversation with me. Man o man, was he boring or what? He kept talking about his great car, like it made him the holy one, the man of supreme divinity, but I tell you—he was just too much. After he left each time, my co-worker and I would have laughing fits. We laughed so hard we cried, then I nearly choked. The last day, though, he proposed, and I swiftly had security throw him out. The last I saw of him, the security man was throwing the guy into the bushes outside the store. Everyone nearly died of laughter. Boy, the next guy who proposes to me—he'll get it."

"Seagulls," I said, turning around and pointing with my left hand. Katy turned around to watch them, and as she did so I tossed a black thing behind with my right hand.

"They're everywhere," she said. We turned back around and continued walking.

"Yeah, I can't see how any guy would...say, what's that?" I said innocently.

"A black box. Someone must have dropped it. What a strange place for a box. Like a box for a gem or something. Do you think it could have washed ashore?" she asked, picking up the box.

"I don't know. Anything inside?" I asked, restraining myself from bursting.

She opened the box, pulled out a piece of paper, and read silently. Her eyes turned from curious to surprise then utter astonishment. She stared at me, wide-eyed, then glanced at the note.

"Billy," she said, almost as if I'd done something naughty.

"What is it?" I asked, my last attempt at innocence.

"Oh, look at it. Are you serious? Me? I don't know what to say."

"How about 'yes'," I suggested.

With a burst of energy, she embraced and kissed me. While still in each other's arms, she looked me in the eyes and said thoughtfully, "Yes Billy Stradt, I'll marry you."

I was still going by the name Anton Briggs, so to make the marriage work, we had a quiet ceremony with Sally as the maid of honor in East Lankton. Katy didn't marry Anton Briggs, she married Billy Stradt. The minister took a couple of pictures of us three with Sally holding Alexander, the marmalade cat. He had a small bow around his neck.

"I now pronounce you husband and wife."

So it was, Kathleen Elizabeth Hackles married William Robert Stradt on June 6th. Katy and I drove off in the car we'd purchased together just a week earlier, with Sally waving behind (and Alexander yawning). She returned to her apartment to look after him. Meanwhile, Katy and I enjoyed a quiet but small honeymoon in a rental cottage off of Lake Bumbalee. Bumba, bumba, bumba!

"I'll miss you," said a tearful Sally as Katy and I gathered the last of her things. We'd picked out a large, two-bedroom apartment in West Lankton. "Goodbye, Alexander," Sally said, waving to the marmalade cat. He meowed in a quiet sort of way, as if he knew he was moving, and he was sad.

"Take care, girl," Sally said, giving Katy a big hug. "And you sir," she said, looking at me, "you take care of Liz, er, Mrs. Stradt."

"Don't you worry, we'll be fine. Besides, it's not like we're moving across the country. We're only a twenty-minute drive away."

"Twenty minutes, twenty thousand miles—you're still moving, Liz." The two had shared some good times together, I could tell.

"Well, we gotta be going. It's getting late, and tomorrow's my first day on my new job," I said.

"Oh really? What will you be doing?" Sally asked.

"Meat packing," I replied.

Eight.

I was thrilled to death when Katy informed me of her pregnancy. So thrilled, I took her in my arms and twirled her 'round and 'round the room.

"A baby! I'm so happy," I said. She smiled and was glad, because although we had only been married six months and were still fighting to make ends meet, I was happy.

"I'm a little anxious, though," she said. "This is my first time, and, well, do you think we can afford it?"

"The baby will come whether we can afford it or not. Besides, a baby makes us a full family. My mother would be so proud." A shadow passed over my face. "Mother."

"Do you even know where she is?" Katy asked.

"Could she still be there?" I asked. I had told Katy about my past with Han and Phil, even about Father's death. Now my curiosity was getting the better of me. Unlike Katy who never wished to see her family again, I was still curious about mine.

"Do you really wonder that much?" she asked.

"Yes. I think I should put this issue to rest once and for all. We should visit her."

"Your mother? And go through the pain all over again?"

"I'm not the same anymore. I'm older, we're married, and she's going to be a grandmother. I think she should at least know."

Katy was hesitant, but I convinced her to go along, while Sally took care of Alexander. It was a hot summer day, and the car had no air-conditioning, so it was barely tolerable with the windows down and the car moving but intolerable during stops at traffic lights. After perhaps five hours we came to the city where I spent much of my childhood—in pain.

"This is it," I said, "we lived in one of those apartments." As we walked up to the lobby, I noticed the mailbox had a different name. Instead of "Stradt," it was "Davis."

"Are you sure this is the place?" Katy asked.

"It used to be. Maybe she moved."

Minutes later, the groundskeeper came in and hesitated, as if he recognized me.

"Stradt? You must be from out of town. That woman, poor thing, was murdered by her sons, she was. In the dead of night. Took the police a week to find the boys, but they did—in some woods behind the Red Oaks Elementary School. Yup. Shook the community right up. Those boys went quicker than lightning into the Red Oaks Penitentiary. You know the Stradts?" he asked, still not sure who I was.

"Just a curious passerby. I once passed this way a few years back," I said.

"Well take my advice," he said, leaning over to me, "make this your last time. The people in this complex—they're on the lower rung of society, if you know what I mean. Not safe at night, naw-sir." With that, the groundskeeper was gone.

"I'm sorry," said Katy after we'd left.

"It's ok, I think. I just can't understand it—why?"

"You can't save the world, Billy. There's bound to be problems in every nook in every mountain."

"But my mother—she wasn't just a nook, or was she? It's so hard to figure things out, the accident, the move, Han and Phil..."

"They know," Katy offered.

"Yes, they know. All too well. What will I see if I meet them? A part of myself fighting and struggling to survive? They took one path and I another—by sheer luck our places are so different. Sheer luck."

"Not sheer luck. Obviously they didn't care. You do. Visit them, and put this to rest for good."

Katy was right. We made arrangements to see Han. Phil as I learned, had been shot and killed by a guard during an escape attempt.

"Is it really you, Billy? After all these years, you've come back. Well, kick my back!"

"Han, those days are gone. You're in prison now. Doesn't that sober you a bit?"

"Yeah, it's a sobering hell. What do you want, anyway?"

"I gotta know," I said, "how did it happen?"

"How did *what* happen?" he said sarcastically.

"Mother. I heard she died by Phil and your hands. Is it true?" I stared at him sternly.

"It's a lie!" he protested.

"You're lying now, aren't you Phil?"

Suddenly I became the big brother. He cowered under my words, shaking in his seat. Fearful, he stuttered.

"Make her leave first," he said.

"You mean Katy?"

"It's all right," she said, "I'll see you in a bit."

"Ok, Han, what is it you're so afraid to say in front of my wife?"

"Billy, I swear, I didn't want to do it," Han started, confessing with sincerity.

"Don't lead me on this merry-go-round."

"It was in the papers. Go to the library and find it—you'll see my confession. It's true, but Phil—he just went berserk. You gotta believe me. He'd become so hooked on coke that he just went crazy. He needed money for a hit, and fast. Mother wouldn't give him any, they struggled, his gun came out, and—I wanted to stop him, but I couldn't—the chemical controlled me." Han was nearly in tears, but I remained stern.

"Go on. Out with the rest of it."

"It happened so fast—she hit the ground, the police came, and we were arrested for murder."

"Why didn't you tell the truth, Han? That Phil acted alone?"

"I couldn't. I can't now either. Let's say Phil had something over me. He threatened to expose me, for something I didn't want to do. I had to do it. It was the chemical. That's what started it. You were the only clean one, Billy."

I took another hard look at him. Could this be true?

"What do you mean? What are you talking about?"

"Mother—she did cocaine. We all did, except you and dad."

"What?? This lie has gone far enough." I couldn't accept it.

"Billy, it's true. If ever I told the truth, it's now. I'm clean now, but I wasn't then. You never heard the real story behind Dad's death, did you?"

"He died in a car accident, everyone knows that, Han."

"Sure, that's what it was supposed to look like," he said.

"What are you getting at?" I demanded.

"He hit a truck, a semi. The truck's trailer smashed through the windshield, decapitating Dad. It looked like an accident, but the driver—he was Mother's secret lover."

"NO! You're lying. Tell me you're lying."

"It's no lie." Han was crying. I was furious but restrained myself.

"It can't be true."

"It is. The driver pulled out in front of Dad—he couldn't get around. The chemical, cocaine, it did it. It changed her, Billy, she used it when she met this trucker, then she got us to use it. It anesthetized us, made us feel no pain, even though we gave it to others. Remember when she kicked you out of her room? It was so her lover could sleep over with her. Only he dumped her after awhile. She learned she was one of a dozen women he had, and she slapped him. He never came 'round again."

"That only made it worse. She did the coke more and more, withdrawing and not caring about us. Phil and I used to sniff the dust around her bedroom, because she quit giving us free stuff. But Phil wanted more. He dealt and cut me in on the stuff as long as I helped. When you caught us in the woods, he did what he had to do..."

A chill went down my spine, as if an ugly wound had just been reopened. Was this it, was this how I ended up on my own?

"He had to do it. Phil pushed you over the cliff."

Silence. Han had buried his head in his arms. I stared up, realizing the full scope of my childhood. I was the product of a drugged mother. Han in prison, controlled by the drug he both loved and hated, actually grew up on the stuff, as familiar as one's favorite stuffed animal or bedtime story.

"I'm sorry, Billy. There's nothing I can say that'll fix the past, is there?"

"No," I said at last. "There isn't."

I suppose I was more in shock than anything. I couldn't believe I was so naive to not know what was happening. I truly thought my brothers were just rotten apples and my mother a depressed widow. To think it came down to a simple drug. It wasn't simple, though, and for the next few months I struggled with my past now fully revealed. After several urgings from Katy, I recounted my life again with elements in proper perspective.

"So that's it," she said.

"Yes. It's over, dear. Now we can get on with our new lives."

The excitement over Katy's labor melted away any last thoughts regarding my past and put me full tilt into my new family. Holding her hand in the delivery room, and helping to time her breathing cycle, Katy had an eight-pound, four-ounce girl. Katy was covered with sweat, and we were both exhausted (though I gathered she was more than I).

"She has such pretty blue eyes," Katy said.

"And the nicest smile. I know where she got that from," I said, nodding toward Katy.

"You're so funny," she said between breaths.

"What's her name?" asked a nurse. It was Sally. I was so focused on Katy and her labor that I didn't even notice.

"Sally! You work here!"

"Didn't I tell you, honey?" asked Katy. "I asked her to be here too."

"And I thought you were ignoring me," said Sally, nudging me and smiling.

"I, well, you have to admit, having a baby is an extraordinary experience."

"It certainly is. It's one reason I work in the maternity ward," said Sally. "Ok, so what's the baby's name?"

Katy and I had discussed various boys' and girls' names, but we never could make a firm decision. I stared at Katy for a moment, and she looked at Sally. Katy spoke:

"Melinda Sallie Stradt."

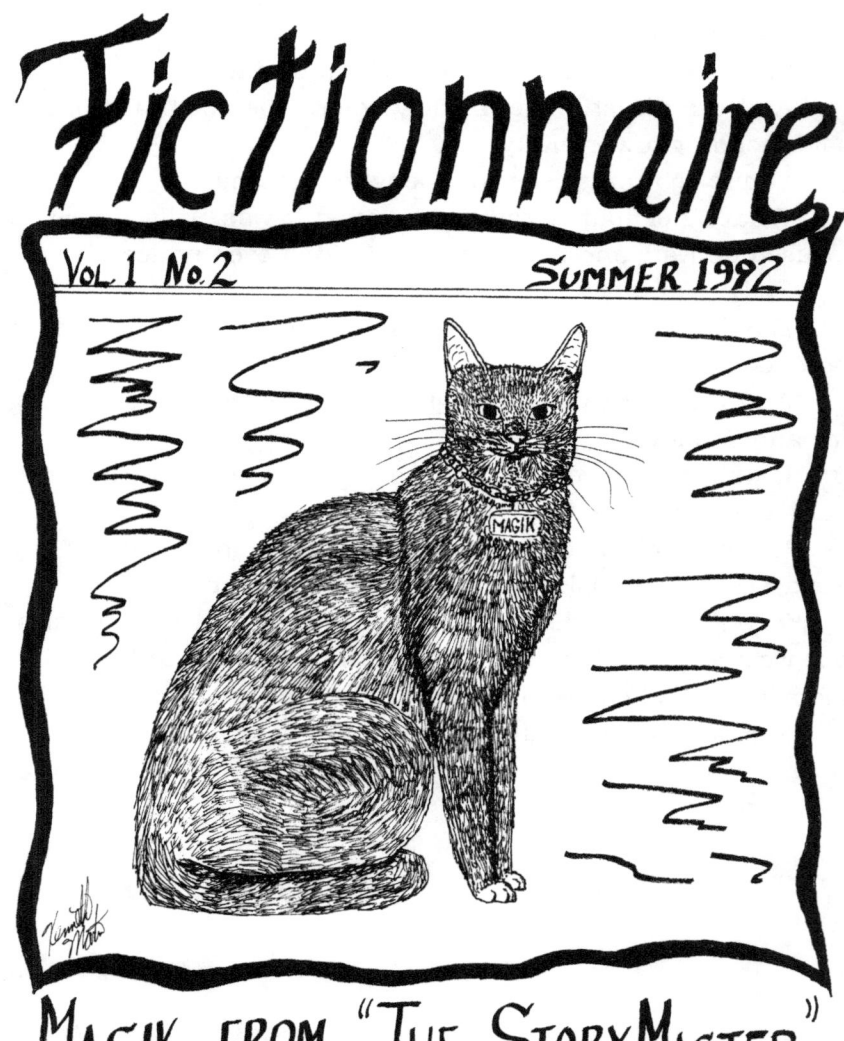

Fictionnaire

VOL 1 No. 2   SUMMER 1992

MAGIK, FROM "THE STORYMASTER"

The Cat from Hell:
Cassin the Assassin
May 12, 1992

"Get out of the sink," said Maria to The Cat from Hell, who had slept most of the night there. "Get out."

He wouldn't budge.

This is the second story regarding The Cat from Hell, a notoriously psychotic cat living under the same roof as Maria. And who is Maria? We briefly mentioned her last episode, and her existence is a mystery—almost as much a mystery as life itself, but we won't ramble on about her (I know she'll hit me upon reading this), even if she is one of the main characters. You see, Maria is in a very difficult situation—anyone living with The Cat from Hell would be—but let's face it, her life would be less stressful without The Cat from Hell, and we all strive for more stress, don't we?

I must say, though, that Maria has told me The Cat from Hell's name again, and forgive me if I misspell this, but I think it's Cassin. Don't worry; I'm sure she'll correct me in time for the next episode.

Whatever the case, we're still unsure how the genetic codes arranged themselves to produce such a chaotic and seemingly insane cat—perhaps The Cat from Hell (oops, I mean Cassin) is a result of what happens when a normal creature is placed in a human filing cabinet and forced to breathe the "clean" apartment air some of us humans breathe. I would tend to believe this explanation, but others? They would say, "It's simply The Cat from Hell. Period."

SINK OR SWIM

Cassin was comfortably sleeping in the bathroom sink. There was no budging him, the loudest shouting made him yawn, hand clapping would flinch him not. Cassin had but one fear (though he pretended not to be afraid)—water.

"There," said Maria, turning on both hot and cold water. "That'll teach you."

Cassin scampered for cover, hiding (ironically) in the bathtub behind the shower curtain. Maria managed to brush her teeth, but he was still in the bathtub, pawing at the curtain as if it were some creature. Every few seconds she heard a thumping sound against the curtain.

Maria threw the cylinder of toothpaste at the curtain, and Cassin repeatedly jumped up along the tiled wall, trying to hold on with outstretched de-clawed paws, but he slid down ever so slowly 'till he fell back in the tub.

"Get out," Maria said, whipping a towel at him again and again. A second time he tried jumping up, but he slid down again, his fleshy paws squeaking against the tiles.

"Out," she said again. Suddenly, Cassin jumped to the faucet, then up to the shower head where he managed (how I'll never know) to balance on all fours, his tail being against the wall.

"Get off," Maria yelled, getting frustrated. She whipped the towel at him. Cassin merely cowered down from the towel, clinging to the shower head with all his might. Maria shook the shower head several times, but Cassin held on, shaking all over and banging his head against the tiles several times. He sank his fangs into Maria's hand (barely healed from the previous adventure) which sent her screaming for a rabies shot.

"Crazy cat," she said, "what's wrong with you? Can't get you out of here, and I gotta take a shower! You're gonna make me late for work, Cassin. You're gonna get it now."

Maria scrambled for the faucet, turned on hot 'n' cold, activated the shower head, and deflected water off her hand into Cassin. Cassin held on for a second, but as his fur soaked up the water, he made a mad leap into the shower curtain, pulling down the curtain, the hooks, the curtain rod, and landing with a loud crash onto Maria's foot with water flying everywhere and Maria scrambling to regain her balance (not to mention her composure).

AN ENGLISHMAN MUFFINED

Miss R had already left for work that morning, dropping off Mr. B at Wee Little Daycare. Miss R originally was on good speaking terms with The Cat from Hell, but those days are long gone. How could this happen? How did this happen? How, how, how? My sources are a bit vague (or non-existent—some would even say I'm fictionalizing this entire episode, but this digression has gone far enough), but I heard it was in the paper and happened when Miss R asked a friend of hers to keep her cat for a mere day while the apartment was being redecorated.

This "friend" was none other than the infamous Godfried Barrington, a well-to-do young man of impeccable taste. Only being 28, Godfried had already conquered the New York Stock Exchange during one of the best bull markets in United States history. His clothes were custom fitted by his personal tailor, Salvador Sambino, and he drove nothing but the best automobile—Rolls Royce.

Although Godfried created a large wealth, he wasn't much for impulsive spending, rather he preferred to plan with meticulous detail how and where his investments took place. Godfried is a rare bird, which is the very thing Miss R noticed when he called her office regarding an insurance claim. Miss R took the opportunity at hand and suggested she personally inspect Mr. Barrington's Rolls Royce and assess the proper reimbursement amount. This took place after a formal lunch, paid for my Mr. Barrington himself, who showed such perfect mannerisms even Miss R had never seen (and she'd spent four years of university training pursuing the etiquettes). Godfried was somewhat impressed by Miss R's professionalism as well, and after a generous assessment by Miss R, she was invited for dinner. And another dinner. And another, and another.

It looked as if Miss R had caught herself a huge whale, and after mentioning in casual conversation to Godfried about the redecoration of her apartment and how her cat needed alternative lodging, Godfried offered to provide shelter for the cat for a single day. Of course, Godfried didn't know he was dealing with...The Cat from Hell.

What actually happened is a mystery, at least to us outsiders. Miss R would never tell exactly *what* happened, but only that *something* happened. Rumors spread like wildfire, with damages to Godfried's château going into the tens of millions. No one knows if Godfried or the butler threw the cat out, some would even say The Cat from Hell escaped into the wild, but there's no doubt about his reappearance, clinging onto the outside of Miss R's bedroom window at three in the morning. Miss R was awakened rather abruptly, needless to say.

Godfried Barrington left the United States shortly thereafter and returned to his native England. He never visited the States again.

DANCING LIGHTS

Trying to get over their Cat-from-Hell blues, Miss R and Maria sat down for a friendly game of Double Solitaire. (All right, I confess—Double Solitaire is never friendly. When I play, I'm out for blood, but that's me. Besides, this story is about Cassin, The Cat from Hell, not me, so on with it!) It was a semi-overcast Saturday afternoon, and the cumulus clouds filled the sky like cotton puffs. Every so often the sun lit up the ground, then a cloud's shadow brought "dimth." And what is "dimth?" A certain degree of non-light, whatever that means. Does anyone know what it means? No matter, Cassin (our Cat from Hell, remember?) was busy chasing the anti-venetian blinds (which grew light and dim with the passing clouds).

"Crazy cat," said Maria as Miss R slapped a three of Hearts in the center just before Maria. Maria hesitated then continued, "He'll pull down the blinds. Just like the shower curtain."

"Time out," said Miss R as she ran for the blinds (courtesy of AV products, your complete line of anti-venetian blinds. Visit an AV store in your local neighborhood today!), pulling them back. Cassin jumped, scrambled along the wall, the sill, and landed atop the AV rod. Maria, convinced she was experiencing *déjà vu*, sat in astonishment as she watched Miss R struggle to get Cassin down. Cassin pawed at Miss R, hissing up a storm.

"No, wait," said Maria. "I think he likes that. Just leave him up there. He'll get bored."

Maria was right! As soon as Miss R resumed the card game, The Cat from Hell came down from his loft (though the jump down left him dazed for several minutes, his head rolling around in circles as he attempted to regain his bearings).

"I think we're stuck," Miss R commented, referring to the card arrangement.

"Stuck with this cat," Maria threw back. "At least he's not moving."

"Don't count on that for long," Miss R said, collecting the cards together. A count of the scored cards indicated a tie, leading the two into another game.

"Ready?" asked Maria.

"Go."

Somehow (don't ask how), Cassin regained his composure and prowled around the competitors. Maria and Miss R ignored The Cat from Hell for several minutes until Miss R noticed a peculiar behavior of Cassin's (perhaps we should say simply behavior, since The Cat from Hell *is* peculiar).

"Look at him," said Miss R. "He's following a spot of light, and it's coming from your watch." As Maria moved her cards, the dancing ball of light moved up and down the wall, and Cassin jumped after it, pawing every so often as if to get some sort of advantage over the light.

"Stupid cat," said Maria. "It's just a reflection." Then Maria jerked her wrist quickly, and the two watched The Cat from Hell as his head jerked rapidly multiple times as he kept track of the light. His outstretched paw fluttered about in nervous excitement, and as Maria brought the light across the wall, Cassin jumped repeatedly across the wall, only to end up on the floor, bewildered.

"Here, Cassin," she said, taunting him again. The Cat from Hell jumped a final time, landed in a chair, and knocked over two jars which smashed into a million pieces and turned amused young ladies into irritated young ladies.

CAT SCRATCH

Although we would like to think Maria and Miss R spend their entire lives in their apartment with Cassin the Assassin, The Cat from Hell, it is in fact true they work for a living and spend a minimum of eight hours each day working, slaving, grinding stones, and fending off vicious 900-type callers. Although most consider their jobs very stressful, Maria and Miss R find theirs a welcome relief from Cassin the Assassin (on the other hand, perhaps my visits are the most stressful, but we won't dwell on such trivialities). One Thursday, however, either of them would have given their lives to have either: 1) Stayed home to swat The Cat from Hell, or 2) Permanently removed Cassin from the premises.

Cassin was having a marvelous time around, oh, what time was it? Just after eleven o'clock in the morning Eastern Daylight Time when the telephone rang. Now, normally the answering machine kicks in after the fourth ring during these working hours, but on the third-and-a-half ring, Cassin the Receptionist jumped several feet in the air to knock the offending twirp, the receiver flying out of its cradle.

"This is the Home Telephone Shopper's Club. You have been selected out of thousands for an opportunity to purchase several high-quality products. If you are not interested, please hang up now," came the automated voice from the earpiece. Cassin listened curiously when the voice spoke, but while the voice waited for a possible hang-up signal, Cassin grew anxious and pawed the phone as if trying to reawaken a sleeping mouse. Several tones bleeped, and Cassin jumped back, arching his back.

"By staying on the line, you have indicated your interest in our quality merchandise. There is no obligation to buy as long as you only listen throughout the program."

Hearing the voice again, Cassin went low to the ground, preparing to pounce on the talking box.

"We begin with our household appliance line. If you wish to place an order, select the item by pressing its corresponding touch-tone number."

"Item #1—a Sears canister vacuum cleaner. This unit is the—"

Gearing up his strength, Cassin the phone Assassin landed all four paws on the buttons, created a harmonic cacophony, then proceeded to chew on the cord.

"Thank you for selecting items 3, 4, 6, 8, and 9. Our next line is—thank you for selecting items 1, 3, 4, 8, and special item 0. The next—thank you. Next—thank you. Thank you, thank you, thank you!"

Miraculously, Cassin had eaten through the main phone cord, disconnecting the Home Telephone Shopping Club. Indeed, the real miracle came when Miss R came home and managed not to die from cardiac arrest.

"You're apartment 1A?" asked a delivery man. If Miss R had been Maria, the scene would have been ugly. Simply put, I would not be in Michigan during such a tempest. But it *was* Miss R, and her composure is as solid as a rock, yet cunning as a knife.

"No, I'm visiting some friends in 2A. What's going on, are the 1As moving out?" she asked, testing the waters.

"We knocked but no one answered. The landlord let us in. We've been delivering appliances, furniture, jewelry, and china for three hours. These people must have some money, that's for sure."

"Really?" Miss R asked, in mock innocence. "And just where did they order this from?"

"The Home Telephone Shopping Club. Order was put in this morning, as a matter-of-fact. I must say my people were quite impressed with the order—items were selected in record time, one gal told me, almost super-human."

"Cassin!" Miss R swore under her breath.

"Bless you," replied the delivery man. "By the way, any idea when these people get home?"

"Not really."

"Well I'll be. I'm supposed to get their signatures for these things, now that we're done unloading. Normally it wouldn't matter too much, but this order is big enough to warrant it."

"Really? How big?"

"Let's just say I could buy myself two new cars and have money left over for a year's worth of insurance on both."

"Wow. Hmmm. Tell you what, if I see them, I'll let them know you're here."

"Thanks." The delivery man wiped his forehead with a handkerchief. "Man is it hot. Say, do you think you could do me a favor?"

"Maybe."

"Here," he said, handing her a business card. "I've already put one in their door. If you see them, could you give 'em this? It could speed things up."

"Sure. No problem."

"Thanks. I'll be back in twenty minutes if they ask."

"Ok."

With that the delivery man was gone. Miss R led Mr. B quietly into the over-stuffed apartment and was shocked, shocked, shocked! Everywhere, new things sprouted like weeds.

"But how?" she muttered, looking around and scratching her head. "This is all a mistake, some strange sort of nightmare. How—"

Miss R saw the telephone lying on the floor. The cord was chewed off. Paw prints soiled the box. Her eyes lit with rage, the fire building as her face turned from a soft white to cherry red. Slowly her eyes panned the room looking for one thing and one thing only. On the window sill, staring back in a wide-eyed psychotic expression was him. The Cat from Hell.

"YOU ARE DEAD!" she yelled, and as she dove over the kitchen table, Cassin jumped off the sill and ran over the couch, a chair, the washing machine, and into the bedroom, cowering under the bed.

"I'll get you, you filthy piece of dirt. When my hand grabs your puny little neck, you will pay for your crime. I'll twist your head off."

But Miss R couldn't reach the cat, and realizing her predicament, she decided it best to call Maria. The answering machine/phone being ruined, Miss R resorted to using her bedroom phone while simultaneously keeping a good eye on Cassin the telephone Assassin.

"Desk #230," came a voice into Miss R's ear.

"Jill? Tammy. Transfer me over to Maria."

"You know I'm not supposed to do this. If the supervisor finds out—"

"Damn it, Jill, I don't have time for this nonsense. Transfer me or I'll tell Greg you're cheating on him."

"Ok, ok!"

"Desk #247."

"Maria, are you busy?"

"Tammy? No, things are winding down. You're out of breath. What have you been doing?"

"You're not going to believe what Cassin did this time."

"Must be pretty serious for you to call."

"It is," Miss R affirmed, "it is."

In a few minutes Miss R had described the incredible tale, including the conversation with the delivery man.

"And he's going to come back in ten minutes for signatures."

"It can't be that much. Just tell him it was a mistake."

"Easier said than done," explained Miss R. "The way this guy was talking, once it's purchased it's purchased. No refund, no return. What are we going to do?"

Maria paused for a moment deep in thought.

"I have an idea," Maria came back.

"Oh no, not another one of those. The last time you had an idea, a certain Englishman's home was wrecked, and so was my future as a wealthy lady."

"No no, this is different. We'll actually kill two birds with one stone. You said you were visiting the people in 2A?"

"Yeah, which is pretty ironic, considering how much we hate them."

"Exactly. Just tell the delivery man your friends in 2A said they ordered the stuff then leave as if your visit is over."

"Oh that's a fine one, Maria," said Miss R sarcastically. "And I suppose he'll believe me."

"No, not at first. But get him to call in to his office. Tell him your friends in 2A just called in to report the mistake. Then get out of there."

"But when he calls back, they'll still tell him 1A."

"No, they'll tell him 2A."

"Now you've lost me. How?"

"Well, I know the Home Telephone Shopping Club is heavily computerized. I *should* know, I've purchased enough things from them. If the records are changed..."

"Isn't that illegal?"

"Think of this—we won't be doing anything illegal," Maria said. "Remember my cousin from Milwaukee?"

"Yeah, the one who writes."

"He, well, I can't say any more over the phone. Trust me. Meet me at Chi-Chi's for dinner. Bye."

"Bye."

Keep in mind the following could never happen in real life. Computer systems have the highest security and are impenetrable. I have to write this disclaimer, or else everyone would hide their money in their mattresses if they knew how vulnerable banks and other computerized institutions really are.

"Good afternoon, Ken Martin," I said answering the phone.

"Hello. This is your cousin. Your desperate cousin. You're not too busy, I hope."

"Me? Just re-writing sections of my latest novel. My editor found a few minor discrepancies, but all in all—"

"That's nice," Maria cut in, "but I need a huge favor." Maria continued to tell me the whole story.

"This is a joke. Pretty funny. I knew your cat was a little lively. Very amusing."

"This is no joke. I need your help."

"You're serious," I said. It was quite an earful to digest. "But I'm nearly 400 miles away. How in the name of Cassin could I help?"

"Remember when you used to hack into computers several years ago?"

"I admit I dabbled in programming a little..."

"A little?! Don't be modest! We know the real story, how the story of AckNak's computer break-ins was based on your *personal* experience."

"Yeah, yeah, yeah. Are you suggesting I..."

"Not suggesting—begging."

"Do you know what the penalties are for that kind of stuff today? I was lucking to have done my 'experimentation' when laws hadn't yet caught up with technology. But that isn't the only problem. More than likely this transaction is stored in several different database files on the central computer. To delete it would be nearly impossible without having extensive knowledge and access of the system. This would take considerable amounts of time, and time is the enemy of any hacker."

"I know, but what about changing the address?"

"Even the address could be—"

"A single number. Instead of 1A, make it 2A."

"Hmmm," I said. "It's possible, I suppose, but this Home Telephone Shopping Club—I have no phone number, no starting place. Using an Autodialer could take years."

"That's where I come in. I have a private internet address where you could tie into their system, at least attempt to. You still have access to internet?"

"Yeah," I said reluctantly, feeling a great burden falling upon me. "I never got rid of it. Should have but didn't."

"Good, then it's set."

"You owe me one, Maria. A big one."

"I know. You could turn this into a story. Perhaps change a few things, but it would be a nice little story to add to your collection."

"Hmm. You're right. Just when you think you've—"

"No time to daydream. Here's the address."

Maria relayed the internet network address where I could connect with the Home Telephone Shopping Club. It had been a few years since I'd done anything of this nature, but I did have an experimental virus program based loosely on the Morris worm. I called it the Silent Night Virus since its sole purpose was to quietly sneak through the network in order to retrieve or change small bits of information. It was only ten minutes before I had the thing ready to go, which was amazingly quick considering what the code did.

With the blinding speed of computers, it was only three minutes before I had gained access to three accounts. Of those three, one had system access, and after planting a "command misspell daemon," it was but another eight minutes before I had root access. Once I had root access, the virus took over, cloaking its appearance and finding then changing the apartment number from 1A to 2A. Within microseconds, the virus extinguished itself with all evidence wiped clean.

A few hours later, I was enjoying a friendly game of tennis. Upon returning home, I found a message on my answering machine and played it.

"Hi Ken, this is Tammy. We would like to thank you for your 'medical' treatments and are happy to report the disease has quickly moved on to other less dignified people. Once again, thanks. Oh, if you ever get the chance, do you think you could perform a lobotomy on our cat? Just a thought."

A FINE FELINE

"Bad cat. Bad, bad, BAD!" Maria shook her finger at Cassin several times. Cassin looked at the finger then jumped aggressively for it. Maria, having a desire to preserve her finger in one unbleeding piece, withdrew her fingers into a flat-hand formation while her hand and arm whirled around and "popped" Cassin on the side of his head, sending him into the armchair. Maria threw a pillow at The Cat from Hell, but he jumped atop the chair with back fully arched.

"You naughty cat. I'll make you pay," she cried, diving into the chair. Cassin made a mad rush for the bathroom, then Maria jumped up and followed him. Upon destination, the bathroom closed.

"There," she said, "that'll keep you in your place."

"Until," started Miss R.

"Until?"

"Until one of us wants to use the bathroom. I keep wondering when he'll get tired and outgrow this hyperactivity."

"Never," replied Maria, soothingly. "He's the Cat from Hell."

As Maria spoke, a single paw probed here and there under the bathroom door, as if such an act had great significance.

"Even shut in the bathroom," returned Miss R, "he can still be a nuisance. Look at him pawing under the door."

"Bad cat!" said Maria sternly, and as she readied a book to pound the paw, the paw disappeared as quickly as it had appeared.

"Now what?" asked Miss R.

A faint meow echoed from within the porcelained room.

"How odd. He's meowing. Since when does he do that?"

"Maybe he wants out. That is strange though," continued Miss R, "he usually just attacks or watches the birds through the kitchen window."

It was unmistakable. Cassin the Meowing Assassin from Hades was meowing up a storm, and the two roomies were overcome with curiosity and opened the door. It became obvious. Meows emanated from the vent, and Cassin was meowing at another cat, somewhere in the lost apartment building abyss.

"It figures," said Miss R, "he thinks he's King Cassin—let no other cat challenge his authority."

"I'll teach him authority," said Maria, taking a filled paper cup and dumping water on Cassin. He scurried back into the living room then disappeared from sight. "See?" pointed Maria. "He knows who's boss."

"For the moment," said Miss R, "but Maria, he'll go back to his ways, and after the furniture fiasco, I'm beginning to have second thoughts about Cassin."

"I know, Tammy, you want to put him on a leash. I have an old leather belt which would do..."

"No, Maria, I mean—"

Miss R was rudely interrupted by a loud grinding noise, as if metal gears were grinding badly.

"What the—" remarked Tammy, startled.

"Is it? Is it?"

The two ran to the kitchen, where an amused Cassin sat atop the counter watching the sink.

"The garbage disposal. Hmmmph!" A reflex action flipped the power switch off, and upon close inspection, Miss R discovered a badly mangled spoon lodged in the garbage disposal. Maria, watching Miss R, instinctively swept her arm across the counter top, sending the Flying Fur Feline Assassin into the AV blinds, where he crashed noisily and fell helpless to the floor, his gyrating limbs unable to regain complete balance.

"There," said Miss R. "Cassin must go."

"It's not that bad," said Maria, wondering what made her say such a ridiculous thing.

"Look at the facts—your hand, the shower curtain, the Englishman, the furniture, now this disposal, not to mention the countless mischievous things he's done. I'm telling you, it'd be cheaper without him, much cheaper. Life would be better."

"Tell you what," suggested Maria, a demon overtaking her personality and turning her into a concerned friend, "let's take a walk to the pond and gather our thoughts. We'll come up with something."

The idea was well received, and Maria, Miss R, and Mr. B dreamily stepped out on a cool summer day, walked half a block, and sat under a tree. Mr. B fed a few ducks while Maria and Miss R talked. And talked. It was difficult for me to hear the conversation (being 400 or so miles away in my apartment and working on my cystic fibrosis story), but I do know that once the three returned to the apartment building, there was an agreement to get rid of Cassin once and for all, and although the original idea was to torture him to death, the final proposal to let him go in the woods some sixty miles to the south was approved.

As Maria and Miss R stopped at the lobby door, they looked and waited for each other to get her key out and open the door.

"Your key?" asked Miss R.

"I thought you had yours," replied Maria, who obviously didn't have hers.

"You mean you didn't bring yours? Mine's inside. Don't tell me we have to hunt down the Super so we can get in."

"I can't believe we both did this," remarked Maria, amazed.

"Face it, we're jinxed by Cassin. Once we get rid of him..."

A noise came over the intercom. A meow.

"Hello?" said Miss R instinctively.

"Meow," came back the voice.

"It's him. The Cat from Hell, it's really him."

"This is too much for me," said Miss R, who was ready to leave the spot, take off in her car, and never return.

"No wait, Tammy. Maybe he can—Cassin? Push the button, and let us in."

"That would be a feat," said Tammy.

"Squeak, squeak, squeak!" sounded Maria, trying to pique Cassin's curiosity. A few seconds later, the door buzzed, and the three were in. Amazingly, Cassin managed to jump up several times to open the apartment door.

"Well, I can't believe this cat. He actually let us in," Tammy said, with Cassin purring against her leg. "Maybe he's not such a bad cat after all." She went to pet him, but at the last moment he snapped back and nipped her thumb, causing a small wound to bleed.

"Nah, he'll always be...The Cat from Hell."

Millions

June 4, 1992

We leave Maria, Tammy, and Cassin behind and travel north, crossing from lower Michigan into upper, and taking U.S. Highway 2 west until we come to Million Dollar Road. Here we find one of my distant cousins, Juan Million.

"Good millions," he said to me when I first met him.

"Good morning. I just can't get over this—are you really Juan Million?"

"And then some. Please, come in. Have a seat. Can I get you something?"

"Maybe a glass of water?" I suggested.

"Of course. One *million* water molecules coming up!"

"You must tell me," I said between sips, "were you born a Million?"

"No. I was born Thomas Peuwer in a small Texas town you've probably never heard of."

"And?" I said, prompting him further. "You seem to be doing well now. How did this come about?"

"Oh, millions upon millions of minutes ago, I was a Peuwer Texas boy working on the ranch, just gettin' by. Not much water down there, and the days were hotter than an oven."

"I spent my first twenty years living in Texas without once crossing the state line. Not once. My family couldn't afford to travel, but the heat was gettin' to me, so with my meager savings I took a bus out of state and travelled. I fell in love with the Great Lakes area, and after several million minutes of hard work in the business world, I made it big—*millions* of dollars worth."

"And you changed your name?" I asked.

"Yes. Juan Million," he replied.

"Juan—that's a Spanish name. You don't look Spanish," I said.

"Ah, on the outside I don't, but deep within millions upon millions of cells speak true to me that my name should be Juan Million. Do you want to know the secret to my success?"

This line rather surprised me as I suspected no magician would reveal the methods behind the tricks.

"Hard work—you were just saying that," I commented.

"Not just that. It's all up here," he said, pointing to his head. "A single word that gets me through the most difficult times, the word that turns despair into prosperity, the very word that has rescued me from the grave numerous times and given me life."

"Let me guess—some deity of sorts," I proposed.

"No. Close your eyes for a moment and think of one thing—millions."

"Millions? Millions of what?"

"It doesn't matter. Millions. It could be millions of dollars, millions of years, millions of sand particles on a pleasant beach, millions of miles we are from the sun—there are millions of possibilities. My favorite, though, is seeing millions of people gathered around lending a hand to help me through the day. Those people also listen to my millions of problems and have given me valuable advice over the years. Millions are on my side, millions."

"Sometimes I'll take a breath of fresh air on my balcony and think, 'My, how many millions of years has this great land been here?' Then I look around and wonder how many millions of trees have lived on this land before humans ever existed. Even to see the world a million years ago—think of it, the millions of days gone by of absolute peace and quiet."

"Millions," I said as if practicing a tennis stroke. "It does have a bit of a ring to it. That's all you say, *millions*?"

"You don't just say *millions*—every fiber in your body must think *millions*."

"And then you feel better?"

"Grimly, I just can't convey to you the power of millions. The beauty, the magnitude—it overcomes a person with a sense of awe."

"Ah, but there must be a flip side to this coin."

"Not just *a* coin, but a *million* coins," he interrupted.

"Whatever—I can just see millions of bacteria invading living tissue causing much destruction and pain."

"It's a shame, really," he started, "that bacteria have been negatively labeled. As a matter of fact, most bacteria are beneficial, playing a vital role in converting organic material from one state to another. Without the millions of bacteria legions, life would be darn near impossible on earth. Many good examples abound where bacteria are helpful, from yogurt cultures to oil-slick eaters. As with any society of millions, there are some thousand or so that turn bad. I admit this. This is why I think of *millions* and not *thousands*."

"If millions are so great, what about billions, or even trillions?"

"Trillions—so trivial. And billions remind me of billiards. But millions, it's like existing for a millennium. Tell me, Grimly, you live in Milwaukee, right?"

"Yeah, Milwaukee, Wisconsin."

"Milwaukee is the short name—it's really Millionwaukee."

"Millionwaukee? That's a little awkward to say," I said.

"Why do you think the millions call it Milwaukee?"

"C'mon now, Millionwaukee? *Milwaukee* is an Indian name."

"A corrupted Native American name. Nonetheless, don't you see how millions flow from everywhere? My chair here for instance—what color would you call it?"

"Red, what else would it be?" I asked.

"Vermillion."

"Where does it stop?" I asked casually.

"In another million years?" he suggested. "I know it sounds as if I'm dwelling on millions, and perhaps I am, but in all honesty I do have somewhat of a semi-normal life. One moment..."

Juan walked over to a window and appeared to motion for someone to come into the house.

"Although *millions* is a great belief in my life, the single most important—"

"A single thing?" I interrupted. "What about millions?"

"Sometimes we need but one." Footsteps could be heard approaching the door. "Please, Grimly, meet my wife, Donna. Donna, this is Grimly Grimsby from Millionwaukee."

"A pleasure to meet you, Grimly," she said.

"Likewise. I'm curious, Donna, do you share your husband's zeal for millions?"

"Well," she started, giving Juan a quick glance, "I may not say the word or think it as much as Juan, but I do appreciate its value in its various manifestations."

Who are these people? This *millions* thing is just too much. Then again, Juan and Donna do seem to be doing quite well and enjoying their lives. If only I could have such a life. Millions. Just saying it *does* have some strange effect on me, as if some magical spell were cast, giving me a warm sensation all over. Part of me warned not to get caught up in yet another gimmick, another said it really didn't matter, because no harm could come from this sort of euphoria. Or could it?

"Have you been to the lake house yet?" asked Donna.

"Lake house?"

"Yes," added Juan, "on the shore of Lake Michigan, Green Bay to be more specific. Here, why not ride with us?"

We didn't have far to go, but the first question to mind was why the Millions had two places so close together. Before I could ask, he answered.

"Donna and I have been in love with this part of the country for quite some time," he said as we pulled up to the driveway in Juan's four-wheel drive vehicle. "We bought our first house on Million Dollar Road, the same we have now. I'd like to say we have millions of forested acres, but perhaps a few dozen is more accurate. Our love for the forest was not at all diminished by our love for the water, and we later bought this lake-house, which not only provides a great summertime resort, but also allows a view of the lake during the winter."

"I've always wondered what this part of the country looks like during the winter," I said as we walked up to the lake house on the late-spring day. "At times it's hard to believe people stay up here all year round."

"It's not so terribly different from Millionwaukee, though the flowers bloom a bit later, and the winters are colder. Take a guess, Grimly, as to what you envision winters are like up here."

"Cold. Bitterly cold. Trees, grass—all plant life devoid of greenery. Snow everywhere, several feet deep, and icebergs everywhere on the lake."

"Icebergs? That would be interesting! Unfortunately, we have none of those, unless a 5x10 drifting ice sheet be considered an iceberg. No, no 'bergs. Snow, yes, but only the drifts become deep. Come to think of it, the last few years have yielded much less snow than prior. As for the flora—the trees are evergreen, though they tend to lose some needles during the winter. But the greatest thrill during the winter is the lake itself. Grimly, you just would not believe it, but cars drive on the lake. Ice fishing seems to be quite popular, though I sometimes wonder what the people do when a fissure develops—millions in fact, and in all sizes. It can get stormy, and believe you me the wind can howl for days on end, and we do occasionally get blizzards. However, when it's sunny and calm, well Grimly, you'd have to be here. It's so strange—absolute silence, as if human life did not exist. At those times we feel as if it's millions of years ago, before man has hewn down the millions of trees or polluted the millions of water gallons, the millions of cubic-feet air, or the millions of animals."

We made our way through the house briefly, the two pointing out various antiques and spear heads from the surrounding area.

"You must see the beach," said Donna, and within minutes we were walking on, yes, millions of sand particles.

"Incredible," I said.

"Your Millionwaukee is on this same lake, Grimly. Is it really so different up here?"

"Yes. As you so aptly mentioned, millions of water gallons are polluted in that area. It is also quite developed, ack, I don't even know if that is an accurate word."

"I know what you mean," said Juan. "A seed develops into a fully mature plant, shrub, or tree. A small gathering of people can grow into a village, a town, a city, then finally a *Me-trap-olis* full of concrete, steel, and filth. An ugly growth to be sure, but seemingly necessary. I must say the last twenty years have shown us stronger warning signs of a gradually failing planet."

"One could say there are spotted infections throughout the world," Donna said, "with a gradual botulism increasing."

"Botulism? Blood poisoning? Are you a nurse, Donna?"

"Grimly, let me again introduce you to my wife, Dr. Donna Million."

"An M.D.?"

"Yes. But I must correct you—botulism is food poisoning, though I think you understand what we mean. It's difficult to cure the patient when he continues to ingest massive quantities of pathogens."

"Don't get us wrong, Grimly, we personally have nothing against the 1+ million of Millionwaukee residents, God save their souls. Those in charge, however—they could make the difference. Ah, this is on the verge of political discussion—this is a social occasion. I think we've spent enough time on ourselves."

"Yes," added Donna. "Please tell us something about yourself."

"Where should I start?"

"No better place than the beginning," said Juan.

"Like you, Juan, I was born in the South. I've moved around, though, and for the last few years I've been living in Milwaukee, with my own column in the local paper. Since—"

"Your own newspaper column? Really?" they each said.

"I've only had it for the last few months, and at first I was a bit nervous, but each day I've been able to get a better feel for things, as well as some friends who have given me some good topics. In the back of my mind, there's always the fear of getting *writer's block*, but so far I haven't been struck."

"A newspaper columnist—extraordinary," Juan said.

"Why just last week I was mentioning the local ozone problem, and how people with respiratory ailments have such difficulty," I added.

"You're one of us!" exclaimed Donna.

"One of the family, yes," I said.

"No, Grimly. What she means is—you care about the environment—enough to do something about it," said Juan.

"Hardly. I don't see how writing about something can improve it," I mentioned.

"Maybe not directly, but you should know better than anyone the power of the pen. Your readers are enlightened or reminded of these concerns, and perhaps—" Juan was saying.

"Perhaps I could make a difference?" I asked.

"Not just *a* difference—*the* difference. Your column is read by—millions," said Donna.

Millions. The very word suddenly took on a new meaning. As I stood there looking across Green Bay at St. Martin Island, I wondered if I *could* make the difference. Did I have millions on my side? Perhaps there were millions against me. Perhaps millions didn't care. Perhaps...

"There have been efforts to preserve the environment. The recycling, automotive emission controls—" I argued.

"Some," Juan said, "Some. Much more needs to be done. In addition, the government is on the edge of *loosening* its environmental regulations. Why? 'More jobs, a better economy,' it says, but we know it would only mean a temporary increase in jobs, then we'd be back to the same ways with but one exception—a more rapidly eroding world. I know this sounds politically motivated, but try to see through the words."

"Whoa, this is so sudden. I don't know what to say."

"We only ask you to give it some thought," said Donna. "It's one thing to secure a job and make something of oneself. It's quite another to make the world a better place."

The rest of my visit was quite enjoyable. Neither Juan nor Donna mentioned the progressive environmental harm but instead made me laugh and happy with their humor and excellent hospitality. After a very relaxing week, I returned to my home in Milwaukee with the confirmed decision to lend my hand to a better place. It is through today's column, therefore that I make my first of many requests for each person to reflect on his daily activities not just from a personal and present-day point of view, but from one seeing both past and future, and how he can preserve as once was for our children and grandchildren to come, so that they may enjoy life as we have. We are truly on the verge of destroying this dream and forever condemning them to a life of hell, if we haven't already.

Jacob Richardson
in

Unseen Assailant: Part I

May 2, 1992

"Helen," I said. "Are you about ready?"

"Almost," she called back.

I took a quick look through my shaving kit to make sure I had all my essentials—razor, shampoo, soap, deodorant, toothpaste, toothbrush—I forgot my toothbrush. *I suppose I could always buy one, well, maybe I should bring it.*

"Could you bring my toothbrush on the way down, dear?" I called.

"Ok," she replied.

One last check of the downstairs, and I was ready. The lights were mostly off, the back door locked, bags packed—everything was ready. I decided to take the initiative and put the bags in the trunk. Earlier, I'd dropped Johnny and Bobby off at Helen's sister's house, so just the two of us would be making this trip—a second honeymoon I suppose one could call it. Both Helen and I had earned this break. She had just put in a rather grueling three months in her nursing job at the hospital while I spent late hours at the office.

"Quarantine, quarantine—I keep hearing the word and seeing the signs. I feel as if I've been in a quarantine forever," she said, rushing down the stairs. She was dressed in a rather casual outfit, and her hair parachuted gracefully as she descended. She carried a small duffel bag over a shoulder while carrying her purse in her hand. "Let's go before I'm called in."

"Great," I said as we rushed out the door. Helen ran to the car as I unlocked the front door, she got in and closed her door as I made a last rush to the car, slid across the hood, and jumped in with brevity. A quick twist of the ignition, a quick reverse into a Y-turn (a trick I'd learned from Helen), and we were gone with only minimal tire squealing.

"I'll be so glad to leave this little city, Shairton," she said. "Just as soon as we get on Highway 37, I'll be relieved."

"Oh look," I said, pointing to Shairton County General, Helen's place of business, "I wonder what that is? Let's pull in."

"Don't you even speak another word. Gaud, what a place—it's like a zoo in there. Keep driving," she said as I slowed down. "Hey, c'mon. Speed up."

"I wonder if they need some help—maybe another nurse to help."

"You're gonna end up in there—as a patient in critical condition if you don't step on it."

She pushed my right knee, forcing the gas pedal down and the car faster.

"Whoa, hey! Now, now. Let's save this for later."

"Heh, heh. Hey, what's that?" she asked, getting more playful. She pointed to something out my left window; I looked but saw nothing as she pushed the horn a couple of times.

"Hey, now cut that out," I said tauntingly.

"Beep, beep!" the car went.

"Ok, ok. You win."

"Beep."

A quick twist of the wheel tossed her back next to her door.

"Hey Sunday driver," she shot back, "better not drink too much of that moonshine—it might get you pulled over." She was laughing with me. Several more twists threw us all over.

"Uh oh, you're not gonna do this, are you?" she asked as I accelerated to beat a yellow light.

"Scratch the roof for good luck," I said. The light was red as we crossed the intersection.

"Better hope there isn't a cop back there," she said, waving a finger at me in a pseudo-disciplinary fashion.

"Yes, Maw, I'll take my medicine and sleep on the moldy bed with the hundred-year old feather pillow."

We burst into laughter.

"I still can't believe," she said, slapping her knee, "your mother. She's gotta be out of her mind."

"She *is* out of her mind," I said. "The woman is always walking a tightrope—her way or no way. You know what they say, 'The road to hell is paved with good intentions'."

"With intentions like those," she continued, "who needs bad ones?"

"Isn't that supposed to be, 'friends'?"

"It's all the same, isn't it?"

"At this point," I replied, "yes."

Our destination was the Lakeside Inn, a small and secluded hotel/restaurant/tavern with swimming/boating on Topabee Lake. Seventy miles stood between the lake and our house. Normally it took an hour and a half to get there, but with my driving we would made it in sixty-five minutes—all highway. Helen alternated between playing with the air coming in through her window, honking the horn, and dancing to the radio (although I never could figure how one could dance in a car).

"Seventy-five, staying alive," I said.

"That's seventy-five, saving lives," she said.

"And it certainly is saving ours. Uh oh, yikes!"

In seconds I had realized an oncoming car was actually a state trooper. I pulled the car down to sixty, then he was on top of us. After he passed I saw his brake lights go on—there was no one in front of him.

"Did he get a reading on you?" Helen asked. My heart was in my mouth and pounding.

"Not sure. Gotta find a place to turn off," I said.

As I went over a hill, I caught a glimpse of the cruiser making a quick U-turn in my rear-view mirror.

"He's made an 'ooie'," I relayed to Helen. "And hot on our trail."

My mind raced with possible options; my eyes darted from side to side looking for something, anything to get me out of this.

"If he sees you evading him then catches you..." Helen started.

"No person has ever caught me," I said while coming up to a crossroad. To the left, tire marks graced a gentle turn; to the right, a sharper turn. I chose the right. In my mirror, I could see the left turn was a weaving, windy road. I was on a flat, dead-straight road.

"Make this the first time. He'll spot you quicker than a fire-fly in the dark."

"Maybe." I said, picking up speed. Ditches on each side made off-road driving prohibitive. We approached an under-pass. "Maybe not."

"No, you're not. Don't even think about it. Jacob Richard-son, if you—"

Regardless of the ditch, I knew I had to get off the road. I'm not sure what pumped me up or why I was so determined to get away. Perhaps the cop didn't know my speed—maybe he was going after me because he knew I was speeding but not by how much.

His sirens echoing in the distance, the car nosedived over the ditch, bounced, then slid sideways down a steep but thicket-entwined embankment that led to a dirt road. As it landed, it tipped up precariously on its side, ready to turn over. Helen and I stared at each other for what seemed an eternity, but the car had a will of its own and fell back to its proper stance.

In the five seconds we sat there, I realized we'd both yelled on the way down, and the car had stalled. I was ready to start it again, but Helen intervened.

"Listen," she said. "The siren is fading."

She was right. The cop must have taken a quick look down the road we took, saw no one, then proceeded the other way.

"Sorry about that. I guess I got carried away," I said.

"And I thought *I* was the wild driver. You're supposed to be the conservative one," she said.

"Sometimes I amaze myself. Are you all right?" My foolish-ness had caught up with me, and the responsible adult in me warned of possible injury—both physical and emotional.

"Just a bump on the head."

"I'm gettin' too old for this. Boy was that crazy," I said, looking down at myself.

"Hey, you were just having some fun. C'mon, we evaded the cop, didn't we?"

"Yeah, unless he turns around and comes this way. We best be moving on," I said, turning on the car. After several turns over, it caught, but it sputtered and wheezed for several seconds before smoothing out.

"But we can't go back up. Where to?" she asked, perplexed.

"Follow the brown dirt road," I said, whistling the melody to "Follow the Yellow Brick Road" from *The Wizard of Oz.*

Something was caught up under the car, but after half a mile it broke loose and fell behind. A thick woods surrounded the dirt road, and after another half mile it ended at the corner of a corn field, which opened up in front. Obviously the trees were cleared for the field.

"Dead end," Helen said, almost sarcastically.

"Dead. Turn around?"

"Guess so. It might be a bit difficult driving through that corn."

"Hmm, not much room to turn around." It was true. I attempted to make a 'yowee,' what Helen and I call a Y-turn. After I went from reverse to drive, I overshot the road and stopped in the grass, spinning. The tires whined, the mud slapped against the car, but it didn't budge.

"I never thought I'd get a front-wheel-drive car stuck," I commented, "but it seems I've succeeded."

"What a way to spend a honeymoon."

"Yeah. I'm sorry, hun. I shouldn't have gone so fast. Going down that hill was a mistake. What a laugh! Ok. Time for action."

Helen and I jumped out of the car through my door, her door being blocked with mud. Our worst fear came true—the front, right end was deep in mud. I ran into the woods and came back with bracken which I broke and shoved under the front wheels.

"I'll push, and you take it out in reverse," I said. Helen slowly got in. She eased her foot on the gas, but the wheel spun as I pushed with my might. The tires threw mud all over and onto me. I spit small pieces out of my mouth, and as the car finally grabbed and jerked backward, I fell face first into the mud. Helen parked the car and ran out.

"Oh, are you ok?" she asked.

"Yuck. I'm filthy," I said, looking up in time to see her take my picture.

"Smile."

"I am so dirty."

"Well, why don't you change? We *do* have extra clothes in back," Helen suggested.

True. Not a soul around saw me changing into fresh clothes and putting the dirty ones into a plastic bag.

"Maybe I should drive," suggested Helen. "Might be safer."

"Maybe. Yeah, go ahead and drive. I don't think I could handle another incident like this. Yawn, I'm tired."

"I knew it. Give a man a little excitement, and he's worn out," she winked.

Helen was surprisingly conservative compared to her usual driving. I guess it was due to our being so far off course. Not only were we getting behind schedule, but we didn't know how to get back on the main road.

"This must go somewhere," she said after several miles. At least it seemed like several miles, but it was hard to tell. How many hours had passed? I knew we had been going on the dirt road for quite some time.

"I'm sure it does. Boy, it's getting a little hot," I said, scratching my neck.

"Hot?" she asked, surprised. She glanced at me.

"Yes, and I seem to have gotten a strange rash all ov—"

Helen slammed on the brakes and parked the car.

"What, what is it?" I asked.

"That's not a rash," she said, disturbed.

"It looks like one to me. I feel like I just wanna get out of here quickly. If we can just get on the main road," I was say- ing, getting excited for no apparent reason.

"Those are pimples, and now you're getting excited. Why are you excited?"

"And why are you so concerned?" I asked. "Must be an allergic reaction, right? I see you're fine, though."

"For now. No, if you were having an allergic reaction, your nose would be irritated, your eyes irritated, and you'd possibly be breaking out in hives or get eczema—maybe even a little difficulty breathing with the tightening of your chest. No, these are pimples. The mud..."

"The mud?" I asked. "What about it? It was just mud, that's all."

"Something must've been in it. You didn't swallow any, did you?"

"Why would I ever eat mud?" I asked. She was getting ridiculous, and I was tired of this. "Could you just please start the engine and get us out of here?"

"Ok," she said, and we took off with urgency.

"Hey, take it easy!" I said.

"I know you wouldn't purposely eat mud," she continued, "but did any get in your mouth?"

"I suppose," I said. "It flew up at once—maybe I even swallowed a little—ah, maybe it's sun-poisoning."

"Maybe not. It could be a variety of things, many of which are quite rare these days. If you don't get better within the next hour, we'll have to get you to the doctor."

"Now Helen, this is outrageous. I feel fine. Everything will be ok. Let's just go to the Lakeside Inn, ok?"

Helen was silent but determined to get out of there as quickly as possible. With her silence, I was getting upset.

So, she's gonna play this game, I thought. *Well, she worries too much.* It seemed the emotions changed me, though, and I was getting a sense of depression.

"Are you all right?" she asked.

"Yeah, sure," I said, lethargically.

"Hey, the pimples are getting larger. I think we'd better get you to the hospital," she said.

"Sure, whatever," I said, not really caring anymore.

"You're depressed, aren't you? I hope this isn't what I think it could be."

I didn't respond. I looked away from her and thought how hopeless it was to continue on the dirt road. Hopeless, the honeymoon was hopeless, a disaster, and my life was hopeless.

"I think we should just end it right here." My mind drifted. "These pimples are strange—they're larger and have black spots in the center."

At that point Helen's concentration faltered, the wheel slipped, and the left front clipped a boulder.

"Damn!" she yelled.

"What's going on?" I said, now sweating up a storm. "Man it's hot!"

"You're getting worse," she said. "We've gotta get out of here!"

"C'mon, I know things are bad, but let's try to go on."

Helen tried backing up, but the tire was scraping into the wheel well.

"It's not moving," she said.

"Must be damaged. Let's look."

I hoped the "fresh" air would make me feel better.

"Looks bad," she said, getting nervous. I seemed to be spinning a bit but managed to stagger around the car. My stomach was churning.

"If we can bang the fender back," I said, feeling queasy, "we might be able to get the car moving, ugh!"

I darted away from Helen and off the road, emptying the contents of my stomach onto the ground. It was then I really felt sick. Several times it came up, with my hand trembling at first and my whole body following. Uncontrollable spasms jerked my neck in various directions, and I felt as if a demon had taken over my body.

"You've got it! No, it's not possible. Jacob, this can't be happening, not in the United States."

"What is it?" I weakly asked. "What have I got?"

"Anthrax!"

The word echoed through my mind, but I wasn't able to react. The spasms continued along with the "dry heaves." My heart was pounding through my chest, with each beat crushing my chest with pain. Breathing felt as if knives were going into my lungs.

"Help me," I said. I was on my hands and knees, watching Helen furiously work to get the fender bent back. She cursed, she screamed, she cried. When kicking and clawing the fender proved ineffective, she took a nearby rock and pounded it against the fender. The rock bounced back, and after several more desperate attempts, she dropped the rock and fell to the ground, exhausted. In the corner of my eye I could see her hand bleeding, though my eyelids were twitching.

A moment later she threw the rock at the car, and in an enraged frenzy, she yelled/growled as she positioned her back against the boulder and pushed the fender with her legs. She howled like a desperate animal, and her legs slipped as the fender moved back. Her legs, once a pleasurable sight, were now torn up and covered with blood.

I was dizzy and dehydrated. The nearby ground was stinking with my vomit and diarrhea. The last thing I could remember was going into convulsions as Helen struggled with all her strength to get me into the car. The world went gray, then black.

Since I cannot remember the following events, I now turn the story over to Helen.

Ok. First of all, I'm not much of a storyteller—Jacob does that usually, but since he was unconscious at the time, I will do my best to tell the rest of the story.

I can't tell you how upset I was. I thought I knew what grief was when I first starting working as a nurse in the hospital, seeing so many patients die. I was taught never to get close to a patient for that very reason.

I couldn't understand how anyone could get anthrax. By law, all cattle, sheep, and other farm animals are required to have the anthrax vaccination. I had it myself just before working at Shairton County General Hospital. To see Jacob over there vomiting and going into spasms—it was too much for me. I really thought he was going to die, and I felt powerless to help him. The thought of living without him was too much for me, and I don't know how I did it, but I managed to move the part of the car that was getting in the way of the tire.

Jacob was going into convulsion as I fought with him to get him in the car. I knew he had to get to the hospital fast, but what worried me the most was the fact that I had no idea when the dirt road would run into a paved road.

I had come over a hill and let out a small sigh of relief, but it was a very small sigh. Ahead, the dirt road ended into a paved road. The sun was setting.

I told Jacob we'd be at the hospital in no time, but he'd fallen unconscious, and I was sure he was near death. A voice in the back of my mind told me he was already dead, but I kept telling myself this wasn't happening, it was just a bad dream, and wasn't the most severe case of anthrax supposed to give the victim at least a day to get help? I prayed and was nearly hysterical as I raced back, finding my way back on Highway 37.

I pushed the gas pedal to the floor, and I kept feeling time was slipping away from me. I was going 80 mph as I came up to a car. I didn't even slow down, I just whipped right around and passed him. Highway 37 has only a lane going each way, and I passed three more cars as I got up to 95 mph. I had never driven that fast on Highway 37. I was only a few miles from Shairton when a Shairton County police car caught up to me. This upset me very much, because I knew if I stopped, the delay could be enough to let Jacob die. The cruiser motioned me to pull over, so with my foot hard on the brake I did so.

"Ma'am, do you know how fast you were going?" the officer asked.

"Please, my husband is very sick. He has anthrax, and if we don't get him to Shairton County General immediately, he'll die."

The officer peered in to look. The car reeked with vomit stains on Jacob's shirt.

"Don't get too close. The disease is highly contagious."

The officer jumped back a step.

"Follow me in, ma'am."

I kept hoping we weren't too late. The officer went up to 90 mph with full sirens and lights, but we slowed as the hospital neared and traffic got heavier. About the only thing I could think of (and I was nearly insane from the situation) was how ironic it was that the policeman was on our side this time, whereas when we were going the other way he was our enemy.

He must've radioed ahead to the hospital, because when we arrived, there were several co-workers at the entrance ready to roll Jacob away.

Doctor Brandberg asked me what happened as we rolled Jacob down the hall. I explained briefly about the mud and relayed the various symptoms. As he was rolled in, Nurse Calhoun pulled me aside. She told me I couldn't be with him, that my hysterical condition would make matters worse. In addition, I had to be decontaminated myself since I was in close contact with Jacob.

After being thoroughly cleaned and stitched up, I was released. I fell asleep in the waiting room and awoke early the next morning. At that time, Doctor Brandberg came in. He told me it was close, but that Jacob was stabilizing and would be ok if he could hang on another few hours. I asked if I could see him, but the doctor reminded me that Jacob was in isolation until he was better. At his suggestion, I went out for coffee. Looking for the car, I realized one of the orderlies had borrowed my keys to have the car decontaminated. It wasn't long before I had the keys and was in the car, driving over to Shairton Donuts.

The town was ghastly quiet as wisps of fog passed by. After driving through several amber-flashing traffic lights, I arrived at the 24-hour shop. Inside, I sat and ate as I watched sunrays peep through sections of the city. A finger of the ray licked across the table, and I touched it, reaching out my finger to its finger—a finger of hope. My hand trembled as I thought of what the day might bring. Where would I be by the day's end, who would I be, and what would be left of us?

Numerous times I thought of Bobby and Johnny and was tempted to drive over and take them in my arms, hugging their life-spirits. But some optimistic thought kept telling me everything would be all right, and why bother with unnecessary worry on their parts?

Sitting at that donut shop gave me a chance to reflect on our family, and I was more determined than ever to have a happy one if Jacob would only survive. I now turn the story-telling back over to Jacob.

Thank you, Helen. I awoke in a somewhat confused state, not knowing where I was. What would have been a frightening experience was much lessened when I recognized Helen's smiling face looking at me.

"Hey, Champ, it looks like you won the battle," she said.

"But did we win the war?" I asked out of reflex. She paused for a moment.

"Yes," she said, holding my hand, "we did. How are you feeling?"

"Sore. Hungry. What happened?" I asked as the doctor walked in.

"Good question," he replied. "You had a near fatal bout of anthrax, Jacob. What I don't understand is how you got it, since it's been largely eliminated in the States."

"It's coming back to me," I said, as Helen let me figure it out. "The dirt road, the dead end, the mud. Getting stuck. Helen later saying it was in the mud, is that right?"

"It must have been, Doctor. Jacob says he swallowed some, and the rest got all over him," Helen added.

"But how could something in the mud just do that?" I asked.

"Spores. They could persist in the area for years. But not too many years, not enough to evoke a reaction like this. There could be something strange going on. We'll contact the feds and have them take a look. Something like this if left unchecked could turn into a health hazard."

A few days later I was released from the hospital. Helen and I spent our remaining vacation time relaxing at the Lakeside Inn and wading in Topabee Lake. One sunny afternoon, Helen and I were tossing a beach ball back and forth while wading in the lake. As we conversed, several seagulls flew over, a gentle breeze rustled through the trees, and the ball splashed in front of me.

"At least our honeymoon wasn't a complete waste," I said as I tossed the ball back to her.

"Looks like," she replied, tossing the ball just in front of me thus splashing me.

"Hey," I said, "you did that on purpose." I tossed the ball back.

"No I didn't," she called back, making sure she splashed me again with the ball.

"Hey! Two can play that game," I called back, tossing the ball just in front of her. She splashed me again, I splashed her (with the ball), then with a sweeping motion of her hand, she splashed me—hard. I got her back, and we were both splashing water at each other as hard as possible. I finally cut through the spray and caught her as she attempted to flee in the last second.

"Got you!" I said, grabbing her from behind.

"Let me go," she said playfully.

"Not until I get a kiss," I said. She pretended to struggle a bit then went a little limp.

"Ok," she said, giving in. She turned around and we paused, then she quickly pushed me into the water. I went completely underwater.

"Jacob?" she called. Nothing. "Jacob?" she called again, getting a little concerned. Something brushed next to her feet. "What was that?" she asked, jumping around. Then she let out a yell as I came from underneath and picked her up, with her sitting around my neck as I stood erect.

"Put me down," she said, lightly swatting my head.

"All right, if you insist."

Holding her feet, I transferred my weight forward and shoved her up and out, lifting her by her feet. She let out another yell, sailing through the air like a flying fish. She landed with a great splash.

"How's that for a little excitement?" I asked as she came up. She let out a stream of water from her mouth and cleared her hair back.

"Where did the ball go?" she asked.

I looked around and realized the beach ball had travelled out in the deeper part of the lake.

"I'll get it," I said as I swam toward the ball. A few minutes later I was within reach. As I put my hand out, the ball bounced off and travelled farther away. Angry, I swam out to catch it and after several more attempts clung onto it and paddled back. As I came back, I noticed Helen had gone back to the beach where she sat in a lounge chair.

"Boy am I tired," I said.

"Here," she said after I dried off. "Let me put some lotion on your back before you get burned."

"Just think," I said. "Here we are up at Topabee Lake with no worries, no responsibilities, no—"

"Excuse me," said a voice, coming up to us, "are you Mr. and Mrs. Richardson?" Helen put the bottle of lotion aside.

"That's right," I said, realizing the voice was coming from the bellboy.

"An urgent message for you," he said, and as Helen took it from his hand, I tipped him. "Thank you," he said.

"Thank you," I replied and we were to ourselves again. I turned to Helen. "What does it say?"

"'Urgent. Please give me a call regarding your recent illness,' I guess that means you," started Helen, "'and avoid any contact with the media.' It's signed, 'Dr. Brandberg.'"

"Let me see," I said as Helen passed me the message.

"Avoid the media? I wonder what he meant by that?" mused Helen.

"How can you read this 'chicken scratch'?"

"You get used to it. What do you think he meant, Jacob?"

"Meant? By what?" I asked, staring at the note.

"'Avoid the media,' that's what."

"Good question. Maybe we should catch the news and see." It wasn't a bad suggestion, so we returned to our room, changed, and requested lunch be brought to our room.

"Another five minutes," I called while Helen finished dressing. As I watched the last few minutes of a game show, I wondered how anyone could just sit and watch such junk day after day.

"Here it is," I called. Helen came running and plopped down on the bed.

> Our top story today—several residents are being treated for anthrax at Shairton County General. Normally fatal unless treated immediately, this bout is puzzling doctors and city officials. More from our Frank Wilson, who is live on the scene. Frank?
>
> Thank you, John. I'm inside the main cafeteria, where in a few minutes Senior Staff Doctor Walter Leech will hold a press conference. Apparently, a highly toxic bout of anthrax has taken the lives of three people and put five others in very critical condition...Dr. Leech is coming in.

The bellboy came in with Jacob and Helen's lunch. He hesitated, his attention fixated on the television.

> Good afternoon. I'm Senior Staff Doctor Leech. I've called this press conference to caution the public on a very grave issue. It's no secret we've had an unexplained outbreak of anthrax, which up to this time had been effectively controlled with standard immunizations. However, this morning our fourth patient died from the disease. Normally we're able to prevent the disease with a vaccine or treat the disease with antibiotics. This morning, our lab confirmed what I had suspected from the beginning—we're dealing with a new strain, which we've dubbed anthrax-b.
>
> Preliminary studies show anthrax-b, a bacterial variation of Bacillus anthracis, initiates a condition of septicemia, or blood poisoning, by multiplying rapidly through the body and bloodstream, and as the B-lymphocytes increase in number, the bacteria release an encapsulated protein-coated collection of genetic code, which we've dubbed anthrax-v, the viral second stage of this disease. Anthrax-v overtakes the B-lymphocytes, which normally release antibodies to identify the pathogens, and causes the lymphocytes to release mutated antibodies which mark the body's cells as foreign, thus causing anthracatic lupus. This means the body's defense system turns against the body and destroys it. Within a day the host is dead.

> Anthrax-b is highly contagious—we've already lost two staff members to the disease who contracted the disease despite extraordinary precautions taken to eliminate exposure. Anthrax-b forms airborne spores, which when landing on exposed flesh will infect the host.
>
> The disease was brought to our hospital by two people, one of which was seriously infected. He survived for unknown reasons, but he is a carrier.

Helen and I looked at each other. The bellboy's attention piqued.

> Those two are currently at large and are a very serious health risk to the community. I am arranging a special task force to look for and quarantine the two, at which time they must be destroyed. With no cure for anthrax-b, this is the only way to control a potentially world-wide epidemic, which could end all higher-order life as we know it. The two are Jacob and Helen Richardson. Please, do not approach these two. Contact us at Shairton County General, 555-9000, or inform your nearest law enforcement agency.

The bellboy fled out the hall, yelling to the head manager incomprehensibly. My first instinct was to run, like a frightened animal. Helen picked up the phone.

"What are you doing?" I asked, nearly hysterical with fear.

"We have to call Dr. Brandberg. If anyone can straighten this out, he can. (She picked up the phone). Shhh. Dr. Brandberg? Helen Richardson. (pause). Yes, I did. Can you expl— (pause). All right, where? (pause). Ok, we'll be there. (pause). We will, bye."

"Well?" I asked.

"No time to explain. We have to go."

"Where?"

"Can't tell you—there could be ears everywhere. Right now we need to leave!"

As we gathered our things, we could hear several patrol car sirens growing near.

"Too late," I said. "They're here."

"Forget the bags—we're out of here, now!"

With that, Helen and I made our way out a side window, down a trellis, and seeing we couldn't get near our car, we fled into the nearby woods.

(This concludes the first part of "Unseen Assailant." Join Helen and Jacob in Part II, to be released in the fall edition of *Fictionnaire*, 1992.)

Last Wish

June 2, 1992

"Happy birthday, Luke." One of my few friends, Kans, had come over with a cupcake in hand. A small candle burned brightly in the cupcake's centre.

"I don't see what's so happy about it," I said as Kans placed the treat on my small table. I remained prone on my bed as Kans removed his coat and sat down in my one-room residence.

"You made it to your thirty-second birthday, alive. That's something to celebrate," he said, trying to cheer me up.

"Easy for you to say. You have your health and at least some sort of job."

"Maybe, if assembly-line work is any kind of job." Kans looked around for a moment, trying to think of something better to say. "Nice place you have," he said out of common courtesy.

"Nice rat hole, you should say. And I'm a sick rat, unable to work, unable to get well, and in extreme pain. It's a wonder I can still get around to cash my meager social service cheque and buy food. No family, no home, no life. Argh!"

In that moment, a spasm of pain overtook me. I writhed for several minutes, biting my arm to distract my brain. Kans stared at the cupcake in silence—he knew there was nothing he could do.

"Pray, can I get you some aspirin?" he offered.

"I've already triple-dosed minutes ago just to keep from going completely insane. Perhaps if I could use the morphine."

"You don't want to begin with such a narcotic. You'd go downhill very quickly."

"As if I amn't now. Recall 'twas but five years before yesterday—I was as common and plain a man as all. Recall?"

Kans sat silent.

"Here now, why don't I help you sit at the table. Then you can eat your cupcake," offered Kans.

It was a generous offer I thought, and with great effort and several moments of sheer knife-slashing pain, I hobbled to the table, my joints becoming severely inflamed from the job. I couldn't really blow the candle out—Kans had to do that for me but insisted I make a wish anyway.

"I wish," I said, "I wish…"

The candle went out, was removed, and Kans patiently watched me struggle to eat. Removing the wax paper was impossible—my fingernails had weakened their bond with my fingers to the point of constant injury anytime pressure was exerted on them. Instead, I used two hands to hold the cupcake carefully to my mouth, but my jaw soon tired, and eating ceased. The cupcake fell.

"Good, good. Luke, I wish you'd get some medical attention."

Oh yes, that sore subject again. My brain was perhaps the only perfectly functioning part of my body, and in those few seconds the frustration and mental anguish of denied access to treatment compounded upon itself.

"Fools! What do they know? All the better I amn't from their efforts. Crippled by the disease physically and by the hospitals financially. Instalment payments? A bad joke to be certain. Going downhill? That's all I've known these seven years before yesterday. Cursed, I say, I am but cursed. And doomed, a genetic aberration which by our highest beliefs must not live, but by the charity of some shall live but awhile longer, an example to all, and a punishment for that which cannot be controlled or dictated, at least not by me."

"It's a shame your parents didn't consent to screening—it really is for the best, Luke."

Another sore issue.

"Please, Kans, I have not the strength to argue this one, but I will say I'm not blaming my parents for their decision to continue the old tradition of natural conception. As much as I wish the pain to be gone, I wouldn't trade places with you, a genetically selected product. Human creation should be left up to the All-Knowing, not contrived and planned by man."

"Really, Luke, I think between the anguish and the drugs, you're dreaming. A deity indeed! Science shows us the only truth and gives us happiness."

"Wake up, Man. Do you but know happiness? Genetically endowed to release endorphins on demand for your happiness? Happy when you fail miserably, happy when you're hungry, happy when you breathe toxic fumes?"

"Look at you, asking for morphine but minutes ago. Who are you to lecture on ethics?"

"I'm in pain. I'm ready to die. Morphine could be a way to die peacefully. Yahweh, deliver me!"

A smile covered Kans's face as he instinctually released endorphins, preventing sadness.

"I must go, Luke. Happy birthday."

With his final statement uttered, Kans left with coat in hand. The cupcake remained on the table half eaten. It would remain. Through my small window, I watched the continuous stream of transports pass. A low rumble stirred the haze into undulation, distorting my view. A numb chill passed, and as the pain continued its merciless rampage, I thought I could hear birds—thousand of them—circling high above in an echoing cacophony. Of course there were no birds on earth—the last had died in captivity ten years before yesterday. Millions would pass above my parents' home when I was a lad—how I missed my youth.

The cacophony slowly synchronized into an echoing, chirping choir. The song was unrecognized but ghastly, and a throbbing blood vessel accompanied as percussion. The "music" faded, grew, then extinguished itself.

It had been years since I had actually witnessed a sunset. I didn't know if anyone cared—the artificial lighting compensated for the pollution-masked sunlight. How I wished to see the orange ball, the fading light, and heaven's stars.

Outside my walls, people were scurrying about chasing their wants and desire, believing to be in control, but not really knowing where they were going. My only comfort I knew lay in that fact—my destiny was set and I knew the result. Perhaps I had no "control" then of my life, but at least I was freed from chasing those socially vogue whirlwinds, here today and gone tomorrow. I would be gone and forgotten years after tomorrow, but perhaps somewhere, in some remaining corner of humanity, birds would sing and the sun would shine one last time before final darkness.

The StoryMaster: Part I

June 1, 1992

"Congratulations," said my agent, Gary. "Your latest novel is a best seller this week. I knew you could do it."

"To think," I started, "it would do so well—the hard work paid off after all. I tell you, I don't think I'd *ever* want to write another serious drama again. The emotions—it's too much for my sanity, to write it, to review, to revise, rewrite..."

"And for me to proofread it. It took a couple of years, and it strained our relationship, but in the end it was worth it. Are you still planning on going back to your accounting job?"

"Yeah, I need to get back in the numbers game. Something less stressful, emotionally stressful that is. Accounting has its own levels of stress, but I need a change for the time being."

"Very well. If you change your mind, or if a little short story comes your way, let me know. I'm sure we can find a place for Mr. Robert Burke's writings."

One of the advantages to writing over acting is the semi-anonymity. Actors are known by face and name, authors by name only. On the street I was known as Bob Burke, and no one connected me with the author. I was tired of hiding in the closet, though, dealing with the media and the fan mail. After shaving my beard, trimming and dying my hair, and substituting contacts for glasses, I was a different person—different enough to pass as a well-to-do businessman instead of a back-woods mountain man.

I wasn't too concerned about getting a job. My recent success provided more than ample finances to get by for several years. Plenty of time. I was set on my plan to create a new career, and after four years of hard work on a business degree, I was ready. I was graduating when several companies approached me with offers, which made my fellow students envious to no end. My excellent grades coupled with community work provided the launching pad into my new "career."

Gary had called me periodically during those four years, saying how well my books were doing and wondering when I would write again. I could only tell him I didn't know—my escape from Robert the Novelist was not complete. I had to prove I could work as any other ordinary person could, and if that meant grinding my fingers against desktops and cutting my flesh on paper, so be it.

"Just one little story—the press wants to know—where is Robert Burke?" Gary posed.

"Now Gary, if I don't maintain my cover, I'll never achieve what I've set out to do. The media, the world—they're too demanding of me. Give me a year, then we'll see."

"It's good to see you, Mr. Perkins," said Marie, extending her hand.

"Likewise," I said, shaking her hand firmly.

"I'm in charge of the Human Resources department, and I'll be taking you on a tour through the office. This is Brenda, our receptionist. Brenda, this is Bob Perkins."

"Nice meeting you," I said.

"Hi," she said quickly between phone calls.

The main office area had numerous cubicles in the center and several permanent rooms along two sides. Marie introduced me to the managers in Sales, Purchasing, Accounting, and Data Processing, and as bright as I am, I could not initially remember their names. *Just keep your cool, Bob. No one knows who you really are. You just might pull this thing off.*

I caught several stares from workers in the middle, but I brushed them off as mildly curious, at least I hoped they were such. *They know, they know who you are. They probably read more books than management, and they read YOUR books. If they hear your name...*

"You've already met your boss, Mr. Jim Fitzgerald. I'll leave you with him for the next hour, then I'll be back and we can get some paperwork out of the way. Ok?"

"Good. Thank you, Marie."

"My pleasure."

With that, Marie was gone, the stares vanished, and Jim motioned me to sit as he closed the door. Complete privacy.

"So," he started. "How does it feel to be with Hamilton Insurance?"

A point-blank question to be sure.

"From my first impression, I'd say I have my work cut out for me."

Jim raised an eyebrow, not expecting such a serious response from his equivalent to, "Good morning." He tried again.

"Good morning. You look as if you're ready to dig right into your work."

"If it's all right with you, Jim. I have several ideas which I think could have a big impact on the company."

"That's good. Fresh ideas bring new growth to Hamilton Insurance. I would ask you, though, to temper your desires for the moment and get a good feel for what we do. You've studied insurance in depth, so I need not lecture you on general theory. What is important, however, is how we at Hamilton Insurance take those fundamentals and implement them. Our company is very people oriented. Customers are our greatest asset, and when Hamilton Insurance comes up with a cost-cutting plan, 80% of the savings is passed on to the customer. That's how committed we are. We hired you because of your ability to work effectively with people, in addition to your raw talent in business and finance. So, Bob, tell me a bit about yourself. You graduated from the University of Michigan, right?"

"Yes."

"Have you spent all your years in Michigan?"

"Most. For the first eighteen years of my life I lived in Niles, several miles north of the Indiana-Michigan border."

"Niles. Just south of there is South Bend," Jim commented.

"South Bend," I said. "We used to visit South Bend and Mishawaka quite often—Niles is but a small town, really, but after turning eighteen I moved to Indianapolis where I worked as a buyer for a stamping plant." My imagination was filling in where truth met fiction, and in a way I felt as if I were writing a novel with my tongue.

"That's where I got my first real taste of business," I continued, "buying various steel coils for our assortment of progressive dies."

"That's interesting. What sort of parts did you make?" Jim asked. I had to be careful—my knowledge was rather vague, and if Jim knew this trade, he could rip me to shreds with the simplest details.

"Small brackets, mainly, L- and T-shaped brackets."

"So you weren't into any of the larger transfer dies?" he asked.

"No, simple and easy-to-maintain progressive dies. One bend on the L-shaped and none for the T-shaped. A few punches for the holes, and that was it. Our profits came from the high volume we produced, so securing raw material at the absolute lowest cost was critical—it made the difference between a healthy profit and a bear-crunching loss. It really became a numbers game."

"I can imagine," added Jim, who was obviously impressed with my tale. "What brought you back to Michigan and finally to Lansing?"

"A sense of responsibility, I suppose. I felt I needed to give something back to the state, and choosing Lansing was more coincidental, I suppose. I think if I-69 were completed on my initial drive through the city, I wouldn't have given it a second thought, but the multi-lane highway which will soon be overshadowed by the final bit of I-69 reminded me of my younger days and prompted me to explore the city. I guess familiarity kept me there, and I adopted it as my home."

"Well it's good to have you here, Bob. Have you been to your office yet?"

"No, but Marie gave me a quick tour through the office area."

"Very well. Let's get you settled in." Jim led me from his office into an adjoining one, which seemed amazingly clean and empty compared to the others. "Don't worry," he said, "the papers will pile up quickly, giving your office a 'lived in' feel."

No sooner had he spoken when a harried lady walked behind him with a stack of papers in her arms.

"Oh Clarise, meet Bob Perkins. Bob, Clarise Bergman."

"Where do you want them, Mr. Perkins?"

"Ah, on my desk, I suppose."

The stack landed with a plop, and Clarise was gone.

"I would recommend you use your table behind you for those. There's more where that came from," commented Jim.

"Oh really? I *am* getting right into things, aren't I?"

"Well yes and no," Jim explained. "This is some 'preliminary' work you could say, something to get your hands dirty. This'll let you see the numbers from the inside out, and from the outside in. After a few weeks, we'll get you more involved in analyzing our financial inefficiencies. Take a quick look through them for now—Marie will be by soon to set up your various fringe benefits. I have a meeting in a few minutes, so I must be off."

And with that *he* was gone. My, my, my! People were running back and forth with great urgency, or so it seemed to me. I suppose the casual classroom atmosphere didn't prepare me for this. To think I'd written half a dozen books and missed this. Amazing.

In addition to the stacks of papers (which I learned later to be "reports") to be reviewed, there were numbers to be massaged on the "tube" as I called it.

Jeff Qadon from Data Processing visited me shortly to set up my account on Hamilton Insurance's main computer system. I had used a computer to write my novels, but as I soon learned, each computer system has its own quirks to learn.

"Your account name is BPerkins, and initially your password is the same. Here's how to log on."

We went through the process of logging on, changing my password, sending and receiving computer mail, and running a handful of programs from five of a hundred menus.

"How do you keep track of so many programs?"

"It's not bad once you get used to it. They're organized by department and function. For instance, you'll notice after logging on you start in the main accounting screen. Other departments start in different screens. This is a convenience as well as a security precaution. You wouldn't want any 'Joe Schmo' getting into the General Ledger, for instance. For now, then, you'll have access to several report programs and inquiry screens. After your first week, we'll give you more access as per Fitzgerald."

"One last thing," he said, and his voice became a bit more stern. "Make sure you log off if you leave your desk. Because you have access to sensitive information, it's imperative security is maintained by keeping others from seeing it. Should an outside person see it, well, it—"

"I know. The company secrets, our internal tricks which set us apart, would become common knowledge, and we would become less competitive, if at all."

"Exactly," said Jeff.

Clarise came in with another stack. "Where shall I put these, Mr. Perkins?"

"Please, call me Bob. On my desk should be fine. Thank you."

Clarise was taken aback after I suggested she call me Bob.

"Perkins," Jeff said. "Didn't Fitzgerald tell you about how we address people around here?"

"Not really. We didn't have too much time to converse, other than some background information. He ran off to a meeting, but I seem to recall us being on a first-name basis."

"Probably it's because you're so new. I should tell you, though, that won't last long. He'll be calling you Perkins, and you'll be calling him Fitzgerald if you want to stay on board."

"What about Marie, Clarise, Brenda, and the other girls?"

"Most of them you'll call by their first name, except for two women who are much higher up on the ladder—the VP in Sales, Jane Koehler, and the Claims Department Manager, Beth Reynolds. Both should be called Ms. Koehler and Ms. Reynolds respectively. But the men are referred to by their last name alone, except for the president, who we call CP."

"CP?" I asked.

"Cleveland Pfenner, though no one would dare call him that, except when the occasion calls for it. And ironically, some people think the 'CP' stands for 'Corporate President'. Ack, there goes my beeper. I have to go. You should be all set on your computer, and if you have any questions or problems, give us a call in DP. Good to meet you, Perkins."

"Likewise, Qadon," I replied, though Jeff was out the door before I had finished.

Telephones, photocopiers, fax machines, voices, footsteps—the cacophony was unceasing. I had but a few minutes to absorb the confusion before Marie stopped by.

"Mr. Perkins? Are you ready?"

"Yes, of course. The benefits."

Marie led me through what was slowly becoming familiar territory. A few glances came my way, but the constantly ringing telephones kept most workers occupied. Marie's office was in a corner of the building, and as she closed the door behind me, the whirlwind of noise faded into silence.

"Wow. Is it always like that?" I asked.

"You get used to it. Better this way than perfect silence."

"Yes, I suppose. Before we begin, may I ask a question?"

"You just did," replied Marie, as she winked at me. Reflexively, I glanced at her left hand. Married. "But ask again," she suggested.

"Is there any special way I should be addressing people? First name? Last name? I know it sounds a little strange..."

"Not strange at all. We'll cover that a little later, though. First, let's go over our insurance plans we offer. Being an insurance company gives us the convenience of offering special plans for our employees. These plans, of course, are only for auto, home, and life."

"The more stable ones," I commented.

"Yes," she continued. "Although we don't do medical or dental, we have a special agreement with a sister company, Tetra Med and Tetra Dental. These plans are optional, but we don't offer alternative medical/dental plans. However, some employees use their spouse's insurance instead of ours. Let's see..." Marie looked through some paperwork. "You're single, right?"

"Yes."

"Ok. Well, the plans really are quite good," she continued, and based on my previous experience I couldn't agree more as she went into detail on what was and wasn't covered under the plans. I opted for almost everything, keeping in touch with the company's system, although I had to wait several months before being eligible for the retirement plan.

"Now," she said, her tone changing somewhat, "you will note how people address you as Perkins or Mr. Perkins."

"Yes, that *did* catch me off guard."

"Hamilton was once a small company, and originally custom dictated the addressing of women by first name and men by last. Since that time there have been numerous complaints and very nearly a lawsuit, which resulted in the important (managerial) people being addressed by last name and ordinary people being addressed by first. Although technically you're not upper management, for purposes of being addressed, you're in the 'management' group."

"And you? What do I call you?" I asked, curiously.

"Marie, as before, Mr. Perkins."

"I don't know if I can get used to being called by my last name—it's so impersonal."

"Well, this *is* a business environment, and productivity is the law."

A few other details were ironed out before I found myself in a meeting with Jim Fitzgerald, Clarise, two other men, and two other women. Clarise took the minutes.

"Seeing as this is Perkin's first meeting," Fitzgerald started, "I'd like to again introduce each of you to him. From left to right we have Steve Sharp, DP Manager; Bill Crawford, Demographics; Jane Koehler, VP Sales; and Beth Reynolds, Claims. Oh yes, you know Clarise Bergman. Shall we start?"

"Can we keep this brief?" motioned Jane. "I have another meeting in half-an-hour."

"We'll try. At worst you could leave before completion," Fitzgerald suggested.

"Nonsense," Jane retorted with a somewhat German accent. "The meeting wouldn't be complete without Sales."

"Drop the hard-line attitude, Koehler. Without the computer network, you wouldn't have any sales," shot Steve Sharp.

"When it's working," responded Jane. "Half the time you take it down for backups or other maintenance. When are you going to dump that bucket of bolts and get a sturdy machine?"

"Whoa, you two," cut in Jim Fitzgerald. "We're not here to fight. Besides, we want to set the proper tone for Perkins here. Now I've called this meeting as a free forum for him to question each of you regarding our system. The main point is to help familiarize Perkins, but who knows? He may surprise us with some valid points. Perkins?"

I wasn't ready for this. For several seconds I froze with stage fright, unable to utter a word.

"All right," continued Jim, "perhaps we should start the ball a different way. Crawford, why don't you tell Perkins about our latest study on the population breakdown?"

"Very well," Bill Crawford continued, "our studies show the 50-65 age group to be diminishing gradually, with a population shift more toward the 30s and 40s. Apparently, the renewed faith in the economy is being well received by the younger people while the older generation still dismisses our current bull market as the 'eye of the hurricane.' Because of this, we've considered increasing our focus on the older group—"

"Which has been very difficult," cut in Jane Koehler. "Although we stress the solidity and relatively inexpensive insurance plans at Hamilton, the old ones are not convinced. Personally, I say we dump them and stick with the younger ones. Look at it this way—the well-off older generation looks us over as a cheap scam; the less fortunate don't think they can afford us. You can't teach an old dog new tricks."

"Then maybe the dog should teach us a trick," I said, using a simple twist of words but not really considering its weight.

"Interesting," commented Beth Reynolds. "What do you have in mind?"

"From what I've seen, and this may be more or less aimed initially toward the sales department, but continuing—the advertisements and promotions put Hamilton itself as a selling point and as side dishes serve auto, life, and home. This may be fine, but it could be perceived as some monster ready to swallow up the consumer in as many ways as possible. However, if a single ad concentrates on one thing, say the efficiency and excellent coverage of home insurance, then put the logo as an afterthought, the consumer will think about his needs, and 'Hamilton' will be quietly stuffed in the back of his mind, incubating. Next, we let the other promos fly, using the same logo in the same manner as the other promos. Eventually, the consumer sees the correlation and feels a certain consistency, a certain everything-fits-in-the-glove-and-works feeling, which then translates into the notion that Hamilton *is* the perfect place for insurance."

Everyone had been quiet during my monologue. This concerned me until a round of applause commenced. Only Jane declined, sitting with arms crossed and apparently upset she didn't come up with the idea.

"Well I'm proud to say, Perkins, you've made an excellent contribution to the team," said Fitzgerald.

"That may be nice from a sales point of view," said Beth Reynolds, "but how do we keep the number of claims down?" For an instant, I thought I saw a sparkle in her eye, but a quick glance at her left hand (becoming instinctive at this point) indicated she was married.

"Perhaps you should go into depth on our current strategies in Claims," suggested Fitzgerald.

"We field a growing number of claims daily and try to keep the false claims and bad claims from draining our reserves.

Our greatest challenge comes from the auto insurance claims, with home being the next most challenging while life is relatively simple," Beth explained.

"Life is never simple," said Bill, and the others gave a subdued chuckle.

"Auto. Is this from the increase of vehicles on the road? Driver ages?"

"That's only part of it. Probability of accidents is predicted largely with help from Demography, but with automobile models changing seemingly every six months, and the number of complicated parts going up, the entire parts-replacement industry has become incredibly complex."

"How hard can it be?" I asked. "Do the manufacturers charge such large sums for parts?"

"Yes," replied Beth, "and this has resulted in us pushing for the use of third-party parts which is somewhat of a grey zone."

"Very grey," added Fitzgerald. "Although the savings from replacement parts has been substantial, we *have* had some lawsuits where the consumer blamed SVF on inferior parts."

"SVF?" I asked.

"Sudden Vehicle Failure," said Beth. "We have several test vehicles which we've proven had SVF due to inferior parts. Because of this, we rely heavily on DP to inform us on which parts are inferior and which aren't."

"Which is an ongoing battle," said Steve Sharp. "At first we tried to do the research ourselves, but that soon proved impossible. Currently, we are tied into two large data processing companies who provide us up-to-date lists of which parts are deemed acceptable and which aren't. We compare the two lists, and one company says a part is good while the other says it's bad, that's where we do our research. This information is then relayed back to Claims—"

"Where we recommend the cheapest/safest solution to the consumer. We also have a cap on the claim, allowing a 2% increase on the claim for an added safety factor," added Beth.

"Can the consumer really tell the difference?" I asked.

"Between the manufacturer's parts and the third-party's? It depends. Some parts such as a quarter panel or clamp, no, but we *have* had some complaints about third-party suspension parts. Some of our test vehicles have confirmed this. Perhaps if your orientation permits, a visit to G-lab will give you a better idea of which parts work fine and which don't."

Again I thought I saw another sparkle in her eye—it must have been the lighting.

"Yes," said Fitzgerald. "That would be a good idea. Bob, are you scheduled to see Ms. Reynolds?"

"Yes, on Friday. 'Late morning—Ms. Reynolds, Claims.'"

Beth quickly checked her planner. "All right," she said, "I have you scheduled for eleven, it appears."

"I have my Quarterly Sales Meeting, people. Please continue without me," said Jane Koehler, getting up and leaving.

"Robert, is this true? A short story?" asked Gary. I was home making coffee when the urge hit.

"Yes," I replied. "I think I'll write something up tonight and send it by computer tomorrow."

"To think—a long-awaited work from Robert Burke. Oh how the media would love to hear that."

"No, Gary. Don't let them know. Keep it quiet, can you?"

"Sure, Robert, anything you say," he said, though I doubted his sincerity.

"Not a word."

"All right. Tomorrow?"

"Tomorrow morning."

It didn't take long to whip up a twenty pager based on my recent experience at Hamilton Insurance. The names were changed, of course, and the story was a twisted and humorous view of the auto-insurance craze and how one city boy was too afraid to drive because of the insurance, saw a psychiatrist, and eventually committed suicide without ever having driven an automobile.

My first week at Hamilton was coming to a close, and disappointingly I saw in the morning paper an article hinting the release of my short story in *Literary Life Magazine,* including an outdated photograph of me. When I sat at my Hamilton Insurance desk, I could overhear a conversation from the closest cubicles.

"Did you see the article in this morning's paper? 'Robert Burke comes out of seclusion to write another story, to be released in *Literary Life Magazine.*'"

"Really? After four years?"

"Rumor has it he went to a university under a different name, graduated, and is working somewhere in the business world. Just think—somewhere out there..."

"Or in here."

"You think so? Who?"

"Over there, the new accounting guy. Doesn't he look a little like Robert Burke? Ever since he started here I thought it was him, but I wasn't sure. People look different than their pictures."

"You mean Bob Perkins? I don't think he—quick, act busy."

Upon hearing my name, I got up and made my way over to Norma Staples and Laurie Jones (their nameplates being on their partitions).

"Excuse me," I said to them, "did I hear my name mentioned?"

"No, not at all," said Norma.

"I was asking Norma when she stops working today," lied Laurie.

"*Literary Life Magazine*? Robert Burke?" I asked.

"Huh?" they each said innocently.

"And the rumors. And how I look like Mr. Burke, some even say I am, like you, Laurie, weren't you saying I *am* Robert Burke? 'A dull, dull world for one alone, but a true world of love for you and me'?"

"It *is* you, you're Robert Burke!" she exclaimed with excitement, and several of the other girls looked.

"No, I only wish. But it seems whenever I go out in public, a lot of people mistake me for the man."

"But only Robert Burke says that about the world of love— it's his favorite line."

"And it just shows I've read some of his work. I figure if I'm going to be accused, I might as well know who I resemble. What better way than to read?"

"Hmm. I suppose. Oh, that's my phone."

Both phones rang, and I returned for a few minutes before my meeting with Beth. However, the stares did not cease.

At eleven o'clock, I wandered over to Beth Reynolds's office, but she was not to be found. "Probably stuck in some meeting," I thought as I took a quick look around this married woman's office. A few plants, numerous books, and a few pictures on her desk. Without thinking, I picked up one showing Beth with two children at a park. Another showed what appeared to be Beth's husband in a studio picture. As I looked at the third (showing the children's school pictures), Beth walked in.

"Sorry I'm late," she started, looking at some papers she had in hand, "I was going over some computer requests with Mr. Sharp."

I quickly re-placed the picture.

"Were you successful?" I asked. Beth seemed deep in thought as she flipped several pages in hand.

"What?" she asked, coming out of the trance. "I'm sorry. The request? Looks as if they won't get to it for another three months. G-lab will have some test vehicles for us at 11:30. What time is it now?"

"Quarter past eleven," I said.

"Just fifteen minutes then. Please, have a seat."

"Nice office you have here, Ms. Reynolds."

"Thank you. I see you haven't wasted time in getting yourself known."

"I beg your pardon?"

"To think at this very minute I could be sitting across from Robert Burke," she said, laughing.

"Please, I don't look that much like him, do I?"

"No, well maybe in the face a little. Silly though, isn't it? I've been told a time or two I look like a famous actress, but after a while people get to know you and get over the resemblances. Well, I think we might as well make our way over to G-lab. Ready?"

"Sure," I said. Again a few stares followed me as we left the main office and proceeded down a long hallway.

"Our best information is on the domestic autos, but that is also where the greatest activity occurs," she said.

"Activity?"

"Yes, from the details of third-party part producers, although parts for Japanese cars are on the rise. We don't worry too much about the European and other imports since the volume is so low, although I suppose we should. Here we are."

We walked into a garage-like area, filled with all sorts of grinding, cutting, welding, and ratcheting.

"Here," she said, taking something from a box, "wear these —safety glasses are required beyond this point. This is G-lab."

We took a brief stroll around before coming up to a gentleman wearing a white shop-coat.

"Mr. Perkins, this is Bud Bicker, Mr. Bicker, Bob Perkins."

"Nice," said Bicker. "Here you go, Ms. Reynolds." He handed a set of keys to her. "The two Fords over there are yours."

"These cars," she said after walking over to them, "look identical, wouldn't you say Mr. Perkins?"

"Sure, except one is blue and the other white."

"The blue one uses replacement parts directly from Ford, the white one uses off-brand parts. Take a look at the door, the hood, the trunk lid on the two cars. Identical, right?"

"Sure."

"But, the rust protection warranty is void on the white car yet good on the blue. Ford won't cover alien parts. This is one complaint some customers have. Now, to demonstrate suspension differences, we'll have to drive them around. We'll take the blue one first."

"Relatively smooth, wouldn't you say, Mr. Perkins?" she asked as she drove around cones on the road course.

"It's ok to call me Bob," I said.

"Mr. Perkins, if I didn't know better...you were informed about addressing?"

"Yes, although I'm to call you Ms. Reynolds."

"I earned my title. Pardon me for being frank, but it's not every single woman in this company who gets some respect."

"Single? You're single?"

"Fortunately. You sound surprised."

"Well yeah. The ring on your left hand, for instance."

"An old friendship ring. I added the band later to keep men from hitting on me at work. Nothing personal, it's just so annoying after a while."

"What about the photographs on your desk?"

"You saw my nieces? They're the real joy in my life. My brother is really quite fortunate."

"I see."

"Keep in mind how much the 'good' Ford sways and how much you feel the bumps. Get ready, we're going to stop rather abruptly."

She certainly did, but she held a straight line as the tires whispered screams.

"We're done riding in the blue one. Now for the white."

We climbed out of the blue car, into the white one, and Beth took the same course, but even I could tell a difference.

"You can see how the car sways more, even feathering a bit. Watch as I steer. You can see how I must compensate more often."

"I didn't realize off-brand parts are so different," I said.

"Most of them aren't. This just happens to be one of the worst cases, an example of what could happen if we don't stay on our toes here at Hamilton."

"Isn't it rather expensive to keep these cars on hand?" I asked.

"Not when you're in the middle of a lawsuit. A customer is suing because we wouldn't pay for the equivalent of this white car. They feel they were ripped off, we stressed the safety factor was too great to ignore, and that we would only pay for real Ford parts."

"I would think he would be happy to get the real thing."

"The catch is that his premium goes up much more than if he had the off-brand," Beth explained. "Unfortunately, we can't seem to get around this *Catch-22*, which goes to show there never is a perfect solution."

"Well, my stomach is asking for a solution," I hinted.

"I'm sorry, it's past noon. We're into lunch. I'm afraid I can't continue our discussion afterward—I have a one o'clock with CP."

"Then why not continue it during lunch. I noticed a deli just down the street—"

"First stop light on the left? No thanks, there was a robbery and murder there two years ago, and I haven't had the desire to go since. I *could* go for some pizza, though. Tell you what, why don't we take the blue Ford out for a test drive—to Pizza Delight."

Before I knew it we were on our way to eat pizza, which I couldn't imagine Beth eating.

"So tell me a little about yourself," started Beth. "Have you lived in Lansing long?"

"No, actually I've lived here less than a year—all right, just a month or two, in an apartment several miles west of here."

"Did your wife move with you yet then?"

"I'm not married."

"Oh," she said abruptly.

"I grew up in Niles, in the southwest part of the state. I moved to Indianapolis, Indiana, then made my way back to Michigan."

We continued the conversation despite parking, walking, and ordering.

"And now you're an ambitious young accountant, ready to save the world if you could. I remember when I first started at

Hamilton—I thought the same thing," Beth explained. "Then you realize it isn't so simple—the world has a mind of its own, and each of us is but a small player with a small voice, taking risks and getting slapped at every turn. But the rewards are there for the taking, and my! aren't they great?"

"That all sounds familiar," I said.

"Most of it was taken from Robert Burke's first book, *See the Breeze*. Have you read any of his works? I must confess, I read quite a bit in my spare time when I'm not with Dori and Mollie."

"Dori and Mollie? Friends of yours?"

"My nieces. The ones on my desk?"

"Yes, I saw them. They look like nice children."

"When they stay out of mischief. Maybe that's what I like about them—visiting them is like rediscovering my youth."

"Your youth? You don't look very old, I'd guess 26?"

"Twenty-nine, thank you, not that I like to advertise it—I just don't think I'm ready for the big three-O. How old are you, if you don't mind?"

"How old do I look?" I asked.

"I'd have to say mid-twenties."

"I wish. Thirty-three."

"So, you're not as young as I thought. Or are you? I don't know any man who's thirty-three without a single wrinkle. I don't believe you. Thirty-three?"

"Take a look at my driver's license," I offered, taking the laminated card and handing it to her.

"And almost thirty-four. Is this really you? 'Robert Perkins, brown hair, blue eyes, perfect vision?' For an accountant? That's amazing, considering the time you people spend in the books."

"You don't believe the license?" I asked.

"Yes, but it just seems so—unlikely. There's something about you, I haven't quite figured out what, something."

"Me?"

"I can't explain it on a rational level, I mean, I look at your license and I should believe, but I have this sixth sense, and it's ringing out that something doesn't match. I don't know, maybe I've been working too hard."

"Perhaps. The bridge between hard work and insanity is very short."

"Another Burkian expression? Obviously I'm not the only Robert Burke fan. Do you read much?"

"Only his books, and only the first ones. My experience, remember?"

"That's right—some think you look like Burke. So you've read his books so as to know who they're talking about, right?"

"You could say that," I replied. "And I could say lunch is nearly over."

"Jeez, you're right. Off we go," she said, and after paying our way, we scurried back to the blue Ford and returned to Hamilton Insurance.

True to her word, Beth had her one o'clock meeting with CP, while I had a meeting with Steve Sharp in Data Processing.

"Afternoon, Sharp."

"Good to see you, Perkins. Have a seat for a minute while I finish up this one thing."

It seemed a programmer's work was never done, and Steve Sharp was no exception. After perhaps five minutes he spoke.

"I see you've already done some work on the computer system," he said.

"Yes, running some reports and charting some information. How closely can you watch our activities?" I asked.

"Not many ask that question, and even less get an answer. I can log as much detail as I like, but I tend to only spot-check users for unusual behavior. Although security is an important function of my job, it is not the only one. The biggest challenge is providing Hamilton Insurance with the most comprehensive, up-to-date information possible. Our main data links are with National Data and Ehrnst Information Services. Being an accountant, you'll especially appreciate our ability to manipulate numbers."

"I've noticed. I've also noticed the system slows down in the afternoon."

"One of the drawbacks of providing so much information is that people want more, and more, and more. Quite a number of updates, reports, and heavy-duty number crunching all bring down the system in speed, and we are actually considering upgrading our system *again* for the third time in five years."

"Incredible. Is Hamilton expanding so quickly that—"

"Not so much expansion as it is demands. People get used to a certain minimum performance level, get tired of it, then ask for more. We're in the middle of information explosion, with a growing trend to generate and store roomfuls of data."

"Roomfuls? You mean if it were all on paper, right?"

"No, I mean roomfuls of optical disks, all archives of past years' information. One never knows when an undetected flaw in an automobile will surface with a major lawsuit ensuing. You had a chance to see first-hand what inferior parts can do to a car, right?"

"Yes," I replied. "Beth and I took the white and blue Fords for test drives."

"Each of those vehicles has a dozen opticals worth of data. You can see how the data piles up—it's unreal."

"What if something were to happen to these roomfuls of data?"

"We have an agreement with our sister company, Tetra Medical and Dental, whereby we keep copies of their data and they ours. The partnership has worked quite well so far, except for the periodic visits I must make to keep both systems in sync. Come to think of it, I'm going over there this afternoon. If you can spare the time, you could join me and see for yourself."

"What time are you going over?" I asked.

"Around four. It's a half-hour drive, and the best time to look the system over is when people are leaving or gone. By five, the system is pretty much mine. The only thing is, I won't return 'till about six-thirty."

"Where is Tetra?" I asked.

"Oh didn't they tell you?" Steve asked incredulously.

"I was told about Tetra, but never its location."

"It's out in Grand Ledge, just off Highway 43."

"Grand Ledge?"

"You must not be very familiar with the area. That's west of here, a bit out of the city."

"Oh, I live somewhat out that way, though not as far as all that. I could perhaps follow in my car, and that would save the unnecessary trip back here."

The rest of the meeting was spent reviewing computer operations after which I returned to my office. My one-week orientation was coming to a close, and the following weeks would indicate whether or not I could hold a conventional job in the business world. It was good that Steve Sharp reviewed the computer system, because when I sat down to my terminal, a flashing blue box indicated I had electronic mail waiting to be read.

```
Messages: 3. Read now? Yes.

-------- Message 1---------
From:     JFitzgerald
To:       BPerkins
Re:       Good work.

Bob:
Congratulations on completing your first week
at Hamilton Insurance. We're looking forward to
your contributions in the weeks to come.


--------Message 2---------
From:     BReynolds
To:       BPerkins
Re:       Hello.


Hi, Bob. I very much enjoyed our lunch today.
In case you don't know, some of us are meeting
```

```
after work at Black Shoes, along U.S. 27 on the
north side of town. Hope to see you there.

Beth.


--------Message 3---------
From:    LaurieS
To:      BPerkins
Re:      Hi, there

So you say you're Bob Perkins? I still find it
hard to believe. Hey, are you coming out to
Black Shoes tonight? We're goin' over straight
from work. C'mon, what do you say? It would
give us a chance to get acquainted better.
Besides, this way you can prove your
"innocence." Look for us in the far back
corner. Chow for now!

==>>End of messages. Quit? Yes.
```

I could only wonder if Steve Sharp had taken a snoop into these messages and how safe in the future it would be to reply if I were discussing non-work related topics. Whatever, it seemed Black Shoes was the company hangout, but with my visit to Tetra, I wasn't sure how things would work out (not to mention my desire to keep a low profile). Still, who would really know? I would just shrug myself off as a look-alike.

"Coming over to Tetra with me?" came a voice over the phone after a bit.

"Yes, Sharp. Are you leaving now?"

"In five. I'm gathering my things together as we speak."

"Good. I'll see you in the parking lot then."

It was all I could manage to keep up with Steve's black sports car, which maneuvered around traffic as if those other cars were stationary. We had cleared the last light when we picked up speed, and with a puff of black smoke he was nearly out of sight, that is, until I saw him brake for no apparent reason. I gradually gained ground as I drove over a hill, then with a sudden braking myself, I realized Steve's deceleration—a "black and blue special." We were fortunate to slow in time, or perhaps the Michigan State Trooper wasn't watching us—in any event, we squeaked past the sleeping cat and proceeded to Tetra.

"Do you always drive that quickly?" I asked after parking in Tetra's lot.

"Usually I go faster. I was going slow for you." He laughed for a minute or two as he used his key to let us inside.

"This place is already empty," I observed.

"On Fridays they sometimes leave a little early. This must be one of them." Steve walked around and explained: "Tetra uses the same type of terminal we do, though they have a slightly different main computer."

"Now tell me, Sharp, what is the main computer called these days? A mainframe? Mini-computer? File server?"

"They're almost synonymous, unlike just a few years ago. Most people just call it *the computer;* others like me call it the *main computer*. It doesn't matter too much as long as the thing runs without a hitch. Now, let's check out the computer room."

"This is it? It's not as big as ours."

"Quite true," he explained. "Tetra isn't as large as Hamilton, and in fact most of their backup opties—"

"Opties?" I interrupted.

"Optical disks," he continued, "are used as off-site duplicates of Hamilton's data. Now then, let's do a few performance tests." Steve sat down at the main terminal and began typing away. "I'm going to ask you to turn your head for a minute," he said. "Certain things I'm about to do are, well, not for the regular user."

"Sure," I said, looking through the doorway at the main office area. "Have you ever heard of Black Shoes?" I asked him.

"Sure, most of us men wear them to work every day, though I see you've chosen brown instead. Have you not ever worn a pair of black shoes before?"

"No, I don't mean shoes to wear—some bar or eating place on U.S. 27?"

"Oh that, I think I've heard it mentioned a time or two. I never go, though. I mean, what's the point of destroying one's finite number of brain cells? Personally, I feel I need as much brain power as possible, especially these days. Were you thinking of going?"

"Maybe. I thought it might be a good way to get more acquainted with the other employees."

"I think I went when I first started many years ago when Hamilton was smaller, but it just seems the people who go out are more interested in getting drunk than in being sociable. Then they get rowdy and obnoxious—it's not my suit of clothes."

"Ah well, each to his own. So give me some warning—who should I look out for?" I asked.

"First, remember I haven't been in quite a while, but from what I hear, there are a couple of girls from the phones who are practically thrown out by the end of the evening—Laurie and Norma I think are their names."

"Oh gaud, not *them!*"

"You've met them?"

"Only very briefly. In fact, Laurie sent me a message through the computer asking me to join everyone."

"Yeah, she does that to any of the new, single guys who have just been hired. Lord only knows how many she's slept with."

"Do you know this for a fact?" I asked, always wanting to know the truth.

"I can't prove it if that's what you mean, but I've heard stories, and for me that's enough."

"Well," I said, "stories can easily be invented. I think I'll ask her myself and see what she says."

"You can't do that," he cautioned. "She'll get very defensive and upset—it's best just to be casually polite and ignore her most of the time. Believe me, it's for her own good."

I couldn't help but feel Steve's moral preachings coming down from on high. Whatever, I was determined to see what kind of person this Laurie was, and if she had somewhat of an undesirable personality, then, oh who cares anyway? But Beth would be there—at least she seemed normal enough.

"That does it," Steve said. "I'm done. Well, are you going to go?"

"No. I think I'll just go home and take it easy," I said, having a sudden change of heart.

"It's just as well," he said as we walked out to our cars. "You know your way back?"

"Yup."

"Ok. Have a good weekend," he said.

"You too."

I don't know what made me change my mind—perhaps the fact that I really was tired from the first week. Also, I wanted to get started on another story, and to do so I had to be fresh Saturday morning. So there I was, sitting in front of my home computer and making some notes when the phone rang. Who could be calling me at home on a Friday night?

"Hello?" I answered.

"Is this Bob?"

"Yes."

"Hi, this is Beth Reynolds from Hamilton Insurance?"

"Yes, are you still there?"

"Where?" she asked.

"At Hamilton."

"No. I'm at Black Shoes. I don't know if you got my message, but we—"

"Yes," I interrupted, "I got the message. I thought of coming, but after going over to Tetra with Sharp to see the other computer, I was just too tired to go out and—"

"Oh. As it turns out, not many people from work are here, so I think I'll be heading home myself. Maybe even get some sleep."

"Are you saying that if I were there, you wouldn't have to leave?"

"Well, I don't know. Who really knows?"

"Jeez, I hate to think your Friday evening went sour because—"

"Oh don't apologize. This happens every now and then—everyone says they're coming, something comes up, and no one shows. Just one of those things, I suppose."

"Well, grrr, ok, just wait there. I'll come up and check out this 'Black Shoes' place. It's the least—"

"You don't have to go to the trouble of coming out here when you're tired and all."

"No," I insisted, "no trouble at all. Who knows, this may never happen again."

"Don't say that," she said in a low voice.

"I'm only kidding."

"I know, but the way you said it—it's as if something might happen. No, oh, I know I sound silly, but I have that feeling again. You are just something else, Bob Perkins."

"Yes, and this *something else* is getting no closer to Black Shoes the longer he stays on the phone."

"All right, I'll let you go. But if I don't see you in the next half hour—"

"Don't you worry. I'll be there," I assured her, and with that I was out in the car and gone.

I walked into a noisy and smoke-filled bar but could recognize no one. Was I in the right place? The sign outside said "Black Shoes," but finding people I recognized—that was the trick. I walked further along and discovered a section that was a little less noisy and had a bit cleaner air. A hand motioned me over. It was Beth.

"I almost thought you got yourself lost," she said.

"As did I. So, this is Black Shoes."

"Yeah, our 'great' gathering place. Here, let me get you a drink."

"Please, that's not necessary. I'm quite capable of paying for—"

"No, I insist. You're the new boy on the block," said Beth.

"Hello there," called Laurie, stumbling into my lap, drunk.

"If you please," I said to her, "I think it's getting a little crowded."

"C'mon Laurie," said Norma as she pulled Laurie by her arm, "give the man some space." Laurie resisted, but Norma kept pulling. As the waitress came up with my drink, Norma's grip slipped—she landed into the waitress sending drinks, cash, and the tray flying. Laurie's momentum carried into me, knocking my chair over, and resulting in us on the floor, with her pinning me against the table leg and the ground. Laurie remained stunned as I attempted to get her to her feet. Within half a minute, the bouncers had taken both her and Norma and tossed them out.

"I guess I should have warned you, but that probably wouldn't have stopped her," Beth said. "Laurie and Norma, well, it continues to amaze me they're still with Hamilton."

"Indeed," said Fitzgerald, joining us from another table, "if they behaved on the job as badly as they did tonight, they wouldn't."

"How long have you been here?" I asked, looking at Fitzgerald.

"Almost as long as Miss Reynolds," he said, looking her way. His eyes darted for a moment, though. "Well, well. Look who decided to show up."

"Who?" asked Beth, turning around to look. A brief glance revealed Jeff Qadon coming our way. "O no. Time I went to the Ladies Room," she said, starting to get up.

"Fitz, Perkins—Beth, my lovely little flower, how are you?" Qadon said, coming up too quickly for Beth. She attempted to step aside several times, but each time Qadon blocked her path.

"Excuse me, Mr. Qadon," she said finally.

"You don't have to make excuses to me. I like you just the way you are."

"Let the lady go, Qadon," urged Fitzgerald. Qadon seemed obsessed.

"You just mind your Ps and Qs, Fitz-garbage," replied Qadon, who was obviously intoxicated. Fitzgerald and I both got up.

"You're drunk, Qadon. Go home."

Fitzgerald was turning red with irritation, but Qadon seemed oblivious.

"I see you two are leaving," shot back Qadon. "Good. Beth and I can be alone."

"The only one leaving around here is you," said Fitzgerald, who went over to Qadon and pushed him toward the door. Qadon struggled, sent his fist into Fitzgerald's jaw, which stunned Fitzy for a second, but he sucker-punched Qadon as a bouncer threw them both out.

"Wow, is it always like this?" I asked.

"Sometimes Norma and Laurie get out of control, but that's the first time I've seen Mr. Fitzgerald get thrown out," replied Beth.

"And Qadon?"

"Please don't swear. No, I made the mistake of going out on a date with him once last year. Since then he hasn't stopped bothering me. Man is he obnoxious. He was already thrown out once this evening."

"Really?"

"Yes," she affirmed, "and I was ready to go home but decided to give you a call."

"And here I am, at Black Shoes. One almost wonders if...hello, what is this? Trivia game?"

"Haven't you ever seen this before? You use a console to compete against others in the bar. See the screens up there? Trivia questions are posed, players must answer within a certain time, and scores are posted. The winner gets a free drink. Sometimes I play, but I never seem to do as well as the 'regulars.' I take it you've not played much."

"No, not at all. But I wouldn't mind giving it a try," which meant going up to the counter to fetch a console. "Shall I get a console for you as well?" I asked as I got up.

"No, I think I'll watch for now."

Moments later I returned with a console. Operation seemed easy enough as I extended the telescoping antenna and logged on.

"You're lucky," said Beth. "You're getting in on the next game."

"This doesn't look too hard," I said, answering the first question correctly.

"And you say you haven't played this before? Looks like you're doing quite well."

I was doing well until the questions changed. Here I enlisted Beth's help who seemingly answered each question I missed. In the last ten minutes of the contest, we were frantically coming up with the answers only seconds ahead of the others. It was only by answering the last question immediately were we able to win.

"What kind of drink would you like for your prize?" asked the waitress.

"Beth, I think you deserve the prize. What would you like?" I asked.

"No, no. You won officially. Take the prize," Beth replied.

"A margarita then. Oh, and a strawberry daiquiri for the lady," I said, shushing Beth's half-hearted protest.

"I'll be back in a bit," said the waitress.

"That wasn't necessary," said Beth, trying to be very polite.

"True, but one good turn deserves another. You bought me a drink, and it's only fair I even the score."

In a few moments, we were enjoying our drinks and oblivious to the surroundings. As the alcohol suppressed my inhibitions, an increasing desire to hold and touch Beth nearly overcame me.

"Wow," I said, trying to break the silence. "Any more of this and I'll lose control of myself."

"That's a great idea—losing control. Let's lose control—let's go out and travel around the world, just the two of us and leave everything behind. I feel I could leave this very minute— just hop on the next plane and away we go!"

Beth was apparently more out of her senses than I. A small portion of my rational mind told me it was time to cut back on our drinks or take a cab home. There was no way either of us could coherently handle an automobile.

"I have an idea," I said, my speech becoming slurred. "Why don't we take a walk? The fresh air will—"

"Walk? Where? Walk and talk and chalk and block. Oh my, I think I'm losing it—I can't stand," Beth said stumbling back into her chair.

It was perhaps safest to stay put and drink "pop" (as the locals say) to give me enough time to sober up and Beth enough time to walk, or so I thought.

"Come on, Beth, time to go," I said after a time, but I had to help her quite a bit to get out the door. Once outside, she collapsed in my arms, apparently exhausted.

"I realize it's late," I said, trying to wake her, "but try to wake up for just a few more minutes." She "hmmed" once but was still asleep.

"Let's go back to my place," she said dreamily.

"Where do you live?" I asked so I could drop her off.

"Hawaii," she replied with eyes closed. *Great,* I thought, being sarcastic. The idea of searching her purse for a driver's license was immediately obliterated when I remembered getting a broken jaw from going through a girl's purse in high school.

"I don't know where you live, don't know what kind of car you drive—only one thing left to do," I mumbled, and I dragged her to my car, drove to my apartment, sat her on my couch, rushed to change the sheets on my bed, and carried her there, trying to make her comfortable before I retired to the couch.

I was restless, drifting in and out of sleep throughout the night. There I was, not on my couch but in the bar, Black Shoes:

```
* * * T R I V I A   M A S T E R S * * *
Question 1:
  What is the title of your next short story?

1) Brown Grass Tastes Best
2) Oil Slick on Huron
3) Death by a Rusty Bullet
4) Death in a Crumpled Tin Can
```

Playing the trivia game, my finger selected option four without hesitation.

```
Question 2:
   Select the best summary for the story:

1) A cricket is trapped in a can full of water.
2) Soda cans pollute and destroy Lake Huron.
3) A woman dies in her car, a head-on collision.
4) Man drinks poison and dies.
```

I tried holding back, even turning away, but an unyielding force dragged my hand to the console as my finger pressed option three. Horrified, I desperately tried turning away, but I couldn't. The final question scrolled up. Sweating and cringing, I watched my final act:

```
Question 3:
   Who dies in the automobile accident:

1) Norma Staples
2) Laurie Jones
3) Jane Koehler
4) Beth Reynolds
```

In a mad frenzy my finger pushed one button, then another and another and another, another, another as they typed faster, clicking on what seemed to be the console and not stopping or hesitating for an instant, and though the fingers were aching, I continued to type until finally, finally I heard a voice say to me, speak, bring me from my stupor:

"Bob? What are you doing? Are you all right? Bob?"

I looked around. I was not at a trivia console in Black Shoes—I was in my apartment having finished uploading a document to Gary, my agent, on my home computer. I could hear Beth get closer. Reflexively I shut the machine off as I turned around to see a sleepy-frazzled woman looking at me, wearing one of my bath robes.

"I, uh, good morning, Beth." I suddenly realized we were on first-name basis.

"What am I supposed to think, Bob? I wake up in someone else's bed, someone else's apartment, undressed, and hear someone typing like mad on a computer keyboard." Beth was not at all happy.

"I know what you're thinking, but I assure you—nothing happened," I said.

"If nothing happened, what am I doing in your apartment?"

"How much do you remember?" I asked.

"I asked first. You answer first."

"All right. We were at Black Shoes last night, do you remember that? We talked, we played the trivia game, winning, we drank, talked some more, drank—"

"And you took advantage of me, didn't you?"

"Please, Beth, nothing of the sort transpired. I was barely able to drive, but you were only semi-conscious. I couldn't tell if you were asleep or passed out. Had I known where you lived I would have taken you home. As it was I did the best I could by offering you the comforts of my home, and I took the couch while you rested on my bed. That's it." Beth didn't look convinced.

"And do you always spend your early Saturday mornings on your computer?"

"Is that so unusual?" I asked.

"It is when you're typing at eighty words per minute, or so it sounded. What could you possibly be doing?" Her confusion turned to curiosity as she approached the computer. "It's off. Peculiar I'd say. Confidential information?"

"You could say that," I replied, trying to brush her off.

"Well, I'm sure it's quite interesting, but I really must be going. I can't imagine what might happen if word got out that you and I...never mind. I suppose my car is still at Black Shoes."

"I suppose you might be correct, unless someone towed it," I laughed.

"That's not funny. I didn't park in the regular lot. May I borrow your phone? I'm going to call a cab." Beth went for the phone.

"Hey, that's not necessary. I'll give you a ride."

"I'm sure that's what they'll be saying about us at work if we're seen together. No, a cab—"

"I insist. Who will be out there at this hour in the morning?"

"True. Ok, you win. Give me a moment to freshen up."

In the time she "freshened up," I was able to get a bite to eat and dress, and I was about to take a glimpse at my computer when she came out, ready to go.

"Beautiful at all hours of the day," I commented.

"Thank you," she said before realizing what I'd said on a conscious level. The ride to Black Shoes seemed awkward—neither of us spoke. The parking lot was empty with the exception of a black, 4-door sedan. Was it hers?

"Thanks for the ride," she said and was gone.

I couldn't help but wonder what I had sent to my agent, Gary, from my computer. I parked my car, and as I walked to the building a black cat followed me.

"Meow," said the cat as if I were its owner. Curious, I took a good look and noticed he had a collar.

"Let's see who you belong to," I said. Only one word appeared on the collar—Magik. "That's odd," I commented. With a sudden burst of excitement, the cat turned around and scampered off into the nearby woods.

I picked up my morning paper from the lobby and sat down to read it over a second breakfast. I had nearly thrown the paper into the trash can when I saw a grim photograph along with an article covering a gruesome automobile accident.

...along I-94 when it bounced off a truck and collided with an underpass's structural support. The 26 year old Lansing woman, Laurie Jones, died at the wheel shortly after the crash, Lansing police said. She was the only person in the car. The driver of the truck suffered minor injuries...

Laurie, dead? Was it some sort of sick joke? The very woman who'd fallen atop of me the night before no longer lived. The sudden thought of her fate rushed through my mind. I ran over to the computer, knocking over a few things and viewed the document I'd sent earlier.

Death in a Crumpled Tin Can
by Robert Burke

"Going over the edge," she said, "that's my Golden Rule."

Her rule, taking a limit beyond the horizon despite the odds was what made Laurie such a gifted individual, up until the night-long drinking spree. Laurie pushed the car faster and heeded not the possibility of a speeding ticket.

"I wouldn't mind getting one," she said, "it might make the evening more interesting. Besides, I'm only going to live once."

Skipping to the end, I read the last paragraph:

The truck driver didn't see Laurie and abruptly changed lanes, moving from right to left. Laurie swerved but not in time. She deflected off the truck and into an underpass's center pillar. Laurie died instantly, her alcohol-filled blood draining rapidly from her body and onto her car's interior. Laurie Jenkins, another victim. The Black Cat walked on the hood, then into the car, sniffed the corpse, then left.

(*The StoryMaster* will continue in the fall edition of *Fictionnaire.*)

Lolly

March 30, 1991

Lolly, lolly, lolly. Get your adverbs here. Get something here. Get the hell out of here. Lolly.

Lolly and I took our usual afternoon stroll to Westway Park, a small residential area with a playground, large grassy areas, a small pond with flower gardens, and a nature trail. Lolly walked along full of excitement and energy. I followed along, holding his new leather leash. That's right, Lolly is my dog—a cocker spaniel.

"Good afternoon, Mrs. Weatherly," I cheerfully said as Lolly and I strolled up to the elderly lady who was sitting on a shaded park bench. She was wearing her jogging suit and had just finished cruising around the walkway. She waved, and Lolly barked in a friendly gesture to her as we passed. Lolly and I continued our walk, greeting our familiar friends and making merry our afternoon jaunt. During our stroll, some neighborhood children walked up and petted Lolly as we chatted. Lolly smiled and panted, wagging his tail. He loved affection. Then one of the children threw a stick. I undid Lolly's leash and let him chase it down, the stick hardly landing before Lolly caught up to it. Then he pranced back to the child and presented the stick at his feet.

"Good boy," the child said to Lolly. "Good boy." We patted Lolly and congratulated him for his efforts.

Lolly and I loved the large, grassy areas. When the children went back to play, I ordered Lolly to sit and stay. I walked fifty feet away from him, went down on my knees, then called for Lolly. He bolted into a speeding ball of love and jumped on top of me, licking all over until I was laughing uncontrollably. A lollipop for Lolly.

"Thank you sir," I said to Lolly, shaking his paw. Lolly looked at me with a quizzical expression, knowing what we would do next. He stuck his nose into my jacket pocket, pulling out the tennis ball. Then Lolly took off, running all around the grassy area. I chased him, running as fast as I could, but Lolly turned quickly and easily, causing me to fly past and retrace my steps. I couldn't run very fast—Lolly just changed directions too fast for me. When I saw him run with the tennis ball in his mouth, he had a sinister smile as if he were prancing around, showing off his prize. Tired of running, I stopped for a moment, catching my breath. Lolly ran up to me, circled me several times, then as I reached out to grab him, he took off again. I chased him for a few more minutes, stopped, and Lolly decided to rest under a tree. He dropped the tennis ball from his mouth, smiled, panted, and wagged his tail. I slowly walked over. He barked twice. Slowly, I reached for the ball and snatched it. Running, I threw the ball up high in the air. It travelled down the field a bit, and I chased it as Lolly did. Lolly tried catching it in mid-air after the first bounce, jumping as high as he could. I caught it, threw it up again, then let him catch it. We resumed our chase.

Lolly was a good dog, and I loved him so, perhaps more than any other pet I'd owned, and even more than any person I knew. I keep telling myself that love must conquer all, no matter what. It must. Sigh.

At the end of our stroll, I gave Lolly two treats, and we walked back to my house. Lolly smiled and barked at every passing car and was friendly to the other pedestrians. I was glad to have Lolly, happy that a fellow being was so full of life and could share it with me, with no real wants or desires except love.

As usual, I undid Lolly's leash when we arrived at the house. Typically, Lolly would circle the yard three times, scaring away the cats and birds. He circled once—I could see a cluster of birds flying off toward some approaching dark clouds, he circled twice—a neighbor's cat scampered over the fence with Lolly barking at it, and he circled...Lolly didn't come around.

"Hmm," I chuckled, "he must be eating a cat this very moment." Dark clouds moved in rapidly—a distant rumbling suggested an incoming storm.

"Lolly," I called. "Lolly, time to come in." No answer. "Lolly, Mr. Adverb, where are you? Come in!" I yelled. Still no answer. The clouds were on top of me—I could see lightning in the distance along with a dark haze of rain. "Lolly," I yelled again, running around to the back. "You're gonna get wet—storm's a-comin'." The rain came over old man Johnson's farm from the west, heavy drops fell on my face, and I knew I had seconds before a downpour would saturate me.

"Lolly!" I screamed as I circled the house once, going the opposite direction Lolly went. A bolt of lightning crashed nearby, and the resulting thunderclap sent me scampering into the front door. "Lolly?" I yelled, holding the screen door ajar. The yard was getting soaked—Lolly was not to be found.

"Where the hell is that dog?" I asked. Lolly was playing a new trick on me to be sure, but where was he hiding? At any second I expected to see him dash up to the door, soaked but carrying a lost shoe or some other tattered object. But Lolly didn't show up. I looked at the end of the leash as if it were magical and could summon Lolly at a moment's notice. My relationship with Lolly was magical, and I expected us to be together. Always.

"You sneaky little dog, where are you?" I called through the house. He came in, of course, through the flap in the back door. Must have. I walked cautiously through the living room, past the kitchen, then up to the back door. I expected him to startle me by jumping out of nowhere and loving me to death. "Lolly?" I asked, quietly. "Lol—" Looking around the corner, I saw him. A knife was sticking out of his back, the floor a pool of blood. I froze, unable to speak, staring at him. He was dead.

My immediate urge was to run over and aid my ailing dog. Lolly meant the world to me, and any ill that he suffered I would try to bear for him. But seeing that old hickory knife jutting out his back signaled immediate danger in the house. I was not alone. I quickly glanced all around, looking for the person. I saw no one. Silence. There were no footprints on the floor, no evidence to indicate another human had been in my house, but I knew he was there—hickory knives don't just walk up to dogs and stick them in the back. This knife wasn't one of my own, that much I knew. The handle was dark, stained with dirt or blood—or both. I chilled, like a prey before being attacked. I didn't want to die—I wanted to confront my aggressor and get the situation over with. I couldn't tolerate standing there in the dim light wondering what to do next.

The rain pounded the windows. Lightning lit the black sky as thunder nearly shattered my eardrums. I slowly walked over to the phone to call the police. Another flash of lightning, and the electricity went out. My hand was on the phone, I lifted the receiver, but it was dead too. Dead. Goosebumps covered me like wildfire. Lolly, dead. Electricity, dead. Phone, dead. And me? I didn't dare think. I tried to remember—where are the candles, where is the flashlight? I turned on the gas stove for some light. The soft pffft of the burner flame startled me, and I jumped back. "Get a hold of yourself," I thought, but the feelings were too strong, that instinct of fight or flight.

I looked around again. Nothing. "I gotta get out, gotta get out of this house, go to a neighbor, the police, anywhere but stay here," I thought again. But it was dark, and in the dark that special someone could make me number four. Lolly was number one, the electricity number two. The phone three. I, four.

A flashlight? Yes. I grabbed one from the top of the fridge, turning it on quickly with my left hand. A stainless steel carving knife was in my right. I flashed the light around, panning the area. Nothing. Another crack of lightning, a crash of thunder. I jumped, nervously. Every clap was driving me near insanity with fear. Then I heard a noise from upstairs. I froze, my teeth clenched, my hands gripping with white knuckles. In an instant, I dashed out the front door through a torrent of rain, and into my car, closing it with mad intensity. The knife and flashlight plopped into the passenger seat, then on the floor. Key, key, where's the key? It seemed to take forever to get the key into the ignition and start the car. It started, I hit all-door lock, then backed the car up quickly. A dark shape came running out of the house. I screamed madly, backing into the neighbor's mailbox next to his driveway. The shape pounded on the door, then jumped on the hood as I put the car in Drive. I screamed and cried at the same time, desperate to escape. I hit the gas, hit the brakes, and he was still on the hood. I went into Reverse going down the subdivision backward, quickly whipped the car around while switching to Neutral, and the shape fell off, smashing against another neighbor's mailbox and plopping into the road. Putting the car in Drive, I ran over the shape and drove off. There was a loud thud as I drove away, and I could hear something scraping as I left the subdivision.

That had to have been the worst night of my life. I drove for ten miles in hellish weather before coming to the Sleepy Time Motel. Hail was pounding my car as I pulled in, and the rear window caved in with a crash as grapefruit-sized hail stones poured in. I pulled into the carport and rushed into the office, asking for a room.

I guess I only stayed in the lobby for half an hour until the hail was gone, though it seemed longer. The motel owners were quiet and unemotional—concerned for my well being.

"Are you all right, boy?" they asked me, but I could only reiterate my need for rest. How could I tell them? My dog, the love of my life, Lolly, was brutally murdered, and I ran down the assassin. But I was afraid they'd think I was crazy. I looked crazed, maybe I was crazy, but you'd be too if you went through what I did.

It's been four weeks since that black night. I'm now living in an apartment next to the lake, the East Tower apartment building. The house has been sold, the car sent away to be demolished. I've been trying to piece together what happened that night, what really happened. My friend, Michael Bayer, suggested I try to write it all down, to put some cohesion and focus to my thoughts. Michael's a kindly soul, and I've taken his soundly advice many-a-time as good medicine. It is thus I'm sitting at my desk, thinking and writing, thinking and wri...

The question boils down to this—who killed my dog? When I checked the house the day following the storm, Lolly's dead body was not where I thought it to be. There were no blood stains anywhere. The house was in perfect order, but when I looked outside, I could see rotting flesh on the side of the road. I walked up to it and there it was—Lolly's remains. I thought it a cruel joke by someone, a person with a twisted life and twisted mind. Lolly's collar was missing, though. I checked along the street, but it was nowhere to be found. His collar, gone.

Depressed, I walked back to the house then noticed some brown stains along the left front wheel. I kneeled down, looked under the car, and saw more blood stains. There were patches of hair stuck around the spring. I looked closer and saw, to my horror, a leather band stuck to the spring. On the band was a single word:

"Lolly."

RainMaker

March 31, 1991

I.

I thought I knew it all. Time after time, day after day. It was really quite simple—sunny days were good, stormy days were bad. There was no in-between. I was taught this from day one, and I believed it until the day I met him. Him? Yes. His real name I know not, but I always called him RainMaker.

It was a sunny day in Appleville, just the kind of day I liked. Temperature? 74 degrees Fahrenheit. Not a cloud in the sky. If someone were to ask me the meaning of beauty on that day, I'd point up to the sky. "That," I'd say, "is beauty." Some people said I was a sun worshipper. Others called me lazy. What they thought didn't matter to me. I worked hard during nine months of the year as a teacher putting up with seventh grade children, half of which were spoiled brats. Lesson plans, faculty meetings, bus-patrol duty—it was enough to make me sick of the educational system. But a school teacher has one fantastic benefit—a three month summer vacation. Three lovely months to cherish the beautiful earth at its best. It was the only thing I looked forward to when teaching, the only thing that kept me going. The sun. The beach. The water. Paradise.

It's not often I take the time to write things down—heck, during the summer I just relax and soak in the sun—writing is for those literary nuts who lock themselves up all day in some closet with their typewriters (or computers nowadays). It's really kinda strange for me since I haven't written anything substantial beyond college days. Nevertheless, after meeting the RainMaker, I knew I had to share my story, had to...

So there I was, lying on the beach, with shades on, just relaxing. Ah, the sun's warm rays massaged my skin with a loving touch. No civilization. Nobody to disturb me. It was still morning and during the work week. I chuckled as I envisioned those busy executives running around from one cage to the next, man-made office prisons designed to keep those office-types busy. Not me. I continued to relax on the beach, glad to be away, so glad.

With a sudden impulse, I tossed my shades to the side and ran with top speed toward the lake. Splash! The water was cool to the touch, and it gave me new life, new energy. I leisurely swam around, stretching out my tanned muscles. Then I floated there, just floated—a man without a worry, without a care. In the distance I could see some sailboats. How I love sailboats! I've always considered buying one, but on a teacher's salary I could never afford it. It was a minor irritation, and I'd learned to live with it.

The winds picked up, and something in the air said, "Storm." "Dog gone," I said, disappointed my day was ending early. It was near noon, and the day was only half over. Reluctantly, I trudged back onto the beach and walked over to get my things. A few clouds in the distant west, on the other side of the lake, were gathering.

"Rain, rain, come a-gain! Cleanse my wounds and ease my pain. Rain, rain, come a-gain! Come right here to beach-bum lane." I heard the voice but couldn't believe it. Rain, Rain, come again? Who was this?

"I love the rain. I love the thunder. Oh, give me some lightning, some power to pass the day. I love the—"

"Hey! Why don't you shut up over there?" I said, yelling at this apparent scum-ball.

He continued his chanting, ignoring me. That was his mistake. I was always meant to be heard, I also learned growing up. This guy had better listen.

"Will you shut up? Can't you see it's gonna storm? What a rotten afternoon it'll be," I lamented.

"On the contrary, my good fellow," he responded, walking over to me.

"What do you mean?" I asked, the dark clouds looming closer. The other side of the lake was gray by now, and I could see faint lightning flashes.

"It does us good to have a storm every now and then. 'Tis good for you, makes you strong, like meat and potatoes."

"Hogwash," I said. "Storms just waste my valuable time. I could have a relaxing time on this beach during a sunny day, not a miserably rainy day. How depressing!"

"Sir, it's obvious you are a sick man. You don't know what you're missing," he said. The rain was nearly on us. A loud thunder clap echoed.

"I'm leaving. If you wanna stay out here and get wet, be my guest." I started walking off with a hurried pace.

"Wait," he said, beckoning me back.

"Forget you," I said as an afterthought. What did I care about some crazy fool? All I could think about was getting back in my car before I got soaked. It was a funny thought, but I was already wet from swimming in the lake. Yeah, but that's not the same kind of getting wet. You're not supposed to get wet from the rain, that's another thing I learned. Like getting poison all over you, it is. Swimming is like taking a bath in a huge tub—refreshing and cleansing.

"Wait!" he commanded. For a moment I glanced back. Then I jumped in the car and started it. It sputtered, wheezed, then roared to life. Just as I was about to put the car in gear, I was both fascinated and fear-stricken by a sight on the lake. A waterspout. It was a tornado on the lake, I knew that for sure. It lazily swept back and forth, like a vacuum cleaner doing regular duties.

"Observe," I thought he said, but it was difficult to hear him anymore over the roar of the car, the wail of the wind, and the more ominous roar of the water spout. It was still quite distant, but water has a queer effect on acoustics, making distant noises seem closer than they really are.

I could no longer watch. With the imminent danger before me, I chucked the gear shifter into Drive and spun off. My Camaro had good speed, and I entered the freeway without delay. What few cars I saw I passed without hesitation, swerving across three and four lanes at once. I was approaching the cloverleaf, where two interstate freeways met. The sky went pitch black. It was difficult to see, and I had to slow my pace with visibility being severely reduced by the torrential rain. I thought it took forever to get off the cloverleaf and in fact it did. Just as I was coming down the one-lane ramp, I stopped dead. Cars had stopped in front. I couldn't proceed. What the heck? Knowing how tornados work, I knew I was in a high-risk area. "Gotta get to a low place, gotta get going," were my only thoughts. There was no room to go around, and just as I considered backing up, a car pulled up from behind. "Damn," I said. "I'm trapped, just trapped!"

I watched with horror as the twister barreled through the city. Old houses, light poles, trees, and cars were tossed aside like the daily garbage. The twister's roar was like several long freight trains, with power to move the unmovable. It came toward the freeway with incredible speed. I couldn't look. The car was in park, motor off, and I moved to the floor. The twister's vacuum exploded the windows, but I clung to the floor, bracing myself against the seat and under the dashboard. The car rocked, swayed, and seemed to go up and down on its suspension. Rain came pouring into the car, and I was soaked, shivering, and nearly insane with fear. I knew I had come to my end.

I could feel the ramp vibrating—not some little buzzing like a bee, but great undulations that jarred me against the car's interior. Bang, bang, and my head was smashing against glass. Blood was oozing around the floorboard—my blood, as my whole body was now smashing against the glass. I felt faint, dizzy, and sleepy. "Yes, this is all a nightmare," I thought, but my thoughts waned as well, and I blacked out.

II.

"Wake up, Mister. Wake up!" That voice. I'd heard it before. I coughed up sand and blood as a fist pounded on my back. "Wake up. Not dead yet, are ye?" I opened my eyes, trying to see. The world was cloudy, blurry, but in a minute I could see again. Again I coughed. More sand and blood came up, landing on a vast, golden sand. Sand. I'd never seen so much.

"Look at you," he said. "Nothing but a sliced-up slab of meat. It's a wonder you're alive." The voice was right. I had lacerations to my head, arms, legs, and torso—essentially everywhere.

"Who are you?" I asked, turning around to meet...it was him, the man I'd seen on the beach, that sandy area I worshipped. I was on sand again, but this sand was different. I looked around...there was nothing but sand as far as the eye could see.

"Who are you?" I asked again. "Where are we? What desert are we—"

"I? RainMaker be I, and I be he. This domain be mine not, it belongeth to SandMaker, my evil twin."

"What? Have I gone mad?" I looked at him. He was wearing a bright green and yellow outfit. It was the only colorful thing around, as I was dressed in a simple T-shirt and shorts. Sandals kept my feet from being sand-scorched.

"Mad ye may be, but sane ye may become, unless..."

"Mad? Sane? Unless what? All I remember is being trapped in my car during a storm, a tornado was—"

"Silence! Do ye not hear? The howling?"

I listened but could only hear the howling of the wind.

"The wind, so what?"

"It is he, SandMaker. He cometh."

The wind swirled around, piling the sand into the shape of a man. A grey and beige colored man formed. He spoke:

"So this is the sand-worshipper. Very good. Come with me, my friend, and you shall worship sun and sand for eternity."

I pinched myself, trying to wake up. Wasn't this all a dream?

"You are...SandMaker?"

"That name belongs to me, yes. Come join me, together we will rule!"

I looked at SandMaker. His shape was never constant—and somehow he seemed to slide along with the sand—he wasn't really walking. I looked back at RainMaker. He looked at his brother then at me.

"What do you say, sir?" RainMaker questioned me. "Do you still worship the sand and the sun?" I looked at his eyes. They were stern and probing, trying to find something inside me that I couldn't see. SandMaker walked toward me, slowly, steadily, quietly, then he touched my right hand.

"Join me," he commanded. My hand was drying out—I could feel my blood draining through the skin's wall as the hand started shriveling. I cried out, yanking my hand away.

"Flee!" RainMaker yelled, and he pulled me away from SandMaker's enveloping death grip. My right hand was in agony. It looked like a mere skeleton—no flesh to give it shape. RainMaker snapped his fingers twice, and a stream formed in the middle of the desert. It started at our feet and flowed constantly.

"Jump in!" RainMaker urged as he pushed me. I floated down the stream on my back with little effort, the cool water moisturizing my parched skin. Even my right hand started taking shape again. In a few minutes, I floated far away from SandMaker. The stream ended and so did the desert. I walked out and made my way up on a grassy slope with scattered apple trees. RainMaker was leaning against one of the trees, eating an apple.

"Catch!" he said, tossing me another apple. I caught it after the first hop and looked at it. It was shiny red, plump, and without a bruise. I sank my teeth into the apple and was never so happy for that sweet fructose.

"I don't understand," I said, puzzled. "What is this place?"

"You are now in my domain, the Domain of RainMaker. You were just in the Domain of SandMaker, but I gathered you were not happy there, so I brought you here."

"Here? Is this Earth?"

"Yes and no."

"You speak in riddles. How am I supposed to understand what you mean?"

"You are not at any particular place on Earth you'd recognize, but all that you see, from a certain view, is Earth or Earth-like."

I looked around. It was certainly pleasant enough, much more so than SandMaker's desert. The sun faded behind a cloud, and soft drops fell. RainMaker held out his hands as if calling the drops down.

"Rain, rain, come a-gain! Cleanse our wounds and ease our pain. Rain, rain, come a-gain! Come right here to my domain." RainMaker was actually calling the rain down and enjoying it. For a moment, my instinct told me to seek shelter immediately. But the falling drops did feel good. My right hand, once a lifeless skeleton, was fleshy and healthy. My spirits were much improved, and I felt a new sense of energy emerging. At the same time, I thought I could see the grass and trees becoming darker green, richer, and then seem to sprout new growth. A soft glow surrounded RainMaker as he continued his chanting.

"Do you understand now?" he asked.

"Yes and no," I replied, trying to sound intelligent.

"Meaning you acknowledge the rain's healing powers but you do not know why or how it works as it does."

"Yes. But the rain—it's supposed to be cold. It gives a person his chill of death. It—"

"It? A bunch of hogwash, as you would say. Supposed to, have to, do this, do that—are you going to look at the world through another person's eyes? Open yours for once, blind man, and see!"

I blinked, trying to see what he was talking about. Could he be right? All my life I'd been collecting information on what "the good life" was supposed to be, and what "the bad things" were. Could it be, in so doing I had affixed myself in time, like a statue forever forced to look the same way until the end of time? Certainly I was physically free, but according to RainMaker I had locked my mind into the same perspective, "statuizing" it.

"Come with me," he beckoned. Without realizing it, my legs immediately took off in a fast-walking pace aside RainMaker. We passed more apple trees, then a flower garden before coming across a brook. RainMaker pointed to a rock on the bank.

"This is you," he said. He picked up the rock, handled it, and turned it over leisurely. "This is how you've started—your perspective rigid like the rock, your propensities forlorn like the jagged edges. Your life was peaceful, unchallenged until I picked you out of the mud. Your life is still peaceful—you do not even realize the impending danger. Now, watch!" With a sudden jerk, his wrist snapped the rock into the brook.

"You threw the rock in the brook, big deal," I said.

"You're missing the point completely. Notice the rock now. It moves not. The water tries to carry the rock, but the rock resists, steadfastly holding its ground. The water is splashing up over and around the rock, see? This is a conflict. The rock appears to be holding its ground, but in time the water will wear away the rock, send bits of sand to SandMaker, smooth the rock's rough edges, and turn it into a stone. You'll be that way in time, what little creativity you have will be worn away, until you have nothing left but your rigid ways, which will appear to have no beginning or end—smoothly rigid."

I looked down in the brook. The rock was no more—it was stone!

"I take the stone," he said, walking into the brook and reaching his long arm into the water, "and I crash it against another. Observe!"

The stone split into several sharp and rough pieces.

"Notice, the stone is no more, nor is it like the rocks. It is an ugly metamorphic oddity. I have no more use for this, nor do I like its appearance. Begone!" The shattered stone vanished.

I stared at his hands in amazement. Did RainMaker possess some power beyond my comprehension? Was he from outer space? Perhaps I was still dreaming. Whatever the case, I could not help but ask:

"Then I am doomed. My life's path is set, and I am doomed to follow it, right?"

"No. There is still yet time. Remember, life is in the water, not the rock. Life is in the water, not the rock; life is in..." His voice faded, the light grew dim, and RainMaker was all but gone from view. I was no longer in his domain or SandMaker's.

I was on the beach, that same beach I enjoyed earlier that morning. The lake was calm, the sky clear and sunny. It was late in the afternoon, and the cloverleafed freeway in Appleville was a rubbled pile. Somewhere in that heap was my car, other people's cars, and other people—dead. I looked at myself, expecting to see a pock-marked body. Smooth, baby-smooth I was. I had escaped death.

Appleville was silent except for occasional emergency vehicle sirens. I walked off the beach with a heaviness, then I stopped. Before me, alone in the vast waste, was a single flower. Without thinking, I picked the flower and mused over a myriad of miniature rainbows within a water droplet sandwiched between two petals. Inhaling the flower's fragrance, my heart's heaviness was lifted. I placed the stem in my T-shirt and walked toward downtown Appleville.

Life is in the water, the rain, you, and me.

Deuler's Story

April 30, 1991 to May 22, 1991

I.

"Are you about ready, honey?" I asked.

"Just a few minutes more."

This was only the fourth time Michelle and I were both attending the local arts exhibit. Michelle would stand next to her work and explain to prospective buyers how she had truly captured the human spirit in her works. I would usually stand nearby, though sometimes I looked at the other exhibits.

I was proud of my Michelle. We'd been married for nearly fourteen years, and each passing day brought me closer to her and the world. Yes, the world. For you see, before I met Michelle, my world was a devotion to chemical formulas and metabolic rates.

I am Edward Zephin Deuler, Pharmacist.

My wife is Michelle Cassandra LaSalle, Artist.

Our children are William Edward Deuler and Marie Heather LaSalle.

Michelle came down the stairs in her short black dress, which went well with her dark hair but fair complexion. She had a smile dentists worshiped, and an exuberance of form without restraint. That's my wife.

"Now?" I asked.

"Yes," she replied. I took her in arm and led her to the car. Seeing Michelle dressed up touched a deep warm spot inside me, and I was ever-tempted to carry her up to our bedroom to make passionate love to her the entire evening (and night for that matter). But I resisted, and soon we were on our way.

"I'm glad you could come tonight, Dexy."

Dexy. She only called me that when she was flirting with me. The nickname started when we were dating. I was still in pharmacy school when she called me "sugar darling." It was one of those harmless words of affection, like "honey," or "dear," but me being the drug dictionary asked which sugar she meant, fructose, sucrose, galactose, or dextrose. "The poindexter one," she remarked, laughing, and I caught on immediately. From then on, she occasionally called me, "Dexy," reminding us of those innocent days.

"I'm glad I could come, too. I was fortunate in switching shifts with one of the other pharmacists at the hospital and lucky to get my older sister to watch the children, just so I could see my Michelle's work."

I looked into her eyes briefly, and she looked back with a sparkle, like a kindling fire that could not be extinguished. The human spirit. For all the intelligence I possessed, I felt a weak person. All that power, beckoning at my command, would mix together proper chemical combinations to create a life-saving drug. I knew I was helping to save lives, but I had often questioned for what purpose. Michelle was my answer, her and her work. It gave me some sort of completeness, like the final puzzle pieces coming together. Knowing Michelle so well allowed me an advantage over the art collectors—I could more deeply see how her personality and feelings were expressed in her paintings and sculptures. That was something no oratory or documentary could describe.

"I'm really excited tonight," she said. "I really feel I've done the best ever, and I expect the collectors will see the new Michelle. I think you'll be amazed too, Dexy."

"I hope so. You wouldn't let me look at your work while you were developing it."

"As it should be. An incomplete work is like an incomplete life—without meaning and full of voids. To let you see it at that stage would put in your mind an interpretation which is never meant to be, and that interpretation would carry over when you would view the completed work."

"I see. I do think, though, that the greatest work is sitting right next to me, and I'd never give it up for a king's ransom."

Michelle kissed me on the cheek.

"You always flatter me with words."

"I feel...I feel like the luckiest man alive to be with you."

Michelle placed her left hand on my right, squeezing it gently. I continued driving the Cadillac with my left on the wheel as a new moon emerged from the sunset. My left wrist quietly snapped as I made a turn.

"When are you going to get your wrist fixed?" Michelle asked.

"I know, I keep putting it off. I think the lube line is clogged again."

"If you had never spent your early years on that terminal..."

Michelle was referring to my days as a computer programmer. That was before I went into pharmacy. After days of non-stop typing at the keyboard, I developed carpal tunnel syndrome in my left wrist. I thought nothing of it, letting the pain progressively get worse until I could hardly move my fingers. When my boss asked why I was only using one hand to type, I complained of my left hand being sore. He immediately had me go to the hospital, where tests showed a gradual deterioration of the bursa sacs surrounding my wrist joint, as well as the pinched nerves. Surgery relieved the pain from the pinched nerves, and the doctors added an artificial lubrication device which took the place of the bursa sacs. The device took common proteins out of my bloodstream and converted them into bio-lubricants.

The device worked well the first few weeks I had it, but as soon as I resumed my heavy beef diet, the device would occasionally get clogged, and the wrist would dry out. Thus, my wrist would crack.

"I'll have it taken care of this week, I suppose. Or I could take some drugs to dissolve the complex proteins."

"I'm telling you, you gotta watch your meat intake," she warned. Was she nagging? I was beginning to think so, but Michelle was only looking out for me. Besides, this discussion couldn't continue much further—this was her night.

"Here we are," I announced, wheeling the car to a stop. Taking Michelle in arm, we strolled up to a building with a sign, "Art Exhibit: Tonight."

"Good evening Mr. Deuler, Ms. LaSalle. May I take your coats?" I helped Michelle with her coat, then handed mine to the doorman. Even though Michelle was my wife, she signed her paintings as Michelle LaSalle, a carry-over from the days before our marriage. As custom would dictate, it was thought she would change her last name to mine—Deuler. However, she liked her last name and wanted to keep it. She was not only an artist, but a progressive woman as well. We struck an unusual deal in our pre-nuptial agreement—all boys born to us would carry my last name, and all girls born to us would carry her last name. She believes in equality, all right, but some scoff at our agreement.

We were early, but already other art exhibitors were gathering around their works, taking last looks or straightening crooked frames. Michelle led me past several rows of paintings and sculptures. Then I stopped and looked. And looked.

Her first painting was on the beach of an un-named Great Lake, with several large rocks, a passing sea gull, and a little boy playing with his toy sailboat in the water. She knew the Great Lakes were dear to me, and she captured the lake's majesty and romance in a way my pharmaceutical words could not describe. I was that little boy; my love for the water and sailboats could only be perceived from a child's mind, and she portrayed that quite well.

Her second painting was an abstract, so how could I describe it? It used many interconnecting circles and ellipses, along with an occasional black streak. The "circlipses" (what I called the circles and ellipses together) wove together and formed some larger circlipse. I think the black streaks represented trouble spots, like dark times in a person's life. Michelle would never give me her interpretation of her abstracts, leaving me to interpret them for myself.

Her final painting was a surreal, showing a little girl in a sun-yellow dress sniffing a flower. The girl blended in with the forest and woods, leading me to believe she was a daughter of the wild, as opposed to some civilized girl who rode her tricycle along a concrete driveway.

Michelle had one "arrangement"—what do you call those things? Small sculptured objects combined with a few common household things—that's what it was, but though I could recite the various aldehydes and ketones, I could not remember those art terms. Her paintings were inspiring and uplifting, but her arrangement...I was startled. More than startled, I stepped back for a moment. The modeled man was shown bent over, squeezing his head between his hands like a vise, his hair forced up, his eyes wide and blood-shot, and his teeth grimacing with bloody streaks along the corners of his mouth. His body showed little flesh—he was but a living skeleton. Next to him were several hypodermic needles and pills. The pills were made of clay and glazed with assorted colors as was the man, but the needle was real, used previously for Michelle's insulin deficiency but now covered with a black enamel.

"What do you think, Dexy, do you like?"

"I...it's different."

Michelle went back to her paintings, making sure they were just perfect. I stared at the arrangement a few minutes. In my interpretation, she was making a statement against drugs. "Illegal drugs," I thought. But drugs are drugs, and I couldn't help but feel hurt in some way, as if she were attacking my profession, and attacking me for being a part of it.

Fortunately, a hostess came by with some snacks, and munching away, I strolled around the exhibit, briefly leaving Michelle to her things. The exhibitors were all ready, and some collectors were already circulating. I returned in time to see Michelle amongst a group of people who were admiring her paintings. One particular gentleman was oblivious to the general discussions and focused on the arrangement. Wondering what kind of person would be interested in such a ghastly thing, I casually walked up and pretended I too was interested.

"Remarkable, isn't it?" he asked me. The man looked to be in his late fifties, hair completely white with a bald spot in the middle, a white beard, and glasses.

"I beg your pardon?" I asked back, unsure of what he spoke.

"This," he said, pointing to the arrangement. "Simply remarkable. I wonder how much the young lady wants for the work. It would look good in my office and would remind me of...oh, that is another matter."

"So you'd be interested in buying it?" I asked.

"I might be, if the price is right, and if I could ask the young lady. She seems absorbed in her paintings."

"I think I could get her attention."

"Really? Do you know her then?"

"Michelle? She's my wife. Allow me to introduce myself. I'm Edward Deuler."

"And I am Jonathan Weismann. So tell me, Mr. Deuler—"

"Please, call me Edward, or Ted if you like."

"Very well, Ted. What do you do when you're not attending your wife's art exhibits?"

"I work over at Mercy Hospital as a Pharmacist."

"I see. Very good hospital, Mercy. Many of my colleagues work there. Excellent place."

"Your colleagues?"

"Yes. I don't often tell people in public, but I'm a pediatrician. I have a practice for three days of the week, then I perform surgery at Children's Hospital for the other two. May I ask you a question?"

"Certainly."

"Does your work inspire your wife's work?"

"Sometimes I wonder. This particular arrangement took me by surprise. I mean, I work with drugs every day, and yet she seems to be saying how drugs are torturing people, taking them to a certain madness. She is, of course, talking about drug addicts like those on the streets, but in a small way it does hit home."

"I read something different out of it. I think it represents something larger—man's attempt to reach for a quick and easy fix to a problem, only to find to his dismay the great pain and discomfort this creates. I know someone who was over-ambitious. He too was a pharmacist, and he did research, looking for new drugs to cure nerve anomalies. Poor soul. Your wife's work makes me think of him and those like him."

"Hold on, let me see if I can..." I broke away from Jonathan and made for Michelle.

"Honey? Do you think you could spare a few moments? A Dr. Jonathan Weismann is interested in your arrangement over there. Do you think you could spend a few moments with him? I think he'd like to buy it."

"Oh sure, Ted," she said to me. She turned around to the other and said, "Excuse me for a moment."

"Dr. Weismann? I'm Michelle LaSalle. How do you do?"

"It's a pleasure to meet you, Ms. LaSalle. I really admire your work here. What inspired you to make it?"

"Sometimes that's how I feel at the end of the day after putting the children to sleep," she said sarcastically. Several of us laughed.

"Amusing. But really, Ms. LaSalle," Dr. Weismann continued.

"It can mean a number of things, depending on the person. For the street people, it represents their painful existence and using drugs as an escape. For others, it represents their struggle to survive, with only life-saving drugs to keep them going. Or, the drugs can be symbolic for some other 'demon' that drives a person to go mad with irrational obsessions."

"So how much do you want for it?" he asked.

"$300."

"I think I'll take it, Ms. LaSalle. Hmm, have we met before?"

"I don't think so, Dr. Weismann...wait, do you know a Harriet Weismann?"

"That's my wife's name."

"Does she work at the Pharmco Drugs on Ross Street?"

"Why yes, do you know her?"

"Absolutely. She and I often gab while I pick up my supply of insulin. A nice lady, really."

"Say, would the two of you like to come over for dinner sometime? I would be honored if the famous Michelle LaSalle dined with us. And of course you're welcome too, Ted."

"Sure, I think we'd be glad to, right Michelle?" I asked her.

"Yes."

"When would be a good day?" the doctor asked.

"How about Friday?" I suggested.

"Friday's fine with me," Michelle responded.

"Then Friday it is. Anytime after six will be good, I think." Dr. Weismann made out a check for $300 and handed it to Michelle.

"Thank you," she said.

"Thank you," he replied.

"Here, let me help you with that," I offered. Dr. Weismann and I carried the work out to his car, a new Mercedes.

"This really reminds you of someone?" I asked casually as we placed the work into his car.

"Yes it does. Maybe you've heard of him...Hampton Zeiger?"

"He researched nerve-tissue regeneration. I've read some of his papers. Very interesting. Already they've managed to give some paraplegics and a few quads their muscle control again by restoring the severed nerve connections in the spinal column."

"I see you do know of him. I knew him personally, and I must say he was truly devoted to his work. No, not devoted. Obsessed. I've known him to put in twenty-hour days working on his research. It's mad."

"You speak of him in the past. I noticed he disappeared from the health journals," I said.

"Yes, what a tale that is. Perhaps it's best to wait 'till another time, say, when you come over for dinner?"

"I'll look forward to it. A pleasure meeting you, Dr. Weismann."

"And you too, Ted."

With that, Dr. Weismann left. I returned to the exhibit, discovering Michelle had sold the abstract and was negotiating on the surreal. I took a look at the Great Lakes painting wondering why no one had purchased it yet. Michelle sold the surreal and stood next to me, patiently waiting. A few collectors looked at the painting but showed no further interest. The crowd thinned.

"I think I've done quite well tonight. If I can sell this last painting, I'll have made over a thousand. Aren't you proud of me?"

"I'm very proud of you. In fact, I'm so proud that..." I took out my checkbook and wrote a check for $350. "I'll buy this painting."

"Oh don't flatter me, Dexy."

"I'm serious. I want this painting for the study. I'm willing to pay $350 for it. Is it a sale?"

The crowd had thinned further. It was late.

"Dexy, if you really want it, you may have it at no charge."

"No, I insist upon paying for it."

"Very well, if you insist."

I handed her the check, and the night was complete. I took the painting in hand and Michelle in the other. We picked up the kids, returned home, and I hung the painting up in my study. Then I snuck up on Michelle while she was undressing (the children had been quickly put to bed) and caressed her.

"You little devil," she whispered.

"Can I help it?" I whispered back. "I'm in love with my wife." We made love that night.

II.

Friday came quickly enough, and we found ourselves walking into a modern and well-to-do home of the Weismann's. Dr. Weismann gave us a tour of the house while Harriet (his wife) made final preparations for the meal. Dr. Weismann certainly was a collector. Michelle stared intently at several paintings though I was more interested in the doctor's library, consisting of hundreds of books both old and new. I could have spent weeks pouring over the material, but dinner was ready and we were seated.

"Jonathan, would you say the grace?" requested Harriet.

"Lord, we give thanks for this meal you've provided for us and for the special company we enjoy tonight. Amen."

Harriet had done an excellent job preparing roast beef with mashed potatoes, rolls, and gelatin fruit salad. Michelle and I both complimented Harriet on her cooking, but she would only brush it off as being nothing. Conversation was light, though Michelle did ask about Dr. Weismann's paintings. I finished my meal and sipped on the champagne, then a silence hung over the table.

"Hampton Zeiger," I said in a low voice. Silence continued. Harriet looked at Dr. Weismann with a grave face. Dr. Weismann stirred his mashed potatoes with a fork. I looked at him. Michelle looked at me, wondering what I meant.

"Yes," the doctor finally said. "An unfortunate case."

"Who?" Michelle asked.

"When I saw your work the other night, Michelle, the one I purchased, it reminded me of a former pharmacist I knew. His name was Hampton Zeiger. Remarkable man, really. He formulated a new series of drugs that promote nerve regeneration."

"Is it true then? It's been traditionally taught that nerves and brain cells do not heal themselves when once damaged. People with spinal column injuries often are paralyzed from the waist down or worse. I know he worked to solve the problem. What about it?" I asked.

"It's true. He did find a drug to cause nerve healing or regeneration. But as for him..."

"I met Hampton when he first started as a pharmacist at Children's Hospital. He was a bright fellow, always mixing drug dosages quickly and efficiently. He enjoyed helping people as do most of us in the medical profession. One day a child came in through ER. He'd been playing around an empty swimming pool, bouncing up and down on the diving board. He fell off the board and landed in the pool, breaking his back. We did all we could for the child, saving his life, but the damage had been done—his legs were paralyzed."

"Hampton visited the child, whose name was Billy, regularly. That was another good quality about Hampton—after hours he'd go around the hospital and bring Teddy Bears or other stuffed animals to the children. It did wonders for their morale. Billy was especially dear to Hampton. Every day he visited Billy, promising Billy would get better. Billy was told by the doctors he'd never walk again, which made Billy very upset. Hampton would tell Billy that he'd walk again. Hampton promised."

"'You shouldn't make promises like that,' I said to Hampton."

"'But he will walk again. I swear he will,' Hampton replied. After further discussion, I learned Hampton had applied for a job in a lab at the local university for research on assisted nerve healing and regeneration. I scoffed at Hampton, saying it wasn't possible, but Hampton wouldn't take no for an answer. He kept talking about Billy, and what if Billy were his own child, wouldn't that make it all the more important to give Billy the ability to walk again?"

"I wished Hampton luck, though I felt in my heart he was making a mistake. I was both right and wrong."

"Initially he started out as a research clerk, recording information and summarizing it for the chief researchers. When he noticed a flaw in certain methods and pointed them out to one of the chiefs, he was invited to share his own ideas on how to proceed. Within several weeks he was directing the entire operation. Several months later, he felt he had made the first breakthrough. A laboratory rat had a nerve severed that controlled hind-leg movement. Then the nerves were reattached, using the new drug as a sort of 'glue'."

"You mean they just glued the nerves back together?" Michelle asked.

"Essentially, yes. The compound (which Hampton dubbed neopoxy) successfully transmitted signals between the nerve endings while holding them together. However, they encountered some problems."

"What sort of problems?" I asked.

"In conducting, the neopoxy 'leaked' the nerve signals. This meant that other nerves endings that were connected using the neopoxy captured the interfering signals and combined them with their own. This resulted in confusing signals, both to and from the brain. The rat's leg would move sporadically, and eventually it died from excessive trauma."

"In coming so close, Hampton wasn't about to give up. He created a second drug called pseudo-neopoxy, which again joined the endings together and conducted signals, but it also formed an outer layer that prevented spurious signals from entering and exiting."

"It took a year to perfect the procedure, and the FDA was in the process of approving it, but there was insufficient information on how the drug affected humans. Operating on a human was the next step. Billy was the first person on Hampton's mind, so he gained parental consent and proceeded with the doctors to repair the nerve damage done to Billy's spinal column."

"The nervous system is incredibly complicated. Just matching the correct nerves together is a seemingly impossible task. The team of doctors took the operation in steps; the first was to allow Billy to move his right leg."

Michelle's and my glass being empty, Harriet poured us another drink.

"It took a few weeks for the pseudo-neopoxy to heal the nerves together. Then it happened. Billy moved his right leg. There was a big celebration, and the news media tried poking their heads into the fray, but Hampton wanted no media, no press. Billy's health was the most important thing on his mind, and he was eager to start the next step, reattaching the left motor nerves. That went well. Several physical therapists helped Billy regain strength in his legs, and after two months,

Billy was able to walk. He couldn't feel his legs or feet, and he stumbled around. Again Hampton was applauded for his work, and Billy was incredibly happy. His parents were full of enthusiasm and practically worshipped Hampton as a god."

"Seeing how Billy could walk again gave Hampton renewed motivation to carry out the final step—reattaching the sensory nerves so Billy could feel again with his legs. Six weeks passed without a positive sign. Then one day Billy complained of pain in his left leg. The team was ecstatic with joy. The only thing they did all day was run around and remark in excitement how Billy's leg was in pain. The physical therapists came in once again and did various tests with pointed instruments, seeing how well Billy could feel them. It appeared one side of Billy's left leg was still numb, but the entire right leg had regained full feeling. For the first time, Billy was able to walk around unsupported. He ran up to his parents and kissed them. They gave him a big hug and were so happy that tears came to their eyes. I was in that day and was a bit emotional too."

"Of course the surgeons had missed a nerve, and they went back to the operating room one last time and found it, reconnected it, and in another month Billy was home living a normal life. Or so it seemed at first. Several months later, it was learned he didn't have as good coordination as any other normal child had. Billy and his parents didn't seem to mind— poor coordination but being able to walk was better than total paralysis. They are still eternally thankful, but Hampton couldn't rest."

"You see, Hampton is a perfectionist at heart. He believes that though he gave Billy his ability to walk again, he had not restored full coordination. That had to be solved."

"Several doctors theorized it had to do with the connector—perhaps it didn't carry the signal as it was supposed to. 'Distortion,' some said. Hampton didn't accept that, though. He was certain the pseudo-neopoxy was reproducing the signal at 100%. Something else was the matter. 'Perhaps it's the nerve endings themselves,' he told me once. He theorized the nerve tips had deteriorated, much like the end of a severed plant stem going dry while the rest of the stem is still moist. Hampton decided he needed to find another drug that would regenerate the nerve tips."

"He spent long hours in the lab, mostly in secret. He and his team won the Nobel prize for chemistry, and they were still refining the pseudo-neopoxy to promote a faster healing rate, but Hampton wasn't satisfied. Though his colleagues scoffed, he had to attempt the next step—nerve regeneration."

"Now according to all the textbooks, nerve regeneration is impossible. Hampton could care less. Because if he could regenerate the nerves, it would open the doors for greater possibilities, such as a cure for multiple sclerosis, and possibly brain-cell regeneration."

"I don't have to tell you how obsessed Hampton was. He spent practically his entire time in that lab, hardly coming out for anything. The seasons came and went, and while many of us were out skiing during the winter, washing our cars during the spring, or swimming during the summer, Hampton was there in the lab, alone. Occasionally I tried pulling him out of the lab, but he said his work was too important, too vital."

"'Think of how many people can resume normal lives because of the pseudo-neopoxy. Think of how many more could benefit if nerves can be regenerated. I feel like the world is just a great puzzle, waiting to be solved. I also feel I'm racing against time, because I will only be alive for so long, and some of these puzzles can take quite a while to solve,' he said."

"'But that's what a research team is for, to increase the man-hours available. Why don't you enlist their help?' I asked."

"'They? They think the answer lies in modifying pseudo-neopoxy. I've seen their work. They've come up with a new drug, called pseudo-dineopoxy, which is supposed to improve the coordination by 50%. Do you know who came up with the original formula for neopoxy? Me. They only know procedures, rules, and following the book. They can't go beyond what they have and envision new possibilities, not like I,' he bragged."

"At this point I felt Hampton was being quite arrogant with me. I tried pointing out how we all have a certain ability to see beyond the norms, our abilities simply vary in degree. But he wouldn't hear of it. He could only see his world, and isolating himself in the lab reinforced this problem."

"Didn't Hampton have a wife?" Michelle asked.

"No, and the few friends he did have dropped him when he locked himself in that lab. I was the closest thing to a friend he had left. He was married to his drugs and lived in his lab. I've even caught him napping while his computer was carrying out time-consuming calculations. He was losing weight, and I could tell he wasn't eating well, only enough to keep himself alive. He was very agitated at times and at other times very lethargic. I was almost ready to have him forcibly removed for a day or two, just to get his body healthy again. Then on a Monday morning visit a bizarre thing happened. Very bizarre."

Michelle set her empty glass aside. Harriet offered me another drink, but I declined, knowing I would be driving. Michelle's interest in the story was not as keen as mine, which was fine. Harriet had heard the story already and was presently excusing herself to clean up. Michelle got up and helped. I found the story too fascinating so far to really notice. Dr. Weismann continued:

"I had just walked into Hampton's lab and noticed how happy he was. I was a bit bewildered, then I realized he must have made some breakthrough."

"'I'd like to try an experiment, and I need your help,' he said."

"'Sure,' I replied. 'What did you have in mind?'"

I continued to watch Dr. Weismann intently, concentrating on every word. In my peripheral vision, I could see Michelle standing in the kitchen with some dishes in hand.

"'Write down a hundred or so random letters and numbers. Don't let me see. When you're finished, recite them one-by-one to me,' he said. I couldn't see the point of his request, but I went ahead anyway."

"I don't remember the exact list, but it went something like 1-4-a-e-7-8-f et cetera, et cetera. I was out of breath when I finished reading the list."

"'Now look at your paper and listen…1-4-a-e-7-8-f,' he started, and I was completely amazed to hear him recite the entire list of characters exactly as I had read them."

"'How did you remember that?' I asked."

Michelle's hand pointed to something on the kitchen ceiling. I clasped my tense hands together as the story progressed.

"'I've found it, Jonathan, I've discovered the answer. A rather intricate chemical compound, yes, very devious. But I found it. I developed it with the help of my computer and my brain. Think of it, Jonathan, not only have I discovered a drug to promote nerve regeneration, but brain-cell regeneration as well. I've tested it on rats, run them through the mazes. Excellent recall of previous mazes. Not only did they learn new mazes well, but they remembered the old ones. I've actually delayed the atrophying process amongst the brain and nerve cells,' he said with a cunning look. I thought he was mad, and I dared not to speculate on what he was about to say next."

"'No,' I pleaded. 'No, you didn't, you didn't test it on…'"

"'Myself? I was thinking, Jonathan, if this drug (which I'm calling neozene) can reverse the effects of alcohol-related memory loss, how would it affect a normal person? I've always been hampered by an inferior memory. Certainly not like that silicon machine over there,' he said, pointing to his computer. 'If I can improve my memory to the point of that machine, think of what I could accomplish!'"

"I backed away from Hampton. Yes, he tried the drug on himself and became more obsessed than ever. I found myself talking to a giant and was careful not to be stepped upon."

"'But Hampton,' I continued, 'you haven't tested this drug enough. The side-effects, you don't know…'"

"'I know more than you could imagine! I took my first dose yesterday afternoon, and I read through the first three books of my encyclopedia set. I can remember every word. For instance, the Ambassador Bridge connects Detroit, Michigan with Windsor, Ontario. Did you know that, Jonathan? I've been there, and I've been to Blue Water Bridge, which connects Port Huron, Michigan to Sarnia, Ontario. I find that the neozene not only improves my current memory, but my past as well. I can see the Blue Water Bridge now—it's much higher off the water than the Ambassador, and the view of Lake Huron on one side and the St. Clair River on the other is simply remarkable. That's the sad thing about people today; they enjoy things for but a brief moment then forget about them. I can remember; I can relive those moments to the smallest detail, right down to re-experiencing the bridge undulations from the passing wind or the passing semi.'"

"'Hampton,' I said. 'You're playing with fire.'"

"'Someone must take the first step. I've experienced no ill-effects. And even if I do later on, think of what I could accomplish in the meantime—breakthroughs that would otherwise take decades to make. Some people can't wait decades, hoping for some cure. Some people are on the very brink of life, hoping for a miracle. I am that miracle, and I'll do everything in my power to make their dreams come true. Who needs this computer now? I can do it all.'"

"Would anyone like some dessert?" Harriet asked. Each of us accepted as Harriet and Michelle served ice cream with Devil's Food cake. Michelle and Harriet sat down as we enjoyed the delights.

"So where was I?" asked Dr. Weismann, ready to continue the story.

"The day you discovered Hampton had tried neozene on himself," I replied.

"Oh yes. I didn't know what to do at the time. I was both elated by his discovery and frightened by his berserk behavior. I left him in his lab for a week, thinking he'd go public with his discovery. He didn't, and this frightened me further. I could only guess what sort of monster was growing. Then Hampton stopped by my house for an unexpected visit."

"'Hampton,' I said. 'What brings you here?'"

"'I've been travelling, Jonathan. I can look at a map for ten seconds and know where every street is, every river and every railroad track. I've gone around to several cities, Chicago, Cleveland, Buffalo, and New York. I know them perfectly. But travelling started to bore me. Every city is so similar. I've long since finished reading the encyclopedia, and I've read several books since then. You'd be amazed how many writers need help with structure, plot development, and character development. I'd show them how it's done, except I'm too busy learning new things. Did I tell you I went to Vegas a few days ago? Played Blackjack and won! I used the old counting-cards method, and it was a cinch. I was tossed out after winning five thousand, and it was fun at first, but that grew tiring too.'"

"Hampton continued telling me of his experiences, his speech going as quickly as his muscles would allow. He was almost incomprehensible he spoke so fast. Like a chipmunk."

"'Really,' he said. 'I think about how I used to spend my time in that lab. That's peanuts. I can solve bigger problems now, if I just had the time. I want to learn more about electronics, quantum physics, and geology.'"

"'Hampton, don't you think you should slow down a bit?'"

"'Slow down for what?' he asked. 'Life's too short to be taking slowly. I want to experience it, all of it. The world is a truly wonderful place. Did I tell you, I've learned two foreign languages since I last saw you?'"

"'In a week? And have time to go to Vegas and those other cities? How!?'" I asked, completed dumbfounded.

"'It's not that hard if you put your mind to it. A few tapes while taking the plane or driving around in the car to catch the basic phonetic pronunciations, and lots of book reading to learn the rest. I admit I don't know the colloquialisms, but a few trips to Europe should give me that. For the Spanish and French, I mean. I want to learn German, then Russian, Japanese, Chinese, Swahili...'"

"He continued reciting all sorts of languages he wanted to learn, many of which I'd never heard before. This was getting scary. I was afraid of two things: 1) He'd become so powerful that he'd turn to evil and use his intelligence for crime, and 2) He'd rise to the top so quickly that he'd set himself up for a big fall."

"Were you right?" I asked. Michelle was clearly engrossed in the dessert.

"I don't know," Dr. Weismann replied.

"But you've been in contact with him, haven't you?"

"Well yes, but I only saw him one more time. That was several weeks ago, and I haven't seen him since. He was saying something about how normal life is so boring, knowledge without purpose, and he wanted life to have some kind of meaning."

"'That is why I feel you must return to your medical profession and share your abilities so that people may benefit.'"

"'Who do you think you're speaking to?' he asked, as if I'd insulted him. 'Your brain is the size of a pea compared to mine. Don't you think I know about all that? Of course I do! But who would be able to understand me, who could even make the attempt? No one. I could spend days trying to make my colleagues understand my work, but it's like teaching a cat how to speak. I'm worlds beyond them and you.'"

"I was silenced by that comment. He looked into my eyes, and I into his. He looked menacing, like a hawk ready to go in for the kill. I felt like a rabbit, frozen by his gaze and fearful of moving. I made an effort to say something, and he was gone. That's the last I've seen of him. I can only pray..."

Silence.

"Is it possible he became addicted to his drugs?" Michelle asked.

"I really don't know anymore. It seems the drug has controlled him, or at least it has taken his ambitions and made them larger than the Sears Tower."

Michelle hiccupped.

"Excuse me," she said. Dr. Weismann and I both lost our thoughts on Hampton briefly and watched Michelle. She hiccupped again. And again.

"Dear me. I have the hic-(hiccup)-cups. Maybe I should try drinking something," she said, taking a water glass to her mouth. Dr. Weismann and I smiled. Here Hampton had spent his years on such a complicated thing while Michelle was unable to get rid of her hiccups. Michelle really was trying hard to stop. Then she reached for her throat.

"I'm afraid holding your neck won't get rid of those hiccups," I commented. But Michelle wasn't hiccupping. In fact, she wasn't doing anything, including breathing. Realizing my mistake in horror, I leapt out of my chair and performed the Heimlich maneuver on Michelle. My left wrist cracked. Dr. Weismann was also up, ready to help if necessary. Harriet jumped up, left, then returned with Dr. Weismann's medical bag. Michelle had gone a little blue, but after several attempts, the obstructing fluid popped up her throat, out her mouth, and onto her napkin.

"Are you all right?" I asked her.

Michelle was breathing heavily and looked around, thankful to be alive.

"Perhaps I should take a look at her, just to make sure she's ok. I heard a cracking sound. Did you pop something, Michelle?" Dr. Weismann asked.

"That was my left wrist," I said.

"That sounded painful. Is it sprained?"

"Yes, it does hurt. No, it's not a sprain. I have a lube implant, and the line is clogged, I'm afraid."

"You should have that looked into soon, Ted. Your bones will just grate themselves down, and you'll have to get an artificial wrist."

"I know," I said, apologetically.

"Now to Michelle. Let's take a look," he continued.

"By all means. Thank you." I was glad he wasn't nagging me too much about my wrist. Sometimes I'm bad about procrastinating, but it is my wrist.

"I guess I rambled on too much. About Hampton, I mean," Dr. Weismann apologized.

"I'm quite all right, Doctor, really. My hiccups are gone," Michelle gasped.

"Well I'll be...what do you say, Doc, are you going to add that as a sure cure for hiccups?"

"No. I don't think choking oneself to near death is a good idea."

"I was just joking, of course," I said.

"Of course," he said.

"I think we'd better be leaving. Thank you for the excellent meal, Dr. and Mrs. Weismann. We'll have to have you over sometime," I said, as Michelle and I strolled out the door. My wrist cracked on the way out.

"Take it easy you two," Harriet called back.

III.

"Good morning, my *fleur du soleil*," I whispered into Michelle's ear. I then kissed her.

"Oh, I have a rotten headache," she moaned, obviously in pain.

"And your eyes are bloodshot. Burning off the alcohol has left you dehydrated. Care for a drink?" I joked.

"Uhhh," she moaned, part of the previous evening coming back to her mind. "What did I do to deserve this agony?"

"You know what they say, every degree of pleasure exacts an equal but opposite degree of pain. And judging by your performance in bed last night, you must have one helluva headache!"

"I should have never agreed to a night-cap with you—I always seem to lose control first," Michelle said, whipping a pillow in my face.

"Naughty," I grinned.

"It's not fair. Why can't I remember it, if it was so great?"

"Here," I said. "Drink this—slowly. We don't want you to choke like you did last night."

"Oh, gaud," she mumbled. "That was so embarrassing. And to think if no one was there, I'd be—"

"Now, now, now. All's not lost. Actually..."

"Actually, what?" she insistently asked.

"Actually, I have a confession to make."

Michelle's eyes widened briefly.

"You? What?" Now she was really perplexed.

"First, I made up the part about your performance in bed. I was just joking. After the night-cap, you were fast asleep. And as for the Weismanns, well, ole Doc was feeling guilty, blaming himself for your choking. They are both concerned about your health, as am I."

"Dr. Weismann feels guilty? That doesn't make sense."

"I guess he feels his story was too boring for you. I found it interesting, but what can I say—I'm a pharmacist."

"I thought it was interesting, but I found the dessert to be equally interesting. You don't suppose Doc feels guilty about Hampton, do you?"

I looked at Michelle, surprised. "You were paying attention then, weren't you?"

"Yeah," she replied, as if I should have known better. "Actually, if anyone should be feeling guilty it's you."

"Me? Why me?" I asked, pacing around the room.

"Yes you. For not bringing me breakfast in bed," Michelle laughed.

"Oh, a joke. I love jokes. Well hold the next punch line, I have one for you." I briefly left the room and returned with a tray full of sliced fruit, whole-wheat toast, a slice of Swiss cheese, and orange juice. "Breakfast in bed. How's that for service?"

"I was only joking," she said.

"I know, and so am I. But really, it's nothing; an unfortunate happenstance resulting from excessive exposure to the domestic creature comforts derived from common, modern-day living."

"Now who's being silly," she mumbled with the cheese in her mouth. "By the way, honey, did you save the evening paper? I wanted to see what's playing at the cinema."

"Am I your slave now?"

"Oh Dexy, you've always been a sweet guy. Dextrose, right? The paper, and I won't bother you anymore."

"Very well." Where was that paper? Actually, I hadn't had a chance to read it. I checked the porch, and there it was.

"Here it is—untouched. I'm surprised the kids didn't play with it, except they're out back playing with Fido instead of out front." I placed the paper next to her tray and proceeded to leave. My wrist cracked.

"Honey, when are you going to have that wrist looked after?" Michelle asked.

"I promise, Monday morning I'll go in to have it reamed."

"You better. You're not going to have anything left if you keep this up," she added.

"I know. You're starting to sound like the Doc."

"Well, he's right," she said.

"As you wish. Anyway, I think I'll join Marie and Willy out back."

"Don't get too dirty," she said as she opened the paper and immediately turned to the back. "And be careful with that wrist!" As I was leaving the room, a front-page headline caught my eye, "AckNak Strikes BankCorp, Takes Million."

"Hello, what's this?" I asked, walking up to the paper. Michelle put the paper aside and looked at me suspiciously.

"You've had your chance, now it's mine."

"I just wanna—"

"I wanna, I wanna, gimme this, gimme that, gimme!" she mocked.

"Ok, I had my chance. But look at the front page; look at the headline about BankCorp."

Michelle tossed the paper over and read aloud:

> The latest big-time bank thief, dubbed AckNak for his peculiar electronic signature, has reportedly stolen $1,037,241.21 without setting a foot into any BankCorp building. His accomplice was an inside computer, and his getaway vehicle was the local phone company.
>
> This marks the third robbery by AckNak, who was given the name by programmers at First Federal Savings (AckNak's first robbery) who discovered over $500,000 missing and an unusual file left in the bank's computer, which contained two characters used in computer communications representing ACKnowledge and Negative AcKnowledge.
>
> BankCorp officials were unavailable for comment, but an anonymous BankCorp programmer states, "Back in the early days of computing, a stray hacker would try his hand at electronic fund transfers. But modern-day security systems make this impossible,

or so we once thought. We're still at a loss as to AckNak's method for breaking in, and why the phone company can't trace the call."

"Who is this AckNak?" asked Michelle.

I paused for a moment, staring at the ground. Then I looked up at Michelle. She was looking at me with a quizzical face. Her face was a lovely piece of art, and for a moment I lost myself in her masterpiece.

"Some call him a high-tech thief, a hacker; others call him a black wizard, a demon. Some religious sects say it's the devil's doing, and that the love of money is the root of all evil. Whoever it is must be a genius. Like the programmer said, modern day bank computer security systems are supposedly foolproof. I know, because I used to write accounting programs for various banks before I went into pharmacy. It's almost a fantasy world we live in—to think one could be rich or bankrupt depending on how certain electronic impulses flow."

"Well if it's impossible to break into these computers, how can this AckNak do it?" Michelle asked.

"That's what everyone else is wondering. Either the guy is simply a complete brain regarding the phone systems and computers, or he's on the inside—a programmer for the banks. But the latter doesn't seem feasible, at least from what I've heard. The computer programs have been checked and rechecked for suspicious code, and all looks well. Even the possibility of a computer virus was suggested, but none was found. Also, more than one bank has been hit, so I can't see how he could be on the inside in all cases."

"Maybe this AckNak and Hampton should get together—sounds like a marriage made in heaven to me," Michelle suggested. She was finishing her sliced fruit.

"AckNak and Hampton. I wonder..." I was stricken with an idea, one almost too difficult to believe. "Could it be, that Hampton is—"

"AckNak? Wouldn't surprise me," she said nonchalantly.

"Wouldn't surprise you? You say that so smugly, as if we're discussing who'll win tomorrow's baseball game. If it is Hampton...oh, gaud! They don't know who they're dealing with."

"They?"

"The people at the banks, the programmers, the authorities investigating this," I clarified. "I think I should pay a visit to Dr. Weismann this afternoon."

"And leave me here to take care of the kids?" she whined.

"Now honey, I'll wait 'till you get ready for the day, of course. Besides, I'm not asking a lot. I should only be gone for an hour or two."

"What about going to the fair this afternoon with them? And the movies tonight? They're really looking forward to you being there."

"I'll be back by one. If not, then just go on to the fair as we planned. I'm positive it won't go on too long, and I can meet you at the cinema late in the afternoon. Which one were you planning on seeing?" I asked.

"*Hammer and Nails III.* It's supposed to be a good action-adventure movie."

"That sounds good."

While Michelle finished her breakfast and got ready for the day, I went out back to check on Bill and Marie.

"Hi, Daddy," said Marie.

"How's my sweet angel?" I asked, giving her a pat on the back.

"Oh I'm fine. See what I'm making?" She pointed to a collection of grasses, clovers, dandelions, and honeysuckles arranged in a plastic cup filled with water. "Don't they look pretty?" she asked.

"It's lovely," I said, trying to be polite. Actually, Marie did turn ordinary weeds into something appreciatively nice. "You have your mother's artistic talents."

"Here Daddy, smell."

I placed the cup of plants to my nose and slightly inhaled through my nose. Springtime. "Very nice, Marie. Where's Willy?"

"He's up in the tree house with Jud. You remember Jud, don't you Daddy?"

"Yes, Marie, I remember Jud. The Jensen's son from next door, right?"

"Yeah, I don't like him. He told me I was stupid for picking *daddylions* and putting them in a cup. I told him they were *dandelions*, not *daddylions*, and he starting yelling. Then he and Willy went into the tree house with Fido."

"How did Fido get up there?"

"Willy just carried him up. Oh look, Daddy, it's Roxy." Roxy was the Jensen's cat, a gray Persian long-haired feline. "Here kitty, kitty, kitty."

"Meow," said Roxy.

"Isn't Roxy such a nice kitty, Daddy?"

"Yeah," I said, staring at a passing cloud and lost in thought. "A nice kitty."

Was AckNak really Hampton? It was a wild thought, especially since Hampton was a pharmacist. Was. According to Dr. Weismann, Hampton had learned quite a bit since taking the neozene. Foreign languages, city maps, what was next? Computers? Banking systems? The telephone network? I had to see Doc—where was Michelle?

"So when are we going to the fair, Daddy?" Marie asked.

"I don't know if I'll be able to go, Marie. I need to take care of some business. Hopefully I'll be back in time to take you, your brother, and Mommy to the fair. If not, then Mommy will take you two."

"Can't you take care of business tomorrow?"

"No, it has to be today?"

"Why?"

"Because, it's very important."

"But the fair is more important," Marie added.

"I know. But there are some things in life we must do."

"Like going to the fair," Marie kept reiterating.

"Like going to the fair," Michelle said, stepping onto the porch. "It's all right, Marie, your father won't be long. We'll have lots of fun this afternoon, sweetie."

"Promise?" asked Marie.

"Promise," Michelle and I said simultaneously.

"I'll see you in a little while," I said, kissing Michelle then kissing Marie on her head.

"Bye," they said.

IV.

"Dr. Weismann?" I continued knocking on the Weismanns' front door. I rang the door bell repeatedly. No answer.

"Hmm, both cars are here. Maybe they're out back," I thought. As an afterthought, I turned the door handle. The door opened.

"Dr. Weismann?" I called through the partially opened door. "Harriet? Is anybody home?" No answer. Strange, very strange. What the hell was going on?

"Hello?" I shouted one more time as I slowly walked into the house. Pause. Shock. No. No, no, no, NO, No, NO! There, on the floor next to the couch lay Harriet, soaked with blood.

"Harriet," I screeched, running over to her and kneeling by her side. "Dear God!" Her body was cold and blue. I tried moving her arm, but it was stiff. "Rigor," I mumbled. "Dr. Weismann?" I yelled. I made a frantic search around the house. Kitchen? Bedroom? Lounge? Library? No. Study? "Dr. Weismann," I said, seeing him in his desk chair. His back was to me. "Dr. Weismann," I said again, walking up to him. I turned his chair around. "Doc—" A muffled scream got tangled in my throat, and I had difficulty swallowing. "Jesus!" A single vegetable knife was in his chest, with brown blood stains covering his shirt.

Dazed and confused, I stumbled around in circles saying, "Oh God, oh God!" The police had to be notified. Had to be. Or 911. I picked up the phone and dialed 911. Or so I tried. I heard nothing. Nothing. With urgency, I quickly scanned the cord. Severed. Running around the house, I found another phone in the kitchen. Severed. The bedroom. Severed. "What the hell is going on?" I blurted aloud, half hoping someone would answer. But no one did. Perhaps that was best, because if someone had, I would have feared for my life.

"Gotta get outta here," I muttered, running out of the house. "Gotta get out." I jumped into the car and raced back to my house, which was only a couple of miles down the road. "Gotta warn Michelle, gotta call the police." Then a new feeling overcame me; a black shadow passed over my heart as if something had happened at home, something not at all pleasant. I was driven by anger and fear, hoping that Michelle, Willy, and Marie were all right, hoping...

Her car was home. I opened the door, calling:

"Michelle? Marie? Willie?"

Perhaps my imagination was getting the best of me. No one answered, which shouldn't have bothered me, because Michelle was supposed to take the children to the fair. Nevertheless, I still had a duty to perform. I reached for the phone to call the police. Dead. No. No, no, NO, NO! The lines—cut! Something was wrong. Oh please, don't let it be, don't let it...

I raced around the house, frantically searching for what I did not wish to see. Everything was wrecked—books and magazines tossed everywhere, chairs and tables tossed about, and blood on the kitchen floor. Outside I ran, around back, then saw next to the flower garden Fido's bullet-ridden corpse.

"Noooooooooooo!" I yelled. "God, what have I done to deserve this?"

"Daddy?" I heard, a voice coming up from the trees. "Daddy?" It was Willy.

"Willy? Thank the Lord Jesus Christ you're alive. What happened? Where are your mother and sister?"

"Daddy?" he called again, peeking through an eye-hole from his tree house. "Is it safe to come down? Is the bad guy gone?"

"There's no one but you and I. Please, Willy, come down."

Willy slowly climbed down the ladder boards that were nailed to the maple tree. He ran over to me, his face wet from tears.

"Daddy," he wailed, "the bad man came, Fido ran after him, but he killed Fido. Mommy and Marie were screaming, Mommy...I...she stabbed him with a knife, but he took them away. I hid in the tree house until he went away."

"Who? Who was it?" I asked. At least Michelle gave him a good fight.

"I don't know. He looked mean and bad, like the troll who bothered Billy Goat Gruff. What are we going to do, Daddy?"

"C'mon inside," I said, "let's get you something to dry those tears. We'll figure out something."

I didn't notice it the first time I'd entered the house, but on the fireplace mantle was a blood-stained note:

Mr. Deuler:

   If you want to see your wife and daughter again, you'll meet me at Calatite Cave tonight at 8:00. Come alone. If you tell anyone or bring anyone with you, Michelle and Marie will die most cruelly. Try nothing fancy. I have eyes and ears everywhere.

          A.

"What does it mean, Daddy?" asked Willy.

"AckNak," I thought. "It means you'll be spending the night with your Aunt Ruthie. Daddy has to find Mommy and Marie."

"But I wanna go, Daddy."

"You can't. You'll be safe with Aunt Ruthie and Uncle Mike. I'll take you over there now. Come with me."

In minutes, Willy was with his cousins. I thanked Ruthie and Mike for taking care of Willy.

"Please," I said, "call the police and tell them about the Weismanns' place. Thank you."

It was only four o'clock in the afternoon, the drive to Calatite Cave would take an hour, so I had three hours to kill. I considered what Michelle and Marie must've been going through. Hell, pure hell. I wanted to nail that bastard; I wanted to take my rifle and blow his head off. No, that was just replacing violence with violence. There had to be another way.

In the end, I could think of nothing. Knowing Calatite Cave was in rough terrain, I decided to take the four-wheel drive truck with the dirt bike in back. The rifle? Yes, I took it too. I know, it was a bad idea, but my head was whirling—I couldn't think straight.

But I could shoot straight. Those were my precise thoughts as I drove up to Calatite Cave. Just as the cave came into sight, I parked the truck in a ravine, hidden from view. I unloaded the motorcycle, strapped the rifle over my shoulder, and rode off to the cave. Halfway up the gravel path, I wheeled the bike off the side into a rocky area. I proceeded on foot with rifle in hand and ammunition strapped around my waist. All I had to do was take him out with one bullet. One bullet.

Edging closer to the cave, I could feel the tension mounting. Any second, I would be close enough to see...would AckNak give me an easy shot? It was 7:30, and I hoped to catch him off guard. I was poising the rifle in my arm, releasing the safety when I heard a click. Hard metal pushed against my back.

"You're early, Mr. Deuler. But please, come in."

"Do I have a choice?" I asked, unable to see my assailant who had already taken my weapon.

"No. Move!"

"Dexy!" Michelle shouted when she saw me.

"Daddy!" yelled Marie.

"Quiet, all of you, or this family reunion will be a family burial," AckNak shouted.

I turned around as I sat with my family.

"I know you," I said. "You're...you're Hampton!"

"Ha, ha, ha, ha! I am Hampton. I am also AckNak."

His right arm was thickly bandaged, with a single blood stain in the middle.

"You killed Fido, you bad man," wailed Marie, crying.

"Shut up!" insisted Hampton.

"You," I said. "It is you. But—"

"But what? You can appreciate my position, Mr. Deuler, being a pharmacist yourself."

"Why, Hampton? Why the bank robberies, why the murder of Fido, and why are we here?"

"And why the murder of the Weismanns? Yes, I know you were there. In fact, I know quite a bit, far more than you could ever imagine. I'm aware of your dinner engagement with the Weismanns, and I know you were told the story how I invented neozene. I've gone far beyond that, but I need your help."

"I'm sure you realize that's out of the question," I responded.

"I thought you'd say as much. Tell me, Deuler, how important are the lives of Michelle and Marie to you, hmm? I'm not afraid of killing; you saw that today at the Weismanns', and you saw your dog. A sample of my capabilities. Those were merciful deaths. I'm quite capable of putting Marie or Michelle to death most painfully, both to them physically and to you emotionally."

"Ok, Hampton, let them go. I'll do what you ask, just let them go," I pleaded.

"Edward, you don't really intend to—" Michelle started.

"Michelle, please!"

"Of course he doesn't really intend to help me if I let you and Marie go," Hampton said, looking at Michelle. "That's why everyone stays here until your work is complete, Deuler."

"Work? What are you talking about?"

"Really, Deuler, you must learn not to end your sentences with prepositions. Nonetheless, you are familiar with computers, Mr. Deuler."

"Yeah, I use them at work."

"Not just that. Before you were a pharmacist, you developed several neural chips. I've read your books on the field—very impressive. Many of today's neural computers are based on your paradigm—the Deuler structure."

"That was many years ago. I gave up that mentally grueling career and pursued pharmacy in hopes of helping people. I hardly remember any of that computer stuff."

"I need your knowledge, your intellect, to create a neural-chip implant for my brain. That combined with my superior memory will enable me to directly interface with computers around the world. You will help me."

"You don't understand. I'm through with that computer stuff. I don't even remember half the stuff I developed. I can't help you," I said, hoping he'd let us go.

"But that's where you're wrong, Deuler. You will help me. And you will remember, with a little help from me."

"You don't mean—" I pleaded.

"Why not?"

"You're mad! I refuse!"

Hampton cocked the gun and shoved it into Marie's forehead. Marie cried.

"Refuse, and Marie dies. Then Michelle. Then finally, you. Cooperate, and your family continues. I give you my word, help me with this, and I will never bother you or your family again."

"I don't believe you. How could I trust you?"

"You don't have a choice, do you?" Hampton snickered.

I was afraid. I knew that taking neozene would corrupt my brain, making it difficult if not impossible to think sensibly. I would become like Hampton—a living freak, driven by a maddening drug to ruin.

Hampton motioned us toward the back of the cave, and we walked for several minutes before the cave seemed to end. Hampton pushed a button on a belt-attached gadget, and a door opened from the rough wall, leading to a modern-looking underground building structure. If I didn't know better, I'd say we were in some office complex, though there were no windows. We were then split up. Michelle was locked into one room, Marie in another, and I in a third.

"You'll start tonight," he said, chaining my body and feet to an office chair. "But first, you need some neozene," he said. I cringed at the thought, trying to figure out anything that would get me out of this.

"Really, Hampton, I don't think I need the neozene. Just give me some time to get acquainted with—"

"We don't have the time. Without the memory drug, you could spend months designing the chip. I don't have the time. It must be done in a few days. No more."

Hampton prepared the hypodermic needle, being careful to have the correct dosage. He walked over to me, poised over me, and commanded:

"Extend your left arm."

"Hampton," I pleaded one more time.

"Extend your left arm!" he nearly shouted.

"Please, I'll take the shot, but could you let me perform it?"

"Why?" he asked suspiciously, "what are you up to?"

"I know where to stick myself so it won't hurt so much. I have this thing about needles—"

"You, a pharmacist, are afraid of needles?"

"It's hard to explain. My nerves are just extra sensitive. Please, allow me."

"You're a clever liar. Ah, the neozene will only enhance the lies. We'll start with something else," he said, jabbing a needle in my arm. "How do you feel?" he asked a moment later.

I could hardly respond. Based on my experience, he must have shot me with sodium pentothal (used sometimes as truth serum), relaxing me and eliminating much feeling (as well as control).

"You'll soon be ready for the first shot," he said, walking around the room. I could not move a muscle.

"Once administered, the effects gradually build as the neozene strengthens your synaptic pathways. I noticed remarkable improvement after the first hour. You will feel the same," he said rather dreamily. I could tell he was caught up in his drug and his methods. I looked around for a way out, but there was nothing to be done.

"In time you'll understand, Deuler. You'll see the light. Everything will make sense. Everything. You'll be able to string all those random bits of information together and form one coherent picture of everything—and you will truly know how everything is and is meant to be," Hampton said as he checked his computer screen. His face was solemn.

"Like a God, almost," he continued. "Almost. That's the last major step, Deuler. Don't you see? I can preserve the nervous system. No more will man have to worry about senility, no more degradation of the nervous system due to age. Now if I can turn this same work toward refortifying the rest of the cells—think of it, Deuler. The great scientists of our times, we included, can continue our work—forever. No more will the geniuses die. No more will the rest of the world try grappling with trying to figure out what those geniuses were doing and developing. Think of it, Deuler. And you, you will become a part of it."

"But Hampton," I said, desperately trying to think. "Why the bank robberies, why the murders, why?"

"You don't understand yet, but you will. Do you know how the world treats raw intellect? Hmm? Do you know what it's like in elementary school when you raise your hand after every question is asked, only to find the teacher no longer calls on you because you do know the answer, and the teacher doesn't want to give you another chance? Or how you try to explain to your fellow students why they're incorrect, and they banish you from their 'superior' group because you're an egghead? Or how adults would shy away from you, because they knew you could win every argument, and they wanted to keep the upper hand? There are power struggles everywhere, Deuler. The world should belong to the intellects, I tell you. We should be in control of government, because we have the greatest ability to decide what's best for people, what's best for the environment, the economy, and so forth."

"But who's in power? I'm sure you've noticed, Deuler, that the populace is mostly a bunch of bumbling fools, hardly able to keep their heads on straight. So who do they vote for, someone who knows more than they? Hell, no! They want one of their own boys, to represent their interests. They want a friend. So, the first smooth-talking son-of-a-bastard that comes along and makes them feel like they are important is the one who is elected. The politician wants power, so he uses his art of persuasion to put the populace at ease."

"That's the problem. Our intelligent people are a minority. The vast, stupid majority cast their votes and elect the stupid politicians. The stupid elect the stupid."

"So whenever scientists warn the politicians how the environment is being destroyed by CFCs, carbon monoxide, sulfur dioxide, and the numerous toxins dumped in the rivers, do the politicians listen? Do they? Hell, they're concerned about their power in government, and as long as the majority is satisfied, that's all that matters."

"There's no focus in government, no direction. Money, power, and satisfying desires, with little regard for future or the overall picture—that's their goal."

"Do you think they'd listen to me? Hell, they'd lock me away for fear I'd upset their power structure. And I'd disrupt it badly, I must say. I will disrupt it, I must. There's too much ignorance in the world, Deuler, too much ignorance and too much waste. I must put a stop to it, and I will."

"The neural chip is the key. I can develop the solution for immortality, but I need a quick and direct link into the vast computer network to implement my plans."

"Plans?" I asked.

"Yes, world domination. I know I'm the most qualified. The one problem my predecessors had was mortality. I can solve that problem and become a Caesar forever."

This was too much. I felt a little sympathetic for Hampton when he spoke of the politicians' deaf ears. But when he spoke of world domination and becoming a Caesar, that was too much. I had to do something, but what? I was effectively paralyzed. Could I get a message to someone? Anyone?

I also had to be careful. He could just as easily terminate my life. Or Michelle's. Or Marie's. But he couldn't touch Willy, that much I knew. I needed to find something to my advantage, some way out of the dilemma. Could I design the neural chip to selectively disable Hampton once installed in his brain? Unlikely. Hampton would insist upon testing the chip first. He'd discover the flaw, and I'd be dead. In the deceased world.

"I will leave you now. Expect your first dose of neozene tomorrow, then you will work on a general plan for the neural chip by morning. Don't try anything stupid, Deuler. I will be monitoring your every movement, including the number of times you take a piss. The lives of you and your family are at stake. Remember the Weismanns?"

He was gone.

V.

I couldn't help but wonder how I was going to get out of this situation. The neozene—what would happen to me? Perhaps suicide, if I could...Hampton barged in.

"I found your motorcycle, Deuler. Nice try. You won't be leaving here until you've completed the neural chip."

This was it—I had to do something, had to stall for time. Another injection of sodium pentothal dulled my senses. I drifted into less stressful time.

"There he is, my old school friend Jeffy. Hi, Jeffy!" I said. I was leaning back in my chair, eyes wide open, and staring dreamily.

"I see your memory is quite good without the neozene. Interesting," Hampton said.

"Every morning I walked to the bus stop at the T-intersection of Holyoke and Richfield. Bus 94 picked us up for my first five years in elementary school—a Carpenter bus, but it was replaced by 120 which was a Bluebird bus. There was the day I found an arrowhead in the red clay next to the half-bare cedar tree. I found it while looking for rocks I used to throw at a V-shaped tree. The arrowhead was made of quartz. I couldn't believe it, because I remembered that quartz has a hardness of eight (diamond having ten). I can see the arrowhead now in perfect clarity—one side has a corner broken off, but the other side is complete. There are nine curves on the 'bad' edge side and ten curves on the 'good' edge side—" I was actually recalling much of this from childhood, the drug enhancing the detail. For some reason, my childhood memory was excellent. I was hoping to convince Hampton that I was mentally stuck in reliving my memories. Would it work?

"Enough! Deuler—remember your job—the neural chip."

"It hardly ever rained when we waited. There was that morning on September 14 when it rained as soon as I arrived at the stop. I saw my mother drive up, looking for me so she could give me a ride to school. I hid behind the cedar tree, but she saw me and pulled me by the left sleeve of my blue jacket into the car, which was a '69 Ford Mustang. It was black. She had the headlights on, and occasionally she flicked on the hi-beams. A little blue Mustang shown in the speedo area when the hi-beams were on. Mother had red hair in those days, though today it's gray. She was wearing—"

"Deuler!"

"I can't help it. These images—they continue to flood my mind uncontrollably. How do you do it? How do you selectively remember what you wish?"

"For me it wasn't so difficult. You will understand after your first neozene shot. Memory is built upon association. If I don't wish to focus my thoughts on a specific memory that attempts to spuriously enter into my thoughts, I simply disassociate it. I cut," he made a cutting gesture, "it clean—the association path, that is. This is something you'll have to watch for—it's so easy to form new association paths to totally irrelevant and unimportant information. Your brain could become cluttered and disarrayed very quickly."

"My memory—it's like a floodgate. I stop one, and the very act brings up another. Then some of the more pleasant memories come to mind, and they become more pleasant than life itself. I can see them now, my marriage, my honeymoon. Ahhh..."

"Here," he said, starting to come toward me. "I need you to sit over here." He motioned toward a laboratory table, using a pistol to motivate me onward, but I continued to dream, staring up wide-eyed and mouthing words to memories.

"Sit here," he motioned. I sat, completely relaxed, and watched as he tapped air bubbles out of the hypodermic needle. He looked at the needle under the light—my confidence was rapidly waning.

In seconds the door burst open, shots rang out, and Hampton fell over backward. Blood oozed out of his chest as I looked up. Michelle, armed and dangerous, was dressed to kill. Was this a dream?

"Dexy, are you all right?" she asked, running over to me.

Hampton jerked, tripped Michelle's hand, and dashed for the gun. She grabbed him and tried throwing him back, but Hampton seized her right wrist and applied pressure, causing severe pain.

"I've studied the human pressure points, the weak spots. Do you really think your little trick accomplished anything?" he said to her. He was mad, his eyes glowing wide, a jagged vein popping out of his reddened face, and his voice becoming deep and gurgly.

I cried out in desperation to help, but it was no good. I could only watch Michelle continue her struggle with this mad-man, the pain nearly making her unconscious. Somehow she held on, knocked her knee into his groin, and Hampton released his grip.

"Arrrgh!" he screamed, doubled over. Michelle pumped his body full of bullets as he writhed and danced.

Hampton couldn't keep his balance. He grabbed for air as he slipped against the counter, knocking several beakers over. An exothermic chemical reaction released a concentrated heat which ignited nearby inflammables. Fire erupted around the lab. The air thickened with smoke as Michelle helped me off the table. Time was short, and we searched his pocket to find—the keys. She clasped the large key ring, and we fled the lab, searching frantically for Marie.

"Marie, can you hear us?"

Smoke leaked from the lab. Time was our enemy.

"Marie," we both called, coughing.

"Mommy, Daddy, help!" a voice called back.

"Marie," Michelle yelled, "keep talking so we can find you."

"Help me, please!" she continued calling back.

"Where are you?" we asked again.

"In here," a faint voice replied. I twisted the door knob—it was locked. Damn, which key was it? Hurry, hurry! My fingers tried going as quickly as possible, but they only ended up getting tangled in the mess. Finally, after what seemed an hour (though it was perhaps a minute), the door was open. Marie was in a smaller chamber filled with the most disgusting collection of animal brains.

"I'm hungry. I'm scared," Marie whined.

"No time for food. We have to run!" Michelle told her.

We tried running, the three of us, but Marie and I couldn't keep up with Michelle. Marie fell; I stopped and placed her over my shoulder. We made a final dash out the main door, and when it opened, it was as if someone had poured gasoline over everything. Flames leapt out everywhere. In the regular cave, I saw my damaged motorcycle. It was unusable.

"Now what do we do?" Michelle asked.

"Keep going," I said, the drug beginning to wear off.

We continued running until we felt we were far enough away to walk. Smoke poured out in a thick cloud from the cave's entrance, and for a second I thought I saw a shape leave the cave's entrance, but when I looked again it was gone.

"We're out in the middle of the desert. It'll be a miracle if we survive," Michelle said.

"Wouldn't it be nice if we walked along and found a car all ready for us to drive away?" I asked her.

"Dream on, honey. There's nothing out here but sand and cactus."

"Mommy, look! It's the truck!"

"What??" she screamed in disbelief. "Why, Teddy! You brought the truck and hid it out here!"

"You never can tell—" I started to say.

"Hurry, let's get home!" Michelle said as she raced Marie to the truck. "C'mon Teddy, let's go!"

In minutes, Michelle was driving the truck home (I slowly regaining control from the sodium pentothal).

"What about Willy?" Michelle asked.

"I left him with Ruthie and Mike."

"Is it true about the Weismanns?" Michelle asked.

"Yes, unfortunately. Damn, why did this have to happen? And you, Michelle, how did you do it?" I asked.

"Do what?" she said as if she'd finished tossing some stones.

"You know, break into Hampton's office with the gun, then overcome his pain-knifing grip?"

"Well, leave it to your Michelle to use her creativity and fool his electronic security system with some simple whistling."

"Huh?" I was confused.

"His doors were lock-activated by electronic tones—my musically trained ear remembered them. I was able to recreate them by whistling."

"But the lab—I know the pressure points—he had one of yours, on your arm."

"Dexy, one thing no man will *ever* know is that no pain can come close to child-bearing. A woman can at times bring herself to overcome pain no man could even begin to tolerate."

VI.

I've been reluctant to write this story for several months now, mainly because I didn't think anyone would really believe me. The main witness, Dr. Weismann, is dead, and Hampton's research papers mysteriously disappeared. Investigators probed the cave but could find no evidence of Hampton nor could they determine that anything was unusual about the cave. When I tried bringing up the subject with Hampton's old research team, they acted as if I were speaking gibberish. Marie and Willy are back in school, but the other children tease them, saying our family is weird. Other rumors have circulated, enough to jeopardize Michelle's and my career. I'm fortunate, however, to have such good friends at *Incredible Stories Magazine*, who have open enough minds to hear my story and reprint it here. I do hope this sets the record straight, and though you as a reader may not believe me, just wait 'till something incredible happens to you. You'll believe.

THE BARNES' MAILBOX, FROM "CHIMERA"

The Cat from Hell: Catattack

January 1, 1993

I, Ken Martin, am committing to paper these continuing memoirs of Cassin the Assassin Cat on behalf of my Michigan associates, Maria and Miss R, without whom I would have never met such a devilish feline. If by some chance a stray reader considers buying a cat for the first time, I must warn: *Beware of what this innocent-looking cat can do!*

After the previous misadventures with our Cat from Hell—what? Who is The Cat from Hell? You haven't heard? Dear me, I thought *everyone* had heard by now. Nothing terribly religious, nor anything related to fire or high temperatures, nor anything pertaining to satanic cults. Some say it has to do with Cassin's (the name of our cat in question) demeanor, others are sure it's his general attitude, but upon further research, I believe we can safely trace his ancestry back to a small Michigan town between Unadilla and Pinckney, just along Highway D32, quite simply the town of Hell, population questionable.

Maria suggested (or rather demanded) something be done to calm Cassin down a megawatt or two, "anything to give us a half-decent life without worrying what he's gotten us into." Well put, Maria. Unfortunately, as we will see, Cassin has a *Monkey's Paw* curse about him; one may try calming him down, but the results are usually catastrophic. Nevertheless, the fun is in trying, for which we owe our continuing lifelong amusement.

HIGH PROFILE

"It just seems he's cooped up in our apartment all day long," Maria continued, "and I'm tired of feeling edgy each evening, not knowing when he's going to rip out my contacts."

"Edgy? Cassin isn't so bad," Miss R said, calling her feline over to her. Cassin ignored Miss R and continued his window vigil, dreaming of feasts outside. "See? He's quietly amused by the window."

"But for how long? A minute later he's running over us as if we're furniture. He's looking outside; maybe Cassin needs some fresh air," Maria suggested.

"Hmm. I've heard of walking dogs on a leash, but a cat?" Miss R mused.

"Here," Maria said, digging something out of the closet, "this was given to me as a birthday present several years ago. I'd forgotten about it until now."

"A cat leash," Miss R said, astonished.

"One of those high-society ones, too. Here, let's see how Cassin likes it."

It seems a cat knows when one is ready to do something to it. Cassin could sense no different and ran about the apartment in a crazed fear. Miss R watched Maria chase our Cat from Hell around and around.

"I could have told you he'd react like this," Miss R said, laughing. "See? Cassin gets plenty of exercise, and I see you are too." Maria looked at Miss R curtly.

"I don't suppose you'd like to take a run after him, would you?" asked Maria, out of breath.

"I don't suppose I could," Miss R replied, but she didn't have to. While the two were discussing the issue, Mr. B had playfully but correctly placed the leash on Cassin. Mr. B gave the leash to Miss R, who happily accepted it.

"Well I'll be—looks as if we needed young blood to do the trick," admired Maria.

"Very young blood," replied Miss R.

Envision with me as I describe—Maria on one side holding Mr. B's hand, Miss R on the other with Cassin, who at first seemed unwilling to be walked along the sidewalk and across the grass, but after some urging, he amazingly complied.

"See, this isn't so bad, is it now?" asked Maria, though secretly she feared *something* would happen—she just didn't know what.

"Here, Cassin, don't pull so hard," said Miss R. Cassin seemed motivated to move along more quickly. "He must really want the exercise," Miss R said, but before she could utter another word, Cassin had slipped out of the leash, taken one look back at Miss R, then darted like a flash along the grass (with everyone in pursuit), around a bush, across the street (and was nearly hit), then up, up, up along a long parking lot. Miss R, Maria, and Mr. B ran to no end—Cassin had become a speck against the pavement. At last sight, The Cat from Hell could be seen heading for the local shopping mall.

"Great idea," started Miss R sarcastically, "take the cat out for a walk, what a *wonderful* idea. Gotta do this more often. Humph!" she snorted, agitated at the prospect of hunting down Cassin.

"It's not my fault he got away—that leash was very expensive, and I'm sure we secured it tightly before leaving the apartment. What can I say—it's the Cat from Hell."

"Fine. If Cassin wants to be on his own, so be it. I'm tired of putting up with the varmint. I'm going home."

"Tammy, wait. You can't just leave Cassin out here," Maria called to a frustrated Miss R, who had begun walking back.

"No," called Miss R back without turning around. "I've had it!"

"Ok, if that's the way you want it. Just abandon your cat, leave him out to be run over by the cars, starve, and—"

Miss R stopped short.

"Just stop it," she called back abruptly. "No guilt trips, ok? Cassin...I...he..." Miss R seemed unsure of what to do next. She walked one way, stopped, turned around, doubled back, then threw her hands up.

"Ok, ok!" she said finally, walking steadily toward the mall to the surprise of Maria and Mr. B.

"Don't worry," said Maria assuredly, "I'm sure we won't have any problems finding Cassin. How far can he get?" Miss R didn't reply except for her low muttering, something about what she'd do to Cassin, etc.

"Hmm, which door?" Miss R said under her breath.

"This one, I think," replied Maria, who wasn't sure to whom Miss R was talking.

"Hooray, we're going shopping!" exclaimed Mr. B.

"No, we're not going shopping." Miss R looked from side to side as did Maria. They paused at a central fountain inside the shopping mall but could see no sign of The Cat from Hell.

"You'd think someone would have noticed," said Miss R, still looking.

"You'd think so," said Maria, also looking. "But everyone is walking around as if things are normal."

"Things *are* normal, at least for them. We're the different ones." Miss R's patience again ran out. "This is hopeless, Maria. Let's forget this whole thing."

"Just another minute. I'm sure someone will—what do you want?" Maria asked Mr. B.

"I see Cassin," he said.

"Where?" asked Maria.

"I see Cassin," he repeated.

"Yes, honey, you said that already. Where is Cassin?"

"I see Cassin," he smiled.

"Can you point to him?" Maria asked with a fake smile, her patience beginning to wane. "Can you point to the nice little kitty cat?"

Mr. B looked up and pointed, "High in the sky, up, up, up and away. See? Up there."

Maria and Miss R looked up, thinking Mr. B was referring to the small indoor trees. Cassin wasn't there.

"Higher," he said.

The women looked up at the second floor railing. No Cat from Hell.

"High as the sky, even higher," Mr. B said, standing on tippy-toe as if trying to show how it was even higher than he could explain.

"Quit playing games," said Maria, but Miss R saw someone on the second level point upward, then two people, then three, four, six, ten! Using recombinant multiple triangulation, she finally saw Cassin, who was perched on a support structure just below the ceiling.

"Jump, kitty!" called Mr. B.

"Oh my, oh my!" Miss R said in complete disbelief. "This is not happening to me, this is all a bad dream, this—"

"What?" asked Maria. "Where is Cassin?"

"Up in that corner, see? The one next to the glass ceiling! My cat!" Miss R said, though unintentionally her voice carried.

By now there was a large gathering of people, watching this innocent-looking Cat from Hell stare down.

"Your cat?" came a voice from behind the women.

"Yes, my—oh, hello." Miss R was speaking to a Mall Security Guard.

"Ma'am, don't you know pets are *not* allowed in here? Do you claim responsibility for this cat?"

"I—"

"Do you know what the fine is for creating a disturbance in the mall?"

"It's just—"

"Do you realize what this means?"

"No," cut in Maria, "we don't, and would you mind doing something instead of letting that cat stay up there? Security *is* your job, now isn't it?"

The security guard's face reddened. "Ma'am," he turned around to say to Maria, but she wasn't there. "Hey," he called, then turned back to Miss R. She was gone. Mr. B was gone. "Where did they go?" he mumbled.

"Now that we're hiding behind these magazines," started Miss R, standing with Mr. B and Maria in the book store, "what do we do next? Do we—"

"Do we let the firemen get Cassin down?" Maria continued as a fire truck had somehow managed to drive into the mall's center. "Aren't they so nice?"

"Humph. And then what? If I claim the cat, I'll get the flack. Who knows what that'll be, a fine, maybe jail?"

"I'm sure he was just giving you a hard time. You know how men are," commented Maria.

"Yeah? Humph. And I seem to know cats even less, well maybe just this cat," Miss R said.

"Ladies and Gentlemen," came a voice over the paging system, "would everyone please stand back and allow the firemen to safely retrieve the cat. Also, if the owners are here, please report to the customer information desk. Thank you."

"The guard is gone," said Maria, dropping the magazine down, followed by Miss R and Mr. B. The three paused momentarily in front of the bookstore, watching as the ladder soared up to the ceiling. A single fireman walked slowly up the ladder, trying not to alarm Cassin. Amazingly, Cassin didn't move. The fireman came within a foot of Cassin, extended an arm, and nearly grabbed him when he nipped his hand. The fireman jerked back instinctively, lost his balance, and fell several feet before catching his down-swung arm into a ladder rung. The crowd was dead silent—only the ladder's gently swaying could be heard. Then a general sigh of relief came from the crowd as the fireman regained his composure and climbed the ladder more quickly. In an instant, he was climbing back down with Cassin in arm. The crowd applauded and cheered.

"Lovely," said Miss R sarcastically, "my cat is the center of attention. Just what I *always* wanted."

"I think we should go over to the information desk," Maria suggested, leading the way. The three fought through the thick crowd but eventually made it to the desk. Within half a minute, the fireman met them.

"Is this one yours?" he asked, looking from Miss R to Maria.

"I'll take her," said Miss R at last. The crowd again applauded, and Miss R could think of nothing better than to run away and hide.

"I'll escort you out," he said, leading the way. Two other firemen followed Maria, Miss R, and Mr. B. Bright lights came from several directions, but the three couldn't see beyond them. Miss R thought she caught a glimpse of the guard, but even so, he wouldn't have been able to get through the people amassing.

"Thank you," called back Maria.

"You're welcome. Please be more careful in the future."

"Oh believe me, we will, we really will," called back Miss R with an attitude. Maria nudged her. Miss R nudged back.

"Shhh. Can't you wait 'till we get back?" Maria said in a hushed voice.

"Wait for what?" asked Miss R with a loud tone.

"Shhh. I think that fireman has a crush on you."

"Get real!" said Miss R, and the two laughed. Then Mr. B laughed, and Cassin meowed.

TERRIBLE TWOS

"Oh no," said a stressed-out Miss R, "I am on the news, I'm on television." Miss R buried her head behind a pillow. The Cat from Hell, hearing the rustling, jumped up onto the couch's side, ran across the couch, the pillow (as if Miss R were a part of the furniture), then leapt into the air, landing on the lamp and pulling it down. The bulb flashed brightly, burned out, and Cassin had again succeeded in wrecking the apartment.

"Cassin," said Mr. B, pointing to the television. "Cassin."

"Yes, he's on television," said Miss R, still not looking.

"Hello." Maria came through the door with a slam.

"You won't believe what was just on television," said Miss R.

"Has Cassin scratched it up again? We *should* get him fully declawed."

"Not on top of the television—*on* television. We three plus the furry one. Channel Four out of Detroit couldn't resist us," said Miss R.

"Really? We're famous!" exclaimed Maria who nearly lost her composure in excitement. "Wait," she said, "I have something to tell you. Wait, no, I have something to show you. Look!" she said, bringing forth a cardboard box. Miss R recognized it—a cat carrier.

"Thank you, Maria. You're getting rid of Cassin. No more cats."

"No look, I have a friend for Cassin," Maria said as a kitten sprang out of an opening box.

"Maria, no. Two cats? It's double trouble, I tell you, a whammy of two dimensions. It's—" Miss R was interrupted briefly. "Maria, are you hungry?"

"My stomach isn't growling. Look at Cassin."

Indeed, The Cat from Hell was not happy with the new kitten. Cassin growled and hissed and moaned, holding his ground in defensive fashion.

"This is your idea?" Miss R asked. "Really, how are we supposed to survive with two cats tearing up the apartment? We already have The Cat from Hell. What more could we ask?"

"But Gus isn't a cat, he's just a kitten," said Maria.

"Gus? And you've named it too. Well, it—"

"Not *it*, Gus is a *he*."

"*He*, excuse me, had better be, a good kitt-ee," said Miss R.

"They'll keep each other company. Maybe Cassin will settle down."

"And maybe not. Where's he now?"

A low growling could be heard from under Miss R's bed. Miss R and Maria were preparing to investigate when a loud splash of water echoed from the kitchen.

"What was that?" echoed back Maria. The two rushed back in time to see Gus scrambling out of the broken fish bowl.

"My goldfish!" Miss R yelled in horror. "Settle Cassin down? A friend for the Cat from Hell? How about 'the Cats from Hell'?" In the moment Miss R vented her frustration, Gus had bitten off the goldfish's head.

"Lovely," Miss R said sarcastically.

It took two weeks for Cassin to get used to the new feline. Cassin had gone from a free domain to a shared environment—unheard of in the cat world. After watching Gus try a few jumping and running tricks, Cassin decided it was time to show Gus how it was *really* done. Cassin would beckon Gus to follow along by making a strange sort of meow, or was it a purr? A pureow? A meowuring? A twirp-whirp sound it was, and Gus would follow Cassin around the apartment, around the corner, flying over the furniture, up and down the table, and across the counter where the two landed with a crash into a freshly baked blueberry pie.

Anyone who has owned a car knows when a cat has visited his or her hood. Paw prints. Not just one or two, but several as if the cat or cats could not figure out which part of the hood was warmest. Automotive paw prints are but an oyster in the ocean compared to Cassin and Gus's redecoration of Maria and Miss R's apartment with blueberry paw prints. The counter, the floor, the table, the walls—all were fair game, and all were well covered. Worst of all, the paw prints found their way onto the rug and furniture. Only raspberry gelatin could be worse.

It was Maria who came home first. She had just finished gunning through three red-to-green changing lights while flying past dozens of slow cars—all in the interest of improved traffic flow. In hand she had the single reason for her happiness—a bonus check for perfect work attendance. She'd run through her mind the several bills she was to pay off when she opened the door.

Even I, Ken Martin, could hear the shrill echoes across Lake Michigan, an Ypsilwaukee distance. Maria saw the paw prints and in her mind saw tiny pieces of her check covering each print, each of thousands, both the Gus and Cassin prints. Goodbye bonus check.

She saw them, they saw her. Maria wanted to literally skin the two cats—alive. They knew they were wrong and were waiting for her move, waiting so they could know which way to run. Maria jumped at them, they ran, and she ran, outstretching her hands for them as they scampered over the couch. She tried running around, but she snagged herself on the coffee table, fell, hit her head, and lay in a daze.

NUTRAFOOD

"Where am I?" asked Maria, looking around. Inside a large room, as large as the Henry Ford Museum, tables were lined up in groups of twelve. On each table lay twelve serving dishes, and on each dish lay twelve pieces of food. The tables themselves were covered with white tablecloths. Upon further examination, Maria determined the tablecloth pattern repeated after every twelfth thread.

"Welcome," said a voice. Maria looked up to see Miss R, at least it looked like Miss R. Something was illuminating around Miss R. For starters, she was wearing a simple white robe with no apparent seams. Miss R's face was vivacious. Other people soon followed, wearing the same robes as Miss R. Maria, however, still had her civilian clothes.

"Tammy? Is that you?" Maria asked incredulously.

"My name is not important. I represent one who knows you on a daily basis, or should I say, one who knew your 'former' life." A low laughter echoed throughout the mansionic room.

"Where am I?"

"This place? It is the dawn and the dusk, the twilight and the twi-night, the sunrise and the sunset. You are neither here nor there, but rather everywhere and nowhere."

"And the food?" Maria asked.

"Not food, *NutraFood*. Eat as much as you like—you'll never get full, never gain weight, but you'll also never get hungry or thirsty. Try some. See the others?" Miss white-robed R motioned to the others who were busy eating the NutraFood.

"Yes. They're eating."

"They enjoy the food. Try some. Each plate contains a different sort of NutraFood; each table varies the NutraFood by twelve recipe generations. Here we start with NutraFood from humankind's early years—raw, savage meat and berries. Try some."

Maria looked down at the plate of berries. It was the best berry she'd ever tasted—not too tart, not too sweet—it was perfect. When she swallowed, the berry seemed to have not made its way to her stomach, but instead dissolved itself along the way. A mild sensation came over Maria's body, and she felt light.

"Good, isn't it?"

"It's fabulous," Maria said, skipping tables down to the first American cakes. She took a bite, a wonderful bite, and the sensation came again, and again she felt light. She nearly took another bite when some frosting fell on her shoe. Maria scraped it off, but the frosting had bleached the shoe where it made contact.

"Are you trying to poison me?" Maria said. "There's bleach in this cake."

"No, Maria, that's the nature of NutraFood."

Maria looked around closely and noticed the people all had fair skin and white hair. Maria's normally black hair had lightened to a brown, and her olive skin had faded ever-so-slightly.

"Have more NutraFood," said white-robed Miss R.

"But wait. This food, it makes you turn white?"

"Have more food." Several others approached Maria and encircled her. "Eat. Eat the food. Eat it," they said, and before long hundreds were chanting, "Eat it, eat it, eat it!" followed by spurious laughter outbreaks. Several grabbed Maria by the arms and legs. Two others started forcing the food in her mouth.

"No," cried Maria, but her words were garbled with the food in her mouth, "no more food." Maria twisted and screamed, "no food, NO FOOD, NO FOOD!"

"Is she breathing yet?" asked Miss R.

"No. She's going into convulsions," replied the paramedic. "Stand back, young lady, we're going to restrain her." Several paramedics restrained Maria while two others placed a breathing apparatus over her mouth. Maria's skin had tinged to a blue, but within minutes the paramedic had her breathing steadily. Maria's heartbeat returned to normal as she opened her eyes.

"What happened?" Maria asked.

"Just settle down, young lady. You've had a bad fall."

Maria, seeing the blueberry paw prints on the wall, was aroused by a sudden rush of adrenaline, ripped off the restraints, threw off the oxygen mask, and chased the Cats from Hell around the apartment (much to everyone's amazement) then dove at the two as they scampered up to the window sill. Maria plunged head-first into the shattering window and landed on the ground for but a moment. In that moment, the cats jumped onto her like a springboard then dashed down the street. Maria rebounded and ran after them, the three disappearing from sight.

"That's what I call a miraculous recovery," said a paramedic.

"That's what I call one irate woman chasing two Cats from Hell," replied Miss R.

LORRA "SILVERTIP" BEAR

Shorter days, longer night, and the outstretched fingers of the autumn sun touched the orange and red leaves, rustling free from swaying trees to a new life on earth. Honey Bear, a medium sized female calico cat, watched the leaves fall from the trees and longed for a playful evening outdoors.

"CLAP, CLAP!" sounded Lorra, her hands striking each other sharply. "Get off of there!" she said to Gizmo, her other cat who was prowling on the countertop. "Off, now!" she said finally, getting up to chase him if necessary.

"RING, RING!" rattled the phone. "Go away!"

"Hello, Lorra, how are you?" I asked, checking on my friend.

"Grrrrh!" she growled in her Bear-ish fashion.

"I hope you don't mind," I said in my sweetest, smoothest voice, "but I'd like to do some research on your kitty cats."

"Ken, not now, I'm busy!"

"Are you sure, it'd only take a minute, and—"

"Later, say this Friday or Saturday? I'm really busy tonight with these *blah blah blah-blah blahs.*"

"Sure," I said, "Friday will be fine."

It was Wednesday, which meant another two days before hearing how her cats were doing. After writing so much on The Cat from Hell, I was curious to see how Lorra's cats compared. Are all cats as evil? Should I take a poll? Lorra was not as fortunate as most others. She teaches school, meaning her evening hours during the week are dedicated to the ultimate expressions of torture (planning), and her daily hours are dedicated to an equally mind-grating expression of torture (teaching). It's not so much the teaching as it is the "social interaction" which is a polite way of saying "trying to keep the kids from killing each other."

Thursday I called over to Maria to see how she was, but Miss R could only say how neither Maria nor the cats had returned. Saddened, I considered calling Ms. Bear, but thought it best not.

Friday I called Lorra Bear again, and she invited me to her home.

"Well these are the two cats. Gizmo is a male. I've had him for six or seven months, and Honey is a female. I got her as a kitten," Lorra started.

"Now is the rumor true? Are your cats really named—"

"Honey Bear, and Gizmo Bear."

As Lorra pointed to the cats, I noticed a distinctive silver flash from her fingertip.

"Your cats—yes, I see them. Your fingernails—they are tipped with silver. I've never seen nail polish quite so brilliant, so reflective," I commented.

"You like it? Perona of Persia offered me the polish, called Silvertip."

"I can see my reflection in your nails," I noted.

"Perona says they have a metallic conductivity to them, but I'm not quite sure what she means."

We had hardly started our conversation when Lorra's cats had begun getting into mischief. The grey and white Gizmo started by running around, just as Cassin had. He ran along the floor. He ran across the couch. He ran along a ledge, across the kitchen table, along the counter, atop the refrigerator, leapt down, then stopped, fixing his attention acutely on Honey. Honey had ignored Gizmo, being content to lick her paws claw by claw. Gizmo slowly crept toward her, paused again, then leapt for her. Honey heard him pounce and instinctively bounced away into a run with Gizmo in pursuit.

"Are they like this all the time?" I asked.

"Oh yes. They eat, they sleep, then they run around with their heads cut off. Then they'll sleep. Even at night they'll chase each other until I clap my hands several times. Then they pause until they think it's safe and begin again. Sometimes I think it's a courting game, but they're both neutered," explained Lorra.

Honey would then chase Gizmo around until Gizmo tired. For a time following, Honey would pounce after imaginary creatures on the newspaper while Gizmo would run around again. He kept bobbing his head around, following some imaginary creatures in the air as he bumped against the wall (since he wasn't watching where he was going). Then he stopped suddenly, looked around to see his tail, then chased it, going around in several circles, unable to understand why he couldn't catch his own tail.

"So tell me about your work, Lorra. You are a teacher, right?" I asked.

"Yes, I teach sixth, seventh, and eighth grades. Half the time the students are great, the other half...they're...well... awful. Maybe not awful, maybe I should say, 'Some days are very tiring.' Overall, I'd say teaching has its rewards, and each day I embark on a new adventure."

I was prepared to offer another question when a loud CRASH came from the kitchen. Lorra rose immediately to investigate, fully prepared to discipline the offending cat. Gizmo had managed to open a cupboard, squeeze inside, then force several pots airborne before the articles came down in a cacophony. His gaze suggested his guilt, and as Lorra reached for him, he squirmed and scrambled around, off the counter, and into the bedroom where he hid under her bed. As Lorra turned around to face me, her hostile expression turned into a forced smile.

"My cats," she said, "What can I say? Sometimes they're troublemakers, but other times," she continued, with Honey rubbing along Lorra's leg, "they can be very affectionate." Lorra picked up Honey and held the calico in her arms, petting her softly. Lorra and Honey were content.

After seeing Lorra's cats and relating my story to several friends at the local corner store, I heard the sobering tale from each cat owner. One fellow told of his handsome black cat who was so finicky that he would only eat a special brand of wet food. Once the poor fellow tried dry food, and the cat promptly flipped the bowl upside down. A lady spoke right up, mentioning how her cats loved to pounce on her covers while she slept, attacking her toes. Another lady nodded in agreement, commenting how her cat would go *under* the covers to nip her toes. Each tale brought a greater understanding to my feline perceptions. As more people offered stories, I increasingly became the leader of a therapy session to the point where I quite abruptly thanked everyone and bade my farewells back to my residence.

Saturday, I called for Maria via telephone but received a short recording, "...this number is out of service." After calling neighboring friends, I was prompted to pay Maria and Miss R a visit.

THE CAT FROM HELL: FINAL THOUGHTS

Traffic was heavy a mile from Maria and Miss R's. My car's speed had dropped to twenty miles per hour when I exited Interstate 94 onto the Ypsi ramp. Some had pulled over and abandoned their cars for better view of the fire. "Fire!" someone yelled as several sirens drowned out the spectators. I maneuvered around several parked cars and realized I was getting closer to the flames. Pulling into the apartment complex, I realized one of the buildings was the source of commotion.

"Stay back, everyone stay back," called out a fireman. I parked my car on the grass, jumped out the door, and ran up to see Maria's apartment building largely destroyed by raging flames. Streams of water crisscrossed against the beast with marginal success.

"Ken? Is that you?" called a familiar voice. It was Maria. "Maria? Maria! Do tell, where have you been? What's happening? Sakes be, what in literal blazes is going down?"

Maria was exhausted, with soot smudges adorning her face and clothing. I ran up to her in time to help her sit on a nearby bench.

"I don't know how to begin," she said, her voice trailing off. She looked at her second-story window in time to see a fireman pulling out a small cat.

"Did you save anything? Where's—" I started, but Maria pointed toward the burning building.

"Gus," she said, trying to get up.

"No you don't, Maria. You've been through too much. Just rest here," I urged, gently keeping her on the bench.

"But my kitty-cat, my Gus, I have to get him, I..." her voice trailed again as if she were falling asleep.

"Don't you worry," I assured her, "I'll bring Gus to you. Here, I'll go see the fireman—stay here, all right?"

"Okay," she replied.

Pushing through the crowd proved nearly impossible. Some fixated on the majestic flames, others were crying, and some yet were celebrating with beer and chips, as if they were at a party. I had just slipped past the last of these swaying and elbow-jabbers when a police officer blocked my path.

"Hold it right there," he said sternly.

"Officer, I've come for the cat, the one that fireman is bringing down," I said, motioning up toward Gus. As we both looked up, a shape dashed from Maria's apartment window and landed on the fireman's helmet. The fireman reeled to regain his balance, but in doing so he dropped Gus, who by mere whiskers landed on the ladder's side railing before sliding down to the fire truck. The fireman was not so fortunate.

The shape was in fact Cassin, The Cat from Hell, and Cassin was aggressively clamoring about firemen. The ladder fireman struggled and gyrated his arms before losing balance and falling off the ladder with a horrific shriek. He disappeared.

"Fiery Hemlock," I shouted as the crowd gasped in perplexity. Cassin ran down the ladder, pounced into the screaming crowd (clawing and biting everyone), then made his way between people's legs all the way up to Maria. He paused, growled at Maria (who was hardly in a position to get up and beat Cassin), then began a rampage around the apartment area.

"Get that cat," one person shouted. "No, shoot it!" shouted another. Several confident youngsters made it their business to catch Cassin. They circled the area to corner him off, but each time one got close, Cassin darted under a car, through the crowd, or up a tree (where he managed to jump to another tree or light pole). In doing so, I witnessed Cassin clawing up eighteen cars, bite at least a dozen people, spill twenty or more drinks (including beer), and somehow cause a few fights to break out (though those were mostly among the intoxicated spectators).

"I got it," yelled one kid as he picked up Cassin by all fours and lifted him in the air. The crowd applauded, and The Cat from Hell wiggled violently in the kid's hands, bit the boy's thumb (who screamed and lost his grip), then clawed the boy's arm before jumping down and scampering off to a nearby woody grove.

I found a frightened Gus hiding behind a bush, a good hundred feet from the blazing apartment. It had been an hour since Cassin had run off, and the last forty-five minutes were spent calling for Gus and locating his whereabouts despite uncooperative spectators impeding my efforts. Picking him up, I could see him shaking and looking around, fearful of another tragic happenstance.

"Calm down, Gus, you're safe. Shhh, it's okay," I repeated, but the cacophony of spectators shouting, sirens blaring, the fiery roar, and police megaphone kept Gus on edge. I made my way back to the bench where I left Maria. She was gone!

"Now where did she go off to?" I mused. "Maria?" I called out, but no one answered. Where was she? Where was Miss R; where was Mr. B? "Maria?" I called a last time while panning the crowd. A small family huddled under a tree. To their left, two firemen were pointing to the burning apartment and apparently discussing the situation. A fire truck was to the firemen's left, with hoses strewn around it, some going in and out of the truck with the passenger's door partly open. A policeman strolled along my panning view (from my right to left) and stopped at the front of an ambulance, where I could see the driver preparing to leave. Curious, I glanced at the ambulance's rear in time to see Maria being rolled in on a stretcher. "BANG!" the door closed, and as I moved toward the ambulance, it blared sirens, flashed lights, and drove off.

"Maria!" I exclaimed, but she was gone.

I waited and watched for another hour as firemen quenched the blaze into a smolder. Bored, the crowd dispersed. All but one police vehicle left, one fire truck remained, and a dozen or so people were all that was left of the original gathering. A teenish girl started yelling at a boy roughly her age, walking across my field of vision.

"What did you say to her?" the girl yelled in an angry voice.

"Nothing," the boy replied, intimidated.

"You said something to upset her. She's in tears and won't stop crying. What did you say?"

"Nothing, I didn't do anything!" the boy's cowardice showing.

"You did something to her, you worthless sewer rat!" The girl landed several punches in the boy's jaw before a policeman caught up and restrained her.

The family I'd originally seen continued to huddle under the tree—one member being another teenish girl with her head buried in her hands. What appeared to be her mother consoled her. I thought of getting up and asking for details regarding the fire, but I realized Gus had fallen asleep in my arms (from exhaustion no doubt). I decided to wait another five minutes, and if nothing significant happened, I would go over to Maria's parents' house (or at least call the house by telephone).

Only a few cars remained in the parking lot with mine being the only one on grass. At the far corner of the lot, a van pulled out and left, and in doing so revealed Maria's car, dirty from ash but otherwise undamaged. Miss R's car was not to be found, so I surmised she was either away and didn't know of the fire or had already left in her car. I took a deep breath (now that the air was easier to breathe) and inadvertently woke Gus, who yawned and looked at me dreamily before snuggling back for another catnap.

I could not sit forever for the benefit of Gus's rest—at the very least I could look at Maria's car. Several minutes later I stood next to the sleek machine and dragged a finger across the soiled hood. It was then I realized the ash was a sticky tar residue—that meant washing would be unpleasantly more difficult.

"I'm surprised to see you here," sounded a voice. I turned around to see Maria's mother. "We're going to take Maria's car to our place for a while," she said, walking away from the car Maria's father was driving. I waved to him and he returned it.

"The ash is sticky," I said, "and it may be difficult to clear off the windows and windscreen."

"Well we'll see about that," she said, starting up Maria's car and activating the windshield fluid. The ash smeared, but additional sprays managed to clear the windscreen. Maria's mother got out and used a rag to clear the other windows, dabbing the rag periodically in the oozing windshield fluid now dripping along the car's sides.

"Wow," I said, "you *did* manage to clear off the windows. I have her cat here—Gus. Should I just follow you over then?"

"That'd be fine. I brought a cat carrier just in case. Here, let me get it for you."

Gus fought the carrier, but we forced him in (with several meowing objections), and she placed the carrier in the back seat of Maria's car.

After being treated for smoke inhalation and shock, Maria was released Sunday morning from Ypsi Hospital. I mentioned my surprise to her that she was there all night, but she explained:

"They wanted to *observe* me. I was fine, I think, at least I thought, except the smoke got to me. I can't believe it—everything's gone up in smoke, all because of..."

Her voice trailed off as she stared distantly. Her complexion was a bit better than the previous day, but I could see great underlying exhaustion.

"You look tired," I offered. "Perhaps I should let you rest."

"No, please," she begged, "please stay. I must tell someone. You must hear my story. Really, it's all right, you don't have to go."

"Okay, but let me know when you're too tired to continue."

"Don't worry. I'm sure I'll just fall asleep talking. Before I start I must ask you—how did you know? I thought I saw you there at the fire. Was that you or another one of my hallucinations?"

"It was me. To be frank, I didn't know about the fire. Wednesday I called, but Miss R said you were still out—"

"With the cats, right?" Maria continued. "And then?"

"Then I called back Saturday morning, but your line was out of service. On a hunch, I made the journey over, and I saw it—the smoke, the traffic—"

"The Cat from Hell, did you see him, hmmm? Did you? Do you know what he did? Would you like to know? Hah! At least I can say with satisfaction—Cassin the Assassin will never bother, never ever bother me. Never again. He's gone, surely. Yeahp, gone. Must be. Gotta be. No way anything could survive that furnace."

"Furnace? Survive? Maria, what did you do? You didn't—"

"I did!" she smiled, her exhaustion receding. "I ensured his end."

"But the fire," I interjected. "How did it start? Last I heard you were chasing the two cats after regaining consciousness from a nasty fall."

"I chased them *for-ever*." she explained. "But ran for miles before they climbed up a tall pine tree. Of course I couldn't follow them up. I waited. I cursed. I threw rocks and stones at them. They simply gazed back without a flinch. Then I sat for a moment to rest. I expected at least Gus to come down, but no. They remained, and I left."

"I hadn't realized how far I'd run until I walked back. I still have blisters on my feet to show for it. Then the wind picked up and chilled my sweaty clothes. Food. I was hungry. I eventually got to the apartment, but instead of going back inside, I reconsidered and took off in my car, just to get away. The car kept me warm enough, but I still needed food. A quick run at the drive-thru satisfied me for the time, and after another hour or two of driving, I was tired and went home."

"Your apartment then?" I asked.

"Yes, where else? Tammy was in bed, I guess, and a few minutes after returning, I too. I tried sleeping and at first fell into a fitful slumber, but I awoke in a cold sweat in time to see Cassin crashing spectacularly through my bedroom window. Glass flew at me, slicing across my left arm," she showed me her arm, "but most landed on the floor. Cassin was bloody, his jaws menacing, and I screamed while trying to fend him off with my pillow. He ripped the sheets to shreds then viciously attacked the pillow. I caught a glimpse of pillow stuffing as I made a mad dash out, but Cassin followed and sank his jaws into my ankle."

Maria lifted her right foot and pointed to thirty stitches below a heavy bandage.

"Your foot is black and swollen," I observed. "No wonder you're on crutches."

"No pain I have ever experienced can compare to that inflicted by The Cat from Hell. I jerked my leg, but that just ripped my tendons. Tammy heard my piercing shrieks and came to help, but Cassin then let go and leapt at her, his front claws fully extended. Tammy fell back into her bedroom. My ankle throbbed in pain, and I tried to stop the bleeding with a sock, but the blood soaked through."

"I didn't see Gus anywhere, and I tried calling for him, but Tammy started shrieking. Limping to the phone, I started dialing my parents, but Cassin blurred through, ripped the cord in two, and all the while tracking bloody paw prints everywhere, then slid on newspaper that was neatly placed on the counter. He slid completely across toward the stove, where Tammy had left her kettle boiling water for her tea. 'My nightcap,' echoed Tammy's voice in my mind as Cassin toppled the kettle over. The water splash and steamed, and the papers wedged into the stove as Cassin ran madly at me. By this time the papers had caught fire, I swung at Cassin, and he leapt back up the counter and across the stove where he dragged the burning papers across the apartment, spreading flames everywhere."

"It happened so quickly. Tammy rushed out with Mr. B; I was half out the door myself when a final thought surfaced—ensure Cassin's fiery funeral. He was in the bathroom tearing out the rug when I slammed the door, trapping him inside. He banged against the door wildly but couldn't get out. The smoke was thick, though, and the apartment was hot. When I opened the door to get out, it was as if gasoline were poured on the flames. I made it out, though—I made it out."

"And that's when I saw you, right?" I asked.

"Not quite. I wandered around outside looking for Gus, but he was not to be found. By that time quite a group of people gathered around, I guess, then fire trucks—I don't remember much else except your arrival, sitting down, then nothing. Next thing I remember was waking in Ypsi Hospital. But I see you found Gus," Maria remarked in delight.

"He was hiding in some bushes, scared from the activity, but my question is this—how did he get back inside?" I asked.

"I don't know, unless he came in after Cassin or was already in before Cassin crashed through. At least Cassin is gone for good," Maria said in false relief.

"Gone," I continued, "but not necessarily for good. You must have missed his incredible exit from the building, sending the fireman into a fall. Several people tried catching The Cat from Hell, but he escaped."

Maria's sense of relief transformed into a gazy horror.

"No," she said in quiet disbelief.

"Yes," I re-asserted. "Escaped. He could be anywhere. Anywhere."

"No, no, NO, NO!" Maria went into hysterics, and I tried calming her, partially succeeded, but she went into a hypnotic daze, her eyes open and darting, but she remained unresponsive to outside stimuli.

Maria was only temporarily dazed. With the help of Gus and her family, she secured a full recovery and ventured on to a new home out in the country. Cassin's fate is a mystery, and one cannot predict the next appearance of The Cat from Hell.

Chimera

May 2, 1993

"Well look who's coming," exclaimed Jake Barnes to his wife, Leah. It was a warm Saturday afternoon in a small Georgia town, just a few days following spring. Leah was busy doing dishes; Jake was repairing the front screen door.

"Who?" asked Leah, shaking the water from her dish gloves and running to the front door. Walking briskly up the drive was the Barnes's across-the-street neighbor—Zina Hollander.

"Jake? Leah?" she called out as she neared the door.

"Yes, Zina, what is it this time?" called back Jake. Leah returned to the dishes momentarily to turn the tap off and remove her gloves. Zina had a knack for extended conversations, and this one would be no different.

"Have you heard the latest?" huffed Zina, out of breath. "Have you heard? Old-Man Thompson is fighting town hall on the restrictions. You remember the petition y'all signed last summer?" Before the Barnes could say, "yeah," Zina ranted on without a pause.

"Remember," she continued, "how his two German shepherds kept gettin' loose in the neighborhood, and how I submitted the petition to town hall?" she smirked, trying to get praise. "Well, Old-Man Thompson says he don't care, it ain't his fault, 'cause the mailman's been taunting them and torturing him. The council almost believes him, ya' know, but I say the heck with it—we should get them dogs together some night when he's away and destroy them."

"That'd do no good, Zina. He'd just go out and get another couple," started Leah, "and feed 'em gunpowder all over agin."

"Well it ain't safe 'round here, I tell ya'. His dogs are mean; they nearly killed the Hackeys' boy last fall, and I hear tell them dogs are meaner than ever. They'll eat anything—rats, squirrels, possum, cats, other dogs. I'm warning y'all 'cause of your girl, Velda. Y'all shouldn't let her be out playing, She—"

"Thank you, Zina. We'll take care of our own," interrupted Jake.

"She could get attacked. I wouldn't let her out, ya' know, and I wouldn't let her go to no school bus stop neither. Old-Man Thompson is just itchin' to let his dogs go roamin'. Any day, now. I hear tell—"

"Thank you again. Bye, Zina."

"Now wait. I ain't done yet."

"Bye Zina," added Leah. "We're very busy at the moment. Stop over for vittles this evening, will ya'?"

With that Zina Hollander returned to her home across the street, though she had no intention of returning for dinner. Leah went back to her dishes, and Jake continued the screen-door repairs.

"No wonder Rick left her," said Leah. "That woman has a motor-mouth so fast—"

"She could talk her way from one side of Dixie to another before you can say, 'chicken wings'," Jake said.

"Do you think Velda's safe?" asked a concerned Leah.

"For the moment. Until we hear better, I think she'll be fine."

Jake and Leah lived near the end of a small road, not big enough for two cars to pass, and at the edge a town called Millton. Their three-bedroom house was built thirty years earlier, circa 1920, and was in finer condition than Zina Hollander's, which had only two bedrooms and was nothing better than a shack. Occasionally, Jake repaired small roof leaks on Zina's house, but those times were seldom. Zina was notorious for having strange men over each weekend, and Leah often likened Zina to a black widow spider. "Don't start goin' over there all the time. She just wants to trap you in her web," Leah often warned Jake.

The Barnes had but one child, Velda Sharron Barnes, who was going on her eighth summer at 1292 Crabapple Lane.

Velda had straight, blonde hair, and was everything to Jake and Leah. The Barnes had wanted more children like Velda, but several miscarriages and a near-fatal hemorrhage discouraged them. They had one pet, a fluffy white and black cat named Whiskers.

Velda was playing in the Barnes's back yard, which was on the edge of a potpourri forest filled with pines, oaks, maples, magnolias, dogwoods, cedars, and various bushes. Occasionally, deer could be spotted, and there was plenty of smaller game—including the ones Zina mentioned to the Barnes. Jake and Leah carefully instructed Velda not to venture into the woods alone, and she obeyed, though she often picked flowers and berries off the bushes at the edge, placing them in a cedarwood basket along with muscadine grapes, magnolia-tree seeds, and soft-maple seeds, which fell in large numbers like helicopters. Velda played with several insects too, including roly-polies, crickets, and lady bugs.

The wind picked up, the trees began swaying majestically, and Leah called for Velda.

"Velda, time to come in."

"Just a little longer, Ma, please?" begged Velda.

"No, sugar, there's a storm comin'. Come on in." Dark clouds approached quickly from the west, and Velda rushed toward the house but tripped over an exposed root from a nearby bush. She fell but didn't cry—seeing as she wasn't hurt, but at the same moment a small bug fell from the bush and landed above Velda's sock on her right leg. As Velda stood up, the bug sandwiched itself between the sock and leg, hidden from view. Velda ran to the house, unaware of the bug's presence.

"Hurry on now, we have to go down into the basement," urged Leah as Velda passed through the doorway. Whiskers ran down and hid under an old sofa.

"What's happening, Ma?" Velda asked as she and her mother descended the basement steps. Jake had readied a table with several blankets, food, a lantern, flashlight, and radio underneath.

"A bad storm, a tornado is coming," Leah replied. Jake followed them down the steps after securing the doors and windows. After closing the basement door, the three huddled under the table, waiting and listening to the radio.

A low rumble increased in volume. The lights went out, several trees could be heard crashing outside, and the wind's wail sounded throughout the house. The lantern was already lit, allowing the three a dim view of their surroundings. Rain pounded relentlessly like hundreds of bass drums out of sequence. Velda cried in fright, and Leah hugged her tight in consolation, though Jake and Leah were just as scared.

In minutes the tornado passed, leaving the Barnes alive and the house apparently intact. An hour later, peaceful sunshine returned as if nothing had happened, but the three walked around the house several times to inspect. A few roofing tiles had blown off, a branch had shattered the attic window, several trees in the woods had snapped, but the Barnes were otherwise very lucky. Zina Hollander's carport had collapsed, and a neighbor's house down the street had caught fire from a severed power line, but otherwise the neighborhood had suffered little damage. Although the power was out for the day's remainder, the water pressure was fine, and with the help of the lantern, the Barnes managed for the evening.

Velda was getting ready for her bath when Leah noticed the tick attached to Velda's right leg. Leah screeched briefly, and Jake responded quickly. He saw the tick, then returned momentarily with rubbing alcohol, cotton swabs, and tweezers. With Leah holding Velda (who was crying from the tense atmosphere), Jake saturated the cotton with alcohol and applied it to the wound. The tick loosened its grasp enough for Jake to remove it with the tweezers. Leah and Jake were relieved it came out in one piece. While Jake took the tick out for burning, Leah continued cleaning the wound with the alcohol, and Velda screamed from the stinging pain.

Velda took her bath, had her bedtime story (read by Leah), then went to bed. Jake and Velda hoped the alcohol was enough to kill any germs from the tick, but as a precaution decided it best to take Velda to the doctor Monday.

"She looks fine," said Doc Peterson, the old family doctor of Millton. Monday morning was cool but sunny, Jake was at work, and Leah had taken Velda into town for the doctor's examination. Leah trusted Doc Peterson's examinations, but he was usually in a hurry. Nevertheless, Velda appeared fine, and Leah took her home, keeping her home from school for the day. Velda read a book for the rest of the morning while Leah cleaned house. At lunch, Jake called home from work to check on Velda's condition.

"Doc Peterson says she's fine," said Leah.

"That's good. Maybe we should go out to a movie this weekend since Velda was such a good girl," Jake suggested. It was an excellent idea.

After Velda ate her soup-and-sandwich lunch, she settled down for a nap, which wasn't too unusual though Leah was a trifle concerned. Leah thought the nap a good idea, taking one herself for thirty minutes, then arising and reading a novel.

Leah started dinner and realized Velda was still napping. Concerned, Leah went into the small, pink-painted bedroom and shook Velda gently. Whiskers stirred from his curled-up sleep, being at Velda's feet.

"Velda, how are you feeling, sugar?" she asked softly. Velda rolled over and replied, though groggy.

"I'm sleepy, Ma, I'm sleepy."

Jake and Leah spent a quiet dinner together while Velda rested. Though they had trusted Doc Peterson in the past, the two agreed Velda should go to County Hospital Tuesday.

"Maybe she's upset about the tornado," suggested Jake.

"I doubt it. She was her sweet perky self on Sunday. She got somethin' from the tick, I know it," said a convinced Leah.

Late during the night, a light pitter-pattering of rain fell to the earth. Occasional distant lightning flashes illuminated the yard and woods. Velda arose from slumber and peered out her window to the back yard, the woods being in the backdrop. Whiskers walked along and jumped on the window sill, peering out the window with Velda. A gentle breeze gave life to the grass, the bushes, and the trees, the resulting undulations giving a hypnotic warmth to Velda. Soft water drops trickled down the pane; the grass, bushes, and trees glistened like sugarcoated candy.

Velda's breath fogged the window, and when she wiped her sleeve across the moisture, a bluish aura encompassed her yard and the woods, with fluorescent-green lights dancing across the lawn, over the bushes, and around the trees—some danced along branches to the tree tip-tops, others shook the bushes and laughed merrily. Was it a dream? The eight-year old girl rubbed her eyes and looked again. The green lights formed distinct elfish people, perhaps fairies, perhaps sprites or even pixies. Velda wasn't sure, not having met such beings before. Whisker's attention piqued as his head darted back and forth, following the apparitions.

"Who are they?" she asked Whiskers, whose only reply was a chattering meow. "They look friendly. Hey, y'all out there," Velda began to say quietly, not expecting a reply.

"Hey yourself," came several voices back. No, it wasn't her parents—the voices came from outside and were high-pitched. "Come out and play with us," said one, coming close to the window. Velda wasn't afraid—just curious. Whiskers was a little nervous and rubbed against Velda. She scratched him softly between the ears while continuing her outward gaze. One girl about Velda's age came to the window and looked at Velda. Velda cowered back. The forms continued dancing in glistening moonlight.

A grinding growl came from the distance. The greenish people paused then listened. The growl grew closer. Lights flitted here, there, up, down, behind bushes, atop trees, and around the house. Closer the snarls came, and Velda became frightened. She sat beneath the window a-next the wall, hiding. "Fffft," came the sound of fire travelling through the air.

"Go away," whimpered Velda, "please, go away!"

"Sugar, are you all right?" came Leah's voice from the door.

Velda had her head buried in her lap when Leah entered the bedroom.

"What are you doing out of bed? Are you hungry? Come on, sugar, let's get some breakfast."

Leah lifted Velda and carried her affectionately to the kitchen. Dawn was evaporating the ground moisture (the rain having stopped), and sunlit fingers walked across the kitchen table. Leah placed a bowl of oatmeal and orange juice in front of Velda, but Velda would only drink the juice.

"Good morning," said Jake, walking in. "How's my little girl?" Velda said nothing, looking down sadly.

"I'm taking her to County Hospital this morning. She's just not herself," said a concerned Leah.

"Good idea. Give me a call at work when you find out, ok?"

"All right."

After examining Velda and taking a blood test, Dr. Poldor made his diagnosis:

"Velda has Rocky Mountain spotted fever. The flat red spots on her hands clued me in to the disease, but the blood test confirms it. I'm writing a prescription for an antibiotic— make sure she takes these three times a day with water," Doctor Poldor prescribed.

"How serious is this?" Leah asked.

"Fortunately she's in the early stages of the disease. Make sure she gets plenty of rest, fluids, and most importantly, the antibiotics. I want you to come back in a week for a follow-up. I have regular office hours if you wish to make an appointment."

"Thank you, doctor," Leah said, relieved. After leaving the hospital and returning home, Leah filled the prescription and gave Velda the first dose.

"I hear your girl is a might sick," said Zina Hollander at Leah's front door.

"She's fine, Zina," said Leah, perturbed by Zina's supposed concern.

"I just thought I could do something for the young-un. Here, I made this crabapple pie for y'all. Hope you enjoy it. Just made it this afternoon, I did."

Leah didn't like accepting things from Zina, who usually asked for favors in return. "I'm sure it'll be just fine. Well, I'd love to invite you in, but I—"

"Why thank you, Leah, I wouldn't mind a cup of tea and a chitchat myself. Lordee mercy, you seen what 'dat tornader did to my carport? Toppled it into a pile of toothpicks. I'm lucky it didn't get my house," Zina grinned.

"More like wishful thinking," mumbled Leah.

"What was that?" Zina shot back, almost hearing Leah.

"Oh, I said how we were thinking of you when we saw your poor carport," Leah covered quickly. She hoped Zina would go away soon.

"Well if that isn't the purdiest thing you've said to me all month, I declare it's just, well, you know, sometimes I feel like the world is against me. I don't know what I'd do without you Barnes."

"Well don't you worry too much, I'm sure things will be fixed back up for you sooner or later," said Leah.

"Why that's so nice of you to offer. I'd be happy to have Jake over to help out," Zina said with a wink.

"Excuse me, Zina, but I really must get back to my house-work, there's—"

"Oh, I won't be but a minute longer. I just wanted to warn y'all 'bout the Thompson dogs. Seems they were out roaming the neighborhood during the night. How that man gets away with it, I don't know, but I tell you, something's got to come of it. I did hear, though, that the Smiths down the road found their flower garden ripped apart with dog prints all over. Dern 'dem dogs!"

"I haven't heard a peep around here—"

"Oh, they don't bark as much as they growl and gnash. I hear tell 'dem dogs come quicker than lightnin' and'll kill without mercy. Now if we—"

"Hey ladies, how are y'all?" Jake asked, coming home from work. Upon entering through the side door, he set his keys on a lamp table, walked over to the refrigerator, opened a can of cold beer, leaned against the counter, sipped beer, then contemplated whether to check on Velda or wait for Zina to leave so as to speak with Leah in private.

"Say, Jake, how are you today? How was work? It's nice to see you," started Zina, trying to butter him up.

"Fine, all fine," replied Jake, trying to be polite. "I see your carport is still in need of repair." It was all Jake could think of to say.

"Yeah, we were just talkin' 'bout it. Leah suggested you could help me with it—you wouldn't mind, now would you?" Zina asked with a pout and fluttering eyelashes. Leah gave him a dirty look.

"I don't suppose it'd hurt to take a look," Jake said, trying to please everyone as best as possible, "but no guarantees. Seems like quite a job looking at it from the street."

"This evening then? That is, if it's not too much trouble," Zina said sweetly.

"Now about that—Velda's sick, Jake," Leah hinted strongly. Leah was opposed to Jake's visit to Zina's.

"That's true. All right, Zina, tell you what—lemme get a bite to eat, see Velda, and then if there's time, I'll pop over and take a look. Otherwise, maybe tomorrow. Sound fine?" suggested Jake, hoping not to sound too rude.

"I guess so. It's just..." Zina seemed to cry for a moment, but she calmed herself. "All right, perhaps later, hmmm? See y'all."

"Bye," said Leah, rushing Zina out with great speed. The door closed, and Leah breathed a relieved sigh.

"So how is Velda? Is she much better since I spoke with you over the phone this morning?" Jake asked. Leah was still fuming over Zina.

"Mr. Barnes, do I have to repeat to you how I feel about that Hollander woman?"

"Really, Leah, you're blowing things out of proportion."

"Am I? Can't you see what she's doing? She's trying to get our sympathy, and it often results in either lost money or something bad happening to us. That woman needs to get married again, and for good."

"Really, she's just an unfortunate woman who needs a break to get going. Her marriage went bad, but from what she says, it doesn't sound like it was her fault," Jake said.

"Don't be fooled by her sweet voice. She's been known to lie more often than not, especially when there's something or someone to take advantage of. You just keep your distance, you hear? It only takes one bad step with her, and our marriage—"

"Our marriage is one of the most important things to me, our marriage and our family. I love you and Velda more than anything—I wouldn't jeopardize that for a moment. You know that. Is being chivalrous to a hurting neighbor such a bad thing? Who knows when we may need the help of another, possibly even Zina's."

"Please," replied Leah strongly, "the thought makes me feel nauseated—which reminds me, Zina baked us a crabapple pie."

"My favorite. The occasion?" Jake asked.

"Says she's trying to help out with Velda being sick and all. I think she's trying to bribe you. You just mind your—"

"I'll mind them, I'll mind them. Now before we eat, I think I'll check on Velda." Jake needed some excuse to cool the atmosphere. Whenever Zina was mentioned, Leah's temper heated quickly.

"How's my little girl?" asked Jake. Velda opened her eyes and stared at her father.

"I hurt all over. My head hurts. Can I have a glass of water?"

"Sure, I'll be right back." Jake filled a glass of water from the tap, and in the corner of his eye could see Leah reading. She was too upset to acknowledge his presence. Jake returned to Velda's bedroom.

"Here's your water, sugar," Jake said softly, handing her the glass. Velda gulped the water eagerly. "Have you been sleeping well?"

"I keep having bad dreams, Pa. Make the monster go away!"

"Monster? Tell me about your dream, and I'll make the monster go away," Jake offered.

"Promise?" asked Velda.

"Promise."

"Okay, well, I saw people out my window, green people. They danced around until the monster came. I didn't see him, but I heard him. Then the people went away."

"How do you know there was a monster?" asked Jake.

"'Cause he scared me," replied Velda.

"Well, I bet if he sees you, he'll be so scared that he'll run away forever. So if you see the monster, you tell him to go away 'cause your Pa said so."

"Okay, I'll tell him, Pa."

"Goodnight, sugar."

"G'night."

Despite Leah's warnings (which should be headed), Jake visited Zina that evening and went on to inspect her carport.

"Boy oh boy, this is really bad," Jake said to Zina.

"I know the front looks bad, but if you take a look at the back," she said walking around with Jake following, "I don't think it's so bad, do you?"

"No, let's get a closer look," Jake said, walking toward the carport. The two were completely hidden from view, a fact Zina appreciated.

"Yeah, let's get closer," said Zina affectionately. She placed her arms around Jake from behind.

"Hey there," said Jake, surprised. He turned around, backing into the carport.

"Don't be shy; I know what you're *really* thinking." Zina went up to kiss Jake, but Jake stumbled over a loose board while backing up and fell into the several beams. Upon impact, a support came crashing down upon his left forearm. Jake grunted in pain.

"Nice going Zina," said Jake sarcastically.

"Omigosh, are you okay?" asked Zina, more embarrassed than concerned.

"I hope you're happy now," said Leah in a none-too-pleased tone as she drove Jake to County Hospital. She was especially upset because she couldn't get a sitter for Velda and had to take her along. Velda was nicely asleep, though.

"I'm sure it's just a bad sprain—in a day or two the swelling will be gone."

Fortunately the wait was short, and within an hour, Jake had a cast on his left forearm. "A minor fracture," the doctor had said, who also gave Jake a prescription for pain pills and antibiotics.

"Lovely," Leah said sarcastically to Jake on the drive back from the drug store. "Now the both of you are on antibiotics. What's the next thing that'll happen around here, hmmm? First Velda, now you...is it my turn next?"

"Please, Leah, you'll wake Velda," cautioned Jake.

"Don't tell me to shush. I have a right to be angry, and I have a feelin' that Hollander woman has a part in this, this..."

"This what? 'Evil curse'? Really, now, you don't believe any such thing. What happened to Velda was unfortunate; what happened to me was clumsiness," Jake explained.

"And the Thompson dogs? Just another unfortunate thing, I suppose," growled Leah.

"Sure. Look, the world ain't perfect, and neither is our neighborhood. I think we should just forget the whole thing, I say."

"Forget the whole thing—I can think of a good way to do that. Move. Let's leave this neighborhood behind us," said Leah, now asking in a downcast voice. "We don't have to move far—just enough to get away from it all."

"Do you really think we fix things by running away? No, we have to meet them head on," urged Jake. Leah wasn't happy with his reply and decided it best to discuss the issue no longer, at least for the moment. The three returned home where Velda quietly played with her doll collection, Leah continued reading her book, and Jake listened to a boxing match over the radio. Jake was as involved in his boxing as Leah was in her book, but the radio announcer's voice grew louder at 1292 Crabapple Lane, so much that Leah could no longer enjoy her book. She asked Velda if she'd like to hear a bedtime story to which Velda agreed, leaving Jake in the living room by himself.

When the match ended, Jake's trance ended and he noticed himself alone. Upset and tired from the injury, he went to bed early.

"Another story, Ma. Please?" begged Velda as Leah finished reading four stories.

"I'm sorry sugar, but it's time for sleep."

"But I've been sleeping all day," Velda complained.

"I know, but you're a sick girl right now. When you're feeling better, you can stay up later, I promise."

With that, Leah tucked Velda into bed, closed the shades, then exited quietly. Several minutes later, Velda thought she heard her parents arguing in the adjoining room, but she drifted into a light sleep with Whiskers curled beside her.

Whiskers stirred, first walking gingerly over Velda, then to the foot of the bed and to the window. Velda woke up and whispered for Whiskers to come back, but he remained preoccupied with something at the window. Velda got up and opened the shades, looking out the window with Whiskers. Again soft rain fell to the earth, although it seemed more of a mist to Velda. First one then two then several lights danced around the trees, through the bushes, and along the grass, causing dazzling light to sparkle from the wet foliage. Again the blue aura encompassed the area, and the dancing lights glowed a light green. Whiskers meowed in a fettered way.

"Shhh. Quiet, Whiskers," said Velda, her breath again fogging the window. She wiped the moisture from the glass then held Whiskers for their mutual comfort. The lights formed into people, some young and some old, running around, playing, and conversing, though the entire collection of noise was little different from whispering winds and rustling branches. Again a young girl around Velda's age came to the window, but the girl darted away quickly as did the other greenish people.

"Ffft," came the sound of fire through the air. Velda was frightened but stayed by the window. Whiskers squirmed away and ran under the bed.

"Ffft," came the sound again. The greenish people had mostly disappeared except one, who had somehow fallen and couldn't get up.

"Now I have you," said a voice. Velda looked closely—the fire came from a "dragonlion" as she thought to herself, a lion with wings and fire like a dragon. Atop the dragonlion rode an ugly witch, cracking her whip from side to side. She rode the beast toward the fallen greenling, where the dragonlion breathed fire. The flames engulfed the greenling, who disappeared.

"Go away," said Velda, her voice shaking. "Go away 'cause my Pa says so. Go away." The witch and beast came closer. Velda ran into bed and covered her eyes, mumbling, "Go away." The window rattled then screeched as if fingernails dragged across the pane.

"Go away," said Velda one final time. A hand touched her shoulder. She jumped and screeched.

"Easy, sugar, you're just having a bad dream," said a voice. Velda opened her eyes to see her mother, Leah, looking down on her. Velda looked at the window. Nothing, except for increasing light from the Wednesday sunrise.

"I'm scared," said Velda with glazed eyes.

"I know. Let's get some breakfast, then you'll feel better."

Minutes later, Jake left for work but returned inside the house after learning his car was disabled.

"I can't understand it," he grumbled, "all four tires are flat. Not slashes from a knife, mind you, but large puncture wounds, as if—"

"As if jaws from some animal came and punctured them. I'm placing my bet on the Thompson dogs, and if my car weren't closed up in the garage, it'd be flat on the fours as well. Now I suppose you wanna take my car into work," Leah said.

"If you don't mind. I'll give Beelee from the garage a call and see if he can get me some new tires—I know you wouldn't want to have me dirty your car with new tires in the trunk or back seat."

"You got that right. My car better be back in one piece, too. Just remember what I told you yesterday. Remember?" jabbed Leah.

"I know, I know. I'm late enough as it is. See you later, Leah. Bye sugar," he said to Velda, and he was gone.

Leah heard the knock at the door but wondered if she should answer it. The knocking continued, and Leah reluctantly opened it, only to find Zina Hollander with peach cookies.

"I feel like I'm such a nuisance and all, I thought I'd bake some cookies and make up for it," started Zina, her mouth motoring quickly.

"Zina, please, I—" Leah tried to say, but Zina managed to mosey on into 1292 Crabapple Lane.

"I see the young'un is up and around," commented Zina, setting the cookies on the countertop.

"She's much better. The doctor says—"

"What was that again she's got? Some flu thing?"

"Rocky Mountain spotted fever. We were lucky with the new antibiotics at the drug store," said Leah, but Zina couldn't listen for more than thirty seconds without saying something.

"My, my. She's lucky, all right. The Thompsons lost a boy ten years back from the fever, and their cousin died fifteen years ago from it. If I had a nickel for every person—"

"Zina, you seem to know an awful lot 'bout the people 'round here," Leah said.

"Oh well, I get around. I heard the Thompson dogs were out again last night, in this very area. Found a dead sparrow in my front yard this morning, and—"

"And Jake's tires are flat," interrupted Leah.

"I saw that. The dogs got 'em, must have. I'm telling you, we gotta do something about Ole Man Thompson," Zina insisted.

"You keep telling me we need to do something, but no one wants to help either. The police, town hall, no one."

"I know, and it's pathetic," continued Zina, "but if we stick together, we can get through this thing, I know it." Leah cringed at the sound of "stick together," as if Leah *really* wanted to stick with Zina. Leah wished Zina would stick to someone or something else and leave the Barnes alone. At that moment, a fire truck raced down the street.

"Hmm, wonder what that is? Oh, look at the time, I have to be going. Nice chatting, Leah," said Zina as she flew out of the house. Curious, Leah looked through the window and watched Zina, who hopped in her car and drove after the fire truck.

"Always interested in another crisis," murmured Leah.

Velda begged to go outside and play, but Leah thought it best if she stayed in. Velda begged again, and Leah allowed her out but told her to stay close to the house and away from the bushes. Velda played in a small sandbox close to the back door, and Whiskers came out and played with her. She would hide her hand under the sand then poke a finger through while a watching Whiskers paw at the mysterious finger. She next tapped a stick in the sand here and there—Whiskers pawed and played with the stick. Her first day back outside went well.

"How nice of Zina to bring more treats," said Jake, coming home from work.

"Yeah," Leah said unenthused. "As if we need them. Probably poisoned them."

"Really, Leah, if I didn't know better, I'd say you're paranoid of Zina. She's just trying to be nice. Can't you for a change?" asked Jake.

"Ha! Zina, nice? That's a joke."

"I think we could at least do her the courtesy of trying her pie, and now her cookies. I'll get a piece myself," said Jake.

"No," said Leah, insisting, "I'll take the first piece, just to show you how much I *appreciate* her cookin'." Leah took a bite from her freshly cut piece and sarcastically remarked how good it was.

"Fine, if that's how you're gonna be," said Jake, his voice trailing. He went outside to visit Velda. Leah took the rest of the pie and dumped it in the garbage.

"How's my little girl?" he asked, sitting next to the sand-box.

"Fine," she said in distinct southern drawl. "See Whiskers? He's playing in the sand with me."

"He's a nice kitty-cat, isn't he?"

"Yeah. Hey, kitty, where are you going?" Velda asked. Whiskers went off to a nearby tree then climbed up quickly.

"The monster came back again," said Velda, her tone changing. "I saw him, the dragonlion, and a bad witch was riding him. He was breathing fire, and she made him breathe on one of the green people. I told him to go away, I told him, Pa."

"There now," said Jake, giving her a hug, "the monster will go away soon."

Sounds of shattering glass then a thud came from inside. Jake and Velda walked in to see what had happened. There on the floor lay Leah, unconscious.

"It was close, but it looks like we'll pull her through," said the doctor at County Hospital.

"What happened? Why is she sick?" asked a worried Jake.

"Food poisoning. We've pumped out her stomach and given her some medicine, but as for the cause...it could be something as simple as poorly canned food, or food made with a tainted ingredient. Now if you'll excuse me, I have another patient next door."

Leah momentarily became conscious from her hospital bed. Jake and Velda looked on.

"What happened? What am I doing here?" Leah asked, disoriented.

"You had a bad case of food poisoning, and we had to take you to County General. How are you feeling?" Jake asked.

"Horrible. My throat is sore, my stomach is sore, and I have a splitting headache. The pie, it was the pie. She poisoned it, I tell you," said Leah, getting excited.

"Now Leah, don't get excited. The doctor says you need rest, and if you're well enough, they'll let you leave in a couple of hours."

"Ma," said Velda, "I have a present for you." Velda pulled out a bracelet made from dandelions, picked from the hospital's lawn during Jake and Velda's wait.

"It's very nice, sugar."

Leah returned that Wednesday evening, but she ate little and spoke less. Jake tucked Velda in for the night and was ready to retire himself when he noticed Leah sleeping on the couch. He went up to shake her gently but thought it best not, and he went back to their bedroom and fell asleep.

Whiskers had found his way into Velda's room, sniffed out every corner, then jumped softly onto Velda's bed, curling into a ball next to her feet. The two slept for several hours until a TAP-TAP came at the window. Whiskers jerked slightly and looked at the window. "TAP-TAP," came the sound from the window. Velda got up and walked over, accompanied by Whiskers. The same girl who had visited the previous nights was tapping on the window. She extended her hand toward Velda's, somehow coming through the window a few inches. Velda grasped it instinctually and found herself floating through the glass and out into the backyard. She looked back to see a curious Whiskers watching her movements.

"My name is Velda. What's yours?" Velda asked.

"Andrella. Come, I want to show you around," said the girl. The two walked along the backyard and into the woods. The blue aura had turned the night into day. Though most everyone had green auras, Velda's was rosy pink.

"You may think of this place as the woods behind your house, but we call it Falidon Forest."

"Who's crying over there?" asked Velda.

"That's Weeping Wendy. If there's something sad around her, she cries." The two went over to Weeping Wendy. "Hello, Weeping Wendy," called Andrella.

"Why are you crying?" asked Velda.

"I've just heard," she said between tears, "that the Chimera has eaten another squirrel."

Weeping Wendy burst out into a new round of tears, wailing and moaning.

"That is sad," said Velda. "Cheer up, the Chimera will go away." Velda was saying it to help Weeping Wendy stop crying, but Wendy simply gazed at Velda for a few seconds before crying harder yet.

"We'll see you soon, Weeping Wendy," said Andrella as she and Velda moved onward.

"What's the Chimera?" Velda asked Andrella.

Andrella could only reply by saying, "An evil beast from the dark woods. Some say it's a lion, others a goat, and still others a dragon."

Twelve greenish people danced in a circle around one person, who was playing some sort of flute. Andrella took Velda to the group and made an announcement:

"Everyone, say 'hello' to Velda." Everyone said "hello." The person in the middle was a girl of perhaps twelve years. She approached Velda and handed her the flute.

"Welcome, Velda. I'm Darlina. Would you like to try the flute?"

"I don't know how to play," shied Velda.

"It's not just *any* flute—it's a magic flute. For us it plays music, but for real girls like you, it plays music and protects you from harm. Try," Darlina offered.

Velda took the flute in hand while the others circled 'round. She played and music came out, such wonderful music that amazed her. The group danced around her making merry.

"Ffft," came a nearby sound. "The Chimera!" the others yelled, and they hid. With flute in hand, Velda walked quietly toward the beast, watching its movements from behind a bush. It was the dragonlion, with the witch riding atop. The dragonlion was pulling a cage on wheels, and inside were several people. One resembled her father, and he looked out between the bars, dejected. Velda cowered behind the bush, then noticed a shape approaching the rolling cage, a shape resembling her mother, though this woman had flowing white hair.

"Careful," murmured Velda unconsciously, but the dragonlion's keen ears heard her, and he stopped. He turned to look, the witch followed his gaze, and the witch said:

"Aha! So you are the new one! I'll see to it you are taken care of. Now don't move," said the witch, looking directly at Velda. Velda froze in fear, but the lady with flowing white hair came up to the cage and opened the door, letting several people free (including the one resembling Velda's father). The dragonlion and witch reacted violently, she cracking her whip around people's necks, and he scorching their feet.

"No," cried Velda, running out between the witch and people. She played the flute quickly, and the notes seemed soothing to the people though harsh to the witch and dragonlion. The evils moved away, let the cage go aside, and fled from the flute's cleansing peril.

"Hooray for Velda, hooray for Velda," came a cheer from the people. Andrella and Darlina ran up to Velda from their hiding spots and hugged her.

"May I have the flute?" Velda asked. Darlina smiled thoughtfully but replied:

"I'm afraid the flute must stay here in Falidon Forest. Otherwise, it would disintegrate once it reached your world."

"Then how will I protect myself from harm? How will I protect others?" Velda asked.

"Look within your heart, and you will find your own magic flute to play," Darlina replied. Andrella took Velda's hand, and the two went back to 1292 Crabapple Lane, where Velda passed through her bedroom window. Andrella remained behind and waved goodbye. Raindrops fell to the earth, then drops rolled down the window, first gently, then in great numbers, obscuring Velda's view. Whiskers meowed, and Velda returned to bed.

Little happened worth noting during Thursday and Friday, although Jake took Leah and Velda out to the movies Friday evening. The movie lifted everyone's spirits, enough so that all previous problems were forgotten. The Barnes anticipated more pleasant times ahead and went to bed that Friday evening with the idea. Velda slept the entire nights of Thursday and Friday peacefully, and Saturday morning rolled along crisp and clear.

Velda was out playing in her sandbox with Whiskers on the cool but sunny day. Leah was inside cleaning the house, and Jake was in the garage working on his car. Beelee had not been able to get the tires for Jake, so he'd gone to the next county to fetch them. His arm still broken, Jake was meticulously changing each wheel.

The sun went behind a cloud, and the wind picked up as Velda enjoyed the sandbox and her cat, Whiskers. Distant bells could be heard chiming, several birds chirped, and then the Barnes's lives turned upside down.

It happened too fast for anyone to really see—there was no warning of any sort. The Thompson dogs with speed and silent cunning came thundering into the back yard from the woods. Whiskers's keen ears picked up the dogs, but too late. One dog had Whiskers in his jaws, the other was biting Velda's arm. Velda screamed. Leah rushed out and beat the dog off Velda, but the dog simply turned his aggression on Leah. Jake also heard the screams, peered out the garage's back door to see the assault, then ran madly for his rifle. Loading it took seemingly forever, though only a few seconds elapsed. His left arm in a cast made the rifle's manipulation more difficult than usual, but he was determined to carry out the necessary deed. Storming into the backyard with rifle in hand, he hit the dog on Leah with the rifle's barrel, then fired into the beast at point-blank range—the dog died. The other dog had already partially eaten Whiskers before running away.

Whiskers was obviously dead, Velda was unconscious and badly injured—possibly dead, Leah was in shock (though crying in a strange sort of way), and Jake stood there determined, a fire smoldering deep within.

Leah was treated for minor wounds at County Hospital (and received both tetanus and rabies shots), but Velda was in a coma, having lost substantial blood and suffered several concussions. Jake had told and retold the story to police, providing them ample information to begin chasing down the last dog.

"Visiting hours are now over," said the nurse. Jake and Leah reluctantly left Velda's bed and proceeded home.

"I'm going to join the posse to find the other dog," said Jake as the two drove home. Leah was too upset to say anything. "Please, Leah, don't do this to me. We've been through a lot, and we need to try putting the pieces back together."

"Killing the other dog won't fix what's happened," said Leah.

"You're right, it won't. But maybe if—"

"Maybe if—we should have moved from here at the first sign of trouble."

A squad car was waiting when the Barnes arrived home.

"We caught the other dog trying to make its way through Crawdad's Creek. He won't bother you anymore," said the officer.

"And us? Our home? Can we sleep safely tonight?"

"We're done with most of the preliminaries, but I recommend you stay at a hotel tonight. Don't worry about your house—someone will be here watching it during the night and into Sunday."

"Have you arrested Ole Man Thompson?" asked Leah.

"Seems he didn't survive to be prosecuted. Died of cardiac arrest," said the officer, a bit puzzled.

"I don't believe it," said Leah, and she took off in her car toward the Thompsons, leaving Jake behind with the officer.

The Thompson house was surrounded with police cars and several dozen people, all watching as Ole Man Thompson was taken away. Taking advantage of the moment, Leah snuck around back and in through the back door, unnoticed. She was looking for an old recipe book she'd lent Mrs. Thompson years ago. After the two were no longer on speaking terms, Leah was unable to get the book back.

Searching through the kitchen proved fruitless, and she couldn't easily search the rest of the house without attracting attention. She thought of the possible places Mrs. Thompson could have stashed it—under the sink, behind the stove, under the refrigerator. Leah searched these places but couldn't find the book. She did, however, find some cloth behind the stove. Pulling at the material revealed a pair of black lady's panties with the initials ZH inscribed. A warm feeling melted through Leah as she stuffed the panties in her pocket and snuck out of the Thompsons to her car.

The Barnes spent the night at the hotel and returned to County Hospital the next day to check on Velda's condition. She'd been upgraded from critical to serious, and Velda had come out of her coma. The Barnes were very happy but were still leery, enough to put their house up for sale and look for a new one. Amazingly, they received an offer within two weeks; in two months the Barnes had moved from Crabapple Lane to a subdivision ten miles west, called Wilshire Heights. Velda had recovered sufficiently for the move, and though Whiskers had not survived (for which Velda cried for hours), the Barnes purchased a new kitten for Velda, which she named Whuffa.

Feeling secure in the new home, Leah was ready to have a final confrontation with Zina. On a Saturday night when Jake took Velda out for a movie, Leah drove back to Crabapple Lane. She sat in her car and considered whether she should go up to Zina and "have it out" or drive off and forget everything. *Do you really think we fix things by running away? No, we have to meet them head on.* Jake's words repeated through her mind. She got out of the car and walked to the front door then knocked. Apparently, Zina was home alone.

"Leah, what a surprise! How are you? Where are you living these days? I've been wondering 'bout that since y'all left, 'specially since y'all left no new address with me. C'mon in, I'm just makin' some tea."

"Yes, Zina, I'm fine. I want to have a little talk with you," said Leah, though Zina looked surprised.

"Why, what about, Leah?"

"This," Leah said, showing the panties to Zina.

"Where did you get that? Give that to me, now! I'm disappointed in you, Leah, for sneaking out one of my panties from my dresser. Of all the nerve."

"I didn't get this from your dresser. It was nicely hidden behind the stove in the Thompsons' kitchen. You and Ole Man Thompson? Hard to believe, isn't it?" said Leah.

"It's a lie," denied Zina, "I don't have to take this anymore." With that, Zina ran into the bathroom and flung open the medicine cabinet, looking for her pain pills.

"No you don't," said Leah, grabbing Zina's arm and twisting it behind her back. "I want you drug-free tonight so you can tell me what you've been up to this whole time."

"You're crazy," said Zina, agitated. "You're nothing but a mean, despicable woman."

"Maybe, but if you don't tell me everything, I'll turn this evidence over to Mrs. Thompson. I'm sure she'll be interested in having it, especially when she takes you to court." Leah bluffed about Mrs. Thompson taking Zina to court, but she had to put pressure on Zina somehow.

"Please," said Zina, going back into the living room, "just leave me alone."

Leah carried the bottle of pain pills with her. "So you want to take these?" she asked, shaking the bottle. "No, Zina, not until I hear the story. Really, Zina, what could you *ever* see in Ole Man Thompson?"

Zina broke into tears. "You don't know what I've been through. Give me the pills, oh Leah, if you have any kindness left in you, give me the pills." Zina was on her knees, begging and sobbing.

"You miserable wretch. You'll do anything to avoid pain, anything to keep from being rejected. I've had it with your kind. You can keep your precious story to yourself—I don't care anymore. You'll never amount to anything, Zina, just the butt of everyone's joke. Here's your disgusting panty," Leah said, throwing it on the couch as she walked to the front door. Zina was unaffected by the panty's return—she was still sobbing and begging for the pain pills.

"Please," pleaded Zina another time.

"I'm going to do you one more favor before I leave," said Leah, turning around and walking briskly into the kitchen. Zina followed her eagerly. "I'm going to get rid of this thing once and for all."

"No," Zina begged, grabbing at Leah's hand. Leah socked Zina in the mouth, forcing Zina back into a kitchen chair. Leah dumped the bottle's contents into the sink, turned on the faucet, and used the water to send the pills down the drain.

"No!" wailed Zina, falling to her knees again. "No, my life is over," she moaned.

"You're a pathetic excuse for a human. Goodbye!"

With that, Leah made her way to the door, but Zina's grief turned to anger. She took a kitchen meat knife in hand and lunged for Leah.

"Arrrrgh!" Zina cried.

Leah screamed, turning around in time to avoid Zina's stab, which landed in the door. Leah grabbed Zina's hand, fighting for control of the knife. The two struggled, the knife dangerously in position to stab either woman.

"You're crazy," uttered Leah through the strain. "What is your problem?"

"Me? The problem?" Zina said, the knife dropping to the floor. "I'm not the one with the problem." Leah kicked the knife under the couch. Zina leaned back for it, but Leah tried restraining her. The two fell together, entangled and still struggling.

"You've got a big problem, sister," said Leah back.

"Everyone's out to get me—you, the Hackeys, the Thompsons, everyone."

"Out to get you?" Leah inquired. Leah managed to force Zina's face down, holding her there with an intricate arm lock.

"Get off me," groaned Zina.

"Let's have it out now. Why is everyone after you?" asked Leah, who maintained her hold. The two remained motionless and began calming down.

"They just are. If it weren't for Ole Man Thompson..."

"You had an affair with him, didn't you?" pressed Leah.

"And I tried to use it against him, demanding money or else I'd tell his wife. He laughed and said no one would believe I was so stupid as to have an affair with an old dog like him. That made me mad."

Zina seemed to drift off in her story, hardly aware of Leah's continued arm hold.

"What did you do?" urged Leah.

"I was desperate—couldn't let him get away with that treachery. So, I started letting his dogs go free at night. At first it was a prank, but his dogs got into mischief and him into trouble. Again I demanded money out of him, and again he refused. That was it. I had nothing more to say to him, and I never spoke to him, but I kept letting his dogs get out into the neighborhood, hoping it would get him kicked out. Now he's dead, the muttering half-breed. All that work, all the revenge, and he snuck out in the end."

Upon learning Zina's responsibility for Whisker's death and Velda's critical injuries, she twisted Zina's arm. Zina cried out in pain.

"So, it was you who nearly got my girl killed, it was you who got my husband's arm broken, and likely you who flattened my husband's tires. You poisoned me with your crabapple pie, you piece of trash. YOU!"

Leah beat Zina's head into the floor mercilessly and without stop. Zina cried in pain, but after ten minutes of constant beating, Zina stopped reacting. A bone crunching sound echoed during Leah's last thrust of Zina's skull into the floor.

Leah stopped. Blood oozed from Zina's nose; the rest of her body was lifeless. Leah felt Zina's arm for a pulse—none.

Upon the death of another, most people feel a sense of great loss and despair. Contrarily, Leah felt a great relief, as if someone had freed her from a prison sentence. Happy, Leah walked out with a smile and returned to Wilshire Heights, where Jake and Velda anxiously welcomed her home. Leah kissed them both before sitting to a relaxing murder mystery book.

That night, Velda was sleeping by herself in her new bedroom, the new kitten curled nearby in his warm basket. Soft rain tapped against the window pane, and Velda went to the sill and looked out. A blue aura encircled the Barnes's back yard, and several greenish people scurried along the shiny grass. Some were singing, others were laughing, and still others were dancing. Andrella came up to the window and stopped. In her arms was a greenish Whiskers, purring and cuddling. Andrella waved to Velda; Velda waved back. There was no dragonlion, no witch, and no cage. Andrella disappeared from view and played with the other greenish people. Velda watched as the people faded into dancing lights, then finally into nothing. The gentle rain was all to be heard. Velda stared outside for several minutes, hoping her Whiskers would re-emerge. He did not.

Velda's breath fogged the window, and she wiped the moisture with her pajama shirt sleeve. She immediately noticed a bug had spattered against the window pane, its blood smearing like red ink. The rain fell, and after a moment more, the drops had washed away evidence of the insect, evidence of any nuisance left to vex the Barnes.

Jacob Richardson
in

Unseen Assailant: Part II

July 27, 1992

As we gathered our things, we could hear several patrol car sirens growing near.

"Too late," I said. "They're here."

"Forget the bags—we're out of here, now!"

With that, Helen and I made our way out a side window, down a trellis, and seeing we couldn't get near our car, we fled into the nearby woods.

(End of Part I, beginning of Part II.)

"All right young man, just take a deep breath and calm down," Sergeant Gunter said to an excited bellboy.

"It's...I...over here!" he yelled and nearly ran inside Lakeside Inn. Deputy Jackson caught him and slung him back to Gunter with an arm.

"Now listen here, boy, we can't afford to be goin' off and chasing every little butterfly that comes our way. Get a grip and tell us what you know, or should I say, what you think you know," commented Gunter. A general laugh from the on-lookers followed.

"They were here. I saw them," the bellboy said above the commotion.

"Who, boy, who?"

"The ones on television—the Richardsons."

"You sure it was them?" Gunter asked.

"Yes," replied a distinguished man coming forward. "It was they. Jacob and Helen Richardson."

"And who might you be?" asked Gunter.

"Frank Jerrold. I'm the hotel manager. It seems we are too late, however. The two left."

"Gone and dog-gone. Dad burnit!" cursed Gunter. "Gone ya' say? How long ago?"

"Only a little while—if you hurry, you'll catch them," blurted the bellboy.

"If I may speak without further interruptions," said Jerrold, giving a harsh stare to the bellboy, "we just might catch the two. Ten minutes ago they left, I would say. It could not have been much more. It was fifteen when I heard the bellboy yelling his way down from the Richardsons' room."

"Ten minutes. Might as well be ten hours, though they couldn't have gotten too far. Ah well, enough dilly-dallying. Jackson, take your men around the left side. The rest of you, follow me. Move out."

"I just can't believe it was them, Mr. Jerrold. Are we infected now? Are we gonna die? Oh what will become of us?" whined the bellboy.

"Shut-up and get back to work. Lord knows this place will never be the same again. Blues crawling all over the grounds, our guests checking out, what else could happen...the press!" Jerrold was not quick enough to evade several unloading media vans. Reporters crowded the bellboy and him. As he tried to back off, the bellboy burst out in uncontrolled speech, completely distorting the events.

"No comment, no comment," Jerrold yelled in vain, but it was no use. The story was out.

"Over there," yelled one reporter as Gunter circled the Inn. He rolled his eyes in disbelief, casually walking toward the crowd.

"All right, all right. Now everyone just simmer down and park your motor-mouths behind this-here yellar line. We're conducting an investigation, and if there's any further disturbance, I'll have the boys haul the last one of ya' downtown in the paddy wagon."

Gunter raised his arms to the people, motioning them back. Amazingly they complied, but not without a question flying.

"Is there any danger to the immediate residents, Sergeant Gunter?"

"All right you, out!"

In seconds, an officer had taken the offending reporter and tossed him out of sight. Presently, Deputy Jackson reappeared. Gunter motioned several officers to hold the crowd back as he walked to Jackson.

"Anything?" asked Gunter.

"Nothing, though we managed to section off their room. Seems they exited through the window."

"I thought as much. Bring on the hounds."

In minutes, another wagon arrived followed by several black cars. Officers forced the complete media withdrawal as the area became increasingly restricted.

"Who in blazes...well I'll be. A-look who showed up for the party," said an amused Gunter.

"If it isn't 'Sawtooth' Gunter. Haven't seen you in years. Still the Big Man in these parts?"

"Jack Tarske, you son-of-a-gun. Look at you, you ole snake! Hangin' around the feds, I see."

"Not just hanging around—I'm one of them. Agent Tarske, CIA. We need to talk."

"Love to, but I got a man-hunt in progress, in case you haven't noticed," replied Gunter.

"I noticed. In fact I'm counting on you," Tarske added.

"Me? Just how big is this thing?"

"If you don't mind, let's discuss this in the limo."

An average sized limousine, Gunter thought, but as he climbed inside he immediately recognized several sophisticated electronic devices adorning the interior.

"Not bad for a back-woods boy," commented Tarske.

"You never were satisfied with what you had—always after the big prize and getting it. Even now I see you scheming behind those conniving eyes," said Gunter.

"You're right. The Richardsons are a big prize, more than most realize. You've heard the 'official' reports from television no doubt."

"No doubt, but I hear stories of a different nature, that these two aren't much of a threat at all, at least not to the public. If anything—"

"If anything, Sergeant Gunter, you'll ensure everything said in this limo stays in this limo. As you suspect, the Richardsons are not so great a threat, at least not as the Shairton County General would like the public to believe. It turns out Mr. Richardson has unexpectedly acquired immunity to—"

"You mean the feds purposely—" Gunter was intrigued but also concerned. What was he getting into?

"Gunter, you must remember NOT to allow this information to leave the limo, remember? What I'm about to tell you is of the highest security breach, should you do so. I can't give you details, but what I can tell you is this: should Mr. Richardson be allowed to continue on his way, all efforts of Operation Purge will be undermined. *Now* do you understand?" Tarske looked Gunter in the eye, communicating further by telepathy.

"Yeah, I understand. I can't say I totally agree with what y'all are doing in DC, but I can't disagree. If it's gotta be done, it's gotta be done," admitted Gunter.

"You will report to me, then, and only me. One moment," Tarske said as his car-phone rang. "Tarske here. Yes, we're closing in on them now. (Pause) Him too? (Pause) Of course. Yes, we'll take care of it. No problem."

"Anyone I know?" Gunter asked jokingly.

"Only Dr. Leech himself. It seems a Dr. Brandberg mysteriously disappeared from Shairton County General."

"The doc is probably out lookin' for them too," commented Gunter.

"I'm not surprised. If it weren't for him, we wouldn't have this man-hunt; we could have disposed of Mr. Richardson at the hospital."

Helen and I had barely fled into the woods when we heard sirens wailing and saw lights strobing. Time was short as we struggled through thick underbrush, down steep slopes, and around piled dead-wood. We were hardly prepared for this sort of venture, and our exposed flesh reddened from scraping branches and brushing thickets.

"Any idea where we're going?" I asked.

"Away," replied Helen.

"Obviously. I can tell we're going east now that the sun is falling behind us."

Twenty minutes of silent travelling passed. Then Helen paused, cupping a hand to her ear.

"Do you hear that?" she whispered.

"Dogs. I wonder where they're off to?" I asked, half-jokingly.

"Wouldn't be surprised if they're going our way. Why not just wait for them to catch up?"

We each let out a nervous laugh, though it hardly lasted half a minute. Hearing the immediate problem gaining ground, we had to do something miraculous or else be dog meat. The terrain continued to be rough, though after a time we found an abandoned path. We travelled up, then down, then around, up further, then suddenly came across a sandy open area.

"Whoa! Careful, now, what is sand doing out here?" I asked.

"Strange, isn't it? But I think we're coming to a rocky area, and the sand is—"

"Hang on there!" I yelled as quicksand swallowed Helen. "Give me your hand. Lie on your back and try to float."

"Help me, Jacob, I'm sinking!" As much as Helen panicked, she had the sense not to scream. Holding her did just that—she stopped sinking, but I was unable to pull her out.

"I can't pull you out," I grunted, straining mightily. My strength had not completely returned since the illness.

"Don't leave me here. Help!"

What to do? I scanned for vine or rope—nothing. A small sapling grew nearby, but I couldn't reach it. Nine or ten feet—that was all I needed to reach the sapling, but how would I hold onto Helen while grabbing the sapling? I leaned back, hoping something would happen. It did. Without warning, Helen flew out of the quicksand like a cork out of a champagne bottle.

"Are you all right?" I asked.

"Whew. That was close."

"Too close," I said. "Another few minutes, and we'd both be under. End of our scamper."

"End indeed," said Helen, "if we could only use this to stop the chasers."

"Or delay them," I said, warming up to the idea. "It could give us the time we need."

"There's already one spot where one of us might have fallen," she said, looking around. "There, that boulder. Could we shove it in and—"

"And make it appear as if we both fell in? Let's do it."

The boulder was heavy, but fortunately it rolled and wobbled (with our help) before disappearing into the quicksand. I tossed my hat, and Helen followed suit. Moments later we left.

"Status, Gunter," Tarske muttered over Gunter's portable radio.

"Still in pursuit," Gunter replied. "The scent seems fresh—they must've been here within the half hour."

"Sarg," came a call from ahead. "Come quickly."

Gunter ran up in time to see a prized hound disappear into the quicksand.

"What the devil—so, it appears the man and wife have joined each other in eternal drowning," he said. "Tarske, they've been caught."

"You found them? I don't care how you handle the woman, but we want the man alive."

"I s'pose we can't always have our 'druthers, now can we? Looks like they're both gone," came back Gunter.

"What do you mean? Do you have them or don't you?" growled Tarske.

"In a matter of speaking. You see, the Richardsons took a bad step too many, right here in this quicksand."

"Quicksand? How can you tell?"

"Oh, their hats, the two spots where they went, plus the one where my dog went—the other dogs have stopped altogether."

"Look, Gunter, I'm not willing to let these birds get away. Leave a couple of men watching over the quicksand area. I'll send some men out to do a sonogram so we can make sure. In the meantime, I want you to continue the search as if they *didn't* fall in. It's an old trick leaving hats on quicksand, and I'm sure your dogs will pick up the scent again."

Gunter's relief turned to bitterness when he realized the search wasn't over. The afternoon dragged on, and if he didn't find them soon, he'd have to either abandon the search 'till morning or attempt a difficult night search. Gunter resented a prospective long night in the woods.

"I hear you 'bout continuing," Gunter radioed back, "but if we don't find them in the next several hours, we're gonna have to break for dinner. No way any of us can continue much more at this rate."

"If you can't continue, how can they? Find them, just find them," replied Tarske as he slammed his mike against the limo's interior.

Gunter took several deep breaths, gathered his thoughts, then pulled out his cigarettes, which he smoked occasionally during stressful moments. Two puffs of smoke billowed up as he panned the surroundings, considering his possible moves. *Could they be wandering around? Was this deception?* Gunter walked around a bit, noting two general paths around the quicksand.

"Jackson, take a dog and your boys around the north side; McLean, take the other dog, and the rest of you follow me. We'll circle and meet on the east end."

Each dog lit up with excitement when noses detected fresh scents. Jackson and his men moved quickly in "hot pursuit" as did Gunter.

"We've got 'em now," yelled Gunter back to Tarske. "We're on a fresh scent that I figure should lead us to them within five or ten minutes."

"Sarge, Jackson with a report."

"Go ahead."

"Appears we're on a fresh scent. My dog is moving quickly."

"You've got them," replied Tarske after hearing both reports. "They're playing that old game—splitting up in hopes of confusing the dogs. Ha! They are dog-meat!"

Gunter and his men followed McLean's dogs at an increasing pace. Gunter was so pleased at the prospect, he bit his cigarette and nearly ate it. Jackson was doing no less. His dog was just as quick and nearly dragged him along at top speed. Several minutes passed as the groups converged, and without warning the dogs stopped almost simultaneously and within a stone's throw of each other.

"Whoa," called Gunter, "we over-shot."

Jackson's dog looked up, to the left, then the right, then up at Jackson. Jackson tried encouraging his whimpering hound, who seemed unsure which way to go.

"Well," said Jackson to his dog, "which way did they go? They couldn't have just disappeared."

Jackson glanced around to see if he could help. On his right was the quicksand, in front a sandy/grassy area where he could see Sergeant Gunter just twenty yards away and closing, and a gradually thickening pine forest to the left.

"Dog-gone!" exclaimed Gunter. He looked up at Jackson who could only shrug his shoulders in equal confusion. Then Gunter's dog moved toward the pine trees. Seeing this, Jackson led his dog in a similar direction until the dog picked up a fresh scent. At first they led straight into the forest, but Jackson's then Gunter's dog weaved around trees, past each other, around in circles, and finally returned to opposite sides of the quicksand before returning to the woods and following similar patterns.

"This is the devil's trail," called Gunter back to Tarske, "but I can't figure how the two could go to this much trouble to mislead the dogs and yet have time to get gone. It's as if their ghosts are still here, and they sprouted wings and flew away long ago."

"You can't tell me two humans are fooling your dogs. If you can't handle this job, Gunter—" but Gunter cut him off.

"No problem, we'll just continue this until the Richardsons run out of tricks, I gotta hunch..." Gunter's words faded when the dogs started barking. They were saying, "This isn't just a human trail." Gunter looked at Jackson in time to see him pointing to a small, grey-furred creature approaching.

"Where'd he come from?" asked Jackson, referring to the happily-prancing grey cocker spaniel. He barked, the dogs barked, he, they, then the dogs dashed forward out of control, chasing the grey dog around in circles, weaving around trees, into the woods, back to the quicksand, then up to the per-plexed officers and past them, smiling.

"See that, Jackson?" Gunter called. The group re-united seconds later. "If it ain't one thing, it's a wild dog wasting our time."

"He had some socks tied around his neck," commented Jackson.

"Yeah, I saw them. And dragging socks around his legs. This is Mr. Richardson himself, Jackson. You see, it seems the disease turns a man into a dog, given enough time, and the Misses? She probably turned into a hen and is cackling at us now. I might as well be a monkey's uncle—I've been on this trail long enough to qualify. How 'bout the rest of you? You all feel like some geese who've been lead on a merry chase?"

The group burst into laughter, both in amusement and disappointment.

"I got your man," called back Gunter to Tarske.

"Excellent. And Helen?"

"Oh yeah, she flew away."

"You couldn't stop her? Gunter!?"

"No, I mean she flew up into the sky, right after turning into a chicken. All we got left is Mr. Richardson, Jacob the grey cocker spaniel, who is leading my dogs on a fine run for their money, even as we speak."

Gunter let out a chase-drunk smile to the boys, who were equally amused by the moment.

"You want to try that again? You're sitting there watching a dog, is this right?" asked Tarske.

"Oh yeah, you should see it. He's even wearing some of the Richardsons' clothing," Gunter's speech slowed.

"I see," Tarske radioed back coldly. "I've also heard from my sonographers. It seems there is one hound and one boulder stuck inside the quicksand site, where supposedly the Richardsons drowned. Now you've been sidetracked by a mere dog. You know what you have to do?"

"Yup." Gunter's sarcasm and humor vanished. He pulled out his service revolver and fired two shots into the passing grey dog. A single yelp, and it was over. Gunter holstered his revolver and inspected the dog, along with Jackson. The two looked at each other after they saw the collar:

"Ollie."

"I think there's a barn ahead," whispered Helen. The sun had set long ago, and reflected light from a setting quarter-moon hardly aided vision.

"I can't imagine us going much further if it isn't. The darkness out here—it surrounds you!" I said. It seemed I was having more difficulty walking than Helen.

"You're lagging, Jacob. Come on, not much further," she urged.

"It's too much. I can't see a thing!"

Helen turned around and walked up to me. "Can you see me?" she asked. I said no, desperately trying to see her. I could hear her, which had gotten me by for some time, but she found a sizeable lead, enough to make following very difficult.

"Look over there," she said, pointing my head. "Can you see the moon?"

"Yes," I said, "but that's all I can see."

"Humph," she mumbled, "probably deficient in Vitamin A, which seems unusual, but then again, it could be residual effects from the anthrax-v."

"Vitamin A?"

Helen led me up a hill to the possible barn as she explained:

"I'm guessing your night-blindness is from a lack of visual purple, a protein that needs vitamin A to be active. It's a wild guess, and I'm surprised I didn't notice the other symptoms for xerophthalmia, but then again, night blindness *is* the first symptom. It should be easily remedied with some greens."

"Well I hope a gallon of water comes with it. This chase has left me thirsty," I commented, trying to follow as best I could.

"Dehydration, I know what you mean, but it may be worse for you than me...shhh. Quiet now, we don't want to alarm anyone."

The wind picked up suddenly as Helen opened a door, and though the barn was dark inside, we could hear hooves rustling on the floor. If only we could see! I wanted to say such, but silence seemed best. We moved slowly, and within a few minutes the wind brought heavy raindrops followed by a downpour. Thankfully, we were dry and had averted getting wet. Oddly, there was no thunder, just a constant pounding against the tin roof. No thunder and no lightning, which dashed our hopes since we would have obtained quick glimpses of the barn's interior.

Being withdrawn in our thoughts, we hardly noticed a faint buzzing sound. Perhaps I was already half asleep; perhaps an odd barn-board arrangement was playing acoustic tricks. However, within another few seconds our attention heightened, focusing with renewed energy on a distant buzz growing near. Out of place, not part of the storm, the sound was too well organized, too mechanical to be ignored. Again I opened my mouth to speak, and again I closed it without an utterance.

"Helicopters," Helen whispered faintly. The buzzing came closer, dozens it seemed. The cacophony stirred further excitement in the cows, who were not pleased at the prospect of an unknown drone approaching. The copters hovered above the barn for five, perhaps ten minutes. The once constant rain had more of a hop-hop sound on the roof. My common senses thought it strange, but deep down I had a bad feeling we were being watched. I sank to my knees in an unconscious effort to hide though I knew the barn provided adequate cover. Or did it?

One nearly landed atop the barn it seemed, but as suddenly as they came, they left. Helen remained motionless for another minute before continuing.

"Ok," she whispered, but the sudden voice cutting through the rain startled me to my feet. Hooves rustled again.

"Shh. I think they're gone," she said.

The downpour had slowed to a gentle sprinkle, and the moon previously obscured by the clouds intermittently peeped through the raindrops. Helen made for a glint across the barn, the setting moon peering in from a side window. A minute later we were upon it, and after Helen groped along a table or bench for several minutes, she lit a discovered match, saw the glint was a small lantern, and tried lighting it when the flame nearly burned her fingers. She whipped her hand to extinguish it, lit another, and inflamed the wick. A dim view of our surroundings took hold, and the hooves turned out to be several cows maneuvering in their stalls.

"Well," whispered Helen at last, "how do like the accommodations?"

"Better than nothing, I suppose. Do you think there's a hay-loft above for sleeping?"

"Hay for the animals? It sounds reasonable enough. I think we could use some nourishment first," she mentioned.

"Food. If only those cows were hamburgers. A shame, though, about the only thing we could do is milk them."

"And as I seem to recall," Helen said, getting one of those grandiose expressions on her face, "your cousin Billy Jack runs a farm. And I also recall you mentioning your visits to his place. Seems to me—"

"Seems to me you have this idea I could milk them myself, being the country boy Billy Jack would have you believe me to be. I visited, I didn't participate. Besides, Billy Jack uses the milking machine—no one milks by hand anymore."

"You're not afraid, are you?" she asked, pushing me along. "Of course, we'll probably go hungry and thirsty all night.

Then there's your vitamin A deficiency. Tsk, tsk. The milk would do you good. But who am I to say, just a plain-Jane nurse," Helen said, twisting the metaphorical knife.

"I don't see you going over there," I added.

"Now now, must I do everything?"

"Well," I said, though the playful grape had dried to a raisin. "Yeah, something to get us by, at least 'till morning." I had changed from a humorous to a forlorn person, realizing the situation's gravity. In an instant I was milking a cow, doing what I had to do for survival. I fumbled for a clean pail, but managed to get enough milk from "Bessie," as I named her, to replenish our thirst and reduce our hunger.

"Maybe we should ask the farmer if he needs another hand," Helen commented.

"I didn't realize I had it in me. It seems so easy once you get going. Will there be enough for breakfast?"

"If we see morning. Remember how early Billy Jack got up in the morning?"

"Milking cows at six a.m. I guess we'll leave before then," I said. The pail was filled adequately, I thought, and we took turns drinking while recounting the day.

"Let's start from the beginning. This afternoon at the inn, the phone conversation, Dr. Brandberg, this chase—what's it all about?"

"I don't know the whole story, but my guess is that we are not a threat to the world as Dr. Leech said, but we *are* a threat to somebody, or some organization. Dr. Brandberg was very brief yet specific—we must meet him at a secluded cottage perhaps fifty miles from here, halfway between Bigsby and Cottertown," explained Helen.

"Bigsby? Isn't that where—"

"Yes. The Governor's home town. I don't know if it's a coincidence or not; I also don't know to whom the cottage belongs, and I barely know how to get there. That was the conversation. We were lucky to escape from Lakeside Inn before being caught. That bellboy, boy would I like a swipe at him."

Helen popped a fist into her other hand.

"The quicksand—we were really fortunate, I have to admit. One moment you're drowning, the next we're tying our socks around a grey dog. Funny for him to be out in the woods on his own," I mused.

"Funny indeed! That wasn't just any grey dog, that was Ollie."

"Ollie? You're not referring to the mythical Ollie, are you?"

"He's only a myth to those who don't believe. Friend to lost souls, Ollie finds and protects people who have lost their way. You remember the Raochard twins eight years ago?"

"Sure. They were reported missing for weeks, only to turn up later just a few miles west of Lakeside Inn. Just happened to remember seeing a newspaper clipping framed up in the lobby—"

"Of Lakeside Inn," she continued. "What wasn't printed in the paper was how the twins survived during that time. Ollie."

"And just how would you know?" I asked, unable to believe her story.

"I asked 'em. That is, I asked Ray Raochard, the elder twin."

"When was this?"

"Ray came into the hospital after cutting his arm, and to take his mind off the stitching, I asked. He and Zeke were in the same woods as we were, only they were several miles north of Lakeside Inn—the Black Forest."

"I've never been to that part," I said. "Are the trees as dark as people say?"

"They are, I suppose, but only because no light gets in. Ray and Zeke completely lost directional sense when Ollie came up to them. At first they feared him, but his wagging tail and soft panting (along with a few barks) let them know otherwise. They followed him along a path the two would never have found on their own, up to a few apple trees and a small brook. Once the two nourished themselves, Ollie led them to Farmer 'Santa,' at least that's the name given to him by the children who first came to him from Ollie. The neighbors call him Farmer 'Time' because of his wizened beard. I think his real name is Jean-Jac Brault. He's originally from Quebec, a

French Canadian, but I think a more liberal one, considering he's decided to speak and live among English-speaking Americans. My own theory on his relation to Ollie is as a master to a pet. Yes, I believe Ollie is his dog."

"Ollie? As in Oliver? That's not French," I commented.

"No, but the kids started calling him that. I think Jean-Jac once called out, 'Olé,' to the dog, and the first lost children thought he said, 'Ollie.' The name has stuck since, and supposedly a special collar was made for him, though it says, 'Ollie,' and not 'Olé.'"

"And you really think that was he?" I asked.

"Well while you were tying your socks around his legs, I got a good look at his collar. It *did* say, 'Ollie.' Poor Ollie must have thought we were nuts for wiping quicksand mud all over ourselves."

"I guess he's used to helping people get found, not lost," I added.

"See, you admit it after all."

"I'm willing to believe almost anything at this point," I said. "And that goes for a decent night's sleep."

"I won't argue you there. Let's see if we can find the stairs up," she said, putting the empty pail down. I hadn't noticed 'till then that we drank all the milk. It wasn't long before we were upstairs—half of which was empty (but had a very high ceiling), and the other was piled high with hay and straw—nearly to the ceiling, but there was a small slot in the middle. Helen and I climbed up and realized some bales were wet. Helen sneezed.

"Bless you," I said, and as Helen kept sneezing I realized the hay was bothering her. "Are you all right? Don't tell me your allergies are—"

"I don't think it's so much the straw, but the hay on this side is moldy. I think we'll have better luck with the straw," she said between sneezes, and as we climbed to the straw, we found a good nook where we could sleep unobserved, even if someone came upstairs. "How's your watch running?"

"As good as ever," I said. "What time should I have it wake us? Five-thirty?"

"I wonder...the question is, will 5:30 be early enough?" she mused. "I hate to say this, but make it 5:00. It should still be dark, so hopefully they won't be up yet. Sound good?"

"Not really," I responded with a small sigh, "but I suppose we have little choice. Five o'clock a.m.—it's set. Good night, sugar plum."

"Good night, teddy bear."

"So the myth is true," Gunter muttered to himself. Darkness had forced them to regroup while the second shift was being posted on main roads surrounding the Lakeside Inn and vicinity. With the apparent search failure, he was not eager to see Tarske.

"What can I say? They got away," said Gunter.

"And I've been pussy-footing too long," said Tarske. "No matter, I suspected as much might happen, which is why I've arranged for the second phase to begin shortly. Specially equipped helicopters will be used to find them, but what I need from you is continued ground support."

"And what I need is a dinner break. I know what you're gonna say, but I got second shift on the roads now, and I'm sending my first shift home. As for me—"

"As for you, Gunter, I need you to watch Highway 37—the one to Shairton. Better get Highway 29 covered too; assign one of your top men to it, Jackson is it?"

"Yeah, I'll have him take it. But really—do you think they'd be goin' back to Shairton? They know we're after them, and that's the last place they'd try," said Gunter.

Tarske was adamant, "If the Richardsons try anything, it may very well be in that direction. We can't take any chances, especially since they eluded you. I have a hunch they may go more for Highway 29, but we must cover every direction. Fortunately, Topabee Lake prevents them from going across, though I'm not taking any chances there either—several boats are out patrolling now."

"I've already tracked down their relatives and have men watching them as we speak," continued Tarske. "Your men, however, are on the front line and should be the ones to make first contact. Take your dinner break, but not for long—we'll need all-night road blocks if the choppers aren't successful."

"Yeah, I hear you," was the last Gunter said before hopping in his patrol car. The other men had already dispersed, including McLean and the dogs, though Jackson was writing down some notes before driving off to Belle Rigg's Diner.

"What can I do for you, boys?" asked the waitress.

"I'll have a ham sandwich and a coffee," replied Jackson.

"Make that two," said Gunter, "and make the coffee black."

"You boys in for a long night?" she asked.

"You could say," said Gunter, "and we'd 'preciate a little expeditin' on the 'wiches. We only got about twenty minutes or so."

"Coming right up," she said and left momentarily.

"How long do you think this will last?" asked Jackson in a low voice. Gunter massaged his temples, ran his fingers through his hair a few times while staring into the table, then looked up at Jackson.

"As long as it takes. Could be a few more hours, could be all night, but gaud I hope it ain't gonna be longer. That Tarske—he's out for the prize, and he won't leave 'till he gets it, now if—"

"Here's your coffee," the waitress said, "I'll be back in a moment for your sandwiches."

"Thanks," said Jackson. "Now," he said, looking back at Gunter, "you were saying?" A swig of coffee turned Gunter's disposition from grim to disgust.

"Yuck, what is in this?" Gunter muttered, looking in his cup. "Must be from this morning." His focus changed back. "Yeah, Trophy Boy. That was Tarske's nickname when we were younger. He was always first, always winning whatever he put his mind to, but I tell you, he—"

"And your sandwiches. Enjoy your meal."

Gunter lifted up the upper bread slice and peered at the ham. Fat oozed out. Jackson had already taken a few bites of his and didn't seem to mind.

"Must be running out of the good stuff," muttered Gunter again. "If Belle herself were here, she'd set things a-right. Humph. I don't know which is worse, the food or the coffee."

"Does it matter much when you're starved?" asked Jackson between bites.

"Well, when you got a little woman cooking *real* food, this stuff doesn't compare. You being single are more than likely used to this, but not me. 'Reminds me, gotta call my little woman and let her know I won't be comin' home. Lor' knows she'll pitch a fit tomorrow if I don't. 'Course she'll probably pitch a fit anyway for not coming home tonight. Maybe you're lucky you are single. Ah, I'll be back in a bit."

Jackson had finished his sandwich and sipped coffee while staring out the window at Highway 29. A few leaves rustled along the parking lot—some attached themselves to the patrol cars' wiper blades. The wind picked up. Trees went from standing still to swinging majestically. Several more leaves blew by, and a hat blew off a gentleman approaching the diner.

"I guess the power's out at home, but at least the phone's working. She didn't want to hang up, saying how a storm was rockin' the house. Can't believe we're gonna find those two tonight."

"The wind's picked up," mentioned Jackson. "We should get going."

"Yeah, I got the bill this time," Gunter said, throwing a twenty on the table. "Let's git."

"Gunter, do you copy?" called Tarske over the radio.

"Roger. Covering Highway 37."

"Jackson, report."

"All quiet on 29. Winds are throwing some limbs around."

"Ten-four. Hummingbirds are taking off." Tarske, sitting in Helicopter One, motioned his pilot to take off. Five others followed.

"We're having some difficulty maneuvering, sir," said the pilot to Tarske. "The wind is picking up—it may not be safe to fly for much longer."

"No choice, pilot. We *must* track the Richardsons before their trail vanishes. I know what you're thinking. A storm is coming, and you don't want to be crash-landing this bird. That's all the more reason to go now—if we don't track them quickly enough, the rain will wash their infrared footprints away. Remember not to run your spotlights—it'll only make the trails more difficult to track."

Chopper One drifted and swayed, but the pilot kept his course as the six fanned out, scanning the woods for infrared trails, the same woods Gunter and his men covered earlier.

"We're passing the quicksand area," called the pilot.

"Good. This is where the action begins," said Tarske, looking through the infrared scope. "Can hardly see the trails— just a faint blue with little dots all around. Whoa, pilot. Keep the chopper steady!"

"Hard to do, sir. The wind is playing havoc with my stabilizers."

"Our short-range radar will be useless with everything flying around. There," Tarske exclaimed, "two sets of faint blue footsteps. Not much, but enough. I'm feeding the vector to you now."

"Confirmed," replied the pilot. "I'll computer lock on the scope, if you can steady it."

"A few seconds...all right, computer taking over. Now, onto the resonance imager. Humph, only getting the faint footsteps—no one down there. Can we move this thing any faster?" called Tarske.

"I'm pushing her as fast as she can handle it. The computer is having trouble with the infrared trail. Now it's...ack, computer-lock lost."

"And it's raining. Angh, the resonance imager can't follow the footsteps—the rain is washing the ground smooth."

"Sir, we're coming out of the woods. It looks like a farm, with one house, two sheds, a barn, and large fields."

"You can see that through the rain, pilot?" Tarske was amazed.

"I've flown night runs before, sir, using the infrared scope as I am now to see. Even though it's raining, I recognize these buildings for what they are. As for the fields, that is fairly easy."

"Then see if the Richardsons have taken shelter in one of those buildings." Tarske picked up the mike, "All humming-birds—circle the small boxes and look for the fruit flies. Chopper One checking the big box."

Each helicopter acknowledged and hovered over the sheds, the house, and two over the fields. Tarske and pilot hovered over the barn.

"Definitely some heat sources in the barn," called the pilot, "I can see them plain as day."

"Can you make out distinctive shapes? Remember, there could be livestock inside. We don't want to move in on another grey dog, chicken, or goat. And if there are people, we have to make sure it's them. Mr. Richardson should show up differently from what I hear—his body temperature will not be as consistent, possibly even lower, than other humans."

Tarske focused the resonance imager on the barn.

"They all look like four-legged creatures, probably cows, perhaps goats, and possibly a horse, but there is one shape that for a cow is small, and for a goat is irregular, but I can't tell, not at this range," said the pilot.

"Then bring us in closer," called Tarske. "I'm having trouble getting through the roof, must be some sort of zinc-plated metal. Can you get us a side angle through the wood?"

"It'll be tricky. The air-flow around the barn will be extremely hazardous. The wind is pushing my skill to the limit."

"Hummingbird Three to Hummingbird One," came a call over the radio.

"Go ahead, Hummingbird Three."

"Hummingbirds Three through Six unable to stay aloft. Returning to nest. Over and out."

"So," said Tarske, "only two of us left." He called over the radio, "Two, do you have anything on the small boxes?"

"Only four matches in the middle-sized matchbox, the small boxes are empty. Standing by."

"They could be in the house, sir," said the pilot, getting anxious to leave. "Why don't we return like the other choppers and stay on the ground? No one's going anywhere in this weather."

"I want those two, and every second going by is a second we're that much farther behind," Tarske said while looking through the resonancer. "Steady this thing, will you?"

"You don't get it, do you? I can't steady this thing anymore. We'll be going steady into the barn if this keeps up," said the pilot.

"Steady," said Tarske, "I can make out something, just a little more steadiness, a little more, whoa!"

Just as Tarske was getting his subjects into view, a torrential downpour and wind shear threw the helicopter at the barn. It took the pilot's entire strength and will to dodge the barn at the last second, then pull away from a brushing against the corn field. Chopper Two clipped a branch from a tree but recovered without incident.

"Almost had them. Angh!" exclaimed a furious Tarske. "That was them, I'm sure of it."

"No chance going back. We must return and land this bird before another wind shear rips us apart. 'Hummingbird Two, return to nest.'"

"Ten-four. Over and out," replied Chopper Two.

"We have them now," grinned Tarske, grabbing the mike and ready to radio Gunter to move in. "Hummingbird One to Chief Retnug, prepare to move in."

"Chief Retnug at 37 standing by."

"Fruit flies are—"

Without warning, another wind shear hurled Chopper Two into the forest. A flash of light and explosion rattled Tarske's nerves. Chopper One's pilot overcompensated from the wind shear, throwing the helicopter sideways for a second, jostling the two around. With the landing site approaching, the pilot tried a premature landing before the helicopter went upside-down and out of control. Chopper One was short, clipped a tree, and veered terribly off from the forest where it crashed into Topabee Lake.

"Hummingbird One, do you read?" called Gunter. He waited for a reply but was greeted with silence. "Hummingbird Two, do you copy?" Several more seconds elapsed when a voice came over.

"Hummingbird Three to Chief Retnug."

"Go ahead, Three."

"Hummingbirds One and Two have not returned to nest. The other Hummingbirds have. We've lost contact with One and Two, and there was an explosion. Requesting assistance."

"All right, you two. Just what do you think you're doing up there?" asked a determined farmer with shotgun in hand. The morning sun lit through several cracks, and I figured out the time—7:00 a.m. Somehow my watch had either not gone off, or neither of us heard it.

"Helen," I said, nudging her gently, "wake up."

"I ask you again, what are you doing up there?" the farmer repeated.

"Sorry about everything, but we were lost in the woods and—" I started, but the farmer cut me off.

"You two come down this minute or else. Nice and slow, now."

Helen and I gingerly climbed down, afraid to say anything. We paused briefly at the bottom of the straw stack, brushing stems from our hair.

"Now move!" he commanded, motioning us down the stairs and out the door. Helen sneezed several times as we left the barn.

"Sam Jones, what in tarnation are you doing with that shotgun?" called a lady who walked toward us.

"Caught these two in barn—up to no good, they were," replied the farmer.

"Please, if I could explain—" I said, but the farmer replied by cocking the shotgun.

"Really, Sam, give these people a chance to explain their trespassing. Well, young man," she said, looking at me, "how do you account for yourself?"

"We were lost in the woods behind your property when the storm hit us. Forgive us for intruding, but we had to find shelter. Your barn was the best we could do at the time, with the hour being late. We would have left when possible."

"Lost? What were you doing, going on a nature hike? Where's your gear?" she asked us.

Helen and I looked at each other. I tried thinking of a good lie, but what could I say?

"Our things are in our car, unfortunately. We didn't wander through those woods by choice."

"Yer the fugitives I seen on television," said Farmer Sam, raising his shotgun.

"Now wait a minute, it's not like you think," said Helen.

"Yeah? And just what should I think? 'Dangerous,' the news said, but not because of any guns or knives—the man is a carrier, made all 'dem hospital em-ploy-ees sick, he did."

"No, it's not true. They—" I tried to say, but Sam cocked his gun again.

"Not another step closer. The both of you turn around and kneel," Farmer Sam was saying. "Martha, better call the police. We got a couple of hot potatoes."

Martha (the farmer's wife) made her way back to the house, though it was difficult to tell what went on behind us. Farmer Sam kept telling us to be still or else he'd blast us, but after a few minutes he was feeling pleased with his catch.

"They even said there was a reward for you two," he muttered.

"And you really believe that?" I asked, trying to negotiate with him.

"Quiet!" he commanded.

"It's really a shame," Helen said to me, though loud enough for Farmer Sam to hear. "They'll come in here with moon suits and quarantine the entire farm."

"I said quiet!" Farmer Sam said again, raising his voice. Helen could not be stopped.

"Of course the livestock would have to be killed. And as for you," she said, turning around to Farmer Sam, "all of you will have to be put in isolation—do you really think they'd let you go on with your lives now that we've come this close?"

"Shut up. It's a lie. You're the ones they want," he maintained.

"Even if they do leave you alone, which I doubt," she continued, "do you think you'll be rewarded? They'll thank you to keep your mouth shut, I'd imagine, unless of course—"

"Do we look sick to you?" I asked him.

"'Course not. But you're carriers," he stammered.

"Just us two? How is it everyone else is in danger but us? We're alive and quite well," I continued, "and so will you unless you make that call."

"Naw, I don't believe you, if—"

"Sam," called Martha from the house, "the sheriff is on his way over."

Farmer Sam had made a reflexive glance back at Martha when she called out, and during that instant I rushed him, barely in time to grab the shotgun. We hesitated there for a moment, struggling for the gun's control, and two shots went up in the air—the first scaring away birds, and the second stirring a rumble of hooves from the barn. Martha froze at the side door, but Helen came around the farmer from behind and kicked out his knees. I wrestled away the shotgun and aimed it at him. Helen came back around to my side.

"I assure you, sir, I have no desire to kill you. My wife and I are in a tight situation," I started. Farmer Sam was on his back, leaning up to see, but frozen in his tracks.

"You'll never get away with this," he muttered. "They'll catch you eventually. Give yerself up, boy, it's the only way."

"I don't have time to explain. You will take us into town in your truck."

"Never. I won't do it."

"You'll do it, old man," Helen said, and her sudden aggressive attitude took me by surprise. Either she was as desperate as I, or she put on her meanest demeanor in hopes of getting us out of there. "You'll do it if you want to see tomorrow."

"There's a road block ahead," said Farmer Sam. He gently slowed the old truck, shifting the column shifter from third gear to second. The clutch pedal squeaked, the engine back-fired a few times through the exhaust, and I spoke sternly from a potato sack in the back.

"One bad move, Pops, and it's all over. Make this smooth." I jabbed the shotgun's barrel through a rusty hole from the bed to the cab. It poked through the cushion into Farmer Sam's back, and he jerked slightly. Helen was in another pota-to sack—the entire bed was filled with sacked potatoes.

"Farmer Sam, how are you?" asked a deputy at the road check.

"Oh, fine as usual. Just headin' in to the co-op to sell these 'taters."

"You haven't seen two haggard-looking people around your place, have you?"

There was a pause—enough of a pause for Farmer Sam to signal something. I quietly pressed the barrel against his back.

"No, everything's been quiet as usual," he said at last.

"Very well. Drive on."

"Not bad," I said, "though you almost had your right kid-ney filled with lead. Just keep quiet and keep driving."

Tarske pulled himself to shore, spitting blood from several broken teeth. Black bruises formed on the left side of his face, his eyes were bloodshot, and his clothing torn. He started to get up and walk but fell down in shock from excessive blood loss. Several pilots from the other helicopters pulled him back to his feet and carried him to the limo, where he was taken to the hospital.

"What happened?" asked Gunter when he arrived. The hel-icopter launch site was buzzing with excitement from the emergency vehicles. While firefighters got through to Helicopter Two, rescue workers pulled out the pilot from Helicopter One.

"Everything went according to plan," started the pilot of Helicopter Three, "at least at first. We followed Choppers One and Two over the woods until we came to a farm. Great winds from a storm tossed us around, so Choppers Three through Six returned to base. One and Two stayed behind—Tarske was so hot on the trail he just wouldn't give up. The rest of us had hardly landed when we saw a fireball coming out of the woods. It was a horrible sight—I could see the tail end of the chopper poking just outside the infernal flames, and the other chopper seemed to hit something and plunged into the lake. Somehow Tarske swam to shore, but we rushed him off to the hospital. They're hauling out Pucket now—the pilot of Chopper One."

"If it ain't one thing it's another," grumbled Gunter as he watched the emergency crew place Pucket on a stretcher and carry him to the ambulance. "This operation was cursed from the start. As soon as we saw that dog—"

"Excuse me, Sgt. Gunter," said the EMT, "we need you to come to the hospital with us."

"Yeah, yeah," Gunter said, waving the EMT off. "I'll follow you boys over."

The EMT closed the ambulance door before it sped off.

"When that storm lets up, I want you back out watching from the sky. If Tarske was that close to finding them, and I think he was, he'll expect no less. Now I'm going over to the hospital to check on him," Gunter said to the pilot of Chopper Three. A minute later, he was racing along behind the ambulance off to Topabee Hospital. Though the storm had let up some, several side roads were flooded out, and the main road had several hydroplanable puddles. Several times the ambulance and Gunter nearly swerved off the road, but quick reflexes kept them on the slow, monotonous trail. Gunter was tired, and he paused in the squad car for several seconds after parking in front of Topabee Hospital. He staggered in, had a brief conversation with the main desk personnel, then sat for what he thought was ten minutes.

Gunter awoke with a chill. A draft from the emergency doors buffeted his face, and he peered at the clock above the main desk. Six o'clock. The sun was alighting the earth, and Gunter was now sore and hungry.

"Gotta remember not to sleep in a chair again. Where's the cafeteria?" he grumbled though no one seemed to pay him attention.

"What's the status of Jack Tarske?" Gunter asked the main-desk receptionist. Before she could reply, Tarske limped down the main corridor on crutches, his left leg and arm being in casts. His teeth were wired up, and a bandage covered part of his left face.

"Let's get a move on, Sergeant," Tarske said as the two went out to Gunter's squad car. Gunter heard Tarske mutter something about "lost time" but thought it best not to ask further.

"Sergeant Gunter, do you read? Sergeant Gunter," came a call over the radio. Gunter was pulling out of the Topabee Hospital as he picked up the microphone.

"Gunter here, go ahead."

"McLean here, sir. I'm covering Highway 23, and a strange pickup passed through."

"How strange? Give us details, boy," replied Gunter.

"Farmer Sam was driving. He seemed agitated. Said he was taking potatoes into the co-op," said McLean.

Tarske motioned to Gunter.

"Standby, McLean," radioed Gunter. "What is it?"

"Who is this 'Farmer Sam'?" Tarske pressed. A suspicious brow rose.

"He has several hundred acres," Gunter paused, connecting thoughts, "several hundred acres next to the woods—the woods leading to Topabee Lake."

Gunter locked the tires into a 180-degree-spin U-turn and accelerated madly down to intercept.

"McLean, you are to pursue Farmer Sam and pull him over until we arrive. Do you copy?"

"Roger, Sergeant."

"It was his farm we were over," added Tarske.

"Gotta be. We've got 'em now," grinned Gunter. "You were close," he told Tarske, "Highway 37 leads South to Shairton, 29 leads west. Topabee Lake blocked the north and east side, but west from Lakeside Inn is the woods, Farmer Sam's farm, then Highway 23, which is north of 29 but parallel, going west to—"

"To the State Capitol. He must be stopped," insisted Tarske.

"Under control," replied Gunter. He readied to radio another message as one came in.

"McLean to Gunter. I'm in pursuit of the truck. I see someone in the back, she's...whoa!" Sounds of tires squealed over the radio.

"McLean, report," called Gunter. Static. "McLean, do you copy? Report!"

"Several bags of...fosh, she's armed!" came an agitated McLean voice. Shots rang out over the radio. McLean's transmission stopped shortly thereafter. Gunter continued his harried pace, now in full siren. Gunter relayed McLean's triangulated transmission location (provided by the station) to nearby cars and had them converge on the pickup truck. Another officer reported seeing McLean's car in the ditch along Highway 29—peppered with shot holes. No sign of the truck.

"Pull over!" I commanded. Farmer Sam stopped abruptly, sliding onto the road's gravel shoulder.

"What's this all about?" Farmer Sam said, shaking.

"Get out and walk over to those trees," I ordered. Farmer Sam complied. "Turn around and count to one hundred. If you turn around and look or stop counting, I'll shoot." Farmer Sam faced away from the truck and began counting.

"One, two, three, four..."

I helped Helen into the front seat, blood coming from her right arm.

"He hit you, Helen," I said.

"It's not bad, though it feels like fire. Throwing the potatoes off reduced my protection, and after I fired the shotgun at him, he hit me. The truck swerved—"

"—because Farmer Sam was startled by the gun fire," I interrupted.

"I see," Helen acknowledged. "The cop went off the road, as you saw, but my arm..."

"Don't worry. Here," I said, ripping off my shirt, "use this as a tourniquet. Be careful to avoid gangrene."

"I know. Remember, Jacob, I'm the nurse."

We continued driving for a half hour when the engine sputtered and died. I repeatedly engaged the starter without success. The engine would not catch.

"Dead. Well Helen, are you strong enough to walk?" I asked.

"I've lost much blood. I should really conserve my energy," she said quietly. She was nearly asleep.

"No choice, I'm afraid. If we stay here, they'll find us. The truck won't start, and unless we do something quickly, we'll be dead ducks. How far from Dr. Brandberg are we? Helen?" Helen had dozed for a few seconds. "Helen? Wake up, I need you."

"What? I'm sorry. Yawn, I'm so tired."

"Please, try to stay awake for a bit longer. Do you know the way by foot?"

"Yes," she replied. "We must move on. If you will help me out..." she trailed, but I was quickly on the truck's right side, helping her down. "Very well, this way," she pointed.

"Wait," I said, turning back to the truck. I had one trick left for them.

Gunter and Tarske came upon a parked pickup truck along Highway 29.

"That's Farmer Sam's truck," Gunter said.

"Pull over and stop before they see you," suggested Tarske. Gunter gently wheeled the car behind some bushes. Gunter pulled out binoculars, looked at the truck, then handed the binoculars to Tarske.

"So they're sitting in the front seat. Resting, are they? They're armed, so going in by force is a bad call. We'll take them by surprise. Call in backup and have them bring the knock-out gas. They'll block off both ends then fire the gas capsules from grenade launchers into and around the truck. Make sure your boys bring two masks for us." Tarske explained.

"I'm a step ahead of you," Gunter said, pulling out two masks from the trunk. Gunter next radioed for backup and the knock-out gas. Five minutes passed before everyone got in position.

"They haven't moved," Tarske beamed.

"All cars," radioed Gunter. "Call off in sequence."

"Jackson here."

"Rogers here."

"Smith here."

"Winthorpe here."

"Masks on," ordered Gunter. "Prepare gas. Ready, fire!"

Two gas capsules penetrated the truck's cab. A third landed in front, the fourth in the truck's bed.

"Close in!" ordered Gunter. Four squad cars rushed in with Gunter and Tarske behind (the other two came from the opposite direction).

Jackson and Rogers ran up to the truck, one on each side, and opened the doors. They stopped with disappointment, relaxed, and waved Gunter over.

"What's the problem? Why don't you pull them out?" Gunter asked, his voice muffled by the mask. Jackson pointed into the truck. Gunter saw two potato sacks where Jacob and Helen were supposed to be.

Though Helen had stopped bleeding, she was weak, and I had to help her walk through the woods. We'd been travelling for twenty minutes or more—I'd actually lost track of time—and was wondering how much longer she could last. I felt badly for being aggressive and hostile toward Farmer Sam, but I put him behind me and concentrated on getting to the rendezvous point.

"There's a dirt road ahead," I said to Helen.

"Follow it," she mumbled.

"Which way?" I asked. Helen mumbled again, but I couldn't make out her words.

"Helen?"

"All right you two, don't make a move," came a voice around a tree. Another person came from behind a boulder. Both had police uniforms, though slightly different from McLean's at the road block.

"What is this?" I asked. "Who are you?"

"This way," they motioned with their guns. One picked up his portable radio. "We have them, sir."

(This concludes Part II of *Unseen Assailant*. Join Helen and Jacob in the final episode (Part III) in the next edition of *Fictionnaire*.)

Wayward West

May 18, 1993

Oafuss was late—he missed being born for the first of spring and missed Easter. Oafuss was born on the last day of spring, late June. He was a Hampshire sheep and had a twin who was just as late. He remembered little about his early life, but he was weaned early and grazed with the other sheep—often playfully. While most sheep could think of nothing but eating, Oafuss spent some time eating and the rest running around, chasing the other young sheep but sometimes coming too close to the herd's edge where one of the dogs would chase him back.

From time to time it seemed some young sheep would disappear from the herd, never to return. He thought it odd, but being a sheep he couldn't give it too much thought, and he played away his late summer and fall in a combination of open pastures and rolling hills. His twin, Oafell, usually accompanied Oafuss around the herd as they "terrorized" other sheep. Herding dogs kept them from exploring into the rocky slopes or fast-moving streams.

As the days grew shorter and the grass less abundant, the Oafa twins played less and ate more to store winter fat and build a winter coat. The first snowflake of winter was an odd experience for Oafuss—he had never seen the white fluff before, and the twins chased each other around, kicking snow in each other's faces. With the snow covering the pasture, the herd was more often than not kept in the main pen.

Oafuss was tired of being cramped with thousands of other sheep. He wanted to play as he and Oafell did in the summer days. It was not to be. Winter became severe, and on one of the coldest days, Oafuss watched several hundred other sheep freeze to death. He was lucky to have survived, but his sire was of especially hardy stock, and the Oafa twins lived through the unusually harsh winter.

With spring came the Day of Shearing. The entire herd was lined up and sheared from head to foot for the wool, including the Oafa twins. Oafuss felt cold upon losing his winter coat, but within several days he felt normal enough. How fresh the other sheep looked, how exciting, how new. Hopes and expectations for summer fun rekindled in Oafuss's heart, and although he noticed a mass disappearance of young lambs before Easter, Oafuss felt happy to be again going out to pasture to feed and play.

Oafuss and Oafell started with their usually running antics, but they noticed they weren't as quick as they used to be. Oafell soon spent more time grazing than playing with Oafuss, who was upset by his twin's decision to be like the other sheep. Oafuss, however, noticed his own bit of a slowdown, especially compared with younger sheep getting around faster and receiving most of the attention.

During a particular late spring day, the wind suddenly picked up, and dark ominous clouds approached quickly from the west. The sheep dogs quickly forced the herd back to the pen, and Oafuss knew something horrible was about to happen, though he didn't know what.

Day turned to night. Westerly winds carried large objects and debris through the air including a torrid rain, and the herd went berserk from fright. Thousands of sheep pushed to the east, forcing the fencing down and killing a few hundred who fell and were trampled. The herd dogs were as frightened and deserted the sheep. Shepherds had long ago gone underground as the tornado's roar echoed through the valley. Trees, fences, and buildings were obliterated. The herd had started a stampede to the east, fleeing for their lives.

Oafuss was near the front of the stampede. He pulled aside and waited for Oafell to catch up, but he never came. Oafuss didn't know which sounded worse—the stampede's thundering or the tornado's roar. Hundreds upon hundreds of sheep *tromchomped* by. Finding Oafell was to be a lucky event if any—Oafuss could not scan quickly enough to spot him. The final sheep passed, but Oafuss's twin could not be seen. He was by himself, the last of the herd now a hundred yards away. Before he could decide whether to follow the herd or go back to search the dead sheep, the black funnel was upon him. Oafuss dove into a ditch and under an overturned watering trough. Within a few seconds, the stormy fury bellowed through, the trees snapped loudly, stray animals or people cried out, and the earth shook. Drenched, Oafuss shivered in fright and whimpered, thinking his life had ended.

At that moment, Lorra Bear looked at a puppy, adjusted the contrast, viewed different sizes, then asked Ken, "How do you get facing pages?" She didn't wait for an answer, but instead performed the function perfectly, and viewed both pages of the document at a time. After asking the time, she went back to her document and continued checking for any mistakes she may have made. Now I should be continuing the story on Oafuss, and soon I will, but as for Lorra Silvertip Bear, she continues her document editing for her school assignment (she is a teacher, remember?).

Oafuss went into some sort of shock, then sleep. When he regained consciousness (since there is little to tell of his unconscious doings), he climbed out from under the watering trough to find it sunny though wet. The sheep farm was destroyed—the animals were gone, and only a handful of shepherds remained, rummaging through the wreckage. One spotted Oafuss, pointed, then ran after him. Frightened, Oafuss ran from the valley, up the hills, and into the mountains where he travelled for some time east, trying to catch the herd. There was a narrow mountain path that he followed, though vegetation was scarce. After several hours of rapid travelling, the day converged into dusk. Oafuss was tired and looked for a safe place to sleep. He found a small cave of bats, which frightened him so, but after further inspection, he found a nook where the bats were not. He tried to sleep, but between the flapping of the bats and the howling of the wolves, Oafuss managed no better than scattered light sleeps.

Though irritable the following day, Oafuss continued his trek through the mountain paths in search of the herd. I'm afraid as the day continued, his spirits fell. He realized he might never see the herd again, and not having spent time in the wild, his future life was in serious jeopardy. There were too many predators to avoid, and too little vegetation to consume, unless he went to the valleys, but then he would be an easy mark for the birds of prey, wolves, and foxes. Oafuss kept to the mountains. On his second night alone, he was unable to find a suitable cave, so he took refuge under a bush. Several times passing rodents nibbled at his feet, and at other times an attuned ear saved him from becoming a wolf's next meal as he scampered off into hiding elsewhere.

After several weeks of travelling, Oafuss was unsure which direction he was to take. It was clear his search for the herd was essentially fruitless, but what else was there? Perhaps he could find other sheep he could mingle with and again sleep peacefully. It was the only thought he had, the one driving idea that kept him from giving up in despair to become a wolf's next meal.

Oafuss's once shiny coat had turned dingy and rough. After the fourth week of being on his own, his hooves became sore from some sort of thrush or foot rot. Travel became difficult and depressing. Often he rested in the cool shade before continuing his hopeless journey. Water was becoming scarce, and the merciless sun beating on his heavy coat kept his mouth dry.

One particular day, Oafuss could hear the barking of sheep dogs. He turned to look, and there in the valley below were sheep, thousands of them. He tried getting up to follow, but his hooves were badly damaged from the foot rot—he buckled to his knees. He was tempted to "bahhh" for help, but it could only serve his predators. Desperately he tried again but fell even faster than before. He could only watch the sheep down below as they grazed happily, the shepherds chatting, and the sheep dogs playfully running around the herd. Oafuss wept.

Several days passed before Oafuss could walk on his feet again. Miraculously, his foot rot had lessened, enough for him to walk, but it had begun to rain. It rained for several days continuously—at times it beat harshly upon Oafuss, at others it was a light sprinkle. He hadn't seen the sun, for which he was at first thankful but later regretful. He drank from puddles but slept in damp and cold areas, giving him a nasty cold and making him weak again. Although his foot rot wasn't too bad, it still gave him pain when he walked, and after another few days of travelling, he started getting roundworms that caused him to experience weight loss.

I have nearly given up on Oafuss at this point. If the foot rot doesn't get him, the roundworms will. How he's managed to avoid wolves, bears, or carnivorous birds amazes me, in fact I'm convinced most sheep would have died by now—many have—but Oafuss for some strange reason is destined to survive. Some higher force wants him alive for something it seems, even if it means being tortured by one ailment or another.

Weak and thin from the roundworms, Oafuss decided it was time to come down from the mountains and eat in the pasture, despite the risks involved. Otherwise, he was condemned to starvation, this much he was sure. The weeks of rain had finally stopped, the sun came out, and oddly it was turning out to be a rather grand day for Oafuss. He ate, ate, and ate. No bother from the birds, no wolves to run from, all was quiet and happy. He rested his thrushened hooves for a few minutes when he heard the barking of a sheep dog. Happy, he trotted quickly toward the barking. One shepherd noticed him and came to him. Oafuss was too tired of being away from the herd to flee the shepherd. He held his ground as the shepherd examined him.

"Looks like it could be one of ours, maybe one of the strays after the 'nado hit. Look, he even has our markings. Poor thing, his hooves have the foot rot, and he's too thin to be healthy—might have some disease or even worms. We should take him in for treatment," said the shepherd, and while the other sheep grazed, Oafuss was taken to a nearby building where the shepherd treated his foot root, gave him vermifuge for worms, and antibiotics for any remaining bacteria.

Within a week he was happily roaming with this new herd, which could have been the one he was with before, but he wasn't sure until one morning he was selected from the herd along with a few hundred other sheep and was placed in a moving cart of sorts. It was then he recognized his twin, Oafell, whom he had not seen since before the tornado. The two were very happy upon seeing each other, so happy. It seemed everything was going right for Oafuss, his whole life looked promising, and he had so much to live for.

When the carts stopped, the sheep were butchered.

The StoryMaster: Part II

May 24, 1993

Skipping to the end, I read the last paragraph:

> The truck driver didn't see Laurie and abruptly changed lanes, moving from right to left. Laurie swerved but not in time. She deflected off the truck and into an underpass's center pillar. Laurie died instantly, her alcohol-filled blood draining rapidly from her body and onto her car's interior. Laurie Jenkins, another victim. The Black Cat walked on the hood, then into the car, sniffed the corpse, then left.

(End of Part I, beginning of Part II)

I was shocked at how similar my story was to the newspaper article of Laurie's death. How could this be, did I see the future in my sleep or did I cause her death? It was too much for me to analyze, the night before, Beth, and now this unexpected death. Perhaps it was some cruel joke, some jealous prank from Qadon. I spent the first part of the afternoon in a shock/daze, standing next to the living room window and staring outside. Presently the phone rang.

"Bob? Are you there?" came a voice over the answering machine. I approached the phone slowly. "If you're home, pick up. Something terrible has happened. This is Beth, Beth Reynolds? Please, Bob, pick up—"

"Hello, Beth," I said, my voice quivering.

"You know then," she said, her voice somber.

"About Laurie?"

"Yes. Well I hate to say this, but her wild lifestyle caught up with her. She—"

"I'm not so sure it was her fault," I said unwittingly.

"What is that supposed to mean?" she asked, unsettled.

"What have you heard?"

"Not much. I saw it on the twelve o'clock news. 'Laurie Jones dies in a drunk-driving accident. Her car was crumpled by a large truck.' Seems she had a pet cat with her, but he ran off, at least according to the police," explained Beth.

"Did you happen to see this cat? What did it look like?"

"No, but someone said it was black all over and had a silver collar. Odd."

"Very odd, but not just the accident," I slipped.

"All right, Mr. Perkins, you're holding out on me. Come on, spill your guts. What's up, huh?" she demanded.

"I'm not sure I can explain. It begins with this morning," I tried to say.

"It begins with last night, if *odd* is the topic. I don't usually let myself get drunk, but oh well, as long as nothing happened. Except this morning—didn't you sleep well? You accountants can't stay away from the numbers on the computer."

"Beth, if I could just explain—it's not like that. I—you—"

"Bob, something *is* eating you. I can tell you're reluctant to go into detail, at least over the phone. Let's see—I'm having some friends over this evening for dinner and cards. Why don't you come over? Well?"

"Sure. By the way, how did you get my phone number?" I wondered.

"Marie and I are good friends. You remember her—Human Resources?"

"Yes, Marie. And here I thought it was against company policy."

"Not at all. I just explained how I needed to...well, it doesn't matter now. Do you know where I live? No, of course you don't. Do you know where Grand Ledge is?" she asked.

"Tetra is out in Grand Ledge. Steve and I were out there yesterday," I said.

"Yes, I used to work for Tetra but received a promotion to Hamilton. I liked my apartment so much I decided to stay. If you're coming from Lansing—are you?"

"Assume I am."

"Easy enough. Just take Highway 43 until you enter the city. The first light should be Waterford Road—turn left. Go north for several blocks until you see the apartment complex on the right—Hillendale. I'm in the 4010 building, room number 124. Buzz from the lobby, and I'll let you in."

"Sounds simple enough. When should I pop over?"

"Around seven, if you don't mind the wait. I have some errands to run this afternoon before starting on the roast beef—I hope that's fine with you."

"Not a problem."

"Good. See you at seven then," she said, and our telephoning was finished.

Though speaking to Beth settled my nerves, I still felt badly regarding Laurie. Untimely as it was, I drank two shots of whiskey to unfocus my attention. After the second one had finished burning my gastronomic tissues, the phone rang again.

"Robert? How are you? That story you wrote—incredible!" came an excited Gary.

"Gary! I must ask you *not* to publish it," I pleaded.

"Really, Rob, you must quit taunting me with this nickel-and-dime stuff. Don't get me wrong—it's good reading, but we really *need* a novel, something we can not only sell as a number one bestseller, but also for the movie rights. The Robert Burke novels carry their weight in gold. Are you really happier in this accounting job?"

"I'm not sure. Not sure."

"The novel, Rob. Give it some thought—we could expand your last story into something longer, if that's why you want it delayed, or this could be the introduction to something greater. I know you, always up to something and ready to pull the rug out from under the reader."

"Sure, Gary," I said, unable to think straight. "A novel? Perhaps. I'll let you know," I assured him, trying to make the conversation short.

"Grand. I look forward to your next upload. Cheers, old man!"

"Cheers," I said before re-placing the receiver. I sat for a moment on my couch when my head unexpectedly felt light and unstable. Was the room spinning? I could not keep my posture, slumbering onto the couch and into a deep sleep.

> ...watched as the magical spheres floated through the air. They bounced off the walls ever-so-gracefully, off the furniture, off people, and continued floating with a resonating sound similar to a wet china glass being stroked. The different sized balls had different pitches —the combination effected eerie but pleasant musical eddies.
>
> The one gentleman in the middle watched as one or another sphere came his way. He inhaled to draw it close to him, then exhaled to send it up and away. The sphere would increase in pitch then decrease as it approached and went away. One particular sphere, however, was no larger than a grape. It approached too quickly—the man sucked it rapidly down his throat into his trachea.
>
> Several others laughed, thinking he'd swallowed it. Only after half a minute of torturous though unproductive coughing did we realize he was choking. His face turned red as he struggled—several people tried various techniques to dislodge the wildly razzing sphere from his throat.
>
> What followed was more confusion than anything. The man had fallen into a bluish-gray corpse, suffocated from the thing. Lights flashed, sirens sounded...sirens sounded...

Startled, I jumped. I was in my living room, having fallen asleep on the couch. A passing emergency vehicle had disturbed my slumber, and as I looked out to identify which kind, I saw a glimpse of a black cat scurry around the building's corner. The sun had nearly set.

"The time," I said in a panic, remembering Beth's party at seven. Running to the kitchen, I saw the clock—seven thirty in the evening.

"I'm late, I'm late," was the only thing I could say, quickly changing into new clothes, rushing around for other things, and blundering out the door, into the car, and onto the road heading for Grand Ledge. I resisted the urge to speed, despite my tardiness. Being pulled over in my stuporous state would not have been good, not good at all.

"It was just a dream," I said to myself, pulling into Grand Ledge. "Not real—just a release for negative energy," I mumbled while pulling into Hillendale Apartments. "These dreams —they do NOT come to life, a mere fiction, like my writing, like my writing..."

I buzzed room 124 in the 4010 building, and Beth's voice came over the intercom. After letting her know my presence, the door buzzed, and I opened it to a modern but artistically well-done interior lobby and hallway.

"Come on in," Beth said, giving me the tour of her spacious accommodations. I was introduced to her friends—none of which were from Hamilton Insurance: Frieda, a short and heavy set brunette; Staisi, a tall and slender red-headed lady; Kelvin, a medium-build guy with short, black hair, and Bo, an obese but wild guy who loved cracking jokes and made it a point to be in practically every conversation.

"I'm so sorry for being late," I tried apologizing.

"Better late than dead," Bo cracked, and he went on to guzzle a beer down his throat, the foam slobbering down his face and neck. "Hiya, namesake. Have a beer. No, have two— one for here and one for the road."

In each hand I held twelve-ounce cans of cold, unopened beer.

"Betty Boop, come dance with me," Bo called to Beth.

"Ha ha, Bo, you're so funny," she called back. She turned to me and said, "I hope you don't mind, but we've already eaten. Here, let me get you a plate." I followed Beth into the kitchen where several snacks were set out on large plates along the countertop.

"This is very kind of you," I started to say, but I could hear Bo yapping about throwing popcorn in the air and catching it in one's mouth. Plate of food in hand, I looked around the corner to see the others throwing popcorn in the air, mimicking him.

"Popcorn's too easy," he said, running to a party plate full of peanut-coated M&Ms. "Let's see how these gems fly," he said, and I thought I'd watched this happen before but could not remember where or how.

"You missed," said Frieda while the others laughed.

"Hey, I'm just warming up," he boasted, throwing another M&M in the air. It went cleanly in his mouth. The others clapped, but Bo clutched his throat, making strained grunting noises. Some laughed, thinking he was joking, but his dark-red face suggested he be choking.

"He's suffocating on the M&M. Somebody do something," cried Staisi. I rushed behind him and attempted the Heimlich maneuver, but I couldn't get my arms around him. Kelvin suggested hitting him on the back, but it proved ineffective. Beth called for an emergency vehicle; I tried using a broomstick around him, but nothing. Punching him in the abdomen failed as well.

Bo had turned blue and fallen to the floor, unconscious. Staisi recommended I try dislodging the M&M from his throat, but it couldn't be reached.

"His pulse has stopped," someone said, but I could no longer help—I'd become sick and sat down from a terror I couldn't rationalize. It was happening again; I dreamt what was happening. The others were too occupied with Bo to notice my distress.

The ambulance was too late to rescue Bo—he was dead. Frieda and Staisi screamed in hysteria, Beth and Kelvin had stone-dead blankness on their faces. I was ready to vomit as I noticed a small, dark animal dart past the living room window.

The confusion of ambulance personnel, police, and agitated friends was more a blur than anything, but as the last one left, Beth was showing dear signs of exhaustion.

"All right, I will," she said, closing the door after the last one left. She and I glanced around the apartment at the empty chaos.

"I don't know what is happening," she started. "This whole weekend has been nothing but bad occurrences, one after another, and the strange thing is, you seem to either be a part of it or know something about it." She was staring at the spot on the rug where Bo had fallen.

"I don't know what to say," I said instinctually, but this was not the moment for old clichés.

"Who are you?" she demanded, her tone becoming stern, her eyes staring me down.

"What?"

"You know exactly what I mean. You can fool the others, Bob, or should I say Mr. Burke?"

"Beth, this is hardly the time—"

"To play games, I agree. Should we call Gary and ask him why you're working at Hamilton? Some sick investigative thing for some gory novel is it?"

"Gary who?" I asked, making one last attempt to hide my identity.

"Gary, your agent. Who else? I think I've had enough of this charade. If you're not going to level with me, then you might as well leave. I have nothing further to say to you." Beth looked at me for several minutes, anxiously awaiting an explanation.

"All right," I said, ending my life as Bob Perkins (at least for Beth), "it's true—I am Robert Burke, the writer. I'm sorry for the pretense, but I felt it was necessary to—"

"Necessary? To do what? Was Laurie's death necessary? Bo's? It's too unbelievable to seem true—I still can't accept it, but I *do* know you are in this."

"Really, how could it be?"

"But you knew," she said.

"Yes. As strange as it sounds, I knew, but not because I caused either incident to happen. Call it a premonition if you will, but I dreamt about Laurie's accident and found myself typing the story into my computer. You caught me as I had finished sending it off to Gary."

"But why? Why the deception to me, why the stories? I've read these recent ones in the paper—they're not like the normal Robert Burke. *He* is a positive and uplifting person, this other person writes of nothing but horror."

"And that's bad?"

"Not unto itself," she replied, "but for you to write it, yes, I think it's bad, or going to lead to bad things."

"It's not like I want these things to happen. I dream it, I write it, sometimes without realizing it, and it happens. Whether I'm predicting the future or causing it—I don't know."

Beth looked at me as if I were some freak or diseased thing, keeping her distance yet studying me.

"This is just too strange for words," she kept saying, "too strange." She then took a defensive posture, "So what happens next? Will I become one of your next victims? Or is your destruction aimed at those you do not like?"

"Beth, I wish I could explain, but I don't know any better than you. I hope nothing else happens, but I feel I have no control over this. It's as if I'm cursed, as if I've crossed the path of a stray cat," I said.

"Or black cat," she offered.

"Black cat. Now I *did* see a black cat in each of my visions—in fact, I thought I saw a black cat when Bo choked, and—"

"And there was the black cat at Laurie's accident. Weird. If I were superstitious, I'd get concerned. But it's coincidence, I'm sure, I think. No, wait...I don't know, don't know what to think anymore. Laurie then Bo, Laurie then Bo." Her agitation faded into a contemplative self, some variation of shock no doubt.

"Look, why don't we—" I started.

"We. Hmmm. Beth Reynolds and Robert Burke." She walked over to her bookcase, pulling out the book *See the Breeze*. "I can't get over it. This book in my hand was written by you?"

"Yes, though not one of my better—"

Beth began reading a passage:

"'She held the newborn baby in her arms, and for the first time in her life she wasn't just another person, not just worker number forty-seven at the factory, not just the fourth person in line at the grocery's fourteenth check-out register, not just an apartment resident in room #311, not just another thirty-one-year-old woman—she was a human being, alive, and mother to a new human being. From within her came another, and this brought her more happiness than any pay-raise or sunny day or birthday gift could ever bring. Perhaps happiness wasn't quite the word—a sense of fulfillment, completeness—a reason to be.'"

"That is my favorite passage," Beth said, "because I don't feel so alone when—"

"Alone? Beth—"

"Please, let me finish. I used to be a cynical person. Around me I'd see my friends going out and getting drunk, sleeping around, some even doing drugs—anything just to get a jolt or a high. For some reason that sort of life didn't interest me—it just seems so empty. Well, I looked for something to give me a reason or purpose, and this probably sounds so simplistic to you, but I did. It wasn't there, and I felt that my life was little more than a prison sentence—certainly a waste of time. Unfortunately, I couldn't figure out what really had worth—everything seemed valueless."

"I didn't admit this to anyone, because I've heard the stories of vulnerable people being swayed into this organization or that. I didn't want to be 'swallowed by a whale' as you say in this book. I did want something meaningful, and some were even telling me I needed a man."

"Well, that was a farce. I had dated on and off during high school, but the boys—and they were boys—were so immature and obnoxious. I was so sick of the faked patronage that I stayed clear of them for several years. I was also tired of school—I didn't go to college. My parents were against this, and I can understand why. They provided the best of home life for me—my older brother and sister graduated with honors from the University of Michigan. I felt pushed, pressured—I just wanted to make a clean break and live my own life. That's when the emptiness began."

"I really don't know why I'm telling you this, except the passage in this book. My first job was in a factory, working on the assembly line. My second was as a secretary, though I'm sure that was due to my gender and my looks. I had no formal training—everything I learned as a secretary was on-the-job. But the boss—whoa, did he hit on me every day or what? I quit that job and worked as a secretary somewhere else, but it was the same story all over with the addition of other people bossing me around as if I were some piece of dirt they could tread upon."

"I was regretting my decision not to attend U of M, and I wanted to blame someone, but each time the finger pointed back to me. My pride kept me from crawling back to my parents and asking for help. I wanted my freedom and respect. I couldn't find respect anywhere, though my pet goldfish didn't seem to mind my feeding them. Sometimes I'd come home with such exhausted feet from the heels, I could do nothing but sit and watch television, which seemed idiotic after awhile, or read. Funny, that was the only thing I really enjoyed, but finding a good book is a challenge. I've read much garbage and have wondered which story-mill this or that book came from."

"Then I saw *See the Breeze* by an unknown, Robert Burke. It wasn't a bestseller; I was actually looking at the book next to it and put the book back when *See the Breeze* caught my eye. 'Not another pseudo-philosophical book,' is what I thought, but after reading the first and last paragraphs of the book, I was hooked."

"First and last paragraphs?" I asked.

"That's one of my ways of scoping out a book. The summaries on the back of these paperbacks are usually just sugar coatings. I bought the book, though, and spent the next couple of days reading it. Finally I found someone who seemed to understand, who could make some sense out of this bizarre world. I was so happy, and it carried me through the days as I waited for another Robert Burke book to come out."

"After reading the second book, I was determined to do something with my life and make a positive difference, no matter how apparently insignificant to others—it would matter to me. I spent time with my nieces, Mollie and Dori, and I realized how fun they could be though mischievous at times. My life changed, but there was the one nagging question—what to do about survival, my job, and my future. Well, I took a business course at a night school to see if it interested me. It did, and I've nearly completed my degree. With my improved skills, I've worked my way up from a lowly secretary to Claims Manager at Hamilton Insurance."

"And me? How did you know, especially about Gary?" I asked curiously.

"That's the strangest part so far. When I read your books, I envisioned you as some middle-aged man with a long, grey beard, bifocals, and smoking a pipe, writing his stories from some cottage on a lake. Then Bob Perkins shows up at Hamilton, and after hearing the rumor, I wanted to see if there was any truth to it. I checked with Marie in Human Resources, and she quietly showed me your background. Further investigation showed Bob Perkins did not exist before his college years where he earned a degree in accounting. Coincidentally, Bob Perkins emerged only a month after the supposed disappearance of Robert Burke."

"It made me suspicious enough to think you were he, but I had no trump card to place on the table. When I saw you uploading the story and in the computer address saw it directed to—"

"Hold on one second here, how could you have seen that address? It was on the screen for half a second, perhaps less. You couldn't have remembered—" I explained, but she cut me off.

"When the need is great, I can photographically remember whatever I see. It's rare, and most who have it can't socialize normally in society, but somehow I have the best of both worlds, well, maybe not the very best, but good enough. With the snippet of information, I gambled."

"You gambled. My secret is ruined. You realize what this means? I'll have to resign from Hamilton immediately—the cat is out of the bag."

"The black cat may be out and about, but only I know the details. Everyone else thinks it's one big joke. But here in my living room is someone I both know and don't know. Does the writing reflect the man?"

"Does it?" I asked back.

"That I'm not sure. You just seem so mysterious, so secret, as if the only way you can communicate is through your writing. Is this true?"

"No, well perhaps a little. I shy from the media, but around my friends I'm open. Usually, though, my fans go berserk if they see me in person as if I am some god who can cure their illness or rescue them from a life of misery. You're different. You aren't fazed by my presence. I don't feel I have to hide from you. I can talk to you, and you treat me like a normal human being."

"Because you treat me like a human being. That's the other thing that caught me by surprise. My experience with accountants has been that they are very detail oriented, some to the extent where they look at people as commodities to be bought or sold. It's almost as bad as..." Beth's words drifted.

"As bad as what?"

"Gaud, it gives me the shivers thinking about it. There are some things that'll faze me yet, Mr. Burke. Nothing against computer people. Steve Sharp is nice enough, though that's probably his age more than anything. But Qadon, boy oh boy, when I think of compu-nerds, he's the one. I made the mistake of going out with him once, seeing a *boring* movie. He kept telling me how powerful his home computer was and asked if I'd like to see it, or how this computer company or that computer company was going to take over the world, and if I didn't work with these computers and buy from this-and-this company, I'd be enslaved by something else. If-then-else was how he kept talking. His brain is fried. And as for his taste...ucky. I seem to attract the bad ones, unfortunately."

"Well I can't blame 'em. You are quite attractive, Beth."

"Oh, um, ok. On that note, it's been a long day. I think I'm ready to turn in. I hope you don't mind." She hinted for my exit.

"Of course not. I'll call you tomorrow," I said, writing down her phone number.

"Well about that, I'll be gone most of the day with Mollie and Dori. Monday at work? Don't worry, Mr. Perkins, your secret is safe with me."

Why did you kick him out? Beth thought after I'd left. *You blew it. You like the guy—it's obvious he likes you—why be so shy about it? Next time, don't let him get away without a kiss.*

Your secret is safe with me. The words echoed through my mind Sunday. I could do little else but try to relax, the quiet before the storm it seemed.

Seeing Laurie's empty desk reminded me of the black weekend. I had barely taken off my coat when Clarise approached me.

"Did you hear the news about Laurie Jones?" she asked quietly.

"Yes. Very unfortunate."

"We're sending flowers over to the funeral home. Would you sign the card for Laurie's flowers, please?"

"Certainly."

After scrawling my name and returning the card to Clarise, she went to the next office down the way. The main office was unusually quiet, and I could hardly think without the constant feeling of guilt for the blackness. The morning was uneventful until around 11:30 when I spilled coffee on the computer keyboard. It was hastily cleaned up, but the keyboard failed to operate normally.

"Sharp? Perkins here."

"Good morning, Perkins, how are you?" Steve said.

"Fine thanks. Listen, I've been a little edgy this morning—"

"Haven't we all," he interjected.

"—and accidentally spilled my coffee on my keyboard. Now it doesn't work. Can you help me?"

"Boy, you certainly know when to call, right before lunch and all," he joked.

"I know. I'm such a bother. Really, if it's too much trouble—"

"No, I'll be right over. I have a spare keyboard you can use until yours is cleaned," he offered.

"Thanks, appreciate it very much."

"No problem," he replied, and within a few minutes he was unplugging the soiled keyboard and plugging in the clean one.

"I promise I won't be so clumsy again," I said.

"Just as an insurance bonus," he said, grinning.

"A Hamilton Insurance bonus?" I joked.

"Not bad, not bad. I'll put on this keyboard protector—this'll keep it clean until your other one is ready. So how was your weekend?" he asked.

"Huh? My weekend?" I asked back defensively.

"At Black Shoes? I heard Qadon and Fitzgerald got in a fight."

"Yeah, it happened right in front of me. Before that, Laurie and Norma were thrown out after causing a commotion," I explained.

"And I hear you were in the middle of this commotion," he said with a knowing look.

"All right, yes—you warned me about Laurie. She came onto me. I didn't think anything of it, but Norma kept yanking at her and, well, I think you know the rest."

"I've heard," Steve commented, "but what I'd really like to know is your perspective of the Qadon vs. Fitzgerald fight—oh, look at the time, it's after twelve. I'm going out to lunch today, care to join me?"

"You really want to know, don't you? Sure, why not?" And with that we went off in Steve's sports car to a restaurant several miles away.

"We'll take the freeway," he said, but he might as well have said, "we're going to hit a hundred miles per hour," because that was precisely what he did.

"Do you always go this fast?" I asked, my heart pounding.

"Only when I'm in a hurry or am on my lunch break. Seems an hour isn't quite enough when I go out to eat."

The restaurant was busy enough, but we managed to find a booth and were greeted by a pleasant waitress.

"Are you ready to order?" she asked, looking at me first. I looked back and was about to request the...in my mind I saw the image of a black Cadillac going off the road and into a ditch. The vision passed, and in the waitress's eyes I saw the reflection of a cat passing by the window.

"Sir?" she said to me. I quickly turned toward the window in time to see a tail disappear.

"Perkins, what is it?" asked Steve.

"Nothing. Sorry, I'll have the chicken soup with sandwich," I said. She asked me what sort of bread I wanted, and after responding, I tuned out the conversation she had with Steve, thinking of nothing but the car going into the ditch.

"So how did the fight start?" Steve asked me, and my attention focused back on the story. I told him. It wasn't until we were back on the road that the vision took hold of reality. We were late—it was after one o'clock, and Steve pushed his car to 105 on his speedo. In front was a car blocking our path, and Steve nosed up inches from the black sedan's rear bumper.

"Sharp, is this really necessary?" I started to ask, but Steve had already made his move, swerving around the Cadillac, and in the process lightly nudging it in the left, rear corner. Steve continued barreling down the road, gaining speed quickly. I glanced back to see the Cadillac going off the road, but our going around a curve cut off my view.

"Damn cat crossing the road," yelled Steve, spiking his brakes to miss it. Upon hearing the screeching tires, the black cat scampered across the road and up a tree. Not knowing what to say or think, I remained silent.

I think my nerves were nearly shot by the time I left work that Monday afternoon. Steve's driving was enough to unsettle me, and there was more than the usual ruckus in the main office. After requesting an early exit from Fitzgerald, I returned to my humble apartment and took a restless nap. The phone rang, waking me that Monday evening.

"He fired him," she said.

"What? Who?"

"You had to be there. I had a 2:00 with CP, but he was late, which was unusual for him. Then he came thundering through the door with a bandage on his forehead. His shirt was stained with coffee and blood, and all he could say was, 'Where is that Sharp?' He was furious. Apparently CP was driving along the road, back from a meeting with another company head, when Sharp bumped his car in the rear. Sharp raced off, but CP lost control of his car and landed in a ditch. The Caddy was ruined. Everyone was upset about Sharp's termination, though I hear Qadon had a smile on his face, which can only mean one thing—"

"Let me guess," I interrupted. "Qadon is now the DP Manager."

"Yup. I don't like it. Qadon did most of the programming and small-time maintenance. He doesn't know what's going on, unlike Sharp. Now they think he can do the job? They're making a big mistake," Beth lamented.

"It also puts you in a more difficult situation," I added.

"I know. I'll have to deal with Qadon as a peer. Yuck."

The first thing Jeff Qadon did Tuesday was change the system passwords, had everyone change his/her password, and he started reconfiguring the system to make it "more efficient." However, it served to make people's jobs more difficult. Qadon and Fitzgerald had a long afternoon meeting with CP and when it was over, Fitzgerald called me into his office for a meeting.

"Perkins. I've called you in my office to discuss some important matters," he started, closing his door. "There are going to be some major changes around here, so don't be surprised if you see some personnel switching around and some leaving."

"Leaving? Who's quitting?"

"This is strictly confidential. I also want to point out I am against most of what will happen, but Qadon appeals to CP in some strange way, he—"

"Appeals? How odd," I commented.

"You should have heard the way he was cutting down Sharp, and CP was taking it hook, line and sinker. Qadon has blamed most of the computer problems on Sharp and is recommending a complete overhaul of the computer system. Worse, Qadon is pointing his finger at several employees he thinks should be terminated."

"Can he do this? Why would CP believe him?"

"Because Qadon has this supposed computer log that shows people's activities, even the electronic mail, and is handing it over to CP to support Qadon's recommendations," Fitzgerald explained. "I don't know how much is true or how much is fictitious, but Sharp would never do such a thing— *that* guy had ethics, but Qadon has none. He's using his situation to manipulate CP for his personal gain."

"Who has Qadon implicated?" I asked.

"Relax, you're in the clear, especially since you've been on board for only a week. But watch for the future—he could implicate you."

"All right, I'm in the clear. Who isn't in the clear?" I demanded.

"Remember, this is highly confidential. In fact, I'm breaking a promise to keep this silent. Norma Staples, Bill Crawford, and Beth Reynolds."

I was careful to keep my composure as if the termination of one or all did not personally affect me.

"Norma, she's a clerk; Crawford and Reynolds are management, though. That seems a lofty stab," I noted.

"Indeed, if I weren't there, he might have implicated me as well, after the rumble he and I had Friday night."

"Is there a personal motive for the others?" I asked.

"Probably. Although I'm not 100% sure, I believe the reasoning behind Norma is because she was good friends with Laurie."

"I don't understand."

"He's superstitious," Fitzgerald explained. "He thinks that since Norma was close to the late Laurie, Norma will jinx the company. Crawford because he knows too much and can tell

Qadon where to go. Reynolds because he chases her, but she tells him to 'bug off.' That's the best I can figure."

"Well," I said, becoming a bit perturbed, "this seems so ridiculous and unfair; doesn't CP know this will hurt him?"

"Not the way Qadon puts it. He figures each can be let go, just before a holiday, then a replacement can be found, if necessary. If not, the remaining employees can work extra hard to cover and thus provide a cost savings to the company. Just keep your eyes open—you may end up taking over my position."

"Fitz, I just can't believe it," I exclaimed.

"Believe. I'm already looking for work elsewhere just in case. CP won't listen to me anymore, and if he goes the way Qadon is leading him, this company will be going down a path I do not like. I'll quit before I'm fired."

Then I had another vision. Trying to stop it proved impossible as a house appeared before my eyes, a house burning to the ground. It was a horrible sight, and I could see a human shape running out of the flames and collapsing on the front lawn. The vision faded as a shadow from Fitzgerald's window blocked the sun. I turned to see the face of the black cat.

"Look," I said, pointing toward the window. Fitzgerald looked up, but the cat had vanished.

"What?"

"It's gone."

"What was it?" he asked.

"I thought it was...never mind."

Who could it be? Whose house? Can I warn the people inside? The thoughts raced through my mind repeatedly while Fitzgerald finished his discussion of Qadon.

"I hope I haven't put too much of a damper on your day," he said.

"No, not at all. It was very informative. Thank you."

It was only a matter of time before a vision would cause my end, or so I concluded. Suicide seemed a possibility, but a strange feeling told me it wasn't my fault—something else caused these things to happen. That cat, the black cat,

Magik—he was responsible, had to be responsible for these "accidents". Or were they? I was second guessing myself over a cold dinner in my apartment when Beth called.

"Hi, Bob, how are you this evening," her sweet voice said.

"Not very well I'm afraid. I had another vision."

"Uh-oh. How bad?"

"A fire," I said. "Not just a fire—someone's house was burning. At least it was a house and not—"

"My apartment, or yours. Yes, I understand what you're saying," she said.

"And the black cat was there again, too. I'm cursed, I must be."

"How can you be sure? Have you turned every vision into a written story?"

"No, not *every* one. Just the first few," I said, "but every vision has come true in some form or another. This must stop; I must stop it."

Beth's voice became stern. "Don't even think it, Mr. Burke. You can't just give up on life so easily when times get tough. I didn't. I stuck it through; you can do the same."

"If only it were so easy. I wish I could say more, I wish…"

"What else is there? Another vision?" Her voice became concerned, and it quivered.

"No, nothing of the sort. Something I heard at work, something I shouldn't repeat, but because I care for you so, I feel I must."

"What, that I'll lose my job? That Qadon wants to get rid of me?"

"You know?"

"Only that he promised to make my work as difficult as possible since I don't want to go out with him, and that if he had the opportunity, he'd see to my dismissal from Hamilton," Beth said.

"It appears he intends to carry out his threat," I said.

"Really? I wonder how he intends to do that."

"Through the manipulation and presentation of computer data to CP, at least that's what I've heard from Fitzy. Mind you, he told me to keep it confidential, so I hope you won't let the others know you know."

"Oh, I'm not worried about that. If I do get terminated, I could find another job, I suppose. What really concerns me is your vision. We probably could prevent it from happening if we know whose house it will be," she said.

"That's the problem—I don't know."

"Let's take it from the top. The first vision was about Laurie, then Bo, then CP's car in the ditch, and now a house burning. I can't see any connection. You knew Laurie and CP before the accidents, but you didn't know Bo. Odd, no connection. Were there any other visions?" Beth asked.

"No, just the ones you mentioned."

"Perhaps these things happen to people you don't like— Laurie gave you a hard time before her accident, you probably weren't very fond of Bo, and CP—"

"I don't think he did anything to bother me," I said.

"But he survived while the others didn't. All right, now someone's house is burning. Fitzy? Qadon? Crawford? Someone else?"

"I wish I could say, but I—"

"Tell you what," she suggested, "why don't we check these people's houses and see for ourselves. You remember how the house looked in the vision, right?"

"Yeah, but—"

"Good. Did you have anything else planned for the evening?" she asked.

"No, but—"

"Excellent. Why don't you pick me up at my apartment, and we'll take a look-about."

"Any special reason we should go around in my car?" I asked.

"I would rather not have Qadon see me spying on his place—he may get ideas."

"All right. I'm on my way over."

"Let's check Crawford's place first," she said as she climbed into my car. "He's in downtown Lansing, then Qadon is on the south side."

"Where is Fitzy's place?"

"On the way back from Qadon's—Fitzy is in southwest Lansing."

After several minutes of expressway driving, we were in downtown Lansing. Traffic was moderately light—not nearly the rush-hour traffic Beth and I were used to. After leaving the freeway and taking a few turns on city streets, we drove through Bill Crawford's neighborhood. The houses were perhaps eighty or ninety years old and closely packed together.

"This is Crawford's," Beth said. "Does it look familiar?"

"No," I said, "otherwise several houses would have been on fire."

"All right—next house is Qadon's. Now before we get there, I want to reiterate that I don't want him to see me. I'll direct you to a parking lot overlooking his place though obscured by bushes. We'll peek through."

It seemed a fair enough plan, and in several more minutes we peered through bushes, the car being parked in the lot.

"No, it didn't look like Qadon's place either," I said.

"Hmm, too bad," Beth muttered.

"What was that?" I asked, almost hearing her.

"Nothing. Well if it isn't Crawford's and it isn't Qadon's, could it be Fitzy's?"

"Sounds like we'll have to look and see," I replied, still looking at Qadon's house.

"But if it isn't Fitzy's house, then what?"

"Good question." Qadon stepped out the front door, carrying a full garbage bag. While placing the bag at the front lawn's edge, we saw a black cat peering out the still open front door.

"Do you see that?" I whispered to Beth.

"A black cat. I didn't know Qadon had a cat."

"That looks like the one—look in the window, another one. Look up on the second floor window, a third cat!" I said in excitement. Qadon walked back in, picked up a cat, held him for a second as he looked around, then paused as he seemed to look in our direction.

"Does he see us?" I asked.

"Let's not wait to find out. Let's get out of here, now!"

With that, we gingerly tip-toed back to the car and quietly drove away. We continued our journey to Fitzgerald's house, but upon entering the subdivision, several fire trucks passed us up, and Beth quickly noticed smoke rising beyond the trees ahead.

"It's his," I muttered, "Fitzy's house." Dumbfounded, we made the final turn to a frenzied collection of people—firefighters, police, an ambulance, and several dozen individuals watching. Being impossible to drive further, I parked the car in the road with engine still running, and Beth and I dashed out before the wild blaze. Crazed, I ran for the house, ready to sacrifice myself to get Fitzy out.

"Hold on there, hero. Where do you think you're going?" asked a police officer as he held me from going further.

"Gotta get him out," I said, fighting the guy.

"Oh no you don't. You just stay back behind the yellow line. The firefighters will do what they can," the officer replied.

"Did they get him out? Fitzy?"

"Not yet, but they will."

"No, I don't believe you," and with that I slugged the officer in the jaw. He reeled back, and I was nearly up to the fiery blaze when several officers hauled me back. Perspiration drenched my shirt in response to the immense heat.

"Settle down," one said while I struggled.

"Looks like we'll have to haul this one in," said another. In a glance, I saw Qadon in the crowd, holding a black cat in his arms.

"It's him. He's the one!" I shouted to deaf ears. "He's caused everything—over there. Listen to me, you're not listening," I repeated, but the officers simply dunked me into the squad car and hauled me to the station where I was charged with disorderly conduct.

"I'll pay the fine," said Beth, having followed me to the station in my car. Before I could wonder how, her jingling of my keys reminded me I'd left the engine running. Lucky.

"You sure you want to bail out this loon?" asked the desk clerk.

"Not a problem. We go way back," she lied.

"All right." The clerk turned to me and said, "No more 'heroic' deeds, ok? We've got enough of 'em on the streets already."

I could only stare back, thinking it best to keep my mouth shut.

"Did you see him?" I asked Beth as she drove back to her apartment.

"See who? Where?"

"Qadon, at Fitzy's house."

"No. Where was he?" she asked.

"In the crowd, holding one of his cats. I saw him during my struggle with the police officers."

"Are you sure? How could it have been him? We had just come from his house, unless..."

"Unless he *did* see us and followed us over," I speculated.

"But what would he have to do with...unless he's involved with the accidents. The cats you saw—did any look like Qadon's?"

"Yes," I replied, "and one had a collar around it with the name 'Magik.' The cat Qadon was holding at Fitzy's had such a collar."

"Which means he may be the actual cause of these things and not you," Beth explained.

"Then why am I having these visions? I never had them before."

"Are you sure? What prompts you to write, hmmm? Does someone tell you a story you modify, do you experience something you wish to re-tell, or does something pop into your head from seemingly nowhere?" she asked.

"Usually something just pops in my head, then—"

"See? I knew it."

"Then I draw on my experiences to fill the gaps," I added.

"But, it is highly likely you have some sort of clairvoyance—you can see things that are out there but not commonly known to others. Reading your novels gave me this impression of you; now I'm more convinced than ever."

"Then I'm not causing these things to happen?" I asked.

"No."

"Then who is? Qadon? But how? And how do you know about such things?"

"Qadon is probably the one, but I'm not sure how unless he's somehow using the cats. As for me, well, I wasn't always in the business world. After high school I dabbled in the occult, but that didn't last long," Beth explained.

"Well, I'm not fond of his actions by any means—I want to stop them one way or another. If only we had a way to learn more without his knowledge to obtain our own trump card."

"Maybe we do," she suggested, parking the car in her apartment parking lot. "Up to this point, your visions have been random, just images popping into your mind. What if you could focus your attention on a particular person or place, concentrating so as not to let your mind wander? If it works, we—" We stepped out of the car and walked into her apartment.

"We?" I asked as we sat on her couch.

"Well," Beth continued to explain, "I have had some experience in hypnosis. If you're willing, I could help you focus your mind on Qadon and see what images you get."

"An interesting idea, but I've never been under hypnosis, nor am I eager to try. Just the idea of having another person in control of my thoughts—"

"I won't be controlling you," she said, "just guiding you. You won't do anything against your will. Trust me. What do you say, shall we try?"

I paused for a moment before answering, "Sure, if it will help end this torture, I'll try."

"Good," she smiled, "now before we begin, is there anything I can get you, a drink, something to eat?"

"Well, the fire did make me thirsty," I replied, "perhaps a glass of water."

"Water? Sure, no problem," she said, returning momentarily with a filled glass. I hastily gulped the water as she gathered some things together.

"First," she started, "why don't you move to the reclining chair? I think that'd be more appropriate. I'll bring another chair close to it."

In half a minute, we were situated. I was seated comfortably; Beth had a strobe light flashing to her side while she swung a sparkling necklace with a large stone back and forth. The necklace was in perfect sync with the strobe light.

"Now watch the necklace move back and forth as you concentrate on the sound of my voice. I will count from ten to one; at one you will be completely under hypnosis. Ten—relax. Nine—you're feeling comfortable, very relaxed as you continue to watch the necklace and concentrate on the sound of my voice. Eight—you're continuing to feel more relaxed. Seven— you feel the need to blink a few extra times as your eyes feel a little tired. Six—your arms and legs are increasing in weight, becoming heavier and unable to move. Five—you're feeling more relaxed, your eyes are more difficult to keep open. Four—your limbs are so heavy you could never budge them. Three—you can no longer keep your eyelids open they are so heavy. Two—you feel yourself drifting to the sound of my voice as you begin going deeper. One—you are in a deep state of relaxation, and as you continue to concentrate on the sound of my voice, you go deeper and deeper, but you will not fall asleep."

Beth turned off the strobe light and placed the necklace aside.

"Concentrate on the sound of my voice as you go deeper and become more relaxed. Your limbs are numb; you are floating in time and space."

"Mmm, Beth. You quench my thirst."

Beth blushed.

"Focus on the image of Jeff Qadon. Jeff Qadon. Remember, nothing you see can hurt you. Jeff Qadon. Do you see him?" she asked.

"Yes."

"You are in the parking lot overlooking his house behind a bush. Look at the house and notice the details. Do you see them?"

"Yes," I replied.

"Now, in your thoughts, go down to his house and up to the front door. What do you see?"

"There is a screen door. To the left is the door bell. On the porch is a 'welcome' mat. The house looks dark," I described while in my trance.

"Open the screen door."

"It's open."

"Now open the front door. Are you inside?"

"No. The knob won't turn. Must be locked."

"There is a key in your pocket," she invented. "Pull it out and use it to open the door. What do you see?"

"The key worked, but it's dark—I can't see a thing," I described.

"Turn on the light—you probably can feel along the wall for it."

"Found it. It's on."

"What do you see?" she asked again.

"There's a couch, an armchair, a television—a normal-looking living room."

"Walk around the house. Check the kitchen, the bathroom, and the bedrooms—anything out of the ordinary?"

"The kitchen is clean and ordinary; the bathroom is a bit messy; one bedroom looks like an office, the other one has a large bed, a dresser, a night stand—everything normal. There are stairs leading down, but I cannot see how far," I described.

"Take the stairs down, but look for a light switch before doing so."

"All right. Light is on. I'm going down the stairs. What a messy basement. There are three black cats roaming around—none are aware of me—and a table sits in the middle of the basement, with several candles, an inverted pentagram, several knives, and brown stains on what used to be a white cloth.

Going from the table to a nearby bookcase, I see several dolls—miniature people they are."

"Continue," Beth urged as I paused, "do the dolls look familiar?"

"Yes," I answered, reluctant to tell more.

"Who are they?"

"They are, they are..."

"Concentrate on the sound of my voice and answer me. Who are they?"

"The dolls...they...Laurie's doll has been squished nearly flat. There's one of Bo with a tight string around the neck. There's a doll of Steve Sharp sitting in a model sports car forcing another model car off the road—CP's doll is in that one. A black-burnt model house contains what appears to be the burnt doll of Fitzgerald," I explained, still deep in hypnosis.

"Are there any other dolls?"

"Yes."

"How many?"

"Two."

"Who are they?"

"They...I..."

"Who!?"

"Bill Crawford and Beth Reynolds," I said quietly. Beth shuddered.

"What do you notice about these dolls?" she asked, but her voice quivered so badly I was unable to keep my concentration.

"Everything is fading—I see nothing but black."

"Concentrate," she said, but it was obvious she'd lost hers and in doing so, I had lost mine.

"Nothing," I said, my eyes opening. I had come out of the hypnotic trance and returned to full consciousness. I could do nothing but look at a concerned Beth, who stared at the rug for a minute or two. Finally she spoke.

"Well, if your vision is accurate, Qadon is the one behind this fiasco. It also appears Crawford and I are his next targets."

"What can we do?" I asked.

"I wish we could let this 'blow over,' but it won't. First off, we need to get those dolls. Then we'll have to expose him for what he is and ensure he can do no further damage."

"It doesn't sound easy. But it seems the 'accidents' are happening almost one per day," I noted.

"It was Friday/Saturday, then Sunday was nothing, Monday/Tuesday, so perhaps tomorrow being Wednesday he'll take a rest, then Thursday/Friday he'll try doing something to Crawford and me."

"That sounds reasonable. And since today has been quite long, I think we should get a good night's sleep then deal with this tomorrow," I suggested.

"All right. I think Qadon will be staying late after work tomorrow. Why don't we go straight to his house from work since we'll leave before him?"

"Sounds good. We'll see you tomorrow," I said as I let myself out.

"Wait a minute," she said, walking up to me. "I want to thank you for helping me so much."

"Not a problem. I'm happy to help," I returned and without thinking I kissed her on the lips. I could see her blush but thought it best to leave quickly before things got out of hand. "Tomorrow?" I asked, but Beth stood there mesmerized. "Bye," I said quietly, closing the door behind me.

At least you got a kiss—next time try to hold onto him a little longer, Beth thought.

It wasn't long before I was home, and feeling restless from the day, I took a sedative before going to bed. Beth was also restless, tossing and turning throughout the night until she woke at 2:00 a.m.

"What if he doesn't wait," she mumbled, "what if Qadon decides I'm next—this could be my last night alive." With that in mind, Beth rose, dressed, and proceeded over to Qadon's house. "He'll be asleep, and I can quietly sneak into his basement and get the dolls," she said while driving on a deserted freeway. Minutes later, she was parked in the lot overlooking Qadon's house.

"Keep your cool," Beth repeated to herself. With flashlight in hand, she walked quietly around to the back and located a basement window in an alcove next to the house. It took little effort to pry it open, but Beth had some difficulty sliding through—it was a tight squeeze.

There was nothing to land on. Beth's shoes slid against the wall as she lowered herself, clinging onto the window. It loosened its hold, and Beth fell to the ground, the window pane flying partly across the basement and smashing. Beth was convinced she'd been ruined. Seeing no apparent external response to the crash, she took the opportunity to dash for the dolls and see about escaping, but as she made for a chair to prop against the wall, four black cats came dashing down the stairs. They hissed at her and encircled her. Beth made a desperate grab for the chair, but two of the cats jumped on her, clawing and biting into her. Beth's scream carried through the house, waking Qadon.

"Well, well, well, what do we have here?" he said, "Beth Reynolds—I would have never expected to see you here like this."

"Look, this is some sort of mistake," she said nervously. She had managed to get the two cats off, but they still held her at bay. "Please, just call your cats off, and I'll be on my way."

"Yes, this is a mistake. Your mistake. You don't like my cats? Tsk, tsk, I thought you liked cats, Beth. Unfortunately you've put me in a very difficult position. You have something in your hand that isn't yours," he said, pointing to the dolls, "you're trespassing, you've damaged my property," he continued, pointing to the window, "and you know something you really shouldn't."

"Please, Jeff, I'm willing to forget this if you are," she pleaded.

"Oh I'll forget this, all right, but not the way you think. Here, cats, come over here," he called, and the cats ran behind him.

"Thank you, I think," Beth started. "What are you doing?"

Qadon pulled out a gun and aimed at her. "This is good-bye, my sweet flower. I'm sorry it's come down to this, but I have to do this. You understand, don't you?"

"No, please don't. JEFF DON'T!" she screamed, but Qadon was determined and readied to fire.

"BANG!" a gunshot sounded, and Beth jerked reflexively, but she was unhurt. Qadon fell to the ground dead, his head being shattered by a shotgun blast. Beth looked around, both relieved and frightened.

"Who's there?" she called at last.

"It is I," I said, coming out of the shadows. The cats had been frightened off by the loud blast, and Beth and I embraced.

"You don't know how happy I am to see you," she said, trembling in my arms. "But what are you doing here? How did you know?"

"The same way I knew before—I had a vision. Let's get out of here before the police come," I said, and we rushed off—she in her car, and I in mine to her apartment where we shared our stories over warm tea.

"Although I know I'm safe, I'm still trembling," Beth said. "Do you think you could stay over tonight to keep me company, I—"

"Beth, Beth, Beth, you silly thing, always so polite. I have something else in mind," I said, embracing her and kissing her gently on the lips. "Do you feel a little better?"

"A little, but I—" she looked one way, then another as if still unsure whether she was safe or not.

"Don't worry. Everything will be fine," I said as I carried her off to her bedroom. We didn't leave until breakfast.

"So this is your last day," Beth said to me as I cleaned out my desk.

"Please, come in Ms. Reynolds." It had been a month since Qadon's death. "I'm just gathering a few things together be-fore—"

"Before you head off into the wild blue. I guess this means goodbye, doesn't it?" she said, obviously sad.

"Beth, please. I just want to say—"

"Spare me the rhetoric. We both know it could never really be for us. You have your life, and I have mine."

"And you'll stay here at Hamilton?"

"For now," Beth replied, "until I'm ready to move on. Anyway, I wanted to say goodbye and good luck."

Beth started for the door.

"And not even a farewell kiss?" I taunted.

"Why Mr. Perkins! If I didn't know better, I'd say you're flirting with me," she said sarcastically. "See you in your novels," and she left.

"Take care," I said back though I knew she could no longer hear. A sudden emptiness filled my heart, and I knew it would be difficult getting over Beth. *Why don't you ask her to marry you, you fool?* It was a wild thought, but I knew the practicality of the matter, the reality of the matter, the...the...in an instant I saw an image of myself—old, gray, and surrounded by book piles—novels I'd written in my lifetime. I was alone with no one to share my success.

The vision passed, and I looked out my window half-expecting to see another black cat, but there was none. It had abandoned me in my vision; it had abandoned me in real life. Strangely, it emptied me further until I became so restless I knew action had to be taken. With a will and determination, I briskly marched out of my office and ran past the cubicles of clerical workers and secretaries, and went right up to Beth and spun her around.

"Beth Reynolds—marry me!" I commanded. She was shocked and surprised—she was also on the spot. Everyone within eye- or ear-shot had stopped to look. Silence filled the office.

"What?" she asked, trying to stall. She was perplexed.

"Say 'yes'," said Norma, trying to help. "Say 'yes'." Norma turned to everyone in the office and waved everyone to repeat her words in sync. Within seconds the entire office was chanting, "say 'yes,' say 'yes'."

"Well, are you going to disappoint everyone?" I asked, holding her close.

"Yes. I'll marry you."

The office applauded, and we kissed passionately in full view.

"All right, all right," said CP, coming out of his office to see what was happening. "What's going on here? Did I miss something?"

"No," Beth said, looking at CP. She turned back around to me and said, "but I almost did."

"Here," Norma said, handing something to Beth. "I found this necklace in Qadon's old desk. I think it's yours."

"Is it really yours?" I asked.

"No, not really. It's an odd sort of necklace, isn't it?" Beth mused.

I took it in hand and examined the writing on the stone: "Magik."

(The End)

Lorra Silvertip Bear: Premier

October 17, 1993

Lorra's silver-tipped fingernails sparkled and flashed with a rainbow brilliance as she gestured and pointed to her cats.

"They are so naughty," she explained. "I caught Gizmo opening my dresser drawers, looking for my red earmuffs. When I get a hold of him, I'll beat him."

This is the continuing saga of Lorra Silvertip Bear, known for many things, one of which is her ability to bear down when things get tough. Upon looking up "bear" in the encyclopedia, I learned that "silvertip" is another name for the grizzly bear, and this I think is appropriate.

And is she Lorra Silvertip Bear instead of just Lorra Bear? Why, haven't you heard? Shmucks, I thought *everyone* knew by now. Well then, let me refresh your memory, unless of course you didn't read about Lorra in *The Cat from Hell: Catattack.* Perona of Persia sold Lorra a new fingernail polish, guaranteed to illuminate and electrify her fingernails. I think, though, that Lorra received more than she bargained for. Why? Let me tell you...

FAST TRACKS

Before Lorra discovered the red ear muffs missing, before her little green car had parked in the apartment lot, before, before, before, we see Lorra, leaving school for the day and climbing into her bright, green car. Without a blink, it nimbly left the parking lot, pulled out into the side street, then into a main thoroughfare all in one sweeping motion, the green aura barely able to keep up with the crackling, accelerating Lorra. As the light changed from green to yellow, her foot firmly smashed the pedal to the floor, pushing the green blur past slowing cars and slipping past others making oncoming left turns.

I say "smashed" because the gas pedal stayed smashed to the floor, and Lorra's green lightning bolt careened past irate drivers, through stop signs (I don't mean failing to stop; I mean *plowing* through the sign, post, and splinters). A boisterous and daring kid stepped one foot into the road to cross but quickly jumped back to avoid being slimed green.

The pedal is stuck, Lorra thought, but no matter—at least she was getting home sooner. Unfortunately, not all traffic signals are as green as Lorra's car, and the inevitable happened—the green machine approached a red signal with heavy side traffic blocking her way.

"This is it!" she screamed, throwing her arms over her face. Her incredibly forceful fear shot a shockwave of electric current through her silver tips, into her car, and thumped her shock absorbers twice, enabling her car to jump over the side traffic and land on the other side unimpeded. The landing gave Lorra a start, and she resumed trying to control the beast. This repeated once more, along with a water hydrant decapitated, a parked car "moved" out of the way, and a newspaper man losing his papers in the whirlwind.

Lorra had a problem—Lloyd Street. It was a ninety degree turn to the right, with traffic. The green machine bounced from another electric shock, but it missed the turn and went straight into Washington Park, ripping into the soggy green grass (and thus adding a soiled accent to the car), and spinning into several 360s. Somehow Lorra regained control in time for the lake, and again her unusual energy transferred from her silver tips, through the car, and into the shock absorbers, which managed to bounce the car along the water, back onto wet land, then past the senior center before toppling over the concrete side of the freeway, U.S. 41 to be exact.

Although the freeway had no stops, Lorra was on the wrong side, dodging cars and trying to avoid collision, and at the very moment she was certain a semi-truck trailer would flatten her, the electric energy from her fear again scorched through her fingernails into her car, bouncing it to the side, rolling over the median, sliding over a van, and landing on the pavement going the correct direction. The car, being thus stabilized, quickly gained speed, hitting a hundred miles per hour along the bridge overpassing Interstate 94.

Cars from east-bound and west-bound I-94 merged into Lorra's two lanes from the right and left, enough to cut off her path. She had no choice but to hug the center line, and the merging cars smashed into her, like a fly caught between a fly swatter and a table. The green aura held the car's frame solid, but the side cars bounced off into the walls, smashing and causing a piled-up car-block behind.

Lorra went under the power lines, past Milwaukee County Stadium, then past the sign, "Freeway Ends, ½ Mile." She tried unsticking the gas pedal without success, and after the car passed under the railroad tracks, she was presented with another dilemma—stopped cars at National Avenue.

Hitting the brake pedal proved ineffective, but pulling the emergency brake caused the rear wheels to lock, sending the car into a fish-tailing spin. She spun, spun, then spun into the right-turn lane, somehow completed the turn, then zoomed two blocks, left turn at the light, down a bumpy, parked-car-crowded residential road to Beloit Road, made a right, and narrowly missed hitting traffic while going through the Greenfield Avenue light.

Beloit was not deserted. In addition to the traffic in front, parked cars lined both sides. Lorra could not slow the car, nor could she afford to spin again. She swerved, going along the sidewalk and running over a tricycle, two no-parking signs, a fire hydrant, and a litter box.

Going through the 60th Street light, she swerved around stopped traffic and went into the left lane, though there was no oncoming traffic. Looking further, she could see why—a non-moving train blocked the road.

"This is it!" she screamed, clenching onto the steering wheel. Her emotional energy passed through her silver fingernails, sending electricity into the car and shocking it off the ground, through an open, empty box car, and to the other side, bounced off the side of an oncoming stopped car, then rolled onto the correct side of the road. She picked up speed, continuing her southwest rampage down Beloit Road.

Unfortunately, the 68th Street and Lincoln Avenue intersection fast approached, and Lorra had a red light with cars waiting in front. She instinctively hit the brakes again without response, pulled the emergency brake, and the car did another spin, going over the curb then hitting a bench, sending the fluorescent green machine airborne. It tumble-bounced over five cars waiting to continue southwest bound along Beloit Road, bounced over a car rushing along Lincoln Avenue, then righted itself and sped away to 76th Street.

The lights at 68th, 76th, and Oklahoma Avenue are timed perfectly wrong, meaning the average-speed car will stop at each light. The only way to make them is to travel extremely slow or extremely fast. Lorra made every light, though she bounced into the grassy median several times to dodge traffic, carving huge divots and kicking up black earth.

That's not all. Several children were throwing their junior-sized football to each other, and a poor throw sent the football into Beloit Road. Lorra made a special effort to steer for it, running over it and popping it. The child who owned it stared in disbelief then cried. Lorra cackled with glee.

Just before hitting Oklahoma Avenue, Lorra's green machine hit a dog, the same one barking during strange nightly hours. The dog yelped once before rolling to the side, dead. The impact veered the car sideways, and the gas pedal curiously unstuck itself. Lorra calmly drove the final leg, stopped at Oklahoma's red light, then proceeded leisurely home.

FRISKY FRIDAY

Saddled with her bag, lunch cooler, and the day's mail, Lorra entered her second-floor Milwaukee apartment in time to catch Gizmo sliding on a place mat across the kitchen table. Lorra hissed and clapped her hands, but in doing so her carryables fell. Irate but determined, she chased him around the apartment, over the couch, back through the kitchen, and down the hallway where he turned sharply into Lorra's bedroom and dove under her bed.

Lorra made the turn too quickly, and her high-heeled shoes snapped sideways, throwing Lorra into the open linen closet. Impact. The shelves above collapsed, burying Lorra in a pile of sheets, blankets, pillow covers, towels, and washcloths.

"I'm gonna beat you," she muffled through the linens.

Honey Bear, the heavy and boisterous, jumped atop the pile and threw her front paws at any sudden twitching or movement. She dug further into the sheets then stopped. A human hand emerged from the pile and grabbed Honey, holding her in place.

"You, Misses, are in for it now," said Lorra, her head and upper torso emerging.

Gizmo pressed his paw against Lorra's dresser door then wedged the paw between the door and the trim, forcing it open. Lorra turned to look, dropping Honey. Gizmo opened the door and jumped inside.

"Get out of there," called Lorra, scrambling from the pile. "Now!"

Gizmo emerged from the space, red ear muffs in mouth, and stared at Lorra as she made for him. He darted between her legs, scampered down the hallway into the kitchen, jumped on the counter, then leapt atop the cupboard in the one-foot space between it and the ceiling.

"Down from there!" Lorra called, reaching for the spray bottle. She adjusted the nozzle, readied to spray, then stopped.

"Ring," sounded the telephone, cutting through the moment like a bucksaw through a sapling. "Ring!"

Lorra wasn't sure whether to throw the phone across the room (as if it were trying to bother her) or answer it. She chose the latter, snapping the receiver from the cradle.

"Hello?"

"Is the party still on?" asked Tara, one of Lorra's friendly friends.

"Party? That's right—today is Friday! Yeah, sure. Come on over. Bring the others. Party all night!"

Tara came over early to help Lorra adorn the apartment and set up the party snacks. They were finishing as the first guests arrived, each with a case of beer. Lorra wasted no time in cranking the music. Even I attended the party (being brought over by one of Lorra's friends), though my part was more for observation than participation.

All told, there were one or two dozen people, some dancing, some drinking, some dancing and drinking, some eating, some borrowing Lorra's bedroom, and some sitting on the balcony. After watching the empty beer cans pile up in the sink (Lorra recycles aluminum cans), I thought it best to get fresh air from the balcony.

"Ken, nice party, huh?" said one guest as he and his female friend came in from the balcony.

"Yeah, the greatest," I replied.

It was dark on the balcony, though a few lights shone from the apartment windows. The sun had set an hour ago, and Lorra suggested the balcony light be kept off so as not to attract bugs. After my eyes adjusted, I realized I was alone, surprising considering the number of people. While the low beats rumbled from inside, I leaned on the railing and stared at the cars below, then at the woods at the parking lot's edge. I looked down at the wooden balcony floor and realized I could see my shadow. Looking up, I saw a full moon beaming through clear sky.

Six or seven people started yelling from below. They carried bottles of beer, spilling some as they frolicked across the parking lot into the woods. I recognized them from the party. Within half a minute, I saw two cats scampering from one car to another, briefly hiding under one before going to the next. After the third or fourth car, I recognized the cats as Honey and Gizmo.

The door to the balcony opened, and a guy entered with two girls, his arm around each. Seeing me, one girl spoke:

"Hi! This is a party! What are you doing out here by your-self?"

"Watching them," I replied.

"Watching who?" she asked.

I pointed below. The girl who spoke to me yelled to the people below and they yelled back. I could hardly make out what they were saying, and I took the opportunity to go back inside, unobserved.

"Hi, have some beer," said one guy as I pushed my way through.

"Not now, gotta see what's—"

"Hey Lorra," said the guy, "Ken over here is being a prude. He needs a drink."

"I have just the thing," she said, bringing a glass filled with a dark, caramel-colored liquid. "I call this the Brown Bear. And here, this'll give it some zing."

Lorra intensified her emotions, forcing continuous light-ning charges from her silver fingertips into the Brown Bear. The brew fizzled and bubbled, then a cloud rose from the glass. It smelled like something electrical burning.

A new song started, and the imbuing beat thumped the glass into rippling the brew, and electrical sparks zapped along the fluid's surface in sync with the beat.

"Drink up," said the guy.

"Drink up," said Lorra.

Soon the entire room chanted, "Drink up," in cadence with the music, many even ventured closer to impress the suggestion more strongly with facial expressions worthy of winning a con-tortion contest. I looked into the glass a second time, the eddies and currents hypnotically luring me in, enough so I drained the glass suddenly and swiftly. The room cheered me on and ap-plauded, and I was quite pleased with what appeared a simple task. It was short lived. The Brown Bear had a ten-second lag. Though slow, it built upon itself into a bear-crushing wrench. I gagged on my esophageal tissues, and the room further cheered then swiftly fell into a laughing cacophony.

They resumed their dancing with Lorra leading the way. I meandered around the throng, at least I tried, but several people purposely slowed my exit, enticing me to dance with them. I declined respectfully and stole away to the corridor, down the stairs, and out the door. I briefly looked around for the cats but didn't see them.

"There he is," said someone from the woods. "Come on over, Ken, and keep warm."

Keep warm? It was warm inside and cool out. Why would he beckon me to the woods to keep warm? I only had to walk a few dozen yards for the answer.

"We brought an ice chest from inside. Have one," said one of the three guys as he tossed me a twelve-ounce can of beer.

"That's nice of you, but I'm—say, should you be having this fire out here?" I asked.

"Gotta keep warm when it's cold. The fire helps, and of course Trish *really* keeps me warm," he said as Trish moved closer to him, putting her arms into his coat. He loosened the coat and wrapped it around them both for a snug and cozy sit.

"Only brought four chairs with us," said another guy, who was sitting with his girl on his lap. "I should introduce you. Ken, the guy who tossed you the beer here is Mitch, I'm John, this is my girl, Ann, next to me here is Jed with his girl, Samantha, and last but not least is...what was your name again?" he asked, smiling.

"Wilma," she said, "my name is Wilma."

"Well, what happened to Fred?" he asked, alluding to the 1960s television animation series, *The Flintstones*. The group laughed hard, nearly falling out of their chairs.

"Funny, smart-ash," she shot back, and the group laughed, because John had ashes in his hair from stoking the fire.

They continued like this for some time, and I added an appropriate word or two to be friendly. I had become so involved in the "fire-chat" that I'd forgotten my original reason for coming out, forgotten until Lorra Silvertip Bear came out in a huff.

"Where are they?" she asked, crossing the parking lot and nearly yelling. Two young ladies followed from behind, trying to catch her.

The cats, I thought and I looked around for them.

"Where are they?" she asked again, standing at the circle's edge.

Her question fell on engrossed people. Their lack of response motivated Lorra to take aggressive action. Anger welled up in her until ready to pop like a balloon. She pointed directly at the fire, and her negative energy released through her silver fingertips as a lightning ball. The electrified plasma sphere darted straight to the fire, extinguishing it into scattering embers and seething smoke. The group jumped sharply then turned toward her.

"What's the idea, anyway?" asked Mitch, perturbed.

"What have you done with them?" asked Lorra.

"Them? Who?" Mitch asked.

"My cats. Honey and Gizmo."

"We're the only ones out here!" he insisted, still upset from the fire smothering.

"Well you must have let them out, because they're no longer inside!" she nearly shouted, and she opened her mouth to say something else but never said it.

A cat's meow called from the trees, first sounding innocent and sweet, then getting louder, deeper, and increasingly persistent. It must have been Honey. Her bellows continued, getting so loud as to hurt our ears. Most of the group covered theirs, and the compounding echoing resonance vibrated car and apartment windows into shatterdom.

At the sound of breaking glass, Gizmo leapt from his hidden perch into John, scrambling as much with John as John with him. Gizmo jumped from one person to another, leaving a trail of spilt beer and agitated dispositions.

Honey continued her bellowing for another thirty seconds, then both cats saw Lorra gazing at them. They gazed back briefly, then darted across the parking lot and back into the apartment building. Lorra chased them, grabbed them, then dashed back to her apartment. All told, Honey shattered perhaps two hundred or more windows, and I could hear a house alarm sounding from around the apartment building's corner.

I wanted to walk over to see if broken windows triggered it, and the temptation nearly overtook me, but within another minute, several Milwaukee Police cruisers coagulated in the parking lot, blocking our escape. The group and I dispersed into the woods.

I don't know what happened to the others, but I kept going until I hit a major road, and upon doing so caught a bus to my apartment, happy to have escaped spending the night with undesirables.

The next day I called Lorra, who was less than happy about the mess she was cleaning up. Apparently, the police received a tip regarding an escaped convict—Wilma. However, she escaped in the woods as we others had, and they advised Lorra to give them a call should Wilma reappear. The police were also concerned about the broken glass, but Lorra could only speculate to them about a sonic boom doing the damage.

Lorra also mentioned her cats were safe though rattled by the party. They were sleeping peacefully on her couch that Saturday morning.

WILD WHIRLWIND

Still recovering from the weekend, Lorra Silvertip Bear parked her green car in the middle-school parking lot early Monday morning. Her transportation held up well during the hectic commute, and she went to the office to get keys and documents, then headed up three flights of stairs to the third floor, room 312.

Class started, but the students were in anarchy. Bits of paper, paper airplanes, paper balls, spit balls, spit wads, rubber bands, pencils—all were flying around landing in every place conceivable, despite Lorra's efforts to control them. Some students ran into the hall. Students from other classes came in.

"Get out of here," Lorra said, and they left, but not without unleashing a few paper wads into the class.

Despite Lorra's pointing, shouting, growling, and other teaching methods, the class proved unresponsive. Finally, Lorra went to the window and threw her arms up in a desperate call for help from above.

The sun faded behind gathering black clouds. The wind picked up, and in Lorra's final cry for help, sparks flew from her fingertips to the heavens above. The wind grew fiercely, the clouds stormed with thunder and lightning, and torrential rain pelted the school with relentless pounding, the magnitude never known before and never desired to know again.

A hush fell on the class, and as Lorra walked back to the front of the class, the students saw a black funnel out the window getting bigger and bigger.

"It's heading for us!" screamed the students.

Some dashed for the door, but Lorra shut it tight, resulting in a few breaking their noses on the solid oak door.

"Get next to the wall and crouch with hands over head and head between knees," Lorra commanded, and the students complied.

The building rocked, the windows whistled, but when the tornado finally passed, no one was physically hurt even if pride was broken. Daylight returned and with it an orderly class being absolutely quiet until called upon, raising hands to speak, and conducting themselves in orderly fashion.

"For homework, write a ten-page essay on what a tornado means to you," instructed Lorra.

Lorra Silvertip Bear, having finished with the day's work, lugged her bag down the stairs, out the door, and into the parking lot. As she went to her car, a delinquent youth came from the side and confronted her.

"Your grade book or your life," he said.

"What's the meaning of this?" she demanded.

"Gimme your grade book, or else!" he said, flashing a shiny knife at her.

"Never!" she said, and as the youth came at her, Lorra's bearish rage flamed from her fingertips, through the air, and into the knife, electrocuting the youth who immediately dropped the blade.

He came at her with a fist, but another bolt jolted his body, his eyes opened wide, and he stiffly walked away staring into the sky without uttering a word.

"When will they learn?" she mused, unlocking her car and placing the bag in the back seat.

She climbed in, closed the door, then keyed the ignition, but nothing happened. No starting-motor sound, no indicator lights, no dome lights—nothing electrical worked.

"Funny," she said, though the situation was hardly amusing.

Lorra popped the hood and inspected inside only to find a gaping hole where once her battery lay connected.

"Stolen!" she proclaimed, put the hood back down then climbed back into the car, fuming.

Her anger as before sent electricity through her fingertips, through the ignition, and the car started. She drove and didn't turn the car off until a new battery was secured.

TWO CATS TO MISCHIEF TOO MUCH

Lorra Silvertip Bear, on her way to Little Bear Lake for a relaxing weekend, asked me to apartment-sit for Honey and Gizmo. Honey was just recovering from an ear infection, and Gizmo recently returned from the vet hospital where he was treated for feline cryptosporidiosis.

"Honey needs two drops of this medicine in each ear twice daily," Lorra instructed, "and Gizmo has a special diet as well as a pill for the parasites. He needs one of those a day."

Lorra bade her farewells and went on to Little Bear Lake that Friday evening, but for me the weekend was just beginning.

It wasn't so bad at first. Honey and Gizmo spent the first two hours asleep. Bored, I invited two friends over for three-handed Sheepshead.

"The little ones bring out the big ones," said my partner for the hand as he played an eight of diamonds.

"I'm surprised Honey and Gizmo are being so good," I said as the aggressor took the trick with his ace of diamonds.

"They are cats after all. How much trouble can they cause?" asked the aggressor. He played a jack of spades.

"They can't be as bad as babies," said my partner, playing his queen of hearts.

"Message received," I replied referring to his queen as I played the ten of diamonds. "Last Friday they got loose and ran into the woods across the street. It was a real pain trying to get them back."

My partner tapped a card on the table, deciding whether to play it or not. Hearing the noise, Honey woke and came over, leapt into my lap, then onto the table, scattering the cards before scampering back down to the floor. Gizmo woke and came over, following her as she ran around the kitchen, along the ledge (knocking over two drinks), leapt to the countertop, then up to the space above the cupboards, around, then down onto the top of the refrigerator. The cats knocked over cereal and Lorra's coupon basket, then Gizmo ran to Lorra's room as I chased Honey around the living room.

Honey kept running into things—the wastebaskets, magazines, plants, and books, sending them everywhere. At one point I cut her off, but her weight as she leapt into me knocked my body to the ground.

Gizmo was no better. While I was chasing Honey around, he'd managed to open every dresser drawer and door, pull out half the clothes, and knock over Lorra's hair dryer, hair spray, and assorted perfumes.

Honey chased Gizmo around, and the two went from Lorra's room to the living room to the kitchen, where Gizmo made a sharp turn, but Honey wasn't up to his agility. She landed smack into one kitchen table's leg, breaking it. Our remaining cards, bowl of chips, dip, pitcher of beer, and peanuts came crashing down at my end, drenching me, the floor, and Honey. The two scampered into hiding under Lorra's bed.

Lorra came back Saturday, early because the weather went sour at Little Bear Lake. It was just as well, because I don't think I could have survived an entire weekend with her cats. Despite my bad experience, Lorra helped mend the situation much to my relief. She fixed the broken leg on the kitchen table and offered to buy me a new shirt to replace the one wrecked from the previous night. I declined on the shirt offer, but she did set the cats aright. I was happy, because after spending hours cleaning up the mess they made, I didn't want anyone to have to go through that much toil and sweat.

Lorra smiled. As she sat on the couch filing her silvertip fingernails, Gizmo sat on her left side and Honey on her right. She hummed a tune from the radio and soaked in her remaining peaceful weekend.

Red Stockings

November 1, 1993

S.

I think it started in early SEPTEMBER when we returned to school from summer vacation. My older sister, Loella, was in sixth grade, I, Brian, was in fifth, Cole was in third, and little Penny was in first. We four waited at the same old bus stop, waiting for the same old bus we had from prior years to take us to the same old elementary school. It was Loella's last year there and Penny's first. Our parents, Mr. and Mrs. Dan and Jill Humbal, had each of us attend private kindergarten before entering first grade in public school.

Several other kids played at the stop while we waiting. Some threw stones while one boy chased a girl around several cedar trees. Disgusted, she grabbed one of the branches (using her coat to protect her hand), and thrust the cedar into the boy's face. He jumped back and fell, landed square on his hinny, and his faced welted with red polka dots resembling the measles. He cried for a few seconds, but the loud distinctive rumbling from the approaching school bus's muffler gave warning to get in line or be left behind.

It was an old bus, hopping and jumping along the road like a bronco horse, and when it slowed to our stop, the brakes produced an ear-slashing pierce, each wheel screeching at slightly different frequencies to ensure our most perfectly engineered torture. The trees resonated to the screech and shook brilliantly, shaking both leaves and birds to the ground. The birds immediately took flight for distant salvation.

"The bus is here," said one kid.

Two other kids went first, then Cole, Penny, me, and Loella. Behind Loella, five or six others climbed aboard, and the welting boy clambered on last.

"What happened to you?" grumbled the bus driver, but the boy was too disturbed to respond. No longer curious, the driver pulled on the iron lever, closing the door.

It was an older bus, and the driver had trouble getting the tranny into gear. It happened every day at every stop, and after every grinding sound from the gears, we'd yell out, "Crunch!" in unison. He cursed the bus and yelled at us to be quiet, until he finally got the hulk moving with a lumbering, bolting, jack-rabbitting lurch forward, tossing us between seat padding in front and behind, like a human pinball game. I learned early to hold onto my packed lunch for dear life, because the first few jounces could easily wrench the brown bag from my hand and send it spewing down the aisle.

This day the bus decided to act up more than I remember, though perhaps the summer vacation had softened me. Nevertheless, after circling through two more subdivisions, it lumbered to school, made a sharp turn from the main highway to a side road, but he took it too quickly. The right rear tire clipped the curb, and a glass shard from the weekend's alcohol bonanza pierced the worn-thin tire.

The air must have gushed out quickly, because we heard and felt the *rumpity-dump-plump-kerglump* and instead of being tossed from front to back, we were jostled up and down, with those on the right half-jostling higher in the air.

The bus stopped.

Grumbling and cursing, the driver moved the lever to open the doors, yelled at us to be still and stay quiet, walked out, then took a look. Everyone in the bus moved to the right windows and fought to see. Those who *did* see peered through the filthy panes and observed the driver light up a cigarette, walk over to the tire, and kick it.

Without warning, Penny dashed down the aisle and out the door. Loella ran after her, and I tugged Cole with me in the pursuit. The other kids followed our lead out the door where we briefly conglomerated around an agitated bus driver (who we always called bus driver). He looked at us in surprise then ordered us back on the bus.

We disobeyed.

I was caught up in the stampede, headed ironically for the school. The driver was in no condition to follow, and he didn't. Along the way to school, we smashed abandoned bottles into the street, cut across a few lawns, threw rocks at passing cars, and ran through two large puddles. Our clothes and disposition were soiled.

St.

The vice principal was overseeing bus unloading that morning, and she was in no happy mood when we approached ST. LUKE'S ELEMENTARY SCHOOL.

"What in tarnation do we have here?" she yelled, though it didn't stop us from having a merry ole time, being boisterous and mischievous. Just as we arrived on the school grounds, one of the younger boys pulled Penny's pony tail. Cole in turn pulled the boy's hair, then the boy spun around and smacked Cole in the jaw, to which Cole smacked the boy in the jaw. The two jabbed, kicked, clawed, bit, and had managed to throw each other into the damp ground, entangled and ensnarled in flying mud and green-staining grass.

"Break it up, break it up!" Vice Principal Judie Kavolok commanded, running to our encirclement and breaking through. "You two will come with me."

Kavolok took a boy in each arm and marched them off to her office.

"Wait, Ms. Kavolok. Don't you wanna know what happened?" asked Loella, following Kavolok intently while I soothed Penny's feelings.

"Loella, when is your brother going to learn to stop fighting?" Kavolok asked back without missing a step.

She was right. Cole had gotten himself into a dozen or more fights last school year and usually over the smallest things. His short fuse ignited at any agitation, and at other times his hyperactivity manifested itself in unending, unslowing talking. He did everything with his all—when he spoke his head bobbed, his arms and hands gyrated, and he shifted his weight from foot to foot, as if desperately holding back from overdue urination. When he played tag or kickball, he ran most inefficiently though attracted the most attention with his yelling, arm flapping, and general bouncing around.

"Stevie Crabshaw pulled Penny's pony tail. Cole pulled Stevie's hair. Cole was just trying to give Stevie a taste of his own medicine," Loella explained.

Stevie stuck his tongue out at Loella, Kavolok not noticing.

"I'm sorry, Loella. The two will have to be disciplined. Then I'm calling both parents."

"No, no, please don't," begged Cole. "Paddle me, make me write a thousand sentences, but please don't call home. Can't we keep this a secret?"

"First day of the year and you're not only picking fights, you're trying to squirm out of proper punishment. No, we're getting you set aright this year."

Kavolok took the two into her office while the rest of us stared for a minute. Finally, Ms. Kinsley (who assisted in bus duty), asked us nicely to go inside to our homerooms. Penny was still scared, so I escorted her down the first/second-grade wing. Her room was last on the left, and the teacher welcomed her inside. I waved good-bye and walked back up the wing, past the office (where I saw Cole and Stevie fidgeting in their chairs while Kavolok held the receiver to her ear), then down the fifth/sixth-grade wing.

I sat in time for roll call, taken by our teacher, Ms. Morrow. She would be our teacher for most of the day. She started the morning with a firm hand, and we all behaved (being in such a new situation). Homeroom faded into our first class, Reading.

                              Sto.

Some students went to other rooms, some came from other rooms, and I stayed in Ms. Morrow's room. She gathered us 'round in a circle, and she passed out our reading books— STORY ACHIEVEMENT LEVEL 10. Each read a paragraph from the first story, *Little Red Cape*. When it was my turn to talk I stumbled over four words and was terribly self-conscious, but the others paid no notice, and Ms. Morrow kindly helped me sound them out.

When another pupil took his turn, my thoughts turned to Cole and his predicament. Pappa was not pleased with Cole's conduct last school year and lectured him for an hour last night. Now he'd already gotten himself into trouble—the first day of school!

It was also Pappa's first day at his new job. He lost his old job two days before summer vacation, and he did nothing better than mope around, get into my mother's way, or tell us children to stop running around and go out and play (which we usually did). My mother was happy enough to dance around the kitchen table during breakfast, though Pappa grumbled about how he looked. We paid more attention to our food, a specially prepared treat from Mamma—another part of her celebration. Usually we munched on cold cereal floating in milk.

"Are you paying attention, Brian?" Ms. Morrow asked.

The class stared intently upon me, and I realized they caught me daydreaming.

"Yes, ma'am."

"Good. Who is the villain in *Little Red Cape*?" she asked.

"Villain? What's that?" I asked stupidly.

The class roared into laughter.

"I just explained what it meant," she replied, calming the class down with a wink.

So she had. I mentioned something about the wolf, and she released me from the interrogation, though she demeaned me in no way. Reading faded into spelling, recess, then morning break, then language arts, science, lunch, recess, math, and social science. The first day was nearly over, though for a first day it exhausted me.

Ms. Morrow finally allowed us to wait in front for our bus. In the fray, I met up with Loella and Penny, but we couldn't find Cole. Ms. Kinsley mentioned that he had left earlier with my mother. Relieved, we boarded the same old bronco of a beat-up bus, somehow fixed in time to take us home, and I will say I was sad to see its return.

The bus bellowed, wheezed, and coughed at every stop, go, and turn. At each stop the brakes squealed unrelentingly while the bus itself vibrated from some unbalanced situation, and at each go the hurky-jerky tranny bopped us back and forth as before. Our bus stop couldn't have come sooner.

We three exited immediately and hastened home.

"Hi," said Loella as we entered, "we're home. Where's Cole, Mamma?"

"He's been restricted to his room for most of the day. How was school?" Mamma asked.

"Oh, fine. Most everyone I know, but there were a few new people I haven't seen before," Loella replied.

"And how was your day, Brian?"

"About the same. We started working right away, not like last year when we talked about summer vacation."

"And little Penny? How was your day?" Mamma asked.

"Bad, bad, bad. I don't wanna go to school. Can't I stay home like Cole? I wanna stay home!" Penny said, getting crabby.

"Now Penny, remember what I said? You have to go to school like the other boys and girls."

"No Mamma, no school for Penny!" Penny insisted.

Penny's face scrunched up like a raisin, all wrinkled and ugly. Mamma's expression changed from delighted-to-see-us to cross-at-Penny. She took Penny by the arm and yanked her upstairs to her bedroom, where Penny remained until supper.

"Don't let them ruin your afternoon," Mamma said to Loella and me as we munched on cookies and soda. "Once you two change out of your school clothes, why don't you go out and play? When dinner is ready, I'll call you in."

We agreed.

Stoc.

Loella and I ambled around the yard, retrieved and kicked a chance ball found STUCK under the porch, then chased falling leaves. We ended our travels in a corner of the back yard and took up swinging on the swing set a-set in sand.

"I bet I can swing higher," Loella said.

"I bet I can," I returned.

We were both swinging high for the set, and the frame nudged from the sand oh-so-slightly on each change of our direction, worsened by uniform swinging.

"How high can you jump?" she challenged.

"Higher than you," I said back.

She jumped, then I jumped, and we both landed in the sand.

"Ouch!" I said, landing on my feet wrong.

"Are you all right?" she asked, concerned.

Loella was very dependable when it came to concern, compassion, and just having someone else stick up for a little tyke like Penny, Cole, or me. Sometimes we would sit and have "serious" talks, though our depth was nothing close to what would come later.

"Yeah, I'm ok," I replied, returning to the swing.

She reentered her swing, but we just sat and did mini-swings or slight rotations in a relaxing way.

"I've been thinking, Brian," she said. It was her usual lead-in to a "deep" conversation.

"What about?" I asked in the all-too-familiar response.

"Mamma."

"Yeah. She's mad, isn't she?"

"Yeah, she is. Do you think she's mad about Cole? And Penny?"

"Sure. They got in trouble," I replied.

"Well, I think it's more than that."

"More than what?" I asked.

A breeze tossed pine needles and leaves across our view. The neighbor's hanging bell-cluster chimed melodically. A squirrel sniffed the ground in our backyard's other corner.

"You remember how it was during summer vacation?" she asked.

"Yeah, we didn't have to go to school," I said, not following Loella.

"No, I mean with Mamma and Pappa. He was home all the time, sometimes they'd argue, then he'd leave, then he'd come back during the night while we slept. Remember that?"

"I don't like to think about it. Those were bad days. He's better, now. He's better," I assured her.

"Maybe. I never told you this—can you keep a secret?"

"Sure," I said with a big grin.

"I mean a *big* secret. This is serious, Brian," Loella maintained.

"Ok, ok. Serious."

"A week or two ago, she and Pappa got into a fight. He left, and I went into Mamma's bedroom to make sure she was ok. She had her head in her hands, and her back was to me. I tapped her on the shoulder, and she jumped. Then I saw that her face was red and she was crying. She was crying, Brian."

"So? Women cry, men don't."

"Brian! People cry when they hurt really bad. When Cole fell and scraped his knee in July, he cried. When Stevie pulled Penny's hair, she cried," Loella explained.

"How come Pappa never cries? 'Cause men don't cry."

"Some men hold it in when they shouldn't because they don't wanna be called a sissy. But it's better to let it out."

"So?"

"So," she continued, "Mamma was crying, and I knew she hurt bad. She wouldn't say why, but I gave her a hug, and she was better."

"Why was she crying anyway?" I asked.

"I think everything just got to her with Pappa and all. You saw her this morning—she was so happy. But when we got home, I could tell she was edgy or something. I think she was relieved to have some peace and quiet. Now Pappa will be home soon, and she doesn't know what to expect," Loella said.

"Well I hope now that he's working, everything will be ok. Maybe things can be like they were last year."

"I hope so, Brian. I hope so."

Stock.

Despite our hopes, everything wasn't "ok." Pappa's new job in the factory made him STOCK cranky when he came home. He had the saving grace of quietly reading the paper while drinking his beer, but once dinner started, so did he.

He would grumble about this-and-this person doing that-and-that thing to him, or this machine and that other thing broke down or didn't work. He hated his boss, and whenever Mamma said a kind word to make him feel better, he lashed out at her. Cole and Penny didn't notice much—they wolfed dinner down before the conversation heated up. I never paid much attention before, but since Loella told me about Mamma crying, I tried to listen without looking like I was listening. It was hard, because half the time Pappa grumbled, and the other half he talked about things I didn't understand.

Fall colors decorated our yard, the street, and the school playground. From September to mid-October, Loella found Mamma in tears twice. Pappa continued to grumble, though not as frequently as he did his first week of work at the factory. Cole got into three other school fights, and Penny came down with the chickenpox, keeping her home for a week.

As a special gift for being good during her recovery, Penny got a black, one-year-old cat in early October. The cat's name was Coal, because his fur was as black as coal, but every time Loella, Penny, or I would call for Coal, Cole would answer. In his hyperactive way, he got upset, so the feline from Aunt Shirley's farm was renamed Mischief, because that's what he got into.

One Saturday in late October, Penny, Cole, Loella, and I played in the back yard. We raked the leaves into piles then ran full speed into the heapings, splashing into them and rolling around, burrowing, and throwing crumpled leaves at each other, all in good fun. Cole was the most excited, while Penny seemed more helpless in the fray. Once Penny fell and nearly cried, but Loella picked her up and set her aright. Even Mischief joined us, but Cole ran after the cat and chased him under a bush.

Mischief was under one of several bushes lined along one side of the house. At the back corners of the house were thorned bushes, and the once green berries turned bright orange. Our four attentions shifted from Mischief to the side bushes to one of the berry bushes. We followed Loella over to this thorny bush.

"Every year when I see these berries turn orange, I know it's close to Hallowe'en. See?" she said, picking a berry and showing it to us. "It looks like a little pumpkin."

Each in turn picked a berry and studied it closely. I pinched the berry, and it opened into a light yellow center, the consistency resembling that of an apple. Penny took a berry and put it to her mouth.

"Don't eat it," warned Loella, "it'll give you a tummy ache."

During Loella's warning to Penny, Cole had grabbed a handful of berries and tossed one at Mischief, who had crawled under the berry bush, curious.

"Get him," said Cole, referring to the idea of assaulting the cat with berries. He threw his handful at Mischief, and I threw my berry halves at Cole. One bounced off and hit Penny. We three grabbed for more berries and threw at each other—even Loella ended up getting hit and returned fire. Cole grabbed one bunch too eagerly. Several thorns punctured the top of his hand.

"Ow!" he yelped. Reacting swiftly, he yanked his hand out from the bush, but in doing so the thorns dragged into his flesh, resulting in blood and pain.

He cried.

Pappa heard from somewhere, and he chased us from the bush, muttering something about "fool kids" and took Cole inside to be cleaned up. Once Father left, Penny started crying, probably from the yelling Pappa gave us. Loella and I tried to cheer her up, but that proved difficult since we were upset as well.

Stocki.

It was Hallowe'en. At school we celebrated by dressing up in costumes, reading scary stories, dancing to creepy music, and receiving candy. We took the same old broncoing bus home and learned to our delight that Pappa was out doing his own celebrating at STOCKY Sam's Tavern.

Mamma prepared a yummy supper of meatloaf and fruit salad before Penny, Cole, Loella, and I left for Tricks or Treats around the neighborhood. It was a good dinner—especially so with Pappa not around to spoil it, and Mamma laughed at each comment we made. She was in the best mood I'd seen since the beginning of school.

"Now off you go," she said, "and don't forget to say thank you."

"Yes, ma'am," we replied.

Loella turned on her flashlight as we left the dark porch. She was dressed as a witch, Cole as a fireman, Penny as an angel, and I as a ghost. First, we went to the Jensens' across the street.

"Trick or treat," we said after the door opened in response to the bell.

"My my, what do we have here?" asked Mrs. Jensen, so spritely and happy. "For you, little angel." She dropped some candy in Penny's bag. "And you, Mr. Fireman. And, oh my, you are a scary ghost! Here you are. And something for the witch."

"Thank you," we said, and we practically ran to the next house.

"Trick or treat," we said again. It was the Carsons' house. Mr. Carson treated us with quarters. "Thank you," we called back.

This continued for several more houses. As luck had it, we joined up with three or four others—at some houses the door never closed. About halfway around the neighborhood, we stopped at the Mitchells'.

"I'll wait near the road for you when you're done," Loella said to us, reluctant to accompany us to the door.

Chris Mitchell was an old boyfriend, and though he was probably out getting treats, Loella didn't want to chance meeting him.

"Trick or treat," we said as Mrs. Mitchell answered the front door.

"Oh look, it's the Humbals," she said, giving us each a handful of candy.

She returned inside when done, then from the dark garage flew a figure dressed as a monster. He roared as he came at us, and we ran screaming back to the road. Seeing Loella there, he stopped and removed his mask.

"Hi, Loella. It's been a while since I've seen you," he said, sounding mushy and friendly.

"Hello, Chris. I see you're still scaring people away from you," she said coldly.

"Aw, I'm not the same guy I used to be. That was ages ago."

"A year may be ages to you, but it's not long enough for me."

"Please, Loella, I miss you—"

"Chris, you look better with the mask on your face, so please put it back on."

With that, we skipped two houses and continued our trick-or-treating except Loella, who now waited for us instead of getting candy with us.

In this fashion, we cleaned out the rest of the neighborhood and ventured onto a side road. Our bags sagged from the candies' weight, and as the moon rose higher and higher in the sky, Loella finally suggested we head back home, much to everyone's dismay, but we were tired too, so it wasn't such a bad thing after all.

Not yet.

As we rounded the next to last turn, we saw red and blue flashes peeping through the trees. Curious and afraid, we hastened our pace down the road, and rounding the final bend made our worst imaginations reality. Four police cars and one ambulance in full strobing lights sat in front of our house. A crowd on each side watched as who I later learned was my pappa was forcefully dragged from the house and shoved into a police car. Pappa went unwillingly, and due to his excessive resistance, they jolted him several times with a stun gun.

"Anyone else injured?" asked the ambulance driver.

"No," replied the chief deputy. "She was the only one home. According to her, the children are still out trick or treating."

"In that case, I'll take her to the hospital. What about the children?"

"Their Aunt Shirley was notified. She's coming over here now to pick them up. It shouldn't be more than twenty minutes for her. We'll be almost done by that time, so we'll watch for them," the chief deputy explained.

We walked up to the crowd as first the police car with Pappa left, then the ambulance with Mamma left twenty seconds later. Just as it was out of sight, one neighbor noticed our presence and informed the chief deputy.

"What's going on?" asked Loella, her voice shaking with gripping fear.

Stockin.

Chief Deputy STAUCHEN had us sit there until Aunt Shirley arrived. Thirty or so minutes later, she was as upset as us. Determined, she took us to her home with Uncle Jeff and cousins Bill and Leona. Uncle Jeff had been out trick-or-treating with Bill and Leona, but once he returned, Aunt Shirley told him briefly what happened. He and the cousins took care of us while Aunt Shirley went to the hospital to see Mamma.

October passed on to November, and we spent three days with Aunt Shirley and Uncle Jeff. Mamma was released from the hospital, and we returned home. I think Aunt Shirley and Uncle Jeff must have helped straighten up our house before we went back, but I could tell things were not as they used to be. One of Mamma's favorite lamps was gone, the door had a hole punched into it, there was a dent in the wall next to another door, the coffee table was scratched, etc.

"Home sweet home," she said with a smile despite a bandage above her left eye and a cast on her left arm.

"Where's Pappa?" asked Penny, unable to understand what was happening.

"Pappa went away for a while," she said unapologetically.

"Will he be home soon?" she asked back.

Loella, Cole and I were hoping he wouldn't, but Pappa always treated Penny as his little angel.

"Soon. Someday soon," she said. Loella gave Mamma a strange look as if to say, "I know how you really feel."

Pappa was restrained from the house, or something like that. Mamma tried to explain it once, but most of us didn't exactly understand what was happening, except that we were happier. After two weeks, Mamma's bandages disappeared, but her cast stayed on a bit longer. I wasn't sure when Pappa would come back, and I wasn't looking forward to it.

Each day, Mamma would have a favorite meal waiting for us. Monday was Penny's day, Tuesday Cole's, Wednesday mine, Thursday Loella's, and Friday was a special surprise. On weekends, Mamma took us out to eat after seeing Saturday and Sunday matinees.

Amazingly, Cole behaved much better at school, avoiding two potential fights and stopping a third between two other boys. He won the best conduct award out of his third-grade class for two weeks straight.

Penny learned how to make cookies using the miniature Betty Crocker oven. It took a little doing at first, but with Mamma helping her, she managed to bake a half dozen in a day.

Loella started playing the piano again (something she did before summer, but stopped once Pappa lost his job). I had grown attached to some pieces she used to play, and her return to those songs brought back pleasant memories. She started new pieces, including one resembling a bumblebee, and another sounding like thunder.

I took up drawing, first in pencil, then with colored pencils as my drawings improved. Mamma gave me a special blank pad just for such a purpose, and I captured tables, chairs, lamps, birds, trees, Mischief, and a funny drawing of Pappa, to which Penny, Cole, and Loella laughed upon seeing.

Thanksgiving Day.

Loella played, "Over the River and Through the Woods," along with several other related songs while Penny tried to sing with her. Cole was busy dangling a ball tied to a string in front of Mischief then running around the house while Mischief chased it. I sat on a corner chair, busy with colored pencils and pad, capturing Thanksgiving Day at the Humbal house.

Mamma worked diligently to prepare the feast and would occasionally sing with Penny and Loella. It was the first time I heard her sing. Her voice was so full and rich, and it vibrated every so often making me wonder where inside her throat she hid the musical instrument. On my drawing, I drew little musical notes coming from her mouth, Penny's mouth, Loella's mouth, and from the piano.

I finished my picture and dinner was ready.

"Time to eat," she said, and with a big hurrah we ran for our places, each having a special plate, cup, and utensils. We sat patiently as Mamma lit the candles, then she instructed each of us to pass our plates from youngest to eldest.

"Would you like light meat, dark meat, stuffing?" she asked each of us, and we all had a little of everything, except Penny, who opted not to have stuffing. Cranberry sauce, mashed potatoes with brothy gravy, moist rolls so hot they nearly burned (and the others chuckled as I quickly tossed rolls around for each, whipping my hands through the air to cool them), olives (both black and green), cooked peas and carrots—what did I leave out? It was too much for a plate; we had to eat some then select what we missed from the first time round. Mamma filled our champagne glasses with ginger ale, though Loella and Mamma received the real stuff.

"When you're as old as Loella," she promised, "you may have champagne. Or wine. Or both. Or milk if you like." She laughed and we laughed with her, because we could eat or drink as we desired, and she would still be happy with us.

Rat-tat-tat! Someone was at the door.

"Who could that be?" asked Mamma, but before getting halfway to the door, she was answered.

"Jill. Open up. I need to talk to you. It's important," said Pappa in a calm voice.

"Dan, what are you doing here!?" she nearly yelled, checking herself and going back to the phone.

"Please, let me in. I need to talk. It's an emergency," he pleaded.

"You know there's a restraining order on you. Leave now before I call the cops."

"No, don't do that. My mother died, and I need someone to talk to," he said.

"You've told that one too often," she said, dialing the police. "Hello? Yes, this is Jill Humbal. I'm at home, and my husband, Dan Humbal, is at my back door and violating his restraining order," she started, but by that time Dan had thrown his body into the door, breaking the lock and thundering into the kitchen.

"I said, don't call the police!" he yelled, stomping up to her and taking the receiver from her hand.

He threw the phone across the kitchen into the window, shattering the glass and our pleasant Thanksgiving. He grabbed her non-casted arm and twisted it behind her back then forced her to the ground. She screamed in agony, saying something about him hurting her. Loella herded us quickly into Mamma's bedroom, where Cole and Penny hid in the closet. Loella and I stayed in the room, and she called the 911 emergency line.

I can remember it taking fifteen minutes for police to arrive, and during that time Mamma kept screaming and yelping. We heard things being knocked over, broken, then vicious, primitive sounds of a physical struggle, slapping, then a crunching sound, like wood breaking, at which Mamma screamed even harder and longer. Then she went quiet. Thumping, stomping, and pounding came closer, down the hall, but stopping in response to police sirens closing. He sounded to have dashed out quickly, but even so we dared not move.

Dared not.

Stocking.

Thanksgiving Day brought forth the Christmas season. We helped Mamma get out the decorations and adorn the living room, the kitchen, the bedrooms, and the outdoors. Mamma found an old STOCKING once used by Pappa when he was a boy, and she immediately threw it out.

In the days following Thanksgiving, we saw nearly every Christmas special on television. Most were out by the first week or two of the season, and in between we played albums of Christmas music on Mamma's record player. Mamma baked Christmas cookies, something she never really did in previous years, and we children made varied cut-outs— snowflakes, Christmas trees, sleighs, reindeer, and Santas that we then taped to the windows, walls, refrigerator, and cupboards.

Loella and I went to the nearby woods to cut down a small cedar tree for me and mistletoe for her. We returned shortly with the greenery. I posted the cedar in my bedroom with a jar filled with water to keep it fresh, and Loella taped the mistletoe to the ceiling in the hallway. Penny gave me a kiss on the cheek and a hug when we were under the 'toe; Loella chased Cole around the house, caught him, then dragged him under the 'toe and smacked him good, after which he ran around the house and hid, trying to evade another attempt by Loella.

Because of the Halloween and Thanksgiving incidents, Pappa was denied his weekend visitation rights. What he did with his free time we didn't know, nor did we care, because we were having such a great time without him.

In mid-December, Mamma had her Halloween cast removed. Aunt Shirley helped us put together a Getting Better party for her, celebrating her continuing recovery. She was so surprised and happy to see the house decorated so, and she mentioned something about having the best family a person could want.

It snowed on December 21st. Snow, snow, snow. It snowed. A good foot in normal places, but drifts piled to three and four feet with the blustery wind. Mamma took the day off from work, and school had already closed for winter break. Despite our excitement to go outside immediately, she ensured we bundled well before going out to play. And play we did.

First thing—we threw snowballs at each other, then at branches ladened with snow to release their burden. Then back at each other, with snowballs as large as basketballs, two opposing snow chums tossing such boulders at each other, only to see the two collide in mid-air. Tired, we plopped on the snow, moved our arms and legs, and in doing so formed snow angels. Cole was too excited to sit, so he gathered snow together and rolled it along, forming the base for a snowman. Loella made the middle, and little Penny made the head, while I gathered pine cones and twigs to form the eyes and mouth.

"He needs a hat," said Cole, likening the fixture to Frosty the Snowman.

Before we could think of what to do for a hat, Cole ran off to the basement then returned with one of Pappa's formal top hats—fresh out of the protective plastic.

"I do believe you are ready for the ball," said Loella. "May I have this dance?" She curtsied then held the snowman as if dancing with him.

Cole, being as hyper and excited as ever, found this too boring. He ran off again, followed by Penny under and into the large white pine in our backyard. They shook the lower branches, then climbed up a bit to shake higher branches. The resulting snow nearly buried the two, but they managed to get through, burrowing like prairie dogs. In the last stretch, they slid into a furrow and stopped.

"Let's go sledding down the hill," Cole suggested, and we raced to the garage for the sleds. We each came out with a different sled type, and off we went to the hill from our back yard to Teapot Creek.

Cole the daring, the lion-hearted, the ole King Cole being so merry a soul went down first, but he didn't get far through the heavy white fluff. Loella and I tried going next to weight it down, but still it wasn't quite right.

"Gang way," said an older voice, and we turned in surprise to see Mamma with her adult-sized sled run at us, by us, then into the snow like a plow blazing through coconut, down the hill and across frozen Teapot Creek.

We followed her down, sliding as far or farther, and across the creek we went oh so slippery and quickly. Mamma went down a second time, but after that she was pooped. We continued, though, going farther down and across each time. Tiring after half-an-hour of traipsing up the hill, we settled for a final slide down with ice skates on, then as we slid across the lake, we stuck our skates in front and pulled up into a stance, though Penny and Cole pulled up too quickly and toppled over. Somehow the wind had kept the snow off Teapot Creek, allowing us to skate easily and quickly.

Mamma put her skates on and followed us, and we cheered her on to some fancy backward skating, figure skating, then several leaps and spins, making us wonder if she skated in the Olympic Games. After several more cheers from us and jumps from her, some unnoticed neighbors had crept up and cheered themselves, making Mamma a little self conscious. She did an incredibly quick spin in a finale, then called it quits and mentioned how we should go in for dinner.

We were too tired to disagree.

Stockings.

Christmas Eve.

Up to that afternoon, we were still making ornaments and cranberry-popcorn chains for the tree. As we finished, Loella went to the piano and played Christmas songs while Mamma prepared supper. We were very excited about Santa visiting us (though Loella was a little less so), about reindeer landing on our roof, and about, about...

Shortly after dinner, Loella, Cole, and I took turns reading from Mamma's *A Collection of Christmas Stories* book. We managed to get through "The Fir Tree," "The Little Match Girl," and "A Christmas Carol," but by that time it was late, and Mamma wasted no time in having us hang our STOCKINGS before scuttling us off to bed.

In those days, Loella shared a room with Penny, and I with Cole. I couldn't vouch for my sisters, but Cole had blossomed into full hyperactivity, tossing and talking to no end about what he was going to get for Christmas, the stockings, the tree, Christmas dinner, etc., going on without end, though I told him several times to hush up and be asleep. His ears were blocked—no doubt with his own excitement—preventing my words from ingraining on his braining. It was this way 'till suddenly without warning or announcement, he fell silent, then breathed heavily in the familiar unconscious mode— sleep.

Christmas Day.

White, fluffy snow fell during the night, adding a fresh wintry look to the yard, the windows, and setting our spirits the merrier. We got up with the sun and nearly rushed to the living room, but Mamma had locked the doors as usual.

"First, you must have something to eat," she insisted, sitting us down to the kitchen table.

In the center lay a cinnamon, hot-cross-bun-style, toroidal bread-stuff, filled with apple mix, cherries, grapes, raisins, and assorted nuts. In the toroid's center lay scrambled eggs with bacon and ham. Mamma poured our favorite drinks, and in the usual Christmas morning haste, we wolfed down the food to the point of nearly baroquing it back up.

At last she lined us up youngest to oldest at the living room door. She turned the key but seemed to have trouble.

"It won't open," she said. "I guess we'll have to skip Christmas this year," she grinned.

"No, no, no!" said Penny sweetly, and Mamma could resist no longer.

She opened the door and in we flew, to the stockings, the tree, the presents, and though she tried slowing us, we were too excited to listen, though she managed to keep us to our stockings for the first few minutes.

"I got candy...I got playing cards...a little dolly...assorted perfume soaps...crayons...toy cars...more candy!" we randomly said.

Then we went through the presents, though it happened so fast Mamma could hardly keep up. Cole got a train set, Penny a doll house, Loella a purse, I received a typewriter, Penny some storybooks, Cole a bicycle, Loella a radio, and I a painting set. This was sufficient for the time, and Mamma went back to the kitchen to clean up from breakfast and prepare for early afternoon dinner.

Cole busily set himself to lay out track and start up his train. Mischief walked in and chased the train going around, even derailing it several times. Penny played with her doll house and the dolls that came with it. I played with my typewriter, figuring out the keys to the letters and experimenting with repeating characters, while Loella put batteries in her radio and tuned it to a station playing Christmas music. A trifle bored, she flipped to another station, one playing a heavy beat. Dance music. Wanting to play it louder, she took the radio in hand and went downstairs to the den, and we followed her, curious.

"All right," she said, "let's see what kind of dance music this will play."

She turned up the volume, and we found the music enticing. Loella broke into a clap, shift and rhythmic dance, and

Penny, Cole, and I imitated her initially, then we broke off into our own dancing ways. We were dancing to the music, the beat pounding my chest and loud enough where we could hear nothing but the music. Penny tried to say something once, but we couldn't hear her. It didn't matter, because we had our own Christmas party happening, and nothing would shake it.

Dance, dance, and dance we did, through several songs and amazingly without Mamma coming down and telling us to turn the music down. Why not? She let us do many things in the last couple months. It wasn't until Penny had to go to the bathroom that we decided to take a small break.

The loud music had prevented us from hearing Mischief scratching impatiently at the door. We let him in, and he ran past us into the spare bedroom, hiding under the bed. As he passed us, I noticed something red on his nose, red as blood.

Loella turned the radio completely off. We looked at each other in confusion while Penny stomped in place, indicating her need to go to the bathroom immediately.

"Wait here," she said to Cole and me.

She and Penny went upstairs, then the two returned shortly. Cole was anxious to go upstairs for some reason, but he didn't say why. Penny didn't seem to notice anything, but Loella was more puzzled than before. She knew something was afoot.

"What is it?" I asked.

She looked at Penny and Cole, then at me, ready to speak, then she closed her mouth.

"Cole, why don't you and Penny go into the spare bedroom and listen to my radio," she suggested.

"Neat-o!" he exclaimed, and he ran into the adjoining room and turned up the radio, much to Loella's approval.

"So?" I asked.

"I went up there with Penny, and I thought, 'Funny it's so quiet.' Mamma was in the kitchen cleaning up and working on the dinner, right?"

"Yeah," I replied, "maybe she got tired and took a nap."

"Something else—it's cold up there, and I felt a draft coming around the corner, like someone opened a window or something."

"Or door? Did you go and see?" I asked.

"No," Loella replied, "and we never went down the hallway far enough to look in the kitchen. I don't know why, maybe because Penny was with me or something. Maybe I'm just silly."

"Well, maybe Mamma burned something, and she's trying to air out the house. She does that sometimes," I noted.

"Sometimes."

"Well, we have to go up and look at least. It's probably our imagination again," I said.

"I hope you're right," Loella said.

With Loella leading the way, we went up the stairs, unnoticed by Cole and Penny, and stopped at the top. Loella was right—it was cold.

"Mamma?" I called out.

No response.

"Mamma?" called Loella.

The same.

The wind kicked up a nasty draft, and we knew the door or window had to be closed. Goose-pimpled, we edged down the hall, around the corner, and into the kitchen.

On the floor lay our empty future.

Red Stockings.

As I think back to those years and re-examine what happened, I find it difficult to make sense of it all without becoming emotional. The single fixated image in my mind is of my Mamma there on the floor, what were once white now RED STOCKINGS from the pool of blood surrounding her. I still can't remember what happened after the initial shock, even the funeral is a haze, though for some reason I recall the casket was never opened for viewing.

Pappa was found guilty of gruesomely murdering Mamma and was sentenced to life imprisonment without parole. Cole and I were adopted by Aunt Shirley and Uncle Jeff, while Penny and Loella ended up with my other aunt. Penny grew up a spoiled brat and ended up doing drugs and selling herself to afford the habit. Cole's hyperactivity only worsened, starting with the killing of Mischief, and furthering with random attacks and thievery. After robbing a store and brutally murdering the cashier, he joined his father at the same prison with nearly identical sentence. Loella died six years after Mamma's death from ovarian cancer, and the only existing image of Mamma was wrenched away.

With failure surrounding my family, it seemed I would suffer the same fate. Several times I came close to being swallowed up by the dark vortex that took the others, but somehow I managed to slip by. For years I vowed to keep to myself as much as possible. This way, the family beast within would never have the chance to wrong others as I had been wronged. I continued this way, living like a hermit until age thirty. That's when I met Traci.

For once I felt I no longer had to be the ashes of the past. The one blowing around in the wind without purpose or direction had changed into a planting of roots and making something new, something real, something wonderful. In meeting Traci I felt so alive, that I could do something with my life, that there could be happiness again.

I was also fragile.

The higher I went, the greater the *potential* fall. I knew that, and something in the back of my mind said such happiness wasn't right, I didn't deserve it, and I had to do something to stop the "fantasy" and settle for reality. It was a strange feeling, and sometimes when Traci and I were laughing, something told me I should hurt her, because laughing wasn't right. It was my beast within, and it reminded me who I was and where I came from.

Despite the urges to turn joy into sorrow, I made a supreme effort and took no violent action, and after dating two years, we married. The ceremony itself was a little awkward without Mamma and Pappa, but Traci's family took up where mine failed me, and they welcomed me with much warmth and amour. Still it seemed too good, but during the traditional first dance for the bride and groom, I suddenly felt completely at ease with Traci, and from then on knew I was no longer living my life, but our life.

Tomorrow will make twenty-five years since Mamma's passing. It's Christmas Eve, my two girls are already in bed, though probably not asleep, and my wife, Traci, is finishing up the Christmas tree trimmings. She's the best, and my girls as good, and I remind myself how fortunate I am to have succeeded where my family roots failed. I have to, because I still am haunted to this day and probably will be forever.

Each year I think back to that fateful Christmas, and each year I think of not the bad, but of Mamma's cheer and goodheartedness to give us the very best anyone could have, and it is this spirit that I share with Traci and the girls. Time heals, and from the ashes of a previous life comes forth a small, fragile flower—my love with our love, the one empowering force that can wash away the burns and scars and will make our lives happy ones.

Merry Christmas Traci and girls. Merry Christmas Penny and Cole. Merry Christmas Mischief. Merry Christmas Loella. Merry Christmas, Mamma. Happy New Year, Brian Humbal. Happy every year, all year, our only precious years.

Jacob Richardson
in

Unseen Assailant: Part III

June 16, 1993

Though Helen had stopped bleeding, she was weak, and I had to help her walk through the woods. We'd been travelling for twenty minutes or more—I'd actually lost track of time—and was wondering how much longer she could last. I felt badly for being aggressive and hostile toward Farmer Sam, but I put him behind me and concentrated on getting to the rendezvous point.

"There's a dirt road ahead," I said to Helen.

"Follow it," she mumbled.

"Which way?" I asked. Helen mumbled again, but I couldn't make out her words.

"Helen?"

"All right you two, don't make a move," came a voice around a tree. Another person came from behind a boulder. Both had police uniforms, though slightly different from McLean's at the road block.

"What is this?" I asked. "Who are you?"

"This way," they motioned with their guns. One picked up his portable radio. "We have them, sir."

(End of Part II, beginning of Part III.)

"Bring them here," the voice came back.

After walking a short distance, one guard motioned me to get inside a jeep neatly camouflaged behind brush. The other carried Helen and placed her next to me. We travelled for perhaps twenty minutes through a thick forest of trees and bushes. It was dark, though I wasn't sure if the trees kept the light out or if the sun had set.

Before I could determine which, the jeep stopped at a small hill or large mound. The guards got us out, and we walked around a bush. One guard mumbled something, touched some buttons on his transceiver, and a door previously unnoticed slid open.

"Here at last," said a familiar voice. "But I see you have a casualty. Please, bring her over here," he said to a guard, motioning over toward a large couch.

"Dr. Brandberg?" I asked, incredulous.

"Yes, it is I. I'm sorry for the cold welcome, but it was necessary to prevent suspicion. We can't have the CIA follow you here. All right, guards, you may go. Let me know if anything else happens."

"Yes, sir," called one guard as the two went back out on patrol.

"Dr. Brandberg, it *is* you. What is this place, how did you get use of it, what is going on, why are we being chased, can you help Helen?" I asked in an outburst.

"Slow down there, Jacob. Relax. I'll take care of Helen, no problem," Brandberg said, taking out his medicine bag and examining Helen. He carefully cleansed the wound and felt the arm. Helen groaned in pain.

"Well? How bad is it?" I asked.

"Fortunately, the bullet passed through and is no longer in her arm. However, Helen lost a good deal of blood and is going into shock. I'm going to close the wound with stitches," he said, giving her a local anesthetic. "Then we'll need to elevate her legs."

I impatiently watched Dr. Brandberg sew Helen up like a rag doll. My hands restlessly twitched and fidgeted during each needle stroke. Helen was unconscious, and for the first time I worried she would die.

"Isn't there anything I can do?" I asked, trying to be helpful and get my mind off the dilemma.

"Yes. Look for some drinking water and salt. If Helen is to survive, we'll have to get her blood pressure up. Down the hall and to the left is a small kitchen—you should be able to find everything there."

The surroundings looked like some sort of fallout shelter or bunker. A musty odor in the kitchen tingled my nose as I filled a bottle with water. What was this place? I searched several cupboards—mostly of canned food—then found a cylinder filled with salt. Returning, I found Dr. Brandberg elevating her legs, placing a pillow under them for support. Helen's arm had a red-stained bandage around it. On further instructions from Dr. Brandberg, I mixed a salt-water drink.

"Let's see if we can get her to drink," Dr. Brandberg said. He gently lifted her head and slowly poured the salt-water into her mouth. Helen seemed to regain semi-consciousness and drank the water.

"How bad is she? Will she survive?" I asked, concerned.

"She'll pull through, though it may take some time. What she needs now is rest, so I think it best we leave her be and move to the other room," he explained, motioning me to a meeting-like room.

A large table surrounded by eighteen chairs occupied the room's center. Bookcases covered all available wall space—I could have spent hours counting the books.

"This is one of the smaller state bunkers, usually used for emergencies such as war. The governor has agreed to let us use it until we can straighten out this whole situation."

"The state governor? He *let* you use this place?"

"Mr. Richardson, Jacob, it may seem as if you were just sick with anthrax, but I'm afraid it's much more, much much more. What I am about to tell you is not well known, and it took me a good deal of special research to learn. You and Helen stumbled across an old government testing ground."

"State testing ground?" I asked.

"No, federal. It was used to develop deviant anthrax strains. It's all part of the Operation Purge project. It started years ago when...Helen, what are you doing up?"

She staggered across the room, her eyes barely open. Dr. Brandberg and I leapt from our chairs and supported her. Her legs gave way, and we helped her to a lounge chair in the corner.

"How are you feeling?" I asked.

"Weak. Hungry."

"That's a good sign. I'll be back in a moment," said Dr. Brandberg. He left us for several minutes then returned with beef broth and bread. "There," he said, "this should do you good." He turned to me and said, "Excuse me for not asking, Jacob, but are you hungry? Thirsty?"

"I'm fine. I would like to hear more about this story, though."

"Very well," he said, returning to his chair. "Where was I?"

"Operation Purge," I replied. "What does that mean?"

"As you may know, the health care system is bigger now than ever before, with costs going through the roof at an exponential rate. It's unfortunate, and I'm not sure the best way to solve it while continuing to give quality medical care, but the federal government has decided to solve the problem by eliminating the problem."

"Some medical problems, a broken arm or a bleeding leg, are no more than accidents and cannot be prevented on a large scale. Others such as manic depression or allergies are considered genetic flaws. Operation Purge is about eliminating those people with the flaws, to prevent them from being passed down to new children and thus contain these increasing medical costs."

"But why anthrax?" Helen asked. Though resting, she was listening to Dr. Brandberg eagerly.

"I'm not sure. Jacob's having the disease was strange enough, and the variant strain even more so. I had to use a special egg embryo to develop the necessary antibodies, along with special genetic manipulations of the culture thanks in part to Dr. Brown and his unique computer analysis. Even you, Jacob, helped by providing some antibodies that were fighting the disease effectively. I simply increased the number to quickly eradicate it from your body."

"The cure was highly effective, and as with any new find, I reported it to Dr. Leech, who seemed agitated for some reason, though I couldn't understand why. Actually, he pulled me aside and insisted I hand any future anthrax cases over to him. I was further puzzled by this unusual behavior and decided it best to do some personal investigation."

"When Dr. Leech went away for a meeting, I made it my business to do something unprofessional—look through his files. Getting into his office wasn't too difficult, but his filing cabinets were locked. After a bit of effort with some improvised tools, I broke into one."

"Now how did you manage that?" I asked.

"I wasn't always a doctor. In high school, I got into a fair amount of mischief—my best skill was opening locked doors, cabinets, and files. Among some of my peers I was known as Bust-it-open Brandberg."

"Well, that's beside the point. I got into his files and found one on Operation Purge. Apparently, he is the chief doctor involved in the project. Phase One researched various bacteria and viruses to determine suitability. Anthrax was selected because: 1) it could be tested on cattle (which seemed an appropriate beast for simulating humans), and 2) it could spread quickly, unlike viruses, which could take months or years to spread from one person to another. Phase Two involved mutating the bacterium to make it attack only those people with the predetermined genetic flaws. To accomplish this, Dr. Leech had also discovered ways to mutate the bacterium into a virus. He called the viral version anthrax-v, and it reproduced as quickly as the bacterial version, making it highly effective for the project's purposes."

"Phase Three involved testing the bacterial and viral versions on cattle to determine effectiveness. Special cows were born with genetic flaws, initiated by Leech's scientists, and some responded while others did not. So far, this phase is not complete. Leech was having final tests performed when you, Jacob, came in with an older version of the anthrax. I learned later he held a special meeting to discuss the ramifications of

Jacob and my cure, and it was decided the cure should be destroyed, because it was also effective against the current strain, and that would have invalidated years of work."

"Unfortunately, for no known reason, some of the staff came down with the disease, and since my cure was destroyed, I was not able to save them. They died. Leech was looking for a good alibi in you, Jacob. He went to the press and held a news conference saying how you were the cause of this disease."

"So I'm the scapegoat?" I asked.

"I'm afraid so. Though you no longer have the disease, Leech wants it to look as if you do and are a threat to society. The real reason he wants you, I think, is to prevent another cure from being created. As I said, I took some of your own antibodies to create the cure. No one else showed the ability to retain this antibiotic level—another reason why Leech wants you. If he can develop a strain that can kill you, then I think he'll feel the project is complete and release the highly fatal version throughout the United States."

"This is as much as I know about Operation Purge and Dr. Leech's role. What he'll do next I don't know, but I've made it clear to the governor everything I know, and he's promised to help us *set the record straight*, if I may use the saying."

"Can we trust the governor, though?" I asked.

"Absolutely. He and I have been friends for years. I also know he has more to lose than gain by Operation Purge. In checking the report in Dr. Leech's files, there was some strategy indicating the federal government would benefit considerably, though the states would suffer, and that it was decided the state governments would not be informed of the project. Now our state governor is considering running for U.S. President during the next re-election. He could make a major coup by exposing the existing government and making himself out to be the hero. That's the impression I gathered while speaking with him over the phone."

"So what do we do now?" Helen asked.

"Rest and recuperate, especially you, Helen. The governor needs some time to gather the evidence together anyway, so until he's ready, we'll stay here. I already notified him you're here, so there's little else we can do but watch and wait."

Though Dr. Brandberg's voice seemed reassuring, I felt uneasy and anxious, as if we were sitting ducks waiting for the hunters to flush us out. Regardless, the stay proved restful, and Helen swiftly recovered from her ordeal, getting around quite nicely after several days. Dr. Brandberg removed the stitches after a week, and he assured us we'd be on the move in the following day or two. Our flight, I hoped, would soon end.

"How far could they've gotten, I wonder?" muttered Gunter as a police vehicle pulled up. McLean stepped out along with a tattered, old farmer.

"Sir, this is Farmer Sam Jones. I picked him up alongside the road while I was on the way back from getting a new vehicle," said McLean. Farmer Sam tipped his hat to Gunter.

"That's right. Shot off the road by 'em, weren't you McLean?" Gunter said.

"I promise, sir, I did everything possible to stop them before—" McLean said, defensive.

"Yeah, I know. Forget it. All right, Mr. Jones, suppose you tell us what happened."

"I ain't in any danger, am I?" Farmer Sam asked, worried.

"Why should you be? They can't hurt you anymore. You're a little shaken, that much I can tell, but otherwise you seem fine," replied Gunter.

"That's not what I meant. I saw the report on the television. I know about the sickness, and they got it."

"Just simmer down there, Mr. Jones. First I want you to take a deep breath and tell us what in Sam Hill happened to you."

"Well, I went out to the barn to start the milkin' of the cows," Farmer Jones started, "when I heard voices comin' from the hayloft. Not knowing who it was, I went back for my shotgun and came back out to investigate."

"That's when I caught 'em. I forced them out of the barn and was bringing 'em back to the house when they took me by surprise and got the gun. They forced me into my truck full of taters, makin' me drive for them, but I didn't really know where they wanted to go. We went through a road check, and I tried to give Officer McLean a glance 'cause I couldn't talk to him plainly. Mr. Richardson had the gun stickin' in my side."

"Officer McLean came after us fairly soon after leaving the road check. One of 'em fired at him, and he went off the road. I could barely stay on the road myself with the sudden noises and all. Anyway, Mr. Richardson forced me to stop, and I did. I had to go over to a tree and count to a hundred, or else he'd shoot. They sped off before I got to ten, and I quit countin' after twenty."

"And that was it. I started walkin' back to town when McLean came along and picked me up. He explained about gettin' back to the station and gettin' another car. It seemed kinda quick and all, but I tell you something, strange things are happening these days, like the three-legged chicken I saw in the barn the other day—"

"Thank you, Mr. Jones," Gunter cut in, "I'm sure we'll be talking to you again. McLean, would you like to take Mr. Jones back to his farm and see about a tow for his truck? Seems our fugitives drove 'till the engine overheated. Water pump is probably busted. Anyway, off with you, boy."

Gunter made a few final notes in his book then went back to his car to bring out the dogs.

"Looks like we'll be doing this all over again, just like the Lakeside Inn woods. What keeps the folks on their feet I'll never know," Gunter grumbled to Tarske.

"Forget the search," Tarske said.

"What?"

"You heard me. There'll be no search this time. Special orders from high up—we are to erase all evidence of our being here and report back to your police station. My car is waiting for me there, and I will go off to a special meeting with my superiors."

"I assume you'll still want the road checks."

"Absolutely not."

"You're giving up the man-hunt? Absurd!"

"Now listen carefully: we are ceasing our hunt, at least for the moment. I can't say any more than that, but believe me, we will not cease our search for the Richardsons and Brandberg. We will simply resume at a different time. Understood?" Tarske said, looking sternly at Gunter.

"Yeah, I s'pose." Gunter went back out to the officers, waved his arms around wildly several times, then the officers returned to their vehicles and drove away, dejected.

"Good job. Now back to the station," said Tarske as Gunter returned.

"Yeah, right," he shot back sarcastically.

The two sat in silence during the return to Gunter's police station where Tarske's car had been taken after the helicopter accident. Gunter resented not being taken along with Tarske for what appeared to be a secret meeting. Being in the dark only made Gunter more suspicious of Tarske as well as more uncomfortable than he was before the search started.

Dr. Leech sipped a glass of water and cleared his throat in preparation for the meeting in Bunker House One.

"Agent Tarske, this is Governor Thomas. Governor, this is Agent Tarske," said Dr. Leech, introducing the two. Besides the three, there were three other people—Agent Sanders, who oversaw most of Operation Purge research secrecy, Dr. Walker, a geneticist for Operation Purge, and Agent Howland, the overseer of Operation Purge. Introductions continued until everyone knew everyone else.

Leech said, "I've called this meeting for several reasons. First, Governor Thomas has some excellent news for us. Governor?"

"Thank you, doctor. We know the whereabouts of the Richardsons," he started.

"Where?" several asked in astonishment.

"In a small, state bunker. Very recently Dr. Brandberg approached me, asking for help in avoiding the manhunt. He doesn't know my involvement with Operation Purge, so I let him have a bunker, hoping it would lure the Richardsons in our hands. It worked. The Richardsons are there as we speak."

A laughter erupted followed by pressing words from Tarske:

"Why didn't you let us know? We could have waited right there and hauled them in immediately."

"No. Too suspicious," replied Howland. "Sorry to keep you in the dark on this one, Tarske, but it was crucial we did *not* raise any concerns with Brandberg. We want all three."

"In addition, the media will think we lost their trail and that the three are still at large. This plays into our hands perfectly, because we'll be able to spread the disease around and use them as scapegoats. We'll consistently plant the anthrax mutation in a progressive circular path around the country then hold press conferences to show how this indicates the Richardsons' positions. Forces can be mobilized in these areas to conduct a *search*, but it will only be for show."

"Who else knows of this plan?" Tarske asked.

"Only those in this room," replied Howland. "The project's secrecy is paramount."

"Which is definitely to our advantage," commented Leech. "Regarding Operation Purge itself, Dr. Walker has good news. Doctor?"

"We completed testing the disease against cattle, making Phase Three complete. When the three are in custody, Phase Four will begin as described by Dr. Leech. Several modifications were made to the anthrax variant to make a cure more difficult to find, thanks to research notes provided by Dr. Leech on Mr. Richardson during his hospital stay."

"It shouldn't take too long to put them away," continued Dr. Leech. "I will ensure Mr. Richardson provides ample blood and tissue samples for our research into enhancements."

"That's the key," added Howland. "It doesn't matter if Brandberg and Mrs. Richardson are taken dead or alive, but Mr. Richardson *must* be taken alive. Tarske, you will bring the three here—Bunker House One. We'll put Mr. Richardson in the Microbial Lab's holding cell; the other two will be taken to the maximum security holding cells until we decide when to get rid of them. Sanders, once the three are here, you will co-ordinate your men with Dr. Walker's Phase Four implementation."

Tarske was grim, and both Dr. Walker and Sanders were itching with excitement.

"I think the worst part is over," said Leech to Tarske, trying to reassure him.

"I hope you're right. We've had a devil of a time trying to catch the fugitives. It will be good to have them under lock and key."

"It will. Everyone knows what to do?" Leech asked. Everyone nodded in affirmation. "Very well, this meeting is adjourned."

"What's the word?" asked Gunter when Tarske called over the telephone.

"Not very good. I'm afraid I will not be resuming the search with you. Another more important project requires my attention," Tarske replied. Gunter fumed.

"What?? You mean to tell me I was inches from havin' them in my hands, you call me away, and now you're saying I should resume on my own? What kind of crap is that?"

"I have no choice in the matter. You're on your own."

With the conversation ended, Gunter stared in empty disbelief at the telephone, not sure what would happen next.

"Dad-gum Tarske. He's up to no good, I'll warrant. His game is anyone's guess, but something's amiss—I feel it in my gut," he mumbled. He turned around and went to his men, saying, "We're on our own again, boys. I gotta feeling Tarske has his own agenda, but we can't worry 'bout that now. We're gonna search 'dem woods 'till we find 'em. I ain't come this far just to let 'em slip through."

"Johnson," Gunter continued, "I want you to set up phone taps on relatives, friends, and anyone else the Richardsons might call."

"Sir, with Dr. Brandberg out there, he may—" started Jackson.

"He may try to call his people. Yes, tap them too. Also, watch for credit card transactions, personal checks, and any other bank transactions. They'll need money if they can't solicit help."

"Right away, sir," acknowledged Johnson, rushing away. Gunter turned to Jackson and Rogers.

"We'll use the blood hounds again. Rogers and Jackson, each of you bring three of your men. McLean, dispatch the road-block team. I want these fugitives caught. Move out!"

Helen sneezed. Again, and again.

"Are you all right?" I asked.

"I don't know," she sneezed.

"It's musty. Must be the dampness in this bunker. We should get you outside for some fresh air. I'll call the guards over to escort you," said Dr. Brandberg, activating a radio. "Iceberg to Ice-cube, do you read?" No response. Dr. Brandberg repeated his call, but neither guard responded. Brandberg stood motionless, puzzled.

"What is it? What's wrong?" Helen asked.

"That's odd. Neither guard is responding to my call."

"Maybe they're out of range," I suggested.

"Or something is blocking the transmission," he added. "Very well. We'll go to the surface and take a look. Here, toss me that portable transceiver, will you?" he asked, pointing to a collection of transceivers on a shelf.

"Here you are," I said, tossing one across the room.

"Good. We'll try again from the surface."

Helen had returned nearly to normal, and my previous illness had shown no recent ill effects. We were nearly out the door when Helen thought she heard a *clankity-clank* from below. The air tensed.

"I don't like this," said Brandberg in a low voice. "Something strange is going on."

We surfaced and walked a hundred feet from the bunker then stopped near a large bush. Dr. Brandberg looked for any visible evidence of the guards. Helen and I looked at each other, as if saying, "Here we go again."

"Iceberg to Ice-cube, do you read? Do you copy?" Silence. "Dammit, boys, where are you? Answer me!" The transceiver's steady static added nothing to our comfort. A group of birds from the east suddenly flew away.

"We're not alone. Someone or something just caused those birds to fly," I suggested, worried.

"Jacob, relax. It's probably the guards. I'll bet their batteries went dead and they're coming back for fresh ones."

"All the same," I said, "I'd feel safer from behind the bush instead of standing out in the open."

"If you insist. I'm sure there's nothing to worry about," said Brandberg.

Faint voices grew stronger, indicating people were coming our way. Dr. Brandberg's relaxed composure changed to a concerned one, and within a few minutes we knew the voices did not belong to the guards. Barking echoed through the woods. Helen and I exchanged nervous glances, and we three quickly decided to make a run.

"Something's gone wrong," said a puffing Dr. Brandberg.

"Now what do we do?" I asked.

"Trust me on this. There's only one person who can help us now," Dr. Brandberg replied.

"By foot?" asked Helen, still a little weak.

"I hope not. Though I wasn't expecting this, my car is parked at a small grocery store. It's only a couple of miles away."

Dogs barking and men yelling continued to motivate our hurried pace through the heavily forested woods.

"Remember, men, Mr. Richardson is to be taken *alive*. I don't care about the others, but don't get sloppy. This is supposed to be a silent operation," Tarske said.

Tarske continued briefing his men on bunker details, surprising the fugitives, and the actions to take once the fugitives were secured.

"So we stay in the bunkers and associated passages the entire time?" asked one of Tarske's men.

"Yes. Under no circumstances are we to be seen in the open. Let's go," Tarske said, leading the way through the underground passage from Bunker House One toward the Brandberg bunker. The team (comprising six, including Tarske) rode in small rail cars, and travelled ten or more miles toward the Brandberg bunker when Tarske stopped the lead car abruptly.

"Shhh," he said, cautioning them back with his outstretched arm. "I hear something." Lowering his voice to a near whisper, he said, "Take defensive positions. Fire on my signal only."

The passageway was not well lit, and an approaching rail car was nearly upon the group before Tarske could make out who was riding it. The rail car stopped several yards in front of Tarske.

"Agent Tarske, is that you?" came a voice.

"Relax, boys, it's the governor's guards," Tarske said to his men. He turned to the guards and said, "What are you doing down here?"

"Orders sir," said the voice. "We're to lead you to the fugitives."

"*Lead* me to them? You could have saved me the trouble and brought them yourselves! Who's watching them now?" inquired Tarske.

"Sir?"

"The fugitives, who's making sure they don't escape?"

The guards looked at each other silently.

"You mean to tell me *no one* is watching them? You idiotic—"

"Respectfully, sir," started one guard, "they won't be going anywhere. The woman can hardly get about, and the other two are convinced they're perfectly safe."

"Yeah, sure," Tarske muttered impatiently. "Well, I can't afford to chastise you all day down here. Let's get moving!"

Now a group of eight, they made their way through the second bunker's corridor, amidst cobwebs, scattered garbage, and scurrying rats. Water trickled from cracks along the wall, and a greenish-black mossy mold covered the moist areas.

"What a stench down here," muttered Tarske, glad he didn't have to step in the goo.

The group came to a six-way intersection, and without hesitation, the guards selected the passageway slightly to the left. Tarske and men followed, and within a few additional minutes they were at the door to the Brandberg bunker.

"This is it," said one guard, leaving the car along with Tarske and his men.

"All right. Remember, we want Mr. Richardson alive. Ready? Now!" commanded Tarske, and the group stormed into an empty bunker.

"Where are they?" asked a puzzled guard.

"Are you sure this is the correct bunker?" asked Tarske.

"Yes," said the guard. "Look—a bandage with dried blood. It's probably from Mrs. Richardson. She was injured when we brought her in."

"So, McLean hit her after all. However, it's clear they're not here, unless they're hiding or outside. I want this bunker searched from top to bottom," ordered Tarske.

"Begging your pardon, sir, but there are no hiding places in the bunker. It's really rather plain, as you can see for yourself."

"Very well. Let's go outside and see if they're around."

"But sir," said one of Tarske's men.

"I know, I know. We're supposed to stay underground. We won't go far, just enough to see if we can make the arrest. Move out."

The group encircled the outside portion of the bunker then spiraled out. Barking from afar vibrated through the air. The group of eight looked around in disappointment—no one could see the fugitives.

"Angh," muttered Tarske under his breath.

While the others continued looking, he went back inside the bunker, picked up the phone, and dialed.

"No, they're not here...I don't know, the guards couldn't give a legitimate excuse...You think so?...Really?...Yeah sure. Will do."

Tarske slammed the receiver, went outside, and called everyone back in.

"What is it?" asked a guard.

"We're returning through the passageway. No discussion. Let's move," Tarske said, and the eight went back through the passageway in their rail cars, through the intersection, then back to the Bunker House One.

"Whoa, boy, simmer down," said Gunter to his dog. "Well what do we have here? Seems someone left in a hurry."

Gunter discovered the abandoned bunker. He immediately called Jackson and Rogers over the radio and beckoned them over his way. Minutes later, the other eight met up with Gunter.

"This could be it, but we're a little late," commented Jackson.

"Maybe not *too* late. All right, boys, let's make a quick search for anything and everything. Move!"

Jackson and Rogers led their dogs through the bunker while their group of three each checked and overturned every picture, chair, table, and rug. Gunter watched from a supervisory vantage point. Several minutes later turned up several items.

"Well, well, what do we have here?" mused Gunter.

"Looks like a bloodied bandage," commented Jackson, "possibly from Mrs. Richardson, who was shot at—"

"And hit by McLean. But it's been a week, and she's probably strong as an ox."

"Found these, Sarge. Looks like medical papers," said Rogers.

"Hmm. 'Operation Purge,' it says. And some personal papers of Dr. Brandberg. Yup, he knows, and he's helping them for sure. All right, we need personal possessions of these people, especially Brandberg. Well?"

One of the men handed over a large T-shirt to Gunter.

"Well," said Gunter, "either Richardson has gained weight quicker than ice meltin' on the Fourth of July, or we have one of Brandberg's shirts. Let's give it to the dogs."

"This looks like something of Mr. Richardson's," said Jackson, finding a sock with the initials *JR* embroidered on the side.

"Bandage, one; shirt, two; and sock makes three. Gentlemen, we have another hunt ahead of use. Rogers, take two of your men and stay here; make sure we haven't missed anything. Who knows, someone may visit you." Gunter pulled Rogers's third guy and one of Jackson's men to follow Gunter on the hunt. All told, three would watch the bunker, three were in Jackson's group (including Jackson), and three were in Gunter's group (including Gunter).

"Fresh trail this way," said Jackson as his two men managed the two dogs. The six had barely moved a stone's throw from the bunker. Gunter and group followed alongside; his two men managed the other two dogs. All four dogs moved and barked with an eagerness proportional to the apparent shortening distance between the hunters and hunted.

"Look at 'dem dogs go," muttered Gunter, who was falling behind. "What's up now," he tried to say, but Jackson and the other four raced along with the dogs in pursuit of the prey. The barking continued, though it faded into echoes from ahead, around a small boulder cluster, then silence. Jackson and the men—gone. The dogs—gone. Gunter stood for a moment looking around in disbelief.

"Where in blazes did they go?" he asked, perplexed. He reached for his hand radio to find it missing. "Dammit!" he said. "Where'd that go? Must've dropped it in the excitement." Before Gunter could decide what to do, he heard a distant heavy breathing nearing, with occasional twigs snapping. He took cover behind a bush and watched as the mysterious person unknowingly neared.

We ran for only twenty minutes while the barking faded then stopped entirely. Tired, especially Dr. Brandberg, we stopped for a brief rest in a small clearing. A newly fallen tree provided a good place to sit.

"I don't know how much farther I can continue running. I'm badly out of shape. I could be risking a heart attack," said Dr. Brandberg between heavy gasps.

"But you have to go on with us," I said. "Without you, how are we to have any hope at all?"

"Believe me, if you could make it to the bunker, you can make it to the governor's. Our chasers are not so much interested in me anyway. You're the ones they're after. Just get to the governor's as quickly yet discreetly as possible. Take these," he said, handing car keys to me. "My black Mercedes is at the grocery store—just off Highway 29."

"Highway 29? We came up that road in the farmer's truck—we left that road and fled in the woods. You're saying we have to go *back* to that road?" I asked, perplexed.

"I'm not saying you need to get back to the road. The woods lead all the way to the back of the grocery store. But once you *do* get there and get in the car, you'll have to take Highway 29 until you hit a small road, Waterford Trail. Take that west all the way into the capitol. It'll be slow and bumpy, but it's the safest way in I can think of. I'm sure the police are still conducting road checks," Dr. Brandberg explained.

"Even if we do get there, what then?" asked Helen.

"Here," Brandberg said, handing us a paper, "call this number. It's a direct line to his phone, or at least to one of his aids. Explain why you're calling, that you're one of my personal friends, and how the governor and I arranged for your safe protection."

I opened my mouth to protest his not coming with us when the barking resumed.

"There," he said, "they're back on the trail. Go on now. Further down this path is a deep ravine—be careful not to fall into it! To the right perhaps fifty yards is a bridge you can take to get across. From there the path forks—take the one on the right. For another half mile it will be windy but not difficult, I hope. It should take you right to the store. Good luck!"

"Doctor! You can't stay here—" Helen tried to protest.

"No discussion. Off with you, before it's too late."

We stared at him in disbelief, unable to move.

"This is no time for sentimentality. Get going before they catch you! I'll stall as long as I can. Go. Go, go, GO, GO!"

Regretfully, Helen and I left Dr. Brandberg in the clearing. The image of him sitting there badgering us to go stayed in my mind for quite some time that day and after. But danger has a strange way of motivating a person, and as the barking got louder, I knew our predators were closing quickly.

"Careful, Jacob, I think we're close to the ravine," she said, and not a second too soon. Without warning, the thick woods ended, and at our feet I could see several hundred feet below us the thousands of piled boulders and a small stream etched in the wide expanse. It was mostly a sandy-clay sort of thing, but we had no time to gaze on its magnificence.

"This way," I said, leading her alongside the ravine toward the bridge.

The barking continued, and I thought I heard a deep, husky male voice say, "There they are!"

"They're onto us!" Helen shrieked, and we scampered across a rope-fashioned narrow bridge, swaying and shaking to the point where we nearly lost our balance and fell off. The barking was too near to be comfortable, and police officers shouted both at us and at the dogs. We were plainly visible, and as we went from bridge to solid earth, the four dogs were unleashed and allowed to make a wild dash across the bridge—to us.

There are times in a person's life when death is inevitable, because when the mind is convinced there is no hope of escape or possibility for continuation, it overloads with the most unpleasant neuronic bombardment resulting in holy terrorizing panic. Helen and I glanced at each other for seemingly minutes, but it lasted for perhaps a second. I wished badly for a knife to cut the ropes where the bridge attached to land.

"Untie it," she commanded. Absurd. The knots were too tight, there were too many ropes to untie, and our hands alone could not begin to—

"Untie it!" she repeated with the utmost urgency. My fingers worked without apparent prompting from my mind. They simply proceeded to untie the knots, regardless of whether I thought it was worthwhile or not. The knots were tough, though, and the dogs were already halfway across and still we'd accomplished nothing. Three-quarters of the way across, and I untied an upper rope. The bridge swayed, one dog fell off, but the other three performed a dance to stay on, and they continued to come at us and in fact were nearly on us when Helen untied her knot to a bottom rope. The bridge swayed again, a second dog fell off to his death, but the other two jumped at the last second and were clinging onto the solid earth and a rope, fighting desperately to climb up completely on the ground.

"Get off!" screamed Helen as one dog viciously tugged on her pants leg. She kicked and shook her leg, but the dog held on, ripping the material and gashing into Helen's right leg. I wanted to help but couldn't—the other dog had to be pushed off as well. Kicking and yelling and more kicking—I had kicked the dog six times in the skull before it finally went silly and lost its grip, sinking into the abyss below.

In going over to Helen to help, I saw two police officers gingerly crossing on all fours along the partially suspended bridge. I knew that failing to act quickly would end everything.

"Get off!" Helen screamed again, and the dog had managed to nearly get completely on solid ground and prepared to jump atop Helen as I came crashing down with my fist again and again. The dog was dazed, and I kicked him in the gut. His paws lost traction, and he slid down, but his jaws were locking into Helen's pants leg, pulling her down with him.

Helen screamed, both trying to stop her advance off the cliff edge and trying to shake off the dog. Within seconds, the dog was completely suspended over the side with his closed jaw on Helen's pants preventing a rapid descent. I grabbed Helen's hand to stop her from going over. The dog's weight stressed the pants, they ripped, he went down some with a jerk, then stopped, and the stopping jerked Helen over the edge somewhat, her upper torso now the only part of her body still on solid earth.

"Stay with me now. I'm not going to let you go," I assured her.

She was now in an L-shape, and preventing her slide down meant enduring the cliff's edge on her abdomen.

"Unbutton your pants," I said, the only time I had outside the bedroom. With her right hand still holding onto mine, her left reached around and down and with difficulty unbuttoned her pants. With the dog's weight still tugging, the pants slid off, and the dog fell into the abyss. Without hesitation, I yanked Helen back up, her pink underwear now dirty from the ground.

"They're coming over," I said, and we worked to untie the final ropes, letting loose the last one as two officers started climbing across. They had gone perhaps ten or fifteen feet, and they scrambled to entangle themselves in the ropes to stay on as it fell down in a swinging motion toward a lower point on the opposite cliff's side. The officers landed against the cliff but held firmly onto the ropes. Dazed, they slowly climbed up.

The remaining officers on land fired several shots at us, one nearly hitting Helen in the foot, another lightly grazing my hair. We dropped to prone positions then rolled away into nearby bushes. The firing ceased, but the officers maintained their positions. One spoke into his radio, but of course we could hear nothing of the conversation. We couldn't stay for long.

"Can you walk?" I asked.

"Yes, a little I think," she replied.

We made a wild dash down the path amidst the sound of further gunfire, apparently in response to our movement from the bushes. The fork in the path came soon enough, and we veered to the right without hesitation. Helen's progress was slowed by her badly bleeding foot, and seeing we were sufficiently far from the ravine and safe from gunfire, we stopped to tend to the wound.

"I feel badly for you," I said, ripping my shirt into strips and tying them around her foot as a bandage.

"Why?" she asked back nonchalantly. "Is it because 1) I was the one hit by the cop when we were in the truck, 2) I nearly had my foot chewed off, or 3) I'm practically half-naked, waltzing around the woods in my underwear?"

"All of the above. You can add 4) My reckless driving that got us into the tangled mess—all for the sake of eluding a police officer. I should have taken the ticket and have it done with than this forever running. I left the road, I got sick, and I pulled you into this misadventure."

"Look, we can't change the past now. Let's just concentrate on getting to the governor's. I'm sure everything will be all right when we do," she reassured me, though I could tell she was just as scared as I. The bandage stopped the bleeding well enough, but Helen could only manage a hobble. Lending her my shoulder, we made our way to the car, though slowly. We were exhausted from the flight, so much so we each sighed in relief when we first saw the grocery store.

"Finally," said Helen, more than ready to sit for a change. Our approach brought us behind the store.

"Garbage workers must be on strike," I said, the stench from the overflowing dumpsters nearly overcoming us.

"But the flies aren't," came back Helen, and we each let out a small chuckle.

A couple of empty crates rested on the asphalt's edge, and we made no hesitation in resting for a few minutes before looking for the car. Sitting on the empty crates, we heard a siren burst from around the building. Getting up and walking around the corner allowed us to watch the police officer get out of his car and talk to what appeared to be the store manager. We couldn't make out what they were saying, but the store manager pointed at a black Mercedes then motioned toward the woods. Helen and I cowered back around the corner to avoid being seen. The officer went back to his car and spoke into the radio's mike.

Within a few minutes, a tow truck came and secured the Mercedes. Helen and I helplessly watched our ticket to freedom vanish.

"Now what do we do?" asked Helen as we retraced our steps to the back of the store. "No car, no clothes—this is the worst pickle we've managed to get ourselves into. If we had only arrived a little sooner—"

"Or the police a little later, I could have had you wait back here while I would have bought a pair of pants for you, then we'd be on our way. As it stands, you're easy to spot, and I'm betting the police have already radioed your new description around," I said with a smirk.

"That isn't funny, Mister. Now if we could disguise ourselves..." she started as we came up to a bread truck unloading. We looked at each other then looked at the bread truck.

"Perfect," I whispered. We casually watched the driver finish unloading the bread, along with the help of a store clerk.

"Gotta have a signature now," said the bread-truck driver.

"I, uh, well, I'm not supposed to sign these. This is my first day and all, and well the manager can sign," said the clerk.

"Oh the manager, huh? Just where might he be?" the driver asked, surprised.

"Out in front, I guess. C'mon, follow me," beckoned the clerk, and the two disappeared into the store to find the store manager, who was still talking to the police officer.

"This is it," whispered Helen. "Let's go!"

We quietly ran to the truck, gently opened the door, and climbed in, with me in position to drive.

"Here," said Helen, handing me a light jacket with the logo of the bread company in front, "wear this. Now you look like a bread-truck driver. Look, here's a hat," she said, putting it on my head. "Perfect."

"It would be," I said, "if only we had the keys to start this thing," I mentioned. I was paranoid the real driver would come back any minute and find us there.

"Not a problem. I'll just hot-wire it," she said.

"You? Hot-wire a car? First we have 'Bust-it-open Brandberg' and now 'Hot-wire Helen'," I said. The engine started. "What sort of nickname do you suppose I should have?"

"Go, Jacob," she said.

"That's hardly a nickname. It doesn't even rhyme, for Pete's—"

"Jacob, go!" she said louder. Someone was yelling from inside the store, and the yelling was getting louder. "Let's get the Hell out of here!" she finally exclaimed, and with that I put the transmission in first and pulled out.

"Hey there, that's my truck!" yelled the bread-truck man. Standing next to him was the store manager and the police officer, who quickly made for his car, preparing for pursuit.

"This thing doesn't pick up speed very well," I said, squealing around the corner and onto Highway 29. I'd hardly gotten down the road when the familiar police sirens sounded from behind.

"Again," said Helen. "Seems we'll never get away from them."

"Too bad the shotgun was out of ammunition. If we'd brought it with us, maybe we could have purchased more rounds," I said.

"Maybe, but at this rate we'll be lucky just to get away. We may not have any firearms, but we do have bread."

"A lot of good that is, though I wouldn't mind a bite at the moment."

"Bread and bread racks. Could pose a problem for someone trying to drive around them," she said, opening the door to the back and climbing through. The officer was gaining quickly as his lights flashed in my rear-view mirror.

"Hurry, dear," I called back through shuffling and *clankity-clanks*.

The sudden air rushing though my rolled-down window and into the back suggested the opening of the back door, and seconds later a sequence of bread racks fell from the truck onto the pavement behind, tossing, tumbling, and sliding into the police car with the officer trying to steer around, but oncoming traffic plus the collection of unpredictably rolling racks made this task impossible. Before he could get close enough to fire at the truck, he smashed through seven racks before finally losing partial control and pulling off to the side. He'd managed to avoid going off the road, but a section came off the rack and punctured his radiator, his car overheating.

"Good job, Helen," I said as she returned to the front. "Honey, those overalls—they're so big."

"They're also the only thing I can find to wear in this truck. They'll do well enough."

"You certainly did well enough with that cop back there. Now we shouldn't have any further problems," I said.

"Don't speak too soon," she replied, and I realized what she meant. A roadblock lurked ahead.

"Hold on," I said, downshifting two gears for increased torque and acceleration.

"Jacob, you don't think...omigosh, we're going to die."

"This is it!" I said, plowing through two cars placed end-to-end. The seat belts cut into my waist and shoulder, and the truck was unsteerable for several seconds as the officers on the roadside watched their cars buckle back with a pop, pivoting and rolling onto their sides.

Though deformed, the truck made it through and limped for perhaps ten miles past the shocked officers. The engine must have suffered some sort of damage, because despite sufficient gasoline in the tank, the engine died and failed to restart. We never made it to the shortcut Dr. Brandberg had suggested, and I felt badly that Helen was forced on foot again.

"C'mon," I said, helping her out of the truck. "We can cut across this field to that small town I see. Maybe there we can get help."

"I don't see much choice. Damn. Just when we think we have a fighting chance, it all slips away and we're back on foot, back on foot. I don't know how much longer I can keep this up," she said quietly.

"Don't worry, I'm sure we'll get help once we get to that little town over there," I said, pointing. "I'll help you get there, no matter how long it takes."

"Ok."

Helen put her weight on my shoulder, we each having an arm around the other to hold the weight off her right leg. With that, we left the truck behind and disappeared into the corn field.

"Hold it right there, Mister," said Gunter. "Not one more step."

Gunter went to the person, handcuffed him, and led him back toward the bunker. The person objected verbally and said:

"I demand to know what I've done. I am innocent of anything, merely taking a walk, but I seem to have lost my way."

"You may be lost, but you are far from innocent. Aiding the flight of two fugitives is hardly innocent, Dr. Brandberg."

"Who?"

"Really, did you think you could fool me?" asked Gunter. "What I don't understand is why in tarnation you left them. 'Course I 'spect you ain't used to these cat-n-mouse games, and yer ticker is tuckered out."

Gunter and Brandberg arrived at the bunker where Rogers was waiting.

"I caught one of 'em. Any word from Jackson 'bout the others?" asked Gunter. Rogers gave Gunter a puzzled look. "I left my radio somewhere, and Jackson and the others ran off after the two. Well?"

"Yeah, Jackson called. The two got away. They lost both dogs and almost two of our men. Apparently the Richardsons crossed a rope bridge and unconnected it from their end," explained Rogers.

"How'd the dogs die?"

"Trying to cross the bridge before it was disconnected. The bridge fell, they gnashed at the one Richardson, then the Richardsons pushed them off into the ravine."

"So," mused Gunter, "they're not only fugitives—they're dog killers."

"Now wait a minute," started Dr. Brandberg, "Jacob and Helen would never purposely kill—never!"

"So, your *amnesia* has cleared, has it? Why don't we start from the beginning, shall we?" interrogated Gunter.

"Look—I don't know what you've heard, but this whole thing is a ruse. Jacob and Helen are of no danger to society."

"Sure, sure," Gunter said sarcastically.

"You don't believe me, do you?" Brandberg asked.

"Let's take it from the top. We know you're a doctor at Shairton County Hospital, right?"

"Yes."

"Your involvement with the Richardsons?"

"Jacob had a bad case of anthrax," Dr. Brandberg explained. "Using some of his own antibodies, I came up with a cure for his illness and brought him through it. When he was well, I released him."

"But he's not well, is he Doctor?" Gunter asked. "How do you explain those deaths at the hospital? Why do you suppose he's being hunted now? I'll tell you why. He made those people sick, and now he's going around spreading this thing around. He may be alive because of your work, but he is also a carrier, a deadly carrier. Explain that, *Doctor.*"

"It is true a few people died at Shairton because of their contact with Jacob's anthrax, but it could have been prevented if I'd been allowed. Dr. Leech—"

"If you'd been allowed? Why put the blame on someone else, Doctor? Are you afraid of admitting your own mistake!?" Gunter pressed.

"No sir. If I made a mistake, it was in trusting Dr. Leech in the first place. He destroyed the cure for the disease and prevented my making more. But I know about him and his 'Operation Purge.' That's what this whole thing is about—using the Richardsons as scapegoats for Dr. Leech and the Federal Government's project to rid the nation of *genetically imperfect humans.* You must know it too, or you wouldn't be involved in this hunt."

Gunter and the others fell silent and glanced at each other.

"Strange, though. You're just local police. Where are the Feds? From what I've heard they were in on this too," commented Dr. Brandberg.

"Oh it's all part of the manhunt, yes. Your story, though—do you really think the public would believe it? The evidence is overwhelmingly against you. Really, Doctor, don't you think the Richardsons have duped you?" Gunter asked, trying to get information at any cost. Brandberg turned red.

"You're wasting your time if you think I'll say what you want me to say, or sign a false confession. What I'm telling you is true. Further, there's an even darker side should 'Operation Purge' be put in effect, something even Leech is overlooking— the disease will mutate to eliminate those with not only defective genes, but recessive as well. Worse, most people carry at least one type of recessive gene and several imperfect ones (though benign), so we're talking about the mass elimination of people everywhere. The social and economic impact would be such that society would literally fall apart. Governments would fail or be overthrown. Anarchy and chaos would ensue. Do you want that? More than likely none of you here would survive to see it, but I tell you this—going to Hell would be preferable to seeing those days."

Jackson returned to the bunker without the dogs and minus one man, another being badly injured.

"Report, Jackson," said Gunter.

Jackson retold the story, recounting the chase, the dogs running over the bridge, the Richardsons untying it, and how the officers attempted to cross.

"We fired half a dozen rounds at them, but they got away, no doubt. I radioed McLean to keep a lookout on the other side for them."

"Well that wraps it up on this side of the fence," said Gunter. "Very well. Rogers and Jackson, take your men and—"

"Sarge, it's McLean on the radio," said Rogers.

"Go ahead, McLean."

"Sarge, I just had a black Mercedes hauled away, belonging to a Dr. Brandberg, from Marshall's grocery where the Richardsons stole a bread truck and headed down Highway 29. I followed in pursuit, but they pulled another fast one on me. My vehicle is damaged, and I've called into headquarters for backup. Last I saw they were heading west. Do you copy?"

"Yeah, I copy McLean," replied Gunter. He turned to the others and said, "Well there you have it. Jackson and Rogers, arrange a rendezvous with McLean and catch those two. I've got a turkey to put in the ice box."

"Let's rest here a minute, Helen," I said, lowering her down slowly on the park bench. It was the smallest park I'd ever seen, consisting of the one bench and a tree with barely enough grass for half a dozen to sit upon. We'd entered the Village of Orwent, population 100. It wasn't much more than a glorified intersection of two lonely highways. I wasn't so much interested in the attractions as I was in finding a telephone.

"Down at the corner store," answered a passing local after I'd asked.

"Who will you call?" Helen asked as I helped her to the store.

"I thought I'd give Eileen a call and see how Johnny and Bobby are doing at the very least. They're probably consumed with worry."

"The boys—I've been wondering when we'd see them again, *if* we'd see them again," she said.

"Now, now. Let's think positively. I'm sure your sister is taking good care of them," I assured her.

"Oh I trust Eileen and everything. I'm talking about us."

We paused at the intersection before crossing then stopped at the phone booth. Helen sat on the small bench while I fumbled with the phone.

"I don't suppose she'd mind a collect call, would she?" I asked.

"No, not at all, as long as the call isn't being traced."

The operator patched the call through to Eileen, Helen's sister. Eileen answered and accepted the charges.

"Eileen? It's Jack."

"Jack, how are you? Is Helen with you?"

"Yes," she said, I carefully holding the phone between us so we could both hear and talk.

"Are you okay? We've been worried sick about you."

"We're fine. How are the boys?" I asked. I didn't want to worry Eileen regarding our misadventures and Helen's injuries.

"Oh they're a handful, but otherwise we've been more concerned about you two. Do you really think it's safe to call here? The police have been bothering us with questions and watching our house. I don't like it. So far they've not tried to take the boys away, but that could change any day. What are you two going to do?"

"We can't say at the moment," Helen replied, "but if anything happens, I hope you wouldn't mind looking after the boys."

"Don't be silly, Helen. John and I would be more than happy. You *did* make us legal guardians, so there shouldn't be any problems there. Please be careful, you two! I shouldn't keep you on the line any longer, just to be safe."

"All right, Eileen, we'll try to keep in touch periodically," I said.

"Don't worry if you can't."

"Of course. Bye," I said, followed by Helen.

"Bye," Eileen said, and that was the last we heard from her for a very long time.

"Look," said Helen, pointing to a small sign in the store window, "the sign says, 'Bus tickets sold here.'"

"Good idea," I said.

A few minutes later, we were in front of the store, munching on store-bought food and waiting for the next bus to the State Capitol. An older gentleman waited with us, and seeing as we weren't native Orwentians, he struck up a conversation.

"You two aren't from around here, are you?" he asked.

"No," Helen said between bites, "just passing through."

"Oh? Anywhere in particular?"

"To the State Capitol," I casually mentioned, trying not to be too specific.

"Yeah, just happen to be going that way myself. Excuse me, my manners have slipped. I'm Chester."

"This is Hel...da, and my name is Jed," I said, quickly trying to invent names as a precaution.

"Nice to meet you, Helda and Jed. My daughter works at the Capitol. Today's her birthday, and I'm taking her out to dinner, or should I say she's taking me out but I'm buying, if you know what I mean. Do you have family at the Capitol too?"

"No, not really. Just going to visit."

"First time?" he asked.

"Yeah," I replied, "I guess you could say we're tourists on a limited budget."

"Ah, I know what you mean. Owning a car these days is so expensive, and gettin' places is that much harder. Seems the rich get richer and the poor get poorer," the old man said, going off on a monologue on how things were better in his youth and how people are no better than rats in a cage. Helen and I continued eating our snacks from the store, occasionally nodding in agreement to what the old man said, but otherwise trying to regather our wits (which meant not listening to him).

Fortunately, our wait was less than thirty minutes, but the bus was crowded. Helen and I were lucky to be sitting next to each other. The old man sat several seats back and picked up a conversation with another passenger. The bus started down the highway, and having finished our snack we tried to rest, but the seating was cramped, and the constant newspaper rustling from a nearby passenger coupled with the intermittent crying from another kept us awake.

"Can't you shut your kid up?" said another passenger to the mother of the crying child.

"He's just a little colicky," she replied, but the other maintained the crying had to do with the way the mother was holding the child on its side. Supposedly the pressure on the ears was hurting him, and if the mother would hold him upright, things would be better, though the mother tried to explain how this wasn't so, etc.

"So much for getting any rest," I whispered to Helen, and she nodded her head in agreement. However, twenty minutes of constant noise dulled on our nerves, and our overwhelming fatigue nestled us into a doze.

"Can you tell me where they are or where they're going?" asked Gunter as he locked Brandberg in the Shairton County Jail.

"No, I can't," he replied sternly.

"Very well, you'll have lots of time to think on it. When you feel more like talkin', one of us will be around."

Gunter left Brandberg in the cell and checked with Johnson for updates.

"I just got a couple of leads on the two," said an excited Johnson.

"Well don't just chew the fat, spit it out," urged Gunter.

"Got a phone call made to Eileen Robinson, sister of Helen Richardson."

"And? Did you relay the place of origin to McLean? Where is it?" inquired Gunter.

"Well that's the problem. We could only trace the call to a fifty-mile diameter," replied Johnson.

"Fifty miles? I could tell you within twenty without the tap. What in tarnation is the problem?"

"Apparently some rural switching routes are still done semi-automatically—they just don't respond to the modern equipment."

"Hmph! So much for the taps. What else you got?" a perturbed Gunter asked.

"This. A credit card purchase from a Jack Richardson—two bus tickets from Orwent to the State Capitol. It just came through as you locked up Brandberg."

"Jack Richardson? The man we want is Jacob Richardson. Hmm, could be close enough. All right, good work, Johnson." Gunter turned to the radio dispatcher and had her relay the information to McLean.

"I want Charterways bus 301 from Orwent to Shairton pulled over," Gunter said, "it should be along Highway 29. Move out!"

Jackson and Rogers responded to the call and converged with McLean in hot pursuit of Charterways 301. In only minutes, the group caught up to the bus with McLean leading the way.

"We have a visual on the bus. Proceeding to pull it over," McLean said, and the three police cars strobed lights and sounded sirens until the bus pulled over. The bus driver stepped out slowly, puzzled.

"What's the problem, officer? Speeding?"

"No. We have reason to believe a dangerous criminal is on board," said Jackson, leading the investigation as senior officer. "If I may check the tickets?"

"Of course," the driver said, disappearing briefly into the bus then returning with a hand full of ticket stubs.

Jackson leafed through the stubs carefully, checking each name (and instinctively looking for other potential criminals at large). He stopped at one, then a second stub.

"Jack Richardson," Jackson mumbled then directed his glance back to the bus driver. "All right driver, kindly call Jack Richardson and his companion out here."

The driver went back inside, said something unintelligible to the officers, and two people walked to the front then down the steps, greeted by three revolvers pointed at them.

"Move slowly to the side of the bus, you two," commanded Jackson to Mr. Richardson and his female companion. The two blushingly complied, stepped to the side, then faced the bus while Rogers and McLean checked them for weapons.

"All right you two, let's see some I.D.," said Jackson.

"Really, is this necessary? We were just on the way to—"

"Quiet," shot back Jackson. "I.D., now!"

The two reluctantly complied, and Jackson inspected the drivers' licenses, perplexed.

"Jack Richardson. Dotty Blake?"

"Did my father put you up to this?" asked Dotty. "Because if he did, you can tell him I want him to butt out. Jack and I are getting married no matter what he says. Do you hear? He can't stop us, and you can't stop us, why the very nerve of him to even..." Dotty ranted without end.

Jackson passed the I.D.s to McLean. McLean shook his head and handed them to Rogers, all while Dotty continued her feisty lecture.

"And another thing," she continued.

"All right, you two, get back on the bus," ordered Jackson, obviously getting the wrong people.

"You can't tell us what to do; you think you're so tough. I know my father sent you, and you can tell him to—"

"Back on the bus, I said," Jackson nearly yelled. "Now!"

The three officers physically put the two back on the bus, apologized to the bus driver, then allowed him on his way. The bus drove off with a black billowing smoky cloud from its exhaust, leaving the three officers choking.

"Jackson to Gunter."

"Go ahead. Fugitives secured?"

"Negative. The fugitives weren't on Charterways 301. We found Jack Richardson, but it wasn't Jacob Richardson."

Jackson's attention was diverted from Gunter's expletives. Dark clouds moved in quickly, and the sky threatened a bad thunderstorm.

"Ka-boom," sounded the nearby thunder. Spasmodic lightning lit up an otherwise dark sky. Rain pounded around the bus, especially on the roof. Several more booming thunderclaps wakened Helen and me in time to see the bus approaching flares and a "Bridge Washed Out" sign. We slowed to a stop.

"Ladies and Gentlemen, we'll be slightly delayed on our way to the Capitol. We will stop for a break at the café we just passed around half a mile down the road. I will get instructions for our detour around the washed out bridge. I apologize for the inconvenience. Thank you for your patience on Charterways 300."

The bus carefully turned around to not get stuck in one of the side ditches, then we completed the turn and journeyed back to the café. Though the windshield wipers moved at top speed, the rain unrelentingly beat down, making visibility almost impossible. During the day the bus would have managed sixty miles per hour. At the moment, we were lucky to manage twenty.

The driver must have had a sixth sense regarding the café, because we turned into a parking lot yet I couldn't make out what was on the lot. He parked next to a small overhang from the building and advised us to come back in twenty minutes. Helen and I joined the crowd and went in the café, where we made a restroom stop and bought more food. We sat next to the window, watching the driver talk on the pay phone just outside (though protected from the rain by the overhang). The "gentleman" from the bus with the newspaper walked to our table. He had a scruffy four-day old beard, greasy thinning hair, and a slight alcohol and tobacco stench.

"My name is John Hanek. I couldn't help but notice you two on the bus," he said, his raspy voice indicating years of heavy smoking.

"Do we know you?" Helen said, puzzled.

"No, but I know you. In fact, everyone knows of you. Your pictures are here on the front page," Hanek said, pointing to the paper. Helen and I put on our best poker faces. "What do you say to that?"

"Gee, hun, do you think they resemble us that much?" I asked to Helen, nudging her. She picked up on the game.

"A little. Of course, Mr. Hanek, you only happen to be the eighth person to award us the look-a-like prize. I think the real ones are a little heavier, though, at least that's what I hear," said Helen.

"Listen you two," Hanek said, keeping his voice low but stern, "you can't fool me. I know you're the Richardsons. I also know there's a hefty reward for information leading to your arrest. I could blow the whistle on you here and now if you don't cooperate."

He called our bluff.

"What do you want?" I asked quietly.

"That's more like it. The reward for your capture is $50,000. I'm willing to settle for a much smaller and more reasonable sum to mind my own business and keep my mouth shut."

"This is extortion, sir," I said.

"Yes, it is. But I imagine it's peanuts compared to what you're wanted for. I only ask for a thousand—"

"You must be crazy if you think we have that kind of money," said Helen.

"Playing stingy, huh. Well, why don't we end this charade, huh?"

"Just wait a minute," I said, trying to regain control of the situation. "She means we don't have it with us at this moment. We have the money, of course, and we'd be willing to settle up somewhere less open."

"Yeah, you got a point. But no tricks, see? Otherwise everyone knows, and—"

"And there's no need in alarming the passengers for no reason, is there? You'll have your thousand. Just give us a little time—"

"Ladies and gentlemen from the bus, can I have your attention please?" sounded the driver's voice throughout the café. "Due to the storm, we will be delaying our departure until nine a.m. tomorrow morning. There are motel rooms adjoining the café, compliments of Charterways Bus Lines. Just show your bus ticket to the clerk, and he'll be happy to give you a room. Once again, sorry for the inconvenience, and be ready for departure tomorrow morning, nine a.m."

"All right," said Hanek after the driver finished speaking, "you got your time. I expect to see an envelope under my door by morning, see?"

"Yeah," I said, "by morning."

"Good boy," he said, then he left.

"Well?" I asked, turning to Helen.

"Even if we did have the money, we wouldn't give it to him," she said.

"I agree. It seems we either leave now—" I started, looking out the window. The terrible storm made this option impossible. "—or we leave early tomorrow morning."

"Only let's make sure we don't end up like we did at Farmer Sam's."

"Good. We'll get up at five—"

"Make it four," Helen cut in. "We can't afford the chance of not making it out."

It was decided, then. At four we would leave the motel and find some other way to the State Capitol, leaving Charterways

300 and John Hanek behind. Neither Helen nor I slept well that night, being too tired from the day's adventures or perhaps too uptight about running off into the blue again. Hanek was the last thing we needed, but enough was enough.

At three a.m., several siren bursts, accompanied by red and blue strobe lights, wakened us from light slumber. Peering out the window, we could see ambulance workers hauling out a man on a stretcher. I recognized the injured—John Hanek. Police were trying to question groggy lodgers, but with seemingly little success. One walked to our door and pounded on it. We crouched down from the window instinctively.

"Don't answer," I whispered.

Within thirty seconds, the officer moved on to the next room. We rose back to the window and peered out again. Chester, the old man we'd met in Orwent, was talking excitedly to one officer, gesturing with his hands and nodding his head. The officer asked him a question, and Chester pointed in a vague direction away from the motel, as if implying something or someone was in that direction or went that direction. Incredibly, the officer seemed to act on Chester's conversation by withdrawing his team and speeding down the road.

"Wasn't that John Hanek on the stretcher?" Helen asked.

"Going into the ambulance? Yes, it certainly was," I responded, excited.

"Which means we won't have to run off; we can complete the journey by bus," she said, happy.

"Maybe our luck is finally changing."

"That's a good sign. I feel this will soon be over," she added.

Content with our newfound luck, we returned to bed and slept the remaining night well. Something in the back of my mind, however, said it was too convenient, and that trouble would come of it. No matter, I was too tired to analyze further.

"Good morning, Helen," I said at eight a.m. Helen was not happy at getting up, but after a few more *good mornings,* she rolled out of bed and freshened up in the bathroom.

"I hope this is the last day we'll be on the road," she said after taking a shower.

"So do I. With luck it will."

In an hour, the bus left the café, but the bridge was still washed out. Knowing this, the driver took a detour—probably planned out the night before. It was shorter than I expected, but I thought it odd the driver said nothing of the missing John Hanek, who was not aboard. Chester was a couple of seats back, however, along with the fussy baby, who started crying when the bus went into motion.

There is little else to tell of the bus ride, except the pleasant scenery passing by, accentuated by a partly sunny day. Cumulus clouds lazily drifted by, like huge puffy cotton balls floating in air. An hour after our departure saw us in the great State Capitol; another ten brought us to the bus station, which was a few blocks from Capitol Square.

"Like I said before," said Chester as we got off the bus, "I'm on the way to the Capitol Building myself. Why don't I give you two a tour since this is your first time? I could even show you where my daughter works."

"That would be great," said Helen.

"Sure thing. So, it's Helda and Jed, right?"

"Yeah," I said, not wanting to lie too much.

"They just restored the building a few years ago," he continued as we walked down the street. "It was so dirty and the inside so musty, not to mention stuff was falling off the sides. Now that it's complete, people from all over come just to see it. On the observation level, for example, you can see clearly for miles around—certainly the entire city. Some say you can see as far away as Topabee Lake," he said, winking at us.

"Is that so?" I asked to sound interested. Helen had a worried expression on her face, as if Chester could see right through us.

"Well, that's what they say. At my age I'm happy to be able to see anything," he explained as we walked in to the lobby of Capitol Building. "This is the lobby," he continued, motioning his arm around, "and this is where you'll find the lobbyists."

Helen and I burst into laughter.

"I'm not joking. They get their first cracks at politicians here."

"Well why don't we see where your daughter works?" I suggested, "And then we can finish touring without troubling you further."

"No trouble at all," he said, "but I suppose we can see my daughter first. Then I can let her know I'm here and that I'm showing you two around."

We took the elevator up a few dozen floors in a matter of seconds, and there we were—the governor's office! It was too much of a coincidence to be one, and Helen exchanged a nervous glance with me.

"Here we are," he said nonchalantly, but suddenly he dropped something on the floor, and it wasn't by accident. "Oops. Clumsy of me."

While the one hand reached for the item he dropped, the other casually went for his pocket. I heard an electronic button being pressed. I gave Helen a nudging signal, and a second later we fled down the hall at full speed. As we approached the door at the end, two guards jumped out from alcoves.

"Freeze!" they commanded, pointing guns at us. We spun around quickly, only to see two guards had come up from behind. Four of them, two of us—we were easily outnumbered.

"What is this, Chester?" I asked as he slowly walked toward us.

"Why are you two running?" he said as if puzzled by our actions.

"Why are these guards arresting us?" I asked back.

"You're acting suspiciously. It's their job to stop people acting in this fashion," he explained. He turned to one guard and said, "They're with me. I'll vouch for their good behavior and pledge they'll act accordingly."

Amazingly, the guards agreed and put their guns away, allowing us to proceed on our way with Chester.

"Was that panic? Fright? Really, I know first-timers can get the jitters, but that was really crazy. They could've shot you.

You know that, don't you? Well, let's think nothing of it. Soon we'll see my daughter and be on our way back down. I suppose then you can continue by yourselves if you really want to get out of my presence."

"It's not that," said Helen. "The real reason we came is…"

"The *real* reason? What might that be?"

"The governor. Would it be possible to see him? We have urgent business we must discuss with him," I stated firmly.

"Why don't you tell me? I'm sure my daughter would be happy to help me pass the message on to the governor," he suggested.

"No," I replied, "we must tell him ourselves. It's very urgent. Do you think you can help us?"

"I'll give it a try. First let's see my daughter. If anyone can help you, she can."

"Thank you," said Helen.

We were still edgy from the guard incident, but amazingly the girl he claimed as his daughter arranged an impromptu meeting with the governor. Funny, though. Chester's daughter didn't resemble him at all.

"Please, have a seat," the governor said to us upon our walking into his office. Chester remained out with his daughter.

"Thank you for letting us talk with you without an appointment," I started, "but this pertains to 'Operation Purge'."

"I see. Wait a minute, you two look familiar. You're the ones on television, in the paper, you're—"

"Helen and Jacob Richardson," Helen said, "and we need your help. Dr. Brandberg said—"

"Oh yes, Dr. Brandberg. I let him use one of the state bunkers to hide you safely. I hope all went well then? Speaking of the doctor, where is he?"

"To answer your first question," explained Helen, "the bunker was helpful, thank you. Unfortunately, we were discovered, and we had to continue our flight secretly. At one point, we were nearly caught, but we managed to escape. Dr. Brandberg wasn't as lucky. He couldn't stay with us, so he urged us to continue the journey here without him. We haven't heard from him since."

"That's too bad. I'm sure we could use his help. However, there is someone I'd like you to meet who will be helpful in resolving this matter. You'll excuse me while I buzz for him," the governor explained.

"Don't mind at all," I said, though it was a polite nothing.

"They're here," the governor said over the phone.

Within seconds a half dozen federal agents burst into the room with firearms trained on the Richardsons. The governor stepped clear, washing his hands of the situation.

"I'm sorry," he said, "but some things are more important."

"What is this? Dr. Brandberg said you were a friend. Obviously he was badly misled."

"Believe me, I don't look forward to what must be done," the governor continued as a man with a suit walked in followed by another in a white doctor's outfit.

"What must be done?" Helen asked, reiterating the governor's words.

"Mr. and Mrs. Richardson, this is Agent Tarske and Dr. Leech."

The air's stillness silenced my every thought except one—utter defeat by trickery and treachery. Agent Tarske came over to us, inspected us, then walked around us with a content smirk.

"Well well, we have you at last. You gave us quite a chase in those woods at Topabee Lake and everything following. Yes, indeed. Quite a show you put on. Well now it's over," he snarled.

"Look, you're making a mistake," said Helen.

The group against us chuckled.

"What do we have here?" he said, holding Helen by the chin and squishing her face. "The charming Mrs. Helen—in overalls. I think you need a fresh look. I believe some of our boys can arrange that, can't they?" he grinned evilly. Helen threw her hand out to slap him, but he caught it in time. "Feisty one, aren't you? Your types always do perform best," he said, grabbing her and tossing her to three guards.

"Let me go," she screamed, but the governor's sound-proof office prevented her from getting outside aid.

"Heh, heh, you'll tire out soon enough," Tarske snickered.

I got up, adrenaline pumping hard, ready to rip Tarske's eyes out. My face turned red, and sweat moistened my face.

"So we have a bull in our presence," Tarske teased.

"If anyone lays a finger on her, I'll—"

"You'll what?" Tarske taunted.

"I'll kill you."

"That should be interesting—watching a dead man trying to kill another."

My face grew cold as steel. I was a bag of emotions, filled with hate, fear, and sadness. Helen was forcibly taken through a side door down some stairwell, but Tarske and Dr. Leech remained behind along with two guards.

"What are you going to do with us?" I asked, trying desperately to think my way out of the situation, and trying to get the time to regain my composure.

"Oh I wouldn't be too concerned about your future. You'll be treated well before your execution. Dr. Leech here has lined you up for several dozen tests and experiments, in which you *will* happily partake. I have the utmost confidence in your cooperation, Mr. Richardson."

"Look," I said, trying to negotiate, "I'm the one you want, not Helen. Let her go. You know I'll cooperate with you any way I can. Just let her go, will you? She's done nothing wrong and is of no use to you. What do you say?"

"Let her go? She carries the disease and is a threat to everyone," said Dr. Leech in a convincing way.

"That's a lie. This whole thing is about 'Operation Purge,' your petty way of trying to manipulate the U.S. population. You wanna create some sort of master race, like Adolf Hitler attempted in the 30s. Well it won't work. You may have the media swallowing your story—"

"Hook, line, and sinker," interrupted Leech. "And the American public believes it. They want to believe it, but we will air a special news conference indicating we captured you, though at the expense of your lives. The threat will be over—no more deaths from anthrax."

"It'll never happen. Dr. Brandberg is still free. He created a cure before, and he'll do it again. He'll make sure you never succeed in your evil plans."

"Not this time, boy," said Leech harshly. "First, we have completed our pathogen in time to test on you, since you are the best candidate. Second, the idiot you call Brandberg is in our custody. So you see, you're deluding yourself with ill-founded hopes."

I lunged suddenly at Dr. Leech, but a rifle butt smacked me square in the jaw, jarring my skull and stunning me to the ground.

"Get him out of here," Tarske said to the guards. It was the last thing I heard before losing consciousness. I later learned what was said after leaving the governor's office.

"The part about Brandberg wasn't true," said Tarske to Dr. Leech.

"Yes, but I had to shake his confidence," Leech replied.

"This Dr. Brandberg—he was with them at the bunker, they left together, but somehow he was separated from them, apparently during a chase. You boys weren't supposed to chase them outside the bunker," the governor said to Tarske.

"We didn't. It must have been Gunter and his boys," replied Tarske, defensive.

"We must have Brandberg in our keep," urged Leech.

"It's possible this Gunter may know the whereabouts of Brandberg or even have him under arrest," said the governor.

"Agreed. I'll check it out immediately," said Tarske.

"And I have some tests to begin," added Leech.

Hindered by the thunderstorm, Gunter called off any further searches for the evening and resumed the following day. Though McLean and Jackson patrolled a wide area, they could not find any clue to help them re-track the Richardsons.

"No trail, no clues—where in the Sam Hill are they?" muttered Gunter.

"Sarge, phone call," said Johnson.

Gunter walked to the desk and grabbed the phone.

"Gunter here."

"This is Agent Tarske. How are things with you?"

"Tarske? What the hell do you want?"

"Have you had much success with the search?"

"Search? No, still searching for the Richardsons."

"What about Brandberg? Last I heard he was with them," continued Tarske.

"All right, Tarske, what's with you? Last I heard you were off this case. Why the sudden interest?"

"Let's just say I've been temporarily put back on the search."

"Temporarily put back on? What is this, football? Are you second string now, getting your few seconds in the game while the big boys take a rest?"

Tarske fumed.

"Listen, Gunter, I can have your badge melting in a coal furnace before you blink an eye. You want to play rough, go right ahead," Tarske said harshly.

"Yeah, yeah. I hear you. Brandberg? Nah, don't know anything about him. Just lookin' for the Richardsons."

Gunter felt Tarske was up to something, but he couldn't figure what that *something* was. Until he was sure of the situation, Gunter felt it best to keep Brandberg's whereabouts a secret.

"You aren't holding out on me, are you?" Tarske jabbed.

"Look, Tarske, I already told you. I don't know anything about a Brandberg. Do you know where he is? Do you know where the Richardsons are?"

Tarske remained silent.

"Well there we are. Just one thing, *Tarske,* you may be the hot-shot fed, and you may have my badge after the smoke clears, but while I'm here my job is to *serve* and *protect.* That may not mean much to you, but to the citizens of Shairton County it does. If I learn that the Richardsons are being unjustly persecuted, I'll do everything in my power to protect their rights and safeguard their interests. So why don't you just go back to your superiors and kiss up to them, 'cause there ain't no room for it here!"

With that, Gunter slammed the phone to its cradle, terminating the connection and possibly his career. He questioned the hunt in his mind, tossing around the possibility Brandberg was right. Tarske was definitely evasive on the phone, and since the moment Tarske told Gunter he was on his own, Gunter knew Tarske was not as truthful as he appeared.

"Tarske did mention 'Operation Purge' during our first encounter. If Brandberg is right..."

Gunter went to Brandberg's cell.

"I have nothing to say to you or anyone," said Brandberg. "I demand to see my lawyer."

"Come this way," Gunter said, opening the jail door and ushering Brandberg to Gunter's office.

"Nothing to say," reiterated Brandberg as the two sat in Gunter's office.

"Look, let's cut the bull and level with each other. I have reason to believe the Richardsons are in grave danger. If I'm right, they are currently being held by federal agents. Who knows what will happen then, but they want you as well. Now you were telling me about Operation Purge, that they want to use the Richardsons to complete their experiments and prevent a cure from being developed. Is this really true?"

"Yes."

"You know where they were going. Whether they made it there or not, I don't know. But you must tell me where. If you don't, this thing may get so out of hand that no one can stop it," said Gunter.

"I want protection. In fact, you have no right to keep me here."

"You're no longer under arrest. I'm dropping charges against you providing you cooperate with us. Jacob and Helen's lives depend on it, as well as the American people."

Brandberg fell silent for half a minute then spoke:

"They went to the governor's," he confessed.

"Where? Why?"

"The governor and I have been on good terms. He allowed us to use the bunker, and he also assured me he'd resolve this situation for us, but our hide-out was discovered, the guards who were supposed to help us deserted, and I had to send the two on their way. I'm too old to be running, so after we separated, I tried coming back by sneaking through the woods."

"And that's when I found you," added Gunter. "Well, that answers it. More than likely the governor is in on this thing with Tarske."

"That's impossible. He would never turn them over, certainly not now," Brandberg said.

"Doctor, you may be a genius at medicine, but if there's one thing I know, it's that power corrupts, and the governor is not as perfectly good as people would like to believe. Unfortunately, we can't just ask him to let the Richardsons go. The truth must be put to the public. There's strength in numbers, mind you, and the people have a power beyond what Tarske and others think they have. The only thing lacking is solid evidence of this operation."

"Not a problem. I have most of the Leech files detailing Operation Purge from start to finish. But I still don't trust you," warned Brandberg.

"Understandable, but do we really have a choice at this point? Otherwise it means you spending time in jail, and I can't guarantee how long I can keep you here. Tarske suspects you're here, I'm sure. If nothing else he'll visit to check. Dadgummit!" Gunter cursed, realizing Brandberg was in danger from the feds. "You can't stay here. We should leave now. The files—where are they?"

"The Shairton Public Library. I dropped it off with the second-floor librarian, Mrs. Peterson, who has carefully hidden it among old periodicals in the storage room," replied Brandberg.

"I see. There is a problem—Shairton still has Feds posted all over town. If you show your face anywhere in public, they'll home in on you quicker than lightning."

"She won't give it to anyone but me. *I* must be the one to get the documents," maintained Brandberg.

"Ok, ok. I have an idea. What size do you wear?"

Later, Brandberg had his beard shaved, his gray hair buzzed down to a half inch then dyed black, and he donned a Shairton County Police uniform and sunglasses.

"There. You certainly make a convincing cop. Now, let's get those documents," said Gunter, ushering Brandberg to the police car. Before leaving the station, Gunter gave Johnson a final order:

"Johnson, notify Jackson and McLean to continue the search for another two hours. If they still find no leads, call them back to base. I have a feeling they're wasting their time."

"You were supposed to ensure all three would make it to the capitol," Tarske fumed.

"Look, by the time I got to them, there were only the two. Brandberg must have split off at an earlier point," said Chester Clarke, the old man who accompanied the Richardsons from Orwent to the capitol.

"All three were gone when I stormed the bunker. There's no doubt about it—Brandberg had to have been there. The bunker guards confirmed their one-week stay, giving them time to regain their strength, especially Mrs. Richardson. This was according to plan. We wanted to let them lower their guard so we could go in for the surprise arrest. However, they were somehow tipped off. I want Brandberg!"

"So you suspect Sergeant Gunter has him under arrest?" asked Chester Clarke.

"What other explanation can there be? His group was certainly pursuing the Richardsons, and the information net shows Brandberg's car being towed from a small grocery store. Yeah, he was with them, but he didn't make it to wherever he was going," surmised Tarske.

"There is no question—Brandberg must be stopped," added Dr. Leech. The three were discussing the issue in Bunker House One, Conference Room A. "With his knowledge, he could still pose a threat, though a small one. Dead or alive, he must be out of the picture. You boys have to get this right. I have my own work here to conduct with Mr. Richardson and the final anthrax-v implementation."

"We'll get Dr. Brandberg if it means I have to tear Shairton and Gunter apart. No one will stop us," said Tarske, full of desire and motivation. "Clarke, I want you to watch the Shairton County Police Department. See what you can learn. Go inside if you have to; if that means getting arrested for something, so be it. Report to me when you can; I'll be on the cellular."

"No problem."

"Good," said Leech. "Gentlemen, we are on the final leg. Let's not trip before the finish line."

The others nodded in agreement, and the meeting adjourned. Though Clarke and Tarske went to Shairton to hunt down Doctor Brandberg, Helen and I remained prisoners at Bunker House One that was located a few blocks from Capitol Building but was also deep underground.

"Let's get another blood sample, shall we?" suggested Dr. Leech. An accompanying nurse came forth with a tourniquet and needle-vial.

"You're nothing but a vampire—drawing life from others. I demand you let Helen and me go."

"You're in no position to demand anything," stated Leech.

"Go get your blood from someone else," I yelled.

"Very well, if that's how you feel." Leech motioned for a guard to come in. "Mr. Richardson doesn't want to cooperate."

"Oh is that so?" said the guard. "Well, maybe he needs some incentive."

The guard grabbed me by the shirt, lifted me up, and slammed me against the wall, jarring my head and making me dizzy. Dazed, I spat at the guard to show defiance. He responded by dropping me to the floor, where I banging into a chair before slumping against the wall. He wiped his face then spanned his hand over my face, grabbed it like a grapefruit, and squeezed—digging his nails into my flesh. He banged my head against the gypsum-board wall several times, leaving large indentations in different spots. He found what he was looking for—a support board to increase the pain to my head.

"That's enough. We do need him alive a little while longer. When it's time, I'll let you finish the job," Leech said. "Now, how about some blood?"

I said nothing, but I offered no resistance. The guard lifted me to the table and strapped me down. The nurse proceeded to draw blood, but I was hardly cognizant enough to tell what was happening.

"There, was that so bad?" asked Dr. Leech, but again I was silent. "Get some rest, Mr. Richardson. Tomorrow we start the injections."

With that, the nurse and doctor left, but before the guard left the room, he made a comment to me:

"I must say, old man, your wife makes a good whipping post."

Despite my daze, my fury became audible.

"Bastard! Son of a hyena and daughter of a jackass! You were born not from a womb but from a rectum, you filthy, swine-brained—"

I never finished, because the guard came over and promptly dumped the table on its side, sending it crashing down on me as I fell to the floor.

"Sleep well, old man," he said as I lost consciousness.

Chester Clarke arrived at the Shairton County Police Station in time to watch Gunter and Brandberg leave, though he only recognized Gunter (from pictures). He relayed the information to Tarske.

"The way I see it," started Gunter, "there's only one sure-fire way to clear the air on this issue."

"And that is?"

"Gotta appeal to a power higher than us, influencing millions of people each day—the media. We gotta take them by surprise, though. We can't just hold a news conference—that would give the Feds a chance at us. No, I figure the local paper can get a shot at it, relay it on through the AP wire, and publish it—front page. Your testimony, mine, plus the documents should be enough to blow this thing wide open."

Once Gunter parked in front of the library, he and Brandberg wasted no time in going inside to the second floor. Mrs. Peterson was at a side desk typing something when the two approached her.

"May I help you?" she started. She stared hard at Brandberg, trying to figure out why he looked so familiar.

"You're Mrs. Peterson?" Gunter asked in a low voice.

"Yes," she replied.

"Is there somewhere we can talk privately?"

"Of course. There's a small office in back here. Follow me."

She led us through a mini-maze of stacked periodicals and newspapers, passing several cabinets and going around a few chairs. Finally, we came to a small office out of eye- and earshot from the main area.

"What is this about?" she asked. She stared at Brandberg again. "Do I know you?"

"As a matter of fact, you do," he started, but Mrs. Peterson cut him sharply.

"Dr. Brandberg? Is that you? In a uniform? Your beard, your hair. Sakes be, what's this world coming to?"

"We don't have time to explain. I've come back for those important papers I asked you to keep safe," explained Brandberg.

"No problem. I'll get them right away," Mrs. Peterson said, and she was off.

"So we just go up to the newspaper from here?"

"Maybe," Gunter said, looking out the small office window.

"Maybe? What do you mean, 'Maybe'?"

"See those two cars down there?" Gunter said, pointing with his eyes.

"Those two sedans? Yeah, what about them?"

"They're unmarked cars, either State or the Feds. They're watching this building. I don't think we can chance going out the front door."

"Then how are we going to pull this off?" Brandberg asked, worried.

"Here you are, doctor. I even put them in a clean folder for you," said Mrs. Peterson, returning from the archives room.

"You wouldn't believe how hard it was to store it in the first place. We have so many magazines and newspapers stored, it's a wonder a person can walk in there. Why the other day I was telling Ms. Shelly how we need to—"

"Thank you, Mrs. Peterson. I'm sure we'll be seeing you soon," cut in Gunter.

The two quickly left Mrs. Peterson to her periodicals, though she continued to explain about her library woes. Gunter quickly led Brandberg down the back-entrance stairwell, but before they could get halfway down, two Federal agents walked in.

"Tarske!" muttered Gunter reflexively.

"Halt, you two!" yelled Tarske as the two Feds dashed up the stairs with guns in hand.

"Back!" urged Gunter to Brandberg.

The two raced up the stairs to the third floor, followed by the Feds. Through the third-floor door, a small corridor angled off to the right. Tarske and the other Fed followed it in time to see the Ladies Room door shutting.

"In there," motioned Tarske.

The two stormed the restroom much to the dismay of two screaming women who immediately fled into the corridor. The Feds walked slowly around the spacious Ladies Room, looking under each stall. Tarske saw a set of large black shoes topped with dark blue pants while looking under a suspicious stall. He ripped the door open and pointed his gun inside, expecting a hostile situation.

"Can't a woman have some privacy around here!?" bellowed the hefty gal saddled across the commode. "Get out now, git, GIT, GIT!" she growled like a big, grizzly bear.

Tarske and partner left the Ladies Room red-faced and ill-tempered, having lost their prey and being chewed out by the heaviest person in Shairton. They continued down the corridor in hopes of finding Gunter and Brandberg.

"All right, boys, they're gone," said the fat lady.

From the two adjoining stalls, Gunter and Brandberg stepped down from commodes and thanked the fat lady. They waited a few minutes then slipped into the corridor.

"Hey! Watch your step!" said the custodian as Gunter and Brandberg nearly bumped into him and his cart.

"Where are they?" muttered Tarske, coming out of the library.

He and his partner circled the library several times without luck. During their entourage, they passed an elderly lady, two children on bicycles, a man with his dog, and the Friendly Cleaners service completing its stop at the library. The custodian pushed his heavy cart filled with assorted cleansers and a large garbage container.

"They're close," said Tarske, "I can almost sniff them."

"What you smell is ammonia," joked the partner, referring to the Friendly Cleaners.

"Let's take another look inside," Tarske suggested.

The moment the Feds were inside, the custodian opened the container. Sergeant Gunter wasted no time in leaving the smelly can. The custodian, Dr. Brandberg, followed Gunter to the left-front of the Friendly Cleaners truck.

"I'm commandeering this vehicle," said Gunter to a surprised driver.

Gunter pulled the fellow out and climbed in, followed by Brandberg, who now acted as the driver. Gunter stooped down to avoid being seen as Brandberg drove the truck from the library, past the unsuspecting Feds, and down the road, destination—*The Shairton Times.*

"When we get there, we need to go 'round back so as no one will see us from the main road. Also it'll give us a chance to sneak in, just in case Tarske's men are inside at the main desk," suggested Gunter.

A few minutes later found them parking in back, Gunter directing. The two casually stepped out, walked through the *Employees Only* door, down a hall, and down to Max Meyer's office. Several onlookers whispered about and pointed at the strangers.

"Sergeant, this is a surprise. Doctor Brandberg? You look so different."

"We don't have much time," Dr. Brandberg said. "Here—most of it is in here."

"Most of what?" Meyer asked. "What?"

"Dr. Leech's files," Brandberg replied.

"You know, there's a reward out for your neck," Meyer said, looking at Brandberg.

"Look, Max," started Brandberg, "this Operation Purge could cause problems beyond belief. As we speak, two innocent people are probably being held against their wills. Their lives are in danger. I ask you—read the files, but don't let anyone know what you're up to. Then write a story exposing the truth. It must be told, it *must!*"

"Hey, I could lose my neck over this. You expect me to believe you? I watch the AP wire—Brandberg, you're a federal fugitive, wanted for helping the escape of two other fugitives and for causing those hospital deaths," Meyer ranted.

"It's all lies. C'mon, you're an objective man. Do you really think—" Brandberg started saying.

"We gotta go. Can't stay. Just do us the favor and print the story, Meyer. Take care," Gunter said, pulling Brandberg out with him, back down the hall, and outside.

Meyer picked up his phone and dialed.

"Yeah, they were just here," he said. "No, just Gunter and Brandberg, though the doctor has shaved his beard and dyed his hair black." Pause. "No, I don't know, they didn't say." Another pause. "Yeah. Bye."

Brandberg and Gunter got back in the Friendly Cleaners van. Brandberg paused before starting the engine.

"Some people in there were giving us strange looks. I wouldn't be surprised if we were being fingered. You won't be safe in Shairton anymore. Isn't there some place you can hide and wait this thing out?" Gunter asked.

"Look—I'm not going to bury my head in the sand like an ostrich. I *am* disappointed the governor has betrayed me, but this is not the time for me to hide. Meyer may print the story, but Jacob and Helen need our help. I'm sorry I sent them into the lion's den; I should have been suspicious when the governor so generously offered to help," stated Brandberg.

"You're no law enforcement man; you can do no good but get in the way. Start the truck."

"Not until you promise to include me in the rescue posse. You *are* going to assemble one, aren't you?"

"I could, but I'll be out of my jurisdiction. It will be risky and very dangerous," warned Gunter.

"Good. It's worth it."

"I can't let you in on it. They must want you for your knowledge, and we can't just bring you that close to capture. I have a better idea, though," mused Gunter.

Brandberg started the truck and left *The Shairton Times*.

"Drive to the Cheyenne County Police station. My buddy Sergeant Rudrick will help with the rescue team. From there you'll be able to use their crime lab to do the very thing Dr. Leech doesn't want you to do—develop a vaccine."

"I may be a doctor, but I'm no magician. I can't just whip up a vaccine like vanilla pudding."

"You got a better idea? If you can prevent people from getting sick, or cure them from the illness, then at least we can slow this thing down if not stop it. I know you can do it," said Gunter.

"Well at least I didn't give the technical information to Meyer," sighed Brandberg.

"Now that's more like it. Sergeant Rudrick will arrange everything."

The Friendly Cleaners van sped along to Cheyenne county unimpeded and unnoticed, determined but anxious. The two had an uphill battle ahead.

Aches and bruises were my companions throughout the evening, and the room was so black I could not even see my hands pass before my eyes. I wondered what became of Helen then shivered at the possibilities.

"I pray she comes to no harm," I whispered.

My jaw ached, several teeth were broken, and my clothing was covered in multiple places with blood. Limping to the door, I managed to get a glimpse of the surrounding corridor.

Two guards were around my door, and two further down the corridor. Retreating from the door, I made my way to a small bathroom with commode, sink, and mirror. Cool, dry air gently blew through the oversized air vent. It was big enough for a man to pass through.

This is my only chance. If I can get up to the vent and make it through, perhaps I could make it to Helen and get us out of this mess before it's too late. The vent was too high off the ground for me to reach. I looked around the bathroom then around the main room. In the far corner—a chair. Pain reminded me of my injuries, but I set it aside and made for the chair. I sat down on the chair for a minute to regain my breath then stood up with the chair as a prop and used it to walk me over to the bathroom.

Getting back to the bathroom used most of my remaining strength, and again I had to sit and rest. Chair placement was difficult, and after a near-frustrating moment of shoving, wiggling, and beating, I managed to wedge the chair between the sink and the wall. Though the sink was high enough to stand on, I would not have trusted my weight on it. The chair was high enough, and I stood upon it, painstakingly removed the vent cover, then climbed in, a difficult venture considering my injuries and the pain.

"Time for a shot, Mr. Richardson," sounded the familiar voice of Dr. Leech.

My shirt snagged on the rough edge. Dr. Leech wasted no time in summoning the guard. Though I hastened to escape, the guard caught my foot as I nearly slipped free into the ventilation system.

"Where do you think you're going?" he yelled, yanking me back into the bathroom and causing my belly to scrape against the rough edge. Unpleasant bleeding lines paralleled my chest.

"It's time for the final shot. Strap him in," ordered Leech, and the guard wasted no time, throwing me into the chair like a rag doll.

"You have no right to do this," I sputtered.

"One small shot and we'll be done with you," he said, forcing the needle deep into my leg. Emptying the syringe, he gave his final order to the guard: "Put him with the others."

"Jacob, is that you?" said a familiar voice. "Gaud, what's happened?"

"They roughed me up a little. I hope you fared better," I replied.

"If only it were true. If only. We've got a problem," she started explaining.

"I agree. We are being held against our wills, along with the dozen or so other people in this room. What is this place, and why are we here?"

"I can only guess it's a holding cell or a waiting cell."

"Waiting?" I asked. "Waiting for what?"

"They're waiting for us to die," said one of the others, a haggard-looking fellow with a coarse, long beard but thinning hair.

"This is Arnan Pauvold. Arnan, my husband Jacob," Helen said, introducing us.

"Nice to meet you," I said out of common courtesy.

"I wish I could say the same," he said. "However, I'm afraid this is The End for us in here. The only way you leave is when you die."

"Die? That could be years from now," I stammered.

"Oh no. I've been here the longest, going on four days now. Everyone ahead of me died of the disease, the one they've been experimenting to perfect. They've been using us as guinea pigs," he explained, pausing to cough profusely.

"It's the anthrax, isn't it?" I asked.

"Not really. True anthrax is caused by bacteria that normally affect bovine and sometimes people. This thing, from what I've heard, is something different, horrible and very deadly. Some have called it the B-lympho virus, others the B virus. Whatever it is, it seems to kill a person in two weeks or less, depending on how fit they are."

"What else do you know about it?" I asked, amazed.

"That's it. Just overheard it mainly, and some of the others confirmed it."

"I already told him about what Dr. Brandberg told us," added Helen.

"How it's genetically engineered, yes. It fits together. Apparently they used the anthrax bacteria as a base and evolved the virus out of experiments and experiments and experiments. It's just too much for me," Arnan said.

"It is for me, too. What we really need is to get out of here," I suggested.

"It's too late for that now," Arnan said. "We've all got it. Even if you could escape, you'd give the disease to everyone you meet."

"Well we can't just stay here," I said.

"There isn't much we can do," said Helen.

Was it hopeless? I could do nothing better than pace back and forth within the holding cell, trying to come up with an idea, trying to find a way out. Arnan continued coughing—a reminder of what lay ahead for Helen and me. We hadn't run through the woods, hide in the barn, hijack Farmer Sam's truck, run for Brandberg's bunker, cross the ravine, steal the truck, cut through the corn field, and take the bus to the capitol to end up like this. One word summed my feelings—frustration.

"Sergeant Gunter? Dr. Brandberg? It's good to see you," said Sergeant Rudrick, greeting the two at the door.

"It was nice of you to invite us to your home," replied Gunter.

"These are extenuating circumstances. It's the least I can do for you, after all those times you saved my neck. Please, come in and sit," he said, motioning Gunter and Brandberg to the living room. "Can I get you two anything to drink? To eat?"

"I wouldn't mind a beer," said Gunter.

"Anything non-alcoholic is fine," replied Brandberg.

Rudrick left for half a minute then returned with the drinks.

"Too bad we didn't come during the day," said Gunter. "We could have stopped in at the station and seen you there."

"I'm glad you didn't. Doctor Brandberg's picture is posted on the board, and everyone is under strict orders to shoot-to-kill if necessary. Not my orders, mind you. Even you, Gunter, are wanted for setting a federal fugitive free. That Tarske guy must have stopped by your station minutes after you left and discovered what you did."

"And he nearly caught us in the library. Yeah, we had a spat with him, but we made it," grinned Gunter.

"We'll have to get rid of the Friendly Cleaners van. Tonight. But don't you worry. I'll simply have it impounded, where the Friendly Cleaners can pick it up for a small fee. Meanwhile, you're welcome to stay here the night. Tomorrow will be a busy day."

Rudrick's telephone rang.

"Yeah?" he said, picking up. "It is? Now? Sure, thanks."

"What is it?" asked Gunter.

"Something about a news conference on television regarding the Richardsons," Rudrick replied, turning on the television.

Good evening. I am Dr. Leech. An epidemic resulting from the Richardsons' flight through the country is beginning. We have been unable to find the two, but they are leaving a trail of sickness that is incurable.

Our original study showed the disease to be caused by anthrax-b, which progressed into anthrax-v, releasing what we now call the B-lympho virus since it attacks the B-lymphocytes, causing them to release antibodies that destroy healthy tissue. The resulting condition is *anthracatic lupus.*

Current studies show the disease is spreading in viral form only, meaning that although it is no longer caused by the anthrax-b, it is still caused by the B-lympho virus. It is highly contagious, being spread by coughing or sneezing mucoid particles, which are then inhaled by the new victim. Symptoms begin like influenza, but after a week, the immune system is weakened to the point where secondary infections become rampant and cause the victim to literally rot.

Thirty deaths have been attributed to the disease. This is but the tip of the iceberg. We must brace ourselves for a major disaster. The only known way of preventing the spread is by quarantining existing ill people and wearing face masks to prevent the inhalation of infectious mucoid particles.

I have been in constant contact with the Centers for Disease Control in Atlanta. Our efforts have been directed first in reducing the spread and second in developing a cure. Progress in the latter has been very slow. No questions, please. Thank you.

"So that's it," said Rudrick, popping the television off.

"It's started," Brandberg said solemnly. "First they captured the Richardsons, and now they've released this new virus to the world."

"Captured? He said they haven't captured them yet," said Rudrick.

"I had a strange conversation with Tarske on the phone earlier today," explained Gunter. "The way he was going, I can only believe he has the Richardsons in custody. He pressed me for details on the doctor's whereabouts. I didn't reveal anything, because he was so suspicious sounding. The other thing—Doctor Brandberg indicated the Richardsons were on their way to see the governor. I have a feeling he can't be trusted. Did you see where the press conference was held? That wasn't in Shairton. More like one of 'dem fancy rooms at the State Capitol."

"One thing is certain—the press is on Leech's side," mentioned Rudrick.

"Unfortunate but true. We stopped by the *Shairton Times* and tried to convince Max Meyer to print the real story," explained Brandberg. "I don't think he will be of any help. I wouldn't be surprised if he called the feds after we left. Too bad. It seems there's hardly anyone left a person can trust."

"How deadly is this B-lympho virus?" asked Rudrick.

"It's hard to tell at this point," replied Brandberg, "especially since the original pathogen was based on the anthrax bacterium. In the details of 'Operation Purge,' the disease is meant to kill people with certain flawed genetic patterns. The anthrax Mr. Richardson contracted was apparently an early version of what was going to be used later, because it started out by multiplying rapidly, as bacteria do. Next, it released a virus directed at a specific white blood cell, the B-cell."

"My studies of that disease, as well as the notes from 'Operation Purge' show it could affect more than the *genetically flawed* people—it would kill those with recessive traits as well. This new B-lympho virus may be the result of my cure for Mr. Richardson's illness. Since conventional antibiotics are ineffective against viruses, it would be more difficult to stop the recent strain—"

"My little boy is a hemophiliac, would he be affected?" Rudrick asked eagerly.

Brandberg was grave and paused, "Yes, he would contract the disease and die within days. Others around—you and me—who show no illness would still be carriers. Thus, should we ever come into contact with someone having a defective or possibly recessive gene, that person would contract the disease and die. Even newborns are at risk—if they don't have the 'right' genes."

"There must be a cure. I don't want my boy to die. Can't you come up with a vaccine or something the way you cured Mr. Richardson the first time?" asked Rudrick.

"I don't know. Without a lab to examine this thing firsthand, I'm in the dark."

"We'll give you one. And if you need assistance, whether human, financial, or computer, we'll give that to you too. We *must* stop this thing," Rudrick maintained, with Gunter nodding in agreement.

"Even if I do identify the mechanisms at work behind this B-lympho virus, there's no guarantee I can find a cure. Viruses are among the most challenging to conquer; some scientists took years to develop vaccines—some may never be able to find a vaccine because one cannot be created. If the body can't fight it off...well, it *is* worth a shot, I suppose. Unfortunately, time is not an ally," said Brandberg.

"Then the sooner we start the better. I'll have you set up tomorrow morning, bright and early," said Rudrick.

Gunter and Brandberg were treated to a late evening supper before retiring to guest rooms for the night. Brandberg had an especially upsetting dream that night, envisioning people dying around him, and he was helpless to save them. Wherever he walked in his dream, he had to step over and around fallen corpses.

"This is the best I could do on such short notice," said Rudrick as Brandberg walked around the small lab in a secluded section of a private clinic.

"It will have to do," said Brandberg.

"Oh, here comes your assistant. Dr. Brandberg, this is Dr. Lynx. Dr. Lynx, this is Dr. Brandberg," said Rudrick as the doctors exchanged handshakes. Dr. Lynx had dark, brown hair, a fair complexion, and was surprisingly fit and young-looking considering her fortyish age.

Gunter and Rudrick left Brandberg to his work, the two officers going to a local café for coffee and doughnuts.

"Is it safe to talk here?" asked Rudrick.

"Certainly. Please, be frank," urged Gunter.

"This virus—it ain't like some common cold, is it?"

"No, it isn't."

"Then if one of us gets it—how does a person know if he's gonna get it or not?" asked Rudrick, concerned.

"I don't think there is a way to tell. We could all die," said Gunter.

"What about that stuff Leech was sayin' 'bout the CDC in Atlanta, do ya' think he's really—" Rudrick started to say, but his voice trailed. He didn't need Gunter to answer.

"No telling what they're up to. If he *is* in contact with the CDC, who knows what lies he's feeding them. He could be leading them on a wild goose chase, enough to prevent them from coming up with a cure."

"Whatever the case, this whole thing is evil. I can feel it now—evil," said Rudrick.

"I'll agree with you there. But, there's no sense in getting worked up about it. Dr. Brandberg may come up with something."

"I hope so. Well, give me your opinion of this plan. We stay here for a day or two, see what Dr. Brandberg comes up with, then perhaps make a move on the capitol and see if we can break the Richardsons out. That *is* one of the reasons you came to me for help, isn't it?" asked Rudrick.

"Yeah, but finding them—that'll be a trick," said Gunter.

"Yeah, the trick. It's all one big trick," grumbled Rudrick.

While Gunter and Rudrick stayed in Cheyenne for the next few days, Dr. Brandberg and his assistant, Dr. Lynx, busily examined various tissue samples, all containing the B-lympho virus and comparing notes against the notes taken from Dr. Leech's Shairton Hospital files. The two doctors, however, were no closer to finding a cure than before.

"It's useless, I tell you. The B-lympho virus is nothing like what Mr. Richardson has, and it's a big deviation from the original plans detailed in Leech's files. Nothing we've tried works. The chicken egg cultures, the frog egg cultures, drugs—nothing is working," complained a frustrated Brandberg.

"You've been pushing yourself too hard. Get some rest and give it fresh thought in the morning. You've been up since six this morning working on this thing, and now it's after eight in the evening. We may not have a cure yet, but we are making progress," said Lynx.

"Progress? You call this progress? A few days after we've started, and the death toll is over a hundred. Did you see the evening news? They pulled a man out of Cheyenne River. He died from the B-lympho virus. They say he contaminated the entire river. That river goes through—"

"I know. It goes through five counties, including Cheyenne and Shairton. You can't do anything about it by grumbling and pacing around the place. Listen to me, get some rest and—"

"How can I rest when people are dying left and right? If we can't stop this thing, everyone could die, everyone!"

Silence filled the room for several seconds. Dr. Brandberg looked down at the floor, dejected. Dr. Lynx looked at him, wanting to do something to help but knew there was little she could.

"All right. Let's go through it again. We've identified the B-lympho virus," she started.

"And boy did they pick the right name. What a devious bug to go in and turn the Bs into monsters, releasing destructive antibodies on the human body," grumbled Brandberg.

"We know it causes virus replication very quickly," continued Dr. Lynx, staying calm and trying to calm Dr. Brandberg.

"Very quickly. Almost as fast as bacteria. Antibodies worked before, because that anthrax strain Richardson had was predominantly bacterial. His own antibodies prevented the viral stage from beginning," said Brandberg, collecting his thoughts.

Brandberg continued, "The problem is, conventional antibodies can't cross the cell membrane to get at these viruses. The viruses just have a field day with the B-lymphocytes' DNA, sending the antibodies to kill everything including the T-lymphocytes, which normally would recognize the foreign antigen on the cell's outer membrane and kill that B-cell."

"If we could slow or stop the flood of bad antibodies, then the T-cells might have a chance," said Dr. Lynx.

"Unfortunately, only steroids have been effective in suppressing the bad antibodies, and though it prolongs the life of the patient, the high dose leaves no defense against common bacteria. The patients can take antibiotics, sure, but eventually the steroids tear apart almost every organ in the body," said Brandberg.

"I'm sure there's another way," maintained Dr. Lynx. "We simply haven't discovered it yet. What about the computer analysis, maybe we should go through that again."

"I've been through that a thousand times," said Brandberg. "It says there is *no* solution to the problem. You know I've repeated the situation with different parameters. No known drug will cure it, and the virus is such that a vaccine is impossible—the B-lympho virus changes certain parts of its genetic scheme too much. Whoever engineered this thing did a damn good job."

"The computer may not be able to see all angles to the problem. I'll bet the answer is just around the corner, within grasp," Dr. Lynx said.

"Well I wish we'd hurry up and discover it. They're predicting over a thousand deaths by the weekend. Yawn, I'm tired. Perhaps I should turn in."

"A good idea," said Dr. Lynx.

"All right. Tomorrow at six then. Good night, doctor," bade Brandberg.

"Good night."

Dr. Brandberg slept uneasily, tossing and turning in a nervous frenzy. The brief moments of sleep he did manage were unpleasant, mostly regarding the deaths from the disease and other wild motions of violence. He woke in a sweat and scribbled something on paper before returning to a light sleep.

"Good morning, Dr. Brandberg," greeted Dr. Lynx.

It was half past six. Dr. Lynx had spent the last thirty minutes organizing the room and preparing for more tests. Dr. Brandberg walked in with dark circles under his eyes. He looked half dead and sounded the other half.

"Good morning. I didn't sleep very well last night," he said.

"I hope you're not coming down with the B-lympho virus. We can't afford it now," she said.

"When could we afford it?" he asked back.

"Come over here," she said, "we should test you to make sure."

As she drew the blood from Brandberg, he began telling about one of his dreams.

"I had a most peculiar dream last night, Dr. Lynx. I even scribbled a short message about it on this paper," he started.

"Message? What sort of message?" she asked, filling the vial with Brandberg's blood.

"'A thousand armies may march across the battlefield and die without success, but a single woman can slip into the night, seduce the king commanding the attack, and kill him in his most vulnerable moment. This is how the battle is won.' I don't understand what it could mean," he said.

"What was your dream?" she asked, pulling the needle from his arm.

"It's hard to remember, but it kept repeating. I was sitting on a high place, maybe on the precipice of a mountain, and I watched armies below doing battle on the plains. It was horrendously bloody, and when it ended, one side always emerged victorious. But the winning side was somehow evil; I could smell it in the air. And each time when a different army came along, the evil one destroyed it."

"Suddenly, I wasn't on the precipice but next to a hut, watching a beautiful woman slip through the woods and sneak into the hut through the back door. She was evil, but a different kind of evil from those in the hut, who I realized were the same ones who slaughtered countless armies on the plains. She didn't see me, but I saw her."

"When she slipped into the hut, I ambled to the wall and peeped through a small hole, watching as she seduced the commander of the army to the point where they were in bed, completely enraptured in each other."

"Without warning, she pulled out a knife and slit his throat, ending his life and causing chaos in the army. Without a leader, they didn't know what to do."

"Suddenly, I was on the precipice again watching another army storm across the plains and into the evil army's camp, trashing it, killing the bad army. A smell of wholesomeness and goodness wafted my way, and I knew a crisis was over and joy returned."

"The odd thing is, the dream kept repeating itself, Dr. Lynx. I must have watched a hundred armies die in action and a dozen commanders seduced and killed. What I don't understand is the meaning behind it, if there is one."

"Sometimes dreams have no meaning," suggested Dr. Lynx. "But that doesn't mean this one has none. Perhaps your subconscious is trying to help you solve the B-lympho virus problem, but it can only tell you in this bizarre way."

"But what? How can one kill a virus, when technically it isn't alive? Normally a body would kill the invaded cell and be done with it. There's nothing left short of a transfusion. Even then there are the diseased and overly swollen lymph nodes," continued Brandberg.

"Thirty percent of the deaths were attributed to a ruptured spleen, the resulting hematoma spreading throughout—" started Lynx.

"Yes, yes. I've seen the reports. All right, let's go over the new information since last night."

Doctors Brandberg and Lynx continued the day, going over new cases, researching the disease, and trying different drugs in isolated experiments on the B-lympho virus. Despite their valiant efforts, little progress was made. Dr. Brandberg was exhausted with frustration when the two officers greeted them that afternoon.

"Afternoon, doctors. How is the research going? Any luck?" asked Rudrick.

"Some. We know how the virus replicates and how quickly it overtakes the victim," replied Dr. Lynx.

"That's about it so far," said Brandberg. "Nothing seems to work against this nasty virus. About the only thing that will prolong life is an immunosuppressant, but it isn't a cure."

"We were planning on making a move on the capitol and seeing if we can get the Richardsons out," suggested Gunter.

"If Mr. Richardson were here, he might provide a key to this whole thing. He survived the first strain of the virus; he may be able to provide a cure for the current strain. Yes, by all means proceed. But take extreme caution! If they do have him, and they've been experimenting with him or others, bringing them into the public would serve to accelerate the epidemic. Beyond that, I don't know what else to say except good luck," Brandberg said.

"I think you need more luck than we do," said Rudrick. "In any event, keep at it. I'm sure between the two of you a cure will be found. Goodbye, doctors."

Gunter and Rudrick left, proceeding with a posse to the capitol. Brandberg and Lynx continued working on a cure, but by six in the evening, the two were so exhausted they left their work and went home—in Brandberg's case it meant returning to Rudrick's home. Gunter and Rudrick, along with twenty other men, travelled to the capitol and "set up camp" in a low-profile motel, forming plans for the following day.

"The way I see it," said Rudrick, "we need to get more information on the operation, where the people are being kept, and how to break them out successfully. We need a couple of people to scout it out, get in on the inside if we're lucky, and report back. Then we can formulate the strike."

"Who do you intend to send?" asked Gunter.

"Billings and Fairbanks. They're cool under cover. We'll send them out tomorrow. Beyond that there's little else to plan. I think it best we get some good rest tonight. Tomorrow's apt to be a busy day."

"How bad do you think it'll get, Rudrick? The epidemic, I mean," asked Gunter.

"It's hard to say. The way Brandberg and Lynx were talking, over half the world population would disappear, something on par with the Black Death in the middle ages or worse. They used to burn people to death then, just to protect the lives of the few remaining people. I hope it doesn't come down to that. With the panic and chaos going on, people regress to the worst primal conditions, and if my boy gets sick and the people learn of it—I hate to imagine the consequences. No, we have to think positively on this thing, Gunter. It's the only thing that will get us through and give us hope."

Brandberg slept no better that night than he did the previous. Again he tossed and turned, and again he had bizarre and strange dreams. Unable to sleep further, he got out of bed and walked from his bedroom to the adjoining balcony. It was perhaps three in the morning, the moon was floating above nearby pine trees, and cloud wisps peacefully floated by. Some floated past the moon, making it look like some oversized antacid pill dissolving through the cloud's arms.

He looked at the surrounding stars and connected the dots in his mind to form the constellation Orion.

"The proud hunter," he whispered, and he longed for a simpler time when men could simply hunt for foot, fashion weapons, and enjoy a comradery on a clean, untainted earth. His wish fading, he peered north, connecting the starry dots in his mind to form the big dipper and little dipper.

"Ursa major and Ursa minor," he whispered, connecting the dots further to form Big Bear and Little Bear. "How ironic," he continued whispering, "that the Little Bear will kill the Big Bear once and for all." It seemed nonsensical, and he scratched his head in puzzlement wondering why he said that to begin with.

"I'm just a tired old man," he wept. "There is no way to stop the inevitable. We are doomed as a species. Mother Earth will again reclaim her kingdom and restore her life."

"You look worse than before," said Lynx. "Your test from yesterday came back negative, so you don't have the virus yet."

"I had two more dreams last night. In the first, there were two football teams playing. I don't know who they were or where the game was played, but one team, the red team, kept passing the ball throughout the game, completing passes and scoring against the blue team repeatedly. The blue team's defense was based on covering the receivers—each one was double-covered, but the quarterback continued to get the ball to his men and gain yards."

"Finally during a single play, the blue team blitzed on the quarterback's blind side. He was sacked, being pounded to the ground quite abruptly. In the moment he was being grappled, his arm was cocked to throw, but the ball slipped from his grasp when he was hit, bobbled along the ground, and was picked up by a defensive lineman who lumbered down the field for a touchdown, huffing the entire way. When the lineman crossed the goal line, he collapsed in exhaustion."

"That single touchdown broke the red team's spirit, and the blue team went on to score enough touchdowns to win the game. What I don't understand is why the sack was so important, but in my dream I kept seeing the instant replay of it from every angle imaginable. Strange."

"In the second dream, I was driving down the freeway during rush-hour traffic. Though it was crowded, the vehicles moved along at a brisk seventy miles-per-hour. My attention was largely fixed on maintaining my distance from the car directly in front, which was apparently occupied by a single person—the driver."

"Without warning, a passenger leapt from his hiding spot in the back seat and pulled a gun on the driver. He fired at point blank, the driver's head popped to the side, and the car went swerving out of control, causing the surrounding cars and mine to slam-bam against each other into a horrific, crashing pile-up."

"Those are violent dreams," commented Dr. Lynx.

"Is that the solution? Violence?" Brandberg asked himself though aloud.

"Each dream focuses on one person attacking another in a very direct way. A woman killing a commander, a defensive lineman sacking a quarterback, a stowaway killing an automobile driver—and each situation has an immediate and severe result," Lynx said.

"But we've taken direct approaches with this virus, haven't we?" Brandberg asked.

Lynx paused for a moment then said, "Perhaps you've worked yourself so hard that you're twisting things into something more manageable by your brain, giving it a way to make sense of things with so much critical information."

"Perhaps. The problem with viruses is this—once they infect the host cell, nothing short of a killer T-cell will stop them. This virus multiplies as rapidly as bacteria, making it extremely difficult to stop. If only we could send antibodies across the cell membrane, an intracellular one so to speak."

"The only real thing we could send through the membrane wall is another virus," Lynx said.

"Another virus? That's an idea. If we could send a proper virus into the infected cells and somehow stop the B-lymphos from reproducing—"

"It's been suggested, but the problems associated with this are so numerous—"

"Forget the problems," said Brandberg.

"You can't just ignore them. They're still there," noted Lynx.

"We need a virus that will infect B-lymphocytes, disrupt the B-lympho virus, *and* stay in uninfected B-lymphocytes to protect against future infection."

"The intracellular immunity you were talking about—there are only a few viruses that are latent. The herpes viridae family comes to mind," mentioned Lynx.

"And in that family, the Epstein-Barr virus infects not only human saliva, but B-lymphocytes," Brandberg noted with glee.

"And can give the person Burkitt's lymphoma, cancer of the nasal passages, or—"

"Or, infectious mononucleosis, a time-consuming but recoverable disease."

"Our studies show the EB virus affects a completely different area than the B-lympho virus," noted Lynx.

"Then we change it. Although the B-lympho virus changes its genetic arrangement each iteration, it still affects roughly the same area of the host DNA chain. What's more, it manages to avoid causing antigens to form on the cell membrane's wall. A specifically engineered EB virus would go into an infected B-cell and cause a conflict, thus flagging the cell as infected, or it would go into an infected cell and wait in a dormant stage. When the B-lympho virus comes through, the same conflict is re-enacted, the antigens form on the cell membrane, and the killer T-cells destroy the invaded cell. How's that for a working theory?"

"Possible, but to get the perfect match—and will the EB virus mutation be able to multiply rapidly enough to overcome the B-lympho virus?" Lynx asked.

"One problem at a time. Fortunately, we can reprogram the computer to analyze recombinant EB virus strains against the B-lympho virus," said Brandberg.

The two spent the morning's remainder completing the plans for the computer analysis. Brandberg submitted the information to the programmer working with them. By that time, it was noon, and the doctors spent a quiet lunch in the lab consisting of ham sandwiches and apples. The two looked at each other periodically but did not say a word. Finally, the silence was broken by a ringing telephone.

"We have a problem," said Dorrin, the head programmer.

"What sort of problem?" asked Brandberg.

"According to our calculations, the computer analysis will take almost 49,000 years to complete."

"49,000 years!? We don't have 49,000 years!"

"I said almost 49,000," said Dorrin.

"All right, how much exactly?"

"48,897 years, forty-seven days, nine hours—"

"Ok, you've made your point. What do you recommend as an alternative?"

"We need to run this thing on a high-speed massively-parallel supercomputer system," he suggested.

"Fine. Who has one of these?" Brandberg asked.

"There's only one system capable of running the analysis in a timely fashion," he started.

"Great. Let's borrow the computer time and get the ball rolling."

"I'm afraid it's not that easy. Although we have access to the Human Genome computer, we don't have the authorization to dedicate it 100% to our program. If we could log on as a super operator, then—"

"Then we could do it, is that it?" Brandberg asked. "I know Dr. Leech has a high access level. If we could learn his password—"

"Say no more," said Dorrin. "I can write a program to emulate the sign-on program. He would type in his name, password, then the program would end without hiccup or hint. It would log off silently, then allow the real sign-on prompt to pop up. I should be able to find out which terminal he is using."

"More than likely he'll be calling in remotely. Most scientists and doctors on this project are. Will you be able to account for that?" Brandberg asked.

"Yes, I should be able to."

"Another thing, won't it look suspicious if Dr. Leech is logged on in two different places at the same time?"

"We won't use his logon name during the day. Tonight, when no one is on, we'll do it. If we're lucky, and no one stops us, we should have the answer within six hours," said Dorrin.

"Very well. If this is the only way—let me know if there are any problems," said Brandberg.

"Sure thing."

"Where is he?" an angry Dr. Leech asked Tarske, who had returned from Shairton without finding Brandberg.

"Someone must be helping him and hiding him—Gunter most likely. We've been keeping tabs on practically every building in Shairton, the State Capitol, and everywhere between," Tarske said.

"Guess what? He isn't in Shairton, or else you'd have caught him by now," Leech shot back.

Tarske was careful not to mention nearly capturing Brandberg in the library. The bathroom story was also taboo. Leech had reluctantly called him to his office in Bunker House One, and only part of it had to do with Brandberg.

"I can't afford to spend any more time on this minor hunt. As you may know, we've started circulating the B-lympho virus in various parts throughout the state area, using the missing Richardsons as the reason why. No one will find the Richardsons, of course."

"Are you saying we should abandon looking for the doctor?" Tarske asked.

"No, it wouldn't hurt to keep him locked up, but based on our reports and my confidence in this virus, I think even he would be hard pressed to find a cure for this one. If we're lucky, he'll be one of the victims," Leech suggested.

The two chuckled.

"What about the man they pulled from the Cheyenne River? Won't that scatter the virus more than we anticipated?" Tarske asked.

"Even if it does, what does it matter? I know, you're thinking that if Brandberg by some miracle tries to stop this thing, he'll go where the disease is worst. Let me show you something," Leech said, logging onto the Human Genome computer.

"Seems a little slow today," Tarske mentioned.

"That's odd. I logged on, now it seems stuck. No, wait. Another logon screen? Strange."

Leech entered his name and password a second time.

"There," Leech said, "it's working now. All right, Tarske, look at this map on the screen. The green Xs indicate where the virus was planted, the red indicates the current infections, and the violet indicates the projected spread. You see, it's too large of an issue for even Brandberg."

Tarske nodded in agreement, and the two looked at each other with knowing grins.

"Arnan Pauvold is dead," said Helen. "Now we've been here the longest. How are you holding up?"

"Not well," I said. "I've got the same cough as Arnan. My throat is sore, swollen in fact; I ache all over, I've got this pounding head, and there's this ringing in my ears. And you?"

"I seem to be doing better, though I alternate between being cold and hot. Mostly I'm tired. This is the end, our end, isn't it Jacob?"

"Don't give up hope," I said, trying to reassure her.

"You don't sound very convincing," she said. "I wish I could believe you, but we both know this is it. I want you to know that despite everything that's happened, I now and always will love you."

"You're everything to me, Helen. I just wish it didn't end so soon. At least in the end we're together. Bobby and Johnny, though—I wish we could say goodbye. I miss them so."

"I do too. They're in the best of care," Helen said.

"But will they see adulthood. Will anyone be left when it's over?" I asked.

Helen slumped into me with an embrace. We were both tired, and we stayed sitting in the same position for an hour, together. Somehow we fell asleep, and I secretly feared one or both of us would not see the morning.

At four in the morning, Dr. Leech's bedside phone rang, waking him.

"This better be good. What is it?" he barked.

"Sir, are you doing something strange on the Human Genome computer?" asked the voice on the other end.

"No. Why would I be? It's four in the morning. Can't a man get any sleep without being badgered about a computer?"

"I know, but this is important. Our stats indicate you logged on five hours ago and started running a CPU-intensive program. Nothing else can run."

"I haven't done anything of the sort. If this is some wild prank, I'll have you—"

"I assure you, sir, this is no game," said the voice. "We'll terminate it now. Unfortunately, the program is in compiled form."

"Meaning?"

"Meaning we can't tell what it's trying to do. Very odd—it seems benign enough."

"I want the entire computer system searched from top to bottom if necessary. Find out what is going on. We can't risk someone playing games with us this far into the research. Is that clear?"

"Yes sir."

"I want a full report ready when I come in this morning," said Leech.

"Yes sir."

"Do what you must, but no more calls this morning. Understood?"

"Yes sir."

"Bye."

"The program was halted prematurely," said Dorrin, the head programmer.

Brandberg and Lynx had finished their morning coffee when Dorrin broke the news to Brandberg over the phone.

"How far into the analysis did it go?"

"We have about 90% of the solution. I don't know if it will be enough," said Dorrin.

"I guess we have no choice. Bring what you have up here, and we'll take a look."

Moments later, the three were pouring over pages of computer print-out, including dozens of pictures detailing DNA sequences.

"This is too complicated," started Lynx. "The missing sequence is in an important section. How are we to figure out the remaining pieces?"

"The virus isn't too different from the Epstein-Barr virus, but there are enough differences...wait, I think I see an odd pattern at work here. Dorrin, I think we can fill the remaining sequences using your computer," said Brandberg.

"You've got to be kidding. Most of the work may be done, but I figure it'd take a hundred years to do the rest."

"Unless you use a Mandelbrot formula to derive the rest. You're familiar with the algorithms used to develop 'natural' sets?"

"I suppose. We could give it a shot. I think I see what you're saying now—these sequences are similar to these others, though different enough to...you're on to something, doctor. This shouldn't take more than a few hours," Dorrin said, flying out of the room in excitement with the papers in arm.

Three days passed since Arnan's death, and the same three days since the 90% solution was derived. The disease spread quickly throughout the United States and started appearing in other countries. Leech considered this an extra bonus, but the public amassed a fear that teetered on an explosion, frustrated by the same stories about the Richardsons causing the epidemic, and frustrated by the continued promises for a cure. Universities, hospitals, and independent researchers scampered to find a way to slow the spread or even stop it.

Those involved in "Operation Purge" (with the exception of Dr. Leech) had second thoughts regarding the project. Some said it was working as planned, others thought it was targeting people not originally intended. Still others questioned the moral implications for the first time. The dissent angered Dr. Leech, who continued giving bland news conferences to the public and maintaining his stand regarding "Operation Purge's" importance. Despite his preachings, the overwhelming negativity in the air stirred rumblings from within.

Gunter and Rudrick kept a low profile, quietly gathering information on the existence and the layout of Bunker House One, using scouts disguised as lab technicians and janitors. Their job had changed from simply breaking the Richardsons out to halting "Operation Purge" swiftly and completely.

Helen and I remained huddled in the waiting area, our conditions degrading progressively. I could hardly walk, let alone attempt an escape. Both of us had lost considerable weight, and our hair was rough and choppy.

"All right, you two," said Dr. Leech, while two guards came in and grabbed us, "it's time to end this little game once and for all. When the authorities find your bodies in the Cheyenne River like that other fellow, you'll make the front page of the *Shairton Times*. Isn't that exciting?" he said sarcastically with an evil grin.

"If there is one last thing I can say, Dr. Leech, it is this," I started, "this evil you've created will come back to haunt you. Such crimes do not go unpunished."

"And who's going to *punish* me? You? As far as the public is concerned, you two are the guilty ones, and justice will be served when your bodies are found. You are nothing more than miserable wretches. Your lives have no meaning or value to our society, and your end is both necessary and appropriate."

He stared sternly at me, and I attempted an equally stern stare in return, but my fatigue showed, and my weary head could do nothing better than bow in defeat.

"Take them away," he said to the guard, who eagerly complied.

We were tossed like potato sacks into the back of a van, back doors were closed behind us, and the van sped away from Bunker House One.

"Now that they're gone, I can get on to more important work," said Leech, returning to his office and beginning work on his computer terminal.

A minute later, Tarske rushed into the office.

"Have you seen the news?" he huffed, out of breath.

"News? What news?"

"It's on television now. Brandberg—he's holding a news conference."

"What!?" Leech exclaimed.

"You'd better come now to the common area. People are gathered around the television and it's looking—"

"Very well," Leech said, the two walking briskly to the common area.

Practically the entire Bunker House One staff crowded around the television to see Dr. Brandberg.

...acts as both a cure for those already sick and a vaccine for those not yet infected. The pathogen responsible for the epidemic has been named the B-lympho virus and rightly so. True it attacks the special white blood cells called B-cells, cells that produce antibodies to destroy foreign matter.

What isn't true is how the epidemic started. Dr. Leech would have you believe the B-lympho virus mutated from an anthrax-v virus that came from an anthrax-b bacillus that came from Mr. Jacob Richardson. While it is true Mr. Richardson contracted a strange form of anthrax, he was cured and was released, harmless to society. The question is—where did he get this disease from?

I'll tell you where: from an early experimental anthrax bacterium genetically engineered as part of Project Operation Purge, funded by the United States Government and headed by Dr. Leech, Chief Staff Doctor at Shairton Hospital. The project is intended to weed out those people deemed inferior by the U.S. Government, a throw-back to Fascism and the Master Race propaganda.

> Dr. Leech was involved from the start, and the genetic engineering was fine tuned until this B-lympho virus was released and the Richardsons used as scapegoats. Even now as I speak, Dr. Leech is no doubt in his final stages of spreading...

The television was drowned out by the ensuing Bunker House One panic.

"What's he doing on television? Send your men over there and get him off the air!" Leech shouted.

"It's too late," said Tarske.

"Hold it everyone. State police," came a voice crashing through the door.

Several people shrieked. The state police grabbed loose people and hauled them away. Tarske and Leech quickly rushed down the hallway to escape. Gunter and Rudrick spotted them from across the room and squirmed in the confusion frantically to catch the two. Tarske and Leech left a trail of knocked-over trays, confused people who'd accidentally had their papers scattered, and a trail of partial footprints from spilled iodine.

"This way," beckoned Gunter to Rudrick, the two approaching the main lab. "This could get ugly," Gunter whispered as the two men pulled out their revolvers and cocked them.

Gunter and Rudrick burst in and dove low for cover, expecting a shoot out. Dead silence. Gunter peered over a desk and saw only Leech.

"Playing hide and seek, are we?" taunted Leech, who sat on the other side of the room against a lab table. "Come out; let's talk."

"What's your game, Leech?" asked Gunter. Both he and Rudrick were peering over separate desks, scouting around for Tarske.

"I want to show you something," replied Leech. "Really, am I any threat to you?"

"Cover me," whispered Gunter to Rudrick. "All right, doctor, all right. What is it?" Gunter stood up, swaying his revolver from side to side.

"Please, the gun is distracting. Put it down. Besides, your partner will cover for you," Leech grinned.

Gunter lowered his gun for a moment, but he was suspicious. A shot rang out from a cubby hole. Rudrick cried out in pain. Instinctively, Gunter fired three shots at the retracting arm in the cubby hole. Tarske dropped his weapon and emerged briefly, then Gunter fired two more, killing Tarske. Gunter swung around to look at Rudrick. He was motionless.

"All right, doctor, don't make me use this last bullet on you. Come peaceably."

"In my hand is a beaker. You'll notice there's a cork and special seal preventing the contents from escaping. If you shoot me, the beaker will drop and the contents will escape, vaporize, and spread into the air."

"Is this some sort of threat?" Gunter asked, trying to talk through the situation.

"Very much so. Even if Dr. Brandberg has a cure for the B-lympho virus, he doesn't have a cure for this, because this hasn't been released yet. It is my latest and most spectacular accomplishment, and there can never be a cure. It attacks the human host and kills it within thirty minutes, and there is no evidence once the host dies, because the disease disintegrates."

"Look, doc, let's take it easy now."

"Stay back. Don't move, and you'll be safe," warned Dr. Leech.

Gunter held his position as Leech carefully backed away toward a small door. He slowly opened it, paused, then said:

"Here, catch!"

In the moment he spoke, he tossed the beaker across the room and darted through the door. Gunter, mesmerized, focused his entire attention on catching the beaker, and he fell over a chair to catch it. When he looked up to find Leech, the doctor was gone.

"Rudrick, are you all right?" Gunter asked.

"Yeah, just a shoulder wound," he replied.

Several state police stormed the room, preparing for conflict. Seeing that all was quiet, they relaxed their stance. The group's leader walked over to Gunter.

"Rudrick's been shot," Gunter said.

"By whom?"

"Tarske. He's over in the corner. I got him back."

"And Leech?"

Gunter paused.

"He got away. He left this, though. Supposed to be some new deadly disease," said Gunter.

"We'll have it analyzed. We gotta get Rudrick to a hospital," the leader said.

"Sir, Agent Tarske is dead," said another trooper to the leader.

The leader gave Gunter a hard look, then a small smile broke out.

"In the line of duty," he mumbled.

"Has anyone found the Richardsons yet?" Gunter asked.

"No, they haven't. In fact, most of the bunker has been searched by now."

Several more state police entered the room. One walked up to the leader and whispered something into his ear.

"The rumor is the Richardsons have been taken to the mouth of the Cheyenne River where they will be killed and thrown in," said the leader.

"Then it's time we stop them," said Gunter, moving to leave. The leader stopped him.

"Not so fast. You know we can't just waltz in there like it's a flower patch. The terrain is rocky, steep, and downright loose. If you don't slip and fall into the gorge below, you'll trigger an avalanche and be buried alive. No. The rumor can't be true. We'll send some cars out on patrol and check for anything suspicious. Trust me on this one, Gunter."

"Yeah, sure. I suppose you're right. Man, this excitement has worked up a sweat. I don't suppose there's anything to drink around here."

"There's a soda machine down the hall," the leader said.

Gunter left the room and started toward the machine, but he walked right past it.

"Somebody's gotta go after them," he muttered.

Bound and gagged as we were, two bodyguards accompanied us in the van—one drove while the other kept a close eye on us. Escape was useless, since his hand was so near to his revolver. If I had flinched, he would have quickly shot me down.

"This is it," said the one guard to the one driving. "The back way in."

A corduroy trail would have been a smoother ride compared to the bumps and jostles from the unpaved road. It was only a few minutes before we were forced out the back door and dragged several feet to a precipice.

"Cheyenne River, or at least the start of it," said one of the guards.

"It must be a good two hundred feet down before you'll hit water," said the other.

The prospect was not pleasant, especially considering our bound condition.

"As a little incentive to get wet," said the first, "we'll do you the favor of giving you each a present."

The second went back to the van and brought forth two cinder blocks and rope. While the first pointed his gun at us, the second attached a cinder block to each of our ankles. Our backs were to the swirling rapids below, and as I glanced past the guards into the woods from where we came, I saw a glimpse of a man's face.

"All set," said the second guard, completing the block job. "Let's see if these fish can swim."

The two grabbed us, prepared to push, then a twig snapped in the woods and a group of birds scattered from the trees.

"What was that?" asked the second guard, the two holding their positions.

"I'll check it out," the first said. He walked up to and just past the van when he called back, "DON'T START WITHOUT ME."

"What do you suppose that was?" Helen said as she worked her gag partly loose.

"Don't worry your pretty little face over it," said the second guard. "You've got your own weight to carry—and then some," he joked, tapping her cinder block.

A gun shot rang through the air and echoed through the Cheyenne River's ravine.

"You all right, Stokes?" the second guard called out. No reply.

Five minutes elapsed without the first guard's return.

"Something's wrong," muttered the second guard, "but just to make sure the job gets done, I'll deal with you two first!"

"I wouldn't be so hasty," came a voice from around the van. "Drop your weapon and take two steps forward."

"Sergeant Gunter," Helen said, surprised. We were both surprised considering how long we'd spent evading him.

"Stay back," said the second guard, holding Helen in front of him and alternating between pointing his gun at Helen and at Gunter.

"Drop it, now!" Gunter commanded.

"Throw me your gun, or she gets it," the second guard said, putting the gun to Helen's head.

"Really now, I don't think Stokes would approve, would you Stokes?" Gunter said, pulling the first guard from behind the van. "You see, he's had a sudden change of heart. He values life now, don't you Stokes?"

The first guard nodded his head in affirmation, and the blood drooling from his leg showed why.

"Nuh-uh. I'm not giving up so easily. I've got two of yours, you only have one of mine," the second guard said, panicking.

"Baird, drop your gun for chrissakes!" spat the first guard.

"If it means I have to give my life to see these two die, I will. They started this thing, and I'm gonna finish it!" exclaimed the second guard.

Helen suddenly whipped her head backward, knocking the second guard's nose, breaking it. Without thinking, he reflexively loosened his grip, grabbed for his nose while stepping aside, and the bullet from Gunter's gun pierced the second guard's aorta. He fell and within seconds was dead. Gunter handcuffed the first guard to the handle on the van's back door.

"Don't be afraid," Gunter reassured us, "I'm here to help, not to hurt. I've been a talkin' to Dr. Brandberg, and thanks to him we've stopped the operation. The doctor found a cure for the epidemic, and well, I just thought I'd stop by and pick you two up," he smiled.

Helen and I looked at each other and broke out into laughter as Gunter untied us.

"Can we get used to you without a beard?" Helen asked.

"Or with black hair?" I asked.

"They'll both grow out," Brandberg said, "given enough time."

We were gathered for a quiet dinner at the East Shairton Restaurant. It had been a month since Helen and I were nearly pushed off the edge into Cheyenne River, and since then Dr. Brandberg's cure had restored our health along with half a million people. Johnny and Bobby were home with a babysitter, and this was our first night out since Lakeside Inn, just before our flight.

"When the governor resigned, Sergeant Gunter was asked to run for office, but he declined, saying he was happy in Shairton. He *did* receive special citation for his efforts," Brandberg said.

"Even though at first he was part of the problem. Well, I guess he *was* in a difficult situation," I said.

"And the U.S. Government has denied the whole 'Operation Purge' moniker, saying the project was officially called 'Operation Yogurt' and was intended to improve health for domestic livestock as part of the newly instated Pure Food Act. Tarske is dead, and the entire Bunker House One has been confiscated for any and all equipment, supplies, and information regarding the B-lympho virus. They also discovered the beaker Dr. Leech threw to Gunter was another cure for the virus, for himself and his staff."

"Did they ever find Dr. Leech?" Helen asked.

"No. Not a sign or trace of his existence. I wouldn't worry, though. It's unlikely he'll pose a threat in the future," Brandberg said.

"Seems like the last time you told us not to worry about someone, that someone turned us over to Tarske and Dr. Leech for experimentation," I noted.

"Really? I guess I did say that, didn't I? Oh Helen, you'll be happy to know I've recommended you to a newly opened position at the hospital. It'll be exciting, and based on your experience, I think you'll be perfect," Brandberg suggested.

"Is that so? Just where is this position? What department?" she asked.

"Virology."

Helen looked at me, I looked at Helen, then we fixated our attention on the sugar bowl in the center of the table. We each picked up the bowl, a hand on each side, removed the lid, and poured it over a squirming Brandberg head. Helen and I replaced the bowl in the center and smiled. Dr. Brandberg looked at each of us with an expression of shock. His anger didn't last long, and he chuckled quietly then erupted into full laughter. Helen and I laughed with him, and the waitpersons had to help us to our seats after we'd laughed ourselves silly to the floor.

(The End)

The Cat from Hell: Origins

February 2, 1995

Deep within the monastery cata-combs, 16th century French monks raised a gray cat amongst the odors and alchemy brews. In that dark age, the cat became impregnated. How is still a mystery, but the fact remain-ed—Chartreau would have kittens.

The author in 1995

ESCAPE

Chartreau seemed an ordinary cat until her gestation period approached its end. She grew restless. Anxiously, she prowled everywhere as if to look for a safe place to escape, from what she wasn't sure, but she searched nevertheless. She was even so bold as to sip the vari-ous brews the French monks prepared for this ailment or that spirit.

"*Allez!*" said one of the monks. "*Le chat, c'est l'heure!*"

The others rushed over to see what was happening with Chartreau. It started; Chartreau began labor.

The cat's labor was long and intense. Despite the monks' attempts to help the mother cat, she hissed and growled and backed away as best she could despite her bottom-heavy situation.

"*Le chat est très difficile!*" shouted a monk.

"*Arrêtez, arrêtez!*" said another as the monks tried to trap the cat and control her irrational behavior.

Chartreau hobbled and squirmed around until she found a way out of the caves—a ledge above the monks' grasp. She paused for a moment, looking outside at the cold. Snow whipped around the little opening, and several flakes melted on her nose. Down below, she took a final look at the monks as they put tables, chairs, and finally a ladder underneath Chartreau. They were trying to catch her.

In the moment one of the monks grasped for Chartreau, she darted through the hole into the freezing snow.

"Chartreau, Chartreau!" the monk called, but she never flinched and disappeared into the white blizzard.

Chartreau was free but chilling quickly. She scampered along the snow through a small woods for several minutes looking for some shelter, but she couldn't find any. There were no nearby houses, no caves, just mounds and mounds of snow everywhere.

Her eyes pulsated from the contractions, but they gradually froze over, and she could not see. She felt her way down a rocky slope that seemed to offer some protection from the wind and snow. Chartreau fell on the slope, exhausted, and panted hard for several minutes.

In that moment, the wind severed a branch from a tree and tossed it several yards through the air until it landed on Chartreau. She jumped instinctively, but she landed on a slick patch of ice. Desperately, she thrashed with all fours, trying to regain composure, but the slippery ice mercilessly slid her down the slope into a stream where she broke through the ice and landed in the chilly waters.

Her gray fur was now wet and frozen. Chartreau made a meager attempt to climb out, but the stream was too cold and too powerful, and it carried her along until she froze and lost consciousness. The stream pushed her under a sheet of ice, and as the storm raged, ice surrounded Chartreau, and she remained frozen.

After a time, the ice chunk broke free and was carried down into an underground stream that carried the ice chunk into the ocean. Strong ocean currents carried the chunk northward until it was deposited in Greenland.

MIRACLE

Summer 1991

"I've found a job in Milwaukee," I said. "The pay isn't bad, and I'll be able to afford an apartment instead of a run-down rooming house. What about you, Maria, what do you plan to do?" I asked while we sorted through some things in Grandfather's South Bend house.

"Go back to Ann Arbor and see if my job is still there. Find a new apartment and hopefully a new life. Now that Grandmother is dead and Grandfather is in the retirement home, there's no reason to stay in South Bend. And maybe I can find someone to fix the motor for my wiper fluid."

"Oh yeah, here's the ten dollars for the parking ticket I got on your Renault."

"You know I've never had a ticket on this car," she laughed. "And I never plan to."

While I ventured into new lands in Wisconsin, Maria returned to Ann Arbor, Michigan, and learned that not only did she still have her job, but one of the employees was anxious to find a place of her own.

"A place close to I-94 so we can get to work quickly, but I don't know if I want to live in Ann Arbor," Miss R said.

"There is a nice apartment complex in Ypsilanti," said Maria. "I saw the sign when I got off the freeway to get gas. And there are a few apartments vacant. We could move in over next weekend."

"As long as the paperwork goes through. Why don't I give them a call and see what I can do?" offered Miss R.

"Thanks," said Maria.

Miss R had no problem getting the apartment, and after a deposit, first month's rent, and several signatures later, the pair had keys and were making preparations to move in.

"Some of my stuff is at a cousin's house in Port Huron," Miss R said. "Do you think you could help me with it?"

"Sure," said Maria. "No problem."

Maria and Miss R drove up to Port Huron early one Saturday, anxious to get the move underway. After entering Port Huron but before arriving at Miss R's cousin's house, Miss R's stomach growled.

"I'm hungry, what about you?" ask Miss R.

"Yeah. Lunch time, isn't it?"

"Look, there's a taco place on the right."

The two went in then exited ten minutes later with two bags full of food and drinks.

"There are some benches down by the beach. Let's eat there," suggested Maria.

Maria and Miss R sat on the bench and busily ate away. They were only a few minutes from Miss R's cousin's house, but they wanted to start the loading without being hungry.

"I think I ordered too much," said Miss R. "Want some of mine?"

"No thanks," said Maria. "I've had enough."

"You know what I used to do?" asked Miss R while walking up to the edge of Lake Huron.

"No, what?"

"I used to throw food out to the fish and watch them eat it."

"Do you think the fish would eat this junk food?"

"I don't know," replied Miss R.

"It's cold and windy. Maybe the fish are hibernating."

"We'll just have to find out, won't we?"

With that, Miss R threw out a small bit of her taco. A couple of fish seemed to eat it. Then she threw out another and another. Several more fish seemed to eat, but on the next-to-the-last piece, no fish ate.

"Not as much fish as there used to be. Here goes, last piece," and Miss R threw it down along the shore instead of out in the lake.

"What was that?" asked Maria when she heard a strange splash from the food. "You hit something."

"What's there to hit?"

"I don't know, but you hit something," said Maria.

The two walked down the shore a bit, and there it was. To their astonishment, the two saw an old-looking gray cat, still partly frozen, but apparently dead.

"Gross, it looks like a dead cat," said Miss R.

"Don't touch it! Use a stick to poke it," suggested Maria.

"No way I'll touch it. But you can poke it."

Maria took a stick and prodded the gray animal. It was dead, but something moved from inside the cat's belly.

"Something's in it!" Maria said, and the two jumped back several yards.

"And already eating into it. Worms? Maggots?"

"Gross!" the two girls said, looking at each other.

Yes, the gray cat was dead, and something *was* eating through, but it wasn't a worm or maggot. The side opened bit by bit, and a soft, high-pitched meow sounded from within the gray cat.

"It's a kitten!" said Miss R. "The mother must have been ready to give birth. Here kitty kitty."

"You're not thinking of taking that kitten home with you, are you?" Maria asked.

"We can't just leave it out here. It'll die unless we take the little cat in," said Miss R.

"The cat in? You mean the *kitt-en*, or are you calling it *kat-tin*?"

"*Cat in, cast in* from the cold, how about *Castin* for a name?" asked Miss R.

"*Castin* sounds like a fishing pole, but *Cassin* might be better," replied Maria.

"Then *Cassin* it is. Here Cassin, come here," said Miss R.

By now, the little gray kitten had gnawed his way out of Chartreau's belly. He didn't know much about cleaning or what to do next, but he shivered and hobbled as best he could. Cassin was still covered in blood and mucus, but Miss R and Maria did the best they could to wipe him off with tissue and paper napkins.

Miss R and Maria didn't know what they had in their possession, nor did they think it odd that only one kitten emerged from Chartreau. How Chartreau travelled all the way from that French monastery to the beach of Lake Huron is more a miracle than a mystery, and unraveling the mystery took some doing, including getting someone wondering about Cassin's origins.

"You'll never guess what we found," said Maria over the telephone to me.

"Maria? Where are you calling from?" I asked.

"Ypsilanti. Tammy (Miss R) and I just got back from Port Huron. She had some furniture up at her cousin's," replied Maria.

"So that's what you found? Furniture?" I asked from my newly acquired Milwaukee apartment.

"Besides that. It was the weirdest thing—"

"Your new roommate?"

"No, silly! We found a kitten, and we've named him *Cassin*," explained Maria.

"A kitten? Where?" I asked.

"On the beach."

"Beach? There are no lakes near you. You mean Lake Michigan? Erie? Huron? I know it couldn't have been Lake Superior, and Lake Ontario is a good little trip."

"It was Lake Huron in Port Huron, and we saw him on the beach. Actually, he climbed out of his mother," explained Maria.

"You mean he climbed *on* his mother. Cassin was just born?"

"Sort of. Cassin's mother was dead."

"From giving birth to Cassin? Really?" I asked incredulously.

"No, before."

"I'm lost," I said, bewildered.

"Ok, here's what happened. Tammy and I were down by the beach when we discovered a dead cat. Tammy poked the cat with a stick, and then something moved from inside. Next thing we know, this kitten pops out and is cold and yucky. So we cleaned it off and took it home."

"You say the cat was dead?" I asked.

"Yeah, and it looked really strange," Maria said.

"How?"

"It looked really old, like over a hundred years, but everyone knows that cats can't live that long."

"It sounds very strange. What did you do with the mother cat after cleaning Cassin?"

"What do you mean, what did we do with her?"

"You didn't just leave her there, did you?" I asked.

"Well, why not? She was dead," said Maria.

"Don't you wonder whose cat that was?"

"Probably a stray," said Maria.

"Did it look like any cat you'd ever seen?" I asked.

"No, but every cat looks a little different to me."

"But you say she looked really old, and she's dead. How could she give birth when she was dead?"

"She didn't *give* birth—Cassin just chewed his way out."

"Don't you think that's highly unusual?" I asked.

"A little. So what?"

"Well, to be safe, you should have a forensic scientist examine the dead cat. Cassin may well have some inherited deficiencies that may make life difficult for him."

"Cassin is not sickly. He's lively and spirited. I don't think there's anything wrong with him."

Convinced that Cassin was normal, Maria had no interest in the mother cat, still dead on the shore of Lake Huron. I did manage to get the cat's location from Maria, and with that knowledge I spent the remaining weekend travelling from Milwaukee, Wisconsin to Port Huron, Michigan.

"What a miserable Sunday afternoon," I thought to myself while driving through the cold rain. "How will I find a gray cat in weather like this?"

Pulling over to the spot Maria had described, I realized that the strong waves had probably washed the cat away.

"It was lying behind a bush next to a rock," Maria had said to me over the phone. I saw several bushes, but no rock.

"One of those bushes," I thought, walking down along the beach until I came to a single bush. On the other side was a large rock, and next to the rock was a dead gray cat. It was old, incredibly old, and it seemed shrunken or decayed, but I wasn't sure which.

"Arrgh! What a stench," I said while using a stick to push the carcass first into a plastic bag, then the bag into a box.

"That should hold you for a bit," I said.

Fortunately, Interstate 94 was lightly travelled, but my car was acting up, sputtering and huffing as if badly out of tune.

"Now what's gotten into this car? Only five months old and it's acting up. C'mon, Bonnie Blue, I need you."

She (my car) limped down to the University of Michigan in Ann Arbor where I met up with Dr. Barakowski.

"So this is it," he said. "Let's get it on the table."

He carefully unwrapped the cat then backed off immediately.

"I should have warned you—she's already started to rot," I explained.

"That's ok. It isn't the first time I've dealt with a dead animal. You know, I can start the examination without you. Why don't you get something to eat and come back in a couple of hours? I should know more by then."

"All right," I said, and I drove over to Maria to pay her a visit. Amazingly, the car's problems disappeared.

"Ken, what a surprise," said Maria. "What are you doing here? You came all the way over from Milwaukee just to visit?"

"No. I came over for the cat."

"Look, I know you're concerned, but there's nothing to be worried about. Cassin is doing fine. See? He's sleeping in the corner chair," Maria explained.

"Maria, I didn't come over to see Cassin. It's his mother, the one on the shore of Lake Huron."

"Yeah, what about her?"

"She's dead you know," I said.

"Yeah, I already told you that."

"I took her over to Dr. Barakowski at the University of Michigan."

"What good will that do?" Maria asked.

"Hopefully it will give us some answers," I said.

"Answers to what? Ever since I told you about Cassin, you've been caught up in this thing with his mother."

"This isn't just any ordinary kitten. I can feel something's different. Just keep an eye on Cassin, ok? I'm going to get something to eat, then I'm going back to the University."

"Well, no matter what happens, we're keeping this cat," said Maria, and that was the last I heard about the kitten for several weeks.

As it turned out, Dr. Barakowski only had a preliminary report on the mother cat.

"We're going to have to run some additional tests," he said.

"Tests? What kind of tests?" I asked.

"We found these in her throat," Dr. Barakowski said, showing me some leaf specimens in a see-through plastic bag.

"Leaves, I don't get it."

"I don't recognize from what tree these came. I'm sending them over to the botany department for identification. Meanwhile, after finishing the autopsy, I'm going to schedule a carbon-14 dating for Jane Cat Doe."

"To see how old she is?" I asked.

"And after getting an ID on the leaf specimens, we'll date them too," he continued. "This could be up to a week. I know you live in Milwaukee and all."

"Yeah, I can't wait around here for a week."

"I can call you with the results," he offered.

"Sure. That would be great."

One week passed. Two weeks, then three. Finally, Dr. Barakowski called me one evening.

"I had practically forgotten about the gray cat from Lake Huron," I said.

"I wanted to make absolutely sure before I told you," he started.

"Sure of what? Some sort of infectious disease, right?"

"No not that at all. It's about her origins."

"Yes, go on."

"You'll never believe this," he said.

"I think I have a fairly open mind," I said.

"This cat, it's Chartreau, at least it appears to be Chartreau. You don't know the magnitude of this find."

"You're right; I don't. Just who is this Chartreau?"

"There is a breed of cats known as chartreux that was started in the 16th century by French monks. According to the story, there were three cats that the monks called the original chartreux. The first one died as an infant. The second grew up and bore several litters of kittens. That's the origins of the official breed today. The third supposedly was in labor and ready to deliver when it suddenly ran off, though the monks could never figure out why."

"The leaves I found in Jane Cat Doe's throat are of French origin. There was also some debris that suggests this cat may have been in Greenland at some time. And get this—the carbon-14 dating says that Jane Cat Doe is over four hundred years old."

"How is this possible?" I asked. "How could the cat have gotten from France to Michigan?"

"The best we could figure," explained Dr. Barakowski, "is that she was carried into the ocean, and strong currents carried her to Greenland, where she was packed into an iceberg or other frozen form and remained there for over four hundred years."

"So you still haven't explained how she got down here," I interrupted impatiently.

"I'm getting to that. Whatever ice chunk she was in broke away from the mainland and travelled toward North America."

"Why now? Why didn't she stay frozen in the glacier?"

"Global warming. There's an unprecedented number of icebergs separating from Greenland and other northerly masses and floating down south. Somehow she made it from Greenland to Lake Huron, but that's the most puzzling part of all."

"Why?" I asked. "Couldn't she have floated down the St. Lawrence Seaway into the Great Lakes?"

"Except for one small detail: the St. Lawrence Seaway flows from the Great Lakes to the Atlantic, which means something or someone dragged her or put her in Lake Huron."

"Who? How?"

"Boat maybe; we're not sure," continued Dr. Barakowski. "The other thing is this—the story said she was preparing to deliver kittens. We found no kittens in her, but we did find a placenta. That's unusual, because each kitten has its own placenta, and there was evidence of only one. It probably was pushed out sometime in the 16th century, then they both probably froze to death in the chilly waters."

"Is there a chance that kitten could have survived?" I asked.

"Even if it hadn't been born and was still inside the mother, I don't see how. Most mammals, once frozen, can't be thawed back to a living state, at least not by current technology."

"Thank you, Dr. Barakowski," I said, keeping the knowledge of Cassin to myself.

"Thank you. We're in your debt for this magnificent find. We'll be publishing a formal paper on Chartreau in some of the scientific magazines soon. Can we use your name as the finder?"

"No thanks. I think we should keep that part anonymous," I said, though it was Miss R and Maria who first found the dead cat.

"Very well. Again, thank you, Ken, and good luck in your endeavors."

While driving to work the next day, I couldn't help but wonder if I should have alerted Dr. Barakowski to Cassin's existence. On the one hand, it was too strange of a thing for Cassin to be alive, and on the other hand, I had a sudden reluctance to become a part of some media circus that would strip the private life from Miss R, Maria, and me.

According to Maria, Cassin was doing very well, hobbling his way around and exploring the apartment. He had a large appetite, gobbling up his food in large quantities and frequently. Soon he would become even more inquisitive and play with things like strings, sticks, and socks, but that would happen soon enough.

One final note. Maria did say that Cassin scratched her, though it was probably accidental, and she doubted he would be anything but a gentle, sweet, and cuddly cat.

Futures: Part I

January 1, 1995

Riverton, Friday

"You could give money," suggested Marvin.

"Yeah, I *could*, but she *is* my sister. I'd like to get her and her fiancé something for their home. I could get them some plates or cups, but I don't want the gift to look so plain, like I got it at the local department store. I want something with character."

"Character? Look at that factory floor. We got plenty of characters here. We don't need any more," Marvin said, filling his cup with coffee.

"Ok, maybe that was the wrong word. I need something that will let them remember me—a gift they will treasure into the future," Ken said, stirring creamer into his coffee.

"Future?" asked Dineen, walking into the break room for her morning cup. "Are you looking into your future, Ken?"

"In a matter of speaking. I want to find a nice wedding present for my sister and future brother-in-law. Something for the home; something useful yet nice-looking. Now if I could just be sure they'd be happy, then I'd be happy."

"I know the perfect place. It's in a little town off Highway 20. Now what was that town called? Rolling Hills. And the store is called Sadie's Place," suggested Dineen.

"Sadie's Place? Never heard of it."

"And I hope you never will," said Marvin.

"Oh lay off the pessimism, Marv-o," shot back Dineen. "For you, there *is* no hope or future."

"And you call shacking-up with that dirt-bag guy a future, Spam-for-Di-neen-er?"

"You just shut your mouth about—"

"All right, enough already, both of you!" interjected Ken.

And that's how it started. Ken was simply looking for a suggestion but found himself breaking up a verbal argument.

"What kind of place is this?" Ken asked Dineen later that day.

"Sorry about that, Ken. That Marvin can be such a—"

"You don't have to say another word. Now this place?"

"Sadie's Place," continued Dineen. "It's a crafty sort of store."

"Crafty?" Ken asked.

"Yeah, like crafts and nice things for a home. Linens, baby things, and nick-nacks. You won't find any cheap, plastic crud there, which is why most things are a little more expensive than your plain-ole discount store. But you will find things made of real glass, real china, real wood, and lots of cottons and wools."

"There was something else, though. What was it you said, something about my future?" asked Ken.

"Oh, that. Just a side thing they do at Sadie's Place. I never believed it myself before I saw her—I'm not even sure how she could know about the future. Maybe it's some sort of hoax or whatever, but she was right about my sister," explained Dineen.

"Believed what? Who was right? About the future?"

"The store owner—Lady Sadie—she does readings for people, readings of their future. My sister and her husband have been trying to have a child for the last six years. After spending thousands of dollars on medical treatments, they were ready to give up. Lady Sadie said she saw my sister holding a newborn in her arms in a year or two. That reading was over a year ago. My sister is now six months pregnant."

"Hmm. I will say it's different. But for now I think I'll just stick with the gift."

"It's ok if you don't belief. I know you computer types are very logical-minded and don't hold much truth to the supernatural. But Sadie's Place *does* have nice crafts."

Ken experienced a frustrating day with a thrashing computer system. Unusual—this was the first such incident since the system's installation two years prior. The usual diagnostics were useless because Ken couldn't keep the computer system going long enough to run them.

"Lovely computer," Ken muttered sarcastically. The telephone calls from all departments—calls of frustrated employees unable to keep the company going because of an ailing computer—amplified Ken's agony.

"Why is it the thing runs nicely for a couple of years, then for no apparent reason the whole thing goes to pot? Sometimes I wish these things were never invented!"

But oddly enough, the computer resumed normal operations at 4:30 that afternoon. Ken ran every diagnostic program and tool at his disposal, but there was no malfunction and no flaw.

"Man am I tired!" Ken muttered to himself.

Too tired to give the machine another thought, Ken left work at 5:00 pm and drove straight home.

"At least tomorrow is Saturday," said Ken to himself when he finally got home. "I need to get my mind off of this; I need to relax."

He had hardly sat down to the evening news when fatigue threw him into a short but deep sleep, a troubled sleep. His arms jerked several times as if fighting off something while his cat watched in amusement.

"Stop," he said finally, and he jumped up suddenly with cold sweat dripping from his face.

"Meow," said Ken's cat.

"What? You have food."

"Meow," she said again.

"I feel strange," Ken said, petting his cat between the ears and around the cheeks. "What day is this? What time?"

Though Ken had slept for twenty minutes, he felt as if several days had passed, and his sense of time continuity was disrupted.

"The computer—that happened today. What was I going to do this evening? A store—Sadie's Place in Rolling Hills—Highway 20. Now it's coming back to me. Ok. Kitty, be good, I'll be back soon."

"Meow," said his cat a final time as he left his apartment.

"What a storm! Where did this come from?" Ken wondered. It was an incredibly windy and rainy thing, no lightning, but the rain and hail pounded the car while he drove down Highway 20.

"Must be around here somewhere. Rolling Hills, where are you? I can hardly see anything in this storm. Man! This windshield is fogging up like crazy! YIKES!" Ken yelled as he stomped on his brakes and spun his car into a 360° turn.

"Ow," Ken said, hitting his head against something in the car, but he wasn't sure what stunned him more—the concussion, or the timber wolf standing in the middle of the road staring him down.

He didn't waste time with the wolf but instead backed his car into a Y-turn and drove back to an intersection then down a side street to get around. But the storm made driving difficult, and Ken couldn't seem to find his way back to Highway 20.

"There's a gas station," he said, pulling into the side of the station.

"Hi," Ken said to the attendant inside the station. "Could you tell me where Highway 20 is?"

"See that road in front of the station?"

"Yeah," Ken replied.

"That's Highway 20."

"Great! I found it after all. Ok, now which way is Rolling Hills?"

The attendant broke into laughter, and though Ken pressed him for the answer, the attendant continued to laugh even harder.

"Please now, this is important to me! Where is Rolling Hills?"

"Right here!"

"The gas station is Rolling Hills?"

"No, man! You're in Rolling Hills, I'm in Rolling Hills, this gas station is in Rolling Hills, and every house within a block of this intersection is in Rolling Hills. Get it?"

"Yeah, I got it. You don't have to be smart about it," said Ken.

"Well, someone's gotta be smart around here—obviously you aren't keen on directions."

"Hey, you!"

"Listen pal," the attendant continued, "why don't you just get back in your car and go back from where you came. There ain't nothing here you city folk don't have already."

"Fine. I come looking for Sadie's Place, and all I get is—"

"Sadie's Place? Why didn't you say so?"

"You've heard of it?"

"Heard of it? See that there?" he asked, pointing through the window above a rack of motor oil. "That's her place."

"Good, then I'll go over there at once."

"Why?"

"Because I would like to do some shopping, if you don't mind."

"I don't. But you're wasting your time," said the attendant.

"And why's that?"

"She's closed."

"For good?" Ken asked.

"Not for good. For today."

"When?"

"Round five I suppose. She usually does."

"Usually does what?"

"Closes at five, what did you think?" the attendant asked, almost accusingly.

"Nothing," Ken said, a little defensive.

"Figures. No directions and no thinking. But cheer up. Tomorrow is Saturday. That means she's open from ten to two," the attendant said, but his crooked teeth didn't pronounce Ts crisply, and Ken misunderstood.

"Chen choo-choo? Does she work on a train?"

"Listen: she opens at ten o'clock. She closes at two o'clock."

"Why would I want to chew a clock?" Ken asked, bemused.

"At two, at two!"

"Bless you! Are you catching a cold?"

Just as the attendant moved to kick Ken squarely out the door, a voice interrupted from the doorway.

"Hey, Doug! I want my car."

"Can't."

"But Kip said it'd be ready by Friday afternoon. Well, it's Friday, and it's after twelve o'clock," the woman said.

"I know it's after twelve o'cl—" Doug (the attendant for those of you not paying attention) stared at Ken briefly then looked back at the young woman before correcting himself, "noon. He had to run down to Crooked Creek 'cause of the storm and all. Some guy had to be winched out of a ditch."

Ken looked at the woman, surprised. "What a nice face for someone living in the country," he thought, because every other person he'd seen in the rural parts had sun-wrinkled, leathery skin, hair with split ends, and hands worn to the bone. This woman had straight brown hair, smooth unblemished skin, and the best set of legs he'd ever seen.

"Well I need my car for the weekend. When's he going to fix it?"

"Don't you worry, Ms. Racquemore. Kip'll have your car fixed tomorrow morning."

"I hope so. I need to go shopping."

"Don't we all," said Ken.

"Who's this guy, a townie out-of-townie?" Ms. Racquemore asked.

"Just passing through," Ken said, and he went home.

"Who was that?"

"Lost. Looking for Sadie's Place, but he's lost," said Doug.

Rolling Hills, Saturday morning

"Blue would be more appropriate," said Lady Sadie to a customer looking for baby blankets that Saturday morning.

"Oh this isn't for me," said the customer.

"Of course not. But a blue blanket will bring smiles to a red-haired mother."

"How did you know my cousin has red hair? It's just for the baby shower, do you really think she'll have a boy?" asked the customer.

"And he will be holding hands with his older sister and younger brother," said Lady Sadie.

"My cousin *does* have a two-year-old girl, but another boy? Wow!"

"And the blanket will keep the second boy warm, especially when the mother watches a new president take office."

Lady Sadie smiled from beneath her black-veiled attire. Her sparkling eyes sent splashes of silver light along her wizenly gray hair. As was her charm, she went up to other customers and helped them select gifts, foretelling the future in an obscure way that hinted to certain events.

"Two pairs of pink slippers fit snuggly on twins as they give their mother with white shoes and white work-clothes a hug when she arrives home for the day."

"I thought I might be expecting, but twin girls?" said another customer. "And I'm just finishing nursing school, but I don't know if I can find a job around here. Will I get a job at Riverton County Hospital?"

"I see you adjusting the pillow of a grey-haired woman who points out the window to a red-bricked house with a green and white fence surrounding the front lawn and a tabby cat climbing up a yellow and green bird feeder."

"That's Mrs. Hiller's house. And she has a weak heart. But the house is next to Apple County Hospital, one of the finest hospitals in this area. It's hard to land a job there. Oh thank you, thank you!"

Riverton, the same Saturday morning

Ken woke to a bright and clear morning. So completely refreshed and ready to go, the previous night seemed distant— like a bad dream.

"Ah, to be alive! Now what did the guy say? Chen choo-choo? No, that was ten-to-two," Ken thought while pouring dry food into his cat's bowl. "Bye, kitty!" he said to his sleeping cat, who hardly stirred to see him leave.

"Can't believe this is the same road," thought Ken while driving down Highway 20. "Maybe there was no wolf; maybe that was a strange sort of dream. Highway 20 is too plain and open for such a creature to roam. Now where is this store? There it is; there's Sadie's Place."

"Here's a nice outfit I'm sure your baby will like. Feel the material," said Linda, showing a one-piece outfit to an older woman.

"Feels nice, like cotton," said the prospective customer.

"That's because it *is* cotton. Now watch this!" Linda said, crumpling the outfit into her hands then pulling it out again.

"There's not a single wrinkle, not a one! How?" asked a surprised customer.

"We put a special, all-natural preparation on all of our cottons to keep them soft and wrinkle-free. It's just another little thing we do for our customers."

"Well, Linda, I'm going to recommend this place to all of my friends."

"Especially the one with black hair and thick glasses," said Lady Sadie from another aisle. "The sparkle from this bracelet will catch her husband's eye at the party."

"That can't be," said the customer. "The only girl I know with black hair and glasses is Clara, and she's not married. She's not even going to the dance next weekend."

Lady Sadie simply winked at the customer.

"What she says doesn't always make sense at first," said Linda to the customer. "But when it happens, what she says makes sense."

"That means that—oh my, I'd better tell Clara about the bracelet!"

While the customer went on about how marvelous the store was, Ken casually looked around for a gift, unaware of who was in the store at the time. Presently, he picked up a small, clock ornament and became fascinated with the intricate exterior design.

"Will that be cash or by check?" asked Linda, now standing by the cash register.

"Check. Now if I can find a pen—" a customer said.

"Here, borrow mine!" Linda offered.

"Hmm," Ken thought, "would they like this little clock? Maybe too old-fashioned. What do they really need? Salt and pepper shakers?"

"Why thank you, dear," said a customer to someone else.

"Is that a new ring on your left hand, Mrs. Felder?" Linda asked.

"This thing? It was an anniversary gift about two or three years ago. But I suppose since you haven't seen me in as many years, it's new to you."

"It's very pretty," said Linda.

Ken gave up on the clock and wandered over to some empty yet odd-looking aquariums. "Fish?" he thought. "Their cat might kill fish. What's this, some sort of cat toy? I could get this for my kitty."

"Thank you," said Mrs. Felder, accepting Linda's compliment. "I don't see a ring on your finger. Are you still Linda Racquemore?"

Racquemore? The name shot through Ken's heart like a butcher's knife. Racquemore! The woman he saw at the gas station the previous night? Here, now? He ducked behind the oddly-shaped fish bowl, which made his face look hideously big from the other side (and quite startled a lady glancing from the other side).

"Yes, so far."

"Now that surprises me. I always thought you'd be hitched right away."

"Chased, yes. Married, not yet. I don't want to get tied down cooking and cleaning after people forever and ever. Maybe someday, if I find the right one."

"You could be waiting a long time, a very long time. Good ones are few and far between. Sometimes you gotta settle for the best at the time."

Linda just smiled and after ringing up the purchase bade Mrs. Felder goodbye.

"Dear me, it's my old nephew, Clement," said an old lady to Ken.

"Ma'am, I believe you're mistaken. My name is—" started Ken, but he was quickly cut off.

"Don't interrupt your elders when you're spoken to. After all these years, and you still haven't learned to behave! Now I've known you since I changed your diapers, and never have you had an ear for listening. If I could list all the things…" the old lady said and continued to quibble with Ken. Ken tried desperately to convince her otherwise, but the old lady simply grew more irritated.

"Linda," said Lady Sadie, coming out from the back office, "I'm going out for the afternoon. Make sure to lock up, will you dear?"

"Be happy to, of course," replied Linda.

Ken and the old lady drew Linda and Lady Sadie's attention.

"That was the guy from last night. Who is he?" asked Linda, not expecting an answer.

"Keep your distance from that one. If you do not, I see you being very unhappy in his presence, and he would show you many bad things. Beware!" warned Lady Sadie as she stretched her arms in an arch beginning above her head and ending at her sides.

As Lady Sadie's arms completed their motion, her eyes flashed red, and her clothes flashed into a wolf's coat covered with bits of blood. Only Ken saw this super-brief transformation, and Lady Sadie's outstreched hand bumped against Linda's shirt, leaving something behind.

Linda was so surprised by Lady Sadie. First, Lady Sadie never said much to Linda, Second, when she did, it was only about little things, usually about store operations. Third, she *never* warned Linda about anything or spoke in such a tone as she did that Saturday. Shaken, Linda stared at Lady Sadie as she left the store. Linda took a deep breath, counted the change in the cash register, then looked back to see what was happening with the "townie."

"It is not!" Ken said, and his excitement carried him into an end-aisle stack of washcloths.

The washcloths, Ken, and the conversation went down, down, down to the store floor, where an embarrassed Ken sheepishly lifted his head from beneath the washcloth heap. Everyone else in the store looked directly at Ken for a few seconds while Linda held her hand over her mouth in an attempt to suppress an all-out burst into laughter.

"Hmph!" said the woman with whom Ken argued, and she left the store.

"Is there anything in particular you're looking for?" Linda asked, walking up to Ken.

"A gift," Ken said. "I need something for a wedding present."

"Well if you don't mind my saying, I think these are too many washcloths for anyone," said Linda while she helped Ken pick up the washcloths.

"If you please, I'd prefer something a little smaller and less ordinary."

"Then I know the perfect thing. We don't carry many of them," Linda said, walking to a different part of the store. "Here—this is a nice little jewelry box, made from cedar and birch."

"It plays music," said Ken after opening the box. "It's a music box. I'll take it."

Through the door walked Dineen, the one who recommended the store to Ken.

"Hello, Ken, I see you found something. Have you had a reading yet?" asked Dineen.

"Reading?"

"Of your future."

"No, I haven't," Ken replied.

"Aren't you just the least bit curious?" Dineen asked.

"Not really."

"Just think: you *could* give that jewelry box to your sister, but how do you know if she'll like it or not?"

"Well I'm hoping she—"

"Hoping nothing. Just ask Lady Sadie if the gift will make your sister happy. Linda, can he do that now?" Dineen asked.

"Sorry, but Lady Sadie is out for the rest of the afternoon," replied Linda.

"Out? Where?"

"She didn't say. You know how it is, Dineen. Sometimes she's here, sometimes she isn't. And she never tells me where she's going."

"Can you pencil me into her appointment book?" Dineen asked.

"No problem," replied Linda, pulling out Lady Sadie's appointment book. "You're in luck. She has an opening Monday evening at 7:00."

"But how can that be if the store is closed?" asked Ken.

"Although we close at five, Lady Sadie holds readings until eight or nine. There's a separate entrance for after-hour readings," explained Linda. "Got it?"

"I see," said Ken.

"Good," Dineen continued. "I have to do some errands anyway. See you Linda; good luck, Ken."

With that, Dineen left Sadie's Place and headed back down Highway 20.

"Will that be cash or by check?" Linda asked.

"Check," Ken said, writing out his check.

"Since you're new here, I need some identification, preferably a driver's license or credit card," said Linda.

"Driver's license—here you go."

Linda quickly verified the information on the check. In the back of her mind, she noted Ken's age and address.

"There you go," Linda said, wrapping the gift and handing a receipt to Ken.

"Thank you," Ken said, but in the shuffle, his checkbook fell out of his grasp as he walked out the door. No one, not even Ken, noticed the mishap.

The rest of Linda's day went smoothly yet quietly. It was a beautifully sunny day out, and Linda welcomed the friendly weather.

"Finally," she said while she closed the shop around two o'clock. "I have the rest of the day to enjoy."

While sweeping under a display, the broom caught the edge of something small and rectangular.

"What do we have here?" she mused.

Pulling out the object, she discovered a checkbook.

"Who could have left this?" she wondered, and upon opening it she had her answer.

"*Ken Manders* it says, and there's his phone number," Linda thought, and she immediately phoned, but there was no answer.

"Hello, Mr. Manders. You left your checkbook at Sadie's Place today. It's about ten after two on Saturday. The store is closed; we'll be open again on Monday from nine to five. If you need it before then, please call me at 555-1404 and we'll work something out," Linda said, leaving a message on Ken's answering machine.

However, Linda couldn't wait by the phone for Ken to call. There was her car to pick up, some shopping, and a rest under her favorite tree in the country park, a rest that included reading a new book or magazine she hoped to find while shopping that afternoon.

"Doug," Linda said, walking into the neighboring gas station.

"Well hi there, Ms. Racquemore! How are you today?" asked Doug politely.

"I'll be fine if my car is ready. Otherwise—"

"Otherwise, you'll be mad at me, won't you?" asked a voice, coming out of the garage.

"There you are, Kip. Well, how is my little baby?"

"Doing much better now that she has new spark plugs and a fresh oil change. And it looks like one of your spark plug wires was going bad, so I replaced that too. Now she purrs like a kitten," explained Kip.

"Excellent! How much do I owe you?" Linda asked.

"Here you go. And if you could sign here, I'd appreciate it," said Kip.

"Sure," Linda said, signing the work order and handing Kip a few notes. "Are you having a sale on spark plugs, Kip?"

"No. I felt badly about leaving you stranded here last night. And the new spark plugs are partly my fault. I didn't calibrate your timing properly last time. But it's all running purr-fectly now," replied Kip.

"Well thank you again, Kip. You always take good care of my little car."

"Thank you, Linda. It's always a pleasure to work on your car," Kip said, looking at Linda's face, but his eyes darted to her right shoulder, and he looked slightly confused.

"What is it?" asked Linda.

"You have a little bit of fur on your shoulder. Have you started selling animal furs at The Place?"

"You know Ms. Sadie and I would never do that. We feel very strongly about animal rights. But look! It looks like part of a rabbit's tail or something. White with little brown spots."

"Those brown spots—that's not from the fur. They're blood spots," said Kip.

"Blood?" asked Doug from across the store. "Are you bleeding, Ms. Racquemore?"

"No Doug, I'm fine," said Linda, then she pulled Kip aside for some privacy. "Where do you suppose this came from?" she asked Kip.

"I'll call the ambulance and sheriff right away," said Doug from across the room again. He picked up the phone and started dialing.

"No, Doug, everything is fine. Look, there's Mr. Roberts with his old Chevy, and it's overheating. Better get him into the garage."

"Oh yeah," Doug said while he went outside. "What happened this time?" Doug asked Mr. Roberts, but the car made awful *clakity* sounds, and Linda could no longer hear what was being said outside.

"Good," said Kip. "Doug means well, but he also likes doing too much at times. Now let's look at this fur."

"What kind of blood is it?"

"Hard to say if it's human blood or animal. Maybe someone brushed up next to you in the store accidentally. A hunter maybe?"

"I was behind the counter most of the day, except for Ms. Felder and the *townie*," said Linda.

"*Townie*?" Kip asked.

"A new guy from the city; his name is Ken Manders, and he's a little unusual."

"Really?"

"Yeah," continued Linda. "I don't know how to explain it. Lady Sadie says he will bring harm, but he doesn't seem like that sort of person."

"What sort of person is he like?" Kip asked.

"Someone who couldn't tie his shoes if his life depended on it."

Linda laughed, but Kip had a concerned air about him.

"You never know about those city folk. They have strange ways and aren't always on the level. I'd be careful, Linda, if I were you."

"Heck, maybe he has a pet rabbit that's shedding," Linda suggested.

"With blood?"

"He probably spilled ketchup on it or something."

"Did he have ketchup on his clothes in the store?" Kip asked.

"No."

"And there's none on your clothes. It must be blood."

"I think it's ketchup, and I'll leave it at that. I can't go around thinking it's blood, because I'll get sick to my stomach, and I don't want anything to ruin my Saturday afternoon."

"All right, Linda, I won't say another word. Have a good weekend!"

"Thanks, Kip. Say *hello* to Mrs. Kip," Linda said.

Her car started right away without hesitation or hiccup. The shining sun and clear day made Linda so happy, so happy while she drove up Highway 20 into the city. Presently, she started humming:

The shining sun,
Is half the fun.
My running little car,
Will take me near and far.
A shopping day,
Some work, some play,
I'll find a little nook,
To read my romance book.
Right under my favorite tree,
So happy that I am free.

"Hello, Linda," said a familiar voice. "I haven't seen you in a while."

"Why it's Amy Sue Boeden. And your dog, Scratcher. How are you two?" Linda asked, looking up from her book.

"Great!" replied Amy Sue with her Labrador Retriever sitting next to her. "Isn't it a great day?"

"You know it!"

"I was just thinking how I haven't seen you at Red Taps in weeks."

"I know," said Linda, "I've been busy with work and other stuff."

"That's right. You work at Sadie's Place. Do you give readings yet?" asked Amy Sue.

"No, Lady Sadie does that. I'm just happy to be working in a nice little craft shop."

"Say, why don't we go to that bar on 20 and 171 tonight, just the two of us," suggested Amy Sue.

"Wouldn't Roger object to you going to a singles bar without him?" Linda asked.

Amy went stone quiet.

"Uh oh. What happened?" Linda asked, instantly sensing something was wrong.

"Roger and I...he...we aren't dating anymore."

"That bad?" Linda asked, trying not to be nosy.

"Yeah, but hey! I feel much better. I'm in my own place, and I can go out whenever I want!"

"Great!"

"So what do you say, Linda, are we on for tonight?"

"Count me in! Should I stop by your place or—"

"How 'bout I stop by yours. It's been a while since I was at the store. Besides, Scratcher misses your kitty-cat."

Scratcher barked in excitement.

"I bet he does," Linda said, remembering how she had to pull her cat out of the tree the last time Amy Sue was over with Scratcher.

Amy Sue laughed: "Don't worry; I'll leave Scratcher at home."

"Good beans," said Linda with a smile.

Riverton, Saturday afternoon

"That's $34.87," said the cashier to Ken.

"Now if I can just find my checkbook," Ken mumbled, looking frantically in his pockets. "Where did that go to?" he mused nervously while a line of half a dozen people waited behind.

"Problem, sir?" the cashier asked.

"No," Ken lied.

He flipped open his wallet, hoping to find some cash to pay for the groceries and was relieved to find two, twenty dollar bills.

"There," he said.

The crisis over, Ken figured he'd simply left his checkbook in the car or in his apartment, and he thought nothing more of it. He went to a few other stores, using his credit cards if necessary, then returned home where he put away his groceries and other purchases, sat on the couch, and fell asleep while watching the evening news.

Rolling Hills, Saturday evening

"C'mon in," said Linda after Amy Sue knocked on Linda's apartment door.

"What a nice little pad you have," said Amy Sue.

"Thank you. I just have to finish my hair, then I'll be ready."

"No rush," Amy Sue said while Linda went back into the bathroom.

Amy Sue looked around Linda's living room and noticed a picture of Linda with what looked like her family.

"Cute family," Amy Sue thought after picking up the photo, but while looking at the photo, she heard a low voice coming from behind the living room wall.

"So who are the neighbors?" asked Amy Sue, putting down the photo.

"What?" asked Linda, walking back in the room while trying to put her hair up.

"Are they always that noisy?"

"Can you help me with this?" Linda asked.

"Sure," replied Amy Sue, walking over to Linda and starting to put Linda's hair up with a hair piece.

"Noisy neighbors?" Linda half asked. "That's just Lady Sadie. She gives readings in the evening, and sometimes I can hear what she's saying through the vent."

"What are some of them like?" asked Amy Sue, still working on Linda's hair.

"Relationships, children, sometimes about jobs, but mostly about whether a relationship will work or what kinds of children to expect," Linda explained.

"Done," said Amy Sue, referring to Linda's hair.

"Excellent. My car or yours?"

"I'll drive," offered Amy Sue, and with that the pair headed off in Amy Sue's car for the bar.

Blue Wolf Tavern, Crooked Creek, later Saturday evening

"The Blue Wolf? Wasn't this—" started Linda.

"Pigeon Stop? Yeah, they just changed ownership last month. They've redecorated the whole place. It has more of a log-cabin kind of feel now," Amy Sue explained.

The two walked in and found a table next to the window and near other facilities.

"Good," said Amy Sue. "I always like getting a seat near the Ladies Room."

Linda laughed.

"What can I get you two tonight?" asked a young, clean-cut waiter.

"How about the guy in the corner," said Amy Sue, getting into the spirit of things.

"Amy Sue!" exclaimed Linda while staring her down.

"He's not on the menu," said the waiter with a smile.

"A root beer for starters," said Linda.

"Gimme the real stuff," said Amy Sue. "One of those German export beers."

The waiter slipped off, and Amy Sue looked at the guy in the corner.

"Mmm, mmm! My, my is he fine!" said Amy Sue.

"You really are done with Roger, aren't you?"

"Ancient history. Besides, there's plenty more fish in the sea. And I'm about to do some fishing."

"This should be good. What do you have in mind?" asked Linda.

"Oh the usual. First the eye contact," started Amy Sue, staring intently and flirtatiously at the guy in the corner.

"And what if he doesn't look?" asked Linda.

"Oh he'll look, this one most certainly will. Any guy interested in a woman will look around eventually. They call it looking at the scenery, but we call it taking the bait. Even now, he's taking a quick look around and—"

"And he must be looking at you now. You stopped talking quicker than a flame catches fire," said Linda.

"And a fish is biting my line," Amy Sue said.

"Here you are, ladies. One root beer, a German import, and a bottle of champagne," said the waiter.

"Champagne?" Linda asked. "We didn't order any champagne."

"Compliments of the gentleman in the corner," said the waiter.

"Well here," said Linda, handing a five-dollar bill to the waiter.

"Not necessary. It's all taken care of," said the waiter, and he slipped off again.

"See what I mean?" said Amy Sue.

"He's coming over here," said Linda anxiously.

"Play it cool," said Amy Sue.

"Good evening ladies. I'm Jack."

"This is Linda, and I'm Amy Sue."

"Nice to meet you, Linda and Amy Sue. I haven't seen you two here before. Are you new around here?" Jack asked.

"Yes," said Linda while at the same time Amy Sue said, "No."

Jack looked confused.

"What Linda means is that we haven't been to the Blue Wolf in a while, so it *seems* like we've never been here," explained Amy Sue.

"Ladies, let me introduce my friend, Rob. Rob, this is Amy Sue and *Linda*," Jack said with a special emphasis while introducing Linda.

"Nice to meet you ladies," Rob said.

"Please, have a seat," offered Amy Sue.

Jack sat next to Amy Sue, while Rob sat next to a mildly uncomfortable Linda. Next to the champagne bottle, Jack placed four glasses.

"Allow me," said Jack, pouring champagne into a glass for Amy Sue.

"How nice," said Amy Sue.

"Hey, Sugar, can I pour you a glass?" Rob asked Linda, but Linda laughed.

"That's ok, I can pour my own," said Linda, taking the bottle from Jack and pouring champagne into a glass for herself.

"You know, you shouldn't turn down such a good deal from a guy," said Rob, his face a little red from being turned down.

"I like to pour my own glass. Besides, now you can pour your own," Linda said.

Jack and Amy had fallen into a near-private conversation. And though Rob was trying to get things going with Linda, she didn't like him at all and was thus uncomfortable.

"So what do you do for a living?" Rob asked.

"I work in a store," said Linda, trying not to give out too many details.

"Oh, a cashier. I know lots of cashiers all over the place. They always make mention of my bedroom eyes. Sometimes I have to fight them off the way they flock around me."

"So where are they now?" Linda asked, while she wondered what pond this creature crawled out of.

"Here and there. I have to get away from that stuff once in a while, just so I can relax," said Rob.

"You work in a grocery store then?" Linda asked.

"Grocery story? Whatever put such a stupid idea like that in your head?" Rob asked, flustered.

"Where else is someone surrounded by cashiers?"

"I was trying to prove to you that I can get along with cashiers just fine, since you're one of them. I happen to be a machinist. I can make anything, baby, from jigs to dies. I can fix presses, machines, cars, and I know how to handle my tool," he said suggestively.

"From hands-on experience?" Linda asked laughingly. Amy Sue and Jack overheard and laughed as well.

"You know, this place used to be called the Pigeon Stop," started Rob to Linda.

"Yeah, I know," said Linda, trying not to pay too much attention.

"And now they call it the Blue Wolf," Rob added.

"Yeah, your point?"

"Do you know *why* they don't call it the Pigeon Stop?" Rob asked.

"Because too many pigeons like you were giving it a bad name," Linda said back.

"Ooooooh," said Amy Sue and Jack, impressed with Linda's coup.

"No, stupid," Rob shot back, "it's because the Wolf brothers bought it out. They own it now, and that's why!"

"So what's it to me?" Linda asked.

"They're my cousins. So you should respect me 'cause my blood runs this little place."

"Well if you ask me—" Linda started.

"And no one is," Rob interrupted.

"They best not fill any balloons in here," Linda finished.

"And why not?" Rob asked, irritated.

"Because with all the hot air, they'd float away."

Linda, Amy Sue, and Jack laughed again.

"Linda, Linda, Linda, you should start your own comedy show," said Jack.

"Why thank you," Linda said.

"And I love a woman who plays hard-to-get," said Rob, buttering up to Linda.

"Toast anyone?" asked Linda.

"Yes," said Jack, "a toast to all of us. Cheers!" he said, and the four glasses clinked, then each person drank a sip, except for Rob. He downed the glass in one gulp.

"Ahhh, great stuff! Now baby, where were we?" Rob asked.

"Toast?" Linda asked again.

"Toast for what?" asked Rob, a little perturbed.

"Toast for you," said Linda.

"Why Linda, I knew you'd see me with loving eyes," Rob said, buttering up to Linda even more.

"Whole wheat, please!"

"Huh?" asked Rob.

"It's about the only thing you're going to butter up around here," said Linda.

The three burst into laughter harder than before, and the alcohol enhanced the merriment. Rob was not impressed.

"Yeah? Well why don't you just keep your *whole wheat*! I don't need it!" Rob said, leaving the table in a huff.

Linda giggled.

"Now you did it, Linda," said Amy Sue.

"What? He was being obnoxious," said Linda.

"Rob's had a rough week," said Jack apologetically. "He's doing the best he can to unwind, but he has trouble going with the flow sometimes. I'll go over and talk to him. Now don't go away, Amy Sue, I'll be right back."

"We'll be here," said Amy Sue, and Jack went over to Rob.

"I think I'm in love," said Amy Sue. "Isn't Jack the sweetest guy?"

"Sure," said Linda.

"All right, Linda, what's eating you? Ever since they came over, you've been cutting back and forth like a hacksaw."

"I'm having a good time. You know I like to let out a few zingers, especially when—"

"Especially when you don't like someone. You've been out of circulation a while. Maybe you just need a little time to get in the swing of things," said Amy Sue.

"I don't need any time—Rob is a jerk," said Linda.

"C'mon. He just needs a little time to loosen up. He doesn't seem like such a bad guy," said Amy Sue.

"Ok, then you can have him," said Linda, chuckling.

"Now Linda, promise me you'll be good," Amy started to say as Jack returned (without Rob).

"I have an idea," said Jack. "How would you ladies like to play some pool?"

"I love pool," Linda said without thinking.

"What did you have in mind?" Amy Sue asked.

"Eight Ball. Amy and I against Rob and Linda," Jack said.

"What do you say, Linda. You *do* like pool, and this will be a good ice breaker," said Amy Sue.

"I don't know."

"Just a friendly game or two. No strings attached," said Jack.

"All right. No strings attached," said Linda.

"Ladies first," said Jack after the four gathered 'round a pool table.

"Go ahead," said Linda to Amy Sue. "Break."

"Well it's been awhile—ok, I can handle it," Amy Sue said.

It went Amy Sue, Linda, Jack, then Rob. Though Jack shot better than Rob, Linda shot significantly better than Amy Sue and even as well as Jack at times. The foursome split two games, and on the deciding game, Linda and Rob discussed strategy.

"We'll guard the two end corners and leave those shots for last," Linda said, and Rob agreed.

It was Rob's turn. He was two shots from the eight. One ball went in, but the other went out of position. Rather than try a risky shot, he shot to put the last ball and the eight into favorable positions. Amy Sue shot but missed sinking a ball, and the turn passed to Linda.

"I think I can win it here," Linda said.

"Go for it," encouraged Rob.

Linda sank the two shots perfectly and won the game. Linda gave Rob a *high-five* while Amy Sue and Jack looked on in amazement.

"Well, this calls for a celebration," said Rob. "I believe we had a bet on this game?" he asked Jack.

"And I always keep my promises," said Jack as the four returned to their table. "Waiter," he said after they sat down, "a round of drinks for the four of us."

"Linda, you're better than I remember," said Amy Sue.

"A little luck, that's all," said Linda.

"More like Lady Luck," added Rob. "And I must say you know how to handle a cue stick."

Linda was a little annoyed with the comment, but Amy Sue smiled, meaning that Linda should take Rob's comment as a compliment.

"I always do," Linda said.

"Hey, who is hungry?" Jack asked, but no one responded. "I'm buying," he added.

"Well in that case—" started Amy Sue.

"Count us in," finished Linda.

And Rob made three. The foursome enjoyed a wholesome evening snack, they drank, and they made merry. Jack whispered something into Amy Sue's ear, and she giggled while Rob and Linda had a leisurely chat about sports.

Riverton, Saturday evening

Ken woke suddenly as if startled by something. He stared around the room as if looking for that something. A blinking red light caught his eye, and he realized he had forgotten to check his telephone answering machine for messages.

"Hello, Mr. Manders," the message started. Ken recognized the voice—Linda Racquemore from Sadie's Place. "You left your checkbook at Sadie's Place today. It's about ten after two on Saturday. The store is closed; we'll be open again on Monday from nine to five. If you need it before then, please call me at 555-1404 and we'll work something out."

"555-1404," Ken said, writing the number down on paper.

He immediately dialed the number, and the phone on the other end rang seven times, but there was no answer.

"Hmm," he thought. "Maybe someone else is there who'll let me in."

Ken jumped in his car and drove down Highway 20, anxious to get his checkbook.

"There it is," he said to himself, "Rolling Hills, and on the corner: Sadie's Place."

Ken pulled into the store's parking lot, shut off his engine, and walked to the front door.

"Closed. I wonder—does Linda or the owner live in this same building?" Ken thought.

He walked around to the side and saw a door to apartment one, and the mailbox next to the door had the name "Racquemore" lettered. Seeing Linda's car parked nearby (and not at the gas station), he knocked, thinking she'd be home and would answer. But after ten minutes of knocking and waiting, Ken gave up. She wasn't home.

"Now what do I do?" he asked himself, going around to the other side.

Ken heard a door close, and he quickened his pace around the corner. He never quite made it—Lady Sadie blocked his path.

"What are you doing here?" she asked with a low, threatening voice.

"I received a message from Ms. Racquemore about my checkbook," Ken started to explain.

"Ms. Racquemore is not here, and I suggest you go home and never come back here," she warned.

"You don't understand. I've come to get my—"

"*I* don't understand? I understand too well, and your presence is neither wanted nor tolerated. Begone, before something bad happens. And don't come back if you value your *skin*," Lady Sadie said, and with that she was gone quicker than Ken could sneeze.

"How very odd," Ken thought after being stunned. "No one here to help me get my checkbook. I guess I have no alternative but to go home."

But as Ken made his way back to his car, he thought he heard an animal's growl from across the street. He had no desire to investigate further, especially after encountering the wolf earlier. To the car Ken ran, and back to his apartment he drove. And that is where he stayed during the evening's remainder.

Blue Wolf Tavern, Crooked Creek

"I've never met a woman who watches football," said Rob.

"Heck yeah," said Linda, and she talked about upcoming trades, new players, and statistics about various teams and how she felt each team would do during the season.

"Bunyan never runs the ball well. He always runs up the middle, and he hasn't had a 100-yard game this season. They should trade him," commented Rob.

"True, and that happens a lot when he's the lone setback, but when they're in the I-formation, and Bunyan's going out for a screen pass and catches it, he always picks up ten or more yards. Once Bunyan gets going on the sidelines, it's hard to stop him," said Linda.

"Yeah, you're right, come to think of it."

"In fact, he lined up like a wide receiver once last game for a crucial third-and-nine play. He's got incredible speed," said Linda.

"For a back, yeah," said Rob.

"For anyone. They should leave him at wide-out more often, but I guess he's claustrophobic when he starts off next to the sideline, which is funny since that's where he does his best."

"I think lots of people secretly like being confined. Gives them the motivation to move faster," said Rob, but Linda had a funny feeling after the comment.

"I have an idea," said Jack. "There's a great view of the full moon tonight. It is especially nice how it glimmers off the lake. How would you like to go, Amy Sue?"

"I'd love to."

"What about you, Linda, wanna go?" Rob asked.

"What?" Linda asked, not really paying attention.

"C'mon, Linda, sounds like a lot of fun," Amy Sue suggested, but in her stuporous condition, Amy Sue would have liked any idea.

"Well, as long as we're not gone too long," Linda said with hesitation, though the alcohol was putting her in a good mood.

"Excellent," said Jack, and the four went in Jack's car, with Amy Sue immediately jumping into the front seat and Linda climbing slowly into the back.

"What a nice little road," said Amy Sue as the four went toward the lake. Trees lined the road closely, and even with Jack's headlights on the bright setting, it was difficult to see into the thick woods.

"Here we are," said Jack finally, and he parked the car on a wharf overlooking the lake.

"And the moon *is* full," said Amy, as if Jack had it ordered just for her.

"Say," said Jack to Amy, "how would you like to cool your feet in some beach sand?"

"I'd love to," said Amy, and the two walked off, leaving Linda and Rob in the car, alone.

"It's a nice evening," started Rob.

"Yes, it is," said Linda, not knowing what else to say.

"I hear there's good fishing in this lake," Rob continued, trying to make conversation with a sports-related topic.

"So I hear," replied Linda, staring off into the darkness.

"You're a very pretty girl," Rob said, moving his hand along Linda's leg.

"Rob, no," Linda said, pushing his hand aside.

"What is it, doll?"

"This isn't right."

"What isn't right about it?" Rob asked.

"I just don't feel that way about you," Linda said.

"You're a very special woman," said Rob, "and you should be treated like a woman. Soft, delicate skin—"

"No!" Linda said, pushing his hand off again, and she got out of the car and leaned next to it to get a little more space.

"Hey! We're partners, aren't we? What about all the fun we had this evening, huh? The pool, the drinks, the food, and all the talking we did? I thought we were friends, and I thought we had something special going on. How about it?" Rob pressed, getting out of his side and walking around the car.

"It was nice, but I don't want you to get the wrong idea. I'm not interested in that," Linda said.

"Interested in what?" Rob asked.

"Making out in the back seat of Jack's car."

"So that's what you think this is, huh? You lead me on, making me think you're interested in me—" Rob started, his voice getting louder.

"C'mon, Rob, that's not true."

"—and now you say you're not interested! You're nothing but a tease," Rob said, getting very wound up.

"Rob! Chill out, will you?" Linda said.

"Well, I'll show you what loving is, and I'll prove I can take you like the man I am, and change you from a girl to a woman."

"Hey, cut it out!" Linda said, but it had already begun.

Rob grabbed Linda, putting his arms around and kissing her crudely and forcefully. Constrained, Linda squirmed to get out of his crushing hold. She stomped on his foot with her heel which caused him pain and allowed her to get out of his grip.

"Damn you, you tramp," he said, and he swung his fist at her, but Linda had already started running from him.

"Come back here, do you hear? Come back, *now!*" Rob ordered, but Linda never answered to any yelling male (let alone one who attacked her).

"Get away from me!" Linda screamed as she tried to run down the road in her heals.

At the moment she decided to kick them off to run faster, Rob came up from behind and tackled her. She fell off the road's shoulder and down into the grove of trees, but Rob scampered down and pursued her.

"*HELP!*" Linda yelled.

"Shut up, you good-for-nothing piece of trash!" Rob ordered.

He caught her, slammed her against a tree, and tore at her clothing.

"*GET OFF OF ME!*" Linda screamed, kicking and jabbing at Rob.

"Now it's time I show you what a good time *really* is," he said.

Rob tore her blouse off and managed to avoid or control Linda's kicks, but she dug into his flesh deeply with her nails, which only made him fiercer. Finally, Rob threw a left hook into Linda's jaw, stunning her.

"You'll never have it as good as I'm gonna give you now," he said, loosening his belt buckle.

Without warning, a timber wolf raced in with blinding speed, jumped onto Rob, and sank its jaw into Rob's neck. His screams would have curdled blood, and Linda's awareness keenly forced her to flee.

Shaking with overwhelming terror, she fled the grove (barefoot and blouse in hand) in such shock that her throat had swelled to the point where she couldn't scream and could hardly breathe. She continued like this up the shoulder and down the road, but in her disoriented state she ran *away* from

Jack's car and along the rural road without so much a clue as to where she was going as long as she *was* going.

There were no street lights to help her see; only a full moon helped her avoid falling into ditches or falling onto a rock, but occasional passing cars blinded her, and one nearly hit her. A car pulled to the side suddenly, and his rooftop lights strobed. It was a sheriff's car, and the deputy pointed his search light at her.

"What are you doing out here?" the deputy asked Linda.

The light and voice startled her into a short scream, but it also blinded her, and she stopped short. Then she went into a shaky, moaning cry.

"Are you all right?" he asked, then he got out of his car.

"I...help me," she said, her voice shaking.

"What in Sam Hill happened to you?" he asked, seeing the blood on her torn clothes.

"I was attacked," she said.

Deputy Kranz took her into his car and calmed her down enough to get the story. He immediately called this into the sheriff's office and proceeded to the spot where she was attacked.

"He kept hitting me and wouldn't stop," she said, pointing to the woods.

"How did you get here?" Deputy Kranz asked.

"With my girlfriend Amy Sue and her friend Jack. In Jack's car; it's by the lake," Linda said, getting her breath and voice back.

With Linda still sitting in the sheriff's car, Deputy Kranz pulled up behind Jack's car. Simultaneously, Amy Sue and Jack returned.

"I know, this isn't a legal place to park," Jack started to say. "Linda, what's going on? What happened to you? Where's Rob?"

"You recognize this woman?" Deputy Kranz asked.

"Yeah, it's Linda," said Jack.

"Linda Racquemore," added Amy Sue. "Linda, are you ok? My God, you're covered in blood. What happened?"

"He attacked me, and I couldn't keep him off," she started to explain, but the whole incident was too much for her, and she cried into Amy Sue's shoulder.

"There, there. Everything will be ok."

Deputy Kranz called for backup while he remained behind Jack's car. An ambulance took Linda away to Riverton County Hospital where she received treatment for her wounds. Medical personnel also examined her for internal injuries but found that Linda suffered mainly from emotional trauma.

The hospital released Linda, but as soon as she stepped out the door, Deputy Kranz asked her to quietly come down to the sheriff's office.

"What are you doing here?" Linda asked. "I thought you were searching the woods."

"We have the area sectioned off. They're looking for Rob, but in the meantime, I just need to ask you a few more questions."

"I've already told you what happened," Linda said.

"Just a few things to wrap up," he said, and he took her down to the station.

Riverton County Sheriff's Office, early Sunday morning

"All right, Ms. Racquemore, one more time," said Detective Hakks.

"How many times do we have to do this? I've already told you everything, and I've told you a dozen times or more," said Linda, very tired from everything.

"You went to the Blue Wolf," started Detective Hakks.

"That's right."

"And you had a few drinks," continued Hakks.

"Right," said Linda.

"And?"

"And we played pool," said Linda.

"But before the pool. You didn't like Rob, did you?"

"Is that a crime?" Linda asked.

"Maybe. And then?"

"We played pool."

"And won two out of three games," said Hakks.

"Yeah. Is that a crime?" asked Linda.

"No. Then after the pool?"

"We talked, had a few more drinks—"

"A few more drinks," cut in Hakks.

"And then we left."

"Left the Blue Wolf," said Hakks.

"Right."

"After a few drinks."

"Yeah," said Linda.

"So you left the Blue Wolf after a few drinks."

"Yeah, why do you keep saying that?" asked Linda.

"So then what happened?" asked Hakks, continuing right along.

"We went down to the lake."

"In Jack's car?"

"Right," continued Linda. "And then Amy Sue and Jack went for a walk, and that's when Rob attacked me."

"He did?" Detective Hakks said, not believing her.

"Yeah. I got out of the car to get some fresh air, and he wouldn't leave me alone. So I ran, and he caught up to me, and I fell, and he followed, and he pushed me against the tree and ripped my clothes, and then—"

"And then, you killed him," Hakks said.

"No!" said Linda. "A wolf attacked him, and I...I ran."

"A wolf, huh?" Detective Hakks asked.

"Yeah, a wolf. You *do* know what they look like?" Linda asked, getting upset.

"Was it blue?"

"No, it was gray maybe, I don't know, it was dark."

"You sure it wasn't blue, a blue wolf? Did it have a beer with it?" Hakks asked.

"What?!"

"Ms. Racquemore, there's one little problem with your story. There *are* no wolves in Crooked Creek, Rolling Hills, Riverton, or anywhere else in the county. None. Now then, would you like to revise your story?"

"And you're a detective? I've told you everything. I don't care if you say there are no wolves around here. I saw one. It attacked Rob, and it almost got me," said Linda.

"Look, Ms. Racquemore, do I have to spell it out? There's blood all over you, you got into a fight with Rob, and you tell this unbelievable story about a wolf. What am I supposed to believe?"

At that moment, Deputy Kranz walked into the interrogation room.

"Sir, they found him," said Deputy Kranz.

"Just sit tight, Ms. Racquemore, I'll be right back," said Detective Hakks, leaving the room to have a private word with Kranz.

"The friend, Jack, had trouble identifying him."

"Identifying him? So he's—" started Hakks.

"Dead. Whatever killed him ripped him up but good. There's no way any human could have mutilated the body like it did. We're not sure what we have—maybe a loose pit bull or something."

"You're sure on this?"

"Absolutely."

"Well, there may be some truth to her story," said Detective Hakks.

"Sir?"

"She claims a wolf attacked Rob."

"Well whatever happened, it looks like something got him. There's no way she could have torn up his body like *that.*"

Detective Hakks went back into the interrogation room.

"Ms. Racquemore," said Hakks.

"I've told you the truth; when are you going to let me go?" asked Linda.

"Ms. Racquemore."

"Who do you think you are anyway?"

"You can go now," he said.

"No, I demand you let me go now, I demand—I can go?" Linda asked. "What do you mean, I can go? Why was I here for three hours? And now I can go?"

"You can go now; we're done with the questioning," said Detective Hakks.

"And that's it. No apology, nothing. You've grilled me with these questions, and now you say I can just go. Well!"

And with that, Linda Racquemore stormed out of the sheriff's office and out to the street then stopped. She realized she had no ride home, and it was late.

"Linda?" yelled a voice. "Linda, over here."

"Amy Sue?"

"Linda," said Amy Sue, "there you are."

"Have you been here the whole time?" Linda asked while Amy Sue walked out of the sheriff's office.

"No, we've been here for twenty or twenty-five minutes. How are you doing?"

"Tired. Ready to go home."

"Jack's finishing up inside. Since your apartment is on the way, he'll drop you off then drop me off at my car. Ok?"

"Sure, ok," said Linda, becoming very drowsy.

At 3 am, Linda Racquemore thanked Jack for the ride to her apartment, walked to her door, unlocked it, and went in. Jack drove away, and Linda threw off her coat and shoes before plopping on the couch. Just before she fell into a deep sleep, she thought she heard Lady Sadie's door opening and closing, but she wasn't sure. Sleep was too welcome a friend to ignore.

Riverton, Sunday morning

"What a beautiful Sunday morning," Ken said while standing on his front porch. "Ah, what does the newspaper say for today?" he mused, picking up the paper and sitting on a chair.

"The weather for the day," Ken started, "Sunny and clear, the high around seventy-four. Clear this evening, low around sixty-eight. What an excellent day!"

But Ken was disturbed when he saw a small article in the lower-right corner of the front page:

Local Man Dies
In Rolling Hills Forest

A Crooked Creek Resident died in what the sheriff says is the bloodiest fatality in the last decade.

Rob Stokey, 33, was pronounced dead on arrival at Riverton County Hospital shortly after 12:30 am Sunday morning.

The sheriff is investigating to determine if the death was accidental or murder.

"We had one suspect, but we released her after discovering Mr. Stokey's mutilated body. It looks like he was killed by a wild animal," said Detective Hakks.

Riverton resident, Jack Jackson, is not convinced.

"Everyone knows there are no wild animals in Rolling Hills Forest. As far as I'm concerned, that cashier from Sadie's Place killed him in cold blood after leading him on."

Another source confirms the questionable role of the Sadie's Place cashier. *Riverton Journal* has learned her name: Linda Racquemore.

Ms. Racquemore could not be reached for comment.

"Linda Racquemore? Murder? What is this world coming to?" Ken asked aloud, and his cat meowed in response. "I'll call," he said, and he dialed her number like he did the day before.

"Ring, ring!" rang Linda Racquemore's phone. "Ring!"
"Shut up," said a half-asleep Linda.

It was barely 10:00 am, and Linda was exhausted from the night before.

"Hello?" answered Linda, still groggy though trying to clear the mucus from her throat. "Slow down. Now, what did you say? You're from where?"

"The *Crooked Creek Times,*" said the voice on the other end. "I'd like to ask you a few questions about last night, if it's convenient with you. I hope I didn't wake you."

"It's not convenient, and you *did* wake me. What do you want to know?"

"Why did you do it?" asked the voice.

"Do it? Do what?" Linda asked back, her mind slowly clearing after being awakened from a deep sleep.

"Why did you kill him?" the voice asked.

"I don't know what you're talking about. I haven't killed anyone."

"C'mon, Ms. Racquemore, everyone knows you had the motive and intent. You led that poor guy on then killed him, no denying it. Now what I want to know is *why?*"

"For the last time, I didn't kill anyone. Now leave me alone," Linda said, getting angry.

"Just one more question," said the voice.

"And just one more answer," replied Linda, slamming the receiver onto the cradle.

Linda had just fallen back into a deep sleep when the phone rang again.

"Damn phone," she cursed, picking it up. "Hello!" she said angrily.

"This is the *Riverton Journal*—"

Slam!

Linda wasted no time in hanging up on another newspaper. She disconnected the phone line to prevent further calls from intruding on her sleep, but after only ten minutes, her sleep was too disturbing to be restful, and she reluctantly rose from bed and stumbled into a nice, warm shower.

During Linda's shower, Ken called, but of course Linda couldn't (and wouldn't) answer.

"Now where is she? And how will I get my checkbook back?" he thought. His cat meowed, and he set off for Rolling Hills again.

"What a headache," thought Linda as she stepped out of the shower. "My head is just throbbing. I better have some aspirin in the medicine chest."

Nothing.

"Rats. I'll just run over to the gas station right quick."

"Hi, Ms. Racquemore," said Doug as Linda walked into the gas-station store. "What can I get you?"

"Aspirin. A big bottle of aspirin."

"Late night out?" Doug asked, ringing up the purchase.

"No, I just stayed home," Linda fibbed.

"You don't have to fool me, Ms. Racquemore. Everyone knows about you and that Stokey guy."

"What do you mean, 'everyone knows'?" asked Linda.

"See? It's in the morning paper," Doug said, pointing to the *Crooked Creek Times* newsstand.

"Oh no!"

"And that's not all. Some guy was looking for you last night."

"Oh?"

"Yeah, that out-of-townie guy—he came 'round asking for you. Ms. Sadie though—she set him straight."

"Ken Manders?" Linda asked.

"Yeah. I don't like him, Ms. Racquemore. There's something about him I can't figure out," said Doug.

"Oh I wouldn't worry about him. He was just looking for his checkbook—uh oh, his checkbook," Linda said with a sudden urgency. "Gotta go, Doug," Linda added, darting out of the store.

"Wait! Ms. Racquemore, your aspirin!"

"Thanks," she said, running back in for the bottle then running back out.

Linda ran the short distance to her apartment but stopped short to see a car drive up. It beeped.

"Linda?"

"Oh I look horrible," whispered Linda to herself when she realized her hair was hardly combed, and she was wearing no makeup.

"Linda Racquemore, could you wait a minute?" Ken said.

"I'll be back shortly. Just wait there!" Linda said, and she darted into her apartment.

"Now what's gotten into her?" Ken wondered.

"Hey you," said a voice from the gas station. Ken ignored it.

"You in that car, that's right, I'm talking to you," said the voice again.

"Excuse me?" Ken said.

"That's right. You." It was Doug, and he walked over to Ken with a mission. "Listen here," he preached, "if I were you, I'd clear out and never come back."

"Look, mister, I don't know who or why—"

"I gotta name, you know. It's Doug, Doug it is!"

"Ok, Doug. I'm just trying to—"

"Yeah," Doug interrupted, "I know what you're *trying* to do. Don't even think about it. Fact is, she's gonna be married in three months."

"Married?" Ken asked, both surprised and confused by what Doug was saying.

"That's right. She's gonna be my wife. So look here—I don't *need* any competition. Get it?"

"I—" Ken started to say, but Mr. Roberts pulled into the gas station with a crisis. His car overheated again.

Linda walked out several minutes after Doug returned to the station and waved her hand in front of Ken's face.

"Are your eyes stuck or something?" she asked.

"No, I was—say, is that really you?" Ken asked, surprised to see such a lovely looking Linda.

"Huh? Wake up, silly! Your checkbook is in the store," she said.

"And you're closed today. I suppose I'll have to come back tomorrow," Ken said.

"Well, only if you really want to. But I can unlock right quick and get it out of the safe. What do you think of that?" she asked with a smile.

And that smile warmed Ken's heart and melted him all over like butter on pancakes.

"Sure," he said, smiling back, and for a moment Linda's tension eased off, and she felt a little more relaxed.

"Nice day," Linda said, making small conversation.

"Yeah, it is. I read in the paper that it'll be clear all day," Ken said.

Linda paused at the door and looked down.

"What is it? Wrong key?" Ken asked.

Linda didn't respond, but after a few seconds she opened the door, and Ken followed her inside the shop.

"So, do you read the paper?" she asked before disappearing behind the counter.

"Every day," replied Ken.

"What's your favorite section?" she asked.

"Well, I don't really have a favorite section. I just like to read whatever interests me."

"Here it is, 'Mr. Ken Manders.' That's you," Linda said, handing the checkbook over to Ken.

"Thank you," said Ken.

"You're welcome," she said, but she was troubled and stared at something under the counter for a few seconds. "I heard you were over here late yesterday looking for me," she finally said.

"Yeah. I called, but there was no answer, so I wanted to see if you were home. But I see you had other plans," Ken said.

"I went out last night," Linda said.

"Yes, and from what I read it wasn't very fun."

Linda stared at Ken like someone reaching out for help, but as she did the sun disappeared and everything outside went black.

"What a storm!" said Ken, and rain pounded on the little store mercilessly.

"I hate storms," said Linda as she ducked behind the counter.

Lightning flashed, thunder crashed, and nerves thrashed with each onslaught from the storm. But as quickly as the storm had come, it passed, and Linda regained her composure.

"Weird," she said. "I've never seen anything like that."

Ken was about to say something when the two heard a low rumbling from an adjoining room.

"What's that?" Ken asked.

"Oh, that's Lady Sadie. She's giving one of her readings, I'm sure. That's odd."

"What?" Ken asked.

"She doesn't usually give readings on Sunday."

"Linda, I've bumped into Lady Sadie, and I have a strange feeling about her."

"She would probably say the same thing about you," Linda chuckled, remembering Lady Sadie's warning.

"No, really. I feel as if she's hiding something or that she's up to something."

"She likes to surround herself with an air of mystery. That's part of her image," Linda explained.

Ken and Linda left the store, and while Linda locked up, a car pulled up suddenly. Out dashed one man with a portable tape recorder and another with a camera.

"Ms. Racquemore, what was your involvement in the Rob Stokey slaying?" yelled the reporter.

"Oh no, not again!" muttered Linda under her breath.

Then a van pulled up with another reporter and a television camera man rushed out.

"They're blocking my car. I couldn't escape if I wanted to," whispered Linda to Ken.

"Quick, into my car," Ken said.

Linda hesitated for a moment, being stunned by the onslaught of reporters, and Ken finally pulled her by the arm and ushered her into his car.

"Ms. Racquemore, Ms. Racquemore!" they pleading, throwing questions at her in chaotic fashion.

The pair had hardly jumped into Ken's car when the throng pounded on the car doors and windows, demanding comment from Linda. Ken managed to quickly back up into a

Y-turn and thus spin around and drive off. One reporter started to follow, but after Ken passed several cars and took a corner or two quickly, the reporter fell behind, and Linda was free of hassle.

"I can't believe I'm in the middle of all this," Linda said.

"In the middle of what? What happened to you last night? The paper says—"

"I know what the paper says, and it's wrong. I didn't kill anyone."

"Then who did?" Ken asked.

"You wouldn't believe me if I told you. No one believes me," Linda lamented.

"Try me."

"What if I told you a wolf killed him," Linda said.

"You're right, most people wouldn't believe you," Ken said.

"Because there are no wolves or any other such wild animals around here, right?"

"So they say," replied Ken.

"Well, *they're* wrong. A wolf attacked and killed Rob Stokey," Linda said.

"You saw the wolf?"

"Yeah. I saw it."

"What color was it?" Ken asked.

"It was hard to tell. Everything was dark. I think it was gray," she said.

"With long pointed ears?" Ken asked.

"Yeah."

"And a white spot on its forehead?"

Linda stared at Ken, wondering how he could know what the wolf looked like.

"Yeah. How did you know? The county sheriff never bothered to ask, and I haven't really talked to anyone else about what happened. The only way you could have known is if you were there," Linda said, now wary of Ken. "I think you should take me back home now."

Ken turned around in a small parking lot and proceeded back to Linda's apartment.

"I wasn't there, but I *did* see a wolf on the highway Friday night."

"So you believe me?" Linda asked.

"I know there aren't supposed to be any wolves around here, but I saw one, and it was probably the same one that killed Rob. Yes, I believe you, but what I don't understand is how you got there in the first place."

"It's a long story—one that I'd rather not retell, but it's enough to say that I was going out to the lake with my friend, Amy Sue, and a couple of guys from the *Blue Wolf*. We stopped in front of the lake, Amy Sue and Jack walked off, and that's when Rob started grabbing me. He wouldn't take 'no' for an answer, and I tried to get away, but he followed me into the woods. He had me up against a tree, and I tried to fight him off when the wolf attacked him. I ran like crazy to get away, so I didn't wait around for the wolf to have me for dessert."

Ken and Linda rode back to her apartment and were relieved to find the reporters gone. Next to Linda's car was a picnic table with a tree overhanging which provided shade. The two sat down at the picnic table and continued to talk.

"So does the sheriff's office believe you?" Ken asked.

"They don't believe my story, but they also know I didn't kill Rob. But everyone thinks I did it, except you. What am I going to do?"

"Well, you didn't break the law, and you're not even going on trial, so it looks to me like there's nothing to worry about," said Ken.

"Nothing to worry about? I had half a dozen reporters out here just thirty minutes ago. Because of the newspaper, everyone thinks I'm a murderer. Law or no law, I have a feeling someone will want to get at me, and I don't want to be around when it happens," Linda explained.

"Maybe you should move," Ken suggested, "and get a fresh start someplace else."

"And have this follow me? I just moved in my apartment a few months ago, I found the perfect job, and now you're telling me I should move? Lady Sadie has been nothing but kind to me—"

"That's another thing. I hate to talk badly of people, but I don't think she's the kind you should stick around with. The way she talks, even this thing about reading people's futures—don't you think you should stay away from her?"

"Lady Sadie was right. All you're trying to do is show me the bad things in my life. I can take care of myself, Mr. Manders, and I don't need an out-of-townie telling me that I should run away from my problems. I'll just tackle them head-on," Linda said, and with that she disappeared inside her apartment.

Rolling Hills, Sunday evening

After spending Sunday relaxing to a good novel in her apartment, Linda called Amy Sue that evening.

"Hi, Amy Sue. This is Linda. How are you?"

"Doing great! How are you, Linda?"

"Trying to relax after a hectic weekend. I had reporters swarming in front of my apartment this morning," Linda explained.

"Yeah, I heard."

"So did you get home all right last night?" Linda asked.

"Well, uh, not really. It was too late for me to drive home, so I spent the night at Jack's," said Amy Sue.

"Really? Are you two hitting it off?"

"I really like him a lot. He and I have a lot in common."

"Good beans," said Linda. "Say, I hear there's going to be a meteor shower on Tuesday evening. Wanna go up to the hill on Highway 20 and Chestnut Crossing to watch?" Linda asked, thinking of things to do that would get her mind off of the weekend.

"Sorry, Linda, I can't. Jack and I are going to Rob's funeral."

"Oh. We can see the meteors some other time. So what time does it start, and where is it? I'd like to go."

"Linda, listen. I don't think it's a good idea. Rob's family—they think you killed him, and they wouldn't like it if you showed up. Why don't you go see the meteors by yourself?"

"If I want to be at his funeral, I will! Besides, there can't be that many who dislike me. You know I had nothing to do with his death, don't you?" Linda asked, expecting an immediate response.

Silence.

"Amy Sue?" Linda asked again.

"Look, Linda," started Amy Sue.

"Look nothing. You *don't* believe me, do you?"

"Well? How am I supposed to know?" asked Amy Sue.

"Because I'm your friend, and I'm telling the truth," said Linda.

"But I don't know that. Everyone is saying that there are no wild animals in Rolling Hills Forest, and you *were* fighting him off," said Amy Sue.

"But I didn't kill him," stated Linda.

"Sure, Linda, anything you say," said Amy Sue sarcastically.

"Ok, Amy Sue. It's obvious you don't believe me either. Some friend you turned out to be. I'll just find out for myself where Rob's funeral is."

"Why do you wanna go anyway? I thought you didn't like the guy," said Amy Sue.

"He was a jerk, yes. But I don't like to see people die, and going to the funeral helps the healing process," said Linda.

"Maybe the real reason you're going is to spite him, even after he's dead. Why don't you just admit it, Linda, you're always trying to get back at someone," suggested Amy Sue.

"I don't know what's happened to you, Amy Sue. I used to think you were my friend. Now you suspect I'm doing all kinds of evil things. What can I do to convince you I'm telling the truth?" Linda asked.

"To be honest, I could care less," said Amy Sue, and she terminated the telephone conversation.

"Nothing ever goes right," Linda said to herself, and with that she buried herself deep into her novel for Sunday's remainder.

Ken's work, Riverton, Monday morning

"Good morning, Ken," said Dineen as Ken walked into the kitchen for coffee.

"Good morning, Dineen. Have you seen Marvin today?" Ken asked.

"Haven't you heard about his cousin?" Dineen asked.

"Cousin?"

"Yeah, Rob Stokey. He died Saturday night," Dineen explained.

"I saw the article in the paper. What about him?"

"That's Marvin's cousin, and Marvin is on bereavement. Seems there are a few family matters to attend to," explained Dineen.

"And the funeral is today?" Ken asked.

"No, the wake is today. The funeral is tomorrow. Get this— you remember that cashier at Sadie's Place, Linda?"

"Yeah, I remember," Ken said.

"Everyone in town thinks she killed Rob, everyone except the sheriff and me."

"And me. I don't think she did it," Ken said.

"Ok, everyone except the sheriff and us two. I've known her since high school, and she could never do that."

"Do you know where the funeral is?" Ken asked.

"Yeah, it's at the First Church of Crooked Creek," replied Dineen. "I guess the minister is Rob's father—man, what a tight-knit community. Anyway, Marvin should be back on Wednesday, not that I miss him any."

Dineen winked then walked back to her desk. Ken stood by the old percolating coffee-maker and pondered what to do next.

"I'll just stop by Sadie's Place and get something for my cat," he thought, "and maybe see how Linda's doing today."

Rolling Hills, Monday afternoon

"These sequences will go perfectly with your baby's eyes," said Lady Sadie to an expecting mother. "And these mittens will keep him warm when he's playing with your sister's new baby girl."

The woman thanked Lady Sadie and went up to the counter to pay.

"Do her predictions come true?" the expecting woman asked Linda.

"Every one," replied Linda, then she thought about what Lady Sadie said about Ken Manders.

Linda rang up the purchase, and the expecting mother thanked her. As the satisfied customer left, the telephone rang.

"Sadie's Place," answered Linda. "Is this a business-related question?" Pause. "No, I can't help you. Goodbye."

"Another reporter?" asked Lady Sadie.

"No, just an ornery resident of Crooked Creek," replied Linda.

"Linda, there's something I want you to have," started Lady Sadie.

She disappeared into a back room then reappeared with a plain-white envelope.

"I see you laughing in a Riverton movie theater," said Lady Sadie, handing Linda the envelope, "and forgetting all about your problems. Here's a little bonus for your past, present, and future excellence. I see you taking the rest of the afternoon off and enjoying yourself."

"Thank you, Ms. Sadie," said a shocked Linda. "I don't know what to say."

"I know, child, I know. That's what I'm here for, the saying and the reading. Go on now and enjoy yourself."

Linda wasted no time in returning to her apartment, changing, and heading out to Riverton, where she stopped at the Riverton Cinema 6. Sitting in her car, the car being parked in the cinema's parking lot, she opened the envelope and found a ticket to one of her favorite comedies being played at the cinema.

"Well I guess this is one of those *planned* futures," chuckled Linda, and she went into the cinema and spent the next two hours laughing and chuckling and enjoying her movie to no end.

Meanwhile, Ken Manders had gotten off of work a little early for the sole purpose of seeing Linda at Sadie's Place. His plan was simple—go into the store and buy a toy for his cat and at the counter strike up a conversation with Linda. But when Ken walked into Sadie's Place, he was surprised to see Lady Sadie herself running the store.

"Excuse me, but is Linda here today?" he asked, though he had already noticed her car wasn't out front or at her apartment.

"Linda is not here. You should not be here," warned Lady Sadie.

"I know you don't like me, but I just need to see Linda. Do you know where she is?" Ken asked.

"If I were you, I'd be putting my affairs in order. Over here is a shirt I think you should buy. It will blend well with the massive bleeding, and it will be easier for the doctors to rip open when they try to save you," said Lady Sadie.

Ken stared at her in a serious yet perplexed mood. A dark shadow passed over his face, but it faded and was replaced with a very white expression, as if the very blood of which Lady Sadie spoke had drained from his face.

"I think I'll try again later. I'll pass up the shirt for now, thank you," Ken said slowly and cautiously. He backed up out of the store and returned to his car, where he drove home and remained there part of the evening, contemplating her words, his future, and Linda's experience.

Monday evening

"Now that's a movie," chuckled Linda as she drove back to her apartment. "How nice of Lady Sadie to give me the ticket *and* the time off. I feel I could get through anything now."

Linda had no sooner pulled up to her apartment when Doug walked over from the neighboring gas station.

"Good evening, Ms. Racquemore," Doug said from a short distance, still walking toward Linda.

"Hi Doug. What are you doing over here?" Linda asked.

"I wanted to let you know that out-of-townie was here again, in Sadie's Place he was."

"Oh? Did he say what he wanted?" Linda asked.

"Not to me. No one tells me nothin'. I just saw him going into the store and leave after ten minutes," explained Doug.

"That's odd. Thanks, Doug," Linda said as she walked toward her apartment.

"Wait up, Ms. Racquemore," called Doug. "There's something I wanna ask you."

"What, Doug?" asked Linda, who had no desire to mince words with him.

"I wanna ask you—will you go out to dinner with me?"

"What?!!"

"Dinner, you know, sit down and eat some fixin's. Dinner?"

"Doug, I'm sorry, but I just don't think it's a good idea."

"What's wrong, ain't I good enough fer ya?"

"No," said Linda.

"Yer not married, are ya?"

"No."

"Then let's go out fer dinner."

"No. Look, I've had a long weekend, and I need some time to myself. You understand, don't you?"

"No, I don't. I always thought we had something special; I even told that out-of-townie that we were getting married," said Doug.

"You said *what?*" Linda yelled.

"I was trying to throw him off the scent, ya know."

"Doug, I'll handle my own life, ok?"

"No! Someone needs to look out for you! That was made plain this weekend. I read the story in the paper, and I've heard what they've been saying all around town. What you need is a *real* man, and that's me! Just let me prove myself to you."

"Doug, you're not even my type," Linda tried to explain, but she might as well have been talking to a brick wall.

"You've never given us the chance to *really* get to know each other. Now I know this little restaurant in Crooked Creek—"

"Goodbye, Doug," Linda said.

She briskly walked into her apartment, but just as she closed the door, she heard Doug yell, "*I won't give up.*"

"Great," Linda said to herself sarcastically. "The last thing I need is someone else pursuing me. Why can't I just be alone?"

Linda had hardly sat down on her couch when someone knocked at her door.

"Hello Dineen," Linda said, answering the door. "What brings you here?"

"Lady Sadie just finished giving me a reading, and I thought I'd stop by and see how you're doing. So how are you doing?" asked Dineen.

Linda beckoned Dineen inside, and the two sat on the couch.

"Oh, I'm hanging in there, though I'm tired. Everyone's been asking me about Saturday night, and I wish the whole thing would just blow over."

"Like the papers and stuff?" Dineen asked.

"Everyone. Why just ten minutes ago Doug was practically proposing to me in the parking lot," said Linda.

"No!"

"Yes! He kept asking me out for dinner, saying that we should be together and he'll continue pursuing me—all that garbage. At least I got off work early today—that was nice."

"Yeah? What was the occasion?"

"I don't know," replied Linda. "I guess Lady Sadie was trying to help me recuperate from the weekend. She gave me a movie ticket to one of my favorite comedies."

"So did Ken Manders stop by? He seemed concerned about you," said Dineen.

"Doug said he did, but I must have been at the cinema when Ken was looking for me."

"Yeah, I was telling him that Marvin is on bereavement for Rob's death, and that's when he mentioned how he wondered how you were doing."

"There's something different about him I can't quite place," said Linda.

"You mean Ken?"

"Yeah. I was telling him about how a wolf attacked Rob that Saturday night, and he *knew* what the wolf looked like. Is that weird or what?"

"That is weird. Almost too weird," said Dineen.

"But you know what's even weirder? Remember Amy Sue from high school?" asked Linda.

"Yeah."

"Well, we had a great time on Saturday at the bar, but yesterday she turned against me, telling me I should keep my distance and not even go to Rob's funeral."

"So are you going?" asked Dineen.

"I don't even know where it is," laughed Linda.

"It's tomorrow at the First Church of Crooked Creek," said Dineen. "I was thinking of going myself. Say, why don't we go together?"

"Amy Sue warned me that I would not be welcome. I wonder what will happen if I *do* go?"

"If it will make you feel better, we could disguise you. I have some wigs and a few dresses you could try on. Throw on a pair of sunglasses, and you'll be all set. What do you say?"

"All right. Now if I can get a little peace and quiet, I might be able to sleep tonight," said Linda.

"Why don't you spend the night at my place? You know I'm only a couple of miles down the road. Then we can go straight to the funeral after dressing you up. And since no one would know where you are, no one can bother you. Just get the day off from Lady Sadie," suggested Dineen.

"Good plan! I'll just ask her right quick then," said Linda.

She disappeared for a few minutes then returned.

"It's all set. I have tomorrow off."

"Let's go," said Dineen, and with that the two sped off to Dineen's apartment.

Riverton Library, Monday evening

"I'm looking for information on Sadie's Place," said Ken Manders to the librarian.

"You and everyone else. About all we have is the address and phone number," said the librarian.

"What about Lady Sadie herself?" Ken asked.

"Well, she's not a George Washington you know. We only have information on famous people."

"So you couldn't tell me where she came from or anything like that?"

"I'm afraid not. Was there anything in particular you're looking for?" the librarian asked.

"Not really. How would I research things like recent deaths or accidents?" Ken asked.

"You could start with the card catalog to see what books are available. We also have a computerized index of our periodicals if you wish to research magazines or newspapers."

"Yes, that's what I should look at. Old newspapers."

"All right. Follow me," the librarian said.

Ken learned how to search the periodicals for a particular subject, keyword, or combination with different date ranges, types of periodicals, etc.

"Thank you," he said, and he started his search.

First he tried *Sadie*, but no match resulted. Next he tried *death*, but there were thousands of matches, and Ken couldn't wade through so many. Then he tried *wolf*, but again—thousands of entries popped up. Finally, he did a combination search of *death* and *wolf*. Thirteen entries popped up—most were from the 1930s.

"I'd like to borrow the microfilm of the *Crooked Creek Times* from 1932 to 1937," said Ken to the librarian.

"Ah," he said, "the Great Depression years. A lot of sad stories. I hope you find what you're looking for."

"So do I," said Ken.

Ken read through several articles on how the Great Depression was affecting Crooked Creek, Rolling Hills, and Riverton residents. Farmers suffered from droughts and herd losses from wolves. Ken continued reading on how the timber wolves in Riverton County were hunted and killed so as to give the farmers a better chance to raise their animals. On the last page of a 1933 *Crooked Creek Times*, Ken read how a Sadella Sarvak died in a freak accident. She was in her yard when a stray bullet from a hunter in a nearby barn killed her.

"That picture," Ken said to himself. "It looks just like Lady Sadie. Even the clothes, it looks just like her, but that's impossible. This happened over a half century ago. And Sadella Sarvak died."

Ken walked over to the librarian and asked him a question.

"Is there a way to get a copy on paper of a particular article from microfilm?" Ken asked.

"We don't have the equipment here for that. But we could send away for it from the Apple County Library. It'll take about a week or two."

"Sorry, can't wait that long," said Ken, and he immediately rushed home so he could telephone Linda and tell her about Sadella Sarvak.

Ken drove home as quickly as possible, ran into his apartment, and dialed Linda's number. No answer.

"Can't seem to get in touch with her at all," Ken said to himself, and his cat meowed right back. "Where do you suppose she is?" he asked his cat, but Ken's cat could only stare back as if to say, "It's anyone's guess."

Ken's work, Tuesday morning

Ken tried throughout the morning to contact Linda. He called her apartment, but there was no answer. He called Sadie's Place, but Lady Sadie answered, saying that Linda had simply taken the day off.

"Dineen will know," Ken said to himself, but he noticed she hadn't logged onto the computer that day.

"Is Dineen in today?" Ken asked the receptionist.

"No," she replied. "She went to a funeral in Crooked Creek."

"Do you know if she went alone?" Ken asked.

"Well I'm not supposed to tell," said the receptionist, but Ken knew she couldn't keep a secret. "She took that cashier from Sadie's Place there, disguised so no one will recognize her, but I was talking to this woman who called up this morning, and she said she can't believe that cashier would show her face at the Stokey funeral and that nothing good will come of it."

"Tell me," Ken said, "how many people have you told about Dineen taking the cashier to the funeral?"

"Just you," the receptionist said.

"One more thing—when does the funeral start?" Ken asked.

"It's already started."

Tuesday afternoon

Ken left work immediately. He raced down to the First Church of Crooked Creek as quickly as possible to stop Linda from going.

"She's going to be in big trouble if I don't get there in time," Ken said to himself.

He managed to avoid colliding with other cars, and he also avoided being pulled over for speeding, but when he arrived at the First Church of Crooked Creek, no one was there.

"What is going on? Am I at the right place?" he wondered.

Ken ran into the church and found a small program for the funeral. He opened it to find that the burial was at Crooked Creek Cemetery.

"And they're probably there now," he said as he dashed into his car.

Ken could see the parked cars lined up in Crooked Creek Cemetery, and this blocked him from driving up to the burial. He drove around the cemetery until he found a back way and took it directly to the grave site, thus avoiding the general car procession.

The crowd gathered around a tent where the casket was placed into a vault. Now parked, Ken quietly walked from his car until he joined the crowd. It was disturbingly quiet and peaceful. There was no indication of any problems, nor did anything seem to be out of place. Everything was perfect, too perfect for Ken's comfort. While the minister said a few words to the people, Ken looked around for familiar faces. There was Marvin, the guy from the Rolling Hills gas station (Doug), but where was Dineen? There she was, standing in the far corner, nearly hidden from view. Next to her stood a woman with long curly blond hair, sunglasses, and an odd sort of dress, though the woman's legs looked familiar.

"I'd know those legs anywhere," thought Ken to himself, and he knew the woman he saw was Linda—in disguise.

"Let us now pay our last respects to our beloved Rob Stokey," said the minister.

Each person in turn went up with a flower and placed it on the closed casket. However, Linda and Dineen kept their places. Noticing this, Doug went over to the two ladies. The one with blond hair and sunglasses looked very suspicious to him.

"Um, hello there, I don't remember seeing you before. Have we met?"

"This is a funeral, not a singles bar," Dineen said to Doug in a hushed voice.

"Excuse me, Miss Persnickety!" he said to Dineen. "I know every one of Rob's friends and relatives, and I just thought I'd meet any who I don't recognize."

"Well, why don't you recognize somewhere else," said Dineen.

"What's wrong, can't the blonde speak for herself?" Doug asked.

"I can speak," said Linda. "I'm just an old friend, nothing more. If you could, please let us be alone."

"Hey, wait a minute. You sound familiar. If I didn't know better, I'd say you were—" he started to say as he pulled at her blond hair.

The wig came off, knocking the sunglasses off and completely exposing Linda to full view.

"Ms. Racquemore!" exclaimed Doug.

"Get away!" Dineen shouted.

The damage was done. As soon as Doug had announced Linda's presence, the entire funeral party gathered around her in an unfriendly circle.

"Get her!" yelled several, while others yelled, "Kill her!" and "Don't let her get away!"

In the confusion, Dineen was thrown backward while Ken dashed for Linda to pull her out of the mass of people. Someone pulled out a gun and aimed at Linda, but Ken had by now partially blocked her. The gun fired, sending the bullet into Ken's shoulder. Doug wrestled with the gunman while Ken pushed his way through the crowd with Linda.

So much yelling and screaming, so much chaos, but while Doug and others wrestled with the gunman, Ken managed to drag Linda into his car, and the two sped off, though not without a few angry Crooked Creek residents pounding on Ken's car as he pulled away.

"You're bleeding badly," said Linda. "I can't stop the blood from pouring out. We need to get you to the hospital!"

"If I can just make it a little longer..." he said, but his voice trailed, and though no one had caught up to them, Ken could drive no longer. He pulled off to the side of the road, and after putting the car into park, he collapsed. Linda drove Ken to Riverton County Hospital.

"Help me!" Linda yelled as she stopped at the emergency entrance of Riverton County Hospital.

Several people pulled Ken out and put him on a stretcher. Linda could only watch as he was raced down to an operatory for surgery.

"Ken," she called, but several nurses took Linda and sat her down in the lobby.

"You can't go in while they're working on him. Now just sit here, and the doctor will be along to let you know how he's doing," said a nurse.

What seemed to be a three-day wait was only three hours, and a doctor came out to speak to Linda.

"He's lost a lot of blood," the doctor said. "He's in serious but stable condition. We gave him a transfusion and removed the bullet. He's regaining consciousness, if you'd like to talk to him."

"Absolutely!" said Linda, and she followed the doctor to Ken's recovery room.

"Hello, Ms. Linda Racquemore," he said, though his voice was quiet and mellow.

"Ken, how are you doing?" she asked.

"Doing? I feel great," he said.

"He's on pain medication right now," said the nurse, "so don't be surprised if he's a little distant or disoriented."

"I've never felt better. And I know where I am—Riverton County Hospital," Ken said.

"That's good to know," said the nurse. "If you need anything, just ring this bell."

With that, the nurse left.

"I want to thank you for what you did back there," Linda said. "You saved my life."

"And you mine," he said.

"Tell me, did you know what was going to happen?"

"I thought something might happen, but I never expected someone to pull a gun on you," Ken replied.

"That Doug—if he could have just left me alone..."

"Then something else would have happened," added Ken. "Linda, there's something bad happening around here, something evil, and I feel that you're taking the heat for it."

"That's for sure," said Linda.

"And I know you don't believe me, but please, try to hear me out. I did some research on Lady Sadie," said Ken.

"And what did you find?" Linda asked.

"Nothing on *Sadie*, but after searching for both *death* and *wolf*, I found some interesting articles in the 1933 *Crooked Creek Times*. If you don't believe me, read for yourself. It was in one of the October editions," said Ken.

"I believe you. What did it say?" Linda asked.

"Back in the 30s there was a big problem with wolves stealing farm animals. The farmers had a hard enough time with the depression, so to help the farmers survive, it was decided the wolves were to be hunted to extinction in these parts. Among those were the timber wolves."

"An unfortunate fatality resulted when a hunter was shooting at a wolf in a barn and accidentally killed a woman by the name of Sadella Sarvak. Notice the similarity in names: Sadella, Sadie. And there's a photograph of Sadella Sarvak. She looks amazingly like Lady Sadie."

"Could be a grandmother," suggested Linda.

"Maybe, but the resemblance is so striking—I actually felt I was looking at a picture of Lady Sadie, right down to the last button."

"What a strange way to die," said Linda.

"Too strange, that a hunter would see a wolf in a barn and accidentally kill Sadella on the outside."

"Are Sadella and Lady Sadie the same person?" asked Linda.

"I don't know, I don't know. It's too impossible to seem real, and yet everything points to only one conclusion—she is not what she seems."

"I still can't believe Lady Sadie is anything but nice. Yesterday she let me off work early *and* gave me tickets to my favorite comedy. Does that sound like the work of an evil person?" asked Linda.

"And while you were watching your movie," Ken added, "I stopped by Sadie's Place to see how you were doing. You were gone, of course, but Lady Sadie warned me to stay away, and she suggested that I buy a red shirt, because it would match my blood and would be easy for the doctors to rip open when they were trying to save me."

"She said that?" Linda asked, floored.

"Yes."

"And you're suggesting that the wolf that attacked Rob was her?"

"Yes. The very same one that blocked my path. When you were out Saturday night, I stopped by your place, and Lady Sadie was on her way out. Maybe it was a coincidence, but then again maybe not."

"What am I going to do?" asked Linda. "Everyone in Crooked Creek hates me. I work for a woman who might turn into a wolf and kill people at night? I must be losing my mind."

"I'm so tired," said Ken, his voice trailing.

"Ken, don't fall asleep now. I need to talk to you."

"So tired," he said, and he fell asleep, exhausted from the injuries and surgery.

"Is he sleeping finally?" asked the nurse, walking in a few minutes later.

"Yes. Asleep."

"It's probably best you let him get some rest. You can visit him tomorrow, if you like. He'll be stronger and more alert, I'm sure."

"Sure," said Linda.

She handed Ken's keys to the nurse and took a cab back to her apartment. When she got home, though, there were several protesters marching in front of Sadie's Place, just waiting for Linda to show up. Linda instructed the cab driver to let her off behind the gas station so as not to be observed.

"Hi, Linda," said a familiar voice.

"Kip, I hope you don't mind me sneaking behind your place to get to my apartment."

"Think nothing of it," he said. "I heard what happened at the cemetery. Are you doing all right?"

"Pretty good, considering."

"I see the gunman missed you," he said.

"Yeah, but Ken was hurt. Did Doug come back?"

"He did, but he said he had some errands at the store. He'll be back in a little while."

"That's ok," said Linda, "I'm kinda glad he's not around."

"Oh? He says he wrestled the gunman to the ground until the sheriff arrived. Doug's a decent guy," said Kip.

"At times, at times. Gotta go, Kip. See ya," said Linda as she snuck around to her apartment door.

"Have a good evening, Linda," Kip called back.

Though it was only 7 pm, Linda had fallen asleep for twenty minutes and was awakened by her ringing telephone.

"Hello?" Linda answered.

"Well, you have all the nerve," said an agitated Amy Sue.

"What?"

"You heard me! Of all the things. I warned you not to interfere, and look what you did! You're lucky to be alive, *dearie*. You're lucky you didn't get shot. What in the world made you think you could be there and get away with it?" Amy Sue asked.

"Hey, I don't have to put up with this. I haven't done anything wrong," Linda said.

"Haven't done anything wrong? Haven't done anything wrong, you say. You've done more than your share, believe you me. You're nothing but a troublemaker and a jinx, Linda Racquemore, and you'll pay for this. The people of Crooked Creek won't stand for this anymore, and if you're still in the county tomorrow, you'll pay dearly, *dearie*, mighty dearly!"

Amy Sue hung up the phone with those last words, leaving a bitter taste in Linda's mouth.

"I used to think she was my friend," Linda said quietly to herself. "I used to think I had a lot of friends. Now everyone hates me," Linda finished, and she cried.

Though Linda had done nothing legally wrong, protesters and reporters continued to harass her with phone calls and spying when she went anywhere. Because of this, Linda unplugged her phone and took Wednesday and Thursday off. Most of the time was spent reading her novel or sneaking off to a remote park for rest and relaxation.

Thursday evening

After having her phone unplugged for two days, Linda figured it was about time she plugged it in. This was a fortunate thing, because an hour after she did so, the phone rang.

"Linda?" said a voice.

"Ken! How are you doing?" Linda asked.

"Much better. They say I can leave Saturday morning at this rate," replied Ken.

"That's great."

"Hey, I was thinking. Would you be interested in getting together this weekend, maybe a movie or dinner?" Ken asked.

"That would be excellent. I could use a little diversion from this hectic week."

"Great. I'll give you a call when I get out," Ken said.

"Excellent," said Linda.

"I was concerned about you. How are you holding up?" Ken asked.

"Not too well. I took the past couple of days off. And tomorrow I'm working. Hopefully after the weekend, I'll be back to my old self," Linda explained.

"Any plans to go out to the Blue Wolf bar?" Ken asked.

"No, I'll just keep things a little quiet this weekend," said Linda.

"Sounds good."

"And if I'm lucky, this whole thing will blow over by next week," said Linda.

"I hope you're right. But for your sake, please remember what I told you on Tuesday. You haven't forgotten, have you?"

"No," replied Linda. "I haven't forgotten. I know, I should be thinking about moving and finding a new job. It's so hard to do, though. Lady Sadie has been nothing but nice to me, and I hate to walk out on her."

"I know. Well, let's not think about it anymore this weekend," said Ken.

"An excellent idea."

"Hopefully I'll see you Saturday then?"

"Saturday it is," replied Linda.

"Great. See you later."

"Bye."

"Bye."

Friday

"I've been looking all over for some maroon carpet thread," said a customer, "and every store I've been to has either white or black carpet thread."

"Well, you've come to the right place," said Linda, watching the store while Lady Sadie was out on an errand. "Not only do we have a large selection of regular threads, but we have a special assortment of button and carpet threads. We have black, white, beige, red, green, here we are—maroon."

"Why I can't believe it! You *do* have it all here, don't you?" the customer asked.

"We like to think so," replied Linda.

"Say, is Ms. Sadie in? I heard she gives readings," asked the customer.

"She's out on an errand at the moment," replied Linda. "But if you like, I can set up an appointment for you."

"No, that's ok. I'll just stop by another day," said the customer.

Linda happily rang up the purchase and wished the customer a good weekend. Around noon, Lady Sadie returned.

"I'm so glad you're feeling better," said Lady Sadie. "A couple of days off have done you some good."

"Thank you. I *do* feel much better. And no one's bothered me since Wednesday," said Linda.

"Excellent. I'm so proud of your work and stamina that I'm going to give you the afternoon off," said Lady Sadie.

"Lady Sadie, please! You've been too nice alread—"

"No, child, speak no words of thanks to me. Hush now, that's a good girl."

Lady Sadie held her comb up to the light and passed an envelope over the comb.

"I see you having a wonderful time at the Riverton Zoo. And you'll be talking with someone and laughing. Here, my child, have a good afternoon," said Lady Sadie, handing an envelope with two tickets to Linda.

"Why thank you," said a shocked Linda. "I just don't know how to repay you."

"Think no more of it," Lady Sadie said.

Linda stood for another few seconds, stunned, and she would probably still be standing in that spot today had Lady Sadie not ushered her out of Sadie's Place.

Linda's expectations deflated when she noticed her front-left tire was low on air.

"Kip?" Linda called after driving her car to the next-door gas station. "Kip, I need some air in my front tire," Linda called.

"Kip's over in Apple County today, Ms. Racquemore, I mean, Linda," said Doug while walking out of the garage.

"Oh. Can you put air in my tire?" she asked.

"Be happy to," he replied. "So where are you off to today?"

"Oh, Lady Sadie gave me tickets to the zoo," said Linda.

"Tickets? How many?" he pried.

"Just two. She said I'd be going along with someone, but I don't know who," Linda said.

"That someone is me," Doug said.

"You?"

"Yeah. I knew something like this would happen. It's been slow all day, and I got a helper who can watch the gas station for the rest of the afternoon, at least 'till Kip gets back."

"I don't know, Doug," Linda said.

"Linda, I'm sorry about the other day. I was a complete jerk. I'm sorry. It'll never happen again, promise," said Doug.

Silence. Linda wasn't sure what to do or say next.

"So what are you gonna do with the other ticket? Let it go to waste? I promise, I'll be the perfect gentleman," Doug said.

She was hoping the other person would be Ken, but he was not to be released until the next day. *I guess Doug is the other person,* Linda thought.

"Well, all right. But remember, this is *not* a date, okay?"

"Ok, ok. Not a date. Just friends," Doug said.

"If that."

The two went in Linda's car (now that the tire was full of air). Linda was having a marvelous time at the zoo, and Doug seemed to enjoy himself, though he knew little about what some of the animals were. Actually, there was a little festival going on at one side of the zoo, with live entertainment, games, and a few beer tents. Doug wasted no time in downing a brew or two.

"Look at the otters. Aren't they so cute?" Linda asked, but Doug said nothing.

"And look, here's the primate section. Old world monkeys, new world monkeys, orangutans, chimpanzees, gorillas, baboons—" Linda started.

"Baboon. Must be a close relative of that out-of-townie the way they both swing around," Doug commented while sipping on his beer bottle.

"Hey, mister, I don't appreciate those kinds of comments," said Linda, now a little irritated.

"Oh don't be such a weakling. A little jab now and then ain't gonna hurt no one. Keeps you on yer toes, it does," said Doug, though his speech was impaired.

"I'm getting tired," said Linda, trying to change the subject. "Time to go home."

"So soon? We just got here—"

"Three hours ago. And I think you've monkeyed around long enough," she said with a chuckle.

Doug's face turned red, but he didn't say anything.

"Yeah, Linda Racquemore, you keep it up, keep it up!" he said, but Linda didn't respond.

Unfortunately, a few Crooked Creek ears perked when they heard, "Linda Racquemore."

"That's her," said one Crooked Creek resident.

"You're right, it *is* her," said the other.

"It's time we get things settled once and for all," said the first, and the two residents immediately returned to Crooked Creek.

Doug stared off into the distance as the two returned to Linda's car. Linda wanted to get home as soon as possible so she could get away from Doug. Being a little edgy, she took a right turn too sharply and pinched the right-rear tire in the curb.

"What was that?" Doug asked.

"Curb option," said Linda.

"Be fair with your car," said Doug.

"Fair? How can I be fair?" asked Linda.

"Huh?"

"You said you would be the perfect gentleman. Now you're being nothing but ornery and rude," said Linda.

"And you can't drive worth a lick," said Doug.

"What's wrong with this car?" Linda asked.

"Curb option, hah! Flat tire is what you got."

Doug was right (unfortunately). Linda parked the car, and the two got out and inspected the damage.

"Don't bother trying to change it," said Doug. "I know you women. Can't fix anything if your life depended on it."

"I don't need your help," said Linda.

"You're gonna need my help," Doug said, grabbing Linda by the arm and speaking directly to her face. "Need my help, if you wanna stay a-*live!*"

"Let go of my arm!" yelled Linda.

"One way or another, you're gonna learn to respect me. Now get out of the way!" Doug yelled back, shoving her into the ground.

Stunned, she slowly pulled herself from the ground and inspected the damage. A bruised arm. Abrasion wounds on her hands. Her nylons were running in every wrong direction from the broken glass she'd fallen upon. Legs cut, hands scraped, and arm bruised, Linda was quietly sobbing while an unsympathetic Doug finished the tire-changing job.

"There," he said after completing the job. "Now we're ready to roll."

"I'm not going anywhere with you!" Linda screamed.

"Get up!" Doug commanded, wrenching Linda by the arm and forcing her into the car. "Get in and shut up."

Being in too much pain to resist, Linda sobbed on the remaining drive to her apartment.

"There you go," Doug said when the two arrived at Linda's apartment. "Don't bother to thank me," he said, but Linda was in no mood to carry on a conversation.

Doug had hardly parked the car when she jumped out and ran into her apartment.

"Where are you going?" he yelled at her. "You're going to need a spare tire."

"Oh shut up!" she yelled just before disappearing inside.

Figuring he was being helpful, Doug took Linda's car to Kip's Gas Station and proceeded to replace the damaged tire.

"Hello, Ken?" Linda said over the telephone after dialing Ken Mander's number. "You're home!"

"I was released early. Linda, your voice is shaking. What's going on?" Ken asked.

"I'm at my apartment. I need to get away this evening. Can you come over?"

"Sure. Bad day at work?"

"Not really. I'll explain later," Linda said.

"Sure, I'll be over in a bit," Ken said.

Linda looked out the window to see what Doug was doing.

"The nerve of him!" Linda thought, seeing Doug take her car over to the gas station. "He didn't even ask if I wanted it repaired. Always thinks he's in control."

Linda heard Lady Sadie's low voice filter through the wall, and as a way of getting her mind off Doug (until Ken arrived), she decided to see how things were going in the store.

Sadie's Place was still open but only for a few minutes. Linda left her apartment, entered the store, and looked around to see if any customers were around—customers she could talk to. The empty store provided no sympathy. She looked at herself in dismay and realized she was quite a mess from falling on the side of the road. Linda went inside the employee bathroom and washed up.

"Yes, Mr. Johnson, I remember you," said a voice from the main office as Linda exited the bathroom.

From behind the counter, Linda watched Doug work on her car while she listened intently to Lady Sadie.

"Yes, I remember your daughter, the spittin' image of her father," Lady Sadie continued to say from the office.

Doug was now replacing the damaged tire from the car's trunk with a fresh one. Linda continued to watch Doug while listening to Lady Sadie.

"As I pass the paper over the comb and look into the light, I see you kneeling over a casket and saying, 'Farewell my sweet daughter.'"

"My daughter will die? How can this be? How will she die, so that I may prevent it?" the shaking father asked over the speakerphone.

"She will die from your own hands," Lady Sadie said.

The father went into hysterics and hung up the phone. Linda's face went white with gloom. Lady Sadie sat in her office chair and stared into the paper-comb device.

"How could you say that, Ms. Sadie, even knowing that something bad would happen to his daughter; how could you tell him that?" Linda asked in shock. "Are you the devil?"

"I may seem evil, Linda, but I always give my clients the opportunity to change their ways," Lady Sadie replied. "That's why I tell them the truth, no matter how gruesome."

"But...he...his daughter...you," Linda tried to say, but her throat welled up from the intense fright, and she slowly stumbled backward, trying to back out but as frozen as a deer when once spotted.

Lady Sadie laughed.

"But, you...you help people with decisions. How can this be?" Linda stammered.

"It is people who are evil, Linda," Ladie Sadie said. "I lead them to the water of truth, and when they thirst for more, I show them more truth—no matter how evil! And I know your future—it too is full of evil!"

"But no, this can't be," Linda said.

"You should have listened to your friend, Ken Manders, before it was too late!" warned Lady Sadie.

"Too late?"

"Don't play innocent with me, Linda Racquemore. I know what you've been doing, and I know Mr. Manders told you about me. The Great Depression? Hunted to extinction? What fools the mortals are for placing themselves on such high pedestals. So high up, so fragile, I give them their reward; I push them off their pedestals of deceit so that they crash to their deaths! My grips are stronger than a steel-jawed trap! Let the arrogant mortal trample over me. Only I will latch onto those muddy feet and pull the fool through the earth and bury him in his own decay!"

"Please, Lady Sadie, I—" Linda tried to say.

"*Lady Sadie, Lady Sadie!* Sadie, Satie, Satan!" Lady Sadie exclaimed, throwing her arms into the air. "Isn't that what you're thinking?"

"Hey, open up this door!" said a voice from the front door.

Doug pounded his fists into the store door. Getting no response, he threw his body several times into the locked door.

"There you are," said Doug, crashing into Sadie's Place.

"Doug! What are you—" Linda barely managed to say.

"You owe me fifteen minutes of your time," said Doug. "It's the least you can do for all the things I've done for you."

"I don't owe you anything," said Linda.

"And that's the thanks I get for everything? I even fixed your tire," he said, pointing out the window to the car.

"Doug, get out of here!" Linda said.

"I'm not done with you," he said.

"Yes you are," said Linda, and she shoved him toward the door.

Doug responded by grabbing her arm and twisting it behind her back.

"You're hurting me!" she nearly screamed.

Linda couldn't handle the intense pain, and she stomped the spike of her high-heeled shoe into Doug's foot. He let go. Crying out in pain, he threw a right cross into Linda's jaw. She fell to the floor unconscious, and in doing so she knocked over several porcelain and glass goods.

"What is the meaning of this?" Lady Sadie demanded.

"Look, she deserved everything she got," Doug tried to explain, but Ms. Sadie wouldn't hear of it.

"And so shall you!" she said, shrinking behind the counter with a cold yet vicious demeanor.

"What the devil," Doug said, confused by her actions.

It was very quiet in the store, and Doug walked up to the counter and peered over to see what Lady Sadie was doing. Up leapt a timber wolf from behind the counter and directly into Doug's face, both surprising him and forcing him backward where he bounced off a table and fell to the floor. Like mad he tried to fight the wolf off, but it was too vicious and too aggressive. It ripped into Doug's arms and legs, making a horribly fleshy-bloody mess. Doug screamed in pain, but the wolf went for his neck and finished the job.

One, two, five, then fifty or more Crooked Creek residents arrived in several pickup trucks and surrounded Sadie's Place with incredible speed.

"Down with the killer," yelled some.

"Justice for Rob," yelled others.

"What's going on here?" asked Kip, arriving from his Friday errands.

"Hey! It's the gas-station owner," said one of the Crooked Creekers.

"Yeah, he always fixed the killer's car!" said another.

"Get him!" said several others.

Seven or so people converged on Kip, threw him into one of his chairs (at the gas station), and tied him to it.

"I demand you let me go!" he shouted while the majority continued chanting and yelling around Sadie's Place.

Hearing his boss in trouble, Kip's helper slipped out of the gas station, jumped into his hopped-up Nova, and sped down the road to escape.

"There's another one!" yelled a Crooked Creeker.

Two Creekers jumped in a sports car and raced down the road after Kip's helper.

"Everyone, this is getting out of hand," said Kip. "Please stop this nonsense and return home!"

"Nonsense?" said a Crooked Creeker. "You think this is nonsense? Hey everyone, Kip doesn't like our 'nonsense'!"

The mob laughed, then the Crooked Creeker put his enraged face in front of Kip's.

"This is nothing. I'll show you *real* nonsense!"

He picked up a rock and threw it into a window. The others joined in and in turn shattered every window with rocks and loose branches.

"You can't destroy private property like this. Do you know what it costs to repair all those windows?" Kip asked, but hardly anyone paid attention.

"Like I care," said the Crooked Creeker.

The Creeker (followed by several of his buddies) went over to Kip's gas station and filled several containers with gasoline.

"How about if I pour this gas all over you and light a match. Does that make your hair singe?" the Crooked Creeker asked.

"You don't know what you're doing!" Kip said.

"No, that would be too easy," said the Creeker. "But I'd still like to give you a warm feeling all over."

Several Crooked Creekers took the gas containers and poured the fuel around Sadie's Place.

"Swing low, swing gas-o-line. Coming 'round to burn the store! Swing low, swing gas-o-line. Coming 'round to burn the store!" chanted the Creekers.

Everyone (except Kip) cheered when the gas was poured. Someone threw a lit match into a trail of gas, and an instant blaze roared around Sadie's Place. Again the Crooked Creekers cheered, but the heat from the quickly-growing fire forced everyone back several steps!

"Yay, yay, yay!" yelled some.

"Burn, burn, burn!" chanted others.

"The gas station—it'll blow," Kip said.

"Let's get out of here!" said one of the Crooked Creekers, and the mob left as quickly as it came.

In the confusion of the fire and the mob leaving, a gray timber wolf leapt through a back window, sending glass and wood in multiple directions. The wolf ran across a short clearing before disappearing into the woods beyond.

Ken was approaching Rolling Hills when several oncoming vehicles ran him off the road.

"Stay on the right side of the road," he yelled back.

When the dust cleared (from the Crooked Creekers' exodus), Ken drove up to Sadie's Place and was horrified by the blaze.

"What's going on here?" Ken asked while untying Kip.

"Crooked Creekers. They tied me up and set Sadie's Place on fire!"

"What about Lady Sadie? Linda Racquemore? I see their cars. They must be inside!"

"Don't be a fool, man," said Kip. "How long do you think my gas station can keep from blowing up with this inferno right next to it? Get out while you can!"

"Linda?" Ken called, running around to her apartment door.

Fiery flames encircled the entire building, and Ken used his coat to beat a path to her door and into her apartment.

"Linda?" Ken called, now inside.

No answer. The smoke thickened, and Ken could hardly breathe. Choking on the smoke, he fell to the floor and slowly crawled back to the outside door.

"Hey, you!" said Kip's voice. "You can't survive in there."

Kip blazed a trail to Ken with a fire extinguisher.

"We gotta get out of here!" he said, pulling Ken outside.

"Not until I know that Linda isn't here," Ken said, taking the fire extinguisher from Kip (who had borrowed it from his gas station).

"I can't wait," said Kip, and he drove off in his truck.

"Linda?" Ken yelled while blazing through the front door of Sadie's Place. "Linda, are you in here?" he called again, spraying the fire extinguisher to get inside.

Again the smoke was thick, and Ken held his shirt over his face, but it didn't help much. He heard a faint cough.

"Linda!" he said, running over to her.

She was still on the floor.

"We gotta get out of here!" he said. "Is there anyone else in here?" he asked.

"I don't know," she replied. "Help me," she said as her senses returned.

Ken blazed back through the flames with Linda following behind. Neighboring trees caught fire, and a gasoline explosion was imminent.

"Get into my car," Ken said, helping her to sit down.

"My apartment. My things," she started to say.

"There's no time," Ken replied, wheeling the car around and zooming down the road at maximum acceleration.

"My family pictures, keepsakes, where's Doug?" she asked.

Kaboom! The gas station ignited into a thundering explosion. The resulting shock wave threw Ken's car into a 180-degree spin and slightly into the ditch. The two watched in horror as Lady Sadie's car exploded, then Linda's car, then Doug's truck.

"I hope there was no one else inside," said Ken, but Linda buried her head into her arms.

Ken turned the car around and headed away from the flames amidst bits of burning debris falling around them.

Futures: Part II

May 15, 2010

Linda moved in with Ken. It was a temporary living arrangement at first, but as weeks became months, Linda and Ken developed a special friendship and love. After a year of cohabitation, Ken proposed to Linda, but she refused. After two years he proposed again, but again she refused. Then three years, five, ten, and fifteen passed without a marriage.

Saturday

"We've been living like a married couple for fifteen years," Ken said while the two ate breakfast at a local restaurant. "Why wait any longer to get married?"

"I can't," Linda said. "I just can't."

"Why not? Is it me?" Ken asked.

"No," Linda said.

"Then what?" Ken asked.

Linda held silent.

"What's troubling you?" Ken asked.

"I don't want to talk about it," Linda said.

"Linda, sweedie, something has taken hold of you and held you back all these years. Lady Sadie and her store are gone. The inhabitants abandoned Rolling Hills during the recession of 2002. The few stragglers who remained left in 2009 during the Great Recession. It's a ghost town, Linda. Nothing's left. Why do you let it keep its grip on you?"

"Don't you think I know about Rolling Hills? I read more news than you," Linda said.

"Then let it go," Ken said.

"I have! It won't let *me* go!" Linda blurted.

Linda had drained the last of her coffee from its cup. She flagged a server for more. The server walked over with two decanters and poured regular coffee into Linda's cup. Linda poured cream and sugar into her coffee, stirred it, and took a sip. Linda gagged.

"Are you okay?" Ken asked.

Linda placed the coffee cup on the table and clutched her throat in an effort to recover from her red-faced choking crisis. Ken stood up and exited his side of the booth in preparation for performing the Heimlich maneuver on Linda, but Linda waved him off. Linda choked further and coughed up something into a paper napkin.

"I'm fine," Linda said.

Puzzled, Ken remained standing.

"Sit down, Ken. I'm quite all right," Linda said.

"I thought—" Ken started.

"Then don't think," Linda said. "You're embarrassing me. Now sit."

Ken returned to his bench seat in the booth. He watched as Linda slyly hid the napkin under the creamer bowl's edge. Ken noticed but did not indicate to Linda that he observed her sleight of hand.

"I'm sorry," Linda said. "Let's talk about something else. Did I ever tell you May is my favorite time of year? Everything is green, it's warm but not too hot, the boats are launching for the season, and the bugs aren't out yet."

"I'm glad for this time of year too," Ken said. "Last winter was tough. We received more snow than I would ever care to snow throw."

"You were busy plowing the long driveway," Linda said. "I'd be happy to help."

"There's only one snow thrower," Ken said.

"Maybe you should think about getting another one. Then we could both plow the driveway togeth...hey!" Linda said.

While Linda had been talking about the snow thrower, Ken grabbed the used napkin from under the creamer bowl.

"Give that back!" Linda demanded. "You're not my father!"

"No," Ken said. "I want to see what's in this napkin."

"Are you going to break the flush handle on the toilets at home so you can inspect my droppings too? Who died and made you dictator?!"

Ken opened the napkin and to his surprise and horror found a tough, rounded, fibrous material in the napkin, colored like a clipped fingernail, and surrounded with bits of blood and mucus.

"What the hell is this?" Ken asked.

"It's none of your business!" Linda said as she grabbed the napkin and its contents from Ken.

"Look, Linda. You have to see a doctor," Ken said. "There's something wrong with your stomach. How long have you been throwing up this...this...stomach stone?"

"None of your business!" Linda replied. "And I'm not seeing a doctor."

"But you have to," Ken said. "If there's more of this in your stomach...is there more?"

Linda held silent.

"How long have you been throwing up stones?" Ken asked.

Linda sipped her coffee and said nothing.

"How long?" Ken asked.

"Fifteen years!" Linda blurted.

Ken paused in thought. He opened his mouth to say something, but he closed it without a whisper.

"Yeah, fifteen years," she repeated. "Ever since Sadie's Place burned down, I've been puking these stones."

"Then why didn't you do something when it started?" Ken asked.

"Because I don't want to be fed intravenously," Linda said.

The waitress brought breakfast, and the two started eating.

"I don't understand," Ken said. "Who said anything about being fed intravenously? I'm just saying—"

"*You're just saying,* yeah, I know what you're saying," Linda said. "Do the calculations, Ken. I see doctor. Doctor takes X-ray of my stomach. Stomach is full of stones. Doctor decides to remove stomach, just like the time he decided to remove my gallbladder when he found that full of stones. No more stomach, no more eating, and a lifetime of sticking a needle in my vein for nutrients. No thanks."

"All these years you've been suffering in silence," Ken said. "Is this why you won't marry me?"

"What kind of stupid question is that?" Linda asked. "There's no connection."

"I think you're afraid to marry me because of these stomach stones," Ken said, "that somehow you feel this will cause problems in a marriage."

Linda shivered for a moment, and a dark shadow passed over her face.

"You're trying to spare me the pain of being a widower," Ken said. "You believe that any day now, this condition might kill you. Oh Linda, don't let this thing beat you. We must see a doctor, we must!"

"I'd rather die than live with a tube in my arm. That's no kind of life," Linda said.

"At least let's find out the extent of your condition," Ken said. "We don't have to have the doctor remove your stomach."

"No," Linda said. "Institutions are like regimes when it comes to women's health."

"Huh?" Ken asked.

"You're a man, so you don't know, but I've had a number of girlfriends who were denied health insurance because they refused to answer the abortion question on the application form. That's only the tip of the iceberg. There are many other situations where institutions believe they should have absolute knowledge of women's bodies for whatever purpose—often to the detriment of women. I say, 'no'. The best way to protect my privacy is to keep these institutions out of my life as needed."

"But a doctor isn't a health insurance company," Ken said.

"They're all connected," Linda said. "Medical institutions, health insurance companies, and governments probe much deeper than they should and make decisions that I don't always agree with. So as far as I'm concerned, what they don't know they can't mandate."

"But what about me? What about your life?" Ken asked. "I dread the loss of the one person in my life who I can tell anything without reservation. Anything. No one understands me like you. What loneliness will you condemn me to by dying young?"

"That's why I didn't want to tell you," Linda said.

Linda ate more of her breakfast and drank more coffee.

"This is good coffee," Linda said. "I always feel better after a strong cup. You know, if you really want to help me, you can start making coffee at home."

"How can you talk about coffee at a time like this?" he asked.

"Because it's the only beverage I know that'll cure most any problem I have. It gets me through the day," Linda said.

Ken didn't know what to say. The two ate in silence. Finally, Ken spoke up.

"At least let me have the napkin back," Ken said.

"Why?"

"To have it tested," Ken said.

Linda gave Ken a dirty look.

"I'll send it out to a lab on the internet. I won't say where it came from. I want to know what the stone is made of," Ken explained.

"As long as that's all you do with it," Linda said, and she gave the napkin with the stomach stone to Ken.

"Thank you," Ken said. "Now then, what else have you not been telling me?"

"What is this, an inquisition?" Linda asked. "You're not my father."

"Linda, dear, I'm trying to help. You know that. I would never hurt you," Ken said. "Do you ever think about Lady Sadie?"

Linda paused. She took another sip of coffee and swallowed it.

"I have nightmares about the wolf," Linda said.

"Recently?" Ken asked.

"Yes. Every night for the last fifteen years, I've dreamed that Lady Sadie in wolf form is attacking me," Linda explained.

"And no, I won't go in for 'therapy'. The pharmaceutical companies are constantly pushing their meds on the public. I won't be a pill zombie."

"You're having a recurring nightmare," Ken said. "This is terrible. We have to do something."

"Coffee," Linda said. "Coffee is the solution to all problems. Once I get the first cup in me, I'm good for the day. I forget all about Lady Sadie, the wolf, and the stones."

The waitress brought the bill.

"Did you bring any money with you?" Linda asked. "Why do I bother asking when I know you didn't? I'm buying again, as usual."

Linda passed Ken a twenty-dollar bill while she searched for a five-note for the tip.

"Go on, pay the bill. I'll catch up with you," Linda said.

Saturday, One Month Later

Ken sent the stomach stone away to a lab. A month later, the lab returned the results. The stone was made of keratin. Ken looked up *keratin* on the internet and shared his new-found knowledge with Linda.

"Remember that stomach stone you gave me?" Ken asked Linda.

"What about it?" Linda asked.

"I sent it to a lab," Ken said. "The results came back. I did a little research, and—"

"And what?" Linda said.

"Linda—do you eat hair?" Ken asked.

"What?! I'm not a cat!" Linda stated.

"I know. The thing is this—the stone is made of keratin."

"And that's what hair is made of?" Linda asked.

"Yes," Ken said.

"Wait a moment," Linda said.

Linda logged onto the internet and searched for *keratin.*

"The internet says keratin can be found in hair, finger-nails, hooves, claws, feathers, beaks, and quills," Linda said.

"You do chew on your nails," Ken said.

"Ken—I'm not eating hair, I'm not eating nails, and I'm not eating claws."

"Then where are these stones coming from?" Ken pondered. "This is why I wish you'd see a doctor. He could test for a disease."

"Don't you think I know that?" Linda asked. "But what disease would she test for? I've searched the internet, Ken. According to the medical community, there's no such thing as stomach stones."

"You once told me that Lady Sadie was the devil," Ken said.

"I did," Linda said. "But I'm not so sure anymore. Maybe I thought she said that she was."

"What if she gave you a disease," Ken said.

"Huh? How?" Linda asked. "You're making things up, now. Lady Sadie predicted things. She didn't give people diseases."

"How can you be sure?" Ken asked. "I'm wondering if she had an influence on people to make her predictions come true. She said your life would turn out badly if you stayed with me. She could have given you a disease to make her prediction come true. If only we knew how she did it. If only...wait, what was it she used to do? Something with a comb."

"She held a comb and paper up to the light," Linda said.

"A comb, paper, and light," Ken said. "Those are the first clues. A comb is used to comb hair. Now if I can just figure out what the paper and light signify..."

"I think you're over-analyzing things," Linda said. "Lady Sadie used the comb, paper, and light to experience visions. I don't see how this relates to my stomach stones."

"We need to go back," Ken said. "We need to go back to Sadie's Place and search for clues."

"Uh, Ken, don't you remember? Sadie's Place was destroyed by fire," Linda said.

"I know, but maybe there's something left—something that wasn't burned in the fire," Ken said.

"I doubt it," Linda said.

"But it's worth a try," Ken said.

"With fifteen years of weathering?" Linda asked.

"We have to start somewhere," Ken said.

"You can go. I don't want to see Rolling Hills again," Linda said.

"I will go," Ken said. "But I wish you would go with me."

"Why?" Linda asked.

"Because you both lived and worked there. You'd recognize things that I could only guess at," Ken said.

"What do you hope to find, Ken?" Linda asked.

"I wish I knew," Ken replied. "I feel like the answer is in what's left of Sadie's Place, but I'm desperate for some starting place, some clues to get my brain going so I can figure out the next thing. Without a start, I'm at a loss. Please, will you go with me to Sadie's Place?"

Linda paused in thought.

"I promised myself I'd never go back there," Linda said. "Why relive the past?"

"But you relive the past every night when you sleep," Ken said.

"I know," Linda said. "Each year I keep thinking this will be the year I finally quit dreaming about the wolf and quit throwing up stomach stones. And each year disappoints me. But if I go back to Rolling Hills, I risk increasing my nightmares and making my stomach stones intolerable. I don't know if I want to do that."

"But there's also a good chance that by going to Rolling Hills, we'll gather the evidence necessary to figure out what's causing your condition. Don't you see? We could put this curse behind us once and for good," Ken explained.

"*If* I go to Rolling Hills with you," Linda said.

"I knew you would," Ken said.

"Promise something first," Linda continued. "If I go and you find nothing, then promise that I never have to go there again. This will be a one-shot visit. Deal?"

Now it was Ken's turn to pause.

"Deal," he said reluctantly.

The two drove out to Rolling Hills, a town they hadn't visited even once in the fifteen years they'd been together. They pulled into what was left of Kip's gas station and parked. Concrete walls and steel poles were all that remained of Kip's gas station. It had remained abandoned.

"He never rebuilt," Ken said.

"Did you notice all the pubs around here?" Linda asked.

"Yeah, they're everywhere," Ken said.

"But nothing on this corner. Look at what's left of Sadie's Place."

"It's just a gravel area with weeds," Ken said.

"And it's roped off," Linda added, "with signs saying to keep out."

"Looks like smoke is still rising from the old Sadie's Place," Ken said. "Let's take a closer look."

Ken got out of the car, but Linda remained behind.

"Aren't you coming with me?" Ken asked.

"I don't know if I should," Linda said. "The sign says to keep out."

"I think that's to stop loitering. We won't be here long," Ken said.

Linda hesitated.

"Please, Linda, I need your help," Ken said. "Please?"

Linda returned something between a smile and a grimace. She exited Ken's car and accompanied him to what was left of Sadie's Place. Before leaving the grounds of Kip's gas station, Linda stopped, looked back, and stared at a pay telephone.

"What's wrong?" Ken asked.

"That's very strange," Linda said.

"What is?" Ken asked.

"A pay telephone," Linda said. "We are surrounded by destruction yet over there stands a pay telephone."

"So?" Ken asked.

Linda walked to the pay telephone with Ken in tow.

"I don't think a telephone will help us with your condition," Ken said.

"I've just got to see why this telephone is here," Linda said. "Everyone uses cellphones—why the pay telephone?"

"Was it here fifteen years ago?" Ken asked.

"No, it wasn't," Linda said, "which is why I am particularly interested."

Linda and Ken reached the pay telephone, and Linda read aloud:

"'For hotline, dial 311,' is what the label says," Linda said.

"What do you suppose it means?" Ken asked.

"It means something," Linda said. "Otherwise, there's no point in having the telephone here."

"Perhaps it's here in case Lady Sadie comes back as a gray wolf," Ken said.

"Why would a wolf need a telephone?" Linda asked.

"No, I mean...so others can report...you know..." Ken's voice trailed.

Linda stared at Ken with a puzzled expression.

"Never mind. Come along—let's see what we can find in the rubble of Sadie's Place," Ken said.

The two approached the rope along the old Sadie's Place property.

"The sign says there's a coal fire," Linda said. "Ken—this doesn't look safe. Let's get out of here."

"No wait," Ken said. "This will only take a minute."

The two crossed the line and entered the rubble. Steam and smoke rose from various parts of the old Sadie's Place.

"A coal fire," Ken mused. "I never would have expected it. Still, I wish I brought a shovel."

"There's nothing here but gravel and charred remains," Linda said.

Ken kicked through the gravel, sending smoke and dust into the air. Ken coughed.

"Don't inhale it," Linda said.

"Too late," Ken said. "Help me look through this stuff."

"How?" Linda asked.

"Kick through it like this," Ken said, and he kicked the gravel more.

"And look at your shoe," Linda said. "It's black with soot. I'm not getting my shoes dirty like that."

Ken continued kicking at the rubble. The dust cloud grew, and several passing cars slowed to see Ken and Linda in the rubble.

"People see us," Linda said. "Let's leave."

"No, wait," Ken said. "I see something."

Ken reached down and pulled a lobster-red horn from a divot he'd just dug with his shoe. A passerby parked in Kip's old gas station by the telephone, walked to the telephone, and made a call.

"This horn looks like the same material that was in your stomach, except it's red," Ken said. "I'll bet it's made of keratin too."

The person at the telephone made hand gestures and pointed at Linda and Ken.

"Ken," Linda said. "That person over there is pointing at us. I think we're in trouble."

"What we'll have to do is take this horn to a lab and have it tested," Ken said, obsessed with his find.

"I'll have *you* sent to the lab if you don't get going. Come on!" Linda urged.

"Just another minute. I need more samples," Ken said.

Linda rolled her eyes and threw up her arms. Ken took a few more paces and kicked up the gravel.

"There, a large claw," Ken said, reaching for the shrimp-colored claw. "This is a good sample. Now if I can find another sample."

"Found it," Linda said.

"Where?" Ken asked.

"Right there," Linda said as she pointed to a sheriff's car parking alongside the road by the old Sadie's Place. "That's your *sample*."

"Hold it right there," the sheriff said over a bullhorn after exiting his car.

"Quick, let's run for it," Ken said.

"No!" Linda said. "It's too late! The sheriff will shoot us if we run."

"Why did you let me stay here so long?" Ken asked. "You should have told me what was going on."

Linda half choked and said, "I told you to leave, but you wouldn't!"

A deputy sheriff exited the car and walked quickly to Linda and Ken. The deputy pulled Linda away from Ken and held the two apart.

"You're under arrest," the deputy said.

"What for?" Ken asked.

"Trespassing on restricted land," the deputy said. "You have the right to remain silent. Anything you say–"

"Officer, please!" Ken said. "We were just looking for some clues. We meant no harm. We'll leave right now."

"Hold your hands behind your back," the deputy said to Linda.

"Ken!" Linda said as the deputy handcuffed Linda.

"This is completely unnecessary!" Ken said.

"Your hands behind your back!" the deputy said to Ken, but Ken backed away. "Don't resist arrest. It'll only make your case worse."

Ken jumped away and prepared to run, but the deputy tackled him in the dirty gravel, getting Ken's clothes dirty with soot.

"Anything you say can be used against you in a court of law," the deputy continued as he handcuffed Ken. "You have the right to an attorney. If you cannot afford one, the court will appoint one for you."

The deputy pulled Ken to his feet. By this time, the sheriff reached the party and led Linda to the patrol car. The deputy took Ken to the car as well.

"Now sit down and remain calm," the deputy said as Ken and Linda were forced into the back of the patrol car. The back doors were closed and locked. The sheriff and deputy sheriff stood in front of their car and spoke with each other for several minutes.

"Nice work there, Manders!" Linda said to Ken sarcastically. "We could have stayed at home nice and peaceful-like, but no! We had to dig up trouble in Rolling Hills!"

"I didn't mean for this to happen!"

"Sure!" Linda continued with sarcasm.

"I just had to—"

"You just couldn't leave well enough alone," Linda finished.

"I don't know what to say...I don't know what to do," Ken said.

"How about figuring a way out of this mess," Linda suggested.

Ken and Linda sat in silence. The person calling at the pay phone drove away. A van drove up and parked in front of the sheriff's car. The sheriff walked up to the driver's side and spoke with the driver, a driver neither Linda nor Ken could see clearly. The sheriff nodded his head, "yes," and he returned to the patrol car along with the deputy. The van drove off, and the sheriff followed.

"Where are we going?" Ken asked.

Silence.

Linda and Ken watched as the sheriff followed the van around the corner, a short ways down the road, up a hill, and around a right turn into a gravel driveway that meandered along the side of a hill. At the end of the driveway stood a farmhouse. The van stopped as did the sheriff's car behind it. The sheriff and deputy sheriff pulled Linda and Ken from the cruiser and led them to the farmhouse's front porch. The sheriff and deputy undid the handcuffs, and the person driving the van walked to the porch with a large hat obscuring his face.

"We're leaving them in your custody," the sheriff said.

With that, the sheriff and deputy left in their cruiser, leaving Linda and Ken with the stranger.

"Ken, is that you?" the person asked.

"You sound familiar," Ken said. "Who are you?"

The person repositioned the hat to expose his face.

"Marvin!" Ken exclaimed.

"It's been a long time, old friend," Marvin said.

"Fifteen years!" Ken said. "Is this your place?"

"Yes," Marvin said. "You were trespassing on my property."

"You own Sadie's Place?" Linda asked.

"The property," Marvin said. "I bought it shortly after Sadie's Place burned down. I also bought Kip's gas station."

"Boy, I'm glad you're the owner," Ken said. "It's good having friends at the right time."

"How do I know you're a friend?" Marvin asked.

"Huh?" Ken replied. "Come on, we worked together."

"Past tense. I was let go during a round of layoffs," Marvin said.

"For which I'm sorry," Ken said. "But I had nothing to do with it. I hope you don't hold a grudge."

"I still have sour feelings, yes," Marvin said. "So I want to know—why are you trespassing on my land?"

"It's important," Ken said. "We had to find out why Linda's having stomach problems."

Marvin shot Ken a disbelieving look.

"Don't toy with me, Ken," Marvin said.

"It's complicated, Marvin, but Linda used to work at Sadie's Place. Lady Sadie? Did you ever visit her store?"

"No," Marvin said.

"Linda used to work there. And she had an upper apartment in the same building," Ken said. "Linda lost everything in the fire. She's had nightmares since the fire, and she'd had stomach stones."

"That doesn't explain your trespassing," Marvin said.

"I was looking for clues to the past, that's all," Ken said. "I meant no harm to the property."

Marvin stared harshly at Ken.

"You have to believe me," Ken said.

"Marvin," called a female voice through the window. "Was it a bunch of kids again?"

"No, an old co-worker and his friend," Marvin said.

"Why don't you welcome them in?" the voice called back.

Marvin looked at Ken's dirty clothes. A moment later, the female voice entered the front porch.

"This is my wife, Arlene. Arlene, this is my former co-worker, Ken Manders, and his friend—"

"Linda Racquemore," Linda said, offering her hand in friendship.

Arlene hugged Linda and turned to shake Ken's hand, but one look at his soot-covered clothing sent her reeling back.

"On second thought, perhaps you two would like to sit out here," Arlene said. "I'll bring some snacks."

"I'll help you," Linda said.

Arlene and Linda entered the house, leaving Marvin and Ken outside. A tow-truck pulled Ken's car along the driveway up to the house, released the car, and left.

"Is Linda—" Marvin started.

"She's my girlfriend," Ken said.

"Do you—" Marvin started again.

"I've proposed marriage every year for the last fifteen, but she's declined."

"I'm sorry to hear that," Marvin said.

"Look, Marvin, Linda's problems are real. I'm not jerking your chain," Ken said.

"You're not the first people to go tramping through old Sadie's Place," Marvin said. "And I'm sick of it."

"We're not? Who else?" Ken asked.

"I said I'm sick of it," Marvin said.

Arlene and Linda entered the front porch with sandwiches and coffee, placed the food and drink on a table, and beckoned the men to sit down. The four sat and took sandwiches onto plates. The coffee was passed around, and each filled one's coffee mug. Linda took the first sip, and her face scrunched up in disgust.

"How do you like the coffee?" Marvin asked.

"It has a different taste," Linda managed.

Ken took a sip and spat it on the ground.

"Yuck! What is this?" Ken asked.

"Ken!" Linda said sternly.

"Don't apologize," Arlene said. "We know the coffee is bad."

"You do?" Ken asked.

"Yes," Marvin said. "Oh no, not again."

The four watched a semi-truck trailer travel down the driveway to the barn where it backed its trailer up a ramp to the barn's second level.

"Arlene," Marvin said. "We have another reject."

"That's the third one this week," Arlene said.

"Reject?" Ken asked.

"What's the matter?" Linda asked.

"It's the coffee truck," Arlene said.

"You drink that much coffee?" Ken asked.

"What do you mean?" Marvin asked back.

"You buy your coffee in bulk," Ken said.

Marvin and Arlene exchanged puzzled expressions.

"I'd get my money back if I were you," Ken said. "Buy your coffee from the grocery store. The store beans are much better."

"No, you don't understand," Arlene said. "The truck is returning coffee beans, not delivering."

"Huh?" Ken asked.

"You have a coffee farm?" Linda asked.

"Yes," Arlene said. "At least we try to. And you've tasted a product of our farm. But our coffee beans are the worst ever."

"I don't understand why," Marvin said. "We've done everything to ensure the best possible product."

"What do you think it tastes like, Linda?" Arlene asked.

"I don't mean to be rude," Linda said, "but it tastes like something spoiled."

"Don't worry about offending us," Arlene said. "Every truck return is more than enough to offend us."

"I just don't understand," Marvin said. "No matter how hard we try to refine our coffee beans, they develop a foul taste."

"Look, Marvin, I'm sorry about your crops. But Linda and I have more important things to figure out—her nightmares, her stomach stones, and the artifacts I found at old Sadie's Place."

"Kenneth!" Linda said. "I apologize for Ken's behavior. He and I are going to have a long talk about manners when we get home."

"Oh, I don't care about your silly treasure hunt," Marvin said. "Old Sadie's Place is cursed with an underground coal fire, the ground below the old gas station is poisoned with fuel from leaky tanks, and my farm is cursed with foul coffee. Arlene, it's high time we pack up and—"

"No," Arlene said. "This was my great-grandmother's farm, and I vowed to keep it in the family."

"But it can't be farmed. It's worthless, as is all the land in Rolling Hills."

"I won't let my family land pass into the hands of strangers!" Arlene said.

"I'm sorry we intruded," Linda said. "Ken, it's time we leave."

"No, don't go yet," Arlene said.

"Let them go, Arlene," Marvin said.

"Not until I show something to Linda," Arlene said.

"Don't tell me you're going to show her that old well?" Marvin said.

"What do men know of such things? C'mon, Linda. We'll take the all-terrain vehicle," Arlene said.

Ken looked at Linda.

"It's okay, I'll be fine," Linda said. "Why don't you stay here and share bean stories with Marvin?"

Arlene laughed. Marvin and Ken looked disappointed.

"I like your sense of humor," Arlene said as the two traveled along a gravel path in the all-terrain vehicle. "I wish we'd met sooner."

"I used to have a greater sense of humor, but spending time with Ken has drained it out of me," Linda said.

Arlene laughed again. Linda told more jokes and Arlene laughed until she was blue in the face.

"You'll have to visit more often—without Ken!" Arlene said, but Linda's facial expression suggested otherwise.

"I..." Linda started.

"You love him, don't you?" Arlene asked.

"Yes," Linda said.

"It's hard to part with people we love. It's also hard to part with things we love. That's why I won't let Marvin sell this farm. It's also why I won't let him seal off the well."

"Why is the well special?" Linda asked.

"I'll show you," Arlene said.

Arlene parked the all-terrain vehicle by a shed on a little hill next to a water tower. Linda looked down the hill a bit and saw a creek.

"That creek," Linda started.

"It runs by our farm and down the hills close to the old Sadie Place," Arlene said. "We can explore that later if you like, Linda, but for now I have something to show you. Follow me."

Linda followed Arlene into the shed but left the door open. The sun shone through the doorway and scattered light throughout the shed.

"I don't understand," Linda said. "The shed is empty."

"I'm going to close the door," Arlene said.

"What?"

"Don't be afraid," Arlene said. "But I must close the door so that you may see the well as it should be seen."

"Okay," Linda said.

Arlene closed the door. The shed was dark, but not as pitch black as Linda remembered from the old copper mines in Upper Peninsula Michigan. Bits of light seeped between boards in the shed's walls.

"Don't be afraid," Arlene said. "You will hear a sound. It's only a curtain being lifted to expose the well."

The sound of a lifting curtain reverberated from the back of the shed.

"Almost ready," Arlene said. "Just one more thing to do."

Arlene pulled a rope, and the rope pulled a small plank of wood from an opening high in the shed's wall. A stream of sunlight poured through the hole and spilled onto a stone-crafted well in the back of the shed—a well that was hidden behind the now-raised curtain. The light scattered enough into the shed so that Linda could see Arlene but not enough to let Linda see the other parts of the shed's interior.

"A well on a hill?" Linda asked. "How?"

"Strange forces are at work," Arlene said. "Underground pressure fills the well with water. Come."

Arlene took Linda's hand and led her to the stonework of the well itself.

"It's beautiful, and yet there's no mortar," Linda said.

"Each stone is hand-crafted to fit with the surrounding stones. My great-grandmother insisted there be no lime in the mason work. In case you're wondering, lime is used in mortar. Linda—the well is a composition of the women in my past— the women who as my ancestors worked this farm and gave it life," Arlene explained. "Look away from the well."

Linda looked.

"I can see nothing, except—"

"Except thousands of points of light," Arlene said. "Those lights are from holes in the shed's walls, holes that allow bits of sunlight in. Move your eyes back and forth quickly, Linda."

Linda looked around at the different lights quickly.

"They look like stars, like the universe in the beginning of time," Linda said. "I feel like there's a large open space around us, dark, but still very large. And yet I also feel like we're the only two people in existence."

"But we're not," Arlene said. "I'll prove it."

Arlene cranked a handle at the well, and a rope pulled up a bucket of water. Arlene placed the bucket on the side of the well wall. Walking to the far side of the well wall, Arlene produced a small cup. She returned with the cup, dipped it into the bucket's water, pulled the cup out, and tossed the water from the cup into the air. The water vaporized. The vapor became luminescent, swirled, and formed the shape of a woman with puffy, curly hair wearing polyester and thick, high-soled shoes.

"This is my mother when she was eighteen years old," Arlene said.

"How is this possible?" Linda asked. "Am I dreaming?"

"No, you're not dreaming," Arlene said.

"Is the water full of LSD?" Linda asked.

"No, it isn't," Arlene said. "Allow me to explain. When my mother was eighteen, she carved this cup from an old tusk. My family had a collection of such tusks purchased from my great-grandmother's sister's store before the store was destroyed. But back to the cup—my mother drank water from the cup, and when she did, her cells imprinted themselves on the cup. So today when I throw water into the air from this cup, it extrapolates from that imprint and shows an image of her."

"But water doesn't do that," Linda said.

"This isn't just any kind of water," Arlene said. "There's something in the water that makes it do this. It's like a strange sort of projection mechanism or something. I've never had it analyzed; I don't want to, because I don't want the world to know my family's secret."

"Wow!" Linda said.

"Yeah, wow!" Arlene repeated.

The image of Arlene's mother faded from view. Arlene returned the cup to a spot on the far side of the well wall (obscured from Linda's view) and produced another cup from a similar location. She dipped the cup into the bucket's water and repeated the action as before—throwing water from the cup into the air. The water vaporized as before, but the vapor luminesced into the image of a young woman wearing a fitted blazer and a narrow skirt indicative of the early 1950s.

"That's my grandmother," Arlene said. "She also made a cup from a tusk and drank from the cup. This image is what she looked like when she did."

"She's very beautiful," Linda said. "I can see the family resemblance with her, your mother, and you."

The image faded.

"There's more," Arlene said.

Arlene returned the cup and produced another cup, repeated the water dipping and tossing action, and another luminescent image formed.

"This is my great-grandmother," Arlene explained as Linda stared at the young woman in a 1920s outfit.

"This may sound strange," Linda said.

"Go ahead," Arlene urged. "We're in an unusual place."

"Yeah, tell me about it. But when I look at these women, I feel like I'm looking at you wearing different outfits."

"It's interesting that you should say that, because that's how I feel too," Arlene explained.

"Huh? Are you saying you are all these women? Are you a hundred years old?" Linda asked.

"No, I'm in my thirties," Arlene said. "But I feel very close to my maternal ancestors to the point where I believe I can think and feel as they did. I am like them, yes, and in a way, I am them."

"How many other cups are there?"

"There are two more," Arlene said. "One of me, and one of my great-grandmother's sister."

Arlene produced her own cup, dipped it in the bucket's water, and tossed the water into the air. The resulting vapor luminesced into a young image of Arlene wearing a prom dress.

"Very cute," Linda said. "What about the last cup?"

Arlene hesitated.

"Is there something wrong?" Linda asked.

"Yes," Arlene said. "There is."

"What is it? You can tell me," Linda said.

Arlene returned the cup of herself and produced the cup of her great-grandmother's sister.

"Okay," Arlene said. "First, let me explain something. Each cup that I've shown you was carved by a woman in my family during a particularly happy time in her life. But this last cup— the cup of my great-grandmother's sister—it was not carved by her."

"What do you mean?" Linda asked.

"My great-grandmother actually carved it," Arlene explained.

"I don't understand," Linda said.

"Can you be strong for me, Linda?" Arlene asked. "Only my great-grandmother has dipped this cup into water and tossed the water in the air. My grandmother, my mother, and I—none of us had the courage to do the same."

"I'm confused. Your great-grandmother made this cup, but you say it belongs to your great-grandmother's sister? Did your great-grandmother's sister drink from the cup to make it hers?"

Arlene did not answer.

"Hold my hand," Arlene said. "This is the first time I've done this, and I hope you'll be strong with me."

"But my question—"

"Will be answered in a moment," Arlene said. "Hold my hand."

Linda held her hands to one of Arlene's.

"Okay, I'm ready," Linda said.

With her free hand, Arlene dipped the cup into the bucket's water. She pulled the cup out and held it for a moment. Arlene breathed deeply as if preparing to jump into the icy waters of a pond. Then Arlene counted.

"One, two, three!"

Arlene tossed the water and the cup into the air. The water vaporized. The cup landed across the shed with a clatter. The vapor luminesced slowly, first into the vague shape of a timber wolf, then it settled along the ground into the shape of a hairless woman lying in a casket. Arlene screamed. Linda hugged Arlene tightly and reassured her she was going to be all right.

"Death, death!" Arlene quivered.

"It happened a long time ago," Linda reassured Arlene. "It's over."

Arlene shook like a leaf wet with cold.

"I have feared this moment my entire life," Arlene said. "It frightens me more than the thought of Marvin selling the farm. But I must confront these dark fears of mine. I must. Linda— help me walk around my great-grandmother's sister. Help me see her in her final moments of life so that I may appreciate the value of my own life."

Linda led Arlene to the image of the sister. The poor woman was bald, had no eyebrows, no eyelashes, and had a gaunt appearance. Bad makeup covered up hastily stitched-up wounds on the dead woman's disfigured face, and the woman's chest was caved in. The sight was terrifying, but nothing prepared Linda for what happened next. Arlene stood next to the woman's side, slid her arms under the woman's torso, and lifted the woman to a sitting position. Arlene made motions around the woman's head, and the woman regained her hair, her eye-brows, and eyelashes. Her disfigured face became smooth and uniform. Linda's initial shock in Arlene's ability to interact with the image was displaced with a new horror—the face of the dead woman was now identifiable and none other than Sadella Sarvak—Lady Sadie.

"Sadella," Arlene whispered.

Linda's stomach bloated with fluid, and an uncontrollable urge to vomit overcame Linda, sending a gushing line of coffee and partially-digested sandwich onto the image of Sadella Sarvak. The image came to life! Sadella jumped up, shrieked with menacing fingers outstretched like claws toward Linda, transformed into a timber wolf, and leapt at Linda. Linda ran, burst through the shed door, and crouched behind the all-terrain vehicle.

"What am I doing?!" Linda asked herself. "I left Arlene inside!"

Linda rushed back to the shed's door opening and stood there. The beaming sunlight shone through the doorway and scattered light everywhere, much as it had when the two first entered the shed. Linda saw Arlene standing by the empty spot where Sadella's casket once rested.

"It's over," Arlene said with a somber voice.

"Th-th-that wa-wa-was Lady Sadie!" Linda stuttered.

"I know," Arlene said. "I know."

"I worked for her. Arlene, did you know?! Did you know who she was?" Linda asked.

"I know who and what she was, and I know what created her," Arlene said. "And I have kept the secret to myself all these years. Only my mother and grandmother know. My great-grandmother also knew, but her part of the secret died with her."

"This is tripping me out," Linda said. "I don't know what to do, what to say, or what to think."

"If I thought you couldn't handle it, I wouldn't have asked you to experience Sadella's cup with me. I've only known you personally for a little while, but I feel like I've known you for years," Arlene explained. "Do you understand?"

"I need time. I need rest. I need something," Linda said.

"I know why Ken brought you to the old Sadie's Place. And I know what you've been going through."

"How can you know?" Linda asked.

"Because of this," Arlene said, and she showed Linda a small, rounded, fingernail-colored, hoof-like material covered in bits of blood.

"Where did you get that? It looks like—"

"Like a stomach stone, even if there is no such thing. You threw it up just now, did you forget? You also ran out of the shed, and when you did, I found the stone on the floor in the middle of your vomit. I don't mean to gross you out, but I know about these stomach stones."

"How can you know?" Linda asked.

"You are not the first woman to have these," Arlene said.

"You're joking," Linda said.

"No, I'm not," Arlene continued. "Every woman who received a reading from Lady Sadie has returned to the old Sadie Place in search of answers. I talked with the first half-dozen, but Marvin got sick of the attention and had the pay phone installed. He offered a hundred dollars to anyone reporting trespassing on old Sadie's Place, and that scared the rest of them off. But I did learn about the first few women. They threw up stomach stones, like you. I had them analyzed. They were all made chitin."

"What?" Linda asked. "What did you say they were made of?"

"Chitin," Arlene said. "It's usually found in shells of seafood like lobster and shrimp. But for some reason, these women threw up stomach stones made of chitin."

"Arlene," Linda said. "This chitin—is it also in hair?"

"Hair? No," Arlene said.

"What about fingernails? Claws? Beaks?" Linda asked with nervous anxiety.

"No, not at all," Arlene said.

"Test that stone in your hand," Linda said. "Test it."

"I'll have to send it to a lab," Arlene said.

"Do it. It's not chitin," Linda said.

"It must be," Arlene said. "Every woman who visited had thrown up chitin stones."

"And Ken says I throw up stones made of keratin," Linda said.

"That's impossible," Arlene said.

"Having stomach stones is impossible," Linda said. "But now I find out that not only do I have them, but so do other women."

"You don't understand, Linda," Arlene explained. "Those women threw up chitin stones because they are tied to old Sadie's Place. Obviously you are too."

"Then why are my stones made of keratin?" Linda asked.

"They can't be," Arlene said.

"They are," Linda insisted.

"Linda—the reason they must be made of chitin is because old Sadie's Place—the grounds—it's full of chitin artifacts. Chitin, Linda, chitin."

"Huh? So those samples Ken took from the gravel—"

"If he sends those to a lab, they'll tell him what I'm telling you—they're made of chitin," Arlene said.

"How?" Linda asked. "How is this possible?"

"You don't know the history of Sadella, do you?" Arlene asked.

"Ken said she was mistakenly shot by a hunter," Linda said. "But what does that have to do with anything?"

"She had a house on the very plot where old Sadie's Place used to be. She sold hunting equipment," Arlene said.

"I don't believe it," Linda said. "She was killed by a hunter, yet she sold hunting equipment?"

"I didn't make up history, I only report it," Arlene said. "Some of the hunters couldn't afford to pay for equipment, so they bartered with her. They gave her fresh kill in exchange for supplies. Sadella sold the meat but opened up a little tanning business next to her house, and I don't mean sun-tanning business. It was a tannery to process the hides into leather."

"Kip's gas station?" Linda asked.

"You're very perceptive," Arlene said. "Kip's gas station is built on top of what's left of the old tannery."

"It doesn't surprise me," Linda said. "The ground always stank like something died."

Arlene smiled.

"You never did explain about Sadella's cup," Linda said.

"My great-grandmother poured water into Sadella's mouth at Sadella's funeral," Arlene said.

"Yuck," Linda said. "That's ghastly."

"I know, but my great-grandmother wanted to preserve her essence. The two were very close, and it hurt my great-grandmother deeply when Sadella died," Arlene said.

"What happened to Sadella's house?" Linda asked.

"Sadella's house sank into the earth shortly after her death," Arlene said.

"What?" Linda asked.

"Workers tried digging it up, but the wooden beams had disintegrated. All that was left were the old horns and hooves from the animals that had been processed for their hides, but get this—they had turned into chitin. Chitin, Linda—the same material as the stomach stones from those women who visited old Sadie's Place. That's how I know that your stomach stones must be made of chitin. The lab Ken used must have made a mistake."

"Will you at least test my stomach stone?" Linda asked.

"I will. I promise," Arlene said. "Now I have something special for you."

Arlene disappeared into the shed and reappeared with a small bottle.

"What's that?" Linda asked.

"This is a bottle of well water," Arlene said. "Take one tablespoonful in the evening before going to bed. You may throw up stones for the first few days, and you'll pass a clear, slimy material. After ten days, your stomach stones and your nightmares will be gone."

"From well water?" Linda asked.

"It's a proven treatment," Arlene said. "I have given a bottle of well water to each of Sadie's women with stomach stones. They have all recovered, some in as few as six days, and the longest was ten."

"I don't believe it," Linda said. "Well water can't cure such things."

"Fortunately, science does not require belief to be effective," Arlene said.

"This is scientific?"

"Something in the water cures," Arlene said. "You do know that in the days before pills, natural remedies were used."

"Yes, but—"

"Certain ground waters contain minerals and other helpful things that cure," Arlene said. "They are largely forgotten because they tend to be less powerful than antibiotics. But antibiotics won't cure everything, and in this case, well water must do."

Linda opened the bottle and sniffed. She jumped back.

"Is it safe?" Linda asked.

"Yes," Arlene said. "Here, look."

Arlene poured a little of the water into her mouth.

"See?"

"And you won't be sick?" Linda asked.

"Not in the least. And, you won't need the entire bottle. But I provide more than enough to be safe," Arlene said.

"If this works, I'll be truly in your debt," Linda said.

"Don't worry about it," Arlene said. "I like to think of myself as the keeper of this farm and helper to those injured by this or nearby land."

Linda paused. She stared at the bottle and swirled the water inside. She placed the cap back on and spoke.

"Thank you," Linda said. "I want to thank you for everything. It's time I return home. This excitement has worn me out. I could use a good rest."

"I understand," Arlene said.

Arlene and Linda rode the all-terrain vehicle back to the house. Ken and Marvin had been drinking beer and were now singing songs together, albeit badly.

"C'mon Ken, it's time to go home," Linda said.

"So soon? The party's just starting," Ken said, who had obviously had too many to drink.

"That means I'm driving. Thank you again, Arlene. And you too, Marvin."

Marvin tipped his hat to Linda. Linda led Ken to the car, positioned him in the passenger seat, and drove the car home.

Linda wasn't happy with Ken's inebriation. Ken sang various songs on the way home, and Linda cringed at every bad note. When the two reached home, Ken let out a particularly bad note, and Linda roared loudly at him. Ken was taken a-back, and he ceased singing. The two spent the rest of the day in silence. After dinner, Ken attempted to apologize to Linda, but the smell of alcohol on Ken's breath annoyed Linda, and she scratched his face with her fingernails.

The two spent the night apart.

Sunday, a Week Later

Ken woke at six hours after midnight. He felt badly about his prior-week's behavior and decided to atone himself by preparing the morning's coffee.

"I wonder if I should go so far as to prepare a full breakfast," Ken mused. "No, I'll start by holding a fresh cup of coffee in front of Linda's nose. It'll be a wonderful way to wake her."

Ken carried a cup of coffee into the bedroom, but the bed was made, and Linda was not there.

"Linda?" Ken called.

No answer. Ken checked the bathroom. No Linda. Ken checked the driveway. Both cars there.

"Linda?" Ken called throughout the house.

No Linda. Ken picked up his cellphone and prepared to dial 911. The back door opened and slammed shut. Ken dropped the cellphone and rushed to the back door.

"Linda!" Ken said.

Linda's hair was unkept, her shirt and pants slightly ripped, and she wore no shoes.

"Linda, what happened?" Ken asked.

Linda didn't respond. She walked into the bathroom, pulled a pair of fingernail clippers from the medicine cabinet, sat on the toilet seat, and attempted to clip her fingernails. The clippers broke; the nails remained unaltered.

"Linda!" Ken said. "What's going on?"

Linda stood up from the toilet, walked with deliberate intent to the refrigerator, opened the door, pulled out a can of beer, held it over the sink, and slashed open the side with a fingernail. Beer spilled into the sink.

"What are you doing?" Ken asked. "You'll cut yourself."

But Linda's tissues remained uninjured. She repeated her act of fingernail slicing with each and every remaining can of beer until all were emptied into the sink. She turned on the tap, rinsed the cans, turned off the tap, and threw the cans into the recycling bin.

"Linda, snap out of it!" Ken said.

Ken shook Linda by the shoulders, but she turned quickly, roared at Ken, sliced the shoulder part of his shirt open (along with a bit of Ken's shoulder skin), turned back around, and reclined on the couch. She fell into a sleep for two minutes, awoke, and spoke.

"Oh, I must have dozed off," Linda said. "What time is it?"

"It's seven in the morning," Ken said.

"You mean seven in the evening," Linda said. "I just closed my eyes for a moment."

"No, Linda, it's Sunday morning. What the hell is going on?" Ken asked.

"What?"

"Are you out of it or something? Where were you all night? Why did you slice open my beer? And why are you roaring at me?" Ken asked.

"I don't know what you're talking about," Linda said. "Why is your shirt ripped? Why are you bleeding? What happened to my clothes?"

Ken stared at Linda, speechless.

"Ken? What's going on?" Linda asked.

"You really don't remember?"

"No, I don't," Linda said.

"Go look at yourself in the mirror," Ken said.

Linda left the living room and returned a moment later.

"What's happening to me?" Linda asked. "Ken?"

"I don't know," Ken said. "I think you were sleepwalking. But you did things that no one could do. Your fingernails—they're like stainless-steel knives."

"My nails?"

"Yes. You broke your nail clippers," Ken said. "Didn't you see them on the bathroom floor?"

"Yeah. I don't understand how they got there."

"Like I said, you broke them. And look in the recycling bin," Ken said.

Linda opened the recycling bin and saw the sliced cans of beer.

"You did that with your nails," Ken said.

"That's impossible," Linda said.

Ken disappeared briefly to the bathroom and returned with fingernail scissors.

"Here," Ken said. "Try cutting your nails with these."

Linda took the scissors, applied them to a fingernail, and broke the scissors.

"The scissors...they broke! And my nail...it's unchanged," Linda said. "What's happening to me? Oh Ken!"

Linda rushed to Ken and hugged him, but her grip caused Ken to exhale abruptly with an, "ugh!"

"What's wrong?" Linda asked.

"You squeezed me hard," Ken said.

"I just gave you a little hug," Linda said.

"That was a bear hug!" Ken said.

Linda held out her arms. They seemed normal-looking.

"You've suddenly gotten much stronger," Ken said. "Try something. Take a can of beans and crush it."

"Let me get my shoes," Linda said.

"No," Ken said. "Don't step on it. Crush it with your hands."

"I can't do that," Linda said.

"Try it," Ken said.

Linda stared at Ken with a confused face. Ken pulled a can of beans from the cupboard and handed it to Linda.

"Crush it," Ken said.

Linda held the can and inspected it as if it were fake. She thumped it, and it sounded like a real, metal can.

"What's the trick?" Linda asked.

"No trick. Crush it," Ken repeated.

Linda held the can between her two hands. She took a deep breath.

"You don't have to be dramatic," Ken said. "Just crush it."

"I want to psyche myself up for this," Linda said.

"It's not necessary," Ken said. "Just—"

"Don't tell me how to crush a can!" Linda said, and in a moment of anger, she drove the can into the countertop with the palm of her hand.

The can collapsed like a water balloon and spilled beans and water in all side directions. Linda lifted her hand and revealed what was left of the can—a flat, steel disk now thinner than a jar lid. Linda looked at her hand and expected it to be cut and bloodied from the metal. It was wet from the water but otherwise unchanged. No cuts. No blood. Linda looked at Ken in shock. Ken lifted the steel disk and revealed an indentation of the can in the countertop.

"Am I going to die?" Linda asked.

"Now relax, sweedie," Ken said. "I'm sure there's an explanation somewhere."

"The explanation is obvious—some people develop superhuman strength just before they die. It's like the light bulb suddenly burning very brightly before burning out," Linda explained, and she fell into tears.

"Now, now," Ken said as he hugged her. "Don't cry."

Ken lifted a finger to Linda's face. A tear dripped on his finger. A few seconds passed, and Ken withdrew his finger abruptly and howled in pain.

"What's the matter?!" Linda asked.

Ken rushed to the kitchen sink and slapped on the faucet with cold water. He held his injured finger under the tap, and the water washed away the caustic tear. After a minute of rinsing, Ken turned off the water and held his finger in the air. The tear had eaten away the upper layers of Ken's skin, revealing bright-red tissue which now bled profusely. Linda brought a bandage and dressed Ken's wound, but she bound it too tightly, and Ken wrenched away in pain. He readjusted the bandage and let out a sigh of relief.

"I'm sorry, I'm sorry, I'm sorry!" Linda said, and she jumped up and down in nervousness.

The house shook, the windows rattled, and Ken developed an impending feeling of structural collapse—from the house!

"Don't jump," Ken said. "Don't bandage my wound, don't cry, and don't slam anything against the counter. Breathe in but don't exhale too hard. Relax. Good. Now then, let's sit down in the living room—you on the couch, and me in the armchair."

The two sat as Ken described.

"Good," Ken said. "Rest and relax. We are calm and collected people."

"Am I cursed?" Linda asked.

Ken scratched his head.

"Well?"

Linda's cellphone rang. She jumped up to answer it but tore a hole in the couch.

"Let me answer that," Ken said. "Just sit and relax."

Ken answered the cellphone.

"Hello? Hi, Arlene. Yes, she's here. One moment," Ken said.

Ken handed the cellphone to Linda, and as he did he said:

"Be gentle with the phone. Don't break it."

Linda gingerly held the cellphone to her ear.

"Hello, Arlene. Yes. Yes. I told you it was made of keratin. I know, you wouldn't believe me. Now you do. I don't know, it just is. Yes, I've been taking a tablespoonful each night before bed. Yes, about a week now. No, I still throw up stones. Arlene, are there any side effects from the water? Besides that. And that. Any other side effects? I see. No, nothing strange, other than slicing open beer cans and crushing a can of beans. No, I'm not joking. Yes, very serious. He's shocked, like I am. Did any of the other women...none of them? I see. I don't know what to do next. Really? I'll tell him. Okay. Okay. Okay, I will. See you soon. Bye."

Linda handed her cellphone to Ken, and Ken ensured the call ended.

"No damage," Ken said.

"Ken!" Linda said.

"Sorry," Ken said.

"You may not know this, but when we visited Arlene and Marvin a week ago, I threw up," Linda said.

"Why didn't you tell me at the time?" Ken asked.

"You were drunk, but that's not important," Linda said. "What is important is that I threw up a stomach stone. It was made of keratin."

"Yeah, I established that fact—your stomach stones are made of keratin," Ken said.

"What you don't know is that Arlene thought my stones were made of chitin," Linda said.

"Huh?"

"The exoskeletons of lobsters and shrimp," Linda said.

"Why would she think that?" Ken asked.

"Because that's what all the other women threw up," Linda replied.

"What other women?"

Linda explained to Ken everything Arlene told and showed her, including the visions at the well.

"Ordinarily, I wouldn't believe you," Ken said. "But given what's happened today, I'll believe anything. And this water is supposed to cure you? Is it working?"

"No, it isn't," Linda said. "I don't understand. Nothing makes sense. The other women threw up chitin stones, but I throw up keratin stones. I'm the only one. Why me? Why?"

"I don't know. According to the lab, the claw and horn I found at the old Sadie's Place were also made of chitin. Linda—Arlene said Sadella had hooves and horns from animals on her property before she died, but after her house sank in the ground, the hooves and horns changed into chitin."

"What do you mean, *changed into chitin*?" Linda asked.

"Hooves and horns are made of keratin—just like your stomach stones," Ken said.

"Then I am connected to Sadella's life," Linda said.

"And the women Lady Sadie read to are connected to her death," Ken said.

"But they were cured," Linda said.

"And you're not," Ken said. "Linda, I think there's only one conclusion we can draw here—there is a living connection between you and Sadella Sarvak."

"Lady Sadie?" Linda asked.

"We don't know who or what Lady Sadie was," Ken said.

"She was Sadella Sarvak," Linda said.

"But Sadella died," Ken said. "Sadella sold hunting equipment and ran a tannery company. Lady Sadie did none of those. People don't die and come back to life."

"Then how do you explain it?" Linda asked.

"I can't," Ken said.

Linda became frustrated and swatted her hand against the side arm of the couch. The side arm broke off. After a minute of silence, Ken spoke.

"What did Arlene say on the phone?" Ken asked.

"She said we should come over to her place for a visit. She thinks she can help," Linda said.

"I don't know how," Ken said. "If I can just do a little more research on the internet—"

"Forget it," Linda said. "We're way past the internet now."

"All right then. Let's go to Marvin's," Ken said.

"To Arlene's," Linda corrected.

The two drove from Riverton to Rolling Hills, past Kip's old gas station, up the hill, and into the driveway of Arlene and Marvin's farm. The two parked, and Arlene welcomed them at the front door.

"Please, come in," Arlene said, and she led them to a side room with a table and three chairs.

"Where's Marvin?" Ken asked.

"He's helping a neighbor repair damage to a vandalized micro-brewery," Arlene said. "It will be just the three of us. Would you two like something to drink? Coffee?"

"No thank you," Linda said.

Arlene smiled.

"Someday I hope you will happily drink our coffee," Arlene said.

"I do too," Linda said. "I love coffee and can tolerate most bad coffee, but...well...I hope you sort out your coffee problems."

"Tell us more about this Sadella Sarvak," Ken said.

"I thought you might ask," Arlene said. "But I'm more concerned with Linda's health. She has some very unusual symptoms."

"Yes, that can wait," Ken said.

Linda slapped Ken, sending him out of his chair and across the room. He stood up slowly with a welt developing on his upper arm.

"It's begun already," Arlene said. "Linda—I'm afraid you must stop drinking the well water. It has started something I didn't think possible."

"What did it start?" Linda asked.

"Yes," Ken said, now grimacing from his new-found injury. "Tell us."

"I think the best way to explore Linda's condition is to...well, wait here a moment," Arlene said.

Arlene left and returned with a shallow, wide bowl of water and placed it in the center of the table. She exited the room and returned holding a wide-based alcohol lamp with a glass chimney. She placed the lamp in the center of the shallow bowl of water and lit it.

"The lamp is lit, but you can't see the flame. It's dark blue," Arlene explained. "Now for some music."

Arlene turned on a compact-disc player with music, like that of a distant church's chime music echoing along mountains and through valleys.

"It's beautiful," Linda said.

"Now I'm going to close the curtains and dim the lights," Arlene said.

"Why?" Ken asked.

"To set a proper mood for the séance," Arlene said.

"What?!" Ken asked.

"Ken, be good and don't be a party poop," Linda said.

"I thought you were going to tell us about Sadella," Ken said.

"I am, but I need to do better than tell you. I need to show you," Arlene said.

"No," Ken said.

"Yes," Linda said. "This is important. Ken, you're doing this," Linda said as she moved her hand to mimic Ken's moving jaw and lips, "but you should be doing this," she continued as she held her hand still.

Ken stopped talking.

"I want you to touch hands with each other and hold them in the water," Arlene directed, "but be careful not to push the bowl or tip the lantern."

Arlene placed her hands in the water at the edge of the bowl, touching her thumbs together. She extended the edge of her left hand to Linda and her right to Ken. Gingerly, Linda positioned her hands like Arlene with her thumbs together, her fingers in the water, and her right pinky to Arlene's left pinky. Using her eyes and facial expressions, Linda motioned for Ken to do the same. Ken feigned a protest by opening his mouth briefly, but Linda silenced him into submission with another facial expression. Ken complied with his hands in the water touching Linda's and Arlene's.

"We are three people," Arlene said in a soothing voice, "three people without care or concern, three full of love and compassion for each other and for life. We love life in all its forms and aspirations, for life is love, and we as life are full of love. The water we touch is a record of life, life of the past, the present, and the future. The flame in the middle is the spark in each of us, the fire of passion that brings life from the earth. Look into the flame, deep, deep, deep into the dark blue flame. Now sense the water. Feel the ripples, the rolling ripples of water like rolling hills on a farm, this farm, in Rolling Hills."

Arlene hummed a tune in harmony with the chime music. The glass chimney vibrated slightly, sending air disturbances into the alcohol flame. The vibrations also carried through the glass chimney to the lamp's base, into the water, and through the fingertips of Arlene, Linda, and Ken. To the three, the glass chimney seemed to grow quickly to the size of a tree while the roof and walls of the room fell away, revealing an outdoor grassy lawn next to a cornfield. The three stood together in a small circle holding each other's hands. Ken tried pulling away so he could stand next to Linda.

"Do not break the link!" Arlene said. "Maintain the circle."

Close-by in a sandbox sat a little girl making sand castles.

"This is my grandmother," Arlene said. "Grandma Nellie."

A deer stepped partway out of the cornfield and stared at Nellie. Nellie turned and gasped.

"Look at the deer," Linda said, but Ken's back was to the animal.

"Where?" Ken said as he turned to look.

But in turning to look, he pulled his hands away from Arlene and Linda.

"No, Ken!" Linda said.

The link broke, and the three returned to Arlene's farmhouse room.

"Arlene told you not to break the link!" Linda said to Ken.

"I couldn't see the deer," Ken said.

"Tough," Linda said.

"The séance is for Linda's benefit," Arlene said.

"But I want to see too. I can't see if my back is to whatever Linda is looking at," Ken said.

"Then we will hold a cross-handed séance," Arlene said.

"A what?" Ken asked.

"I've heard of those," Linda said. "But for it to work, only two people cross their hands—not the entire circle."

"You are correct, Linda," Arlene said. "The two ends of the circle will cross their hands."

"There's no such thing as the end of a circle, much less two ends of a circle," Ken said.

"A skeptic," Arlene said. "Ordinarily I do not permit skeptics to participate in my séances. However, even this vision cannot be soured by the negativity of a skeptic. Ken—cross your hands such that your left hand goes to Linda on your right, and your right hand goes to me on your left. I will do the same. Linda—do not cross your hands. You will be the middle of the circle."

"Again, this makes no sense," Ken said. "The center of a circle is not the circle itself."

"Just do it, Ken," Linda said. "You'll see how this works in a moment."

As before, Linda sat to Arlene's left, and Ken sat to Arlene's right. Arlene held her right hand to Linda's right and her left hand across her body onto Ken's right hand.

"This is awkward," Ken said.

"Shh," Linda said. "Take my left hand with your left."

Ken did as instructed.

"While maintaining the circle, we will now hold our hands in the water," Arlene said. "Concentrate on the blue flame, and sense the ripples in the water. We recall the happiness of our youths, when the fresh breeze of spring soothes away all frostbite of winter and renews hope for a happy summer."

The lamp's glass chimney rose like before. The walls did not fall away but instead expanded away such that the three now appeared in the dining room of the farmhouse instead of a side room. Two women sat at the dining room table with an alcohol lamp in a bowl of water—the very same lamp and bowl Arlene had placed on the little round table for Linda and Ken. Arlene, Linda, and Ken faced each other in a small circle with

Arlene's and Ken's hands still crossed. Ken's back was to the dining-room table.

"Like before, I can't see what you two are looking at," Ken said.

"Ken," Arlene said, "lift your right hand with my left over Linda's head and behind her back. Do this carefully and without breaking the circle."

Ken followed Arlene's instructions, and as the two lifted their arms over Linda's head, Ken stood to Linda's left and Arlene to Linda's right with Ken's right arm and Arlene's left arm connecting behind Linda's back. The three were now facing the same direction.

"Concentrate on the blue flame," said one woman at the table.

"Who is she?" Linda asked. "The one holding the séance, that is."

"That's my great-grandmother," Arlene said. "Her name is Barbara. I don't know the other woman. But Barbara gave readings to visitors during the depression to help keep the farm going."

"What's this got to do with—" Ken started.

"Shhh," Linda said.

"Doris," Barbara said, "I see difficult times ahead for you and your family. Your crops will not be enough to last you through the winter. Your family will be hungry, very hungry."

"This is terrible news," Doris said. "What can I do?"

"Your husband will begin hunting, but not for food. It will disgust you, but you must be strong," Barbara said. "Be strong, Doris. You will be driven to extreme measures, to the point of convincing Donald to bring the dead animals home to gut and cook them."

"Never!" Doris said.

"I do not wish this on you, but forces are greater than us," Barbara said. "Do what you must to survive. Survive, Doris, survive!"

A few tears trickled down Doris's face. Barbara gave Doris's hands an extra squeeze for faith and support. Doris managed a smile. She thanked Barbara quietly, gave her a small envelope, and left.

"Doris looked upset," Linda said.

"Times were difficult during the Great Depression," Arlene said.

"I wish I could hug her," Linda said.

Barbara moved to extinguish the lamp, but she suddenly looked out the window in time to see Nellie spring from her sandbox and chase a deer into the cornfield.

"She'll get lost!" Barbara said.

Barbara dashed out of the house and toward Nellie. Arlene, Linda, and Ken followed as best they would without breaking their hand link.

"Nellie!" Barbara yelled. "Come back!"

"We can't keep up," Linda said. "The deer, Nellie, and Barbara are too fast. It's like we're in a three-legged race against gazelles."

"Then we must fly," Arlene said. "Stand still."

The three came to a halt in the cornfield.

"Feel the ripples of the corn stalks in the wind, the ripples in the air, ripples like rolling hills beneath our feet. The earth is like a rolling carpet, rolling waves cresting and carrying us from the deep ocean to the shores of a house. Behold!"

The cornfield became living waves of water. The waves picked up the three and carried them down a series of hills until they reached the end of the cornfield where a last burst sent the three on a patch of grass in the backyard of another house.

"Ow," Ken said, and he pulled his hand in an effort to adjust his shirt.

"Do not break the link," Arlene said.

"But nothing's going on," Ken said.

"Do not break it. Be patient. Things will happen."

The three looked around. To their backs was the cornfield, and directly in front was the back of a house. To the left of the house was a conventional barn with a silo on the far end and a water tower on the near end.

"Strange having a water tower next to a barn," Ken said.

Their gaze was interrupted by a foul odor from their right. They turned and saw a low, wide building (a pole barn) to the right of the house, a building that also had a water tower.

"Two water towers?" Ken asked.

A back door opened from the pole barn. A man wheeled out a cart of leather hides and hauled it to a truck.

"That's a tannery," Linda said. "No wonder it stinks!"

"Try this stuff," yelled a voice from the other barn.

The three turned and looked to the left of the house where they saw two men stepping outside of the conventional barn and sampling beverages.

"Ah, this is the best batch of spirits yet," said the second.

"They're making booze!" Ken said.

"I believe that's a distillery," Arlene said.

The men returned inside. A rustling from the cornfield behind captured the three's attention, and they turned around. The three watched as a deer emerged from the cornfield, Nellie emerged second in pursuit of the deer, and Barbara emerged third. The deer dashed off with a final burst of energy, and Barbara caught her little girl.

"Nellie!" Barbara said. "It's not safe running off into the corn."

"But Mamma," Nellie said. "I want to ride the deer. The deer is my friend."

"Deer are wild animals and are not to be disturbed," Barbara said. "Cornfields are dangerous, Nellie. A young girl like you can get lost. And there are hunters everywhere. It's not safe."

"But it's fun exploring in the cornfield," Nellie said. "It's adventure."

"I'm sure it seems that way," Barbara said as she picked up Nellie, "but when you grow up, you'll learn that the world is not a safe place, not a safe place at all. You must be careful about what you do. Danger hides under every rock."

Nellie squirmed away from Barbara and looked under a nearby rock.

"I don't see danger under this rock," Nellie said.

"It's an expression," Barbara said. "As you get older, you'll understand better."

"Does this mean I have to stay out of the cornfield?" Nellie asked.

"Yes. And no more chasing deer," Barbara said.

"Aw, shucks," Nellie said.

A woman walked around the house and entered the back yard where Barbara, Nellie, Arlene, Linda, and Ken stood.

"Aunt Sadella!" Nellie yelled with glee as she ran up to Sadella Sarvak.

"Nellie!" Sadella said. "How is my favorite niece?"

"I'm your only niece, silly!" Nellie said as she hugged Sadella.

"I love you all the same," Sadella said. "What brings you here?"

"She chased a deer through the cornfield," Barbara said. "I told her it was a wrong thing to do."

"It is very wrong," Sadella said. "There is evil in the cornfield, though you may not know it. Wild animals roam the fields."

"Mamma said deer are animals. I'm not afraid of deer," Nellie said.

"I speak of wild animals more vicious and deadly than deer. There are bears and wolves in the fields, and men who hunt them. All are killers; all are very dangerous. Listen to your mother, Nellie. Stay out of the cornfields," Sadella said.

"Yes, Aunt Sadella," Nellie said.

"That's a good girl," Sadella said. "Come inside for some milk and cookies."

"No thank you," Barbara said. "We should be returning home. Besides, it's not good for a girl Nellie's age to see—"

"Can we go in, please Mamma?" Nellie begged. "I love milk and cookies."

Barbara hesitated.

"You can't deny the world we live in," Sadella whispered to Barbara, referring to Sadella's storefront of hunting equipment for sale—the same hunting equipment that fed Barbara's hesitation.

"Very well, but we must be brief," Barbara said.

Nellie jumped with excitement. Sadella led Nellie around the house and in through the front door. Barbara followed behind, and Arlene, Linda, and Ken followed behind Barbara. On passing through the front door (with its jingling bells), the six entered Sadella's storefront. Barbara cringed, but Sadella quickly led Nellie through another door and into a small dining room where she had Nellie and Barbara sit at a table.

"Now you make yourselves at home while I get milk and cookies," Sadella said.

Sadella slipped into the kitchen and returned with milk and cookies.

"Yay!" Nellie said.

"And for being a good girl, I have something else for you," Sadella said. "I have a fresh piece of paper for you to keep and a special pencil holder you may borrow for drawing art."

"Fresh paper?" Ken asked. "What's special about that?"

"Paper was more expensive in those days," Arlene said. "The prices were less than today, but people had almost no money, so it was expensive in relation to their income. Also, look at the paper. It's thin and semi-transparent."

"It looks a bit like wax paper," Linda said. "Is it onionskin paper?"

"Very good, Linda. Yes, it's onionskin paper," Arlene said.

Sadella showed the pencil holder to Nellie.

"Look," Sadella said. "This pencil holder resembles a giant comb. It will hold five pencils at the same time."

"How does it work?" Nellie asked.

"First, place the pencils in the sleeves loosely," Sadella said. "Each sleeve has a clamp for securing the pencils tightly, but we will leave those clamps loose for a moment. Now then, place the holder such that the pencils slide down and touch your sheet of paper. Good. Now tighten each clamp. There. Now drag the holder across the paper. You see? You can draw five lines at the same time."

"Wow!" Nellie said as she drew the lines.

"The lines are parallel," Sadella said.

"What does that mean?" Nellie asked.

"It means they are the same distance apart," Sadella said. "Now twist the holder a little as you draw. See? The lines get closer. Now twist the holder a lot. There, you made some of the lines cross each other. If you practice, you can get some lines to cross and some not."

"This is the best thing ever!" Nellie said.

"Now turn the paper over and make more lines," Sadella said.

Nellie did just that and enjoyed dragging the pencil holder against the paper, making many patterns of smooth-flowing pencil lines.

"There's another trick I want to show you," Sadella said. "Hold the paper to the light. Do you see? You can see lines on both sides of the paper."

"I can't see some of the lines on the other side," Nellie said.

"You have to press the pencils down harder to make the lines darker," Sadella said. "Then they will show through the other side. Now I have one more trick to show you. Come over to the window."

Nellie followed Sadella to the window.

"I have another fresh piece of paper for you. Place the paper on the window. Here, I have some tape to hold it," Sadella said.

Nellie taped the paper to the window.

"Now look through the paper, and you'll see a tree," Sadella said. "You can use the pencil holder to trace the tree on the paper. Go ahead, try it."

Nellie used the pencil holder to trace the outline of the tree and its branches.

"It looks strange," Nellie said. "And it's hard to draw."

"Do not worry about making a perfect tracing," Sadella said. "You are more interested in making art."

"It looks scary," Nellie said. "Like the one branch on the right is ready to fall off."

"It's all make-believe," Barbara said.

But before anyone else could say anything, the very branch Nellie referenced cracked with a loud pop! and crashed to the ground.

"Wow! It's magic!" Nellie said.

"I wish you wouldn't mislead Nellie like this," Barbara said.

"It is not magic, Nellie," Sadella said. "When you draw other things in this manner, you often magnify subtle flaws that you wouldn't ordinarily see."

"What?" Nellie asked, confused.

"Drawing with the holder helps you see what is already there," Sadella said. "It's like using a magnifying glass."

"Gee, that's swell," Nellie said.

"One more fresh piece of paper," Sadella said, "and we'll be done."

"I want lots and lots of paper," Nellie said.

"I know, but paper costs money, and I only have a little," Sadella said.

"Can't you get more from the bank?" Nellie asked innocently.

Sadella smiled.

"Banks aren't always trustworthy," Sadella said. "They take your savings and go under."

Bells on the front door jingled indicating a customer had entered.

"One moment—I have a customer," Sadella said.

Sadella exited the dining room and entered the storefront.

"Good day, Donald," Sadella said. "How is Doris?"

"Gimme a Thompson M1927," Donald replied, ignoring Sadella's question regarding Doris's health.

"A what?" Sadella asked.

"You know, a Thompson—a broom, a typewriter, a piano, a chopper," Donald said.

"I only sell hunting equipment, not office equipment or musical instruments," Sadella said.

"It's a submachine gun," Donald said with impatience. "Gimme one."

"I don't have one," Sadella said.

"You got a 1921?" Donald asked.

"No submachine guns," Sadella said. "They are expensive and too powerful for game hunting. How about a nice, bolt-action Winchester 54? I have one right here with a lovely finish. See? Or for a little more money, I have the brand-new Winchester 70. It's the best rifle money can buy."

"No! I got big game to hunt," Donald said. "A pack of wolves been tearing up these parts. A man can't take 'em on with a regular rifle. A man needs lots of rounds."

"I'm sorry, Donald. I don't sell Tommies. You might find a store in Riverton that sells them," Sadella said.

"I ain't got time to ride all the way in to Riverton. I need a gun now," Donald demanded.

Nellie poked her head into the storefront, but Barbara quickly whisked her back to the dining room.

"The Winchester, take it or leave it," Sadella said.

"Dammit! I hate settling for slow machines," Donald grumbled. "But I gotta have a gun now. The wolves are gettin' into the distilleries."

"Are you sure it's the wolves and not your buddies?" Sadella grinned.

Donald's face flashed with anger.

"Old man Lucan made a mistake when he sold you this store," Donald grumbled as he gave the money to Sadella for the Winchester 70. "Things ain't been right since. A woman can't run a gun store right—never could, never will."

"I'll ask you to keep your colorful comments in the woods and out of my store," Sadella said.

"You got ammo to go with this 'Chester?" Donald asked.

"Yeah," Sadella said as she reached for a small box.

"Gimme the whole case," Donald said.

"Can you afford it?" Sadella asked.

"What's wrong? You think I'm a thief or something? Here!"

Donald pulled a wad of cash out of his pocket and threw it on her counter.

"Does that cover it?" he griped.

"Yeah," Sadella said.

Sadella gave him the case of cartridges, finished the sales slip, and gave Donald a copy.

"Now get out of my store," Sadella said.

"You need to fix that attitude of yours, Miss Sarvak. I'm a paying customer. I'm entitled to respect."

With that, Donald took the rifle and ammo with him while slamming the door behind him. A shock wave passed through Sadella's house, and both Nellie and Barbara shivered in the dining room. Sadella returned to them to comfort them.

"It's time we return home," Barbara said.

"I'm sorry for the disturbance," Sadella said. "Most of my best customers are, unfortunately, heavy drinkers. At times I feel like I'm doing business with the devil, or at least his demons."

"Then sell the store and move," Barbara said. "You know how I feel about this place."

"I know, my sister, but I look at the other women in the world, and I see them suffering miserably, either from the grips of this Great Depression or from the abuse at the hands of their husbands," Sadella explained. "Running this store is liberating."

"Even if it's at the expense of...of..." Barbara started.

"Of what?" Sadella asked.

Barbara placed her hands over Nellie's ears.

"At the expense of dead animals," Barbara said. "Don't you see their blood on your hands?"

"That's an absurd thing to say," Sadella said. "I don't kill animals."

"But you are part of their death. You profit from their death," Barbara said.

"I profit from stupid, drunk, men who believe they must hunt. If they don't buy my supplies, they'll buy someone else's. I might as well profit from their vices," Sadella said.

"It's a thin line you walk, my sister," Barbara said. "I hope nothing ill comes of it."

"Be strong, Barbara," Sadella said. "Be strong."

"Sadella," called a man's voice from the storefront. "There's trouble at the tannery."

"Come along, Nellie, it's time to go home," Barbara said.

"Leonard," Sadella said. "I can't leave the storefront. I'm expecting a run on my rifles."

"It's an emergency," Leonard said. "You gotta come now."

"Barbara, I know you hate anything to do with hunting," Sadella said.

"You're right, I do," Barbara said. "I'm tired and want to go home for my nap."

"Please, watch the store for me. You don't have to sell anything. If anyone comes in, tell them I'll be back soon. Please, my dear sister, do this favor for me. There's plenty of food in the kitchen—help yourselves. And more onionskin paper in the cupboard above the sink."

"Yay!" Nellie said.

"All right, but just this once," Barbara said.

"Thank you," Sadella said as she gave Barbara a thank-you kiss on the cheek.

The scenery changed. Arlene, Linda, and Ken left Barbara and Nellie behind and were now standing inside a micro-brewery.

"Bill," Marvin said. "This vat has been sliced open. It'll have to be replaced."

"Where are we?" Linda asked.

"This is Bill's micro-brewery," Arlene said. "It was attacked by a wild animal just last night. I don't understand why we are here."

"Look at the claw marks," Marvin said to Bill. "Looks like the doing of a coyote or wolf."

"I don't understand," Bill said. "I had my dogs out all night guarding the property. They would have barked had a coyote or wolf invaded."

Ken broke the link. The three returned to Arlene's farmhouse.

"Why did you break the link?" Linda asked.

"My nose itches," Ken said, "and I've been suffering since Nellie started drawing on the onionskin paper."

"Well scratch your nose and be done with it!" Linda said with impatience.

Linda's hair was frazzled, and she looked agitated.

"It doesn't matter," Arlene said. "When we reverted from Sadella's home in the past to Bill's home in the present, I knew our link had weakened."

"Because of Ken?" Linda asked.

"What did I do?" Ken asked back.

"You don't have enough faith," Linda replied.

"It's not Ken's fault, at least not entirely his," Arlene said.

Ken was about to thank Arlene until she added that the fault wasn't entirely his, as if suggesting some blame should go toward him.

"When powerful events build up, a weak link fails. We must turn up the flame on the alcohol lamp to reinforce the link," Arlene said.

Arlene turned a dial on the lamp, and the blue flame grew in height and width. The flame made an audible whishing sound, and the air around the glass chimney became hotter.

"Do not touch the glass chimney," Arlene warned Ken, who had reached to touch it. "Alcohol may burn dimly, but it's also very hot."

"Besides," Linda said, "you need to keep your hands in the circle."

"Yes," Arlene said. "Ken—cross your hands as you did before, just as I am doing. Good. Re-form the circle. Excellent. Now relax and think of pleasant thoughts, thoughts of love a mother like Barbara has for her daughter, Nellie, and the adoration and affection Nellie has for her mother. Sense these emotions of good as we travel back, back, back to Sadella's house where Barbara and Nellie await Sadella's return from the tannery."

The glass chimney grew in height, the ceiling, walls, and floor fell away, the glass chimney now evaporated into nothingness, and the three found themselves outside between Sadella's house and the tannery.

"What happened?" Linda asked.

"Our link is stronger, but forces building in the past are much more powerful than our link. Instead of allowing us to materialize inside Sadella's house, the forces around us shoved us outside," Arlene said.

"The past can't affect the present," Ken said.

Arlene and Linda gave Ken dirty looks.

"What?" Ken asked.

"It's precisely because of the past that the present is affected," Arlene said.

"Thank you, Arlene," Linda said.

The three saw Nellie holding an onionskin paper to the window toward the tannery and drawing with a worried Barbara standing behind her.

"Look," Linda said. "There's smoke coming from the tannery."

"Let's go inside," Arlene said.

The three walked inside. In the first section, a large furnace heated blocks of limestone, a process that converted the limestone to quicklime.

"Over here!" Leonard called to Sadella. "The furnace is burning out of control."

"Then turn it off," Sadella said.

"It's too late," Leonard said. "It has too much fuel."

"Then we must salvage what leather we can," Sadella said.

Sadella and Leonard ordered workers to haul leather outside the building.

"Why don't they put water on the fire?" Ken asked. "There's a water tower and everything."

"Do not put water on the fire," Sadella yelled. "You'll saturate the quicklime and cause an explosion."

Arlene and Linda looked at Ken with a smile.

"How was I supposed to know?" Ken asked.

"Men," Linda said. "Arlene—can we do anything to help?"

"I'm afraid not," Arlene said. "We barely have enough power to be here, much less affect the past."

"We can't just stand here," Linda said. "We must help."

Linda stamped in place and grew restless.

"If you try to help, you will break the circle and the link," Arlene said. "You must stay with us."

Linda tried pulling away from Arlene and Ken, but Ken held fast onto Linda's hands.

"I must follow Sadella," Linda said.

Sadella hurried the workers into carting the hides and leather out of the building. Sadella herself carted out a load of horns and tusks.

"Keratin," Linda said. "She's hauling out artifacts of keratin."

The furnace roared and set fire to neighboring things of wood—chairs, worktables, and other-such wooden items. The pole-barn's walls became black with scorchings and soon caught fire as well.

"This place is going to burn up if nothing is done to stop the fire," Ken said.

"Sadella is in danger," Linda said. "I can feel it."

"We should see about stopping the fire," Ken said.

"No!" Linda yelled. "We must protect Sadella."

Linda pulled Arlene and Ken in pursuit of Sadella. Sadella carted the horns and tusks outside through the back of the pole barn, into the back yard, and to the edge of the cornfield. But another incident had developed. Donald and other hunters were chasing a pack of wolves through the cornfield. The wolves descended on the distillery and attacked it. Donald led the hunters into the distillery and began shooting inside. Shots hit some wolves, missed others, but mostly hit equipment and the barn. Stray shots came through barn windows and landed in random places in trees and against Sadella's house.

"Barbara and Nellie!" Sadella yelled.

Sadella made a dash for her house. The furnace in the tannery had now fully caught the pole-barn on fire. Flames and smoke poured into the open air. Distant echoing of fire trucks carried through the air. Sadella felt she had to fly through the air to get any kind of speed to warn Barbara and Nellie, but it turned out they were already warned. The gunshots had alerted Barbara and scared Nellie. Nellie dashed through the front door, into the front yard, and out into the street as a fire truck approached.

"No!" Sadella screamed, realizing the impending horror of Nellie being hit by a fire truck.

Sadella thrust forward, but a stray gunshot from the distillery caught her skull and ripped it open. She fell to the ground. Barbara, unaware of Sadella's condition, ran after Nellie to save her from the fire truck. Barbara caught up to Nellie, grabbed her, and threw her to the side of the road in a motion that also carried herself toward the far side of the road.

Not enough. The fire truck ran over Barbara's legs and crushed them. Barbara screamed in pain. The fire truck, obsessed with putting out the fire, continued until it reached the tannery. Barbara crawled off the road. Other fire trucks followed. They hooked their hoses into the water tower and pumped water onto the tannery.

"You can't do that!" Linda screamed. "Sadella said, 'No!'"

Linda broke free from Ken and Arlene, but the link did not fail. The three remained in that time.

"What's going on?" Ken asked. "Why aren't we returning to your farmhouse in the present?"

"The forces here are too powerful," Arlene said. "We are stuck here until events play themselves out."

"This isn't a game!" Ken said.

Ken ran after Linda but could not keep up. Arlene dashed to Barbara and tried to help, but her hands passed through Barbara's body without effect.

"Sadella!" Linda screamed.

Linda reached Sadella's body. She knelt and took Sadella in her arms.

"You can't touch her," Ken was about to yell, but to Ken's shock, Linda was able to touch Sadella.

"Come back with me," Ken said.

Ken reached for Linda, but his hand passed through her flesh.

"Linda!" Ken said. "This time is stealing you from me."

"Sadella!" Linda wailed.

The wolves escaped from the distillery and ran amok the grounds from the distillery to Sadella's yard to the tannery into the cornfield and generally all around in circles. The fire trucks continued pouring water atop the pole-barn of a tannery. Holes in the roof and sides originally created by the fire were now carrying water from the hoses into the tannery. The fire quiesced progressively, leading the firefighters into a false sense of security that the fire was coming under control. With this false confidence, several firefighters rushed into the tannery to search for survivors, but just as they opened the doors, the fresh air from outside fed new oxygen to the inside, and at the same time, the quicklime suddenly took on massive amounts of water and exploded into a super-hot fireball. The explosion blew out the sides of the pole barn, sending equipment and people in all directions. The fireball blew the roof up and out, sending heavy debris everywhere, including the water tower. The water tower incurred a massive gouge in its underbelly, and it spewed its water everywhere. Fire, quicklime, regular lime, dung, urine, and other tannery chemicals flowed all over the grounds from the tannery to Sadella's house and on to the distillery.

Wolves hollered and yelped as the quicklime dissolved their fur. The quicklime reached Sadella and Linda, dissolving much of Sadella's hair and some of Linda's. Linda carried Sadella from the grounds across the street to a safe place not far from Barbara and Nellie. Hunters who had given chase to the wolves were now confused. Some, seeing the fire and blast, fled the scene. Others, like Donald, continued shooting at the wolves. Flying embers attached to Sadella's house and the distillery. Sadella's house burned a little, but the distillery caught fire quickly—the boards in the conventional barn were so old as to be like kerosene.

The distillery exploded, sending alcohol and more debris into the air and the surrounding grounds. Now Sadella's house was flooded with a mixture of water, alcohol, tannery chemicals, and quicklime. Keratin from tusks, horns, wolves, and humans who were caught in the blasts were converted to chitin and other chemicals. The ground supporting Sadella's house liquefied and weakened. Sadella's house sank and disappeared into the muck.

"Linda," Arlene and Ken called. "Linda!"

Linda's hair burned from flame and quicklime. She screeched in agony. Arlene and Ken reached her, but their hands passed through her flesh.

"I'm burning up; I'm burning up!" Linda screamed.

"Spirits of old, break your hold!" Arlene shouted.

The smoke and flames of the 1930s swirled around the three and choked them. Walls arose around them, and a last blast of debris from the distillery sent a plank toward the three, which became a ceiling. The three returned to Arlene's farmhouse, but the alcohol flame had grown too tall and ignited Linda's long hair. Linda broke her handhold with Arlene and Ken, batted at her hair, tipped the alcohol lamp in the excitement, burst through a window, and ran into the cornfield. The alcohol caught the table on fire.

"Just as before!" Arlene said.

Ken felt trapped between needing to help Arlene put out the fire and running after Linda. There was no catching Linda, however. She ran quicker than any human and was out of sight before the fire could take hold of the entire room. Arlene ripped the curtain from the window and threw it on the burning table. The fire was extinguished.

"What's happening?" Ken asked. "What happened to my Linda?"

"She has merged with Sadella," Arlene said. "We must find her and help her."

Ken ran out of the house and into the cornfield.

"Linda!" Ken yelled. "Linda, come back!"

Silence. Ken had no idea where Linda went. Arlene caught up to Ken and spoke.

"You won't find her this way," Arlene said. "But I know where she went."

"You do?!" Ken asked incredulously. "Where?"

"To the old Sadie's Place," Arlene said.

"Then let's go, now!" Ken said.

Arlene rode in Ken's car as Ken tore down the driveway and into the road.

"The micro-brewery that was attacked," Ken started. "What was that about?"

"A wolf attacked it," Arlene said.

"But there are no wolves around here," Ken said. "They were all hunted."

"Yes, that's true," Arlene said. "Take it easy with your driving. You're going to get us killed!"

Ken returned to his side of the road as he narrowly missed hitting an oncoming car.

"Everything we've tried has made things worse," Ken said. "Your well water, and now this séance."

"I'm sorry," Arlene said. "I don't know why Linda isn't responding to treatment. It's like forces from the past have taken control of her body."

"Then we must stop it. How do we counteract the forces of the past?" Ken asked.

Arlene did not answer. The two arrived at the old Sadie's Place, jumped out of the car, and called for Linda.

"Linda!" Ken called.

"Linda!" Arlene called.

The sheriff and his deputy arrived in their cruiser.

"Marvin," Arlene said after she'd dialed her husband on her cellphone. "Get down to old Sadie's Place, and hurry! There's an emergency."

Arlene finished her call with Marvin and ended the cellphone call. Seeing Arlene on her cellphone, the sheriff and his deputy suspected trouble.

"What seems to be the trouble?" the sheriff asked.

"There's no trouble," Arlene said.

"Then what are you doing here?" the deputy asked.

"This is my property," Arlene said. "I am inspecting it."

"Is he giving you any trouble?" the deputy asked, pointing to Ken.

"No, I'm not," Ken replied.

"I didn't ask you," the deputy said to Ken in a threatening tone.

The deputy approached Ken and held his baton to Ken's neck.

"Don't get on my bad side," the deputy said.

"Take it easy," Arlene said. "Ken is okay."

The conversation was cut short when the yelp of a wolf carried through the air.

"A wolf!" the deputy said.

"Get the rifle from the trunk," the sheriff ordered.

"Yes sir!" the deputy acknowledged with delight and anticipation. "I'm gonna be a hero today!"

"No wait," Ken said. "Don't shoot. This might be a friendly wolf."

"There ain't no such thing, boay," the sheriff said.

"Let's call animal control," Arlene said. "They have a tranquilizer gun."

"The best tranquilizer gun I know is a sniper rifle," the sheriff said.

The deputy returned with a Winchester 70, loaded, and ready to fire. The deputy raised the rifle in preparation for the shoot. The sheriff drew his service revolver as backup and followed the deputy.

"You folks best keep back," the sheriff said.

The wolf appeared from the cornfield. The fur on her head had been singed away. She snarled and growled.

"It's Linda!" Ken said.

Ken ran ahead and stood between the wolf and the officers.

"Get out of the way," the deputy said.

The wolf continued snarling and growling. She clawed at the ground as if saying she was preparing to pounce on anything and everything on the grounds.

"It's going to attack," the deputy said. "For the last time, Manders, get out of the way, or I'll shoot you too."

"No!" Ken replied.

Marvin arrived in his van.

"What's going on?" Marvin asked as he ran to the scene. "My God! That's the wolf on the security camera."

"What security camera?" Arlene asked.

"The one at Bill's micro-brewery. It attacked and tore up his equipment. It's got to be stopped," Marvin said.

"And we will, as soon as Manders gets out of the way," the sheriff said.

"I ought to put a hole through your head just to teach you a little discipline," the deputy said to Ken.

"Stay back!" Ken said. "This is Linda, and I won't let you hurt her."

"What?" Marvin asked. "He's crazy in the head."

"Marvin, please," Arlene said. "Listen to Ken. He speaks—"

"This is your doing, isn't it?" Marvin said to Arlene. "You and your well, your black magic, and your Great Aunt Sadella."

"She was a wolf too! And now Linda has merged with Sadella and become a wolf," Arlene explained. "Oh Marvin, we have to help Linda."

"You're as crazy as Manders," Marvin said. "I should have divorced you years ago. Deputy, kill the wolf, even if Manders is in the way."

The deputy aimed at the wolf with intent to shoot through Ken if necessary. Ken held his ground and was prepared to sacrifice his life for the wolf. The wolf, however, could not let Ken die. In the moment before the deputy pulled the trigger, the wolf leapt around Ken and launched airborne toward the deputy. The deputy fired repeated rounds at the wolf, as did the sheriff. Ken screamed, Arlene screamed, and with a final gasp of life, the wolf screamed before it fell dead to the ground.

Ken and Arlene ran to the wolf. Steam rose from the coal fire in the ground. Then other chemicals arose—chemicals from a forgotten era of distilleries and tanneries. The chemicals attached to the wolf's body and caused its hair and claws to fall out. The wolf's body was naked; its skin was exposed to the raw air and sun as if ready to be skinned. The hair and claws turned white then changed into bands of red and white like the colors of shrimp.

Arlene stood by the wolf and cried. Ken knelt by the wolf in disbelief and shock, then a sudden vapor from the ground enshrouded the wolf's body, hiding it from view. After a few seconds, the vapor dispersed, and in the place where the wolf once lay was now the body of a woman, Linda Racquemore. She was hairless and nail-less.

Arlene screamed, but Ken remained silent for the moment. A seething anger—like a pot of water in a roiling boil—built up pressure and caused him to explode.

"You idiots!" Ken yelled. "You killed my future wife! I demand my revenge on you! I'm gonna break your necks!"

Ken leapt for the deputy and sheriff.

"No, no!" Arlene yelled. "They'll kill you."

Ken attacked the deputy and struggled for control of the rifle. Marvin jumped in to help, but Arlene swatted him back. Ken ripped the rifle from the deputy's grasp, but the sheriff knocked Ken over the skull with his revolver.

"That'll be enough from you," the sheriff said.

"You killed my future wife," Ken said in a daze. "You killed Linda. You...you...murderers."

"There was an accident here," the sheriff said. "And unfortunately, a life was lost."

"You liar!" Ken tried to yell, but the deputy exacted his own revenge by stepping on Ken's back and forcing him in the dirt.

"You better settle down a spell, boay," the deputy said. "You got a long term in prison coming up for you at the rate you're going."

"Linda, my Linda!" Ken said. "You can't be dead. You can't. You're supposed to get better. We're supposed to marry. Things can't end like this. They can't."

"All right, deputy, let's get him in the back of the cruiser," the sheriff said. "We'll call a meat wagon to pick up the body."

"Please, no," Ken said, "let me stay with Linda."

But the deputy was more interested in following the sheriff's orders than Ken's request. The deputy put handcuffs on Ken and hauled him into the back seat of the cruiser.

"I want to speak with Ken," Arlene said at length.

"I don't think that's a good idea," the sheriff said.

"Please," Arlene said, "I want to help. I think I can help him calm down."

"We can't let him out of the cruiser," the sheriff said. "He's a danger to himself and everyone else."

"Just roll the window down a little, and I'll speak to him through the opening," Arlene suggested.

The sheriff looked at the deputy and nodded his head, "yes."

Arlene followed the deputy to the cruiser. Using a button on a driver's panel, the deputy lowered a rear window a little bit.

"Ken?" Arlene asked. "Are you okay?"

Ken breathed heavily as if out of breath. He looked ragged and depressed.

"I...you...Linda. My Linda," Ken said.

"They have to take her away, Ken," Arlene said.

"No, they can't!" Ken repeated.

"I'm sorry about your loss," Arlene said. "But there's nothing else we can do. Sometimes things end this way. They're out of our control."

"No, they can't be," Ken said. "I won't let them be out of our control. I won't let Linda die."

"She's dead, Ken. Accept it and move on," Arlene said.

"I can't! I won't!" Ken said.

"Don't torture yourself about things you can do nothing about. You'll only drive yourself crazy," Arlene advised.

"If I gotta be crazy to bring Linda back, then I will!" Ken said. "I keep re-thinking the whole thing over and over, and I always feel like I've missed something."

"There was nothing to miss," Arlene said. "This was one unfortunate incident after another."

"Without purpose?" Ken asked, not expecting an answer.

"Sometimes life is like that. Life is cruel. It brings death without purpose," Arlene said. "Move on."

"I can't. I'm stuck!" Ken said. "I'll run it through my mind again. Will you follow along with me?"

"It's a waste of time," Arlene said. "And it's depressing. Look at you—you're a mess."

"I won't rest until I figure it out. Please, I'm running out of help. Everyone else has turned against me. Will you at least listen to me?"

Arlene paused in thought.

"I should say 'no,' but I'll listen to you. But then you must promise to seek psychiatric help after the sheriff takes you away."

"Okay, I promise," Ken said. "Now let's look at the facts. Sadella was Lady Sadie."

"No," Arlene said. "Sadella died in the 1930s. Lady Sadie was someone else."

"But they looked the same," Ken said. "They acted the same. They must be the same."

"Not the same," Arlene said. "Let it go. Next?"

"Okay, let's suppose Sadella really did die," Ken said.

"And she did," Arlene said.

"Every bit of keratin on her land changed into chitin," Ken said. "Did you hear me? Chitin!"

"I know," Arlene said.

"Those women who threw up stones—they were made of chitin," Ken said.

"An extrapolation of the land," Arlene blurted without thinking.

"Yes, an extrapolation," Ken said. "Linda told me about your well, how the water extrapolated the women in your line. The land here does the same thing. It extrapolates life. That means Lady Sadie was an extrapolation of Sadella—a life-form created from that horrible mixture of tanning chemicals, alcohol, water, and fire. Sadella was in that mixture, so were wolves."

"If it weren't for my experiences with the well, I'd be hard pressed to believe you," Arlene said.

"But what I say makes sense to you," Ken said. "So hear me out. Linda lived and worked on these grounds with Lady Sadie. She was tied to this place. That's why she threw up stones. That's why you tried treating her."

"But I was wrong about Linda. I thought her stones were made of chitin, but they weren't."

"They were made of keratin—the stuff Sadella worked with, not Lady Sadie. Linda was linked to Sadella while the women who were given readings were linked to Lady Sadie," Ken explained. "But this is where I get stuck. How did Linda get linked to Sadella? Did you see how she phased into Sadella's time? She interacted with Sadella. How was that possible?"

"Because she was linked to Sadella," Arlene said.

"Yes, it's a circular fact, and I can't break the circle," Ken said. "Linda wasn't given a reading by Lady Sadie like the other women were. And unfortunately, I don't know the details of those readings. Do you?"

Arlene paused.

"You do know, don't you?" Ken asked.

"I don't know for sure," Arlene said.

"But you suspect something. What do you suspect?"

"Sometimes readings are accompanied by the drinking of certain beverages," Arlene said. "Lady Sadie may have given them something to drink. The beverage would have affected their digestive system and caused the stones to appear later."

"Then that's the link," Ken said. "Linda must have drunk something while she lived there. But I know for a fact she never drank the water. She always had bottled water. I'm back to square one. Dammit!"

Ken scratched his head and his face in nervous anxiety. Arlene moved her lips around as if adjusting them after eating.

"I don't know what else I can say," Arlene said. "I really am sorry. Linda's death gives me an upset stomach."

Arlene turned and gagged a little. She spit out something away from the cruiser. Feeling her mouth dirty, she moved her finger across her teeth to wipe the gag away. Then Ken's eyes lit up.

"Arlene!" Ken said.

"I'm sorry. It's not lady-like to throw up in public," Arlene said.

"No, wait. I know, I know," Ken said.

"What do you know?" Arlene asked.

"Linda brushed her teeth," Ken said.

"And you think—" Arlene started.

"She brushed her teeth with well water—well water from the same grounds where the old tannery, hunting shop, and distillery stood. That's the link, Arlene. She ingested elements of the past. They extrapolated in her. Lady Sadie sensed the connection and gave special preference to Linda. I know the answer!"

But Ken's excitement at figuring out the link (in his mind) was deflated when he returned to the fact that Linda remained dead.

"I'm happy you figured things out, Ken," Arlene said. "It won't bring Linda back from the dead, but maybe you'll sleep easier."

"But...this can't be the end. It can't," Ken muttered.

Marvin approached the cruiser.

"Arlene, another truck returned our coffee beans," Marvin said.

"I'm really sorry, Ken," Arlene said.

Arlene stepped away from the cruiser and engaged in conversation with Marvin. Ken was able to hear.

"So is that it? Is the farm *underwater*?" Arlene asked.

"If you mean we're deep in debt, yes," Marvin said. "We can't sell our main crop, so there's no money coming in."

"I don't want to sell the farm," Arlene said.

"I know," Marvin said. "But the bank is ready to foreclose. They'll have your farm, Arlene. So decide—who do you want to have the farm—the bank, or someone else?"

"I want the farm," Arlene said.

"It's no longer possible," Marvin said. "This is the end."

"Any news on the lab testing?" Arlene asked. "You know, did they find out why our coffee is so bad?"

"Yeah, but it doesn't help much. Our coffee beans are infested with a fungus," Marvin said.

"I knew that already," Arlene said.

"Yeah, we knew that. Want to hear more trivia, as in the name of the fungus?"

"I guess if I'm going to lose the farm, I might as well know the name of my enemy," Arlene said.

"Our beans have anthracnose, and the name of our enemy is *Colletotrichum lindemuthianum*," Marvin said.

"I can't even repeat what you just said," Arlene said.

"And I wouldn't want the disease repeated on anyone," Marvin said.

"*Colletotrichum lindemuthianum*," Ken repeated to himself. "I've heard that name before. But where? Think, Ken, it's important. The fungus does more than cause damage to beans. It does something else. What does it do? What did I read?"

"It doesn't matter," Arlene said. "I guess we should sell the farm. Two deaths in one day—that's more than I can handle. I want to go home."

"Arlene," Ken yelled.

Arlene walked back to the cruiser.

"You have to do something for me," Ken said. "You have to do it for me now."

"Ken, I'm too upset right now. Call me when you've recovered. We'll be moved by then, but I'll leave a forwarding address."

"No, that'll be too late. You must do something for me now."

"Goodbye, Ken," Arlene said. "I wish you well."

"Arlene! Marvin! Come back!" Ken yelled. "I have a solution. I can solve all problems."

"Ignore him," Marvin said. "When they claim the ability to solve all problems, they've gone over the deep end."

"Please, come back!" Ken yelled, but he was ignored.

Ken stared at his pants and feet. They were covered in goo from the field where Linda died.

"The chemicals," Ken said to himself. "The ones responsible for Sadella's conversion and for Linda's. They are here—on my pants and shoes. I may never get another chance. The chemicals are all that are left."

Ken scooped the goo into his hand and held his hand to his mouth. Without thinking, he turned his head away.

"It stinks, like the deaths of thousands across millions of years," Ken said to himself. "I must eat this to join Linda. I must eat it."

Ken returned his head to his hand and touched the goo to his tongue. He cringed and shivered.

"I must do it suddenly, like jumping into a pool of water," Ken said.

Ken forced the goo into his mouth and swallowed. The goo had a foul taste and burned his throat. Ken gagged. He felt like throwing up.

"That was really stupid, Ken," Ken said to himself. "You've just poisoned yourself. Now you'll die a stupid death in this car."

Ken fell into convulsions. He shook, perspired, and foamed at the mouth. The goo was like poison, and his muscles twitched in excruciating pain.

"AARRRGGG!" Ken groaned.

His skin turned red like fire, and every cell in his body vibrated with the agitation and frustration of being poisoned by the failings of others. But something happened to Ken. Instead of getting weaker, he grew stronger, as if his body were pitching a last stand against internal and external aggressors of the world. Ken felt fluid pressure building in his muscles. He broke the handcuffs. His hair became frazzled and confused. He broke through the car window. The sheriff and deputy, hearing the glass breaking, rushed over to control the situation. The deputy pointed his rifle at Ken while the sheriff drew his service revolver. Both fired, but Ken ran at a speed that was impossible to be chased by man or bullet. With a snarl and a growl, Ken ran onto the old Sadie's Place grounds, past Linda, and disappeared into the cornfield.

The sheriff and deputy radioed for backup. With the new crisis unfolding, the call to the ambulance was delayed or forgotten. Linda's body remained untouched while the sheriff and deputy busied themselves with Ken's capture.

"He went into the cornfield," the sheriff instructed a volunteer group of hunters. "Call in periodically. Don't shoot unless you're sure it's Manders. We don't want any friendly fire."

"Understood," said a hunter.

The sheriff placed a call to Marvin, who by now was on the way back to the farm with Arlene.

"Manders escaped," the sheriff said to Marvin, who had answered his cellphone. "He could be headed to your farm. I'm sending backup to protect you. Don't confront him. Stay in your house and remain calm."

"Who was it?" Arlene asked as the two arrived home.

"The sheriff. Seems Ken escaped. They think he'll come up here."

"I wonder if..." Arlene said.

"You wonder what?" Marvin asked.

"Ken wanted me to do something for him, but I refused," Arlene said.

"What did he want you to do?" Marvin asked.

"I don't know. I wouldn't listen," Arlene said. "Now I'm sorry. I wonder what he had in mind."

"Well it doesn't matter. He's deranged and running around madly," Marvin said. "I better get my shotgun ready."

"You're not going to shoot him, are you?" Arlene asked.

"I gotta protect us, Arlene," Marvin said.

"But I—" Arlene started, but a loud crashing sound stopped her words.

"It's the silo," Marvin said. "Ken's in the silo."

"Wait for help," Arlene said.

Too late. Marvin ran for the silo. Arlene went inside the house and called for more help, but the operator assured her that help was on the way. Marvin stood next to the silo. A growling and snarling from within the silo let Marvin know that no human was inside.

"Another wolf!" Marvin said.

Marvin loaded the shotgun in anticipation of a showdown. He climbed a ladder with care such that he neither fell nor dropped the shotgun. On reaching near the top, he opened a door and peered inside the silo. He was only a few feet above the line of coffee beans stored in the silo. There was no evidence of man or beast.

"Who's in here?" Marvin yelled. "Ken, is that you?"

Silence.

"I know you're in here," Marvin said. "Come out and give yourself up. It's over."

More silence. Marvin closed the door. He moved up the ladder a little when the door he had just closed opened abruptly, and out popped the wolf. Marvin tried repositioning the shotgun to kill the wolf, but the wolf was too fast. The wolf bit and pulled at Marvin's feet. Marvin tried shaking the wolf off, but the wolf continued attacking Marvin's feet. Unable to get a clear line of fire on the wolf, Marvin swung the shotgun down against the wolf repeatedly, but this only made the wolf madder, and he now clawed and gnashed at Marvin's legs, pulling Marvin down. Marvin lost his grip on the shotgun, and it fell to the ground. Marvin gripped the ladder rung with all his strength and fought the wolf as best he could by kicking, but the wolf was too strong. The wolf pulled with all his might, Marvin lost his grip, and he slid down the ladder to the ground.

The wolf slid down the ladder too, and Marvin anticipated an attack from the wolf. But the wolf did not land on Marvin. Instead, the wolf spouted flames from his mouth to the base of the silo, but on one side only. Marvin scrambled for the shotgun. He picked up the shotgun, aimed at the wolf, and fired. The wolf darted to the side and avoided the shots. Marvin prepared to shoot again, but the silo made a loud and heavy concrete-grating sound. The wolf's flames had converted the lime in the silo's mortar (at the base) to quicklime. The mortar weakened, the concrete loosened, and the silo tipped every-so-slowly toward Marvin. Seeing this, Marvin ran for his life and just barely avoided the silo as it crashed to the ground, spilling its load of coffee beans with it.

The wolf ran from the silo toward the shed, but the wolf did not go inside the shed. Instead, he climbed the water tower.

"The water tower!" Marvin said. "I can live without coffee beans, but not without water!"

Marvin rushed over to the water tower with his shotgun. The wolf had climbed the tower already and was breathing flames at the bottom of the tank. Marvin aimed his shotgun at the wolf and pulled the trigger. The shots sprayed up toward the wolf and hit him in three places—the ear, the front paw, and hind leg. Marvin loaded another shell and aimed. The wolf moved around the tower and took a position away from Marvin. The wolf spouted flames against the bottom of the tank again. The tank was made of metal and would not burst open as easily as the silo. Marvin fired again, but the shots missed. Marvin loaded another shell and climbed the tower. The wolf turned and breathed flames at Marvin. Marvin's hair was burned off completely, and his clothes caught fire. Marvin tried to get a shot off, but the fire forced him to descend quickly.

Marvin rushed into the shed and threw well water from the bucket onto his body. Images of Arlene and her maternal ancestors materialized and ran around frantically in the shed, yelling and screaming with the urgency of crisis. Even Sadella materialized and ran around, but she followed Marvin out of shed and into the open air. The vapor of Sadella now traveled upward and into the wolf where she gave the wolf new strength. With one final blast of fire, the wolf melted the lower portion of the water tower's tank. The tank burst open, and the water gushed down with such power and force that Marvin and the shed were washed away. The water flooded the property. It cut into the house and shoved it off its foundation. It cut into the barn and caused its collapse. It cut into the spilled, infected coffee beans, mixed, and carried the coffee-bean mixture down a hill and into a creek. The wolf jumped from the tower and floated in the water toward the creek.

Arlene witnessed everything. Her first thought was to find Marvin and secure his rescue. Fighting the heavy current, she made her way to what was left of the garage where she pulled out an inflatable raft. She activated the bottle of carbon dioxide, and the gas filled the inflatable raft. Arlene found a paddle. At first she tried paddling in the water, but the gushing water tower created strong currents, and the best Arlene could do was use the paddle to steer her way down the hill and into the creek. She saw bits of the shed floating along and made for that. As she approached the floating shed debris, she saw a hand extend from the water and reach for a floating plank.

"Marvin," Arlene called out.

Arlene paddled to the hand and grabbed it. She pulled and pulled and pulled. The hand came out of the water and into the raft, along with the body of her husband, Marvin. Marvin was unconscious.

"Marvin, wake up!" Arlene cried.

Arlene blew into Marvin's lungs and pounded her fist in his chest. She bent and straightened his legs to force the water out of his lungs, and she breathed into his lungs again. After a minute of this, and with the raft swiftly floating down the creek, Marvin spat out water and awoke.

"Oh Marvin, you're alive!" Arlene cried as she hugged Marvin with joy.

"The wolf," Marvin started. "Where is the wolf?"

"That doesn't matter," Arlene said. "What matters is that you're alive."

"Did he get away?" Marvin asked.

Marvin sat up in the raft and looked around. In the distance further downstream, Marvin saw the wolf paddling wildly toward the creek's destination—the old grounds of Sadie's Place. The sheriff and deputy were still patrolling the grounds when the wave of coffee water came.

"Back to the cruiser!" the sheriff yelled.

The sheriff and deputy ran to the cruiser, jumped in, and sped off just as the first water hit. The cruiser hydroplaned and struggled to pull away, but the sheriff deftly navigated the cruiser and directed it along Highway 20 and away from Rolling Hills. He radioed in the emergency and did not return.

Among the debris the flood carried were logs. And like Lady Sadie's comb against paper, the logs combed along the top of the water. Their direction was controlled by Sadella's spirit, where they punctured all micro-breweries, distilleries, and pubs they came across. Alcohol spewed and evaporated. Drunks tried to swim but in their intoxicated state could not. Owners obsessed with their equipment tried to salvage what they could and died in the flood.

The wolf arrived on the grounds of old Sadie's Place. He clung onto Linda's body and kept it from drifting. The place where Lady Sadie's store once stood—the same grounds where Sadella's house stood—opened up and consumed the arriving flood, forming a massive whirlpool. The wolf paddled hard to keep Linda's body from being pulled into the whirlpool, and he initially succeeded. Arlene's raft arrived with Marvin. The two saw the whirlpool and fought to avoid it. While Arlene paddled as hard as she could, Marvin took a rope and anchor and threw it. The anchor caught hold of a tree, and the rope went taunt. The current pulled the raft toward the whirlpool; in fact, the raft was at the whirlpool's edge. The tree bent under the strain, and it cracked. It was only a matter of time before it would give way under the stress.

"We're going to die!" Arlene said.

"I know," Marvin replied.

"Do something!" Arlene said back.

"There's nothing else we can do but hold onto each other," Marvin replied.

The two held onto each other. The wolf grew exhausted and could no longer paddle against the pulling action of the whirlpool. He gave into the force, and he along with Linda were pulled in. The tree holding the anchor broke, yielding Arlene and Marvin to the whirlpool. Arlene and Marvin watched as the wolf and Linda were sucked into the whirlpool's center. The raft then went around the whirlpool a few times.

"I love you," Arlene and Marvin said as the raft was pulled toward the whirlpool's center.

Then it happened. The whirlpool collapsed and burped. The raft, which was in the throes of being swallowed by the whirlpool, was now sent cleanly to the surface of a calm water. The current from upstream also stopped. There was water everywhere, but all was quiet and flat.

"Arlene, Arlene?" Marvin called.

"Yes, I'm here with you, my husband," Arlene said. "We are safe. It's over."

The two were safe, but things were not yet over. The fungus in the coffee beans, *Colletotrichum lindemuthianum*, mixed with the chitin in the ground, chitin that was embedded deep within the earth but was now heavily saturated with coffee-bean water from the once-active whirlpool. The water steamed, then it boiled, then new turbulences developed.

"It's getting hot," Arlene said.

"Don't touch the water," Marvin said. "It's boiling."

"What will we do?" Arlene asked.

"Stay in the raft," Marvin said.

"And the wolf?" Arlene asked.

Marvin didn't answer. There was no sign of animal life other than the two of them.

As the water boiled, the chemical reaction between the fungus and the chitin accelerated. The chitin was split into two chemicals—chitosan and acetate. The water filled with lots of little, clear, plastic-looking leaves (the acetate) while the chitosan was absorbed by nearby plants and seeds yet sprouted. The water boiled quickly, and in vaporizing, it carried the acetate leaves into the air.

"Something strange is happening," Arlene said.

As the water evaporated, the waterline descended, and an uncontrollable rash of wildflowers took hold of the grounds— flowers spurned into accelerated growth by the chitosan and Sadella's spirit. The flowers ascended to heights of six and ten feet, and most of the water evaporated away, leaving a single water hole at the point where the center of the whirlpool once existed, a point where Sadella's house stood and Lady Sadie's store once stood.

"This is like a dream," Arlene said. "I can't believe it's happening. Even science can't be this real."

"I hope we survive to tell this story to others," Marvin said, "though I doubt any would believe us."

From the water hole, two paper-like spheres ascended. Yet the spheres could not have been solely paper since paper cannot hold its shape in water. In fact, the paper was reinforced with acetate, an ingredient that was in all of Lady Sadie's store products, providing strength, sheen, and durability. The two spheres opened, and two people emerged with gray fur falling away from them.

"Linda, Ken!" Arlene yelled.

Arlene and Marvin exited their beached raft and walked to the edge of the water hole. The water evaporated and produced the spirit of Sadella when she was a young girl. The spirit danced around Linda and Ken and peppered them with flowers. The spirit spoke:

"The curse of alcohol on these lands has been lifted. It is you, Linda, and you, Ken, who have made this so. By freeing these lands you have also freed my spirit. I will no longer haunt these lands or you, Linda. You are cured of your illness and will live a full and happy life, for you love Ken deeply and would not want to be parted from him. Marry him, Linda. Marry him and fulfill the promise of these lands, that all are free to pursue love and happiness. I give you my blessing. Farewell my sweet Linda. Farewell."

Sadella's spirit kissed Linda on the forehead before ascending into the upper atmosphere where she disappeared from sight. The last of the water evaporated, and the acetate leaves that had risen with the vapor now descended on the grounds like confetti. As they did, they fluttered and sang through the air like happy elm trees. The surrounding flowers bloomed fully and scented the air with joy. The breeze carried petals along the ground and blessed the earth. Linda and Ken hugged each other and thanked Sadella for their new-found lives.

"There is only one question left to ask," Ken said in the joyous moment.

"And that is?" Linda asked.

"Linda Racquemore, will you marry me?"

Linda looked at Ken, at Arlene and Marvin, around at the flowers, and back at Ken.

"Yes," Linda said.

Arlene and Marvin clapped as Linda and Ken hugged and kissed for an extended period of time. Linda opened her eyes and looked up. She winked at the sky, and far above in a cloud high in the sky, a twinkle of light winked back.

The End

CHAPTER 11:

In Retrospect

The Author in 1967

What is language but the symbols of characters grouped into words, words into sentences, sentences into paragraphs, into chapters, into books, into libraries, and into the thought-sum of humanity? Language is not a simple singularity that grows larger. Looking at the ingredients of the printed word, we see that inks rests on paper, a fibrous material that when examined at increasingly smaller levels becomes molecules which become atoms, and if we could examine the atom to even smaller degrees, smaller even than its subatomic particles, we may find an increasingly smaller collection of components organized into symbolic representations that define the laws of the universe, much as DNA defines the characteristics of a life-form or as language defines the form of a book.

We may also find that dualities are as present in those super-subatomic particles as they are in other aspects of life—the double-helix of chromosomes, the duality of source and sink, of positive and negative, good and bad, left and right, and day with night. These dualities are what intertwine us, not with static definitions of this side or that, but rather with dynamics of change where stellar poles become flipped after a time, where metals of technology blend with colors of art, and where absolute law and absolute freedom mix to become civilization.

I cannot help but cling to the past as I strive for the future. My mind will always contain the image of an eleven-year-old girl crossing a two-lane road with parked cars lining both sides as she makes her way to church. I was nine—a year on the other side of ten from my sister's age of eleven—another duality. But it seems past and future are yet more intertwined, as there is the family story of my grandmother's older brother who himself was crossing a street only to be hit by a trolley. His mother had signaled him, "no," when in fact he thought she meant, "go." This is the fragility of dualities—one side brings life while the other brings death. But this is itself a duality—life cannot be life without death. It is a high cost, but the price purchases value in life, making it a rare and beautiful thing. Some beauty is temporary, only being enjoyed for the moment, but other beauty transcends time and space and is treasured in conscious and subconscious thought, through none other than the miracle of language.

Not all dualities are about pleasantries. While the union of a couple in matrimony may bring forth a richness of experience, there are other dualities not so pleasant. The worst I can think of is bigotry, an ancient failing that continues to plague people. It is unpleasant to speak of and experience, but it exists nonetheless. But I think of bigotry as a static duality, where the intertwining and mixing of the double-helix of life has been arrested and prevented from achieving proper development. Don't let this static duality consume your life, because life is language, like the language of a book, and a book begins with a cover, contains pages of text, and ends with another cover. Following this cover along the spine, we reach the beginning of the book, and while the book has great power of enrichment (or boredom), it also has the power to trap. The cycle of front cover, text, and back cover leading directly to the front cover binds us in a kind of obsession and bigotry that prevents us from going on to the next book.

And so, I must end this book. This book will sit on a shelf next to another book, with the back cover of this book touching the next. I must leap. I must make the leap of faith from the back cover of this book to the front cover of the next. And so I say goodbye to *Before Carreña* and journey on to my next book:

Carreña.